OXFORD WORLD'S CLASSICS

THE IDIOT

FYODOR MIKHAILOVICH DOSTOEVSKY was born in Moscow in 1821, the second in a family of seven children. His mother died of consumption in 1837 and his father, a generally disliked army physician, died, apparently murdered, on his estate two years later. In 1844 he left the College of Military Engineering in St Petersburg and devoted himself to writing. *Poor Folk* (1846) met with great success from the literary critics of the day. In 1849 he was imprisoned and sentenced to death on account of his involvement with a group of utopian socialists, the Petrashevsky circle. The sentence was commuted at the last moment to penal servitude and exile, but the experience radically altered his political and personal ideology and led directly to *Memoirs from the House of the Dead* (1861–2). In 1857, whilst still in exile, he married his first wife, Maria Dmitrievna Isaeva, returning to St Petersburg in 1859. In the early 1860s he founded two new literary journals, *Vremia* and *Epokha*, and proved himself to be a brilliant journalist. He travelled in Europe, which served to strengthen his anti-European sentiment. During this period abroad he had an affair with Polina Suslova, the model for many of his literary heroines, including Polina in *The Gambler*. Central to their relationship was their mutual passion for gambling—an obsession which brought financial chaos to his affairs. Both his wife and his much-loved brother, Mikhail, died in 1864, the same year in which *Notes from the Underground* was published; *Crime and Punishment* and *The Gambler* followed in 1866, and in 1867 he married his stenographer, Anna Snitkina, who managed to bring an element of stability into his frenetic life. His other major novels, *The Idiot* (1868), *Demons* (1871), and *The Brothers Karamazov* (1880), met with varying degrees of success. In 1880 he was hailed as a saint, prophet, and genius by the audience to whom he delivered an address at the unveiling of the Pushkin memorial. He died six months later in 1881; at the funeral thirty thousand people accompanied his coffin and his death was mourned throughout Russia.

ALAN MYERS has translated a wide variety of contemporary Russian prose and poetry, including poems, essays, and plays by Joseph Brodsky. He has also produced a volume of facsimile versions from the golden age of Russian poetry, *An Age Ago*. His translations of Dostoevsky's *A Gentle Creature and Other Stories* and Pushkin's *The Queen of Spades and Other Stories* are also in Oxford World's Classics.

WILLIAM LEATHERBARROW is Professor of Russian at the University of Sheffield. His publications include *Fedor Dostoevsky: A Reference Guide* (Boston, 1990) and *Dostoevskii and Britain* (Oxford and Providence, 1995).

OXFORD WORLD'S CLASSICS

*For almost 100 years Oxford World's Classics have brought
readers closer to the world's great literature. Now with over 700
titles—from the 4,000-year-old myths of Mesopotamia to the
twentieth century's greatest novels—the series makes available
lesser-known as well as celebrated writing.*

*The pocket-sized hardbacks of the early years contained
introductions by Virginia Woolf, T. S. Eliot, Graham Greene,
and other literary figures which enriched the experience of reading.
Today the series is recognized for its fine scholarship and
reliability in texts that span world literature, drama and poetry,
religion, philosophy and politics. Each edition includes perceptive
commentary and essential background information to meet the
changing needs of readers.*

OXFORD WORLD'S CLASSICS

FYODOR DOSTOEVSKY

The Idiot

Translated and Edited by
ALAN MYERS

With an Introduction by
WILLIAM LEATHERBARROW

OXFORD
UNIVERSITY PRESS

OXFORD
UNIVERSITY PRESS

Great Clarendon Street, Oxford OX2 6DP

Oxford University Press is a department of the University of Oxford.
It furthers the University's objective of excellence in research, scholarship,
and education by publishing worldwide in

Oxford New York

Athens Auckland Bangkok Bogotá Buenos Aires Calcutta
Cape Town Chennai Dar es Salaam Delhi Florence Hong Kong Istanbul
Karachi Kuala Lumpur Madrid Melbourne Mexico City Mumbai
Nairobi Paris São Paulo Singapore Taipei Tokyo Toronto Warsaw

with associated companies in Berlin Ibadan

Oxford is a registered trade mark of Oxford University Press
in the UK and in certain other countries

Published in the United States
by Oxford University Press Inc., New York

Translation and Notes © Alan Myers 1992
Introduction © William J. Leatherbarrow 1992

The moral rights of the author have been asserted

Database right Oxford University Press (maker)

First published as a World's Classics paperback 1992
Reissued as an Oxford World's Classics paperback 1998

British Library Cataloguing in Publication Data

Data available

Library of Congress Cataloging in Publication Data

Dostoevsky, Fyodor, 1821–1881.
[Idiot. English]
The Idiot / Fedor Dostoevsky : translated by Alan Myers : with an
introduction by William Leatherbarrow.
p. cm.—(Oxford world's classics)
Translation of: Idiot.
"First published as a World's classics paperback 1992"—T.P. verso
I. Myers, Alan. II. Title. III. Series.
PO3326.13 1992 891.73'3—dc20 91–29143

ISBN 0–19–283411–8

3 5 7 9 10 8 6 4

Printed in Great Britain by
Cox & Wyman Ltd.
Reading, Berkshire

CONTENTS

INTRODUCTION

NOTE: Readers who don't want to know the plot of *The Idiot* beforehand might prefer to read this Introduction after the book itself.

Between 1865 and his death in January 1881, Fyodor Mikhailovich Dostoevsky wrote four incomparable novels—*Crime and Punishment* (1866), *The Idiot* (1868), *Devils* (also known as *The Possessed*) (1871–2), and *The Brothers Karamazov* (1879–80)—as well as *A Raw Youth* (1875), a work equally ambitious in both size and philosophical scope, but now generally recognized as less successful artistically. These works represent the very pinnacle of the nineteenth-century realistic novel, and they have exercised an immense influence on the subsequent development of the genre in the twentieth century. Of these novels Dostoevsky retained a special regard for *The Idiot* and for its hero, the saintly Prince Myshkin, even though its publication had a considerably more muted reception than that of *Crime and Punishment*, and even though Dostoevsky himself came to regard it as an artistic failure in which he had wasted a long-cherished idea. Indeed, the spectre of failure accompanied Dostoevsky throughout his work on this novel. From the outset he approached his task with reluctance and a sense of foreboding, writing to his niece in January 1868: 'The idea of the novel is my old favourite one, but it is so difficult that for a long time I did not dare attempt it; and if I have attempted it now, it is really because I found myself in a desperate situation . . . I am terribly afraid it will be a positive failure.' A few days later he wrote to his friend, the poet Apollon Maykov: 'For a long time now a certain idea has tormented me, but I have been afraid to make a novel from it, because the idea is too difficult and I am not ready for it, even though it is most tempting and I love it . . . Only my desperate situation has compelled me to use this premature idea.' This fear of failure certainly derived in part from the appalling personal circumstances under which Dostoevsky wrote *The Idiot* and the importance for him of the novel's idea and hero. But it could also be argued (and this is a far more intriguing possibility) that it arose because in a very fundamental sense this was to be a novel *about* failure.

The special significance which *The Idiot* and its hero held for Dostoevsky is suggested by the fact that it is in some respects the most personal of his novels, drawing deeply from the well of his own experiences and articulating some of his most cherished convictions. The gauche, self-effacing, and unworldly Prince Myshkin is far from being an actual self-portrait of a writer who was in reality touchy and self-absorbed, and who had a remarkable history of participation in the political and intellectual currents of mid-nineteenth-century Russia. But in some important ways he is a sort of idealized self-projection. He is afflicted with the same disease, epilepsy, that marred much of Dostoevsky's life and which made his work on *The Idiot* such a nightmare; he embodies the same Christian conviction, love of children, and faith in humility and compassion that were the corner-stones of the writer's own philosophical stance; he describes in great detail the feelings of a man condemned to execution, in terms which recall Dostoevsky's own experiences in 1849 when, convicted of participation in a plot against the regime of Nicholas I, he too faced the firing squad for several agonizing minutes before his sentence was commuted to hard labour and Siberian exile. Myshkin is also drawn into a nerve-racking relationship with a proud and sensual woman, Nastasya Filippovna, which has much in common with Dostoevsky's painful affair with Polina Suslova, with whom he had travelled in Europe in the early 1860s and who drove him to extremes of passionate jealousy comparable to those experienced by Rogozhin in the novel. Other details, too, suggest autobiographical influences: like Dostoevsky, Myshkin is fascinated by calligraphy (the pages of Dostoevsky's notebooks are filled with extravagant examples of Gothic script); Myshkin's return to a strange and unfamiliar Russia after his years of enforced 'exile' in a Swiss clinic recalls Dostoevsky's own return from Siberian exile in 1859; and the views on beauty, Catholicism, socialism, and the spiritual bankruptcy of the contemporary age with which he confronts his often bemused listeners are almost verbatim transcripts of convictions Dostoevsky himself had expressed in his earlier journalistic articles and which he continued to explore in his personal correspondence.

If, as the evidence so clearly suggests, *The Idiot* is a repository for Dostoevsky's most intimate memories, cherished precepts, and personal details, then this can only be because the novel was the sole focus of all his hopes for salvation during an extremely trying period in his life. On Good Friday 1867, only a month or so after his second marriage, Dostoevsky left St Petersburg for Europe with his new wife, the 20-year-old stenographer Anna Grigorevna. Dostoevsky had met Anna in the autumn of 1866, while working on *Crime and Punishment*, and he had employed her shorthand skills in order to dash off in less than a month the novel *The Gambler*, and thus meet a contractual obligation with the unscrupulous publisher Stellovsky. The professional relationship blossomed into an unlikely, but highly successful, marriage. The European trip, however, was no conventional honeymoon; it was an attempt to escape from debts and importunate relatives, which were threatening the newly-weds with financial ruin. Despite the success of *Crime and Punishment*, Dostoevsky still owed large sums of money as a result of the collapse of his periodical, *The Epoch*, in 1865 and the burden of supporting the family of his brother Mikhail, who had died in 1864. He had barely escaped debtors' prison, and the flight abroad was made possible only by the redoubtable Anna's financial acumen and willingness to pawn her dowry. The trip was planned to last for three months, but the Dostoevskys were not to return to Russia until July 1871. Their journey took them first to Berlin and Dresden, where the writer's xenophobia and aversion to Germans in particular were only partly offset by the cultural riches offered by the Royal Picture Gallery in Dresden. There he took Anna to see Raphael's *Madonna* and Claude Lorrain's *Acis and Galatea*, both of which embodied for Dostoevsky that ideal beauty which sustained man through the difficulties of an imperfect existence, affording glimpses of a harmony and perfection that normally eluded him. This aspect of Dostoevsky's aesthetic convictions is summed up in *The Idiot* in the assertion, attributed to Myshkin, that 'the world will be saved by beauty' (Part III, Ch. 5), and the theme of the redeeming power of beauty is central to the novel's philosophical design.

The Dostoevskys led a rather difficult life in Dresden. Fyodor Mikhailovich's anxiety about the age-difference between himself and his wife was matched by Anna's jealousy of her husband's continued correspondence with Polina Suslova. Moreover, the couple's financial difficulties were exacerbated by Dostoevsky's pathological addiction to roulette, an addiction which Anna must have anticipated as she took down the novelist's dictation of *The Gambler*. Occasional visits to the casino at Homberg did not satisfy his craving, and in July the couple set off for Geneva via the gaming tables of Baden-Baden. They passed seven disastrous weeks in Baden, during which Dostoevsky lost everything, borrowed extravagantly until his credit ran out, and met and quarrelled with the Russian novelist Ivan Turgenev, who remained a bitter foe until the very last months of Dostoevsky's life. Dostoevsky disliked Turgenev's foppishness and condescendingly aristocratic manner; he envied him the wealth and material comfort that allowed him to compose and refine his novels with no regard for pressing deadlines or financial hardship; but above all, he was opposed to Turgenev's liberalism and admiration for all things European. Turgenev had spent much of his life in the West, where he moved easily among European literati. By conviction he was a *Zapadnik* or Westernizer, a term first applied in the 1840s and 1850s to those Russian intellectuals who dismissed indigenous Russian culture as inferior to that of Western Europe, and who argued that Russia's salvation lay in catching up with the cultural and technological advances made by the West. Turgenev's Westernism took the form of a preference for French over Russian, an admiration for the liberalism and individualism enshrined in much European political thinking, and a tendency to consign Russia to the historical dustbin. Such ideas were anathema to Dostoevsky, who had moved far from the political liberalism of his youth. The young conspirator who had faced execution in 1849 for subversion and plotting the overthrow of the Tsarist regime had 'died' in Siberia. Firsthand experience of the criminal mind had convinced him that earthly paradise was not to be achieved through rational progress or liberal social reform. The sort of depraved human souls he had encountered in prison would not respond to enlightened humanism; they could be retrieved only by the complete moral transfiguration of the sinful individual through religious experience. What was needed were not 'good' institutions or 'good' political systems, but positively good men. Through the darkness of his Siberian torment Dostoevsky had been sustained by his copy of the New Testament and his developing religious conviction. He had returned to freedom as a writer with a religious mission, anxious to persuade his compatriots that the religious spirit, lost in the West's headlong pursuit of political and material progress, was still alive in that same unspoiled Russian past so scornfully dismissed by Turgenev.

Stung by his encounter with Turgenev, anxious to have his say in a major new novel of his own, but prevented from working by financial hardship, Dostoevsky moved on with Anna, who was now pregnant. They left Baden in late August for Basle, where Dostoevsky was profoundly struck by Hans Holbein's painting of *Christ in the Tomb*, which depicts with harrowing realism a corpse which has already begun to decompose, and in which there is no sense of imminent resurrection or of life eternal. Dostoevsky remarked that such a painting could make a man lose his faith, and similar words are put into Myshkin's mouth in *The Idiot*. In fact, Holbein's painting has an almost anti-iconic significance in Dostoevsky's novel: a copy of it hangs in Rogozhin's house and a full description of its horrific effect is given by the dying Ippolit Terentyev:

The picture shows Christ, just taken down from the cross. I believe artists usually depict Christ, whether on the cross or taken down from it, as still retaining a trace of extraordinary beauty in the face; they seek to preserve this beauty in him, even during the most terrible agonies. There was no hint of beauty in Rogozhin's picture; it is an out-and-out depiction of the body of a man who has endured endless torments even before the crucifixion—wounds, torture, beatings from the guards, blows from the populace, when he was carrying the cross and fell beneath it, and finally the agony of the cross . . . In the picture the face is terribly mangled by blows, swollen, with terrible, swollen, bloody bruises, the eyes open and unfocused; the whites wide open, gleaming with a kind of deathly, glazed lustre. But it's odd; as you look at this corpse of a tortured man a most curious question comes to mind: if a corpse like that (and it must certainly have been exactly like that) was seen by all his disciples, his future chief apostles, and seen by the women who followed him and stood by the cross, by all in fact who believed in and worshipped him, how could they have believed, looking at such a corpse, that the martyr would rise again? The compulsion would be to think that if death was so dreadful, and nature's laws so powerful, how could they possibly be overcome? How could they be overcome when even he had failed, he who had vanquished even nature during his lifetime, he whom nature obeyed, who said '*Talitha cumi!*' and the girl arose, who cried '*Lazarus come forth!*' and the dead man came forth? Looking at that picture, one has the impression of nature as some enormous, implacable, dumb beast, or more precisely, strange as it may seem—in the guise of a vast modern machine which has pointlessly seized, dismembered, and devoured, in its blind and insensible fashion, a great and priceless being, a being worth all of nature and all her laws, worth the entire earth—which indeed was perhaps created solely to prepare for the advent of that being!

(Part III, Ch. 6)

If we remember that in his approach to *The Idiot* Dostoevsky was preoccupied by both the fear of failure and his conviction that salvation could be achieved only on the basis of good men, rather than good institutions, then it becomes clear that he found in Holbein's painting of a defeated Christ an idea that allowed him to reconcile these two conceptions, that galvanized his thinking and came to dominate his novel: that of the failure of the positively good man.

Dostoevsky began work on the first draft of *The Idiot* in the autumn of 1867. An already difficult task was made worse by family tragedy (the death of his infant daughter Sonya) and by further travel, which took the couple first to Geneva and then on to Vevey, Milan, and Florence, where Dostoevsky finally finished *The Idiot* at the end of 1868. Dostoevsky's epilepsy was also at its worst during these months, and frequent fits, punctuated with painful periods of recuperation, rendered his work on the novel haphazard and confused. In the light of this it is hardly surprising that the evolution of this novel from original conception to final form was particularly tortuous and trying. On his own admission Dostoevsky felt unready for the task, as he confessed to Maykov in January 1868:

Many embryos of artistic thoughts flash in my head and in my heart . . . But they only flash, when what is needed is a complete embodiment, which always comes suddenly and unexpectedly, and you can never tell when exactly. And then, having received the complete image in your heart, you can proceed to its artistic realization.

To his niece Sonya he wrote: 'If only you knew how hard it is to be a writer, and to carry such a burden! I know for certain that if I had two or three stable years for this novel, as Turgenev, Goncharov, and Tolstoy have, I would write a work they would talk about for a hundred years!' Yet it is clear that during his work on *The Idiot* Dostoevsky had neither such peace of mind nor the 'complete image' he described to Maykov. Quite the contrary, in fact: financial pressures compelled him to publish the first part of the novel at a time when he had no idea of how to continue!

Dostoevsky's working notebooks for *The Idiot* have survived, and they show very clearly the confusion in his mind. The work went through no fewer than eight different drafts, each quite different from the others. Indeed, the first six are hardly recognizable as preparation for *The Idiot*. They suggest that Dostoevsky's original intention was to write a novel about the Russian family and its decline through an over-emphasis on material, rather than spiritual, values. This idea came to dominate Dostoevsky's thinking in the 1870s, when it provided the conceptual framework for his two last novels, *A Raw Youth* and *The Brothers Karamazov*; but it also survives after a fashion in *The Idiot*, in Lebedev's apocalyptic indictment of contemporary materialism (Part II, Ch. 2), and in Ganya Ivolgin's conviction that all men are usurers at heart and that money can make even the most ordinary person interesting (Part I, Ch. 11).

What is not recognizable in these early drafts is the figure of Myshkin. Initially, the central character was to be the epileptic illegitimate son of a family that was to evolve into the Ivolgin family of the finished novel. But this figure has nothing but his epilepsy in common with Myshkin. He emerges as a dark and passionate character, burning with pride and egoism and indifferent to the hurt he inflicts on others. In the final novel these characteristics are to be attributed to the figures of Rogozhin and Ganya Ivolgin. In the subsequent drafts there gradually developed a new idea: the novel was to be the one Dostoevsky promised in the Epilogue of *Crime and Punishment*, an account of the moral and spiritual regeneration of a proud and demonic soul. In these pages of the drafts the 'Idiot' is still a vengeful and violent figure, but he is now possessed of 'a spontaneous thirst for life' which will allow him to develop 'a high moral sense' and a nature capable of compassion: 'He could have evolved into a monster, but love saves him.' An important catalyst in this change was to be a new figure—the legitimate son of the family—who is meek, virtuous, and simple-minded. (In the final novel, of course, the legitimate son of the Ivolgin family is the distinctly unvirtuous Ganya.) This 'new' Idiot, a lost soul burning with the desire for salvation, at times bears a striking resemblance to Stavrogin, the hero of Dostoevsky's later novel *Devils*, and this reminds us that the titanic artistic struggle that eventually gave rise to *The Idiot* also produced valuable fragments that were to mature and then lodge in the novels of the 1870s.

It is clear that the figure of Myshkin was beginning to emerge in the meek and childlike legitimate son of the 'Ivolgin' family. But the real breakthrough came at the end of Dostoevsky's sixth plan, written in November 1867. Of the central figure Dostoevsky suddenly remarks: '*He is a Prince!*' and 'Prince *Yurodivy*. (He is with the children)?!' The *yurodivy*, or God's fool, was a distinctive phenomenon in Russian Orthodox Christianity, a crazed but saintly figure who sought salvation through meekness and self-abasement. The association of his hero with this figure, along with the image of him surrounded by children, allowed Dostoevsky to develop in the seventh and eighth drafts a more complete picture of a forgiving, compassionate, Christlike prince, fully recognizable as the Myshkin of the final novel. It would seem that Dostoevsky reached a creative crisis in the sixth draft, after which he abandoned his earlier work on the novel and proceeded to write the final version of the first part in only twenty-three days. This crisis was brought about by a problem that had confronted Dostoevsky before, in the Epilogue to *Crime and Punishment*: how to depict in art the mysteries of a soul's salvation and spiritual regeneration. Then he had, frankly, avoided the issue by deferring the problem until a later novel. Now, too, in his work on *The Idiot* he shrank from the difficulties of the task before him. The theme of the spiritual rebirth of a sinner was put aside for his later, unrealized project, 'The Life of a Great Sinner', and the depiction of a positively good man, already fully developed, became the focus of *The Idiot*. This new focus was clearly defined by January 1868, when he wrote the following to his niece:

The main idea of the novel is to depict the positively good man. There is nothing more difficult than this in the world, especially nowadays. All writers—not only ours, but European ones too—who have set about depicting the *positively* good have always shirked the task. It is because this is a task that is immeasurable. The good is an ideal, and neither we nor civilized Europe have yet succeeded in working out such an ideal for ourselves. There is only one positively good man in the world, and that is Christ. The appearance of this immeasurably, infinitely good figure is therefore in itself an infinite miracle ... Of all the good figures in Christian literature, Don Quixote is the most complete. But he is good only because he is at the same time ridiculous. Dickens's Pickwick (an infinitely weaker conception than Don Quixote, but still immense) is also comic and succeeds because of this. Sympathy is aroused for the good man who is ridiculed and who does not know his own worth, and this sympathy is aroused in the reader too. This arousing of sympathy is the secret of humour ... I have nothing of the kind, absolutely nothing, and therefore I am terribly afraid that [my novel] will be a positive failure.

The emergence of a 'positively good man' from the confusion of the creative process provided Dostoevsky with the central dramatic confrontation his novel required. Into an almost apocalyptic depiction of a contemporary Russia beset by the evils of materialism, egoism, and political opportunism, and dominated by the ethics of self-interest and personal wealth, Dostoevsky introduced the idealized figure of Myshkin, untouched by these failings and driven by the conviction that 'meekness is a mighty force' (Part III, Ch. 6) and that compassion is 'the most important, perhaps sole law of human existence' (Part II, Ch. 5).

Dostoevsky's portrait of contemporary Russia is informed by the anti-European sentiments and Christian belief he acquired in Siberia. His distaste for Western capitalism, sharpened by his travels abroad, is evident in the important role played by money in *The Idiot*. In this novel Dostoevsky's attack on the spiritual poverty of modern man is centred on his seduction by the power of finance. The arrival of the destitute Myshkin provokes amused contempt in Russian society, until he suddenly inherits a fortune, from which point he is regarded as a man of substance. Money is indeed the primary determinant of social worth in this novel; the characters at the top of the social pile are those who are skilled in investment: the businessman Totsky; the financier General Ivolgin; and the vulgar but well-heeled money-lender Ptitsyn. The would-be usurer Ganya Ivolgin articulates the hidden ethos of this world when he confesses: 'Once I've got my hands on a fortune, you'll see I'll be extremely original. The most disgusting and hateful thing about money is that it even endows people with talent' (Part I, Ch. 11). In the society depicted in *The Idiot* nearly all are mesmerized by money. One of the most striking features of this novel is that many of the characters Myshkin meets on his arrival from Switzerland introduce themselves with a remark about money. In the opening scene on the train Rogozhin speaks of his recent inheritance and quizzes Myshkin about the cost of medical treatment in Switzerland; later, when Myshkin lodges in the Ivolgin household, he is warned not to lend money to the General; the other lodger, Ferdischenko, peers around Myshkin's door to ask for a loan; the 'progressive' Burdovsky and his henchmen try to deceive Myshkin out of his inheritance; and the rivalry between Ganya and Rogozhin for the favours of Nastasya Filippovna culminates in an auction where the two try to outbid each other. Rogozhin's winning bid of a hundred thousand roubles is, significantly, wrapped in a copy of *The Stock Exchange Gazette*.

It is the minor character Lebedev who invests this depiction of widespread acquisitiveness with a profound philosophical significance. At Myshkin's birthday gathering (in Part III, Ch. 4), Lebedev, a self-styled interpreter of the Apocalypse, is goaded into an intemperate attack upon the spiritual vacuum at the heart of modern society: '. . . the whole thing, sir, altogether accursed, the entire spirit of these last centuries, in its scientific and practical totality, is perhaps really accursed, sir.' In Lebedev's analysis, contemporary man, driven by greed and self-interest, has lost the spiritual basis of his existence. In a comically irreverent anecdote, Lebedev goes on to tell of a twelfth-century monk who, after twenty years of cannibalism, confessed and went to the stake. What was it, asks Lebedev, that drove him to confess despite the punishment that awaited him?

There must have been something much stronger than the stake, the fire, even the habit of twenty years! There must have been an idea more powerful than any disaster, famine, torture, plague, leprosy, and all that hell which mankind could not have borne without that one binding idea which directed men's minds and fertilized the springs of life! Show me anything resembling that power in our age of depravity and railways . . . Show me a force which binds today's humanity together with half the power it possessed in those centuries . . . And don't try to browbeat me with your prosperity, your riches, the rarity of famine and the speed of communications! The riches are greater but the force is less; there is no more a binding principle; everything has grown soft, everything and everyone grown flabby!

(Part III, Ch. 4)

Lebedev's anecdote is absurd, but it serves a serious purpose, disclosing Dostoevsky's own vision of modern Europe, devoid of spiritual purpose or strength, distracted by empty materialism, and poised on the brink of Armageddon. Lebedev finds a symbol of mankind's state in the vivid apocalyptic image of the four horsemen:

. . . we're in the time of the third horse, the black one, the one that has the rider with scales in his hand, because in our age everything is weighed in the balance and settled by agreement, and all men seek only their own due: 'one measure of wheat for one denarius and three measures of barley for one denarius' . . . as well as wanting to have freedom of spirit, a pure heart and a sound body, and all God's gifts added thereunto. But they cannot have these things by right alone, and the pale horse will follow and he whose name is Death, and after him, Hell . . .

(Part II, Ch. 2)

The apocalyptic atmosphere, created by Lebedev and by the novel's emphasis on money and materialism, provides the crucible in which Myshkin's Christian ideals are tested. Both literally and metaphorically, the prince is from another world. Afflicted with an illness that has always kept him apart from his fellow men, he has spent his formative years not amidst the pressures of contemporary life, but in the sterile environment of a Swiss clinic. He is a man of 27, but his emotional and spiritual growth has been arrested, and he retains the heart and mind of a child. His ideals remain bright and intact, for they have never before been challenged by experience. In these respects he is clearly analogous to Cervantes's unworldly hero in *Don Quixote*, and it is clear that Dostoevsky intended his hero to be read, on one level at least, as a contemporary restatement of the quixotic knight-errant, intent on transforming the iron age of nineteenth-century materialism into a golden age of chivalry and Christian virtue. When Aglaya Yepanchina receives a letter from Myshkin, she conceals it in her copy of *Don Quixote de la Mancha*, and she also reads aloud Pushkin's poem 'The Poor Knight', whose theme clearly parallels Myshkin's self-denying love for Nastasya Filippovna.

As well as suggesting the figure of the chivalrous knight, Myshkin also appears as a Christlike figure, preaching the same virtues of meekness, truth, and compassion. At the time of his work on *The Idiot*, Dostoevsky had been reading Renan's *Life of Jesus*, and many of the details of Renan's account of Christ's ministry are incorporated into Myshkin's personal history. Both Christ and Myshkin enter the world from other, very different, ones in order to preach their ideals. Indeed, Myshkin confesses to the Yepanchin sisters that he regards himself as a philosopher who has come to teach. Moreover, throughout the novel he continues to look upon Switzerland as a sort of paradise, where his innocence was intact and his faith unshaken by the complexities of Russian reality. It is to there he longs to retreat when the pressures of his new life become too much for him. The anecdotes Myshkin relates about his period in Switzerland also offer parallels between his life and that of Christ. His story of his friendship with the young girl Marie, who had been seduced by a travelling salesman and spurned by the whole village, and who was rehabilitated through Myshkin's compassion, is clearly designed to be read as an allegorical reworking of the tale of Christ and the fallen woman, Mary Magdalene. Myshkin's friendship with the children of the Swiss village, whom he teaches and to whom he refuses to lie, much to the annoyance of the village elders, recalls another biblical image—that of Christ surrounded by the children.

As with Christ, little is known of Myshkin's formative years. He dimly recalls that when he was taken into Switzerland to be treated at Schneider's clinic, the only thing he heard through his epileptic confusion was the braying of an ass. This suggests, albeit faintly, Christ's entry into Jerusalem on an ass. The first people Christ encountered in Jerusalem were the merchants and moneylenders on the steps of the Temple: Myshkin's arrival in Russia is marked by his immediate acquaintance with merchants (Rogozhin and Totsky, for example) and moneylenders (Ptitsyn). In an episode that runs parallel to Christ's retreat into the wilderness, Myshkin flees from St Petersburg for six months, between Parts I and II of the novel, in order to collect his thoughts. There are many other examples of such parallels with the life of Christ, and these are complemented by the many occasions when the other characters discern Christlike qualities in the prince.

Yet, if Myshkin is a Christ he is a flawed one, and his mission is doomed to failure. His Christian meekness and compassion, which translated so effectively into positive achievements in Switzerland, have disruptive and ultimately lethal consequences when practised in the 'real' world of nineteenth-century Russia. In Switzerland his innocence and simplicity win the trust of those he meets; in Russia the same qualities breed mistrust, embarrassment, and hatred. The honesty and truthfulness that win him friendship in Switzerland only serve to offend those he encounters in Russia. The compassion that served to resurrect Marie provokes the insane jealousy of Rogozhin and leads to the death of another fallen woman, Nastasya Filippovna. In Russia Myshkin discovers, for the first time in his life, the gulf between ideals and reality and the impossibility of achieving paradise on earth. His epilepsy becomes a metaphor for this tragic discovery: it provides him, in the aura which precedes the fit, with his greatest insights into beauty and harmony, but these divine moments are instantly wiped away in the darkness and chaos of the fit itself. At the end of the novel, the Myshkin who arrived in Russia hopeful of recovery and anxious to please, and who pledged himself to the salvation of Nastasya Filippovna through Christian love, is found gibbering unintelligibly alongside her mutilated body in the company of her murderer. All are destroyed by the passions unleashed by the 'positively good man'.

Yet, as we have seen, this is a failure which Dostoevsky anticipated. He drew back from the challenge of presenting a flawless hero, for he knew that such a figure would not be human, but would be, like Christ, divine. Myshkin's decline from innocence and idealism to renewed idiocy and complicity in the death of Nastasya is the device Dostoevsky chooses to convey his acknowledgement of man's imperfect state, and his lack of faith in human perfectibility. Paradise on earth is, indeed, an unrealizable dream, and the Myshkin who arrives from Switzerland carries within himself, in the form of his epilepsy, the seed of his eventual destruction. Prior to his arrival he is not, in Dostoevsky's eyes, a human being at all, for he has not known sin. He is the product of a retort, a homunculus bred in the protection of Schneider's clinic. From the moment he enters Russia and is exposed to the passions and intrigues of the real world, he begins his inevitable decline as his humanity, suppressed by the years of his isolation, asserts itself. Myshkin, of course, resists his fall, but the process is unstoppable and the end-result inescapable; for only Christ, and not a merely Christlike figure, is without sin. Thus, Myshkin's Christian love for Nastasya Filippovna is gradually compromised by a growing sensual love for Aglaya; his initial belief in the goodness of men yields to his realization that Rogozhin is bound to kill Nastasya; and his purity of heart, suggested by his total lack of material wealth, is darkened by his highly symbolic inheritance. Myshkin inherits far more than money—he acquires also his due legacy of human weaknesses.

Myshkin is indisputably the thematic and structural centre of *The Idiot*, serving to articulate Dostoevsky's lack of faith in paradise on earth, and acting as a catalyst unleashing the dramatic forces latent among the other characters. But the novel's secondary characters are equally effectively drawn and invested with a strong symbolic charge. The reader is alerted to Dostoevsky's approach to characterization in this novel at the beginning of Part IV, where the narrator observes:

In their novels and stories, writers for the most part try to take certain social types and present them vividly and skilfully—types who are very rarely encountered in real life precisely as they are drawn, but who are nevertheless almost more real than reality itself . . . In real life the typical characteristics of people seem to get diluted . . .

(Part IV, Ch. 1)

The characters in *The Idiot* are, indeed, 'more real than reality itself'. They function as convincing social and psychological types, certainly; but they are also endowed with a compelling mythical or allegorical significance. The merchant Rogozhin, for instance, is clearly contrived as a dark *alter ego* to Myshkin. In the opening scene on the train they are brought together, only to be contrasted in every respect: Myshkin's Christian compassion is thrown into relief by Rogozhin's satanic passion; the prince's fair complexion, physical weakness, and tranquil demeanour are strikingly contrasted with Rogozhin's darkness, robust physicality, and passionate unease; in a clearly symbolic detail, they occupy the same carriage but sit on opposite benches. This contrapuntal relationship between the prince and Rogozhin is continued to the end of the novel, when we see the two making their way to their final vigil over the body of Nastasya, walking in step but on opposite sides of the street. The young consumptive Ippolit Terentyev is also symbolically bound to Myshkin. He too is a condemned man, afflicted by an uncaring Nature with a destructive illness; but, whereas Myshkin reacts to his epilepsy with Christian resignation, Ippolit makes his condition the justification for profound rebellion against a malign God.

If Rogozhin and Ippolit are designed to represent the qualities of passionate sexuality and rebellious egoism from which Myshkin has been protected during his earlier existence, then the sensual and unpredictable Nastasya Filippovna subverts Myshkin's most fundamental beliefs that 'the world will be saved by beauty' and that 'meekness is a mighty force'. Her beauty unleashes only destructive passions, and her apparent 'meekness', as she parades herself as 'Rogozhin's slut' and seeks self-abasement, is far from being Christian meekness: it conceals a vast reservoir of pride. Her complex psychology, as she pursues the goal of self-destruction, discloses the inadequacy of Myshkin's hopelessly naive view of human nature.

The destruction of the 'positively good man' through his increasing intimacy with such symbolically charged characters marks *The Idiot* out as much more than merely another social novel of the nineteenth century. The trappings of the realistic novel conceal a core of myth; the critique of nineteenth-century Russian society yields to a complex apocalyptic allegory, in which the author's deepest beliefs are explored. Yet, Dostoevsky's

unerring artistic sense and penetrating psychological insight
ensure that *The Idiot* also succeeds as a novel. He was right to
anticipate the moral failure of his hero, but wrong to fear the
artistic failure of his work. Out of the chaos of the creative
process and the disorder of his personal existence, Dostoevsky
succeeded in contriving a great novel which has indeed lasted for
a hundred years, and which will no doubt continue to captivate its
readers for centuries to come.

W. J. LEATHERBARROW

NOTE ON THE TRANSLATION

THE chief problem facing the translator of Dostoevsky lies in coming to terms with the novelist's idiosyncratic style, with its feverishly accelerating sentences and mixture of styles ranging from bureaucratese to the classical cadences of gentry prose. It is a style which has made Dostoevsky the only Russian writer to be recognizably parodied in English (memorably, by Woody Allen and S. J. Perelman).

Russian readers are also familiar with Dostoevsky's solecisms, such as using the word 'again' five times in four lines, or 'suddenly' six times in ten lines, both examples taken from *The Idiot*. To complicate matters, there are Russian usages which are actually unique to this novel!

Bearing in mind the novelist's breathless readability in his native language, the translator must strive to preserve this distinctive style, while maintaining a convincing natural flow in the English translation. I have aimed at scrupulous accuracy with regard to the original, repetitions and all, unless the effect was outlandish enough to draw attention to itself and hinder the reader's appreciation.

It should be noted that the characters always gravitate towards *polite* literary speech. Even people outside the upper-middle-class milieu adopt the speech-patterns of their betters, and usually fail through being either over-genteel or over-literary. Raciness is explicitly eschewed—the prince is taken to task by Aglaya for using two colloquial expressions! The characters may speak of their emotions in a very direct and disconcerting manner, but no one employs common, rough, or uneducated language.

As money plays an important role in *The Idiot*, it may be helpful to establish that the Russian rouble in the novel is roughly equivalent to £2 sterling (or $3) in present-day money.

Russians often use the contracted form of the patronymic in conversation, Ivanich for Ivanovich, for example, or Ardalionich in place of Ardalionovich. I have followed this practice where it

occurs in Dostoevsky. Diminutives denoting affection or
familiarity should be clear from the context. The most frequent
use of this form is in relation to the Ivolgin family. Gavrila
Ardalionovich Ivolgin, for example, is usually referred to as
Ganya, or even Ganka. His little brother Nikolai is called Kolya,
while his sister Varvara Ardalionovna becomes Varya.

SELECT BIBLIOGRAPHY

CATTEAU, JACQUES, *Dostoyevsky and the Process of Literary Creation*, trans. by Audrey Littlewood (Cambridge, 1989).

DALTON, ELIZABETH, *Unconscious Structure in 'The Idiot': A Study in Literature and Psychoanalysis* (Princeton, 1979).

FRANK, JOSEPH, *Dostoevsky: The Seeds of Revolt 1821–1849* (Princeton and London, 1976).

—— *Dostoevsky: The Years of Ordeal 1850–1859* (Princeton and London, 1983).

—— *Dostoevsky: The Stir of Liberation 1860–1865* (Princeton and London, 1986).

—— *Dostoevsky: The Miraculous Years 1865–1871* (Princeton and London, 1995).

JONES, MALCOLM, *Dostoevsky: The Novel of Discord* (London, 1976).

KJETSAA, GEIR, *Fyodor Dostoyevsky: A Writer's Life* (London, 1988).

LEATHERBARROW, W. J., *Fedor Dostoevsky* (Boston, Mass., 1981).

—— *Dostoevsky: The Miraculous Years 1865–1871* (Princeton and London, 1995).

MOCHULSKY, K., *Dostoevsky: His Life and Work*, trans. by Michael Minihan (Princeton, 1967).

PEACE, RICHARD, *Dostoyevsky: An Examination of the Major Novels* (Cambridge, 1971).

WASIOLEK, EDWARD, *Dostoevsky: The Major Fiction* (Cambridge, Mass., 1964).

CHRONOLOGY OF FYODOR DOSTOEVSKY

Italicized items are works by Dostoevsky listed by year of first publication. Dates are Old Style, which means that they lag behind those used in nineteenth-century Western Europe by twelve days.

1821   Fyodor Mikhailovich Dostoevsky is born in Moscow, the son of an army doctor (30 October).

1837   His mother dies.

1838   Enters the Chief Engineering Academy in St Petersburg as an army cadet.

1839   His father dies, possibly murdered by his serfs.

1842   Is promoted Second Lieutenant.

1843   Translates Balzac's *Eugénie Grandet*.

1844   Resigns his army commission.

1846   *Poor Folk*
        The Double

1849   *Netochka Nezvanova*
        Is led out for execution in the Semenovsky Square in St Petersburg (22 December); his sentence is commuted at the last moment to penal servitude, to be followed by army service and exile, in Siberia.

1850–4 Serves four years at the prison at Omsk in western Siberia.

1854   Is released from prison (March), but is immediately posted as a private soldier to an infantry battalion stationed at Semipalatinsk, in western Siberia.

1855   Is promoted Corporal.
        Death of Nicholas I; accession of Alexander II.

1856   Is promoted Ensign.

1857   Marries Maria Dmitrievna Isaeva (6 February).

1859   Resigns his army commission with the rank of Second
        Lieutenant (March), and receives permission to return
        to European Russia.
        Resides in Tver (August–December).
        Moves to St Petersburg (December).
        Uncle's Dream
        Stepanchikovo Village

1861   Begins publication of a new literary monthly, *Vremia*,
        founded by himself and his brother Mikhail (January).
        The Emancipation of the Serfs.
        The Insulted and the Injured
        A Series of Essays on Literature

1861–2 *Memoirs from the House of the Dead.*

1862   His first visit to Western Europe, including England
        and France.

1863   *Winter Notes on Summer Impressions*
        Vremia is closed by the authorities for political reasons.

1864   Launches a second journal, *Epokha* (March).
        His first wife dies (15 April).
        His brother Mikhail dies (10 July).
        Notes from the Underground.

1865   *Epokha* collapses for financial reasons (June).

1866   Attempted assassination of Alexander II by Dmitry
        Karakozov (April).
        Crime and Punishment
        The Gambler

1867   Marries Anna Grigorevna Snitkina, his stenographer,
        as his second wife (15 February).
        Dostoevsky and his bride leave for Western Europe
        (April).

1867–71 The Dostoevskys reside abroad, chiefly in Dresden, but
        also in Geneva, Vevey, Florence, and elsewhere.

1868   *The Idiot*

1870   *The Eternal Husband*

1871   The Dostoevskys return to St Petersburg. Birth of
            their first son Fyodor (16 July).

1871–2   *Devils* (also called *The Possessed*)

1873–4   Edits the weekly journal *Grazhdanin*.

1873–81 *Diary of a Writer*

1875   *An Accidental Family* (also called *A Raw Youth*)

1878   Death of Dostoevsky's beloved three-year-old son
            Alesha (16 May).

1879–80 *The Karamazov Brothers*

1880   His speech at lavish celebrations held in Moscow in
            honour of Pushkin is received with frenetic enthusiasm
            on 8 June, and marks the peak point attained by his
            reputation during his lifetime.

1881   Dostoevsky dies in St Petersburg (28 January).
            Alexander II is assassinated (1 March).

LIST OF CHARACTERS

Prince Lev Nikolayevich Myshkin (The Idiot)

Nastasya Filippovna Barashkova, *Totsky's ex-mistress*

Parfion Semyonovich Rogozhin, *a merchant's son, now fabulously wealthy*

General Ivan Fedorovich Yepanchin, *a financial dealer*
Lizaveta Prokofievna (Madame Yepanchina), *his wife*
Alexandra ⎫
Adelaida ⎬ *their daughters*
Aglaya ⎭

General Ardalion Alexandrovich Ivolgin, *retired officer*
Nina Alexandrovna, *his wife*
Varvara Ardalionovna Ivolgina (Varya), *their daughter*
Gavrila Ardalionovich Ivolgin (Ganya), *their son, secretary to General Yepanchin*
Nikolai Ardalionovich Ivolgin (Kolya), *their younger son*

Ippolit Terentyev, *Kolya's friend*

Lukyan Timofeyevich Lebedev, *a rogueish amateur lawyer*
Vera, *his daughter*
Vladimir Doktorenko, *his nephew*

Antip Burdovsky, *friend of Doktorenko*

Ferdischenko, *a lodger with the Ivolgins*

Afanasy Ivanovich Totsky, *a rich man of business*

Ivan Petrovich Ptitsyn, *a money-lender*

Darya Alexeyevna, *a friend of Nastasya Filippovna*

Keller, *a pugilist*

Yevgeni Pavlovich Radomsky, *a friend of the Yepanchins*

Prince S., *his kinsman, a progressive man of affairs*

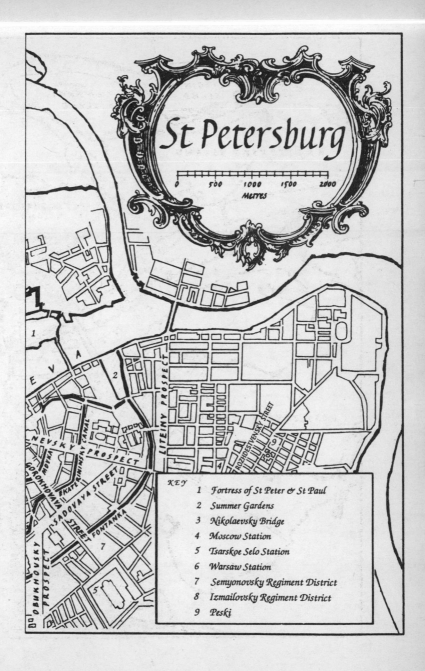

St Petersburg

0   500   1000   1500   2000
METRES

KEY
1 Fortress of St Peter & St Paul
2 Summer Gardens
3 Nikolaevsky Bridge
4 Moscow Station
5 Tsarskoe Selo Station
6 Warsaw Station
7 Semyonovsky Regiment District
8 Izmailovsky Regiment District
9 Peski

PART ONE

1

At around nine in the morning towards the end of a thawing November, the Warsaw train was approaching Petersburg at full steam. The weather was so dank and misty that it was a long time getting light; anything beyond a dozen yards to left or right of the track could hardly be made out from the carriage windows at all. Among the passengers were some returning from abroad, but it was the third-class compartments which were really crowded—for the most part with ordinary folk and business-people, not travelling long distance. As usual, everyone was tired and heavy-eyed after the night, everybody was chilled through, their faces wan-yellow to match the fog.

In one of the third-class carriages, two passengers had found themselves opposite each other by the window since day-break—both young men, both travelling light, both plainly dressed, both with rather striking features, and both at length desirous of engaging the other in conversation. Had each been aware of what was remarkable about the other at that particular moment, they would naturally have marvelled that chance had so curiously placed them opposite one another in a third-class carriage of the Warsaw–Petersburg train. One was a shortish man of about 27, with curly dark hair, almost black; his grey eyes, though small, were fiery. His nose was broad and rather flattened, and he had prominent cheek-bones; his thin lips were permanently set in a sort of insolent, derisive, almost malevolent smile; his forehead, however, was high and well formed, redeeming the unprepossessing lower portion of his face. Most noteworthy in that face was its deathly pallor, which gave the young man's otherwise strongly formed features a gaunt appearance, along with a kind of passionate, almost anguished intensity, wholly out of keeping with that coarse, insolent smile and truculently complacent expression. He was warmly wrapped up in a capacious overcoat lined with astrakhan, and had kept warm overnight, while his shivering neighbour had had to endure all the delights of a raw Russian November night, something for which he was manifestly unprepared. He was wearing a rather broad, thick, sleeveless cloak, with an enormous hood, just like winter travellers often do abroad in far-off places like Switzerland or Northern Italy, not reckoning of course on stretches as long as from Eidkuhnen to Petersburg. What had answered perfectly satisfactorily in Italy, however, turned out not to be altogether suitable for Russia. The owner of the hooded cloak was a young man, also of 26 or 27, a little above medium height, and very fair-complexioned with masses of hair; his cheeks were sunken and he had a wispy, pointed little beard, almost white in colour. His eyes were large and pale blue, and their intent gaze held something at once gentle and saturnine, filled as they were with that odd expression by which some people can detect epilepsy at a glance. For the rest, the young man's face was pleasant, refined, and clean-cut, though lacking in colour—even bluish now from the cold. The meagre, faded-silk bundle dangling from his hands appeared to contain all his travelling effects. He wore thick-soled shoes and gaiters, all very un-Russian. His dark-haired neighbour in the sheepskin coat eyed all this, partly from having nothing else to do, before enquiring at length, with that tactless smirk which sometimes so openly and carelessly expresses people's pleasure at a neighbour's misfortune:

'Chilly?'

And wriggled his shoulders.

'Very', replied his companion with the utmost readiness. 'And it's still thawing, isn't it? What if it was a real frost? I never thought it could be as cold as this at home. I'm not used to it any more.'

'Been abroad, have you?'

'Yes, Switzerland.'

'Whew! You have been on your travels!'

The dark-haired individual gave a whistle and laughed.

Conversation got under way. The fair young man in the Swiss cloak was remarkably willing to answer all the questions put by his dark-featured companion, without suspecting in the least how

completely casual and idly random some of them were. He
disclosed in passing that he had actually been away from Russia
for a long time, four years or more, that he'd been sent abroad for
health reasons, some mysterious nervous complaint to do with
epilepsy or St Vitus's dance, involving tremors and convulsions.
As he listened, the dark man grinned several times and broke into
a laugh when his question: 'Well, and did they cure you?' elicited
the reply, 'No, they didn't.'

'Ha! I expect you paid them a deal of money for nothing, and
here we still go on believing in them', the dark man remarked
caustically.

'That's absolutely right!' The intervention came from a
wretchedly dressed gentleman sitting nearby. He looked to be an
official, hardened by long years of quill-driving; he was about 40
and strongly built, with a red nose and pimply face. 'Absolutely
right, sir. All they do is bleed Russia dry and give nothing in
return!'

'Oh I'm afraid you're much mistaken in my case', rejoined the
Swiss patient in a quiet, conciliatory tone. 'Of course I can't
argue, there's a lot I don't know, but my doctor paid for my ticket
here from the little he had left—after keeping me at his own
charge for almost two years, what's more.'

'Why was that? Wasn't there anyone to pay for you?' asked the
dark man.

'You see, Mister Pavlischev, who was supporting me, died two
years ago; I wrote to Madame Yepanchina here, she's a distant
relation of mine, but I never got an answer. That's why I've come
back.'

'Come back where exactly?'

'You mean where will I stay? . . . Well, I really don't know as
yet . . . just . . .'

'Not made up your mind yet?'

At this, both listeners burst out laughing again.

'I suppose you've got all your worldly goods in that bundle?'
asked the dark young man.

'I wouldn't mind wagering you're right', put in the red-nosed
official, with an expression of considerable satisfaction, 'and
there's nothing else in the luggage-van, I'll be bound, though
poverty is no crime, one must never ever forget that.'

He turned out to be correct again: the fair young man at once confessed as much with unusual alacrity.

'That bundle of yours does have a certain significance all the same', the official went on, when their fits of laughter had subsided (it was singular that the bundle's owner had also begun to laugh eventually as he looked at them, which added to their hilarity), 'although it's a fair bet there's no bags of gold Napoleons in there, or Fredericks either, not to mention Hollanders,* all of which we can deduce from the gaiters wrapped round your foreign shoes if nothing else, still . . . if one adds in a relative like Madame Yepanchina for example, that bundle takes on quite a different meaning, assuming of course that Madame Yepanchina really is your relation and you haven't just made a mistake about that . . . which could happen to anybody, anybody at all, having, shall we say . . . an over-fertile imagination?'

'Ah, you've guessed right again', the fair young man seized on this, 'I really am nearly mistaken, I mean she's nearly not a relation; in fact I wasn't at all surprised really when I didn't get an answer in Switzerland. I expected that.'

'You wasted your money on the stamp then. Hmm . . . still at least you're open and good-natured about it, that's to be commended! Hmm . . . one does know General Yepanchin, of course sir, he's a public figure; as also the late Mr Pavlischev who supported you in Switzerland, assuming he was Nikolai Andreyevich Pavlischev, because there were two cousins. The other one's still living in the Crimea, but Nikolai Andreyevich, the deceased, he was a man of position, well connected, owned four thousand serfs in his time, sir . . .'

'That's right, he was called Nikolai Andreyevich Pavlischev', and so saying, the young man surveyed the knowledgeable gentleman with keen curiosity.

You come across these know-alls occasionally, quite often in fact, at a certain level of society. They know everything; all the restless curiosity of their mind and faculties is directed irresistibly in one direction, for want of any more important opinions or interests in life of course, as a contemporary thinker would put it. In saying 'they know everything', it should be understood, however, that their field is somewhat restricted: where so-and-so is serving, what his circle of acquaintance is, how much he's worth, where he was governor, who his wife is, how much the dowry was, who his cousin is and his second cousin, and so on and so forth, all that sort of thing. As a rule, the know-all goes round out-at-elbows and earns seventeen roubles a month. The people they know in such minute detail, of course, would never guess at this ruling passion of theirs, and yet with a good many of them the amassing of this information (a whole science in itself), acts as a positive solace; they achieve self-respect, supreme spiritual contentment even. It's a tempting field of study too. I've seen scholars, literary men, poets, political figures, all seeking and finding their highest ambitions and satisfactions within this same branch of science—actually to the extent of basing their entire career on it.

Throughout this conversation the dark young man yawned and gazed idly out of the window, impatiently anticipating the end of the journey. He was preoccupied, very much preoccupied, indeed almost on edge, as his behaviour began to verge on the odd: he would listen then not listen, look then look away, at times laughing without realizing it or knowing why he had done so.

'But permit me, whom have I the honour . . .', the pimply gentleman suddenly addressed the fair young man with the bundle.

'Prince Lev Nikolayevich Myshkin', the other responded with complete and ready frankness.

'Prince Myshkin? Lev Nikolayevich? I don't know it, sir. I can't say as I've even heard of it, sir', the official replied dubiously. 'That is, I don't mean the name, the name's historical, you can find it in Karamzin's *History*, must be there, no, it's the person, sir, and somehow you don't come across the Princes Myshkin anywhere, not even hearsay.'

'Oh, I should think not!' replied the prince at once. 'There aren't any Prince Myshkins left at all now, apart from me; I think I'm the last. As far as the older generations are concerned, some were just yeomen. My father was a sub-lieutenant in the army, incidentally, after cadet college. I've no idea how Madame Yepanchina came to be a Princess Myshkina, last of her kind as well . . .'

'Heh-heh-heh! Last of her kind! Heh-heh! That's nicely put.' The official giggled.

The dark-haired man also grinned. The prince was a little astonished at having managed to utter a witticism, however feeble.

'Imagine, I said it quite without thinking', he explained at length, surprised.

'That's plain to see, sir, plain to see', assented the official genially.

'And you studied things, Prince, with that professor of yours?' asked the dark young man all of a sudden.

'Yes . . . I studied . . .'

'Well, I've never studied anything.'

'Well I was the same, just one or two things', the prince added, almost apologetic. 'They weren't able to teach me systematically because of my illness.'

'Know the Rogozhins?' the dark man asked quickly.

'No, not at all. I know very few people in Russia, really. Are you a Rogozhin?'

'Yes I am, Rogozhin, Parfion.'

'Parfion? Not by any chance one of the Rogozhins who . . .' the official began, more solemnly than before.

'Yes, them, one of those', the young man interrupted him, brusquely impatient. He had never spoken to the pimply official once, incidentally, addressing himself exclusively to the prince from the very start.

'But . . . you mean?' The official was positively rigid with astonishment, eyes popping: his face at once assumed an expression of servile reverence, fear even. 'The son of Semyon Parfionovich Rogozhin, hereditary honorary citizen, who passed away leaving two and a half million net?'

'And just how did you find out that he left two and a half million net?' interrupted the dark young man, even now not deigning to glance at the official. 'Just look at him!' (here he indicated him with a wink for the prince's benefit). 'Just what do they expect to gain by toadying up straight away like that? Still it's true, my father has died and I'm coming home from Pskov a month late practically barefoot. My rascal of a brother didn't send me word and neither did my mother, and no money either—nothing! Like a dog! I had a fever for a whole month in Pskov.'

'And now you're going to get a cool million and a bit at the very least, heavens!' The official threw up his hands.

'Well, I ask you, what's it got to do with him?' Rogozhin nodded towards him, irritated and angry. 'I wouldn't give you a kopeck if you walked on your hands in front of me.'

'And I'll do it, I'll walk on my hands.'

'You see! And you'll get nothing, nothing, you can dance about for a week!'

'That's right! Give me nothing, that's what I deserve! And I'll dance. I'll leave my wife and little children to dance before you. Grovel! Grovel!'

'Get out of my sight!' spat Rogozhin. 'Five weeks back I was just like you', he addressed the prince, 'ran away from the old man to my aunty in Pskov with nothing but a bundle; that's where I caught the fever and took to my bed, so I wasn't there when he died. A stroke got him. God rest his soul, but before that he practically beat me to death! Believe me Prince, honest to God! If I hadn't run away then he'd have simply murdered me.'

'Had you made him angry over something?' responded the prince, regarding the millionaire in the overcoat with a somewhat singular curiosity. Now although the million and its inheritance might have been noteworthy enough in themselves, what surprised and intrigued the prince was something else; Rogozhin himself was extremely keen to engage the prince in conversation for some reason, though his need seemed to be automatic rather than something willed; somehow more out of preoccupation than actual candour, and prompted by anxiety and agitation—just so as to have someone to look at and something to chatter about. He still seemed to be ill, or feverish at least. As for the official, he continued to hover close to Rogozhin, fearing to breathe, catching and weighing every word as if searching for diamonds.

'Yes, well, he was angry of course, and maybe he had good reason', replied Rogozhin, 'but it was my brother who really got on my nerves. Mama's all right, she's an old woman, reads the lives of the martyrs and sits round with the other old women. What brother Senka says goes. And why didn't he send word in time, eh? Oh, we know don't we? All right, I was delirious. There was a telegram sent as well, so they say. But it comes to my aunty, you see. Been a widow thirty years and spends her time with the holy fools from morning till night. Worse than a nun, worse than a nun. Anyway, she was frightened by the telegram and took it to the police station without opening it, that's where it's been ever since. Konyov, Vasili Vasilich, came to the rescue and sent me a report. One night, my brother cut the tassels off the brocade on the old man's coffin, solid gold they were: "They cost a mint of money" says he. He could end up in Siberia just for that if I'd a mind, that's sacrilege, that is. Hey you, scarecrow!' he addressed the official. 'What's the law on that? Is it sacrilege or not?'

'Oh yes, sacrilege!' assented the official at once.

'You get Siberia for that?'

'Oh yes, Siberia! Siberia straight away!'

'They still think I'm ill', Rogozhin went on to the prince, 'but I sneaked into this carriage and away, better or not, and no word to anybody: open up the gates, dear brother Semyon Semyonich! He slandered me to my father, rest his soul, that's something I do know. Still, it's the truth, I did annoy the old man over Nastasya Filippovna. That was all my fault. Led into temptation.'

'Over Nastasya Filippovna?' mumbled the obsequious official, as if something was dawning on him.

'You don't know her, do you?' Rogozhin shouted at him, exasperated.

'Indeed I do!' replied the official triumphantly.

'Oh, really? There's plenty Nastasya Filippovnas in this world! And you're an impudent creature, I may say! There you are, I knew some creature like this would fasten on to me before I could turn round!' he continued, addressing the prince.

'Perhaps I do know her, sir, for all that!' the official was much agitated—'Lebedev knows! You, your highness, are pleased to speak harshly, but what if I can prove my words? Is it not that same Nastasya Filippovna who caused you to be chastised with a hazel rod by your father? Her surname's Barashkova, and she's a lady of quality, so to speak, also a princess of some kind, and she associates exclusively with a certain Totsky, Afanasy Ivanovich, a very wealthy landowner, director of various companies, and a great friend of General Yepanchin on that account . . .'

'Oho, so that's your game, is it?' Rogozhin was at last genuinely surprised. 'Well damnation, he really does know.'

'Everything! Lebedev knows everything! Your highness, I

spent two months going about with Alex Likhachov after his father died as well, so I know it all, all the ins and outs; it got so that he wouldn't stir a step without Lebedev. Nowadays he's in the debtors' prison, but at that time I had the opportunity of getting to know Armance and Coralie, and Princess Patskaya and Nastasya Filippovna too, and got to know a good many other things besides.'

'Nastasya Filippovna? You don't mean Likhachov and her . . .' Rogozhin stared grimly at him with pale and tremulous lips.

'N-not at all! N-n-nothing! Nothing as I live!' the official recollected himself and hurried on, 'I mean no amount of money could get Likhachov what he wanted! Not like Armance. It was just Totsky, he's the only one. Well, she used to sit in her own box at the Bolshoi or the French Theatre. There's plenty of talk among the officers there, but even they can't prove anything: "there she is, that's the famous Nastasya Filippovna", and that's about it; as for anything beyond that—nothing! Because there isn't anything.'

'That's just how it is', confirmed Rogozhin, scowling morosely. 'Zalyozhev used to tell me the same thing at the time. I was running across Nevsky Prospect, Prince, wearing my father's three-year-old fur jacket, just as she was coming out of a shop and getting into her carriage. I went hot all over. Then I come across Zalyozhev, he's nothing like me—he goes round looking like a barber's assistant, with a monocle in his eye, while we live it up at my old man's in our dubbined boots, eating cabbage soup without meat. She's not on your level, says he, she's a princess, says he; her name's Nastasya Filippovna, surname Barashkova, and she lives with Totsky. He doesn't know how to get rid of her, because he's reached a good age now, 55, and he wants to get married to the most ravishing beauty in Petersburg. Then he gave me the idea that I could see Nastasya Filippovna that very day at the Bolshoi ballet, sitting in her own box at the side of the stalls. Just try and get out of my old man's house to go to the ballet—I'd catch it for certain, he'd kill me! Still, I did sneak out on the quiet for an hour and saw Nastasya Filippovna again; I didn't sleep a wink that night. In the morning, the old man, God rest him, gives me two five-per-cent bonds, five thousand each. Sell them, says he, and take seven thousand five hundred to

Andreyev's office, pay it over and bring what's left straight back to me, no dilly-dallying; I'll be waiting for you. Well, I sold the bonds but I didn't go near Andreyev's, I went straight to the English shop and chose a pair of ear-rings with a sweet little diamond the size of a nut in each one. I was four hundred short but they trusted me when I gave them my name. Over to Zalyozhev's with the ear-rings: out with the story and let's away, friend, to Nastasya Filippovna's. We set off. I haven't the slightest recollection of where I walked, what was in front of me or to either side. We went straight into her entrance hall and she came out to us herself. At the time I didn't let on it was me: "from Parfion Rogozhin", says Zalyozhev, "to mark his meeting with you yesterday; please deign to accept this." She unwrapped it, peeped inside, and smiled: "Thank your friend Mister Rogozhin for his kind thought", she says, then said her goodbyes and went out. Well! Why didn't I just die on the spot? I mean I only went because I thought I wouldn't come back alive! I felt the most annoying part was that beast Zalyozhev taking all the credit himself. I was dressed like a lackey and I'm not very tall either; there I stood speechless and shy, just staring at her, while he was dressed up to the nines, primped and pomaded, all pink in his check cravat, bowing and scraping—why she very likely took him for me! "Well", I said as we left, "just don't go getting any ideas in that quarter, understand?" He laughs: "And how exactly are you going to settle your account with Semyon Parfionich?" To tell the truth I was on the point of throwing myself in the water there and then, without going home, but I thought: "What do I care, really?" I returned to the house like a damned soul.'

   'Oh! Oh dear!' the official made a wry face as a shudder ran through him. 'You know the deceased used to hound people to death for ten roubles, never mind ten thousand', he nodded to the prince, who in turn surveyed Rogozhin curiously; the latter seemed even paler at that moment.

   ' "Hound to death"!' Rogozhin broke in. 'What do you know about it? He found out', he continued, addressing the prince, 'and in any case Zalyozhev was blurting it out to everybody we met on the way. The old man got hold of me and locked me in upstairs, then laid into me for an hour. "That's just a foretaste, I'll be back to bid you goodnight as well." And what do you think?

The old chap went round to Nastasya Filippovna's, bowed to the ground, weeping and pleading with her; in the end she brought the box out to him and snapped: "There's your ear-rings then, old greybeard, and they're worth ten times more to me now that I know the risk Parfion ran in getting them. Take my greetings to Parfion Semyonich and thank him." Meanwhile I borrowed twenty roubles off Seryozha Protushin with Mama's blessing and got the train to Pskov, where I arrived in a fever; the old women started reading the saints' days out over me with me sitting there drunk. Then I went the round of the taverns spending my last kopeck and lay about the streets all night dead to the world. By morning I was really ill, and the dogs had been worrying at me in the night as well. I had a hard time coming to.'

'Never mind, sir, never mind, Nastasya Filippovna will sing a different tune now', tittered the official, rubbing his hands, 'what are ear-rings to us, sir, we'll make it up to her for those ear-rings . . .'

'If you utter one more word about Nastasya Filippovna, then by the good lord I'll thrash you, whether you went round with Likhachov or not', Rogozhin shouted, seizing him powerfully by the arm.

'If you do thrash me, it means you're not rejecting me! Go on! If you do, it seals . . . Ah, we've arrived!'

And indeed they were pulling into the station. Although Rogozhin had said he'd gone off without telling anybody, several people were waiting for him. They were shouting and waving their caps in the air.

'Look at that, and Zalyozhev's here as well!' Rogozhin muttered; his smile as he surveyed them was both triumphant and sardonic; he turned abruptly to the prince. 'I don't know why I've taken a fancy to you, Prince, maybe it was just the time and place, but then I met him too' (he indicated Lebedev) 'and I certainly don't feel that way towards him. Come along to my house, Prince, we'll have those silly little gaiters off you, get you into a marten coat, first class, you shall have a frock-coat, first class, white waistcoat, whatever you want, I'll stuff your pockets full of money and . . . we'll go off to Nastasya Filippovna! Will you come or not?'

'Listen to him, Prince Lev Nikolayevich!' urged Lebedev with weighty solemnity. 'Don't miss the opportunity! Oh, don't miss it!...'

Prince Myshkin half rose and politely extended a hand to Rogozhin, saying courteously:

'I shall come with the greatest of pleasure and I am most grateful for your regard. I may come today even, if I am able to, because I tell you frankly, I'd taken a great liking to you, particularly when you were telling me the story of the diamond ear-rings. Even before that, though you have such a gloomy face. I thank you also for the promised clothes and the overcoat, as I will certainly have need of them soon. As for money, I have hardly a penny to my name at the present moment.'

'There'll be money by evening, come along!'

'There will, there will!', Lebedev took it up, 'by evening and on until dawn there will!'

'And are you a great admirer of the female sex, Prince? Tell me in advance.'

'I? N-n-no! You see, I'm ... Perhaps you don't know, but because of the illness I was born with, I have no experience of women at all.'

'Well, if that's so', Rogozhin exclaimed, 'you're an out-and-out holy fool, and God loves the likes of you!'

'Such as these the Lord God loveth', echoed the official.

'And you follow me, pen-pusher', said Rogozhin to Lebedev as they all left the carriage.

Lebedev had finished up by gaining his ends. Soon the noisy throng was moving off in the direction of Voznesensky Prospect. The prince's route lay towards Liteinaya. It was raw and dank; inquiries from passers-by established that it was two miles or so to his destination, and he made up his mind to take a cab.

2

GENERAL Yepanchin resided in his own house just off Liteinaya, towards the Church of the Transfiguration. Besides this splendid dwelling, five-sixths of which was rented out, the general possessed another huge house on Sadovaya which also brought in a vast income. In addition to the two houses, he had an extensive and highly profitable estate outside the city; there was a factory of sorts too, in Petersburg province. It was common knowledge that, many years before, General Yepanchin had been a tax-farmer. Nowadays his voice carried weight in a number of reputable business concerns. He passed for a man of considerable wealth, with large responsibilities and influential contacts. In certain quarters, including his own department, he had been able to render himself absolutely indispensable. And yet it was also common knowledge that Ivan Fedorovich Yepanchin was the uneducated son of a private soldier; certainly this latter circumstance could only redound to his credit, but the general, intelligent man though he was, did have a number of minor pardonable weaknesses and disliked any hints in that direction. Nevertheless, he was intelligent and astute, that was undeniable. It was his way, for example, never to push himself forward where it was better to remain in the background, and many people valued him for this unassuming behaviour, the fact that he always knew his place. If only those judges could have known what sometimes went on in the heart of that same Ivan Fedorovich who knew his place so well! Although he certainly possessed a good deal of practical experience in day-to-day affairs, along with a number of remarkable abilities, he liked to convey the impression of being the executant of someone else's ideas rather than a man with a mind of his own; to play the 'loyalty without flattery' role—even, such are the times we live in—the heartfelt Russian patriot. In this latter connection he had gone so far as to get himself involved in a number of amusing incidents, but the general never repined, however amusing the situation; besides he was a lucky man, even at cards, and played for enormously high stakes. Far from wishing to conceal this supposed little weakness for the pasteboards, so materially useful to him on so many occasions, he actually flaunted it. He moved in mixed circles, but of course always among 'first-rate' people. Everything lay ahead of him, there was no hurry, never any hurry, all would come to him in its own good time. After all, General Yepanchin was, as they say, in the very prime of his years, not a day over 56, a flourishing age certainly, an age when *real* life can truly be said to begin. His state of health, facial coloration, firm (though blackened) teeth, the stocky, thick-set build, the grave morning expression at work in the department, the genial one in the evening at cards or attending his highness—everything contributed to his present and future success and strewed his excellency's path with roses.

The general was possessed of a flourishing family. True, not all was roses there, but there was a great deal else on which his excellency had for long been seriously concentrating his fondest hopes and ambitions. Indeed, what ambitions in life are more important and sacrosanct than parental ones? What should one cleave to if not to one's family? The general's family consisted of his wife and three grown-up daughters. He had got married long ago, when he was still an army lieutenant, to a girl of about his own age who possessed neither beauty nor education and brought only fifty serfs with her all told—though these had formed the basis of his later fortune. The general had never subsequently grumbled about his early marriage, never referred to it slightingly as a rash youthful infatuation, and respected (and occasionally feared) his wife to the point of actual love. The general's wife was a Princess Myshkina, of a very ancient though hardly brilliant lineage, and piqued herself greatly on her ancestry. A certain man of influence, one of those whose patronage costs them nothing incidentally, agreed at that time to concern himself with the young princess's marriage. He opened doors for the young officer and pushed him through—though he didn't need pushing even, a single glance would have been amply sufficient. Barring a few occasions, the pair had passed their long life together amicably. In her very early years the general's wife, being a born princess and the last of her line, as well as through her own personal qualities perhaps, had contrived to secure herself a number of patronesses in high places. Later on, through the wealth and official position of her husband, she began to feel somewhat at home in these exalted circles.

In recent years the general's daughters, Alexandra, Adelaida, and Aglaya had grown to maturity. True, all three were only Yepanchins, but they were descended from princes on their mother's side and had considerable dowries. Their father had prospects of achieving a very high position himself and, what is also quite important, all three were remarkably pretty, including the eldest, Alexandra, who was already over 25. The middle daughter was 23, while the youngest, Aglaya, had just turned 20. This youngest one was a great beauty in fact, and beginning to attract considerable attention in society. Even this wasn't all; the three were remarkable for their cultivation, wit, and accomplishments. They were well known for the great affection they bore one another and for standing by their sisters. There were even stories of the two elder girls making sacrifices for the sake of their youngest sister, the idol of the whole household. Rather than wanting to cut a figure in society, they were somewhat too modest and retiring. No one could accuse them of being haughty or supercilious, though people were aware that they had their pride and knew their own worth. The eldest was musical and the middle one was a fine artist, but no one knew this for many years; it had only been discovered very recently, and that by chance. In a word, a very great deal was said in praise of them. Still, well wishers were not universal. The number of books they read was commented on with horror. They were in no hurry to get married, and though they valued a certain circle of acquaintance, it was in a restrained fashion. This was all the more remarkable in the light of what was generally known of their father's character, desires, and ambitions.

It was already nearly eleven o'clock when the prince rang the bell at the general's apartments. He lived on the first floor and occupied rooms on as modest a scale as possible commensurate with his dignity. A liveried servant opened the door to the prince, and lengthy explanations followed, as at first the fellow looked suspiciously at him and at his bundle. Finally, after repeated and precise declarations that he really was Prince Myshkin and had urgent and immediate business with the general, the puzzled man conducted him into a small ante-room nearby, close to the study and leading into the actual reception-room itself, before handing him on to another fellow whose morning duty it was to announce visitors to the general. This second man, who wore a tailcoat and a grave expression, was past 40; he was his excellency's study-attendant and announcer, and in consequence had a high opinion of himself.

'Wait in the reception-room and leave your bundle here', he said, slowly and solemnly seating himself in his armchair; he looked at the prince with severe astonishment as the latter at once disposed himself next to him, his bundle in his arms.

'If you will permit me', said the prince, 'I would prefer to wait here with you, what would I do there on my own?'

'You cannot wait in the ante-room, because you are a visitor, in other words a guest. You wish to see the general in person?'

The servant clearly couldn't reconcile himself to admitting a visitor like this, and made up his mind to inquire yet again.

'Yes, I have business . . .', the prince began.

'I am not asking you what business precisely—my duty is simply to announce your presence. Until the secretary arrives, however, I have said I will not do so.'

The man's suspicions were apparently intensifying by the minute; the prince was too much a departure from the norm of day-to-day visitors, and although fairly often, almost every day in fact, the general had perforce to receive guests of the most varied nature at a certain hour, especially on *business*, the servant was very dubious, despite this flexible discretion; he had to have the secretary's sanction for the announcement.

'And you're sure . . . from abroad?' he felt almost compelled to ask at length—and lost the thread at once; perhaps he wanted to ask: 'Are you really Prince Myshkin?'

'Yes, just off the train. I think you were going to ask if I was really Prince Myshkin, but you restrained yourself out of politeness.'

'Hmm . . .', grunted the lackey, disconcerted.

'I assure you I didn't lie to you and you won't have to answer for me. My appearance and my bundle are nothing extraordinary: at the present moment my circumstances are none of the best.'

'Hmm. That isn't what I'm concerned about, as a matter of fact. I am obliged to announce you, and the secretary will come out to you directly, unless you . . . Well, that's the long and short of it, that "unless". You haven't come to ask for money, if I may be so bold as to ask?'

'Oh no, you may be quite easy on that score. I have other business.'

'You must forgive me, but I was going by your appearance. Just wait for the secretary then; he is engaged with a certain colonel at the moment, and the . . . company secretary is due also.'

'If I'm to wait a good while, I would ask you then if there is anywhere I can smoke here? I have a pipe and tobacco with me.'

'Sm-o-ke?' the attendant threw him a glance of amazed contempt, as if unable to credit his ears. 'Smoke? No, you may not smoke here, moreover you should be ashamed to entertain such a thought. Heh . . . the idea, sir!'

'Oh, I didn't mean in this room; I know what's expected; I meant I'd go outside somewhere, wherever you said, I've got the habit, you see and I haven't had a smoke for three hours or so. Still, as you like, there's a saying, you know: when in Rome . . .'

'Well, how am I going to announce someone like you?' the lackey couldn't help muttering. 'Firstly, you shouldn't be here at all, you should be sitting in the reception-room, because you're by way of being a visitor, otherwise a guest, and I'll be held responsible . . . And do you intend living here, is that it?' he added, again looking askance at the prince's bundle which was obviously still causing him unease.

'No. I don't think so. Even if I were invited, I shouldn't stay. I've just come to introduce myself, that's all. No more than that.'

'What? Introduce yourself?' asked the servant, surprised and by now doubly suspicious. 'Why did you say at first that you'd come on business, then?'

'Well, hardly business! I mean, there is one matter if you like, just a case of asking advice, but I'm really here to introduce myself, since I'm Prince Myshkin and Madame Yepanchina is also the last of the Myshkina princesses; apart from us, there are no Myshkins left.'

'So you're a relation as well?' The lackey started, by now thoroughly alarmed.

'That's hardly true either. Still, to stretch a point, we are kin, but so distant that really it can't be counted. I did once write to the general's wife from abroad, but she didn't reply. All the same, I decided I had to get in touch on my return. I'm explaining all this to resolve your misgivings, as I can see you're still uneasy: just announce that it's Prince Myshkin and that in itself will explain the reason for my visit. If they receive me, all well and good, if not, perhaps that will be all to the good as well. I don't think I'll be rejected though: Madame Yepanchina will surely want to see the senior and only representative of her line, she is very proud of her ancestry—that I've certainly heard of her.'

To all appearances, the prince's conversation was simple and straightforward; the simpler it was, however, the more absurd it became in the present instance. The experienced servant could not fail to be aware that what was perfectly acceptable man to man was absolutely unacceptable between *guest* and man. Since servants are a good deal brighter than their lords and masters usually take them for, it dawned on him that one of two things applied here: either the prince was simply some kind of vagabond and had certainly come round begging, or he was a simpleton lacking any sense of self-respect; what self-respecting intelligent prince would be sitting in an ante-room telling a lackey about his private affairs? Either way, would he not be called upon to answer for him?

'All the same, you would be better waiting in the reception-room', he pointed out as urgently as he could.

'Well now, if I'd been sitting there, I wouldn't have been able to explain everything to you', the prince laughed blithely, 'and you would still have been anxious, looking at my cloak and bundle. So now perhaps there's no need to wait for the secretary, you can go and announce me yourself.'

'I can't announce a visitor such as yourself without the sanction of the secretary, especially since I was instructed just now that they were not to be disturbed on any account while the colonel is there; only Gavrila Ardalionich goes in without announcement.'

'He's an official?'

'Gavrila Ardalionich you mean? No. He works for the company on a private basis. At least put your bundle over here.'

'I was thinking of that myself, if it's all right. Can I take my cloak off as well?'

'Of course, you can hardly go in there with a cloak on.'

The prince rose and hastily took off his cloak, revealing a worn but tolerably decent and well-cut jacket. His waistcoat displayed a steel chain. From it hung a silver Geneva watch.

Although the prince was a simpleton—the lackey had already decided this—it seemed improper on the part of the general's attendant to pursue this conversation between himself and the visitor, despite the fact that he felt drawn to the prince for some reason, in his own fashion that is. From another point of view, however, he aroused in him a decided feeling of outright indignation.

'And when does Madame Yepanchina receive guests?' the prince enquired, seating himself in his former place.

'That is not my affair, sir. Different times depending on the visitor. Her milliner comes at eleven. Gavrila Ardalionich is received before others, sometimes to early lunch.'

'Your rooms are warmer in winter than they are abroad', the prince observed, 'although it's warmer outside there, a Russian can't stand it indoors in winter, he's not used to it.'

'Don't they have heating?'

'Yes, but the houses are constructed differently, the stoves and windows I mean.'

'Hmm! Have you been travelling long, sir?'

'Four years. Actually I mostly stayed in one place, in the country.'

'You've got out of the way of things here then?'

'That's certainly true. Believe it or not, I'm amazed I haven't forgotten how to speak Russian. Here I am talking to you and thinking to myself: "Aren't I speaking it well?" Perhaps that's why I'm talking so much. Really, since yesterday, I keep wanting to speak Russian.'

'Hmm! Ahem! Did you live in Petersburg before then?' Despite his firm intentions, the lackey found it impossible not to go along with a conversation as polite and courteous as this.

'Petersburg? Hardly ever, just passed through occasionally. I knew nothing about the place before and now I hear there's so much new happening, that people who were well-informed before now have to re-learn it all, so they say. There's a good deal of talk about the courts.'

'Hmm! . . . Courts. Courts there certainly are. And are the courts fairer over there or not?'

'I don't know. I've heard a good deal said in praise of our courts. Then again we don't have capital punishment.'

'They have that there?'

'Yes. I saw it in France, in Lyons. Schneider took me there with him.'

'Do they hang them?'

'No, in France they always cut their heads off.'

'Do they shout out or anything?'

'Heavens, no! It's instantaneous. They put the man in position and this broad knife drops down, it's mechanical, they call it a guillotine, it's a heavy drop, lots of power . . . The head jumps away so fast you'd miss it if you blinked. The preliminaries are grim. That's when they announce the sentence, get the machine ready, bind the prisoner, and take him up to the scaffold, that's the horrible part! The crowds come rushing round, even the women, though they don't like women to see it.'

'Not the thing for them.'

'Of course not! Of course not! Agony like that! . . . The criminal was an intelligent man, strong, brave, getting on in years, his name was Legros. Well, I tell you, believe me or believe me not, he mounted the scaffold—and wept, white as a sheet. Is that possible? Isn't that a horrible thing? Who on earth weeps because they're afraid? I had never conceived that anybody could weep from fear, not a child mind you, a man of 45, who'd never wept before. What on earth must be taking place in the soul to convulse a man like that? It's a violation of the soul, nothing less! It is written: "Thou shalt not kill"; because he killed, should he be killed as well? No, that's wrong. I saw it all of a month ago and I can picture it to this day. I've dreamed about it half a dozen times.'

The prince had grown more animated as he spoke, and a faint flush came into his pale face, though his voice was no louder than before. The flunkey observed him with sympathetic interest, unwilling, it seemed, to take his eyes off him; perhaps he too was a man with an imagination and some reasoning ability.

'Still, it's a good thing the agony's not prolonged', he remarked, 'when the head comes off.'

'Do you know', the prince seized on this warmly, 'everybody makes exactly the same point that you have, that's why the machine, the guillotine was invented. But something occurred to me when I was there: what if that's actually worse? You may think that's silly, ludicrous even, but with a little imagination even an idea like that can flash into your mind. Just think: if there was torture, for instance; there'd be suffering and wounds, bodily agony, all of which would distract you from the mental suffering, you would only have the torment of your physical injuries right up to the point of death. After all, the greatest, the most intense pain lies not so much in injuries perhaps, so much as the fact that you know for certain that in an hour's time, then in ten minutes, then thirty seconds, then now, at this moment, the soul will take wing from the body and you will cease to be a man, and that this is certain to happen; the main thing is that it's *certain*. You put your head under the blade and you hear it sliding towards you, it's that quarter of a second which is the most terrible of all. It's not just some fancy of mine, you know, lots of people have said the same thing. I'm so convinced of this that I'll tell you straight out what I think. To kill for murder is an immeasurably greater evil than the actual crime itself. Judicial murder is immeasurably more horrible than one committed by a robber. Someone killed by a robber, knifed at night in a forest or somewhere, certainly keeps hoping for rescue right up to the last second. There have been instances of people whose throats have been cut still hoping, or running away, or pleading for their lives. But all this final hope, which makes dying ten times easier is taken away by that *certain*; the sentence is pronounced and the whole agony resides in the fact that there's no escape. There's no greater torture in the world than that. Fetch a soldier and stand him right in front of a cannon during a battle and fire at him, he'll go on hoping; but read out a *certain* death sentence to that same soldier and he'll go off his head or burst into tears. Who can say that human nature can bear a thing like that without going mad? Why this disgusting, pointless, unnecessary mockery? Perhaps there exists a man who has had his sentence read out to him and been allowed to suffer before being told: "Be off, you've been pardoned." That man could tell you perhaps. Christ himself spoke of such agony and terror. No, a man should not be treated so!'

The servant, though he could not have expressed all this like the prince, took in the gist at least, as his softened expression clearly showed.

'If you really want a smoke', he said, 'you can, I dare say, if you're quick about it. They might just call you and you'd not be there. You see the door under the stairs there. Go through that and there's a box-room on your right: it'll be all right in there but be sure to open the window, it's not allowed you see . . .'

The prince, however, had no time to go off for his smoke. A young man holding some papers suddenly came into the ante-room, and the lackey began helping him off with his fur coat. The young man looked narrowly at the prince.

'This gentleman, Gavrila Ardalionich', began the servant, confidential to the point of familiarity, 'says he is a Prince Myshkin, a relation of the mistress, he's come from abroad on the train, with just a bundle in his hand, only . . .'

The prince heard no more as the servant started whispering. Gavrila Ardalionovich listened carefully and glanced at the prince with considerable curiosity; finally he stopped listening and came eagerly over to him.

'You're Prince Myshkin?' he enquired with the utmost courtesy and grace. He was a very good-looking young man of about 28, slender and fair, of medium height with a small imperial beard. His face was both intelligent and strikingly handsome, but his smile, for all its politeness, had something slightly too refined about it; the teeth it displayed were just a little too even and pearly white; his gaze, for all its apparent unaffected geniality, was just a little too keen and searching.

'When he's alone I expect he looks quite different and perhaps never laughs at all', the prince sensed somehow.

The prince made his explanations as best he could, briefly recounting more or less what he had told the servant, and Rogozhin before him. Gavrila Ardalionovich meanwhile appeared to be recalling something.

'Was it not you', he asked, 'who was good enough to send a letter a year ago, or perhaps more recently, to Elizaveta Prokofievna, from Switzerland if I remember rightly?'

'I did indeed.'

'Then they know you here and will surely remember. Have you come to see his excellency? I'll announce you directly . . . He'll be free presently. Only you should . . . you should wait in the reception-room till then . . . Why is the gentleman here?' he addressed the lackey severely.

'I kept telling him but he didn't want to . . .'

At that moment the study door suddenly opened and a military man with a briefcase in his hand emerged, still conversing loudly as he took his leave.

'Are you there, Ganya?' came a shout from the study. 'Come in here please!'

Gavrila Ardalionovich nodded to the prince and hurried through into the study.

A couple of minutes later the door opened once more and Gavrila Ardalionovich's voice was heard, affable and sonorous: 'Please come in, Prince!'

3

GENERAL Ivan Fedorovich Yepanchin stood in the middle of his sanctum and watched with considerable curiosity as the prince came in; he even took two paces towards him. The prince advanced and introduced himself.

'So then', the general responded, 'how may I be of service?'

'I have no pressing business at all; my intention was solely to make your acquaintance. I would not wish to incommode you, since I do not know your receiving hours or other arrangements . . . but I'm just off the train myself . . . from Switzerland.'

The general was within an inch of smiling but bethought himself and managed to suppress it; on further reflection he narrowed his eyes and surveyed his guest once more from head to foot, before swiftly motioning him to a chair and sitting down himself at a slight angle; he then turned towards the prince, impatiently expectant. Ganya stood in the corner by the bureau, leafing through some papers.

'I have little time available for making acquaintances as a rule', said the general, 'but since you have some purpose of your own, of course, then . . .'

'I felt sure', the prince interrupted, 'that you would see some set purpose behind my visit, but I assure you that, apart from the pleasure of making your acquaintance, I have no private end to pursue.'

'The pleasure on my part of course is very considerable also, but life cannot be all relaxation; sometimes, you know, there are affairs to attend to . . . Besides, so far I cannot for the life of me see that we have any common interest . . . any reason, so to speak . . .'

'No reason, certainly, and of course, little in common. Since if I am Prince Myshkin and your wife is of our lineage, that does not constitute a reason of course. I quite understand that. However, that is my sole pretext for this meeting. I have been away from Russia for nearly four years, longer even; and when I left I was off my head! I knew nothing then and know less now. I am in need of well-disposed people; I even have a certain business matter on my mind and I don't know where to turn. Back in Berlin I thought: "They're practically kinfolk, I'll start with them; perhaps we'll be of use to one another, they to me and I to them—if they are good people." I had heard that you were good people.'

'I'm obliged to you, sir.' The general was disconcerted. 'May I enquire where you are staying?'

'I have nowhere to stay as yet.'

'So, it's straight from the train to me? And . . . with your luggage?'

'My luggage is only one small bundle of linen, nothing else; I usually just carry it. I'll find a room by evening.'

'So you still intend to seek a room?'

'Oh yes, of course.'

'Going by what you said, I might have thought you were coming straight to me.'

'That might have been the case, but not otherwise than by your invitation. I have to confess that I shouldn't have stayed even if invited; no particular reason, it's just . . . the way I am.'

'Well, it's a good thing I didn't invite you then, nor will I now. Permit me further, Prince, to clear matters up once and for all: since we agreed just now that there is nothing more to say between us on the score of family ties—though of course it would have been extremely flattering to me, it remains . . .'

'It remains to get up and leave?' The prince half-rose, laughing cheerfully, despite the obvious difficulty of his situation. 'And to be really truthful, General, although I know precisely nothing about local manners, or people's way of life here, things have turned out between us exactly the way I thought they would. Well, perhaps that's how it ought to be . . . I got no reply to my letter that time either . . . Well, goodbye and I'm sorry to have inconvenienced you.'

The prince's expression was so kindly at that moment, his smile so devoid of the faintest hint of ill feeling, that the general halted all of a sudden and looked at his guest in a different manner; the alteration in his expression was instantaneous.

'Look here, Prince', he said in quite a different tone, 'I don't know you, after all, but Elizaveta Prokofievna might like to see her namesake . . . Wait a while if you wish, and if time isn't pressing.'

'Oh, I have plenty of time; my time is absolutely my own' (at this the prince placed his soft round hat on the table). 'I confess that I was relying on Elizaveta Prokofievna perhaps remembering my letter. Just now, while I was waiting, your servant suspected that I had come to beg money from you; I noticed it and no doubt you have issued strict instructions on that score; honestly, I haven't come on that account, truly I've simply come to make contact with people. Only I do rather feel that I've inconvenienced you and it makes me uneasy.'

'Well, Prince', said the general, smiling jovially, 'if you really are the man you seem, it will indeed be a pleasure to make your acquaintance; but as you see, I'm a busy man and I've got to sit down presently and look through some papers and sign them, then I have to go off to his highness, then to the department, so the upshot is that, though I'm glad to see people . . . decent people, that is . . . but . . . However, I'm so convinced you are a person of excellent breeding that . . . How old are you, Prince?'

'Twenty-six.'

'Is that so? And I was thinking you were much younger.'

'Yes, they say I've got a baby-face. I'll soon learn not to get in your way, because I hate to inconvenience people myself . . . After all, it seems to me that we're such different people to all appearances . . . for all sorts of reasons, that we just can't have many points in common, but, you know, I don't believe that last idea myself, because it often just seems that way, that there are no points of contact, but they are very much there . . . it's people's laziness that makes them categorize each other on sight, so they can't find anything . . . Perhaps I'm boring you?

You seem to . . .'

'Just one thing, sir: do you have means of support of any kind? Or do you intend taking up any line of work? Forgive me for being so . . .'

'Heavens, I appreciate your question and understand your implication. I have no means of support for the present and no work, also for the present. I must see about that. The money I had wasn't mine; Schneider, the professor who taught and treated me in Switzerland, gave me enough for the journey and no more, so I only have kopecks left. There is one matter I need advice about, but . . .'

'Tell me, what exactly do you propose to live on for the moment, and what are your plans?' the general broke in.

'I want to work at something.'

'Ah, but you're a philosopher; still . . . have you any particular skills or abilities, preferably the kind you can earn your daily bread by, pardon me again for . . .'

'Oh, no need to apologize. No, sir, I don't think I possess any talents or any special aptitudes; the contrary in fact, because as an invalid I never had a proper education. As regards bread, it seems to me . . .'

The general interrupted once more to put further questions. The prince told him what has already been narrated. It turned out that the general had heard of the late Pavlischev and had even been personally acquainted with him. Why Pavlischev had concerned himself with his welfare the prince was unable to explain—perhaps it was simply a matter of friendship between him and the prince's late father. The prince had been orphaned while still a small child and had spent his whole life growing up in various villages, as his health demanded country air. Pavlischev had entrusted him to the care of some old lady landowners, relatives of his; a governess had been engaged for him to begin with, and later a tutor; he stated incidentally, that although he recalled everything, he could explain little satisfactorily, as there was much he had not been aware of. The frequent bouts of his illness had made almost a complete idiot of him (the prince's own word). He concluded by saying that Pavlischev had met Professor Schneider in Berlin one day, a Swiss specializing in this very type of illness; he had an establishment in Valais canton in

Switzerland, where he used his own methods to effect cures in cases of idiotism and madness, involving cold water and gymnastics. He undertook to teach his patients and supervise their overall spiritual development; Pavlischev had sent him to Schneider some five years before, and had died suddenly himself two years ago, without having made any further arrangements. Schneider had kept him on and continued treating him for almost two more years; he had not cured him but had helped him a great deal, and had now finally sent him back to Russia at his own request and as a result of certain unforeseen circumstances.

The general was greatly surprised at all this.

'And you have no one in Russia, absolutely no one?' he asked.

'At the moment, no one . . . but I have hopes, besides I have received a letter . . .'

'At least', the general intervened, missing the mention of the letter, 'you did learn something and your illness won't prevent you taking on some straightforward work—in an office, say?'

'Oh certainly not. As regards work, I'd be very pleased; I very much want to see for myself what I'm capable of doing. I was studying all the time over the four years, though not really properly, it was the professor's special system; I did manage to read a great many Russian books in that time.'

'Russian books? That must mean you can write without mistakes?'

'Oh, I certainly can.'

'Splendid, sir; and handwriting?'

'My handwriting is excellent. I do have a talent there, if you like; I'm a real calligraphist. Allow me to write something for you now as a specimen', said the prince with enthusiasm.

'Please do. It would be useful even . . . And I do appreciate this willingness of yours Prince, you really are most kind.'

'You have such beautiful writing materials, all these pencils and pens, this beautiful thick paper . . . It's a beautiful study you have! I recognize this landscape; it's a Swiss view. I'm sure the artist painted from nature and I'm sure I've seen the place: it's in Uri canton . . .'

'Very possibly, though it was bought here. Ganya, give the prince some paper; here's pen and paper, on this table if you will. What's this?' The general addressed Ganya, who had meanwhile taken a large photographic portrait from his briefcase and handed it to him. 'Bah! Nastasya Filippovna! Did she send this to you? Did she? Herself?' he asked Ganya, consumed with curiosity.

'She gave it to me just now, when I was wishing her a happy birthday. I've been asking her for one for a long time. I don't know if it wasn't a hint on her part that I came with empty hands, no present on a day like this', added Ganya, smiling unpleasantly.

'I doubt it', the general interrupted with conviction. 'What a strange cast of mind you have, really! She wouldn't bother hinting . . . anyway she's not in the least mercenary. What would you think of giving her in any case? You'd need thousands! Not a portrait anyway! Incidentally, she hasn't asked you for a portrait yet, has she?'

'No, not yet: perhaps she never will. Of course you remember the party this evening? You are one of those specifically invited.'

'I remember, I remember, naturally, I'll be there. It's her birthday after all, 25! Hmm . . . you know, Ganya, I think I'll let you into a secret, prepare yourself. She's promised Afanasy Ivanovich and myself to give her final answer this evening: to be or not to be! So be ready, you've been warned.'

Ganya was disconcerted all of a sudden, and even turned a little pale.

'Did she promise for certain?' he asked, his voice unsteady.

'She gave us her word the day before yesterday. We both pestered her so much we forced it out of her. She just asked us not to let you know in advance.'

The general was staring at Ganya; the latter's embarrassment was clearly not to his liking.

'You will recall, Ivan Fedorovich', said Ganya, nervous and hesitant, 'that she gave me complete freedom of decision until such time as she had made her own mind up, and after that it was still up to me . . .'

'But you surely don't . . . you surely aren't . . .?' The general was suddenly alarmed.

'I haven't said anything.'

'But good lord, what are you trying to do to us?'

'Oh I'm not refusing. Perhaps I didn't express myself very well . . .'

'I should think you're not refusing!' snapped the general, no longer bothering to conceal his exasperation. 'It's not a question of your *not refusing*, it's a matter of your willingness, your pleasure, your joy in accepting her consent . . . how are things at home?'

'What's there to say? My word is law at home, it's just my father playing the fool as usual, his behaviour's really outrageous these days; I'm not speaking to him actually, but I keep him on a tight rein; really, if it hadn't been for mother I'd have shown him the door. Mother's always in tears of course, and my sister's in a foul temper, but I told them once and for all that I'm the master of my fate and that in the house I wish to be . . . obeyed. At least I impressed that on my sister in mother's presence.'

'Well, dear fellow, I still can't understand it', the general remarked, shrugging slightly and spreading his arms. 'Remember when your mother came to see me the other day, moaning and groaning? What's the matter, I ask her. It turns out that they see it as some kind of *dishonour*. What dishonour can there possibly be, may I ask? Who can reproach Nastasya Filippovna with anything or say anything against her? Surely not that she lived with Totsky? That's really utter nonsense, especially in the given circumstances! "You", she says, "won't let her associate with your daughters, will you?" "Well! Really! Come now, Nina Alexandrovna! How can you fail to grasp, how can you fail to grasp . . ."'

'Your own position?' suggested Ganya, seeing the general in difficulties. 'She does; you mustn't be angry at her. I gave her a good talking to at the time, by the way, for meddling. Up to now, however, everything at home is only holding together because the final word has not yet been spoken; the storm is looming, though. If the final word is spoken tonight it means everything is bound to come out.'

The prince overheard all this conversation as he sat in the corner working at his calligraphic specimen. He completed it and came up to the table to deliver his sheet of paper.

'So that's Nastasya Filippovna?' he said, taking a close and curious look at the picture. 'She's astonishingly pretty!' he at once added warmly. The portrait certainly depicted a woman of extraordinary beauty. She had been photographed in a black silk dress of exquisite simplicity; her hair, apparently dark auburn, was done up simply, domestic-fashion; the eyes were dark and deep, the forehead pensive, while her expression was passionate with a touch of hauteur. She was rather thin in the face, perhaps, and pale ... Ganya and the general looked at the prince in amazement ...

'What, Nastasya Filippovna? Surely you don't know Nastasya Filippovna too?' asked the general.

'Yes; twenty-four hours in Russia and I know a great beauty like this', replied the prince, and at once told them of his encounter with Rogozhin and recounted the latter's story.

'Now, this is something new!' The general was once again troubled after listening to the prince with rapt attention. He gave Ganya a searching glance.

'Probably just some wild prank', muttered Ganya, also somewhat taken aback. 'A merchant's son kicking over the traces. I've already heard something about him.'

'So have I, dear fellow', said the general. 'After that ear-ring business Nastasya Filippovna retailed the whole story. Still, it's a different matter now, you know. There really is a million involved perhaps, and ... passion, wild and foolish it may be, but it smells of passion all the same, and we know what these fellows are capable of when their blood is up! ... Hmm! ... Let's hope nobody gets involved in scandalous gossip over this!' concluded the general thoughtfully.

'You're worried about the million?' grinned Ganya.

'You aren't of course?'

'How did it strike you, Prince?' Ganya addressed him suddenly. 'Did you think he was a serious sort of man or just a desperado? Your own opinion?'

Something peculiar was taking place in Ganya as he posed the question. It was as if some strange new idea had flashed into his brain and glittered eagerly in his eyes. The general, for his part, was genuinely and openly uneasy; he also glanced sideways at the prince, though appearing to expect little from his reply.

'I don't know how to put it', answered the prince, 'but it seemed to me that there was a great deal of passionate feeling in the man, even morbid passion. And he seemed quite ill himself, as well. He could very possibly take to his bed in his first few days in Petersburg, especially if they fill him up with drink.'

'Really? You thought that?' The general clutched at this idea.

'Yes, I did.'

'Still, a scandal could erupt before evening, never mind in several days' time, today even something might happen', Ganya grinned at the general.

'Hmm! . . . Of course . . . It really all depends on what she takes it into her head to do', said the general.

'And you know how she can be sometimes, don't you?'

'And what on earth do you mean by that?' the general burst out again, by now thoroughly distraught. 'Listen Ganya, just don't keep contradicting her today, try to be, you know . . . humour her . . . Hmm! . . . Why twist your mouth up like that? Now listen to me, Gavrila Ardalionich, it would be very much to the point to ask: what are we trying to do here? You realize that whatever personal advantage I stand to gain in the matter was guaranteed long ago; whatever happens, I shall resolve the business in my favour. Totsky won't go back on his decision, I am totally confident. If I wish for anything now, therefore, it is solely for your benefit. Judge for yourself; don't you trust me, is that it? Besides, you're a man . . . a man . . . well, a man of intelligence, and I've been relying on you . . . in the present instance, it's . . . it's . . .'

'The main thing', Ganya finished for him, once again rescuing the general, as he twisted his lips into the most sardonic of smiles with no attempt at concealment this time. His blazing glance was directed straight at the general, as if willing him to read there all that he was thinking. The general went crimson with anger.

'Well of course, intelligence is the main thing!' he conceded, looking sharply at Ganya. 'And you're a funny chap, Gavrila Ardalionich! I can see you're really glad this merchant cub has appeared, aren't you? It's a way out for you. This is where brain should have been applied from the start; it was just at this point you should have realized and . . . and dealt honestly and openly with both sides, or if not . . . given warning in advance so as not to compromise others, especially as there was plenty of time to do it; there's still time enough now' (here the general raised his eyebrows meaningfully) 'even if it is only a few hours . . . You understand my meaning? Do you? Do you want to go through with it or not? If not, say so and—that will be that. No one is stopping you, Gavrila Ardalionich, no one's forcing you into a trap, if that's the way you see it.'

'I'm willing.' Ganya's voice was low but steady as he dropped his eyes and fell gloomily silent.

The general was satisfied. He had lost his temper and clearly regretted having gone too far. He turned suddenly towards the prince, and it seemed as if the uneasy thought passed across his face that the latter had been present and had heard everything. He was instantly reassured however: one glance at the prince was reassurance enough.

'Oho!' the general exclaimed, looking at the calligraphic specimen proffered by the prince. 'Now that's real writing for you! And very unusual at that! Have a look, Ganya, the skill!'

On the thick vellum sheet, the prince had written in Russian medieval characters:

'The humble Abbot Paphnutius hath set his hand hereunto.'

'This', elucidated the prince, highly elated, 'is the personal signature of the Abbot Paphnutius copied from a manuscript of the fourteenth century. They had splendid signatures, all our old abbots and metropolitans, such exquisite style sometimes and such care! Surely you have Pogodin's edition at least, General? After that I've written using different lettering: this is a large, rounded, French script of the last century, some characters were written in different ways even, it's a script of the market-place, used by public scribes and taken from their specimens (I used to have one)—you'll agree it has its virtues. Look at these rounded 'd's and 'a's. I've written the Russian letters in the French style, which is very difficult, but it's come out well. Here's another beautiful and original script, the phrase here: "Zeal conquers all." It's a Russian script, a clerk's or, if you prefer, military clerk's script. An official letter to an important personage would be written in this way. It's also a rounded script, splendid and *black*, written in black but with excellent style. A calligraphist would not have allowed these flourishes or rather these attempted flourishes, these unfinished half-tails here, you see, and yet taken altogether they have a character of their own, look, really the entire soul of the orderly clerk peeps out: it wants to spread its wings and the skill is there, but the military collar is tightly fastened, discipline comes out in the script as well, wonderful! I was really struck when I came across a specimen like that not long ago, guess where? Switzerland! Then there's this simple, ordinary, clean-as-clean English script: elegance can go no further, it's pure delight, like a pearl necklace; that's perfection, but here's a variation, French again, I got it from a French commercial traveller: the same English script, but the black line's just a touch blacker and thicker than in the English, so the balance of light and shade is disturbed; note also: the oval is altered, just a touch rounder and a flourish has been permitted—the most dangerous thing of all! A flourish demands rare taste; but if it succeeds, if the proportion should be found, then this script is incomparable, one might even fall in love with it.'

'Oho! You're going into the fine detail aren't you', the general laughed. 'Dear fellow, you're not just a calligrapher, you're an artist, eh, Ganya?'

'Amazing', said Ganya, 'and aware of his vocation too,' he added, with a sarcastic laugh.

'Laugh away, laugh away, there's a career in this, you know', said the general. 'Prince, now we'll give you papers to write to a certain important person, do you know who? You can reckon on thirty-five roubles a month just to start with. However, it's already half-past twelve', he concluded, glancing at his watch. 'To business, Prince, as I have to hurry and we may not meet again today! Please sit down for a moment; I've already explained that I cannot receive you very frequently, but I really would like to help you a little, just a little, it goes without saying, in the areas of most need—after that it rests with yourself. I'll arrange a little job in the office for you, not too arduous, but accuracy will be essential. Now further: in the house, the family that is, of Gavrila Ardalionovich Ivolgin, this young friend of mine here, whom I hereby introduce, his mama and sister have set aside two or three furnished rooms in their apartments and rent them out to highly recommended lodgers, meals and service included. I'm sure Nina Alexandrovna will accept my recommendation. In your case, Prince, it's invaluable, as you won't be starting off on your own but in the bosom of a family, so to speak; in my opinion, you shouldn't be on your own at first in a city like Petersburg. Nina

Alexandrovna and Varvara Ardalionovna, her daughter, are ladies I hold in the highest respect. Nina Alexandrovna's husband, Ardalion Alexandrovich, is a retired general, a former comrade of mine in my early army service; for certain reasons we are not on terms, which doesn't prevent me from respecting him in my own fashion. I am telling you all this, Prince, so that you understand I am recommending you personally, as it were, and so vouching for you in a way. The terms are extremely reasonable and I trust your salary will soon be ample to the occasion. Of course a man needs spending-money, if only a little, but you won't take offence, Prince, if I suggest that you'd be better off without spending-money, or any money at all, in your pocket. I'm saying this from my impression of you. But as your purse is absolutely empty at the moment, allow me to offer you these twenty-five roubles to begin with. We'll settle up later on, of course, and if you're the sort of honest and principled fellow your words seem to indicate, there won't be any difficulties between us there. If I'm taking this much interest in you, I do have a certain end in view; you will learn what that is later. So, you see, I'm being perfectly straightforward with you; I trust, Ganya, you have nothing against the prince residing in your apartments?'

'Oh, on the contrary! And mama will be very pleased too . . .' confirmed Ganya, courteous and complaisant.

'I believe you've only got one other room occupied at the moment. That, what's-his-name, Ferd . . . Fer . . .'

'Ferdischenko.'

'That's it; I don't care for that Ferdischenko of yours, he's a foul-mouthed buffoon. I don't understand why Nastasya Filippovna encourages him, he's not really a relative of hers, is he?'

'Oh no, that's all nonsense! Not even twice removed.'

'Well, to blazes with him! Now then Prince, what about you, are you satisfied or not?'

'I thank you, General, you have treated me extremely kindly, especially considering that I asked for nothing; I don't say that out of pride, I really didn't know where to lay my head. True, Rogozhin did invite me a while ago.'

'Rogozhin? Ah, no; I would advise you as a father, or if you prefer, as a friend, to forget all about Mr Rogozhin. In fact, my advice would be to stick to the family you are about to enter.'

'As you are so kind', the prince began, 'there is a certain matter. I've received notification . . .'

'Now you must excuse me', the general broke in, 'I haven't a moment to spare. I will tell Lizaveta Prokofievna about you presently: if she wishes to receive you at once (I shall try to recommend that she should), I advise you to use the opportunity to get into her good graces; she could be very useful to you, since you are her namesake. If she doesn't, don't press the matter, some other time will do. You, Ganya, take a look at these accounts, Fedoseyev and I got nowhere with them just now. We mustn't forget to include them . . .'

The general left the room and the prince had still not managed to discuss the matter he had tried to raise three or four times already. Ganya lit a cigarette and offered one to the prince, who took it but said nothing for fear of interrupting; he fell to examining the study. Ganya, however, barely glanced at the sheet of figures the general had indicated. He was preoccupied; it seemed to the prince that his smile, his pensive appearance, had become a great deal more sombre now that they were left alone together. Suddenly he came over to the prince, who at that moment was again standing over the portrait of Nastasya Filippovna, scrutinizing it.

'That sort of woman appeals to you, does she, Prince?' he enquired all of a sudden, fixing him with his stare. It was as if he had something important in mind.

'An astonishing face!' responded the prince. 'And I'm sure her life has been no ordinary affair. The face is cheerful, but she's suffered dreadfully, hasn't she? The eyes say that, these two little bones just here, the two points under the eyes where the cheekbones start. It's a proud face, dreadfully proud, and I just don't know, is she a good woman or not? I do hope she's good! It would redeem everything!'

'Would *you* marry a woman like that?' Ganya pursued, keeping his burning eyes fixed upon him.

'I can't marry anyone, I'm a sick man', said the prince.

'And would Rogozhin marry her? What do you think?'

'Well I suppose so, he could marry her tomorrow; marry her and perhaps murder her a week later.'

As soon as the prince had said this, Ganya gave such a start that the prince almost cried out.

'What's the matter?' he said, seizing his arm.

'Your highness! His excellency requests your attendance upon her excellency', announced a footman, appearing in the doorway. The prince set off after him.

4

ALL three Yepanchin girls were sturdy young ladies, tall and blooming, with magnificent shoulders, powerful bosoms, and strong, almost masculine arms; as a consequence of their health and strength they naturally enjoyed eating well on occasions, something they took no pains to conceal. Their mama, the general's wife, Lizaveta Prokofievna, sometimes looked askance at their frankly hearty appetites, but since many of her opinions, despite the show of respect they were accorded by her daughters, had long since lost their pristine and indisputable authority over them—to the point, indeed, where the three girls' firmly united conclave had begun to prevail time after time—she found it more convenient to yield rather than argue, as far as was consonant with her own dignity. True, her temperament very often failed to comply, and declined to submit to the dictates of reason; with each passing year Lizaveta Prokofievna became ever more fretful and intolerant, even to the point of eccentricity, but as she had an obedient and well-trained husband close at hand she would usually vent her accumulated excess of exasperation on his head, after which harmony was restored in the household and everything went on as well as could be.

Madame Yepanchina had not lost her own appetite either, incidentally, and at half-past twelve normally partook of an ample lunch, resembling a dinner almost, along with her daughters. Still earlier, the girls each had a cup of coffee in bed at exactly ten o'clock, the moment they awoke. They had grown to enjoy this and it had become an established custom. At half-past twelve, then, the table would be laid in the small dining-room, close to mama's rooms, and if time allowed the general himself would attend this intimate family luncheon. Besides tea, coffee, cheese, honey, butter, cutlets, and Madame Yepanchina's favourite special fritters and so on, a rich hot broth might also be served. On the morning when our story began, the whole family had gathered in the dining-room in expectation of the general, who had promised to appear at the appointed time. If he had been as much as a minute late he would have been sent for at once: he appeared punctually, however. As he came up to greet his wife and kiss her hand, he noticed on this occasion a most peculiar expression on her face. Although he had had a presentiment the previous evening that such would be the case today, on account of a certain 'incident' (as he habitually expressed it), and had felt uneasy about it on going to bed, he nevertheless felt himself quailing now. His daughters came up to kiss him; though they were not angry with him, there was something odd about them also. It was true that the general had his reasons for becoming over-suspicious, but as an experienced and resourceful husband and father, he took measures immediately.

Perhaps it will do no harm to the main elements of our story if we pause here to clarify certain matters, in order to present a precise and straightforward picture of the relationships and circumstances obtaining in the general's household at the beginning of our narration. We have already said just now that the general, though not really an educated man—on the contrary he used to describe himself as 'self-taught'—was an experienced and resourceful husband and father. Among other things, he had adopted the strategy of not hurrying his daughters into marriage, not nagging at them or worrying them too much with his paternal affection and concern for their happiness, as time and again happens, naturally and unwittingly, even in the most worldly-wise families who happen to have an abundance of grown daughters. He even succeeded in winning over Lizaveta Prokofievna to his strategy, though it had been a difficult task—difficult because unnatural; but the general's arguments were extremely cogent and based on palpable facts. If the girls were left completely free to decide for themselves, they would naturally make their own minds up in due course and then matters would move rapidly, as they would be acting according to their own desires, readily

setting aside any tendency towards being flighty or over-
fastidious; all that would remain for the parents to do would be to
keep a vigilant, and as far as possible unsuspected, watch-out for
any odd choice or unnatural aberration, then, seizing a suitable
moment, assist and guide the affair with all their strength and
influence. Finally, the fact that their wealth and social status grew
in geometrical progression with every passing year meant that the
longer time went on, the more the girls gained, even as
prospective brides. Upon these incontestable facts, however,
obtruded another: suddenly and quite unexpectedly, as is
invariably the case, the elder daughter, Alexandra, turned 25.
Almost at the same time, Afanasy Ivanovich Totsky, a man of the
social élite, with the most exalted connections and immense
wealth, had once again announced his long-felt desire to marry.
He was a man of about 55, elegant and with a rare refinement of
character and taste. He wished to marry well and he was a
remarkable judge of beauty. Since he had been for some time on
the closest terms of personal friendship with General Yepanchin,
reinforced by joint participation in certain financial dealings, he
informed him of his wishes, so to speak, and requested friendly
advice and counsel: would a marriage proposal to one of his
daughters be acceptable or not? Clearly an upheaval was about to
occur in the delightfully even tenor of General Yepanchin's
family life.

The undoubted beauty of the family was, as has been stated
already, the youngest, Aglaya. Even a man of such overweening
egoism as Totsky, however, realized that he would be wasting his
time there and that Aglaya was not destined for him. Perhaps the
somewhat uncritical love and the excessive attachment of the
sisters for one another had exaggerated the matter, but Aglaya's
future, as had been settled quite openly between them, was not to
be any ordinary future; it was to resemble an attainable version of
the earthly paradise. Aglaya's future husband was to be a paragon
of virtue and accomplishment, not to mention wealth. The sisters
had even come to an arrangement, without making too many
bones about it, regarding the possibility of sacrifice on their part
for Aglaya's sake: Aglaya's dowry was to be enormous, something
unheard of. The parents were aware of this agreement between
the two elder sisters and so, on hearing Totsky's request for

advice, they had barely any doubt that one of the two elder sisters would certainly agree to crown their desires, more especially since Afanasy Ivanovich could hardly make difficulties about the dowry. The general, with his characteristic worldly wisdom, at once placed a high estimation on Totsky's proposal. Since Totsky himself, as a result of certain peculiar circumstances, was observing extreme caution in his actions for the time being and was doing no more than exploring possibilities at the moment, the parents consequently represented all this to their daughters as no more than a remote possibility. The answer they obtained was, if not quite definite, at least reassuring—a declaration that the eldest, Alexandra, was unlikely to refuse. She was a strong-minded girl, but kind-hearted and sensible and very accommodating; she might indeed be very willing to marry Totsky, and if she did give her consent she would stand by it. She was not fond of display, and would sweeten and soothe her husband's life rather than threaten him with fuss and upheaval. She was very pretty, though not in an immediately striking way. What could be better for Totsky?

However that might be, the matter continued to proceed in a tentative manner. It had been agreed mutually and amicably between Totsky and the general that they should avoid any premature formal and irrevocable step. Even the parents had not yet begun to talk to their daughters completely frankly about it; something approaching discord was beginning to develop: Madame Yepanchina, as mother of her family, was becoming displeased for some reason, and that was a very serious matter. It involved a certain complex and troublesome circumstance, which was frustrating progress and might ruin the whole negotiation irretrievably.

This complex and troublesome 'circumstance' (as Totsky himself used to describe it) had begun a long time before, a matter of eighteen years since. In one of the central provinces, adjoining one of Afanasy Ivanovich's richest estates, lived a certain miserably poor landowner on his tiny property. This man was noted for the constant stream of proverbial disasters which befell him. Filipp Alexandrovich Barashkov was a retired officer of good family, rather superior to Totsky's own in point of fact. Up to his neck in debt and mortgaged to the hilt as he was, he finally succeeded in setting his small property more or less to rights by dint of cruelly hard, almost peasant-like toil. The smallest success would elate him tremendously. Encouraged, and radiant with hope, he went off for a few days to the district township, to meet one of his chief creditors and, if possible, come to a final agreement. On the third day of his stay there, his village elder rode in with his cheek and beard burned, bringing news that 'the house of his fathers had burned down' the day before at the stroke of noon; moreover, his wife had 'been burned as well, but the little children were safe and sound'. Even Barashkov, inured to the 'buffets of fortune' as he was, could not withstand a shock like this; he went off his head and died of a fever within a month. The gutted farmstead, along with its masterless peasants, was sold up to pay the debts, while Afanasy Ivanovich Totsky magnanimously took upon himself the expense of rearing Barashkov's two little girls, aged 6 and 7. They began to be brought up alongside the children of Totsky's German estate-manager, a retired civil servant with a large family. Soon only one little girl, Nastya, was left; the younger had died of whooping-cough. For his part, Totsky resided abroad and soon completely forgot about them both. About five years later, Afanasy Ivanovich was passing the neighbourhood and took it into his head to look in on his property; he suddenly noticed, living with the German's family, a delightful little girl of about 12, a clever little thing, winsome and spirited, already giving promise of extraordinary beauty; in this regard, Afanasy Ivanovich was an infallible judge. On this occasion he spent only a few days on the estate, but contrived to make all necessary arrangements; a considerable alteration came about in the little girl's education. A respectable, middle-aged Swiss governess, experienced in advanced girls' teaching, was engaged; she was a cultured woman and taught French as well as various other subjects. She took up residence in the house, and little Nastasya's education grew enormously in scope. After four years this educational process ceased; the governess left and a certain noblewoman, also a landowner and a neighbour of Totsky's, but this time in a distant province, came and took Nastya away with her on the instructions and authority of Afanasy Ivanovich. There was a small but newly built wooden house on the little estate, furnished with the utmost elegance, and the hamlet itself, as luck would have it, was called Gladdening. The lady brought Nastya straight to this little house, and since she was a childless widow and lived less than a mile away, she moved in with her. An old housekeeper and an experienced young maid also materialized near Nastya. The house contained musical instruments and an exquisite young girl's library, pictures, prints, pencils, brushes, paints, and a marvellous little greyhound. A fortnight later Afanasy Ivanovich himself came visiting . . . After that he seemed to develop a particular fondness for this remote, steppe-land hamlet of his, dropping in every summer and staying for two or even three months. Thus passed a considerable length of time, about four years, in peace and happiness amid elegant and tasteful surroundings.

One day around the beginning of winter, about four months after one of Afanasy Ivanovich's summer visits to Gladdening, this time only for two weeks, a rumour went the rounds, or to be more precise, a rumour chanced to reach Nastasya Filippovna, that Afanasy Ivanovich was getting married in Petersburg to a wealthy society beauty—in a word, he was making a prudent and brilliant match. Subsequently this rumour turned out not to be altogether well founded: the marriage was then only being considered and everything was still very much in the air. Nevertheless, from that time on Nastasya Filippovna's existence underwent a remarkable transformation. All of a sudden she exhibited unusual resolution and a most unexpected strength of character. Without the slightest hesitation she abandoned her little country house and suddenly appeared in Petersburg, all on her own, and went straight to Totsky. He was amazed and tried to talk to her; it turned out, however, almost from the first word, that he would have to alter his mode of address completely, along with his tone of voice and the topics of agreeable, elegant discourse he had employed up till then with such success; his logic, too—everything, everything! It was a totally different woman who sat before him, bearing no resemblance to the one he had known hitherto and had left in Gladdening only that July.

In the first place, it transpired, this new woman both knew and comprehended a great deal, so much in fact, that it was a matter of profound astonishment whence such knowledge could have proceeded and how she could have worked out such precise formulations for herself. (Surely not from her girl's library?) Moreover, she possessed an extraordinary grasp even of legal affairs and had a definite knowledge, if not of the world, then at least of how certain matters are arranged in that world; secondly, her character was quite different from what it had formerly been, no longer demure or schoolgirlishly tentative, sometimes enchanting in her unpredictable spirited innocence, at other times sad and pensive, astonished, mistrustful, tearful, and restless.

No: it was an extraordinary and startling creature who sat laughing in front of him now, stinging him with venomous taunts as she told him straight to his face that, in her heart, she had never held him in anything but the most profound contempt, contempt verging on nausea, which had begun immediately after her initial shock and surprise. This new woman declared that she was perfectly indifferent whether, when, or whom he married, but that she had come to prevent this union out of sheer spite, for the sole reason that she felt like it and consequently so it must be, 'if only so that I can laugh at you to my heart's content, because now at last I want to laugh as well'.

That, at least, was how she put it; all that was in her heart she perhaps did not express. While the new Nastasya Filippovna was laughing as she made her declaration, Afanasy Ivanovich was pondering the situation and gathering his somewhat shattered thoughts as best he could. This pondering of his took a considerable time; he spent nearly a fortnight cogitating before finally making up his mind, but at the end of those two weeks he had come to his decision. The fact of the matter was that Afanasy Ivanovich was by then nearly 50, a decidedly staid man, set in his ways. His position in the world and society had long since been established on the firmest of foundations. He cherished and prized above all else on earth his own person, his creature comforts, and his peace of mind, as indeed was appropriate for such a highly respectable man. Not the smallest violation, not the tiniest tremor must be allowed to disturb what had taken a lifetime to stabilize in so perfect a form. On the other hand, his experience of life and deep insight told Totsky swiftly and very accurately that he was now dealing with a wholly extraordinary creature, a woman who would carry out whatever she threatened, and, what was most important, would assuredly stick at nothing, particularly as she assuredly cared for nothing in this world and was thus immune to inducements. There was clearly something else at work here, some kind of mental and spiritual ferment, a sort of wild romantic indignation, goodness only knew why or directed against whom, some insatiable feeling of contempt, going far beyond accepted norms—in short, something utterly absurd and inadmissible in polite society, and which for any decent person to encounter was to endure whips and scorpions. Naturally, with his wealth and connections, Totsky could easily have perpetrated some wholly blameless little villainy to rid himself of this unpleasantness. For her part, however, it was clear that Nastasya Filippovna herself was in no position to do any harm, in the legal sense, for example; she couldn't even raise a scandal of any proportions, since she could be so easily restrained. All this, however, depended on whether Nastasya Filippovna had made up her mind to act like the generality of people in similar situations, that is, without stepping too freakishly far beyond the bounds of acceptable behaviour. This is where the accuracy of Totsky's insight came to his aid: he was able to divine that Nastasya Filippovna herself realized perfectly well how innocuous she was in the legal sense, but that she had something altogether different in mind . . . and in her flashing eyes. Caring for nothing, least of all herself (it needed a good deal of intelligence and insight to realize at that moment that she had long since ceased to care about herself, and for him as a sceptical and cynical man of the world to admit that feeling genuine), Nastasya Filippovna was quite capable of ruining herself scandalously and irrevocably, risking hard labour in Siberia, just as long as she could jeer at this man for whom she harboured so inhuman an aversion. Afanasy Ivanovich had always admitted to a measure of cowardice, or to put it more flatteringly, he was extremely conservative by temperament. If he knew, for example, that he was going to be murdered during his wedding or that something utterly indecent, absurd, and unpleasant of that sort was going to happen in front of company, he would be alarmed of course, but not so much because he would be killed or severely wounded or his face publicly spat on, and so on and so forth, as that it would happen to him in such an unnatural and disagreeable manner. And it was just that which Nastasya Filippovna was threatening, though she was saying nothing at the moment; he knew that she had studied and understood him through and through and consequently knew where to strike the blow. So, since the marriage was still really only a matter of intention, Afanasy Ivanovich resigned himself and yielded to Nastasya Filippovna.

There was one other factor which assisted him in coming to his decision: it was hard to imagine how much this new Nastasya Filippovna differed facially from her former self. Previously, she had been just a very pretty girl, but now . . . it was a long time before Totsky forgave himself for having spent four years looking without seeing. True, sudden inner alteration on both sides can make a great deal of difference. He recalled, however, that there had been moments even before when strange fancies had come to him as he looked at those eyes, for example: how he sensed in them a kind of darkness, profound and mysterious. Her gaze rested on him, seeming to propound a puzzle. Over the last two years he had often marvelled at the girl's change in facial coloration: she had become terribly pale—and oddly, the more beautiful for it. Totsky, like all gentlemen sowing their wild oats, had at first regarded the immature spirit he had obtained so cheaply with contempt; recently he had altered his opinion somewhat. At all events, as long ago as last spring, he had intended marrying her off quickly and well, with an ample dowry, to some sensible and respectable gentleman serving in another province. (Ah, how horribly, how malevolently Nastasya Filippovna had laughed at that now!) At the present moment, however, Afanasy Ivanovich, seduced by the novelty of the situation, thought he might exploit this woman once more. He made up his mind to settle Nastasya Filippovna in Petersburg and surround her with luxurious comfort. If he couldn't have one thing, he would have another: he could flaunt Nastasya Filippovna and even boast about her in a certain circle. Afanasy Ivanovich valued his reputation in that regard, after all.

Five years of Petersburg living had now passed, and it goes without saying that much had become clear in that time. Afanasy Ivanovich's situation was unenviable; the worst thing about it was that, having once played the coward, he was never able subsequently to come to terms with himself. He was afraid of her—and didn't know why—he just feared Nastasya Filippovna. For a while, during the first two years, he had begun to suspect that Nastasya Filippovna wanted to marry him herself, but that overweening pride kept her silent, waiting doggedly for his proposal. It would have been a strange claim on her part; Afanasy Ivanovich frowned and pondered deeply. To his considerable and (such is the heart of man!) somewhat disagreeable surprise, an incident occurred which convinced him that, even if he had proposed, he would not have been accepted. For a long time he was unable to understand this. Only one explanation seemed possible to him, that the pride of the 'humiliated and fantastical woman' had reached such a level of fury that she took more pleasure in venting her scorn through a rejection than in regularizing her position permanently and attaining untouchable eminence. The worst of it all was that Nastasya Filippovna had achieved so signal a triumph. She did not succumb to any financial inducements either, however large, and although she had accepted the proffered comfort, she lived very modestly and saved almost nothing over the five years. Afanasy Ivanovich risked a most cunning approach in order to break free of his fetters: with imperceptible skill he began to seduce her with the help of able accomplices, and sundry ideal temptations were placed in her way. The embodiments of these ideals, however—princes, hussars, embassy secretaries, poets, novelists, socialists even—none made any impression on Nastasya Filippovna. It was as if her heart was made of stone, and her emotions had withered and died once and for all. She lived alone for the most part, reading, even studying; she liked music. Her circle of acquaintance was small: she spent much of her time with certain poor, rather ridiculous civil-service wives, knew a few actresses and old women, and had a great affection for the multitudinous family of a certain respectable teacher; the family loved her in return and were always pleased to welcome her. Quite often of an evening some half-dozen acquaintances would call on her, not more. Totsky appeared with frequent regularity. Recently General Yepanchin had made her acquaintance, not without difficulty. At the same time a certain young official had done the same thing quite easily and without any difficulty at all; his name was Ferdischenko, a coarse purveyor of indecent jokes, and a hard drinker with pretensions to wit. She also knew a certain odd young man called Ptitsyn, a neat, modest, rather dapper figure, who had risen from poverty and become a money-lender. At length she was also introduced to Gavrila Ardalionovich . . . The end result was that Nastasya Filippovna gained a rather curious reputation: everyone knew of her beauty, but that was all; nobody was able to boast with regard to her, and nobody had any stories to tell of her. A reputation like that, her upbringing, her elegant manners, her wit—all this finally confirmed Afanasy Ivanovich in his projected strategy. Here began General Yepanchin's active and prominent participation in the story.

When Totsky had so courteously applied to him for friendly advice with regard to one of his daughters, he simultaneously made a full and frank confession, in the most chivalrous fashion. He revealed that he was resolved to *stop at nothing* to gain his freedom; he would not rest even if Nastasya Filippovna herself declared that from henceforth she would leave him in peace; words were not enough for him, he required the fullest guarantees. They reached agreement and resolved to act in concert. Initially it was decided to employ the gentlest of means and touch, so to speak, only the 'noblest strings of the heart'. Both of them went to see Nastasya Filippovna, and Totsky began bluntly by making clear the intolerable burden of his situation; he blamed himself in every respect, saying frankly that he could not repent of his initial conduct towards her because he was an inveterate sensualist and unable to control himself, but that now he wanted to marry and the whole fate of this eminently suitable society marriage was in her hands; in short, he was depending on the generosity of her heart. Then General Yepanchin began to speak in his capacity as the father; he spoke judiciously, avoiding pathos, mentioning only that he fully acknowledged her right to decide the fate of Afanasy Ivanovich, while adroitly parading his own humility by pointing out that the future of his daughter, possibly all three daughters, now depended on her decision. To Nastasya Filippovna's question: 'What exactly do you want of me?', Totsky confessed, with the same absolutely unadorned directness, that he had been so intimidated five years before that even now he could feel no peace of mind until Nastasya

Filippovna married someone herself. He added at once that the request would have been quite absurd on his part had he not possessed certain grounds for making it. He had noticed, and indeed knew for a fact, that a young man of name and most respected family, to wit Gavrila Ardalionovich Ivolgin, whom she knew and was in the habit of receiving, had long been deeply enamoured of her and of course would give half his life for the mere hope of gaining her favour. Gavrila Ardalionovich had confessed as much himself to him, Afanasy Ivanovich, long ago out of friendship and a pure young heart, and General Yepanchin, his benefactor, had long known about it. Finally, unless Afanasy Ivanovich was very much mistaken, Nastasya Filippovna was well aware of the young man's affections and regarded them indulgently. Of course it was harder for him to talk about it than anyone else. But if Nastasya Filippovna was willing to allow that he, Totsky, besides selfishness and a desire to further his own ends, had at least some desire for her good also, then she would realize how strange and distressing it had been to look upon her loneliness for so long: her existence was a formless obscurity, a total lack of belief in the renewal of a life, which could have had such a wonderful resurrection in love and a family and thus taken on a new direction; it was a waste of talent, perhaps brilliant talent, to give herself up to the contemplation of her own anguish, it was a kind of romanticism in fact, worthy neither of Nastasya Filippovna's common sense nor her noble heart. Reiterating that it was more difficult for him to speak than others, he concluded by saying that he could not abandon the hope that Nastasya Filippovna would not reply with scorn if he expressed his sincere desire to provide for her future by offering her the sum of seventy-five thousand roubles. He added by way of explanation that this sum was already earmarked for her in his will; in other words, it was not a kind of compensation . . . and, finally, why not allow for and excuse his human desire to salve his conscience, and so on and so on, everything that is said on such occasions on subjects of this nature. Afanasy Ivanovich spoke eloquently and at length, adding in passing, as it were, the very curious information that this was the first time he had ever hinted at this seventy-five thousand, and that even General Yepanchin himself sitting nearby didn't know; in a word, *nobody* knew.

Nastasya Filippovna's reply astounded both the friends. There was not the faintest trace of her former sneering manner, her former hostility and hatred, the laughter which sent cold shivers up Totsky's spine at the mere recollection—no, on the contrary, she seemed glad to be able to talk to someone amicably and frankly. She admitted that she herself had wanted to ask for friendly advice for a long time, and only pride had prevented her. Now, since the ice had been broken, nothing could suit her better. Smiling sadly at first, but then gaily breaking out into playful laughter, she confessed that at all events her stormy scenes were a thing of the past; she had long ago changed her view of matters, and though her heart remained unaltered she had been compelled to accept many things as a *fait accompli*; what was done could not be undone, what was past was past; she was surprised, even, that Afanasy Ivanovich should still be so fearful. Here she addressed the general and declared, in an attitude of deepest respect, that she had long been hearing a good deal about his daughters and was in the habit of thinking of them with profound and sincere esteem. The very thought that she might be of service to them, would be, of course, a source of happiness and pride. It was true that she was depressed and dull at present, exceedingly dull; Afanasy Ivanovich had divined her dreams correctly; she would like to renew herself, if not through love then through a family, as a new end in life. As to Gavrila Ardalionovich, however, she could say nothing. It was probably true that he loved her; she sensed that she could fall in love herself, if she could be convinced of the firmness of his affections; still, even if sincere he was very young; it was a hard decision. What pleased her most, incidentally, was that he was employed, and toiled to support his entire household. She had heard that he was a man of energy and pride who wanted a career, was anxious to get on. She had also heard that Nina Alexandrovna Ivolgina, his mother, was a splendid and most estimable woman, and that his sister, Varvara Ardalionovna, was a very fine and energetic girl; she had heard a good deal about her from Ptitsyn. She had also heard that they were bearing up under their misfortunes; she would much like to make their acquaintance, but there was the question of whether they would welcome her into their family. On the whole, she had nothing against the marriage, but it needed careful consideration; she hoped they would not press her. Regarding the seventy-five thousand, it was a pity Afanasy Ivanovich had felt it so difficult to mention it. She knew the value of money and would accept it of course. She was grateful to Afanasy Ivanovich for his tact in not mentioning it even to the general, let alone Gavrila Ardalionovich, still, why shouldn't he know about it in advance? She had no reason to feel shame about accepting it on coming into their family. At all events she had no intention of asking anybody's forgiveness for anything, and wished them to know that. She would not marry Gavrila Ardalionovich unless she was convinced that neither he nor his family harboured any reservations on her account. In any case, she didn't regard herself as guilty of anything, and it was better that Gavrila Ardalionovich knew on what basis she had been living in Petersburg for the last five years, what her relationship with Afanasy Ivanovich had been, and whether she had amassed any personal wealth. Finally, if she were accepting money now, it was certainly not as payment for her maidenly shame, in which she was blameless, but simply as a recompense for her ruined life.

Towards the end, she had become so ill-tempered and irritable in making all this plain (as was only natural) that General Yepanchin was very pleased and regarded the matter as concluded; the thoroughly unmanned Totsky, however, was mistrustful even now, and long feared to find a snake under these flowers. Nevertheless the negotiations began; the point on which the entire strategy of the two friends was based, namely the possibility of Nastasya Filippovna being attracted to Ganya, had gradually begun to take clearer and more convincing shape, so that even Totsky at times started to believe in the possibility of success. Meanwhile, Nastasya Filippovna had discussed the matter with Ganya: few words were spoken, as if her modesty found the subject painful. She acknowledged and permitted his love, but insisted that she had complete freedom of action; she reserved the right to say 'no' right up to the wedding itself (should there be one), even at the very last minute; she allowed absolutely the same right to him. Soon Ganya learned by chance that Nastasya Filippovna certainly knew the broad details of his family's hostility to the marriage and to her personally, evidenced by domestic scenes; she never spoke of this to him, though he was in daily expectation of it. It would be possible to mention a great deal else concerning the history and circumstances surrounding this matchmaking and the accompanying negotiations, but we have run on ahead as it is, and in any case some of the circumstances were no more than the vaguest hearsay. Totsky, for example, was supposed to have found out somewhere that Nastasya Filippovna had entered into some vague secret relations with the Yepanchin girls—a most improbable story. On the other hand, there was another nightmarish rumour he felt compelled to believe: he heard for a fact that Nastasya Filippovna was perfectly well aware that Ganya was marrying her for money, and that he was a blackguard—envious, intolerant, and voracious, a monster of self-regard; that formerly Ganya had indeed passionately sought to conquer Nastasya Filippovna, but when the two friends had made up their minds to exploit this reciprocal passion for their own ends and buy Ganya by selling him Nastasya Filippovna as his lawful wedded wife, he had conceived a poisonous hatred for her. Passion and hatred seemed strangely intermingled in his heart, and although he agreed in the end, after agonizing hesitations, to marry the 'awful woman', he swore in his heart to wreak bitter revenge on her for it and 'make her smart', as he was supposed to have put it himself. All this Nastasya Filippovna was supposed to be aware of, and she was thought to be hatching something up in secret. Totsky was so unnerved that he had ceased confiding his anxieties to Yepanchin; there were moments, however, when like any weak man he took heart again and his spirits rose quickly: he was immensely cheered, for example, when Nastasya Filippovna finally promised both friends that on the evening of her birthday she would make her decision. On the other hand, the oddest and most unlikely rumour of all, which concerned the highly respected Ivan Fedorovich Yepanchin himself had turned out, alas, to be more and more probable.

At first glance, the whole thing seemed utterly preposterous. It was hard to credit that Ivan Fedorovich, in his honourable old age, with all his outstanding intelligence and worldly wisdom, and so on and so forth, could be infatuated by Nastasya Filippovna himself—but that was what was being said; indeed, infatuated to such an extent, the thing seemed almost to border on passion. It was hard to imagine exactly what hopes he entertained in the matter—perhaps he was even counting on Ganya's co-operation. Totsky was beginning to suspect something of the sort at least, to suspect the existence of some kind of tacit agreement almost, between the general and Ganya, based on their mutual understanding of one another. Still, it is well known, of course, that a man carried away by passion, especially at an advanced age, is quite blind and ready to detect hope where none exists; he loses his reasoning powers, moreover, and acts like some silly child, whatever his intellectual equipment. It was common knowledge that the general was intending to give Nastasya Filippovna a wonderful pearl necklace of enormous value for her birthday and had taken great trouble over the gift, though he knew that Nastasya Filippovna was not a mercenary woman. On the eve of her birthday he was almost in a fever, though he concealed his feelings adeptly. It was of this same necklace that Madame Yepanchina had heard rumours. Elizaveta Prokofievna had long experience of her husband's waywardness, was even used to it to some extent, but clearly this was too much to let pass: the pearl rumour vastly intrigued her. The general had got wind of this in good time; there had been words between them the day before and he foresaw that a thorough explanation of his conduct was inevitable. This was the reason why he was decidedly disinclined to go and have lunch in the bosom of his family on the morning this story began. Even before the arrival of the prince he had intended to plead pressure of work and avoid doing so. For the general, avoiding things sometimes meant fleeing from the house, pure and simple. He just wanted to get this day over, especially the evening, without unpleasantness. And suddenly here was the prince's opportune arrival. 'God must have sent him!' thought the general, as he went in to his wife.

5

MADAME Yepanchina was jealous of her lineage. Her feelings may well be imagined on learning, bluntly and without preparation, that this Prince Myshkin, the last of her line and a man of whom she had already heard something, was no more than a pitiable idiot, almost a beggar, accepting alms. The general had been at pains to create an effect which would grip her attention at once and divert it somehow away from him.

In moments of crisis Madame Yepanchina was wont to open her eyes very wide and lean her body back slightly, staring vaguely before her without uttering a word. She was a tall, lean woman, of about her husband's age, with abundant dark hair, heavily streaked with grey, a somewhat aquiline nose, sallow sunken cheeks, and thin puckered lips. Her forehead was high, if narrow; her grey, rather prominent eyes occasionally held a most surprising expression. At one time she had been prone to think her glance extremely striking, and the conviction had remained unshakeably with her.

'Receive him? You mean receive him now, this instant?' Here Madame Yepanchina strove to widen her eyes at the general fidgeting before her.

'Oh, as far as that goes, one can dispense with the formalities, just as long as you wish to see him, my dear', the general hastened to explain. 'He's an absolute child, one feels so sorry for him; he has fits of some kind; he's back from Switzerland, just off the train, dressed rather oddly, sort of German-fashion, and literally not a kopeck to his name; practically in tears. I gave him twenty-five roubles and I want to get him some sort of clerking job in the office. I would ask you, *mesdames*, to offer him some lunch, because it appears he's hungry as well . . .'

'You astonish me', his wife pursued. 'Hungry and fits! What sort of fits?'

'Oh, they don't happen very often, besides he's almost like a child—educated though. I would like you, *mesdames*', he addressed his daughters again, 'to put him through an examination, it would be useful to know what he's good for after all.'

'Ex-am-ination?' drawled his wife and began rolling her eyes from husband to daughters and back again in profound astonishment.

'Ah, my dear, don't misunderstand my meaning . . . well, as you wish; I meant make a fuss of him and make him feel at home, it's almost an act of charity.'

'Feel at home? From Switzerland?'

'That could come in useful; still, as I say, just as you wish. I am suggesting this in the first place because he's your namesake, perhaps even a relative, and secondly because he doesn't know where to lay his head. I had thought it might be of some interest to you, as he bears the name.'

'Of course we should, *maman*, if it's informal; besides, he's hungry after his journey, why not give him something to eat if he has nowhere to go?' said the eldest, Alexandra.

'A complete child as well, we could play blind-man's buff with him.'

'Blind-man's buff? How do you mean?'

'Oh, *maman*, please do stop putting on an act', Aglaya cut in, vexed.

The humorous middle daughter, Adelaida, couldn't help bursting out laughing.

'Call him in, papa', Aglaya decided. '*Maman* gives her permission.' The general rang for the prince to be summoned.

'But only on condition he ties a napkin round his neck, when he sits down to table', his wife decided. 'Call Fedor, or let Mavra . . . to stand behind him and see to him while he's eating. Is he quiet during these fits at least? Doesn't wave his arms about?'

'On the contrary, he's been very nicely brought up and his manners are beautiful. He's just a trifle too simple sometimes . . . But here he is! So then, may I introduce Prince Myshkin, last of his line, your namesake, and perhaps relation, do welcome him and make him feel at home. Lunch is being served, Prince, do us the honour . . . You will excuse me, I'm afraid I'm late, I must dash off . . .'

'We know where you're dashing off to', said his wife heavily.

'I'm in a hurry, my dear, and I'm late, I'm late! Do show him your albums, *mesdames*, and get him to write something for you; you've never seen such a writer! A real talent; the way he noted down for me out there in old-fashioned lettering: "The Abbot Paphnutius hath put his hand hereunto" . . . well, then, *au revoir.*'

'Paphnutius? Abbot? Wait a moment, wait, where are you off to and who's this Paphnutius?' cried Madame Yepanchina to her absconding spouse, her dogged exasperation verging on alarm.

'It's all right, it's all right, my dear, it was in olden times, an abbot . . . I'm off to the count's, he's been expecting me, long ago, and the thing is, he fixed the time himself . . . *Au revoir*, Prince!'

The general made off, stepping swiftly.

'I know, I know, count indeed!' said Elizaveta Prokofievna brusquely, and transferred her petulant gaze to the prince. 'What was I saying just then?' she began, tentative and peevish, struggling to bring it to mind. 'What was it again? Oh, yes: what abbot was that again?'

'*Maman*', began Alexandra, while Aglaya went so far as to stamp her little foot.

'Don't interrupt, Alexandra Ivanovna', snapped Madame Yepanchina. 'I want to know too. Sit here, Prince, here in this armchair opposite, no, here towards the sun; move nearer the light so I can see you. Well now, who is this abbot?'

'Abbot Paphnutius', responded the prince, earnestly attentive.

'Paphnutius? That's interesting: well what about him then?'

Madame Yepanchina questioned him abruptly, quick and eager, keeping her eyes fixed on him; when the prince replied she nodded after every word.

'Abbot Paphnutius lived in the fourteenth century', the prince began. 'He was the head of a monastery on the Volga, in present-day Kostroma province. He was well known for his righteous life and used to travel to the Horde* to help in the management of affairs in those days; he signed a document and I've seen a photograph of that signature. I liked the style of writing and learned how to do it. When the general wanted to see my writing just now, to decide if I was suitable for employment, I wrote a number of sentences in different scripts, among them "The Abbot Paphnutius hath set his hand hereunto", using the hand-writing of Abbot Paphnutius himself. The general liked it very much, that's why he recalled it just now.'

'Aglaya', said Madame Yepanchina, 'remember that: Paphnutius, better still, write it down, I'm always forgetting things. However, I thought it would be more interesting than that. Where is this signature then?'

'It's still on the table in the general's study, I think.'

'Send someone to fetch it at once.'

'It might be better if I wrote it for you some other time, if it's more convenient.'

'Of course, *maman*', said Alexandra. 'We should have lunch now; we're hungry.'

'Very well', decided Madame Yepanchina. 'Let us go, Prince; are you very hungry?'

'Yes, I do feel hungry now and I really am most grateful to you.'

'I'm very glad you're well-mannered and I can see you're not at all the . . . eccentric you were made out to be. Come along. Sit yourself here opposite me.' She fussed about seating the prince when they arrived in the dining-room. 'I want to look at you. Alexandra, Adelaida, look after the prince. He's not at all . . . an invalid, is he? Perhaps we can dispense with the napkin too . . . Did they use to tie you a napkin on at mealtimes?'

'Formerly, when I was about 7, I think they used to do that, but now I normally put it on my knees when I'm eating.'

'Quite right. And the fits?'

'Fits?' The prince was somewhat surprised. 'I have fits quite rarely these days. I don't know though, they say the climate here won't be good for me.'

'He speaks very well', remarked Madame Yepanchina, addressing her daughters and continuing to nod after every word of the prince's. 'I didn't expect that at all. It must have been all stuff and nonsense, as usual. Help yourself, Prince, and tell us where you were born and brought up. I want to know everything; you interest me greatly.'

The prince thanked her and, while eating with great relish, began relating what he had been obliged to repeat several times that morning. Madame Yepanchina's pleasure increased. The girls also listened with a fair amount of interest. They discussed their degree of kinship and the prince turned out to have a good knowledge of his family tree; however hard they tried, though, it seemed there was hardly any blood relationship between him and Madame Yepanchina at all. There might have been some distant connection among the grandfathers and grandmothers. Madame Yepanchina enjoyed this kind of dry stuff; she got few opportunities of talking about her pedigree, however much she wanted to, and rose from the table much elated.

'Let's all go to our sitting-room', she said, 'and they'll bring the coffee in there. We have this little common-room', she told the prince as she led him out, 'just my little drawing-room where we sit together when we're on our own and everybody gets on with their own work. Alexandra here, my eldest daughter, plays the piano, reads, or sews; Adelaida paints landscapes or portraits (and never finishes anything), and Aglaya just sits and does nothing. I'm all thumbs as well: can't get anything done. Well now, here we are; sit over here, Prince, by the fire and talk about something. I want to hear you tell a story. I want to be fully convinced, and when I see the old Princess Belokonskaya I'll tell her all about you. I want them all to take an interest in you as well. Come along now, say on.'

'*Maman*, that's a very funny way of having to talk, you know', observed Adelaida, who had adjusted her easel meanwhile and taken up her brushes and palette to resume copying from a landscape print. Alexandra and Aglaya seated themselves together on the small sofa and, with arms folded, prepared to listen. The prince became aware that singular attention was being directed towards him from all sides.

'If I was ordered to do it like that, I wouldn't say anything at all', remarked Aglaya.

'Why not? What's odd about that? Why shouldn't he talk? He's got a tongue. I want to know how well he talks. Anything will do. Tell us what you thought about Switzerland, your first impression. You'll see, he'll start in a minute and very well too.'

'I was greatly struck . . .' the prince began.

'There you are', Lizaveta Prokofievna seized on this eagerly, addressing her daughters, 'he's started, hasn't he?'

'At least let him talk then, *maman*', Alexandra stopped her. 'This prince may be a great fraud, and not an idiot at all', she whispered to Aglaya.

'Very likely. I could see that ages ago', answered Aglaya. 'And it's mean on his part to pretend. What does he think to gain by it?'

'I was greatly struck by my first impression', repeated the prince. 'When I travelled out of Russia through various German towns, all I did was stare in silence, and I remember asking no questions. It was after a long series of severe and agonizing bouts of my illness, and I would always fall into a total stupor whenever the illness was intensifying or attacks came one after another. I lost the power of remembering things altogether, and although my mind went on working it was as if my capacity for logical thought was disrupted. I couldn't string more than two or three ideas together at any one time. So it seems to me. Whenever the attacks subsided I grew well and strong again, just like now. I remember feeling unbearably sad; I felt like crying even; I was in a continual state of wonderment and anxiety: it affected me terribly that all this was *alien*: that much I realized. It was this sense of the alien which was crushing me. I shook off this blankness completely, I recall, one evening in Basle, as we were entering Switzerland, and what roused me was the braying of an ass in the town market. That ass really astonished me; it greatly took my fancy for some reason, and at the same time my head seemed to clear suddenly.'

'An ass? That's odd', remarked Madame Yepanchina. 'Though what's odd about it, one of us could well fall in love with a donkey', she remarked, glancing angrily at the giggling girls. 'It happened in mythology. Continue, Prince.'

'Since then I've been extremely fond of donkeys. There's a kind of common chord between us. I began asking questions about them, because I'd never seen them before, and I became convinced at once that they are the most useful of creatures, hard-working, strong, patient, cheap, and long-suffering; and through that donkey, I suddenly began to like everything about Switzerland and my former sadness passed off completely.'

'All this is very strange, but you can leave off about the donkey; let's get on to something else. Why are you still laughing, Aglaya? And you, Adelaida? The prince told us about the donkey beautifully. He saw it himself, and what have you seen? You've never been abroad.'

'I've seen an ass, *maman*', said Adelaida.

'And I've heard one too', added Aglaya. All three laughed again. The prince began laughing along with them.

'It's too bad of you', remarked Madame Yepanchina. 'You must excuse them, Prince, they're good-hearted really. I'm always scolding them, but I love them just the same. They're scatter-brained and flighty. Mad things.'

'Well, why not?' laughed the prince. 'I wouldn't have missed the chance in their place either. I'm still on the side of the ass though: the ass is a good and useful creature.'

'And are you good? I'm just being curious', asked Madame Yepanchina.

Everyone burst out laughing again.

'That wretched donkey again: I wasn't thinking of that at all!' cried Madame Yepanchina. 'Please believe me, Prince, I wasn't . . .'

'Hinting? Oh, I believe you, really I do!'

And the prince continued laughing.

'I'm very glad you can laugh about it. I can see that you're a most good-natured young man', said Madame Yepanchina.

'Not always', the prince replied.

'Well I am', put in Madame Yepanchina unexpectedly. 'If you want to know, I'm always good-hearted, it's my one failing, because one shouldn't be, not all the time. I very often lose my temper, with them, for example, and with Ivan Fedorovich especially, but the awful thing is, I'm kindest of all when I'm angry. Just now, before you came in, I lost my temper and made out I didn't and couldn't understand what was going on. I tend to do that sometimes, just like a child. Aglaya taught me a lesson; thank you, Aglaya. It's all nonsense though. I'm not as silly as I seem or as my daughters like to make me out. I have a mind of my own and I'm no shrinking violet. I'm saying this without malice, by the way. Come over here, Aglaya, and kiss me, there . . . that's enough', she remarked, when Aglaya had kissed her feelingly on lips and hand. 'Do go on, Prince. Perhaps you can remember something more interesting than a donkey.'

'I still don't see how anybody can tell a story straight out like that', said Adelaida again. 'I wouldn't know how to start.'

'But the prince will because he's extremely clever, at least ten times more than you, maybe twelve. I hope you'll realize it after this. Prove it to them, Prince; do go on. The donkey can be left out of it, really. Well now, what did you see abroad apart from that?'

'It was clever about the donkey as well', observed Alexandra. 'What the prince said about his illness was very interesting, how he started liking everything after one external shock. I've always been interested in how people go mad and then recover their wits. Especially if it happens suddenly.'

'Really? Really?' cried Madame Yepanchina. 'I see that you can sometimes be clever as well; that's enough laughing now! You had got up to the Swiss scenery I think, Prince, now then!'

'When we got to Lucerne, I was taken out on the lake. I thought it was splendid but I felt wretched at the same time', said the prince.

'Why?' asked Alexandra.

'I don't know. I always feel wretched and uneasy when I see nature like that for the first time; happy and uneasy at the same time; however, I was still unwell at that time.'

'Oh no, I would love to see it', said Adelaida. 'I don't know when we're going abroad. I haven't been able to find anything to paint for two years:

Both East and South have long been pictured . . .

Find me, Prince, a subject for a picture.'

'I don't understand anything about it really. It seems to me you just look and paint.'

'I don't know how to look.'

'Why talk in riddles? I don't understand this', Madame Yepanchina broke in. 'What d'you mean, "I don't know how to look"? You've got eyes, use them. If you don't know how to look here, you won't learn abroad either. Better if you tell us how you looked yourself, Prince.'

'Now that would be better', Adelaida said. 'The prince learned how to look when he was abroad, didn't he?'

'I don't know, really I just recovered my health there; I don't know if I learned to look or not. Incidentally, I was very happy almost all the time.'

'Happy! You know how to be happy?' cried Aglaya. 'So how can you say you never learned to look? You could teach us.'

'Yes, teach us please', Adelaida laughed.

'I can't teach anything', said the prince, laughing in his turn. 'I lived in that Swiss village practically all the time I was abroad; an occasional short trip outside—what have I got to teach you? To start with it was just pleasant, and I soon began to recover my health; after that every day became precious to me, the more so the longer time went on, so that I began to notice it. I used to go to bed very contented, and rise even happier. Why all that should be so, I should be hard put to tell you.'

'So you never felt like leaving, you felt no urge to go elsewhere?' asked Alexandra.

'At first, at the very beginning, yes, there were times when I used to have very restless moods. I kept thinking how I was going to spend my life; I wanted to test the future that awaited me. There were certain moments when I used to feel restless; you know how those moments come, especially when you are alone. We had a waterfall there, quite a small one, dropping high off the mountain in a delicate thread, almost vertical—white, pattering, foaming; it fell from a great height but it seemed quite low, it was a good half-mile off, but it seemed only fifty yards away. I loved to listen to it at night; it was in moments like those that I sometimes reached a peak of anxiety. Also at mid-day sometimes, on mountain walks, I'd be alone among the mountains, pine-trees all around me, ancient, tall, resinous; up there on the rock an old castle, medieval and ruinous; our village far away below, barely visible; the sun bright in the blue sky, a fearful silence. It was there that I used to sense a something that kept calling me elsewhere, and it seemed that if I walked straight ahead for a long long time, past the line, that line where sky and earth meet, the whole puzzle would be resolved and I should see a new life, a thousand times more vital and tumultuous than ours; I kept dreaming of a big city like Naples, all palaces, life, the thunderous noise . . . What didn't I dream! Then it seemed to me that even in prison one might discover an immense life.'

'I read that last laudable sentiment in my school anthology when I was 12', said Aglaya.

'It's all philosophy', observed Adelaida. 'You're a philosopher come to teach us.'

'Perhaps you're right', smiled the prince. 'I am indeed a philosopher, and who knows, perhaps I really do mean to teach people . . . That's possible; indeed it is.'

'And your philosophy is exactly the same as Eulampia Nikolavna's', Aglaya rejoined. 'She's a civil service widow, comes to us, a sort of hanger-on. Her one concern in life is cheapness; how cheaply one can live; all her talk is about kopecks and yet she has money, you know, she's a complete fraud. It's the same with your immense life in prison, and perhaps your four years' happiness in the country that you sold your Naples for—at a profit too, it seems, if only a few kopecks-worth.'

'As regards prison life there is room for disagreement', said the prince. 'I heard the story of one man who had spent nearly twelve years in prison; he was one of my professor's patients. He had recurrent fits and he would get restless sometimes, used to cry—and once even tried to kill himself. His life in jail was very grim, I can assure you, but by no means to be measured in kopecks. And yet all the companionship he had was a spider and a sapling growing under his window . . . But better if I tell you of another man I met last year. He had a very strange story to tell—strange because an incident like that happens only very rarely. This man was led out along with others on to a scaffold and had his sentence of death by shooting read out to him, for political offences.* About twenty minutes later a reprieve was read out and a milder punishment substituted; however, during the interval between the sentences, twenty minutes, or quarter of an hour at least, he lived with the certain conviction that within minutes he would suddenly die. I was extremely eager to listen whenever he recalled his emotions of that time, and I started asking him about it on a number of occasions. He remembered everything with the utmost clarity and he used to say that he would never forget anything of those minutes. About twenty yards from the scaffold, near where the people and soldiers were standing, three stakes had been dug into the earth, as there were several criminals. The first three were taken to the stakes and bound before being dressed in the death garments (long white smocks), and white hoods over their eyes so that they couldn't see the rifles; then a party of soldiers was lined up opposite each stake. My acquaintance was number eight, so he was due to go to the stake in the third group. A priest went round everyone with a cross. It worked out that he had five minutes to live, no more. He used to say that those five minutes seemed to him an eternity, an immense richness. It seemed that in those five minutes he could live through so many lives, that there could be no thinking now of the last instant; he divided his time up. He calculated the time in which to say farewell to his comrades and allotted some two minutes to that, then two more minutes to reflect upon himself and then look about him for the last time. He clearly recalls making these dispositions and the way he calculated them. He was dying at 27, healthy and strong; in bidding goodbye to his comrades he remembered asking one of them a somewhat irrelevant question and even being very interested in the answer. Then, after he had said goodbye to his comrades, came the two minutes he had set aside for *thinking about himself*; he already knew what he was going to think about: he kept wanting to imagine as swiftly and vividly as possible how on earth it could be that now he existed and was alive and in three minutes' time he would merely be *something*—something or somebody, but who, though? And where? He thought he could resolve all this in two minutes! A church stood not far off and its gilded roof sparkled in the sunshine. He remembered staring with an awful intensity at that roof and the sunlight glancing from it; he couldn't drag his eyes away: it occurred to him that those rays were his new state of being, and that in three minutes he would somehow merge with them . . . His revulsion at the unknown and the new, now that it was inevitable and imminent, was dreadful, but he says that nothing was more terrible at that moment than the nagging thought: "What if I didn't have to die! If life was returned to me—what an eternity it would be! And it would all be mine! I would turn every minute into an age, nothing would be wasted, every minute would be accounted for, nothing would be frittered away!" He used to say that this thought finally roused him to such a pitch of anger, that he wanted them to hurry up and shoot him and have done with it.'

The prince suddenly fell silent; everyone waited for him to go on and draw some conclusion.

'Have you finished?' asked Aglaya.

'What? Yes', said the prince, rousing himself from his momentary reverie.

'But why did you tell us about all this?'

'Just . . . it came back to me . . . it seemed relevant . . .'

'You're very abrupt, Prince', remarked Alexandra. 'You probably wanted to demonstrate that one shouldn't value a single instant in mere kopecks, and that sometimes five minutes can outweigh a fortune. All very laudable, but if I may ask, this friend of yours who told you about his sufferings . . . he had his sentence commuted, didn't he? So he was presented with that "eternal life". So what did he do with those riches afterwards? Did he "account" for every minute?'

'Oh no, he told me himself, I asked him about that; he didn't live like that at all and wasted an awful lot of minutes.'

'So it follows from your example, it follows that one can't really live one's life "counting every minute". It's just impossible, for some reason.'

'Yes, for some reason it's just impossible', the prince echoed, 'that's what I thought myself . . . But somehow I just can't believe it all the same . . .'

'That means you think you're going to live more wisely than anyone else?' said Aglaya.

'Yes, I thought that too sometimes.'

'And think so now?'

'And . . . think so now', replied the prince, smiling gently and almost timidly at Aglaya; then all at once he laughed out loud again and looked brightly at her.

'Modesty indeed!' said Aglaya, almost nettled.

'And how brave you are, really, here you are laughing and I was so shaken by all he told me I dreamed about it, just those five minutes . . .'

He again gave his hearers an earnest and searching look.

'You're not angry with me for any reason are you?' he enquired suddenly, apparently disconcerted but managing to look everyone straight in the eye.

'What for?' cried all three girls, astonished.

'Well, because I keep lecturing you . . .'

Everyone laughed.

'If you are angry, don't be', he said. 'I'm well aware that I've less experience than others and I'm less worldly wise than anybody. Perhaps I talk very strangely at times . . .'

Now he was definitely at a loss.

'If you say you were happy, that means you lived more, not less; why do you wriggle and try to apologize then?' began Aglaya, severely censorious. 'And please don't worry about lecturing us, you've nothing to be superior about. One could fill a hundred years of happiness with your sort of quietism. Whether you saw an execution or a little finger, you would draw equally laudable conclusions and still be happy. That sort of living's easy.'

'What you keep getting so angry about I fail to understand', said Madame Yepanchina, who had been observing the speakers' faces for a long time. 'And I don't understand what you're talking about either. What's all this nonsense about a finger? The prince talks beautifully, though a bit on the sad side. Why are you discouraging him? He was laughing when he started and now he's quite depressed.'

'It's all right, *maman*. It's a pity you never saw an execution, Prince, I wanted to ask you something.'

'I have seen one', responded the prince.

'You have?' cried Aglaya. 'I should have guessed! That's the finishing touch. If you have seen one, how can you say you lived happily all the time? Well, aren't I right?'

'They didn't execute people in your village, did they?' asked Adelaida.

'I saw it in Lyons, I went there with Schneider, he took me. I came across it as soon as I arrived.'

'Well then, did you enjoy it? Was it very edifying? Was it instructive?' asked Aglaya.

'I didn't enjoy it at all; I was rather ill afterwards, but I admit I was riveted by the sight, I couldn't tear my eyes away.'

'I couldn't have either', said Aglaya.

'They're very much against women going to watch, they even write about such women in the papers.'

'If they say it's not suitable for women, by the same token they're saying it's all right for a man and so justifying it. I congratulate them on their logic. You think the same way too, of course?'

'Tell us about the execution', Adelaida interrupted.

'I would much prefer not at the moment . . .' The prince was troubled and frowned slightly.

'It's as if you begrudge telling us', Aglaya reproached him.

'No, it's because I was telling someone about this execution just now.'

'Who?'

'Your footman, while I was waiting . . .'

'What footman?' came from all sides.

'The one who sits in the entrance-hall, with the greying hair, reddish face; I was sitting there before going in to see General Yepanchin.'

'That's an odd thing to do', remarked Madame Yepanchina.

'The prince is a democrat', Aglaya put in bluntly. 'Well if you've told Alexey, you can't refuse us, now can you?'

'I would certainly like to hear it', Adelaida repeated.

'A little while ago, actually', the prince addressed her, quite animated once more (he seemed to get excited in a very quick and unaffected way), 'when you asked me to give you the subject for a picture, I actually thought of this one: draw the face of a condemned man in the minute before the guillotine falls, while he's still standing on the scaffold before lying down on the plank they have.'

'The face? Just the face?' asked Adelaida. 'A strange subject, and what kind of picture would that be?'

'I don't know, why on earth not?' the prince insisted with some heat. 'I saw a picture like that in Basle not long ago. I'd very much like to tell you . . . I'll tell you some other time . . . It made a great impression on me.'

'You must certainly tell us about the Basle picture later', said Adelaida, 'but now explain this execution picture for me. Can you tell me how you imagine it yourself? How should one draw that face? Just the face, yes? What kind of face is it, then?'

'It is exactly a minute before death', began the prince perfectly readily, at once carried away by his recollection and apparently oblivious to all else, 'just when he has climbed the stair and set foot upon the scaffold. That was when he glanced in my direction; I looked into his face and understood it all . . . But how can one convey it? I would be terribly pleased, terribly pleased if you or anyone else could draw that face! Best of all if it were you! At the time I thought a picture would do a lot of good. To do it one really has to imagine everything that had taken place earlier, every single thing. He had been living in prison and expecting to wait at least a week before execution; he had been reckoning on the usual formalities, the documents being sent somewhere and taking a week to come back. But this time, for some reason, the process was curtailed. At five o'clock in the morning he had been asleep. It was towards the end of October; at five o'clock it's still cold and dark. The prison governor came in very quietly with a warder and touched him gently on the shoulder; he raised himself on one elbow and saw the light: "What's the matter?" "The execution is at ten o'clock." Still half-asleep, he didn't believe it and started to argue that the document was only due in a week's time, but when he was fully awake he stopped arguing and went quiet. That's what they told me. Then he said: "Still, it's hard like this, all of a sudden . . .", then fell silent again, there being nothing more he wanted to say. Then three or four hours go by on the usual things: the priest, breakfast for which he gets wine, coffee, and beef (well is that a mockery or not? Just think how cruel that is and yet on the other hand, honestly, these innocent people do it out of the goodness of their hearts, convinced they're being humane), then comes the dressing-up (you know what that involves for a condemned man), then finally they take him through the town to the scaffold . . . I imagine he thinks he still has an eternity left to live while they're taking him . . . I imagine he probably thought as he went along: "It's a long time yet, three streets yet to live; after this one there's the next, then the one after with the baker's on the corner . . . it'll be ages before we reach the baker's!" All around there's the crowd, shouting, noise, ten thousand faces, ten thousand eyes—all that had to be borne, and then worst of all, the thought: "There's ten thousand of them and not one of them is being executed, but I am!" Well, all that is by way of preliminary. The ladder is put up against the scaffold; suddenly he begins to weep in front of it, this strong and courageous man, a great evil-doer, so they said. All this time the priest has been inseparable from him, travelling with him in the cart, talking all the time, though hardly heard: he would start to listen, then fail to comprehend more than two words. It must have been so. Finally he began to mount the ladder; his legs are bound so that he walks in tiny steps. The priest, a perceptive man no doubt, stops talking and just keeps offering him the cross to kiss. At the bottom of the ladder he had been very pale, but after he had climbed it and stood on the scaffold, he became as white as a sheet all of a sudden, as white as a sheet of writing paper. Probably his legs had gone numb and were giving way, then came nausea—as if his throat was being constricted and almost tickling him—have you ever felt like that when you've been frightened or in moments of terror, when your reason remains perfectly clear but is no longer in control? I would think that in some inescapable disaster, like the house collapsing about you, for example, one would have an awful desire to just sit down, close one's eyes, and wait—what will be will be! . . . Just then, when this weakness was beginning, the priest with a swift gesture silently placed the cross to his lips; it was a little, silver, four-ended cross and he kept putting it to his lips every minute. And as soon as the cross touched his lips he would open his eyes and come to life again, as it were, and his legs moved on. He kept kissing the cross avidly, hurrying to do so, as if anxious not to forget to take something with him just in case, but he would scarcely have felt anything religious at that moment. And so it went on right up to the board itself . . . It's odd but very few people faint in these last seconds! On the contrary, the brain is fearfully alive and active, must be working, working, working, ever so hard, like a machine; I can imagine all kinds of thoughts hammering away, all half-formulated, perhaps even absurd, irrelevant thoughts like: "That one staring—he's got a wart on his forehead, the executioner there, he's got a rusty bottom button" . . . yet all the while you know and remember everything; there is a certain point you cannot forget, and you must not faint, and all things move and revolve around that point. And to think, this goes on till the last quarter of a second when your head is lying on the block and waiting and . . . *knowing*, and all at once it hears the iron sliding above! You would certainly hear that! Speaking for myself, if I was lying there I would deliberately listen for it and catch the sound! There might only be the tenth part of an instant, but you would certainly hear it! And just imagine, people still argue that perhaps the head when it flies off knows for a second that it has done so—what an idea! And what if it were five seconds! . . . Draw the scaffold so that the very last rung only can be seen clearly and close to; the felon has placed his foot on it: the head and face as white as a sheet, the priest is holding out the cross, while the other greedily protrudes his blue lips, and stares, and *knows everything*. The cross and the head—that's the picture; the faces of the priest, the executioner, his two assistants and several heads and eyes from below, all that can be drawn in as distant background, indistinct, subordinate. That's the sort of picture it should be.'

The prince fell silent and regarded them all.

'That's not much like quietism, of course', said Alexandra to herself.

'Well, now tell us how you fell in love', said Adelaida.

The prince stared at her in astonishment.

'Listen', Adelaida hurried on, 'you have still to tell us about the Basle picture, but just now I want to hear about your being in love; don't try to deny it, you were. Besides, as soon as you start telling a story, you stop being a philosopher.'

'As soon as you stop speaking, you're ashamed of what you've been saying', Aglaya remarked suddenly. 'Why is that?'

'Now that is just silly', said Madame Yepanchina sharply, with an indignant look at Aglaya.

'Not clever at all', confirmed Alexandra.

'Don't believe her, Prince', Madame Yepanchina told him. 'She does that on purpose out of spite; she's not as bad-mannered as that; don't pay any attention to their teasing. They're probably up to something but they already like you. I can read their faces.'

'And I can read their faces too', said the prince, emphasizing his words.

'What do you mean?' asked Adelaida curiously.

'What do you know about our faces?' the other two enquired.

But the prince was silent and grave; everyone awaited his answer.

'I will tell you later', he said, softly and earnestly.

'You're really trying to intrigue us', cried Aglaya, 'and so serious!'

'Well, all right', Adelaida once more hurried on, 'but if you're such an expert on faces, then you must have been in love; that means I was right. Tell us the story, do.'

'I was never in love', said the prince, quietly earnest as before. 'I . . . was happy in a different way.'

'How, then, in what way?'

'Very well, I'll tell you', said the prince, apparently deep in thought.

6

'HERE you all are', the prince began, 'looking at me with such curiosity that if I didn't satisfy it, you would probably be very angry with me. No, I'm just joking', he added hastily, smiling. 'There ... there it was children all the time. I spent all my time with children, just children. They were the village children, the whole crowd of them at school. I didn't actually teach them; oh no, there was a schoolmaster to do that, Jules Thibaud; I did teach them a little bit as well, but I mostly just spent time with them all the four years I was there. I wanted nothing else. I used to tell them everything, keeping nothing back. Their parents and relatives used to get very angry with me because their children couldn't do without me in the end, always crowding about me; the schoolmaster finally got to be my worst enemy. I made a lot of enemies there, all because of the children. Even Schneider took me to task. What were they all so afraid of? You can tell a child everything—everything; I've always been struck by how little adults understand children, even their own fathers and mothers. Nothing should be kept from children on the pretext that they're little and it's too soon for them to know. Such a sad, wretched idea! Children themselves are well aware that their parents regard them as too small and uncomprehending, when actually they understand everything. Adults don't realize that children can give extremely valuable advice in the most difficult situations. Heavens! When that pretty little bird looks at you, so happy and trusting, you are ashamed to betray it! I call them little birds because the earth holds nothing finer than a bird. Still, the main reason everybody in the village was angry with me was because of a certain incident ... Thibaud was simply jealous of me; at first he kept shaking his head, wondering how it was that the children understood everything I taught them and practically nothing he did. Later on he started laughing at me when I said that neither of us would teach them anything, they would teach us. How could he be jealous of me and tell stories about me when he lived among the children himself! The soul is healed through contact with children ... There was one patient in Schneider's establishment, a most wretched individual. His plight was so dreadful that it can hardly be paralleled. He had been sent there to be treated for insanity; in my view he wasn't insane, he was simply terribly distressed—and that was the extent of his illness. If you only knew what our children came to mean for him in the end . . . still, better if I tell you about that patient some other time; what I'll tell you now is how it all began. At first the children didn't take to me at all. I was so big and awkward; I know I'm not very good-looking either . . . and I was a foreigner to cap it all. They made fun of me at first, and later on they even started throwing stones at me when they caught sight of me kissing Marie. And I only kissed her once . . . No, don't laugh', the prince hastened to restrain his smirking audience, 'it wasn't anything to do with love. If you only knew what an unhappy creature she was, you would feel as sorry for her as I did. She was from our village. Her mother was an old woman who was permitted by the village council to partition off one of the two windows of her ramshackle little house and sell laces, thread, soap, and tobacco for coppers enough to live on. Her health was poor and her legs were all swollen, so she always sat in the one spot. Marie was her daughter, about 20, a feeble slip of a thing; she'd been developing consumption for long enough, but she still kept going round the houses as a daily, doing heavy cleaning work—washing floors, doing laundry, sweeping out yards, and mucking out livestock. A French commercial traveller passed by, seduced her, and carried her off; a week later he abandoned her alone on the road and quietly disappeared. She arrived back home, begging her way, all begrimed and ragged, her shoes worn through; she had walked for a whole week, sleeping out in the fields and catching a severe chill; her feet were bleeding and her arms swollen and chapped. Even before that, incidentally, she had been nothing to look at, though her eyes were placid, kindly, and innocent. She was a terribly quiet girl. Once, before all this, she suddenly started singing and I remember everybody being astonished and laughing: "Marie singing! Did you ever? Marie singing!"—and she got horribly self-conscious and kept quiet ever afterwards. People were still affectionate towards her then, but when she came back all ill and bedraggled, nobody showed her the slightest sympathy! They are so cruel over that sort of thing! Their views are so rigid! Her mother was the first to treat her with angry contempt: "You have dishonoured me now." She was the first to expose her to public disgrace: when the news got round the village that Marie had come back, everyone came running to have a look at her and practically the whole village crowded into the old woman's hut: old men, children, women, girls, everybody in such jostling, eager hordes. Marie was lying at the old woman's feet, hungry, ragged, and weeping. When everybody ran in she just hid her face in her dishevelled hair and pressed herself face down on to the floor. Everyone around regarded her as some sort of vermin; the old men condemned and berated her, the young folk laughed even, the women scolded and blamed her, looking at her contemptuously as if she had been a spider. The mother let all this go on, just sitting there nodding her approval. Her mother was very ill at that time, practically dying; in fact she actually did die two months later; she knew she was dying yet she still had no thought of forgiving her daughter till the time she died; she didn't say a word to her and chased her out to sleep in the passage, hardly giving her anything to eat. She frequently had to stand her diseased legs in warm water and every day Marie washed her legs for her and looked after her, but she accepted all these services in silence and never gave her a kindly word. Marie put up with everything and I noticed later, when I got to know her, that she approved of all this herself; she thought of herself as the lowest of creatures. When the old woman finally took to her bed, the old women of the village came in turns to look after her, as the custom is there. At this point they stopped feeding Marie altogether; in the village they used to chase her away and nobody even wanted to give her work, as they had done before. It was as if everyone despised her and the men stopped regarding her as a woman even, saying all manner of vile things to her. Sometimes, though very rarely, when the drinkers had had their fill on a Sunday, they used to throw down coppers for her, just like that, straight on the ground; Marie would pick them up in silence. She was coughing up blood even then. At length her old clothes became so tattered that she was ashamed to show herself in the village; she had gone about barefoot since the time of her return. It was now that she began to be tormented, especially by the children, the whole gang of them, about forty or more, and even had filth thrown at her. She implored a herdsman to let her look after the cows, but he drove her away. Then she began going out with the herd all day, without permission. Observing that she was extremely useful to him, the herdsman didn't chase her away this time, in fact he would sometimes give her the leavings from his own dinner, bread and cheese, regarding this as a great kindness on his part. When the old woman did die, the local pastor did not shrink from holding Marie up to public disgrace in church. She was standing over the coffin just as she was, in her rags, weeping. A good many people had congregated to see her crying as she followed the coffin; then it was that the pastor—still a young man, filled with hopes of becoming a great preacher, addressed them all, pointing to Marie. "She was the cause of this worthy woman's death" (which was untrue because she'd been ailing for two years), "behold her standing before you, not daring to look because she has been marked by the finger of God; there she is, barefoot and in rags, an example to all who lose their virtue! Who is she, then? That woman's daughter!" and much more in the same vein. Can you imagine, this vile stuff was much to the taste of practically all of them, but . . . now something extraordinary happened; the children took her part, because by this time they were all on my side, and had begun to feel affection towards Marie. It came about like this. I felt I must do something for Marie; she was in great need of money, but I never had a penny while I was there. I did have a small diamond pin, which I sold to a second-hand dealer who used to go round the villages trading in old clothes. He gave me eight francs for it, though it was worth all of forty. I tried for a long time to get Marie on her own; at length we did meet behind a tree by the fence outside the village, along a side-path leading up into the mountains. I gave her the eight francs and told her to take care of it because I wouldn't have any more. Then I kissed her and said she mustn't think I had any evil intentions, that I was kissing her not because I was in love with her, but because I was very sorry for her and had never thought her guilty from the very first, merely unfortunate. I really wanted to console her there and then and assure her that she shouldn't see herself as beneath everyone, but I don't think she understood me. I could see that at once, though she said practically nothing the whole time, standing in front of me with her eyes cast down, dreadfully ashamed. When I had finished, she kissed my hand and I seized hers at once and made to kiss it, but she hastily pulled it away. It was then that the children caught sight of us, the whole crowd of them; I found out later that they had been keeping watch on me for a long time. They started whistling, clapping their hands, and laughing, while Marie took to her heels. I tried to talk to them but they began pelting me with stones. That day everybody knew, the whole village, and Marie took the brunt of it all again: they detested her more than ever. I heard it said they even wanted to have her legally punished, but nothing came of that, thank goodness; still the children wouldn't let her be and tormented her worse than ever, pelting her with mud, chasing her as she ran from them breathless with her weak chest, shouting abuse after her. Once I even rushed in to fight them off. After that I began talking to them; every day I talked to them, whenever I possibly could. Sometimes they would stop and listen, though they still kept abusing her. I told them how unhappy Marie was; soon they left off reviling her and went away in silence. Little by little we began to get talking and I concealed nothing from them; I told them everything. They listened to me very intently and soon began to feel pity for Marie. Some of them began to greet her kindly when they met her; it's the custom there if you meet anybody—whether you know them or not—to bow and say: "Good day." I can imagine how surprised Marie must have been. One day, two little girls got hold of some food and took it to her. After they gave it to her, they came to me and told me. They said Marie had burst into tears and that they were now very fond of her. Before long everyone else began to love her—and me too, suddenly, along with her. They started coming to me often, asking me to tell them stories; I think I did this well because they all liked to listen to me. Later on I studied and read everything just so as to have something to tell them afterwards. And I did this for all of three years. When I was accused—by Schneider too—later on for talking to them like grown-ups, hiding nothing from them, I used to answer that it was shameful to tell them lies, and they knew it all anyway, however much you kept from them, and they would find things out in a squalid sort of way, which was not the case with me. People should just recall how it had been when they were children. They didn't agree . . .

'I kissed Marie a fortnight before her mother died; by the time the pastor preached his sermon, the children were all on my side. I immediately told them what the pastor had done and interpreted it for them; they were all angered at him and some went so far as to smash his windows with stones. I stopped them doing it because that was wrong; still, everybody in the village got to know about it and started accusing me of corrupting the children. Then they found out that all the children loved Marie, and were terribly alarmed; but Marie was happy by now. The children were forbidden to see her even, but they used to run to her on the sly out to the herd, quite a way off, almost a mile from the village; they took her presents, while others just ran to hug and kiss her and say: "*Je vous aime, Marie!*" before racing back again. Marie almost went mad from such unexpected happiness; she had never so much as dreamed of this; she was overjoyed, though bashful, but the main thing was that the children, the little girls especially, were very keen to run and tell her how much I loved her and how I was always talking to them about her. They said I had told them everything and that now they loved and pitied her and would always do so. Then they came running along to me with such joyful, flustered little faces to announce that they had just seen Marie and that she sent her greetings. In the evenings I used to go to the waterfall; there was a place there completely secluded from the village side, with poplars growing all around; it was there they came running to find me of an evening, some of them in secret even. I think they found my love for Marie terribly enjoyable, and yet it was the one thing in all my life there in which I deceived them. I didn't disabuse them of the idea that I loved Marie, that I was in love with her I mean, rather than merely being very sorry for her; I could tell that this was the way they wanted it, the way they had imagined it and settled it among themselves, so I kept quiet and pretended that they had guessed right. Those little hearts were so tactful and kind: it seemed impossible to them that Marie should be barefoot and so poorly dressed, when their kind Leon loved her so. Just imagine, they got hold of shoes and stockings for her, and underthings, and even a dress of some sort; how they had contrived to do this I have no idea; the whole crowd of them had a hand in it. Whenever I asked them about it, they just laughed gleefully and the little girls clapped their hands and kissed me. Sometimes I would go secretly to see Marie myself. She was very ill by now and scarcely able to walk; she had finally given up working for the cowherd, but still went out with the cattle every morning. She would sit down some distance away; there was a ledge under a sheer, overhanging rock, and she would sit there right in the corner, secluded from everyone, almost motionless the livelong day, from morning till the cows were moving off home. By then she was so weak from consumption that for the most part she sat with her eyes closed, leaning her head against the rock, dozing and breathing heavily; her face was emaciated and skeletal, and sweat stood out on her forehead and temples. That was how I always found her. I used to come for a minute or so and had no wish for anyone to see me either. As soon as I appeared Marie would at once start, open her eyes, and fall to kissing my hands. I didn't withdraw them now, since it made her happy; all the time I sat there she would tremble and weep; several times she actually started saying something, but it was difficult to make anything out. She seemed demented at times, terribly agitated and ecstatic. Occasionally the children would come with me. When that happened they used to stand not far off, guarding us from something or somebody; they got enormous pleasure from that. When we left, Marie was alone again, motionless as before, her head pressed against the rock, perhaps dreaming. One morning she could no longer go out to the herd and stayed behind in her empty house. The children found out about this at once and practically all of them came to visit her that day; she lay all on her own in bed. For two days it was the children alone who looked after her, trotting in to her by turns, but later, when the village heard that Marie was actually dying, the old women began to come and sit by her. The village had begun to take pity on Marie, at any rate they no longer tried to check the children or scold them as they had done formerly. Marie was drowsy all the time, her sleep restless: she coughed dreadfully. The old women chased the children away but they used to run up to the window, sometimes only for a moment, just to say: "*Bonjour, notre bonne Marie.*" When she caught sight of them or heard them, she revived and, ignoring the old wives, struggled to rise on her elbow to nod her thanks to them. They brought her gifts as before, but she hardly ate anything. Because of them, I assure you, she died almost happy. Through them she forgot her own black misfortune, accepting absolution through them, as it were, because to the very end she continued to regard herself as a great sinner. Like little birds, they beat their wings against her windows and shouted to her every morning: *"Nous t'aimons, Marie."* She died very soon after. I had thought she would live much longer. On the eve of her death, I called in to see her before sunset; she seemed to recognize me and I pressed her hand for the last time; how shrivelled it had become! Then suddenly in the morning they came to tell me that Marie had died. The children couldn't be held back now: they decked her coffin with flowers and placed a garland on her head. In church, the pastor did not shame the dead this time; there weren't many at the funeral in any case, just a few out of curiosity; but when it was time to carry the coffin, the children all rushed forward at once to bear it themselves. As they couldn't carry it, they did their bit to help, and all of them ran behind, weeping. Since then the children have revered Marie's little grave: they deck it with flowers every year and have planted roses round it. But it was after the funeral that I was most persecuted by the village on account of the children. The pastor and the schoolmaster were the chief ones behind it. The children were strictly forbidden even to meet me, and Schneider undertook to see to this. Nevertheless, we continued to see each other and communicated by signs. They used to send me little notes. Later on things were patched up and settled, but even at the time it was all right: the persecution brought me even closer to the children. During my final year I almost made my peace with Thibaud and the pastor. Schneider talked a good deal to me, arguing about my "harmful" system with the children. As if I had a system! At length Schneider told me of a very strange notion he had conceived—this was just before my departure—he told me he was firmly convinced that I was a complete child myself, an absolute child, that it was only in the face and build that I resembled an adult, but in development, spirit, character, and perhaps intelligence I was not a grown-up and I'd stay that way, even if I lived to be 60. I was very amused: he's wrong of course, a child indeed! But he was right about one thing, I really don't like being among adults, grown-up people; I've noticed that long since. I don't like it because I can't cope with them. Whatever they say to me, however kind they are to me, I never feel at ease with them for some reason, and I'm always terribly glad when I can get away to my friends—and my friends have always been children—but not because I am a child myself, it was simply because I have always been drawn to children. At the beginning of my time in the village—when I used to go off to brood alone in the mountains—and I came across the whole band of them sometimes, usually at noon when they were let out of school, making plenty of noise as they ran along with their little satchels and slates, shouting and laughing as they played their games, my soul began suddenly to reach out to them. I don't know, but I began to experience an intense sensation of happiness whenever I encountered them. I would stop and laugh from sheer gladness as I gazed at their little flashing legs, always running, at the little boys and girls running together, at their laughter and tears (many of them contrived to fight, burst into tears, make up again, and start playing before they got home), and I would forget all about being depressed. Afterwards in fact, for the next three years, I simply couldn't understand how and why people could ever be depressed. My whole life became centred on them. I never reckoned on leaving the village, and it never entered my head that I would one day come here to Russia. I thought I should always be there. But one day I realized that Schneider couldn't very well go on keeping me at his own expense, and a certain matter turned up, so important, seemingly, that Schneider himself urged me to go, and wrote a letter on my behalf. I'll look into all that and discuss it with somebody. It may be that my life will be completely changed, but that's not the main thing. The main thing is that my life has already changed utterly. I left a lot behind there, a very great deal. It's all disappeared. As I sat in the railway carriage, I thought: "Now I'm on my way to be among people. Perhaps I don't know very much, but a new life has begun." I resolved to conduct myself honestly and firmly. I might be bored and miserable among people, but my first decision was to be polite and open with everyone; no one could ask more of me than that. Perhaps they would look on me as a child here as well—let them! Everybody regards me as an idiot for some reason—I really was ill enough at one time to resemble an idiot; but hardly now, when I'm well aware that they think of me as one? I come in and I think: "Now they regard me as an idiot, but I'm intelligent really, they just don't realize . . ." I often think like that. When I was in Berlin and got some little letters they had already managed to write—it was only then I realized how much I loved them. It was very distressing to get that first letter! How sad they had been seeing me off! That had started a month before: "*Leon s'en va, Leon s'en va toujours!*" We would gather every evening by the waterfall like before, and talked constantly of our parting. Sometimes it was as jolly as it had been before; when we separated for the night, though, they had taken to hugging me warmly, something they hadn't done before. Some of them used to run and see me secretly by themselves, just so as to hug and kiss me on their own, not in front of the others. When I was finally setting off, all of them together flocked to see me off at the station, which was about a mile from the village. They tried to stop themselves from crying but many of them couldn't manage it and wept aloud, especially the girls. We were hurrying so as not to miss the train, but first one then another would rush out of the crowd just to embrace me on the road with his little arms and kiss me, so holding up the whole procession; even though we were in a hurry, everybody stopped and waited while he said his farewells. When I got in the carriage and the train started moving, they all shouted out "hurrah!" and stood for a long time till the train was completely out of sight. And I was staring too . . . Do you know, when I came in just now and saw your nice faces—I look closely at faces now—and heard your first words, I felt my heart ease for the first time since then. I was already thinking just now that perhaps I was one of the really lucky ones: after all, I know that one doesn't often meet people one takes to at first sight, but I have met you straight away as soon as I got off the train. I am very well aware that everyone is shy when it comes to talking of their own feelings, but here I am talking to you and not being shy at all. I'm not a sociable person, and perhaps I won't come to see you for a long time. I don't mean it like that: I didn't say that because I don't think highly of you—and don't imagine I've taken offence at anything. You asked me about your faces and what I saw in them. I will tell you with great pleasure. You have a happy face, Adelaida Ivanovna, the nicest face of all three. Aside from the fact that you're very pretty, one looks at you and thinks: "She has the face of a kind sister." You have a straightforward, cheerful manner, but you can quickly understand a person's heart. That's how your face seems to me. Your face, Alexandra Ivanovna, is also beautiful and very sweet, but perhaps you have a secret sadness; you have the kindest of hearts, no doubt of that, but you are not high-spirited. You have a certain something in your face reminiscent of the Holbein Madonna in Dresden. Well, so much for your face; am I a good guesser? You said I was yourselves. But as for your face, Lizaveta Prokofievna', here he addressed Madame Yepanchina all of a sudden, 'from your face I do not have to think, I am perfectly certain that you're an absolute child in everything, everything, for good or ill, even though you're the age you are. You aren't angry with me for saying that? After all, you know my opinion of children! And don't go thinking I'm saying all this about your faces out of simplicity; oh no, not at all! Perhaps I have my reasons too.'

7

WHEN the prince had concluded they all looked brightly at him, even Aglaya, and especially Lizaveta Prokofievna.

'Well, you've certainly put him through an examination!' she exclaimed. 'So then, dear ladies, you thought to take him under your wing like some poor little soul, but he hardly deigned to accept you himself, and even then with the proviso that he'll only visit occasionally. We're the ones to look foolish and I'm glad of it; Ivan Fedorovich comes out worst of all. Bravo, Prince, we were instructed to put you through your paces just now. And what you said about my face is absolutely correct: I'm a child and I know it. I knew that even before you told me; you put my thoughts in a nutshell. I believe your character is just like mine, and I'm very pleased; like two drops of water. Only you're a man and I'm a woman and I've never been to Switzerland; that's the only difference.'

'Don't be too sure, *maman*', exclaimed Aglaya. 'The prince says he had a motive of his own in all his confessions, he wasn't just talking for talking's sake.'

'Yes, yes', laughed the others.

'Don't make fun of him, my dears, he might be a bit craftier than all three of you put together. You'll see. But Prince, why didn't you mention Aglaya? She's waiting and so am I.'

'I can't say anything now; I'll tell you later.'

'Why? Isn't she striking?'

'Oh, indeed she is; you are extraordinarily beautiful, Aglaya Ivanovna. You're so pretty, one is afraid to look at you.'

'Just that? No qualities?' Madame Yepanchina pursued.

'It's hard to judge beauty; I'm not ready yet. Beauty is a puzzle.'

'That means you've set Aglaya a puzzle', said Adelaida. 'Solve it then, Aglaya. She is pretty though, Prince, isn't she?'

'Marvellously!' the prince replied feelingly, his glance drawn to Aglaya, 'almost as pretty as Nastasya Filippovna, though the face is totally different! . . .'

They exchanged astonished glances.

'Like wh-o-o?' Madame Yepanchina brought out. 'Like Nastasya Filippovna? Where have you seen her? Which Nastasya Filippovna?'

'Gavrila Ardalionovich was showing Ivan Fedorovich her portrait just now.'

'What, he brought Ivan Fedorovich her portrait?'

'To show him. Nastasya Filippovna gave her portrait to Gavrila Ardalionovich today, and he brought it to show.'

'I want to see it!' Madame Yepanchina burst out. 'Where is this portrait? If she gave him it, he must have it with him in the study. He always comes in to work on a Wednesday and never goes before four. Call Gavrila Ardalionovich at once! No, I'm not exactly dying to see him. Do me a favour, dear Prince, go along to the study, get the portrait from him, and bring it here. Say we just want to see it. If you please.'

'He's nice but a bit on the simple side', said Adelaida, when the prince had gone out.

'Yes, rather too much so', said Alexandra. 'It makes him a bit ridiculous even.'

Neither of them seemed to be saying all she thought.

'Still, he got out of the face business well enough', said Aglaya, 'flattered us all, even *maman*.'

'No clever remarks, please!' cried Madame Yepanchina. 'He wasn't flattering, it was I who was flattered.'

'You think he was being crafty?' asked Adelaida.

'I fancy he's not so simple.'

'Get away with you', said her mother, bristling. 'I think you're more ridiculous than he is. Simple, maybe, but he's got his wits about him—in the best sense of course. Exactly like me.'

'Of course it was awful of me to blurt that out about the picture', the prince was thinking to himself as he entered the study, his conscience troubling him somewhat. 'But . . . perhaps it was for the best . . .' An odd idea, still rather vague, had begun to take shape in his mind.

Gavrila Ardalionovich was still sitting in the study, engrossed in his papers. He obviously wasn't paid his company salary for nothing. He was horribly embarrassed when the prince asked for the portrait and related how the others had found out about it.

'E-e-ch! Why did you have to blab about it!' he cried in savage annoyance. 'You know nothing about all this . . . Idiot!' he muttered to himself.

'I'm sorry, I did it absolutely without thinking; it just slipped out. I said that Aglaya was almost as pretty as Nastasya Filippovna.'

Ganya asked for a more detailed account and the prince obliged. Ganya gave him a derisive look.

'You've got Nastasya Filippovna on the brain . . .', he muttered, but fell to thinking before finishing the sentence.

He was clearly distraught. The prince reminded him about the picture.

'Listen, Prince', said Ganya suddenly, as if struck by an idea, 'I have an enormous favour to ask of you . . . But I don't know, really . . .'

He paused, embarrassed; he was making his mind up about something and engaged in an internal struggle of some sort. The prince waited in silence. Ganya stared at him again, intently, searchingly.

'Prince', he resumed, 'just now the people through there . . . because of something really strange . . . ridiculous too . . . and I'm not to blame . . . well, irrelevant anyway, those people are a little cross with me, so I don't want to go through there for the

time being unless they call me. And I badly need to speak with
Aglaya Ivanovna. I've written a few words in case of need' (a
small folded paper appeared in his hand), 'but I just don't know
how to deliver it. Would you, Prince, undertake to pass it to
Aglaya Ivanovna, but only to her, I mean so that no one else sees,
you follow me? It's not much of a secret, there's nothing out of
the way . . . but . . . you'll do it?'

'I'm not very happy about it', replied the prince.

'Oh, Prince, it's a case of desperate need!' Ganya began
imploring him. 'She might answer, perhaps . . . Believe me I
would only have asked you in the most urgent, the most pressing
circumstances . . . Who else can I entrust with it? It's extremely
important . . . Terribly important for me . . .'

Ganya was miserably afraid that the prince would refuse, and
gazed into his eyes with timid entreaty.

'Very well, I'll do it.'

'But make sure no one notices', the delighted Ganya begged
him. 'The thing is, I'm relying on your word of honour here,
aren't I?'

'I shan't show anybody', said the prince.

'The note isn't sealed, but . . .' Ganya blurted, over-anxious,
then halted in embarrassment.

'Oh, I shan't read it', said the prince quite simply, as he took
the portrait and left the study.

Ganya, left to himself, put his head in his hands.

'One word from her and I . . . and I really might break it
off! . . .'

The excitement and suspense prevented him sitting down to
his papers again, and he began wandering round the room from
one corner to another.

The prince walked back, a prey to reflection; the commission
troubled him, as did the thought of Ganya writing notes to
Aglaya. Two rooms away from the drawing-room on his way
back, however, he stopped short, as if recalling something,
looked about him, then went over to the window nearer the light
and began to study Nastasya Filippovna's portrait.

It was as if he was trying to resolve some mystery hidden in that
face which had struck him earlier. That recent impression had
hardly abated, and now he was in haste to verify it once more.

The extraordinary beauty of the face, along with something else about it, struck him even more forcibly now. It seemed to contain a boundless pride and scorn, almost hatred, and yet at the same time something trusting, something astonishingly ingenuous; the contrast prompted a feeling approaching compassion in him as he gazed at those features. That dazzling beauty verged on the intolerable, the beauty of the pale face, the almost hollow cheeks, the burning eyes; a strange beauty indeed! The prince gazed for a minute or so, then suddenly bethought himself, looked about him, then swiftly brought the portrait close to his lips and kissed it. When he walked into the drawing-room a minute later, his face was perfectly composed.

As soon as he entered the dining-room, however (two rooms before the drawing-room), he almost collided with Aglaya coming out. She was alone.

'Gavrila Ardalionovich asked me to give you this', said the prince, handing her the note.

Aglaya halted, took the note, and gave the prince a rather odd look. There was no hint of embarrassment in her glance, apart from a glimmer of surprise, and that directed at the prince alone. Aglaya's gaze seemed to demand some explanation from him—how had he got mixed up in this affair with Ganya?—a demand that was cool and lofty. They stood opposite one another for several seconds; at length a look of faint derision came into her face; she gave a slight smile and walked past him.

Madame Yepanchina studied Nastasya Filippovna's picture for some time in silence, evincing a certain disparagement as she held it at arm's length in showy affectation, as far from her eyes as she could.

'Yes, pretty', she brought out at length. 'Very pretty even. I've seen her once or twice but only from a distance. Does that kind of beauty appeal to you?' she suddenly addressed the prince.

'Yes . . . that kind . . .', he replied, with a certain effort.

'You mean just that kind?'

'Just that kind.'

'Why?'

'In that face . . . there's a great deal of suffering . . .', the prince went on, somehow reluctantly, seeming to be talking to himself rather than answering the question.

'I dare say you're talking nonsense', decided Madame Yepanchina, and with a lofty gesture tossed the picture away from her on to the table.

Alexandra picked it up, and as Adelaida came over both began to scrutinize it. At that moment Aglaya returned to the drawing-room.

'Such power!' cried Adelaida suddenly, gazing avidly at the picture over her sister's shoulder.

'Where? What power?' Lizaveta Prokofievna asked sharply.

'Beauty like that is power', said Adelaida warmly. 'With beauty like that one could turn the world upside down!'

She walked thoughtfully over to her easel. Aglaya glanced only fleetingly at the picture, blinked, and pushed out her lower lip as she sat down to one side and folded her arms.

Madame Yepanchina rang.

'Call Gavrila Ardalionovich, he's in the study', she ordered the servant who had entered.

'*Maman!*' cried Alexandra significantly.

'I just want a word or two with him, that's all', Madame Yepanchina snapped, silencing the protest. She was plainly irritated. 'As you see, Prince, we're all full of secrets here. Full of secrets! That's the done thing, a sort of etiquette; it's stupid. Especially in a matter which needs the utmost frankness, openness, and honesty. There's marriages in the air and I don't like the sound of them . . .'

'*Maman*, do you have to?' Alexandra again hastened to stop her.

'What's the matter, dear daughter? Are you saying you like it yourself? What if the prince does hear, we're friends after all. At least he and I are. God seeks good people, of course, and he has no use for the wicked and wayward; the wayward ones especially, who decide one thing today and talk differently tomorrow. You follow me Alexandra Ivanovna? They say I'm a queer one, Prince, but I can tell people apart. The heart is what matters, the rest doesn't count. You need brains too of course . . . perhaps that's what matters, after all. Stop smiling Aglaya, I'm not contradicting myself: a foolish woman with a heart and no brains is as bad as one with brains and no heart. Old but true. I'm the fool with the heart and no brain, you're the other way round; we're both miserable and we both suffer.'

'What are you so unhappy about then, *maman?*' Adelaida couldn't help asking, as the only member of the company who retained her good spirits.

'In the first place from having clever daughters', snapped Madame Yepanchina, 'and since that's reason enough, there's no need to go into the others. There's been quite enough chatter. We'll see how the two of you (I don't count Aglaya) manage to extricate yourselves with all your cleverness and long words, and whether you'll be happy with your fine gentleman, my dear Alexandra Ivanovna . . . Ah!' she exclaimed, seeing Ganya enter the room, 'here comes another nuptial union. Good day!' she responded to Ganya's bow, without asking him to sit down. 'Are you contemplating marriage?'

'Marriage? . . . What? . . . What marriage?' Gavrila Ardalionovich mumbled, aghast. He was dreadfully taken aback.

'Are you getting married, I'm asking you, if you prefer that expression.'

'N-no . . . I . . . n-no', lied Gavrila Ardalionovich, shame flooding his cheeks with colour. He shot a swift glance at Aglaya as she sat apart, and quickly averted his eyes. Aglaya's cool, calmly intent gaze was fixed upon him as she contemplated his confusion.

'No? Did you say no?' pursued the implacable Lizaveta Prokofievna. 'Very well, I will remember that today, Wednesday morning, you answered "no" to my question. It is Wednesday today, isn't it?'

'I believe so, *maman*', responded Adelaida.

'They never know what day it is. What's the date?'

'The twenty-seventh', Ganya replied.

'Twenty-seventh? That's good for another reason. Goodbye then, I expect you are very busy, and I have to dress and go out; don't forget your portrait. Give my regards to poor Nina Alexandrovna. *Au revoir*, dear Prince. Come and see us often, and I'll drop by on old Princess Belokonskaya specially to tell her about you. And listen, my dear: I believe that God has brought you from Switzerland to Petersburg just for my sake. You may have other things to attend to, but I'm the main reason. It's God's purposes at work. *Au revoir*, my dears.

Alexandra, come to my room, dear.'

Madame Yepanchina went out. Ganya, crestfallen, distraught, and in a foul temper, picked the portrait up from the table and with a twisted smile addressed the prince.

'Prince, I'm going home now. If you're still minded to live with us I can drive you, otherwise you won't know the address.'

'Wait a little, Prince', said Aglaya, suddenly rising from her chair. 'I'd like you to write in my album. Papa said you had a fine hand. I'll just bring it . . .'

And she left the room.

'*Au revoir*, Prince, I must be going too', said Adelaida.

She squeezed his hand hard, smiled at him with cordial affection, and went out. She did not look at Ganya.

'It was you', grated Ganya, rounding on the prince as soon as they had all gone. 'It was you letting on to them that I was going to get married!' he muttered in a swift undertone, his face working and his eyes furious. 'Shameless blabbermouth!'

'I assure you, you're mistaken', the prince replied, calmly polite. 'I didn't even know you were getting married.'

'You heard Ivan Fedorovich talking about everything being decided tonight at Nastasya Filippovna's, that's what you told them! Don't lie! How could they have known? Who the devil could have told them apart from you? The old woman was dropping the hint, wasn't she?'

'You know better than I who told them, if you think the hint was directed at you, I never said a word about it.'

'Did you hand over the note? Any answer?' Ganya interrupted, hotly impatient. But Aglaya returned just at that moment, and the prince was unable to reply.

'There you are, Prince', said Aglaya, placing her album on the table. 'Choose a page and write me something. Here's a pen, it's a new one too. Does it matter if it's got a steel nib? I've heard calligraphists don't use steel nibs.'

As she spoke to the prince, she appeared not to notice Ganya's presence. But while the prince was adjusting the pen, choosing a page, and making his preparations, Ganya walked over to the fireplace where Aglaya was standing close to the prince's right, and in a faltering, trembling voice spoke almost in her ear:

'One word, just one word from you and I'm saved.'

The prince turned swiftly and looked at them both. Ganya's face registered genuine despair; he seemed to have uttered the words without thinking, on a sudden impulse. Aglaya regarded him for several seconds with precisely the same expression of cool astonishment she had directed towards the prince a little while before; it seemed this cool astonishment of hers, this bewilderment, this apparent total incomprehension of what was said to her, was for Ganya at that moment more terrible than the most withering contempt.

'What shall I write then?' enquired the prince.

'I'll dictate it to you', said Aglaya, turning to him. 'Are you ready? Very well, write: "I do not bargain." Now write the day and month underneath. Show me.'

The prince gave her the album.

'Excellent! You've done it beautifully; you have a wonderful hand! Thank you. Now *au revoir*, Prince . . . Wait though', she added, as if suddenly remembering something, 'come with me, I want to give you a keepsake.'

The prince followed her, but as they came into the dining-room, Aglaya stopped.

'Read this', she said, handing him Ganya's note.

The prince took it and looked at Aglaya in bewilderment.

'I know very well you haven't read it and you can't be in that man's confidence. Read it; I want you to read it.'

The note had evidently been written in haste:

'Today my fate is to be decided, you know how. Today I have to give my irrevocable word. I have no right whatever to your sympathy and do not dare to nurture any hopes; but once you spoke a word, just one word, and that word lit up the black night of my life and became for me a beacon. Speak one more such word to me—and you will save me from disaster! Just tell me: *break the whole thing off* and I'll do it this very day. Oh, does it cost so much to say it? I only ask for that word as a token of your sympathy and pity for me—only that, only that! Nothing more whatever, nothing! I dare not cherish any hope, because I am not worthy of it. But after a word from you, I will take up my poverty again and rejoice to endure my desperate plight. I will take up the struggle and rejoice in it, I will be reborn, with strength renewed!

Send me that word of compassion (compassion alone, I swear)! Do not be angry at the presumption of one in despair, a drowning man who

nerves himself to make one last effort to save himself from perishing.
                                                                G. I.'

'This man assures me', said Aglaya harshly, when the prince
had finished reading, 'that the words "break the whole thing off"
will not compromise me and commit me to nothing; he gives me a
written guarantee himself, as you see, in this note of his. See how
naively quick he is to lay stress on certain words and how crudely
his real intent shows through. And yet he knows that if he had
broken it off by himself, without any word from me—not even
telling me, and with no claim on me at all, then I would have
altered my opinion of him and perhaps become his friend. He is
perfectly aware of that! But he has a mean soul: he knows and yet
he can't bring himself to act; he knows and still he asks for
guarantees. He's incapable of acting on faith. He wants me to give
him hopes of my hand, in exchange for the hundred thousand. As
for the word he talks about in the note, that I once spoke and
supposedly lit up his life, it's a barefaced lie. I just felt sorry for him
once. But he's bold and has no sense of shame; it immediately
struck him that here was a semblance of hope; I realized that at
once. Ever since, he's been angling for me; he's still at it. But
enough is enough; take his note and give it him back, this minute,
when you get out of the house of course, not before.'

'What answer shall I give him, then?'

'Nothing, of course. That's the best answer. So you intend
living in his house?'

'Your father recommended that himself this morning', said the
prince.

'Well be on your guard against him, I warn you; he'll never
forgive you for giving him his note back.'

Aglaya squeezed his hand lightly and left. Her expression was
grave and frowning, she did not even smile as she nodded her
farewell to the prince.

'I'm coming, I'm just getting my bundle', said the prince to
Ganya, 'then we'll be off.'

Ganya stamped his foot impatiently, his face darkening with
fury. At length they both emerged into the street, the prince with
his bundle in his hands.

'The answer! The answer!' Ganya turned on him. 'What did
she say to you? Did you give her the letter?'

The prince silently handed him the note. Ganya froze.

'What? My note?' he cried. 'He didn't give her it! Oh, I should have guessed! Oh, d-da-damnation . . . Of course she didn't understand a thing just now! But why, why, why on earth didn't you give it to her? Oh, double damn . . .'

'I'm sorry, on the contrary, I managed to give her your note straight away, the moment you gave it to me, exactly as you wished. I have it now because Aglaya Ivanovna gave it back this minute.'

'When? When?'

'As soon as I'd finished writing in the album, when she asked me to go with her, as you heard. We went into the dining-room and she gave me the note, told me to read it, and to return it to you.'

'Re-e-ad it?' cried Ganya almost at the top of his voice. 'Read it? You read it?'

He again halted in the middle of the pavement, stupefied, his mouth wide open in astonishment.

'Yes, I read it just now.'

'And she gave it to you to read, herself?'

'Herself, do believe me, I wouldn't have looked at it without her invitation.'

Ganya was silent for a minute, in an agony of thought, then suddenly exclaimed:

'It's impossible! She couldn't have told you to read it. You're lying. You read it yourself!'

'I am speaking the truth', replied the prince in a completely imperturbable fashion, as before, 'and believe me, I am very sorry to see it upset you so much.'

'Wretched creature. But at least she said something to you at the same time, didn't she? She made some sort of reply, didn't she?'

'Yes, of course.'

'Then tell me, tell me, dammit! . . .'

Ganya twice stamped his galoshed right foot on the pavement.

'As soon as I'd read it, she told me you were angling for her; you wanted to compromise her into giving you hope, and relying on that hope, abandon your hopes for the hundred thousand without risk. That if you had done that without bargaining with her and broken the thing off yourself without asking guarantees from her in advance, she might possibly have become your friend. I think that's all. Yes, one more thing: when I had already taken the note, I asked her what answer I should give you then, and she said no answer was the best answer—I think that was it; I'm sorry if I can't remember her exact words, I'm saying it as I understood it myself.'

Ganya was seized by a boundless rage and his fury burst out, unrestrained.

'So! That's the way of it!' he ground out. 'Throw my notes out of the window! So! She won't bargain—but I will! Then we'll see! I've a trick or two up my sleeve yet . . . we'll see! I'll show her who's master! . . .'

He had turned pale, his face working and his lips frothing; he shook his fist. So they walked on a few yards. He made no attempt to observe the niceties as far as the prince was concerned, and behaved as if he were alone in his own room; he regarded him as a complete nonentity. All of a sudden, however, he was struck by a thought and recollected himself.

'But how on earth', he asked the prince abruptly, 'how on earth could you' (an idiot, he added to himself), 'how could you be on such confidential terms two hours after meeting them for the first time? How did it happen?'

Only jealousy had been wanting to make his torment complete. Now it suddenly pierced him to the heart.

'That I can't explain to you.'

Ganya looked at him grimly.

'It wasn't to present you with her confidence that she called you into the dining-room was it? She intended to give you something, didn't she?'

'I can't account for it otherwise.'

'Then what was it, for God's sake? What did you get up to in there? Why did they take such a fancy to you? Look', he was acutely fidgety (everything within him at that moment seemed to be in a seething turmoil, he simply couldn't collect his thoughts), 'look, can't you just remember something of what you talked about in there and put it in some sort of order, what exactly you talked about, all the words from the very beginning? Anything you remember noticing?'

'Oh, I can certainly do that', responded the prince. 'To begin with, after I'd come in and been introduced, we started talking about Switzerland.'

'Oh, to hell with Switzerland!'

'Then about capital punishment . . .'

'Capital punishment?'

'Yes; it just came up . . . Then I told them about my living there for three years, then a story about a poor village girl.'

'Oh to hell with the poor village girl! Get on with it!' Ganya was bursting with impatience.

'Then Schneider's opinion about my character and how he made me . . .'

'Confound Schneider and damn his opinions! Get on!'

'After that I got on to faces, facial expressions I mean, and said that Aglaya Ivanovna was almost as pretty as Nastasya Filippovna. That's when I let it out about the portrait . . .'

'But you didn't tell them, you surely didn't tell them what you'd just heard in the study? Did you? No?'

'I tell you again, I did not.'

'Then where the devil . . . bah! Aglaya didn't show the note to the old lady?'

'I can completely reassure you on that point; she did not. I was there all the while; she didn't have time either . . .'

'Still you might not have noticed . . . Oh, wre-tche-d idiot!' he exclaimed, now absolutely beside himself, 'he can't even tell a story properly!'

Having once started swearing without encountering remonstrance, Ganya gradually cast off all restraint, as is invariably the case with some people. A little while longer and he might well have begun spitting, such was his fury. And yet it was this same fury which blinded him; otherwise he would have noticed long before, that this 'idiot' he was berating was sometimes capable of very swift and subtle understanding, and could give a perfectly adequate account of events. But all of a sudden something unexpected occurred.

'I must point out to you, Gavrila Ardalionovich', the prince said suddenly, 'that formerly I was so ill that I actually was almost an idiot; I recovered from that a considerable time ago, however, and it is somewhat unpleasant when I am called an idiot to my

face. Although you may be forgiven, bearing in mind your
disappointments, you have already abused me twice in your
annoyance. I don't like it at all, especially just like that, suddenly,
on first acquaintance; since we are standing at a crossroads,
would it not be better for us to part: you turn right towards your
house and I to the left. I have twenty-five roubles and I'm sure to
find some lodging-house.'

Ganya was horribly embarrassed and even blushed for shame.

'Forgive me, Prince', he cried hotly, abruptly altering his
abusive tone to one of extreme politeness. 'Do please forgive me!
You see the trouble I'm in! You still know practically nothing
about it, but if you knew everything, you would surely forgive me
at least a little; though of course it was inexcusable . . .'

'Oh, there's no need for any profuse apologies', the prince
hastened to reply. 'I do understand how unpleasant it is for you,
and that's the reason for your rudeness. Well, let's go on to your
house. I'll come with pleasure . . .'

'No, I can't let him go now just like that', thought Ganya to
himself, glancing savagely at the prince as they walked on. 'This
rogue squeezed it all out of me, then suddenly dropped the
mask . . . There's something behind all this. Well, we'll see! All
will be decided, everything! This very day!'

By now they had reached the house.

8

GANYA's flat was on the second floor, reached by way of a clean,
bright, and spacious staircase. It comprised six or seven rooms,
large and small, nothing special in themselves but rather beyond
the means of an office-worker with a family, even one earning
two thousand a year. It had been taken over by Ganya's
household some two months before and had been laid out, to
Ganya's utter disgust, as separate flatlets with board and service,
at the insistent request of his mother and sister who had wanted
to make themselves useful and increase the family income by
however little. Ganya would scowl and call it outrageous to take
in boarders; subsequently he began to feel somewhat ashamed in

polite society, where he was accustomed to cut a figure as a young man with prospects and a certain polish. All these concessions to necessity, and the consequent exasperating feeling of constriction, were deeply wounding to Ganya's spirit. Of late he had begun to get intensely, disproportionately, upset over trifles; if he was willing for the moment to resign himself and show patience, it was only because he had resolved upon altering and refashioning the situation in the very near future. Meanwhile this very process of change, the escape-route he had decided upon, was presenting no small difficulty; it was a problem whose resolution bid fair to be more troublesome and agonizing than anything which had gone before.

The apartment was divided by a corridor which led from the hallway. The three rooms for letting 'to specially recommended' lodgers were on one side of this corridor; there was also a fourth room, smaller than the others, right at the end by the kitchen, where lived the retired General Ivolgin himself, the head of the family. He slept on a broad sofa and, in order to enter or leave the flat, was obliged to go through the kitchen and down the back-stairs. Gavrila Ardalionovich's 13-year-old schoolboy brother Kolya lived here as well; he had to squeeze himself in to do his studying, and sleep on another sofa, ancient, narrow, and short, with a sheet full of holes; above all, he had to look after and keep an eye on his father, who was becoming more and more dependent on such attention. The prince was allotted the middle room of the three; the first one, to his right, was occupied by Ferdischenko, while on his left, the third stood vacant for the moment. Ganya initially conducted the prince into the family half of the apartments, however. This consisted of a hall, converting at need into a dining-room; a drawing-room, which fulfilled that function only in the mornings, however—it turned into Ganya's study cum bedroom later on in the day; and finally a tiny third room which was always kept locked: this was the bedroom of Ganya's mother and sister. In a word, everything in the apartments was cramped and constricted; Ganya just had to grit his teeth; although he was and wished to be respectful towards his mother, it was obvious from the first moment that he was the tyrant of the family.

Nina Alexandrovna was not alone in the drawing-room. Her

daughter, Varvara, was sitting with her; both of them were busy knitting as they conversed with a visitor, Ivan Petrovich Ptitsyn. Nina Alexandrovna seemed about 50, with a pinched, sunken face, very dark under the eyes. She had an ailing look about her and an air of mourning, though her face and expression were quite attractive; her first words bespoke a serious nature full of genuine dignity. Notwithstanding her melancholy look, one could sense a firmness in her, resolve even. She was dressed extremely modestly in something dark, old-lady fashion, but her deportment, conversation, her whole manner in fact, pointed to her as a woman familiar with a better class of society.

Her daughter, Varvara, was a girl of about 23, of medium height and rather on the thin side; her face was not exactly pretty but possessed the secret of being winning without being beautiful, and was really remarkably attractive. She was very like her mother, even sharing her strong disinclination to dress ostentatiously. Her grey eyes might sometimes have been very gay and affectionate, if they had not been more often grave and pensive, sometimes too much so, especially of late. Strength and resolution could be seen in her face too, but one got the impression that her strength could be much more dynamic and resourceful than that of her mother. Varvara was rather quick-tempered, and her brother went somewhat in fear of that temper. Among those who shared this apprehension was their present visitor, Ivan Petrovich Ptitsyn. He was still quite a young man, around 30, elegantly though unobtrusively dressed, with manners which were attractive but somehow a little too solemn. His small, dark-brown beard indicated that he was not in the government service.* His conversation was clever and interesting, but more often than not he was silent. On the whole he made a pleasing impression. He was clearly not indifferent to Varvara Ardalionovna and did not hide his feelings. She treated him in friendly fashion, but some of his questions were not to her liking and she delayed before answering; Ptitsyn, however, was far from being discouraged. Nina Alexandrovna was nice to him, and of late had begun to confide in him to a considerable extent. It was common knowledge, though, that his main activity was lending money at high interest on more or less reliable security. He was exceedingly friendly with Ganya.

After an abrupt, though circumstantial, introduction by Ganya (who gave his mother the coldest of greetings, ignored his sister, and at once led Ptitsyn out of the room) Nina said a few pleasant words to the prince and told Kolya, who was peeping in at the door, to take him to the middle room. Kolya was a pleasant boy with a cheerful face and a trusting, unaffected manner.

'Where are your things, then?' he asked as he led the prince into the room.

'I've just got a bundle; I've left it in the hall.'

'I'll fetch it directly. We only have the cook and Matriona, so I help out as well. Varya supervises everything and gets cross. Ganya says you arrived from Switzerland today?'

'Yes.'

'Is it nice there?'

'Very.'

'Mountains?'

'Yes.'

'I'll go and bring your bundles.'

Varvara Ardalionovna entered.

'Matriona will make your bed presently. Do you have a suitcase?'

'No, a bundle. Your brother's gone for it; it's in the hall.'

'There's nothing there apart from this little one; where did you put them?' asked Kolya, returning.

'There aren't any apart from that', the prince announced, taking his bundle.

'Ah-h! I thought Ferdischenko might have carried them off.'

'Don't tell lies', said Varvara severely; she was barely polite even to the prince, and spoke extremely coldly.

'*Chère* Babette, you might treat me more affectionately, I'm not Ptitsyn you know.'

'You're lucky to escape whipping, you're so silly. Ask Matriona for anything you want; dinner is at half-past four. You can eat with us or have it in your room, as you wish. Come on, Kolya, don't get in the way.'

'Let us go then, oh woman of decision.'

As they left they encountered Ganya.

'Is father in?' Ganya asked Kolya, and on receiving an affirmative reply whispered something in his ear.

Kolya nodded and went out after his sister.

'A word, Prince, I forgot to mention about this . . . business. I have a favour to ask: would you oblige me, if it isn't asking too much, by not mentioning here what has passed between me and Aglaya—or speak at the Yepanchins' of what you may find here; because things are at a pretty pass here too. Still, to hell with it . . . At least restrain yourself for today at least.'

'I do assure you, I said a good deal less than you think', said the prince, somewhat nettled by Ganya's reproaches. Their relations were clearly becoming more and more strained.

'Well I've gone through a lot today because of you. Anyway, I'm asking you.'

'I must point out also, Gavrila Ardalionovich, that I was in no way bound not to mention the portrait this afternoon. You didn't ask me did you?'

'Phew, what a horrid room', remarked Ganya looking about him disdainfully, 'dark and a view of the yard. You've come at an awkward time for us in every way . . . Well, that's no business of mine; I don't let the apartments.'

Ptitsyn looked in and called Ganya, who hastily deserted the prince and left, despite having something more to say; he was obviously ill at ease and nervous about coming out with it, finding fault with the room in his embarrassment.

Scarcely had the prince washed and managed to tidy himself up somewhat, when the door opened and a new personage peered round it.

This was a gentleman of around 30, stocky, broad-shouldered, and with a huge, ginger-curled head. His fleshy face was florid, with thick lips and a broad, flat nose. His small eyes were bleary and mocking as if perpetually winking. The overall impression was one of insolence. His clothes were rather grubby.

To begin with, he opened the door just enough to insert his head. The head surveyed the room for about five seconds, then the door began to open gently and the entire figure appeared; the visitor, however, did not enter. He stayed regarding the prince from the threshold. At length he closed the door behind him, approached, sat down on a chair, seized the prince firmly by the hand, and placed him on the sofa almost opposite.

'Ferdischenko', said he, with a keen and searching look at the prince.

'Yes?' responded the prince, almost laughing out loud.

'Lodger', said Ferdischenko again, staring as before.

'You wish to be acquainted?'

'E-ech!' said the visitor, sighing as he ruffled his hair. He began staring at the opposite corner of the room. 'Have you got any money?' he addressed the prince all of a sudden.

'A little.'

'How much exactly?'

'Twenty-five roubles.'

'Show me, then.'

The prince took the twenty-five rouble note from his waistcoat pocket and gave it to Ferdischenko. He unfolded it, examined it, then turned it over and finally held it against the light.

'It's rather odd', he spoke, as if ruminating, 'why should they go brown? These twenty-fivers sometimes go really brown and others fade completely. Here.'

The prince took his note back. Ferdischenko rose from his chair.

'I came to warn you: first don't lend me money, because I'll certainly be asking you.'

'Very well.'

'You intend to pay here?'

'I do.'

'And I don't; thank you. I'm the first door on the right from you, did you see? Try not to come and see me too often; I'll come to see you, never fear. Have you seen the general?'

'No.'

'And not heard him?'

'Of course not.'

'Well, you will see and hear him; he tries to borrow money from me even! *Avis au lecteur.** Goodbye. Can one really live with a surname like Ferdischenko? Eh?'

'Why ever not?'

'Goodbye.'

And he walked to the door. The prince learned later that this gentleman had taken it upon himself to astonish everyone with his originality and high spirits, though it never quite came off. He even impressed some people unpleasantly, a fact which grieved him but did not prevent him pursuing his task. In the doorway he managed to recover lost ground, as it were, by stumbling against another gentleman who was coming in; as he let this new visitor, unknown to the prince, into the room, he gave several warning winks from behind his back and thus contrived to make a reasonably effective exit after all.

The new arrival was a tall man of about 55 or a little older, rather stout, with a fleshy, purplish-red face whose flabbiness was framed in bushy grey side-whiskers and moustache. He had large, rather prominent eyes. His figure would have been quite dignified had there not been something neglected and slovenly, even grubby, about it. He wore an ancient, out-at-elbows frock-coat and his linen was also soiled, in a round-the-house fashion. Close to, there was a slight whiff of vodka; his demeanour was striking, nevertheless, though rather studied and obviously designed to create a dignified impression. He approached the prince slowly with a welcoming smile, silently took his hand and, while retaining it, peered into his face for some time, as if recognizing familiar features.

'It's him! Him!' He spoke with quiet solemnity. 'To the life! I hear them repeating the dear familiar name and I recall the dead past . . . Prince Myshkin?'

'It is indeed.'

'General Ivolgin, retired and wretched. Your first names, if I may be so bold?'

'Lev Nikolayevich.'

'That's it! That's it! The son of my friend and childhood companion, Nikolai Petrovich?'

'My father's name was Nikolai Lvovich.'

'Lvovich', the general corrected himself, but unhurriedly and with complete confidence, as if it had been a mere slip of the tongue rather than forgetfulness. He seated himself, and taking the prince's hand, sat him down beside him. 'I carried you in my arms, sir.'

'Really?' said the prince. 'My father died all of twenty years ago.'

'Yes; twenty years; twenty years and three months. We went to school together; I went straight into the army . . .'

'Yes, my father was in the army too, a sub-lieutenant in the

Vasilkovsky regiment.'

'The Belomirsky. He was transferred to the Belomirsky just before he died. I stood there and blessed him to his eternal rest. Your dear mother . . .'

The general paused, as if in sad reflection.

'But she died as well, six months later from a chill', said the prince.

'Not from a chill. Not from a chill, take an old man's word. I was there at the funeral. It was from grief for her prince, not a chill. Yes, how I remember the princess! Ah, youth! It was because of her that the prince and I, lifelong friends, almost became each other's murderer.'

The prince began listening with a certain scepticism.

'I was still passionately in love with your mother when she was betrothed—betrothed to my friend. The prince noticed and was shocked. He comes to me one morning at seven and wakes me up. I get dressed, astonished; not a word on either side; I understood. Takes out a brace of pistols from his pocket. Across the handkerchief. No witnesses. What need of them if we were sending each other into eternity in five minutes' time? We loaded, spread the handkerchief out, braced ourselves, and aimed at the heart as we looked one another in the face. Suddenly, tears flooded from our eyes and our hands shook. Both of us, both, at the same time! Well, then came the embraces of course, each of us outdoing the other in generosity. The prince shouts: 'She's yours!' I shout: 'Yours!' Well, in short . . . in short . . . you've come here . . . to live?'

'Yes, for a time, perhaps', said the prince, seeming to hesitate slightly.

'Prince, mama asks you to come and see her', cried Kolya, glancing in at the doorway. The prince half-rose to go, but the general placed his right palm on his shoulder in friendly fashion and sat him down on the sofa again.

'As a true friend of your father, I want to warn you', said the general. 'As you can see, I am the victim of a tragic misfortune; but no court involved, no trial! Nina Alexandrovna is a rare woman. Varvara Ardalionovna, my daughter, the rarest of daughters! Circumstances compel us to let out rooms—an unheard-of degradation! Me, who could have been a governor-

general! . . . You we are always glad to see. But there is tragedy in
this house, all the same.'

The prince looked at him inquiringly, his curiosity greatly
aroused.

'There's a marriage in the offing, and no ordinary one. It's a
match between a woman of dubious reputation and a young man
who might have risen to a position at court. They are bringing
that woman into the house where my wife and daughter are
living! But over my dead body! I'll lie down on the threshold—
she'll have to walk over me! . . . I hardly speak to Ganya these
days, in fact I keep out of his way. I'm giving you advance
warning; if you're going to live here, you'll witness it all anyway.
But you're my friend's son and I have the right to expect . . .'

'Prince, be so good as to come into the drawing-room', called
Nina Alexandrovna, now appearing in the doorway herself.

'Just fancy my dear', exclaimed the general, 'it seems I used to
dandle the prince in my arms!'

Nina Alexandrovna glanced reproachfully at the general and
inquiringly at the prince, but did not utter a word. The prince set
off after her, but no sooner had they seated themselves in the
drawing-room, and Nina Alexandrovna had begun talking to the
prince in a rapid undertone, than the general himself came in.
His wife at once stopped talking and bent to her knitting in visible
annoyance. The general also perhaps observed her vexation, but
it failed to dampen his excellent spirits.

'The son of my friend!' he cried, addressing Nina Alexandrovna. 'And such a surprise! I'd long since given up thinking
about it. My dear, surely you remember the late Nikolai Lvovich?
You met him in . . . Tver?'

'I don't recall a Nikolai Lvovich. Is he your father?' she asked
the prince.

'Yes, but he died in Elizavetgrad I believe, not Tver', the
prince observed diffidently. 'I heard it from Pavlischev . . .'

'Tver it was', confirmed the general. 'He was transferred to
Tver just before he died, even before his illness developed. You
were too young to remember either the transfer or the journey; I
dare say Pavlischev was mistaken, splendid fellow though he
was.'

'You knew Pavlischev as well?'

'One of the finest, but I was an eye-witness. I blessed him on his death-bed . . .'

'My father died awaiting trial', the prince observed again, 'though I could never find out exactly what for. He died in military hospital.'

'Oh, that was over the Private Kolpakov business, and the prince would have been acquitted without a doubt.'

'Really? You're sure about that?' asked the prince with marked curiosity.

'I should say so!' exclaimed the general. 'The trial ended without a decision. The case was ridiculous! Mysterious even, one might call it: Lieutenant Larionov, the company commander dies; the prince is appointed acting commander; right. Private Kolpakov is caught stealing a comrade's boot-leather and selling it for drink; right. The prince—and note this was in the presence of a sergeant and corporal—gives Kolpakov a roasting and threatens him with a flogging. Very good. Kolpakov goes off to the barracks, lies down on his bunk, and in fifteen minutes he's dead. Excellent, but the situation is unusual, almost incredible. However that might be, Kolpakov is buried; the prince reports the matter, and Kolpakov is taken off the roll. What could be better, eh? But exactly six months later, Private Kolpakov turns up in the third company of the second battalion of the Novaya Zemlya infantry regiment, same brigade, same division, just as if nothing had happened!'

'What!' cried the prince, in stunned amazement.

'It isn't so, it's a mistake!' Nina Alexandrovna addressed him suddenly, her look almost anguished. '*Mon mari se trompe.*'*

'Now, my dear, *se trompe* is easily said, but try and sort a thing like that out yourself! Everybody was baffled. I would be the first to say *qu'on se trompe*. Unfortunately, I witnessed it and was a member of the commission myself. All who saw him testified that it was the very man, the same Private Kolpakov who had been buried six months before with the usual parade, drums beating. A really odd case, almost impossible I agree, but . . .'

'Papa, your dinner is served', announced Varvara Ardalio-novna, entering the drawing-room.

'Now that's splendid, excellent! I'm famished . . . That case though, psychological you might say . . .'

'The soup will be cold again', said Varvara impatiently.

'Coming, coming', muttered the general as he went out. 'Despite all the inquiries . . .' was still audible from the corridor.

'You will have to overlook a good deal of my husband's behaviour if you stay with us', Nina Alexandrovna told the prince, 'though he won't bother you much; he even has his dinner on his own. You'll agree, everybody has their shortcomings and their . . . peculiarities, sometimes more than those who tend to have the finger pointed at them. One thing I would beg of you: if my husband should approach you in any way for the rent of the apartment, tell him you've given it to me. I mean anything you give him would be taken off your bill, I'm only asking you so that I can keep things straight . . . What is it, Varya?'

Varya had returned and silently handed Nastasya Filippovna's portrait to her mother. Nina Alexandrovna gave a start, then studied it for some time, at first with something like alarm, which gave way to feelings of overwhelming bitterness . . . At length she looked questioningly at Varya.

'It's a personal gift to him today', said Varya. 'Everything's to be settled between them this evening.'

'This evening!' echoed Nina Alexandrovna in a despairing undertone. 'Well then, no more uncertainty and no hope left either: she's made her announcement through the portrait . . . Did he really show it to you himself?' she went on, surprised,

'You know we've hardly exchanged a word for a good month. It was Ptitsyn who told me all about it; the portrait was lying on the floor by the table and I just picked it up.'

'Prince', Nina Alexandrovna suddenly addressed him. 'I wanted to ask you, in fact why I asked you in here, have you known my son long? I think he told me you had just arrived today from somewhere?'

The prince gave a brief account of himself, leaving out the greater part. Nina Alexandrovna and Varya heard him out.

'I'm not asking you because I'm trying to worm out anything about Gavrila Ardalionovich', Nina Alexandrovna said, 'you mustn't misunderstand me. If there is anything he doesn't want to tell me himself, then I don't want to find out behind his back. What I mean is that, just now when you were present and later when you'd gone out, Ganya told me when I asked about you:

"He knows all about it, you needn't mince words with him!" What on earth does that mean? I mean, I'd like to know to what extent . . .'

At this point, Ganya and Ptitsyn came in; Nina Alexandrovna stopped talking at once. The prince remained in his chair next to her, while Varya moved away; Nastasya Filippovna's portrait lay in the most conspicuous place, on Nina Alexandrovna's work-table, directly in front of her. Ganya scowled on seeing it and crossly took it from the table and threw it on to his own writing-desk at the other end of the room.

'Tonight is it, Ganya?' asked his mother abruptly.

'What is?' Ganya gave a start, then suddenly turned on the prince. 'Ah, I see—you're here as well! . . . What on earth's the matter with you, some sort of disease is it? Just can't keep a thing to yourself? Let it be understood once and for all, your excellency . . .'

'I'm the one to blame, Ganya, no one else', Ptitsyn broke in. Ganya looked at him inquiringly.

'It really is for the best, Ganya, especially since the matter's been decided on one side', muttered Ptitsyn, moving away to sit by the table, where he took out a piece of paper covered in pencilled writing and began studying it intently. Ganya stood bleakly by, anxiously anticipating a family scene. He had no thought of apologizing to the prince.

'If everything's settled, then Ivan Petrovich is right of course', said Nina Alexandrovna. 'Please don't frown so and don't be cross, Ganya, I shan't inquire about anything you don't tell me yourself; I assure you I'm completely resigned, so please don't worry.'

She went on working as she spoke, apparently quite placid. Ganya was astonished, but maintained a wary silence while he looked at his mother and awaited clarification. He had suffered too much from family scenes already. His mother observed his caution, and smiled bitterly as she added:

'You still have your doubts and can't trust me; don't worry, there won't be any more tears or entreaties, at least on my part. My only wish is that you should be happy, you know that; I am resigned to what will be, but my heart will always be with you, whether we stay together or part. Naturally I can speak only for myself; you can't demand the same from your sister . . .'

'Ah, her again!' cried Ganya, giving his sister a look of sneering hatred. 'Mama dear, I swear to you again what I have promised already: no one shall ever dare to show disrespect to you while I am here, while I live. Whoever it is, I shall insist on the height of respect being shown, whoever crosses our threshold . . .'

Ganya was so delighted that his expression as he looked at his mother was conciliatory, almost tender.

'I feared nothing for myself, Ganya, as you know; I was never worried or anxious on my own account all this time. I hear it's all to be settled this evening? What's to be settled exactly?'

'This evening, at her house, she has promised to announce whether she consents or not', replied Ganya.

'We've been avoiding that topic for nearly three weeks now, and that was for the best. Now that everything's settled, I will permit myself just one question: how could she give her consent and even send you her portrait, when you don't love her? Surely a woman so . . . so . . .'

'Experienced, you mean?'

'I didn't want to put it that way. How could you pull the wool over her eyes to that extent?'

There was a sudden note of intense exasperation in the question. Ganya stood thinking for a moment and went on, not bothering to conceal a sneer:

'You've got carried away again, mama, just couldn't help it, that's the way it always starts flaring up with us. You said: there'll be no questions, no reproaches, now here they are starting already! Better leave off; no, really; at least the thought was there . . . I shall never leave you for anything; anyone else would have run away from a sister like that—look at her staring at me now! Let's leave it there! I was just feeling cheerful too . . . And how do you know that I'm deceiving Nastasya Filippovna? As for Varya, she can do as she likes and there's an end of it. This has all gone quite far enough!'

Ganya's temper had risen with each word as he paced aimlessly about the room. Talk like this touched every member of the family on the raw.

'I said that if she comes here I go, and I mean it', said Varya.

'Out of sheer pig-headedness', cried Ganya. 'You refuse to get married out of pig-headedness as well! What are you snorting at me for? I don't give a damn, sister of mine; you can go straight away if you like. I'm sick of you. What, you've decided to leave us at last have you, Prince?' he shouted as he saw the prince rising from his place.

Ganya's voice rang with the exasperation of a man almost revelling in his own anger, letting himself go with a sort of increasing enjoyment, regardless of the consequences. The prince turned in the doorway to make some reply, but realizing from the contorted face of his tormentor that only one more drop was needed to make the cup run over, he turned back and went out in silence. A few minutes later he could hear by the voices in the drawing-room, that the conversation had become even noisier and more outspoken in his absence.

He walked through the hall into the lobby to reach the corridor and from there his own room. Passing close to the front door, he could hear someone trying to ring the bell with all their might outside; the bell mustn't have been working; it merely trembled slightly, but no sound came. The prince undid the latch, opened the door, and—stepped back in astonishment, thoroughly startled: before him stood Nastasya Filippovna. He recognized her at once from her portrait. Her eyes flashed in annoyance as she saw him; she passed quickly into the hallway, shouldering him out of the way, and remarked testily as she flung off her fur coat:

'If you're too lazy to mend the bell, you should at least be sitting in the lobby when people knock. There, you've gone and dropped the coat, you oaf!'

The coat was certainly lying on the floor; Nastasya Filippovna, without waiting for the prince to help her off with it, had flung it into his arms behind her without looking and the prince had failed to hold it.

'They should get rid of you. Get along and announce me.'

The prince was about to say something, but was so taken aback by all this that nothing came out, and he went on towards the drawing-room, still holding the coat he had picked up.

'Now look, he's carrying the coat! What does he want to do that for? Ha-ha-ha! Are you out of your mind or what?'

The prince came back and looked at her like a dummy; when she began to laugh he grinned also, but still couldn't utter a word. When he had first opened the door to her, he had been ashen, now the colour flooded his face.

'What kind of idiot is this?' cried Nastasya Filippovna angrily, stamping her foot at him. 'Well, where are you going? Who are you going to announce then?'

'Nastasya Filippovna', he mumbled.

'How do you know who I am?' she asked him swiftly. 'I've never seen you before! Get along, announce me . . . What's all the shouting?'

'They're quarrelling', responded the prince, and walked towards the drawing-room.

He entered at a rather critical moment: Nina Alexandrovna was on the point of forgetting that she had 'resigned herself' to it all; she was, in fact, defending Varya. Ptitsyn was standing near Varya as well, having abandoned his pencillings. Varya herself was not cowed either, timidity was not in her nature; her brother's rudeness, however, was becoming coarser and more insufferable with every word. In such situations she usually stopped talking and merely stared fixedly at her brother, silently taunting him. This proceeding, as she well knew, was capable of goading him beyond all endurance. It was at this very moment that the prince strode into the room and announced:

'Nastasya Filippovna!'

9

THE silence was total: everyone was staring at the prince, apparently unable to comprehend—and not wishing to do so. Ganya was numb with fright.

The arrival of Nastasya Filippovna at this particular juncture was the strangest and most worrying surprise for all of them. There was the fact that this was her very first visit; up till now she had held herself aloof, and in her conversations with Ganya had expressed no desire whatever to meet his relations; indeed of late had stopped alluding to them altogether, as if they did not exist.

Ganya was quite glad to be relieved of a trying conversational topic, but had set this haughty attitude against her in his heart. At all events, he expected sneers and sarcasm at the expense of his family rather than a visit; he knew for a fact that she was aware of what was going on in his household with regard to his marriage-plans and in what light his relations regarded her. A visit *now* after giving him the portrait on her birthday, the day when she had promised to resolve his future, was almost tantamount to the answer itself. —

The bewilderment with which they all looked at the prince was of short duration: Nastasya Filippovna herself appeared in the doorway, again brushing the prince lightly aside as she entered.

'Well, at last I've managed to get in . . . Why do you keep your bell tied up?' she said brightly, giving her hand to Ganya as he rushed to meet her. 'Why the gloomy face? Introduce me, do . . .'

Ganya, completely flustered, introduced her first to Varya; the women exchanged an odd glance before taking one another's hand. Nastasya Filippovna laughed in fact, and hid her feelings beneath a show of good humour. Varya, however, had no desire to dissimulate and looked at her with grim intensity; her face was devoid even of the faint smile that simple politeness demands. Ganya was aghast; there was no point in pleading with her, and indeed no time to do so, but he threw her a glance of such menace that it compelled Varya to realize what this moment meant for her brother. Thereupon she decided, it seemed, to relent and give Nastasya Filippovna the faintest of smiles. (All the family were still very fond of one another.) Nina Alexandrovna partially retrieved the situation as Ganya, who was completely flustered by now, introduced her after his sister and even led her up to Nastasya Filippovna. But no sooner had Nina Alexandrovna begun on her 'particular pleasure' than Nastasya Filippovna, without waiting for her to finish, turned swiftly to Ganya, and seating herself (without invitation) on a little sofa in the corner by the window, cried:

'Where's your study, then? And . . . where are the lodgers? You do take lodgers don't you?'

Ganya flushed horribly and was stammering some sort of reply when she added immediately:

'Where on earth can you keep lodgers here? You haven't even

got a study. Is it a paying business?' she abruptly addressed Nina Alexandrovna.

'It's quite a bother', she began. 'Naturally it should be profitable. Actually we've just . . .'

But Nastasya Filippovna had once again ceased to listen: she was laughing as she looked at Ganya, and shouting out to him:

'What sort of a face is that? Good heavens, what a face you've got this minute!'

Several seconds of this laughter ensued, and Ganya's face actually was a good deal contorted: his rigid stance, his comic, weak-kneed confusion had all of a sudden left him; he was terribly pale, however; his lips were working convulsively and he stared grim-faced and intent at his visitor, who carried on laughing.

There was another observer present who had likewise not shaken off his near stupefaction at seeing Nastasya Filippovna; although he remained standing ramrod-stiff in his former position by the drawing-room door, he still managed to note Ganya's pallor and the ominous change in his features. That observer was the prince. Almost in fright, he suddenly stepped instinctively forward.

'Have a drink of water', he whispered to Ganya. 'And stop looking like that . . .'

It was obvious that he spoke on the spur of the moment, on impulse, and with no particular ulterior motive; his words, however, produced an extraordinary effect. It was as if Ganya's entire fury suddenly turned against the prince: he seized him by the shoulder and stared into his eyes with mute, vengeful hatred, seemingly incapable of uttering a word. A general commotion ensued: Nina Alexandrovna even gave a small shriek. Ptitsyn took an anxious pace forward, while Kolya and Ferdischenko, who had appeared in the doorway, halted in amazement: only Varya looked askance as before, while watching closely. She did not sit down, but remained standing to one side, near her mother, arms folded.

Ganya recovered himself at once, however, virtually as he moved, and gave a nervous laugh. He had himself completely in hand.

'Are you a doctor then, Prince?' he cried, trying hard to sound unaffectedly cheerful—'You quite frightened me; Nastasya Filippovna, let me introduce a most priceless individual, though I've known him only since morning.'

Nastasya Filippovna stared at the prince in bewilderment.

'Prince? Is he a prince? Imagine, just now in the lobby I took him for a footman and sent him here to announce me! Ha, ha, ha!'

'Never mind, never mind!' put in Ferdischenko, approaching quickly, relieved that they had begun to laugh, 'no harm done: *se non e vero . . .'**

'And I was on the point of giving you a good scolding, Prince. Please forgive me; Ferdischenko, what are you doing here at this hour? At least I didn't expect to find you here. Who? What prince? Myshkin?' she inquired of Ganya, who had contrived to introduce him, still clasping his shoulder.

'Our lodger', Ganya repeated.

Clearly the prince was being presented as a *rara avis* as well as a convenient way for everyone to escape from their false position, and almost being forced upon Nastasya Filippovna; the prince even heard the word 'idiot' distinctly whispered behind him, probably by Ferdischenko explaining matters to Nastasya Filippovna.

'Tell me, why did you let me go on making that awful . . . mistake about you, just now?' pursued Nastasya Filippovna, scrutinizing the prince most unceremoniously from head to toe; she awaited his reply eagerly, as if utterly convinced that it would be laughably foolish.

'I was too surprised, seeing you so suddenly . . .' the prince began muttering.

'But how did you know it was me? Where had you seen me before? Can it be . . . it's as if I'd actually seen him before. And may I ask, why were you stunned just now? What is there so stunning about me?'

'Come along, now, come along!' Ferdischenko said, grimacing away. 'Come now, what wouldn't I say to a question like that! Come on . . . What a slowcoach you are, Prince, to be sure!'

'And in your place I could have said lots of things too', laughed the prince. 'A little while ago I was very much struck by your portrait', he went on to Nastasya Filippovna, 'and then I talked to the Yepanchins about you . . . and early this morning before my train got to Petersburg, Parfion Rogozhin told me a good deal about you . . . At the very moment I opened the door you were in my thoughts, then all of a sudden, there you were.'

'But how did you recognize that it was me?'

'The portrait and . . .'

'And what?'

'And because you were exactly as I had imagined . . . As if I'd seen you before too somewhere.'

'Where? Where?'

'I've certainly seen your eyes somewhere . . . but that's impossible! I'm just talking . . . I've never even been here. Perhaps in a dream . . .'

'Bravo, Prince!' cried Ferdischenko. 'No, I take back my *se non e vero*. Still . . . still, he says it in all innocence', he added regretfully.

The prince had said his few words in a tremulous voice, faltering and frequently pausing for breath. Everything about him betrayed an intense agitation. Nastasya Filippovna was regarding him curiously, though she had stopped laughing. At this moment a loud new voice, audible beyond the press of people round the prince and Nastasya Filippovna, parted the crowd as it were and divided it in two. Before Nastasya Filippovna stood the head of the household in person, General Ivolgin. He was wearing a frock-coat and his shirt-front was clean; his moustaches were dyed . . .

This was too much for Ganya.

Vain and self-regarding to the point of morbid fastidiousness, he had been seeking over the past two months for some point of support to give him the appearance of decency and gentlemanly conduct. Sensing his lack of experience on the path he had chosen, and indeed that he was likely to be unsuccessful in it, he had resolved to brazen things out at home where he was a despot, though without having the temerity to do so in front of Nastasya Filippovna. She, meanwhile, had kept him in suspense till the last moment, mercilessly retaining her dominance over him—the 'impatient beggar' as she herself called him, according to report. He had sworn by every oath that she would pay bitterly for all this afterwards, yet at the same time he sometimes dreamed, childlike, of making ends meet and reconciling opposites. Now he had to drain this dreadful cup too—and at this of all moments! One more unforeseen torment, the most terrible of all for a vain man—the torture of blushing for his own kindred in his own house—had fallen to his lot. 'Is the game really worth the candle, after all?' flashed through his mind at that moment.

What was occurring was something which had been giving him nightmares for these two months, making him go cold with horror and hot with shame: at long last the meeting of his father with Nastasya Filippovna. To tantalize and torment himself he had occasionally tried to visualize the general during the marriage ceremony, but had always failed to picture the agonizing scene properly and hastily abandoned the attempt. Perhaps he was exaggerating the extent of the disaster, but that is always the way with vain people. Over these last two months he had come to the conclusion that, whatever happened, he would get rid of his father at least temporarily, even get him out of Petersburg, whether his mother agreed or not. Ten minutes before, when Nastasya Filippovna entered, he had been so stunned, so thunderstruck, that he had completely overlooked the possibility of Ardalion Alexandrovich's appearance on the scene and had taken no steps to prevent it. And here the general was, in front of them all, solemnly got up in evening dress what's more, at the very moment when Nastasya Filippovna was 'just looking for the chance to shower him and his household with ridicule'. (Of that he was convinced.) After all, what could this visit of hers signify otherwise? Had she come to establish friendly relations with his mother and sister, or insult them in his own house? Considering the attitudes of both sides, there could be no doubt as to which it was: his mother and sister were sitting out of the way, humiliated, while Nastasya Filippovna seemed even to have forgotten that they were in the same room with her . . . And if she was behaving like this, she had her reasons!

Ferdischenko took hold of the general and led him forward.

'Ardalion Alexandrovich Ivolgin', announced the general in dignified fashion, bowing and smiling, 'a poor old soldier and head of a family, happy in the expectation of welcoming such a charming . . .'

He did not finish; Ferdischenko quickly placed a chair behind him and the general, somewhat unsteady at that post-prandial moment, flopped, or rather fell, into it, without, however, losing composure. He seated himself directly opposite Nastasya Filippovna and, with a pleasant simper, slowly and affectedly brought her fingers to his lips. The general was a hard man to disconcert. His appearance, despite a certain slovenliness, was still quite presentable, and he was well aware of it. Formerly he had moved in very good society, and had been finally dropped only some two or three years before. Since then he had given himself up rather too freely to certain of his weaknesses; his easy and agreeable manners had not deserted him, however. Nastasya Filippovna was apparently delighted at the appearance of Ardalion Alexandrovich, of whom she had heard much at second-hand.

'I have heard that my son . . .', began the general.

'Yes, your son! You're a fine one too, Papa! Why do I never see you at my house? Do you keep yourself hidden away or won't your son let you out? You can come and see me without compromising anyone, you know.'

'Children of the nineteenth century and their parents . . .' began the general.

'Nastasya Filippovna! Please let Ardalion Alexandrovich go for a moment, he is wanted', said Nina Alexandrovna loudly.

'Let him go! Forgive me, I've heard so much about him, I've wanted to see him for ever so long! What business can he have? He's retired is he not? You won't leave me, general, you won't go away?'

'I give you my word he will come and visit you himself, but now he needs his rest.'

'Ardalion Alexandrovich, I'm told you need a rest!' cried Nastasya Filippovna, making a peevish, resentful face, like some fretful little girl deprived of a toy. The general at once tried to make even more of a fool of himself.

'My dear, my dear!' he said reproachfully, turning solemnly to his wife, hand on heart.

'Won't you come away, mama dear?' Varya asked in a loud voice.

'No, Varya, I'll sit it out to the end.'

Nastasya Filippovna could not fail to hear both question and answer, but it seemed only to intensify her gaiety. She at once began peppering the general with questions, so that within five minutes he was in high good humour, holding forth amid the loud laughter of those present.

Kolya tugged at the prince's coat-tail.

'Can't you get him away at least? Can't you? Please!' Tears of indignation shone in the poor boy's eyes. 'That blasted Ganya!' he added to himself.

'I was certainly on close terms with Ivan Fedorovich Yepanchin', the general gushed on in answer to Nastasya Filippovna. 'He and I and the late Prince Lev Nikolayevich Myshkin, whose son I embraced today after a twenty-year separation, were three inseparables, a regular cavalcade, you might say, like Athos, Porthos, and Aramis. But, alas, one is in his grave, struck down by bullet and slander, the second stands before you, still fighting those same two enemies . . .'

'Bullets!' cried Nastasya Filippovna.

'Here in my chest; I got them at Kars and I get twinges in damp weather. Otherwise I live like a philosopher, go for walks, play draughts in my café like a retired businessman, and read the *Indépendance.** But with Yepanchin, our Porthos, I've had absolutely nothing to do since the lap-dog scandal on the railway three years ago.'

'Lap-dog! What on earth was that?' asked Nastasya Filippovna, vastly intrigued. 'A lap-dog? Really, and on the railway! . . .' She seemed to be trying to recall something.

'Oh, it was a silly story, not worth repeating even: it all had to do with Princess Belokonskaya's governess, Mistress Schmidt, but . . . it's not worth repeating.'

'Do tell it at once!' cried Nastasya Filippovna gaily.

'I've never heard it either!' put in Ferdischenko. '*C'est du nouveau.*'

'Ardalion Alexandrovich!' Once again came Nina Alexandrovna's beseeching voice.

'Daddy, someone wants to see you!' shouted Kolya.

'It's a silly story, it can be told in no time', began the general complacently. 'Two years ago, yes it was! A bit less, just after the opening of the new railway—I was on some personal business of great importance in connection with giving up the service (I was already in mufti at the time). I got a first-class ticket, got in, sat down, and had a smoke. I mean I carried on smoking the cigar I'd started earlier. I was on my own in the carriage. Smoking wasn't forbidden, but it wasn't allowed either; it was sort of half-allowed, the usual thing, depending who it was. The window was down. Suddenly, just before the whistle went, two ladies got in with a lap-dog just opposite me; they were late; one gorgeously decked out in blue; the other quieter, black silk with a cape. Not at all bad-looking, gave me a rather haughty look and talked in English. I just carried on smoking of course. That is I thought about it, but I went on smoking anyway, out of the window as it was open. The lap-dog was resting on the blue lady's knees, it was the size of my fist, little black thing, white paws, you don't see many of them. Silver collar with something written on it. I just sat. I noticed the ladies getting annoyed, about the cigar of course. One stared at me through her lorgnette, tortoiseshell. I still didn't do anything: because they didn't say a thing! If they'd said something, given me warning, or just asked me, there is such a thing as human speech after all! But not a word . . . All of a sudden, as I say, without the slightest indication, not a hint of a warning, just as if she'd taken leave of her senses, the blue lady grabs my cigar and out it goes through the window. The train races on, me staring like a half-wit. The woman was wild; really wild, in a savage state; a well-grown woman, incidentally, tall and stout, fair-haired and rosy-cheeked (too rosy even); her eyes were flashing at me. Without a word, and with extreme courtesy, the most perfect, the most exquisitely refined courtesy, I leaned over to the dog, picked it up delicately by the collar with two fingers, and slung it out of the window after my cigar! One squeal! The train goes rushing on . . .'

'You monster!' cried Nastasya Filippovna, laughing and clapping her hands like a little girl.

'Bravo, bravo!' Ferdischenko was shouting. Ptitsyn grinned too, though the general's appearance had dismayed him considerably; even Kolya began laughing and joined in the shouts of 'Bravo!'

'And I was right, I was right three times over!' continued the exultant general warmly, 'because if cigars are against the rules in railway carriages, dogs are even more so.'

'Bravo, papa!' cried Kolya ecstatically, 'wonderful! I would certainly have done the same, certainly!'

'But what about the lady?' Nastasya Filippovna asked eagerly.

'Her? Well now, that's where all the unpleasantness comes in', the general went on, frowning. 'Without saying a word and without the slightest warning, she ups and smacks me across the face! Wild woman, really wild!'

'And what did you do?'

The general lowered his eyes, raised his brows and shoulders, pursed his lips, then said after a short pause:

'I got carried away!'

'You hit her? Hit her hard?'

'No I didn't, honestly I didn't. There was a scene, but I didn't hurt her. I just pushed her away once, just to defend myself. But the devil of it was that the blue lady turned out to be an Englishwoman, a governess or companion of some sort in Princess Belokonskaya's household, and the one in black was the eldest of the Belokonskaya daughters, an old maid of around 35. Everybody knows how close Madame Yepanchina is to the Belokonskaya family. All the princesses swooning, tears of mourning for the pet lap-dog, shrieks from the six princesses, shrieks from the English lady—it was bedlam! Well of course I went to say sorry, ask for forgiveness, wrote them a letter, but they wouldn't receive either me or my letter; quarrelled with Yepanchin, ostracized, banished!'

'But really, general, how can this be?' Nastasya Filippovna asked suddenly. 'Five or six days ago I read the exact same story in the *Indépendance*—I read it regularly—the very same story! It happened on one of the Rhine valley trains, with a Frenchman and an English lady in the compartment: the cigar snatched away, the lap-dog thrown out of the window, just the same as you, and it all ended as it did with you. Even the dress was blue!'

The general flushed horribly, Kolya also went red and clutched his head with his fists; Ptitsyn swiftly turned away. Only Ferdischenko carried on laughing as before. There are no words to describe Ganya: he had been standing the whole time in mute, intolerable agony.

'I do assure you', muttered the general, 'that the self-same thing happened to me ...'

'There was some unpleasantness between Papa and Mistress

Schmidt, the Belokonskys' governess', cried Kolya. 'I remember.'

'What? Exactly the same thing? The same incident at opposite ends of Europe, identical in every detail down to the blue dress!' pursued Nastasya Filippovna mercilessly. 'I'll send you the *Indépendance Belge!*'

'But bear in mind', the general went on insisting, 'it happened to me two years earlier . . .'

'Ah yes, there is that!'

Nastasya Filippovna was laughing hysterically.

'Papa dear, please come outside for a word or two.' Ganya spoke in a quavering, exhausted voice as he took his father automatically by the shoulder. His eyes blazed with a limitless hatred.

At that very instant came an extremely violent ringing of the bell in the hallway, so loud the bell might have been wrenched off altogether. It could presage no ordinary visit. Kolya ran to open the door.

10

THE hallway had suddenly become extraordinarily noisy and crowded; from the drawing-room it seemed as if a number of persons had come in from the courtyard and more were still arriving. Various voices were talking and shouting at once; there was more talking and shouting on the staircase, as the front door which led on to it had not been closed. This seemed a most peculiar visit. They all exchanged glances as Ganya rushed out into the reception room to find several people already there.

'Ah, here he is, the Judas!' shouted a voice familiar to the prince. 'How are you, Ganka, you dirty dog?'

'That's him, that's what he is!'

The prince could not be in any doubt: one voice belonged to Rogozhin, the other was that of Lebedev.

Ganya stood in apparent stupefaction on the threshold of the dining-room, silently staring and making no attempt to obstruct the entry of some ten or twelve people filing in after Parfion

Rogozhin. The company was motley in the extreme, and notable for disorder as well as diversity. Some were coming in just as they were from the street, in coats and furs. Nobody was completely drunk, however, though they were all rather tipsy. They seemed to need each other's support to actually enter; not one had the temerity on his own, they all seemed to be pushing one another in. Even Rogozhin was stepping cautiously at the head of the throng, but he had something on his mind and seemed irritable and morosely preoccupied. The rest of them only made up the chorus, or rather the gang of his supporters. Besides Lebedev, there was the wavy-haired Zalyozhev, who had discarded his fur coat in the hallway, and came in dandified and jaunty along with two or three like him, evidently scions of the merchant class. There was a man who wore a semi-military greatcoat; another was short and extremely fat, continually laughing; there was a giant of a man, over six feet, also very stout, grim and silent, clearly one who put much faith in his fists. There was a medical student among those present and a little, cringing Pole. Two ladies peered in from the staircase without venturing inside; Kolya slammed the door in their faces and hooked it shut.

'How are you, Ganka, you dirty dog!' repeated Rogozhin, reaching the drawing-room and halting opposite Ganya in the doorway. 'What, didn't expect Parfion Rogozhin?' But just at that moment he caught sight of Nastasya Filippovna across the room. Clearly it had never occurred to him that he might encounter her here, as the sight of her had an extraordinary effect upon him; he went so pale that even his lips took on a blue tinge. 'So it's true!' he said softly, as if to himself, the picture of despair. 'It's the end! . . . Well . . . You'll certainly answer to me for this now!' he grated suddenly, looking at Ganya with furious hatred . . . 'Well . . . ach!'

He was fairly gasping for breath and could scarcely get his words out. He moved on into the drawing-room automatically, and once inside caught sight of Nina Alexandrovna and Varya; he came to a standstill, somewhat embarrassed in spite of his agitation. Lebedev followed him in, sticking to him like a shadow, and by now exceedingly drunk, then came the medical student, then the gentleman with the fists, then Zalyozhev, bowing extravagantly to right and left and, bringing up the rear, the short fat man squeezed himself in. They were all somewhat inhibited by the presence of the ladies, a powerful restraint upon them of course only until things got *started*, till the first excuse arrived to begin kicking up a row and get *started* . . . Then all the ladies in the world wouldn't bother them.

'What? You here as well, Prince?' said Rogozhin vaguely, somewhat surprised at coming across him. 'Still in those wretched gaiters, e-ech!' he sighed, dismissing the prince from his mind at once as he transferred his gaze once more to Nastasya Filippovna, moving steadily towards her as if drawn by a magnet.

She too was regarding the visitors with uneasy curiosity.

Ganya at length recovered himself.

'But look here, what on earth is the meaning of all this?' he began loudly, surveying the newcomers sternly and addressing himself principally to Rogozhin. 'You're not in the stables, you know, my mother and sister are here . . .'

'We can see it's your mother and sister', Rogozhin said through his teeth.

'It's obviously your mother and sister', seconded Lebedev, keeping his end up.

The gentleman with the fists, doubtless thinking his moment had arrived, began growling.

'But hang it all!' Ganya's voice rose suddenly, over-loud, explosive. 'First of all, I want everybody out of here into the other room, then kindly inform me . . .'

'Fancy, he doesn't recognize me', Rogozhin grinned malevolently, not budging. 'You don't recognize Rogozhin?'

'I suppose I must have met you somewhere, but . . .'

'Fancy, met me somewhere! Why, I lost two hundred roubles of my father's money to you just three months ago. The old man died without finding out; you dragged me into it and Knif cheated. Don't recognize me? Ptitsyn's a witness, aren't you! If I took three roubles out of my pocket just now and showed you them, you'd crawl to Vasilyevsky Island for them on your hands and knees, that's the sort you are! Your soul's like that! I've come to buy you off for cash, never mind looking at these boots, I've got money, friend, stacks of it, I'll buy you out lock, stock, and barrel . . . I could buy you all out if I wanted! Buy everything!'

Rogozhin was getting very heated and seemingly more and more drunk. 'E-ech!' he shouted, 'Nastasya Filippovna! Don't drive me away, just say one little word: are you going to marry him or not?'

Rogozhin asked the question like a desperate man supplicating some deity, but with the recklessness of one condemned to death who has nothing more to lose. He awaited the reply in a deathly anguish.

Nastasya Filippovna measured him with her taunting imperious stare, but glanced at Varya and Nina Alexandrovna, then looked at Ganya and suddenly altered her tone.

'Of course not, what are you talking about? Whatever possessed you to ask a thing like that?' she answered, quiet and serious, and apparently mildly surprised.

'No? No!!' shouted Rogozhin rapturously. 'So you're not, then?! And they told me . . . ach! Well! . . . Nastasya Filippovna! They told me you were engaged to Ganka! Him of all people. It couldn't be true, I tell them. Why I could buy him for a hundred roubles, if I gave him a thousand, say three, to withdraw, he'd clear off on the eve of his wedding and leave his betrothed to me. It's true Ganka, you swine! You'd take the three thousand! Wouldn't you! Here it is, look! That's why I came, to get your signature on it; I said I'd buy you off—and so I will!'

'Get out of here, you're drunk!' shouted Ganya, flushing and growing pale by turns.

His outburst was abruptly followed by an explosion of several voices: Rogozhin's crew had long been waiting for the first challenge. Lebedev was earnestly whispering something in Rogozhin's ear.

'True enough, clerk!' Rogozhin responded. 'True, you drunken devil! Ech, well here goes. Nastasya Filippovna!' he cried, looking at her as if half-crazed, nervous at first, then suddenly emboldened to the point of insolence. 'There's eighteen thousand!' He tossed a white paper packet tied up with string on to the table in front of her. 'There! And . . . there's more where that came from!'

He couldn't nerve himself to say what it was he wanted.

'No-no-no!' Lebedev started whispering to him again, his face registering considerable alarm; it could be guessed that the magnitude of the sum had terrified him and he was suggesting a very much lower starting-point.

'No, my foolish friend, you're out of your depth here . . . yes, and I'm no better, that's clear enough!' Rogozhin pulled himself together as he trembled before Nastasya Filippovna's flashing eyes. 'E-ech! I've made a mess of it, listening to you', he added with intense regret.

Nastasya Filippovna laughed suddenly as she regarded Rogozhin's crestfallen face.

'Eighteen thousand, for me? There's a yokel talking!' she added suddenly with a brazen familiarity and half rose from the sofa as if about to leave. Ganya observed the whole spectacle with a sinking heart.

'Forty thousand then, forty, not eighteen!' shouted Rogozhin. 'Vanka Ptitsyn and Biskup promised to deliver forty thousand by seven. Forty thousand! Hard cash.'

The whole thing was becoming outrageous, but Nastasya Filippovna continued laughing and made no move to go; it seemed as if she was deliberately prolonging things. Nina Alexandrovna and Varya had also risen from their places and were waiting in silent dismay for what might transpire; Varya's eyes glittered, but her mother was taking it all very badly; she was trembling and seemed likely to faint at any moment.

'Well if that's the way it is—a hundred! One hundred thousand this very day! Ptitsyn, lend me it, you're on to a good thing!'

'You're off your head', Ptitsyn whispered suddenly, coming over to him swiftly and laying hold of his arm—you're drunk, they'll be sending for the police. Where do you think you are?'

'It's the drink talking', said Nastasya Filippovna, seeming to taunt him.

'No word of a lie! The cash will be there by tonight. Ptitsyn, lend it to me, little usurer, take what you like as security, just deliver one hundred thousand by tonight; I'll prove I'm as good as my word!' Rogozhin was all of a sudden in an ecstasy of excitement.

'Now, hang it, what is all this?' shouted an angry Ardalion Alexandrovich belligerently as he moved towards Rogozhin. The old man had kept quiet until now, and the unexpectedness of his outburst smacked of the comic. Laughter broke out.

'Where did you spring from then?' Rogozhin laughed. 'Come with us, old man, we'll make you drunk!'

'Now that's rotten!' shouted Kolya, fairly weeping with shame and exasperation.

'Isn't there one among you to take this shameless woman out of here?' shouted Varya suddenly, shaking with anger.

'Here's me being called shameless!' parried Nastasya Filippovna with cheerful contempt. 'I'm the one who came here like a fool to invite them to my party! See the way your sister treats me Gavrila Ardalionovich!'

Ganya stood for some time as if thunderstruck by his sister's outburst; seeing, however, that Nastasya Filippovna was really leaving this time, he rushed frantically over to Varya and grabbed at her arm in a frenzy.

'What have you done?' he shouted, looking at her as if to incinerate her on the spot. He was utterly beside himself and unaware of what he was doing.

'What have I done then? Where are you dragging me off to? You aren't going to ask me to apologize to her for insulting your mother and coming here to disgrace your house, are you, you contemptible man?' she shouted again, staring at her brother in defiant exultation.

They stood facing one another thus for several seconds, Ganya still holding her by the arm. Varya tugged once, then again with all her might, but lost control and suddenly, goaded beyond endurance, spat in her brother's face.

'Now there's a girl for you!' cried Nastasya Filippovna. 'Bravo Ptitsyn, I congratulate you!'

Ganya saw red and, completely forgetting himself, he lashed out at his sister with all his strength. The blow would have caught her full in the face had not another hand seized Ganya's in mid-air.

Between his sister and himself stood the prince.

'That's enough, that will do!' he said insistently, though trembling all over himself, apparently severely shaken.

'Are you for ever going to get in my way!' roared Ganya, releasing Varya's arm and in an extremity of fury, using the full force of his free hand to strike the prince across the cheek.

'Oh!' cried Kolya, throwing up his hands. 'Oh, my God!'

There were exclamations from all sides. The prince went ashen. He looked Ganya directly in the eyes with an oddly reproachful expression; his lips trembled as they strove to say something; a sort of strange, utterly incongruous smile played upon them.

'Well me perhaps . . . but her . . . I won't let you! . . .' he said softly at length, but broke down suddenly and released Ganya, covered his face in his hands, and went off into a corner; facing the wall, he spoke in a faltering voice:

'Ah, how ashamed you're going to be for what you've done!'

Ganya was indeed standing utterly crushed. Kolya rushed across to embrace and kiss the prince; behind him pressed Rogozhin, Varya, Ptitsyn, Nina Alexandrovna, all of them, even the old man Ardalion Alexandrovich.

'It's all right, it's all right', murmured the prince to everyone in general, still with the same incongruous smile.

'He'll rue the day!' cried Rogozhin. 'You'll be ashamed Ganka for insulting this . . . sheep!' (He couldn't think of any other word.) 'Prince, dear heart, leave these people; damn the lot of them, come away with me! You'll find out what Rogozhin's friendship means!'

Nastasya Filippovna was also much taken aback, both by Ganya's action and the prince's reply. Her normally pale and pensive face, which all along had seemed out of keeping with her affected laughter, was now clearly stirred by a new emotion; she still appeared reluctant to betray it, however, and the mocking expression seemed determined to cling to her features.

'I've certainly seen his face before!' she said, suddenly quite grave, as she recalled her recent question.

'And aren't you ashamed of yourself! Surely you're not what you've been pretending to be? Can that really be possible?' the prince cried all of a sudden in profound, heartfelt reproach.

Nastasya Filippovna was surprised at this and smiled, though seeming to conceal something behind the smile; she shot a somewhat confused glance at Ganya as she left the drawing-room. Before reaching the hallway, however, she came back, went swiftly up to Nina Alexandrovna, took her hand, and brought it to her lips.

'I'm not like this really, he's right', she whispered quickly and vehemently, suddenly colouring; she turned and this time left so quickly that no one realized why she had returned. All they saw was that she whispered something to Nina Alexandrovna and appeared to kiss her hand. Varya, however, heard and saw everything, and followed her with astonished eyes.

Ganya recollected himself and darted after Nastasya Filippovna, but she had already left the apartment. He caught her up on the stairs.

'Don't see me out!' she cried to him. '*Au revoir*, till this evening! Be there, you hear!'

He came back bemused and thinking hard; a painful uncertainty oppressed his spirit, even worse now than before. There was the prince too . . . He was so sunk in reflection that he barely noticed the whole Rogozhin entourage spilling past him, even jostling him in the doorway, as they hastily vacated the apartment in Rogozhin's wake. They were all talking in unison about something. Rogozhin himself had been walking with Ptitsyn, insisting on some matter of urgent importance.

'You've lost, Ganka!' he shouted as he went by.

Ganya gazed after them uneasily.

11

THE prince left the drawing-room and shut himself in his own room. Kolya at once came running in to soothe him. By now the poor boy couldn't keep away from him, it seemed.

'You were right to come away', he said. 'Now there'll be a bigger row than there was before; it's like that every day here, and it all started because of that Nastasya Filippovna.'

'You've got all sorts of extremely painful problems here, Kolya', the prince remarked.

'Yes, that's true. No denying that. It's our own fault. Still, someone I know well is even worse off. Would you like to meet him?'

'Very much. Is he your friend?'

'Practically a friend. I'll explain all that later . . . But Nastasya

Filippovna is pretty, don't you think? I'd never seen her before, you know, though I've tried hard enough. Just dazzling. I'd forgive Ganya everything, if he were doing it for love; but he's after the money, that's the whole trouble!'

'Yes, I don't much like your brother.'

'Well, I should think not! You of all people, after . . . You know, I can't stand all these ideas people have. Some fool or madman or some villain in a frenzy slaps your face and you're dishonoured for the rest of your life and can't wipe it out except in blood, or unless he goes down on his knees and begs for pardon. It's absurd I think, a sort of slavery. Lermontov's play *Masquerade** is based on that, and in my opinion it's silly. I mean it's unnatural. Still, he wrote it when he was practically a child.'

'I liked your sister very much.'

'Spitting in Ganka's mug like that. Varka's got nerve! But you didn't do that and I'm sure it wasn't for lack of courage. And here she is, talk of the devil. I knew she'd come; she's a grand girl, though she does have her faults.'

'And you shouldn't be here', Varya pounced on him first of all. 'Off you go to your father. Is he bothering you, Prince?'

'Not in the least; on the contrary.'

'Look out, big sister's getting started! That's the trouble with her. Incidentally, I thought father was sure to go off with Rogozhin. I expect he's feeling sorry he didn't now. Better go and see how he is anyway', he added as he went out.

'Thank heavens, I got mama away to bed without another flare-up. Ganya's feeling sheepish and doing a lot of thinking. He's got good reason to. It's been a sharp lesson for him! . . . I came to thank you again Prince, and ask you a question: you didn't know Nastasya Filippovna before?'

'No, I didn't.'

'What made you tell her to her face that she wasn't "like that"? And guessing right apparently. It seems she really isn't like that, perhaps. Anyway, I can't make her out! She came here bent on humiliating us, that's obvious. I'd heard a lot of strange things about her previously, too. But if she came to issue an invitation, why did she start treating mama like that? Ptitsyn knows her very well and he says he couldn't fathom her behaviour today. And what about Rogozhin? You can't talk like that if you have any self-respect, in the house of your . . . Mama's very worried about you as well.'

'It's all right!' said the prince, with a wave of the hand.

'The way she obeyed you . . .'

'How do you mean?'

'You told her she should be ashamed and she changed completely all of a sudden. You have an influence over her, Prince', Varya added with the ghost of a smile.

The door opened and Ganya walked in absolutely unexpectedly.

The sight of Varya caused him no hesitation; he stood for a moment on the threshold before resolutely approaching the prince.

'Prince, I have behaved despicably, forgive me, my dear man', he said abruptly, strongly moved. His face was anguished. The prince regarded him with astonishment and made no immediate reply. 'Come, forgive me, forgive me, please!' urged Ganya impatiently, 'I'll kiss your hand if you like, this minute!'

The prince was much overcome and silently put both arms round Ganya. They kissed each other with sincere feeling.

'I had no idea, not the slightest, that you were like this!' said the prince at length, drawing breath with difficulty. 'I thought you were . . . incapable of it.'

'Of apologizing, you mean? . . . Now where did I get the idea this morning you were an idiot! You notice things other people never would. I could talk to you, but . . . best not to say anything!'

'There's someone else you should apologize to', said the prince, indicating Varya.

'No, they're all my enemies. Rest assured, Prince, there's been many an attempt made; no sincere forgiveness here!' Ganya burst out vehemently, turning away from Varya.

'That's not so, I forgive you!' Varya said suddenly.

'And you'll go to Nastasya Filippovna's this evening?'

'I will if you want me to, but don't you think it's out of the question for me to go now?'

'She's not like that you know. You see what puzzles she's setting us! It's her tricks!' and Ganya laughed grimly.

'I know she isn't, and all about her tricks. Besides, Ganya, do you realize what she must take you for? All right, she kissed mama's hand. The rest might just be her idea of fun, but you know she was laughing at you all the same, wasn't she? It's not worth seventy-five thousand, believe me brother! You've still got honourable feelings in you, that's why I'm telling you. Now then, don't go there yourself! Just you be careful! It's bound to end badly!'

So saying, Varya quickly left the room, much agitated.

'That's what they're all like!' laughed Ganya. 'Surely they can't think I don't know all that myself? I know a lot more than they do, don't I?'

Ganya sat down on the sofa, plainly wanting to prolong his visit.

'If you know it yourself', asked the prince, somewhat timidly, 'how is it that you've chosen this torment, knowing it isn't worth the seventy-five thousand?'

'I'm not talking about that', muttered Ganya. 'Incidentally, tell me, what's your opinion, I really would like to know: is this "torment" worth the seventy-five thousand or not?'

'In my opinion, no.'

'Well, now we know. And this is a dishonourable marriage?'

'Most dishonourable.'

'Well, I want you to know then that I'm going to marry her, now it's settled. I was in two minds but now I'm not! Don't say anything! I know what you're going to say . . .'

'I wasn't going to say what you think, but I'm surprised at your sheer confidence . . .'

'In what way? What confidence?'

'That Nastasya Filippovna's sure to marry you and that all that's settled, and secondly that even if she does, that the seventy-five thousand will find its way straight into your pocket. Of course, there's a lot I don't know about the business.'

Ganya moved briskly nearer the prince.

'Of course you don't know everything', he said. 'Why do you think I'd take on such a burden?'

'It seems to me it happens all the time: people marry for money and the money stays with the wife.'

'N-no, it won't be like that with us . . . there are . . . certain circumstances . . .' mumbled Ganya, pondering uneasily. 'But as for her answer, there's no doubt about that now', he added swiftly. 'What makes you think she'll refuse me?'

'I know nothing beyond what I've seen; and what Varvara Ardalionovna was saying just now . . .'

'Oh, that's just talk, they've run out of things to say. As for her, she was making game of Rogozhin, be sure of that, I was watching. It was obvious. I was a bit alarmed this afternoon but I can see it all now. Or do you mean the way she behaved towards my mother and father, and Varya?'

'And you.'

'If you like; but that's just the age-old way women have of getting their revenge, nothing more than that. She's a frightfully suspicious woman, touchy and proud. Like an official passed over for promotion! She felt like showing off and demonstrating her contempt for them . . . well, and me too; it's true, I don't deny it . . . But she'll marry me all the same. You have no inkling of the tricks that human vanity can get up to: so she thinks me despicable because I'm openly taking her, someone else's lover, for her money, at the same time she has no suspicion that another man would deceive her even worse: he'd keep on at her, spouting liberal-progressive notions and dragging in the woman question, so she'd be putty in his hands. He'd assure the proud fool (no trouble at all!) that he was taking her purely for her "nobility of heart and her misfortunes", but it would be for money just the same. I cut a poor figure in all this because I don't want to play the hypocrite; though I should. But what is she doing herself? Doesn't it amount to the same thing? So what right has she to despise me and get up to these games herself? Just because I show some backbone and won't give in. Well, we'll see about that!'

'Surely you didn't love her before this?'

'I did to begin with. Well, enough of that . . . There are women only fit to be mistresses and nothing else. I'm not saying she was my mistress. If she wants a quiet life, then she'll have it; if she starts making trouble, I'll throw her over straight away and take the money with me. I don't want to appear ridiculous; above all, I don't want to appear ridiculous.'

'I keep thinking', the prince observed cautiously, 'that Nastasya Filippovna is an intelligent woman. If she sees this torment ahead of her, why should she walk into the trap? She could marry someone else after all. That's what makes me wonder.'

'That's where her reasons come in! There are things you don't know in all this, Prince . . . There's . . . besides, she's convinced I'm madly in love with her, I swear it, and you know, I have a strong suspicion that she does love me, in her own fashion I mean, you know the old saying: you always hurt the one you love. All her life she'll look on me as a cheap adventurer (and perhaps she needs to do that) and still love me in her own fashion; she's preparing herself for that, that's her nature. She's a thoroughly Russian woman, I tell you; and, well, I've got a surprise of my own in store for her. That scene a while ago with Varya wasn't deliberate, but it's to my advantage: it's convinced her of my devotion and she's seen that I'm prepared to break all ties for her sake. So we're no fools either. By the way, you don't think I'm usually such a chatterbox do you? I may be doing the wrong thing in confiding in you, my dear Prince, but it's really because you're the first noble-minded person I've ever come across and I just fell on you, if you'll excuse the pun. You're not angry at what happened just now are you? I'm speaking from the heart for the first time in maybe two years. There are terribly few honest people round here; Ptitsyn's the best of them. Do I see you laughing or not? Rogues love honest men—didn't you know that? After all I . . . anyway, how am I a rogue, tell me honestly? Why do they all follow her lead in calling me that? You know, because of them and her, I call myself a scoundrel as well! That's as contemptible as can be!'

'I shan't ever regard you as a scoundrel now', said the prince. 'A little while ago I thought you an outright blackguard, then you suddenly made me feel so glad—a real lesson for me: not to judge without experience. I can see now that you shouldn't be regarded as a wicked man, nor even a very corrupt one. I believe you are the most ordinary man that ever was, except for being very weak and not having a grain of originality.'

Ganya smiled caustically to himself but said nothing. The prince saw that his judgement had caused offence, and also lapsed into an embarrassed silence.

'Has my father asked you for money?' Ganya asked suddenly.
'No.'

'If he does, don't give him any. I remember he was a decent enough fellow, you know, had the entrée to the best society. How quickly they go to pieces, all these decent old folk! A slight change in their circumstances and there's nothing left, as if their powder's all burned out at once. He never used to tell lies like that, I can assure you: he used to be just a bit over-excitable—and see what it's all come to now! Drink's his trouble, of course. Do you know he keeps a mistress? He's not just a harmless old fibber now. I can't understand how mother puts up with it. Has he told you about the siege of Kars? Or when his grey off-side horse started talking? That's how far it's gone.'

And Ganya suddenly rocked with laughter.

'Why are you looking at me like that?' he asked the prince.

'Oh, I was surprised at your genuine laughter. You've still got a childlike laugh, really. A while ago you came in to make your peace and said: "I'll kiss your hand if you like", just like a child would make up. That means you must still be capable of words and impulses like that. Then you start lecturing about this dark business and the seventy-five thousand. Really, it's all rather absurd and it mustn't go on.'

'So what do you think then?'

'Aren't you acting too recklessly and shouldn't you look about you first? Varvara Ardalionovna could be speaking the truth.'

'Ah, morality! I'm well aware that I'm still a little boy', interposed Ganya hotly, 'if only because I started this conversation with you. Prince, I'm not going into this murky business just for mercenary motives', he went on, blurting it all out like a young man wounded in his pride. 'I'd certainly come to grief if I did, my mind and character aren't hardened enough yet. I'm going through with it because I passionately want to, I'm bent on it; I have a most important aim in view. You're thinking that as soon as I get the seventy-five thousand I'll go straight out and buy a carriage. No, sir, I'll be wearing out my three-year-old coat and dropping all my club acquaintances. There aren't many self-disciplined characters about—though there's no shortage of money-lenders—and self-disciplined is what I want to be. The main thing now is to bring it off—the whole enterprise! Ptitsyn was sleeping in the street at 17, selling penknives; he started with coppers; now he's worth sixty thousand, but what an obstacle-course he had to go through! So I'm going to jump clear over the obstacles and start with the capital straight away; fifteen years from now, they'll say: "There goes Ivolgin, the King of the Jews." You say I haven't any originality. But mark this, dear Prince, there's nothing more annoying for a man of our time and race than to tell him he's not original, a weak character with no special talents, ordinary in other words. You didn't even deign to regard me as a genuine rogue, I felt like killing you for that just now, you know that? You insulted me worse than Yepanchin; he thinks me capable of selling him my wife!—just like that, mark you, out of the goodness of my heart, no sweet words, no inducements. I've been furious over that for a long time, my friend, and I want the money. Once I've got my hands on a fortune, you'll see, I'll be extremely original. The most hateful and despicable thing about money is that it even gives you talents. That's the way it will be till the end of the world. You'll say all this is childish, romantic even, well then, so much the pleasanter for me and it'll be done anyway. I'll go through with it and keep my head. *Rira bien qui rira le dernier!** Why does Yepanchin insult me like that? Out of ill will? Not at all, sir. It's simply because I'm of so little consequence. Well, sir, but then . . . Still, enough of that, time to go. Kolya's stuck his head in twice already, he's calling you to dinner. I'm going out. I'll drop by your room now and again. You'll be all right here with us; they'll look on you as one of the family now. Watch you don't give me away. I think we two are going to be either friends or enemies. What do you think, Prince, if I'd kissed your hand just now, as I genuinely offered to do, would that have made me your enemy afterwards?'

'It certainly would, but not for always; you wouldn't have kept it up, then you'd have forgiven me', decided the prince after some thought, laughing.

'Oho! You have to be handled with care. Damn me if you haven't put a drop of venom into that as well. And who knows, perhaps you're my enemy too? Incidentally, ha, ha ha! I forgot to ask: was I right in thinking that you're very much taken with Nastasya Filippovna, eh?'

'Yes . . . I like her.'

'In love?'

'N-no.'

'He's gone all red and embarrassed. Well, never mind, it's all right, I won't laugh; *au revoir.* You know she's a virtuous woman don't you—can you believe that? You think she lives with him, Totsky? Oh no! Not for ages. And did you notice how terribly gauche she is and how flustered she was several times back then? It's true. Those are the ones that love to lord it over everyone else. Well, goodbye then!'

Ganya went out a good deal more jauntily than he had come in and in a pleasant frame of mind. The prince remained motionless for some ten minutes, deep in thought.

Kolya put his head round the door once more.

'I don't feel like dinner, Kolya; I had a big lunch at the Yepanchins not long ago.'

Kolya came right into the room and handed a note to the prince. It was from the general and was folded and sealed. Kolya's face showed how painful it had been for him to carry out the commission. The prince read it, rose, and took his hat.

'It's only a little way off,' said the embarrassed Kolya. 'He's got a bottle in front of him. How he manages to get credit there I can't imagine. Dear Prince, don't mention it to the family that I delivered you a note! I've promised a thousand times not to do it, but I feel so sorry for him; oh yes, and don't stand on ceremony with him: give him a few coppers and have done with it.'

'I'd been thinking of it myself, Kolya; I need to see your papa ... about a certain matter ... let's go then ...'

12

KOLYA conducted the prince the short distance to Liteinaya, to a café-cum-billiard room; it was on the ground floor with a door on to the street. To the right, Ardalion Alexandrovich was sitting in a separate cubicle in the corner, like some ancient *habitué*; there was a bottle in front of him on the table and the *Indépendance Belge*, no less, in his hands. He was waiting for the prince; as soon as he caught sight of him, he laid aside his paper and started on a heated and voluble explanation, of which the prince understood almost nothing, since the general was already far from sober.

'I haven't got exactly ten roubles', the prince broke in. 'Here's twenty-five, change that and give me fifteen, otherwise I'll be left without a penny myself.'

'Oh, certainly; and rest assured, this very minute . . .'

'Besides which I have a certain favour to ask of you, general. You've never been at Nastasya Filippovna's, have you?'

'I? I not been? Is that what you're saying? On several occasions, my dear fellow, several!' exclaimed the general exultantly, in an access of complacent irony. 'I gave up going myself in the end, not wanting to encourage an unseemly union like that. You saw for yourself, you were a witness this afternoon: I did everything a father could do—a mild and indulgent father that is; now another kind of father's going to take the stage, then we'll see, we certainly shall: will the old and honoured warrior defeat the intrigue, or is some shameless Camille to gain entry into a most noble household?'

'What I actually wanted to ask you was whether you could take me to Nastasya Filippovna's this evening as a guest? It has to be today; I have a reason, but I've no idea how to get in. I was introduced today but not invited: the party is by invitation, but I don't mind disregarding a few of the niceties or even being laughed at, as long as I can get in somehow.'

'You've hit upon my idea exactly, my young friend', exclaimed the general rapturously. 'I didn't ask you to come here because of this trifle', he went on, taking the note, however, and transferring it to his pocket, 'I actually called you to invite you to accompany me on an expedition to Nastasya Filippovna's, or rather against Nastasya Filippovna! General Ivolgin and Prince Myshkin! Imagine what she'll think of that! Under the pretext of a courtesy visit on her birthday, I shall let my will be known at last—indirectly, not straight out, but just as effectively. Then Ganya will see how he stands: it's either his father, honoured and . . . so to speak . . . and so forth, or it's . . . Well, what will be, will be! Your idea is a capital one, first class. We'll set off at nine o'clock. There's plenty of time.'

'Where does she live?'

'A long way from here: by the Bolshoi Theatre, in the Mitovtsov's house, practically on the square, first floor . . . It won't be a large party, even if it is her birthday, and they'll break up early . . .'

The evening was getting on; the prince was still sitting waiting as the general started on countless stories without getting to the end of any of them. When the prince came in the old man had ordered another bottle and finished it in an hour, then asked for another and finished that as well. In the course of all this he must have got through the story of his life. At length the prince rose and said he could wait no longer. The general drank off the last dregs from the bottle, got up and walked outside, very unsteadily. The prince was in despair. He couldn't understand why he had been so stupidly taken in. In actual fact that had never been the case; he had been reckoning on the general solely as a means of getting to Nastasya Filippovna's, albeit at the cost of some impropriety; what he had certainly not reckoned on was a major scandal: the general was decidedly drunk, borne along on a tide of emotional eloquence, talking tearfully and incessantly. The interminable burden of all this was that, because of the reprehensible behaviour of every member of his family, everything had gone to rack and ruin, and it was finally time to call a halt to this. They emerged at length on to Liteinaya. The thaw was continuing; a warm, damp wind whistled dismally along the streets, carriages splashed through the mud as the horses, high-steppers and nags alike, rang their hooves against the cobblestones. Damp, dispirited crowds of pedestrians wandered along the pavements, with here and there a drunk.

'You see all these first-floor windows lit up', the general was saying. 'My old comrades live all round here, while I, I, the most senior and battle-scarred of the lot, trudge along on foot to the Bolshoi Theatre, to the apartment of a woman of doubtful reputation! A man with thirteen bullets in his chest . . . you don't believe me? Why, it was entirely on my account that Pirogov left besieged Sebastopol for a while to telegraph Paris, and Nelaton, the court physician managed to get a safe-conduct in the name of science and turned up in Sebastopol to examine me. The highest authorities know about it: "Oh, that's Ivolgin, the one with thirteen bullets in him! . . ." That's how they talk, sir! See that house, Prince? An old comrade of mine lives there, General Sokolovich, with his most noble and numerous household. That

house and another three on the Nevsky and two on Morskaya—
that's the circle of my acquaintance nowadays, my own personal
acquaintance that is. Nina Alexandrovna resigned herself to
circumstances long ago. I still keep the memory green . . . and
relax, so to speak, in the cultivated society of my former comrades
and subordinates, who adore me to this day. This General
Sokolovich (I haven't been there or seen Anna Fedorovna for
ages, incidentally) . . . you know, dear Prince, when you don't
entertain yourself, somehow you find you stop visiting others.
However . . . hm . . . you seem not to believe me . . . Anyway,
why shouldn't I introduce the son of my best friend and
childhood companion to that charming family household?
General Ivolgin and Prince Myshkin! You'll see an astonishing
girl, no two, three even, the very ornament of metropolitan
society: beautiful, cultivated, progressive . . . the woman question, poetry—all rolled up into one happy mixture, not to mention
a dowry of around eighty thousand, cash, with every one of
them—never comes amiss, whatever feminine or social questions
are involved . . . in short, I must certainly introduce you, it's my
bounden duty. General Ivolgin and Prince Myshkin!'

'Now? This minute? But you've forgotten', began the prince.

'It's all right, it's all right, I haven't forgotten, come along! This
way, up this magnificent staircase. I wonder why there's no hall-
porter, still . . . it's holiday time and he'll have gone off
somewhere. They haven't fired the drunken devil yet. This
Sokolovich is indebted to me for the entire success of his life and
career, to me, no one else, but . . . here we are.'

The prince followed him up submissively, no longer protesting
against the visit in order not to irritate him, fervently hoping that
General Sokolovich and his entire family would little-by-little
evaporate like a mirage and turn out to be non-existent, and they
could ever-so calmly go back down the staircase. But to his
horror he found this hope was failing him: the general was
conducting him up the stairs like someone who really did have
acquaintances here, every moment adding more biographical and
topographical details, with mathematical precision. At length,
when they had reached the first floor and halted on the right in
front of the door of a luxurious apartment, and the general had
grasped the bell-pull, the prince finally made up his mind to flee;

however, an odd circumstance made him pause for a moment.

'You've made a mistake, general', he said, 'it's got Kulakov on the door and you wanted Sokolovich.'

'Kulakov . . . that doesn't mean a thing. It's the Sokolovich apartment, and that's why I'm ringing; to hell with Kulakov . . . ah, they're opening up.'

The door actually was opening. A footman peered out and announced that 'the master and mistress are not at home, sir'.

'Just my luck, what a pity, what a pity', repeated Ardalion Alexandrovich, desperately disappointed. 'Just tell them, my dear fellow, that General Ivolgin and Prince Myshkin wished to pay their respects in person, and are extremely sorry, extremely . . .'

At that moment another face peeped out through the open door, apparently that of a housekeeper or perhaps a governess, a lady of about 40, wearing a dark dress. She approached with mistrustful curiosity on hearing the names of General Ivolgin and Prince Myshkin.

'Maria Alexandrovna's not at home', she spoke, eyeing the general closely, 'she's gone with the young lady, Alexandra Mikhailovna, to the grandmother's.'

'Alexandra Mikhailovna gone too, oh dear, that's terrible! Would you believe it, madam, this always happens to me! May I humbly beseech you to convey my greetings and remind me to Alexandra Mikhailovna . . . in short, pass on my best wishes for what they wished themselves last Thursday evening, listening to Chopin's ballade; they'll remember . . . My most cordial greeting! General Ivolgin and Prince Myshkin!'

'I shan't forget, sir', said the lady, less suspicious now as she took leave of them.

They descended the staircase, the general's enthusiasm undiminished as he continued to lament that they had failed to catch the family at home and that the prince had thus been deprived of such a charming acquaintance.

'You know, my dear fellow, I'm a bit of a poet at heart, have you noticed? However . . . however, it does seem we didn't call at exactly the right flat', he concluded quite unexpectedly. 'I've just remembered, Sokolovich lives somewhere else and I believe he's in Moscow at the moment anyway. Yes, I made a bit of a mistake there, but it . . . doesn't matter.'

'There's only one thing I want to know', the prince remarked gloomily. 'Should I stop relying on you altogether, and go on my own?'

'Stop? Rely? On your own? But whatever for, when this is such a major undertaking for me and so much of the future of my family depends on it? My dear young friend, you little know Ivolgin. To say "Ivolgin" is to say "stone wall": you can rely on Ivolgin like a stone wall, that's what they used to say back in the squadron where I began my service. I must just drop in for a minute at a house along the way, where for several years now my soul has found repose after trials and tribulations . . .'

'You want to go home?'

'No! I want to go . . . to Captain Terentyev's widow, he was my former junior officer . . . friend even . . . At the widow's I revive my spirits, I bring all my worldly and family troubles here . . . And since I have a great load on my mind today, I . . .'

'I think I've already made one terrible mistake in bothering you this evening', murmured the prince. 'Besides, now you're . . . Goodbye!'

'But I can't let you go my young friend, I just can't!' cried the general. 'The widow is the mother of a family and her heartstrings resonate through my whole being. Visiting her would be a matter of minutes, it's a second home to me, I virtually live here. I'll have a wash, tidy myself up a bit, then we'll get a cab to the Bolshoi Theatre. I assure you, I have need of you for the whole evening . . . In this house here, we've arrived already . . . Ah, Kolya, you're here? Is Martha Borisovna at home, or have you just got here yourself?'

'Oh no', replied Kolya, who had bumped into them in the doorway, 'I've been here ever so long, with Ippolit—he's taken a turn for the worse, he was in bed this morning. I was just going down to the shop for some cards. Martha Borisovna is waiting for you. But papa, what a state you're in! . . .' concluded Kolya, looking closely at the general's walk and stance. 'Very well then, let's go!'

This encounter with Kolya inclined the prince to accompany the general to Martha Borisovna too, though only for a minute. The prince needed Kolya; he had resolved to abandon the general in any event, and couldn't forgive himself for imagining he could place any reliance on him that afternoon. It was a long climb up the back-stairs to the fifth floor.

'Do you mean to introduce the prince?' asked Kolya as they went.

'Yes, my dear, introduce him: General Ivolgin and Prince Myshkin, but what . . . how is . . . Martha Borisovna . . .'

'You know, papa, it might be best not to go in there! She'll kill you! You haven't shown your face for three days and she's waiting for her money. Why on earth did you have to promise her that money? You're always the same! Now you'll have to get out of it somehow.'

On the fourth floor they halted in front of a low door. The general, visibly quailing, pushed the prince in front of him.

'I'll stay here', he mumbled, 'I want to make it a surprise . . .'

Kolya went in first. A lady of about 40, heavily rouged and painted, wearing slippers and a dressing-jacket and with her hair in plaits, peered out of the door; the general's surprise abruptly evaporated. As soon as she caught sight of him, she immediately started shouting:

'There he is, the nasty horrid man! I knew it in my bones!'

'Let's go in, it's all right', muttered the general to the prince, still innocently trying to make light of it all.

But it wasn't all right. No sooner had they passed through the low, dark hallway, and into the narrow sitting-room with its half-dozen wicker chairs and two card-tables, than the lady of the house at once continued in what must have been her habitual tone of assumed tearfulness:

'And you're not ashamed, are you, cruel tyrant of my household, barbarian, monster! Rob me of everything, suck me dry, and still not satisfied! How much longer am I going to put up with you, you shameless, dishonourable man!'

'Martha Borisovna, Martha Borisovna! This is . . . Prince Myshkin. General Ivolgin and Prince Myshkin', mumbled the general, flustered and trembling.

'Would you believe', the widow abruptly addressed the prince, 'would you believe that this man without shame does not spare my orphaned children? He's robbed me of everything, taken it all away to sell or pawn, and left me nothing. What am I supposed to do with your IOUs, you cunning, unscrupulous man? Answer, you deceiver, answer me, you insatiable devil: how shall I feed my orphaned children, how? Here he turns up drunk, he can hardly stand up . . . What have I done to provoke the wrath of the lord God, you horrible, disgusting rogue, answer!'

But the general had other things on his mind.

'Martha Borisovna, twenty-five roubles . . . that's all I can manage, thanks to the help of my most noble friend. Prince! I was cruelly mistaken! Such . . . is . . . life . . . And now, forgive me . . . I feel weak', the general went on, standing in the centre of the room and bowing in all directions, 'I feel weak, forgive me! Lenochka, a pillow . . . sweetheart!'

Lenochka, an 8-year-old girl, at once ran for a pillow and placed it on the tattered oilcloth of the hard sofa. The general sat down on it, intending to say a great deal more, but as soon as he touched the sofa he immediately bent over sideways, turned to the wall, and sank into the sleep of the just. The widow Terentyev, with sad solemnity, motioned the prince to a chair by the card-table and seated herself opposite, leaning her right cheek on her hand, and looked at him in silence, sighing. Three little children, two girls and a boy, of whom Lenochka was the eldest, came up to the table; all three placed their hands on it and all three began staring at the prince. Kolya appeared from the other room.

'I'm very glad I met you here, Kolya', the prince told him. 'Could you help me I wonder? I have to get to Nastasya Filippovna's urgently. I asked Ardalion Alexandrovich a while ago but here he's gone to sleep. Can you take me there, as I don't know any of the streets or roads. I do have the address, however, it's near the Bolshoi Theatre, the Mitovtsov house.'

'Nastasya Filippovna? Oh, she's never lived near the Bolshoi Theatre, and father's never been at her house, if you must know; it's funny you should expect anything of him. She lives near Vladimirskaya, by the Five Corners, much nearer here. You want to go there now? It's half-past nine. If you like, I'll take you.'

The prince and Kolya left at once. Alas, the prince had no money for a cab, so they had to walk.

'I wanted to introduce you to Ippolit', said Kolya. 'He's the eldest son of the widow in the jacket. He was in the next room; he's not well and he's been in bed all today. But he's a queer character; he's awfully touchy and I couldn't help feeling he'd be ashamed to see you, coming at such a moment . . . I'm not so ashamed as he is, because it's my father—but it's his mother. There's a difference there you know, because a situation like that isn't seen as discreditable for a male. Still, it might just be prejudice that one sex is more privileged in this respect. Ippolit's an excellent chap, but he's a slave to certain prejudices.'

'He's got consumption, you say?'

'Yes, so it seems; best if he dies quickly. In his place I'd certainly want to do that. He feels sorry for his brothers and sisters, the little ones I mean. If it were possible, if only there was enough money, we'd rent a separate flat and stay clear of both our families. That's what we dream about. You know what, when I told him just now about what happened to you he got really annoyed, and said that anybody who let himself be slapped on the face and didn't insist on a duel was a scoundrel. Anyway, he's frightfully quick-tempered and I've stopped arguing with him now. So then, Nastasya Filippovna immediately invited you to come and see her did she?'

'That's the trouble, she didn't.'

'How can you go though?' exclaimed Kolya stopping short in the middle of the pavement, 'and . . . looking like that, to a formal party?'

'I honestly don't know. If they let me in, all right, if not, then I've failed. As for my clothes, what can I do?'

'Have you got some business in mind? Or are you just going to pass the time in "polite society"?'

'No, I really . . . that is, I do have some business . . . I can't explain, but . . .'

'Well whatever it is, it's your affair: what matters as far as I'm concerned is whether you're forcing yourself into the charming company of trollops, generals, and money-lenders. If that's the way it was, excuse me, Prince, but I would laugh at you and start despising you. There are awfully few decent people hereabouts, there's really no one you can respect unreservedly. You can't help looking down on them, and yet they all insist on respect; Varya most of all. And have you noticed, Prince, how everybody's on the make these days! Here I mean, in Russia, in this beloved country of ours. How it all came about, I've no idea. Everything seemed to be so solidly based, but what's it like now? That's what everybody talks about and people write about it everywhere. They expose things. Everybody exposes things here. Parents are the first to go on the retreat and feel ashamed at their former moral values. In Moscow now a father tried to persuade his son to *stop at nothing* when it came to making money; it was in the papers.* Look at that general of mine. Well, what's he turned into? And yet, you know, I really think my general's a decent chap; really, I mean it! It's just the mess his life's in, that and the drink. Honestly, I mean it! I even feel sorry for him, only I'm afraid to say so in case everybody laughs; but I really do. And what about the others, the clever ones? They're all money-lenders, every last one! Ippolit defends money-lending, he says it has to be that way, economic crisis, the ebb and flow of capital, blast it. I hate to hear it from him, but he's all embittered. Just imagine, his mother, the widow, gets money from the general and then lends it back to him at high interest; what a dreadful disgrace it is! And do you know, mama, my mama I mean, Nina Alexandrovna, helps Ippolit with money, clothes and everything and partly provides for the children as well, through Ippolit, because the widow neglects them. Varya helps as well.'

'There you are you see, there aren't any decent, strong-minded people about, everybody's a money-lender according to you; but now you have principled people, your mother and Varya. Lending a hand here in the circumstances is a mark of moral strength, isn't it?'

'Varka does it out of vanity, just showing off and keeping up with mother; well, mama really . . . I respect her. I respect what she does and approve of it. Even Ippolit feels that, and he's got a grudge against the world. At first he was inclined to laugh and thought it demeaning of her, but now he's beginning to feel it sometimes. Hmm! That's what you call strength is it? I'll make a note of it. Ganya doesn't know about it or he'd call it cosseting.'

'So Ganya doesn't know? There's a good deal Ganya doesn't know besides that', the prince let slip as he mused.

'You know, Prince, I like you a lot. I keep remembering that business this afternoon.'

'Well I like you very much too, Kolya.'

'Look, where are you thinking of living here? I'll soon be

working and earning a bit of money, let's all live together, you, me and Ippolit, we'll get a flat; we can invite the general.'

'I should be delighted, still we'll see. At the moment I'm very . . . very upset. What? There already? In this house . . . what a splendid entrance! And a hall-porter. Well, Kolya, I don't know what's going to come of this.'

The prince stood looking forlorn.

'You can tell me about it tomorrow! Don't be too intimidated. Good luck anyway, because I think as you do about everything! I'm going back to tell Ippolit. And of course, they'll receive you, don't worry! She's awfully unconventional. Up this staircase, ground floor, the porter will show you!'

13

As he went up the steps, the prince was much troubled and tried his best to cheer himself: 'The worst they can do', he reasoned, 'is to turn me away and think ill of me, or perhaps let me in and laugh at me to my face . . . Eh, never mind that!' And in fact that part of it caused him little disquiet; but to the question of why he was going and what on earth he would do there, he was quite unable to find any reassuring answer. If it had only been possible for him to say to Nastasya Filippovna somehow: 'Don't marry that man, don't destroy yourself, he doesn't love you, it's your money he loves, he told me so himself, and Aglaya Yepanchina told me, and I've come to tell you', it would hardly be right and proper, even if he were to get the opportunity. There was yet another unresolved question, so crucial that the prince was afraid to think about it or even dare to admit its existence; he didn't know how to formulate it, and flushed and trembled at the very thought. In the end, however, in spite of all these doubts and misgivings, he went in and asked for Nastasya Filippovna.

Nastasya Filippovna's flat was magnificently appointed, though not excessively large. During the five years of her Petersburg existence there had been a time, at the beginning, when Afanasy Ivanovich had been particularly open-handed; he had still cherished hopes of her love and thought to win her over, chiefly with comforts and luxuries, knowing how easily luxurious habits are inculcated and how difficult they are to shake off later, when, little by little, they have become necessities. In this respect, Totsky had remained faithful to the good old traditions in every particular, having limitless faith in the invincible power of sensual influences. Nastasya Filippovna had not rejected this luxury, had enjoyed it even, but—and this seemed to him most odd—she never succumbed to it; it was as if she could always get along without it; she even attempted to say so plainly on several occasions, much to Totsky's discomposure. In fact there was a good deal about Nastasya Filippovna which disconcerted Afanasy Ivanovich and eventually led him to despise her. Besides the unseemly sorts of people she would sometimes consort with, and hence must have found congenial, there was evidence of other strange propensities: a certain barbarous mixture of two tastes, a capacity for making do with and being content with things and expedients whose very existence one would have thought foreign to any decent and well-bred person. Indeed, to give an example, if Nastasya Filippovna had suddenly displayed a dainty and refined ignorance of the fact that, say, peasant women couldn't afford the kind of cambric underwear she herself wore, Totsky would probably have been extremely pleased. His education programme for Nastasya Filippovna had been designed to produce this sort of outcome from the first—Totsky was a very shrewd man in this respect—but alas, things had gone awry. Despite this, there was and had always been something about Nastasya Filippovna that made Totsky marvel at her extraordinary and fascinating originality, a power which sometimes drew him even now, when his former calculations concerning her had come to nothing.

The prince was met by a maid (Nastasya Filippovna's servants were always female) who, to his surprise, was not at all startled at his request to be announced. The muddy boots, the broad-brimmed hat, the sleeveless cloak, his flustered appearance, none of this occasioned the least hesitation. She took his cloak and requested him to wait in the hall while she went off at once to announce his arrival.

The company gathered at Nastasya Filippovna's consisted of her usual friends and acquaintances. Indeed, compared with the anniversary gatherings of previous years, the guests were few in number. First and foremost, Afanasy Ivanovich Totsky and Ivan Fedorovich Yepanchin were present; both were polite but both were secretly rather uneasy in their barely concealed expectancy over the promised announcement concerning Ganya. Ganya was there too, of course, also very sullen and preoccupied, even to the point of being 'unamiable', standing by himself for the most part, away from the others, saying little. He had not ventured to bring Varya, but Nastasya Filippovna did not allude to the fact; on the other hand, as soon as she had greeted him she did refer to the scene that day with the prince. The general, who hadn't heard about this, began to evince interest, whereupon Ganya related everything which had occurred in a calm, restrained fashion, omitting nothing, including the fact that he had already·been to the prince to apologize. At the same time he expressed the fervent opinion that it was odd and unaccountable for the prince to be called an idiot; he thought him quite the opposite, he was a man with all his wits about him. Nastasya Filippovna listened to this tribute with close attention, watching Ganya curiously, but the conversation at once passed to Rogozhin, who had figured so prominently in the events of the afternoon and in whom Totsky and Yepanchin showed intense interest. It appeared that Ptitsyn had something of significance to say about Rogozhin, having been with him and active about his affairs till nearly nine that evening. Rogozhin had vigorously insisted on getting hold of a hundred thousand roubles that very day. 'He was drunk of course', observed Ptitsyn, 'but it seems he'll get his hundred thousand, however hard it may be; I just don't know whether it'll be today or whether it'll be the full amount. Lots of people are working on it, Kinder, Trepalov, Biskup; he doesn't care about the interest he pays: of course it's the drink talking and the first careless rapture about his legacy . . .', concluded Ptitsyn. All this was received with interest, of a bleak sort in some quarters; Nastasya Filippovna was silent, clearly not wishing to express an opinion, Ganya likewise. General Yepanchin was secretly more disturbed than almost anyone else: the pearl necklace he had presented that morning had been accepted with an excessively chilly politeness, and even a peculiar hint of mockery. Ferdischenko alone of all the guests was in high spirits and festive mood, laughing loudly on occasion for no particular reason, and then only because he had assumed the role of court jester. Totsky himself, who had the reputation of a subtle and elegant raconteur, the life and soul of the party on former occasions, was clearly not in the vein, uncharacteristically perplexed. The other guests, few as they were, included a poor old schoolmaster, unaccountably invited, a very young man unknown to the company, terribly shy and silent the whole time, a sprightly, actressy lady of around 40, and an extremely beautiful young girl, very well and richly dressed and very taciturn. Not only were they unable to enliven a conversation, they simply didn't know what to talk about at times.

Thus the appearance of the prince was opportune indeed. The announcement caused bafflement and several odd smiles, especially when Nastasya Filippovna's astonished expression made it clear that she had had no thought of inviting him. After the initial surprise, however, Nastasya Filippovna at once looked so pleased that the majority promptly prepared to meet the unexpected visitor with laughter and high spirits.

'It's probably just his innocence', pronounced Ivan Fedorovich Yepanchin, 'and it's rather dangerous to encourage such tendencies, but it's no bad thing he took it into his head to call at this moment, unconventional or not: he may cheer us up, at least if I'm any judge.'

'Especially as he invited himself!' Ferdischenko at once put in.

'Why, what has that to do with it?' the general enquired coldly. He detested Ferdischenko.

'Because he'll have to sing for his supper', explained the latter.

'Well, Prince Myshkin is no Ferdischenko all the same, sir', the general couldn't help observing, still not reconciled to being on equal social terms with Ferdischenko.

'Ah, general, don't be hard on me', came the smirking reply. 'I have my privileges, you know.'

'And what privileges may they be?'

'I had the honour of explaining it in detail to the company the last time; I will repeat it once more for your excellency. You see, your excellency: everyone has wit, but I have none. As compensation, I have been granted permission to speak the truth, since everyone knows that only unwitty people speak the truth.

Besides, I'm a most vindictive person, also a consequence of lack of wit. I can meekly put up with anyone's insults, but only till my tormentor comes to grief. As soon as that happens I remember it at once and get my own back somehow, I kick, as Ivan Petrovich Ptitsyn has said of me; he, it goes without saying, never kicks anyone. You know Krylov's fable, your excellency: "The Ass and the Lion"? Well, that's the two of us to the life, it was written about us.'

'You're talking nonsense again, it seems, Ferdischenko,' the general flared up.

'But why get upset, your excellency?' rejoined Ferdischenko, who had bargained on getting another chance to rub it in. 'Don't worry, your excellency, I know my place: if I said that we were the Lion and the Ass in Krylov's fable, naturally I assume the role of the Ass, your excellency is the Lion, as Krylov says:

> The mighty Lion, scourge of the woods,
> Had lost his strength as he grew older.

And I, your excellency, am the Ass.'

'I agree about the last part', the general blurted out incautiously.

All this was crude of course, and deliberately engineered, but it was accepted that Ferdischenko was permitted to play the jester's role.

'That's the only reason I'm allowed in here and not thrown out', Ferdischenko had once exclaimed, 'so I can talk just like this. Now is it possible to receive someone like me, I ask you? I realize that myself. Can such as Ferdischenko be sat next to a refined gentleman like Afanasy Ivanovich? There's only one conceivable explanation: I'm put there because such a thing is impossible even to imagine.'

But although it was crude, it could also be scathing, sometimes very much so, and it was this which appealed to Nastasya Filippovna. Those who very much wanted to visit her had perforce to endure Ferdischenko. He had guessed the real truth, perhaps, realizing that he was received because from the first his presence had been intolerable to Totsky. For his part, Ganya had undergone an infinity of torment at his hands, and in that way he had contrived to be very useful to Nastasya Filippovna.

'The prince will start by singing us a popular song of the day', concluded Ferdischenko, glancing to see what Nastasya Filippovna would say.

'I don't think so, Ferdischenko, and kindly control yourself', she remarked shortly.

'Aha! If he's under special protection, I relent as well . . .'

But Nastasya Filippovna ignored him as she rose and walked out to greet the prince.

'I was sorry', she said, suddenly appearing before him, 'that in the heat of the moment today I forgot to invite you and I'm very glad you have given me the opportunity yourself of thanking you now and congratulating you on your resolution.'

As she spoke she stared intently at the prince, striving to gain some inkling of his motive in coming.

The prince might have have said something in reply to her gracious speech, but he was so dazzled and overwhelmed that he couldn't utter a word. Nastasya Filippovna was pleased to see this. That evening she was in full evening dress and produced a stunning impression. She took his arm and led him towards the guests. At the door to the drawing-room the prince halted abruptly and whispered hurriedly, in high agitation:

'In you everything is perfection . . . even being thin and pale . . . no one would wish to see you different . . . I wanted to come to you so much . . . I . . . forgive me . . .'

'Don't apologize', laughed Nastasya Filippovna. 'That would be too ordinary and conventional. They're right then, when they call you an odd person. So you think me perfection, do you?'

'Yes.'

'You may be an expert at guessing, but this time you're wrong. I'll remind you of that later . . .'

She introduced the prince to her guests, a good half of whom knew him already. Totsky at once made some polite remark and everyone seemed to liven up somewhat, talk and laughter broke out immediately. Nastasya Filippovna seated the prince by her side.

'Well now, what's so astonishing in the prince turning up?' Ferdischenko raised his voice above everyone else's. 'It's as clear as day, speaks for itself!'

'Too clear and speaks too much for itself', the silent Ganya abruptly put in. 'I've been watching the prince virtually all the time today, right from the moment he set eyes on Nastasya Filippovna's portrait for the first time on Ivan Fedorovich's desk. I well remember what I thought at the time, and now I'm firmly convinced; the prince confessed as much to me himself, incidentally.'

Ganya said all this perfectly gravely, with no hint of jocularity, morosely even, which seemed rather strange.

'I made no confessions to you', the prince replied, going red, 'I only answered your question.'

'Bravo, bravo!' cried Ferdischenko. 'Honest at least; crafty and honest!'

There was general loud laughter.

'Do stop shouting, Ferdischenko', Ptitsyn told him in a disgusted undertone.

'I wouldn't have looked for initiative like that from you, Prince', said Ivan Fedorovich. 'I'd expect that sort of thing from someone else altogether. And here was I thinking you were a philosopher! Still waters run deep, eh!'

'And to judge by the way the prince blushes at a harmless joke, just like an innocent young girl, I conclude that as a well-brought-up young man, he has the most honourable intentions in mind', the toothless septuagenarian teacher, hitherto totally mute, suddenly spoke up, or rather mumbled, quite out of the blue, since no one had expected him to open his mouth that evening. Everyone laughed even more. The oldster, most likely thinking they were appreciating his witticism, began laughing even louder as he looked at them, till a cruel paroxysm of coughing cut him short; at this point Nastasya Filippovna, who for some reason was inordinately fond of eccentric old men and women, even including holy fools, set about making a fuss of him, kissing him a good deal and ordering more tea. When the maid came in she asked for a shawl to be brought for her; she wrapped herself in it and had more logs put on the fire. When asked what time it was, the maid replied that it was already half-past ten.

'Gentlemen, wouldn't you like some champagne', offered Nastasya Filippovna suddenly. 'It's ready and waiting. It might cheer you up. Please don't stand on ceremony.'

An invitation to drink, especially couched in such naive terms, sounded queer coming from Nastasya Filippovna. Everyone recalled the high degree of formality which had prevailed at her previous parties. Indeed, the party did liven up, but in a rather unusual fashion. Nobody refused the wine, however: first came the general himself, then the sprightly lady, the old man, then Ferdischenko, followed by the rest. Totsky took his goblet too, hoping to modulate the new tone the evening was taking by giving it, as far as possible, the character of a pleasant joke. Ganya alone drank nothing. It was difficult to make any sense of Nastasya Filippovna's oddly brusque, rapid outbursts, as she took her wine and announced that she would drink three glasses that evening, or her hysterical, pointless laughter, abruptly interspersed with silence and moody depression. Some guests supposed she was feverish; they began to notice at length that she too seemed to be expecting something, frequently consulting her watch and becoming irritable and preoccupied.

'You seem to have a little fever?' enquired the sprightly lady.

'A great deal, not a little, that's why I'm wrapped in this shawl', replied Nastasya Filippovna, who had in fact grown paler and seemed to be suppressing a violent shivering.

All present grew concerned and stirred uneasily.

'Should we not permit our hostess to rest?' said Totsky, with a glance at the general.

'Most certainly not, gentlemen! I particularly wish you to remain seated. I have special need of your presence tonight', announced Nastasya Filippovna, with meaningful emphasis. Since virtually all the guests had found out that a most important decision was due to be made that evening, these words seemed extraordinarily significant. The general and Totsky exchanged glances once more. Ganya made a convulsive movement.

'It would be nice to play some kind of parlour-game', remarked the sprightly lady.

'I know the most marvellous new parlour-game', said Ferdischenko. 'At least it's only been played once, and it didn't work then.'

'What was it?' asked the sprightly lady.

'Some of us got together one day, we'd had a few I admit, and somebody suggested that each of us, without getting up from the table, tell something from his own life that he honestly considered to be the worst action he had ever performed in his life; but he had to be honest about it, that was the thing, to be honest, no lying!'

'Curious idea', said the general.

'Couldn't be more so, your excellency, that's the beauty of it.'

'Ridiculous idea', said Totsky. 'Still, one can understand it: it's a sort of exhibitionism.'

'Perhaps that was what we had in mind, Afanasy Ivanovich.'

'That sort of game's more likely to make you cry than laugh', the sprightly lady remarked.

'The thing's unthinkable and absurd', opined Ptitsyn.

'But did it work?' asked Nastasya Filippovna.

'Well, that's the trouble, it didn't; it was a flop. Everybody did come out with something, a lot of us told the truth, some even enjoyed the telling, if you can imagine that, but later we all felt ashamed, we couldn't keep it up! On the whole though it was great fun, in its way.'

'But really, that would be splendid!' observed Nastasya Filippovna, suddenly all animation. 'Really, let's try it, gentlemen! We're rather dull somehow aren't we? If each one of us agrees to tell something . . . like that . . . voluntarily of course, no one's forced to do it? Maybe we can keep it up? It's terribly original at least . . .'

'Pure genius!' said Ferdischenko. 'The ladies are excused, incidentally, the men have to start; we'll draw lots, like we did then! Oh yes, we must, we must! If anyone really doesn't want to, he needn't—but that's being a spoil-sport! Your lots here, gentlemen, into the hat; the prince can draw them out. Nothing could be simpler, tell us about the worst action you've ever performed in your life—simple as can be, gentlemen! You'll see, if anyone does happen to forget, I'll undertake to remind him!'

The idea appealed to no one. Some frowned, while others smiled craftily. Some objected but not very forcefully—the general for example, not wishing to cross Nastasya Filippovna since he noticed how much the bizarre idea had taken her fancy. Where her own desires were concerned, Nastasya Filippovna had always been relentlessly single-minded once she had resolved to make them known, however whimsical and pointless they might be, even to her. Now she was in a state verging on hysteria,

bustling about, convulsed by fits of laughter, especially at
Totsky's nervous protestations. Her dark eyes glittered and two
red spots had appeared on her ashen cheeks. The glum and
squeamish air of some of her guests appeared to inflame her
mood of mischief. Perhaps it was the cynicism and cruelty of the
game which appealed to her. Some of those present were certain
she had a special reason for it all. At all events, they began to fall
in with the idea: it was intriguing at least, and to many of them an
alluring prospect. Ferdischenko was more restless than anyone.

'What if it's something that can't be told . . . in front of ladies?'
said the reticent youth timidly.

'Then don't tell that one; there must be plenty of other nasty
deeds', replied Ferdischenko. 'Ah, you young people!'

'Well I really don't know which action of mine is the worst',
put in the sprightly lady.

'Ladies are not obliged to take part', repeated Ferdischenko,
'but they have the option; if anyone's inspired to confess, so be it.
Men are also exempt if they have a really rooted objection.'

'But what's there to prove I'm not lying?' asked Ganya. 'And if
I am, the whole point of the game goes. Is there anyone here who
won't lie? Of course nobody's going to tell the truth.'

'That's one of the fascinating things, seeing what sort of lies a
man tells. Anyway, Ganechka, you've nothing much to worry
about if you do lie, everybody here knows what your worst action
is in any case. Now just you think, gentlemen', cried Ferdischenko with an air of inspiration, 'with what eyes we shall look
upon each other later, tomorrow for instance, after the tales have
been told!'

'Can this really be happening? Is all this really serious,
Nastasya Filippovna?' asked Totsky with dignity.

'If you're afraid of wolves, stay out of the forest', she remarked,
smiling ironically.

'But permit me, Mister Ferdischenko, how can one make a
parlour-game out of this?' pursued Totsky, becoming more and
more alarmed. 'I assure you, such things never work; you say
yourself it's already been a failure once.'

'What do you mean, failure! I told my story last time about
stealing three roubles, I just upped and said it!'

'No doubt. But surely there was no possibility of you telling it in such a way as to have it believed as the truth? And Gavrila Ardalionovich has quite properly pointed out that the whole game falls flat if there's the slightest hint of falsehood. Truth can only be incidental to someone's exhibitionist mood, which would be in the worst possible taste and quite unseemly and unthinkable here.'

'You are indeed a most subtle man, Afanasy Ivanovich, you positively astonish me!' cried Ferdischenko. 'Imagine gentlemen, by pointing out that I couldn't tell the story of my theft so as to be believed, Afanasy Ivanovich is hinting ever so subtly, that I couldn't really have done it, since to mention that sort of thing aloud would be indecent—though he may be perfectly convinced in his heart that Ferdischenko is only too likely to have been a thief! But to business, gentlemen, to business, the lots have been collected and yours is in too, Afanasy Ivanovich, that means no one has refused! Prince, draw!'

The prince silently put his hand into the hat and drew out the first lot—Ferdischenko, the second—Ptitsyn, the third—the general, the fourth—Afanasy Ivanovich, the fifth—his own, the sixth—Ganya, and so on. The ladies had not participated.

'Dear me, what awful luck!' cried Ferdischenko. 'Here was I thinking that the prince would have the first turn, and the general next. Still, thank heaven, at least Ptitsyn is after me, and that will make up for it. Well, gentlemen, of course I am bound to set a good example, but my greatest regret at this moment is that I'm such an undistinguished nobody; even my rank in the service is the lowest possible; what's really interesting about Ferdischenko's having done something nasty? It's an *embarras de richesse*. Do I really have to talk about that thievery again, just to convince Afanasy Ivanovich that one may steal without being a thief?'

'You're convincing me, Mister Ferdischenko, that one can derive huge enjoyment from relating one's own dirty deeds without being asked ... However ... Your pardon, Mister Ferdischenko.'

'Do make a start, Ferdischenko, you've got a lot to say for yourself; is there no end to it?' commanded Nastasya Filippovna, irritably impatient.

Everyone noticed that after her recent fits of laughter she had all at once become gloomy, peevish, and irritable; nevertheless, she stubbornly and despotically insisted on her impossible whim. Totsky was going through agonies. General Yepanchin was exasperating him as well: there he was sitting drinking champagne as if there were nothing untoward, even perhaps considering a contribution of his own when his turn came.

14

'I'VE no wit, Nastasya Filippovna, that's why I chatter so much!' cried Ferdischenko as he commenced his story. 'If I had as much wit as Afanasy Ivanovich or Ivan Petrovich, I'd have just sat here today and not said a word, like Afanasy Ivanovich and Ivan Petrovich. Allow me to ask your opinion, Prince, I can't help thinking that there are a great many more thieves in the world than non-thieves, and the supremely honest man who has never stolen anything in his life simply doesn't exist. That's how I see it, from which, however, I certainly do not conclude that everyone's a thief, though I swear there are times when I'd dearly love to think so. But what's your opinion?'

'Well, this is a silly way of telling a story', protested Darya Alexeyevna. 'What nonsense, it can't be that everybody's stolen something; I've never stolen anything.'

'You have never stolen anything, Darya Alexeyevna; but what says the prince, who has gone all red suddenly?'

'I believe you are right, but you greatly exaggerate', said the prince, who had indeed blushed for some reason.

'And you've never stolen anything yourself, Prince?'

'Well, this is ridiculous! Bethink yourself, Mister Ferdischenko', the general intervened.

'It's as plain as plain; when it comes to the point, you're ashamed to tell your story, so you try and drag the prince in, because he doesn't stand up for himself', snapped Darya Alexeyevna.

'Ferdischenko, either get on with your story or keep quiet and mind your own business. You're exhausting everybody's patience', said an annoyed Nastasya Filippovna sharply.

'At once, Nastasya Filippovna; but since the prince has confessed, and I maintain he has, what would anyone else have said, I name no names, if he had wanted to tell the truth? As far as I'm concerned, gentlemen, there's nothing more to tell: it's all very simple, stupid, and nasty. But I can assure you I'm no thief; I just unaccountably stole something. It was three years ago at Semyon Ivanovich Ischenko's villa, a Sunday it was. He was having a dinner party. After the meal the ladies withdrew. It occurred to me to ask Maria Semyonovna, the daughter of the house, to play something on the piano. As I walked through the corner room, there were three roubles lying on Maria Ivanovna's writing-desk, a green note: she'd got it out to pay some household bill. Not a soul about. I took the money, and put it in my pocket, I've no idea why. I can't explain what came over me. I went back quickly and sat down at the table. I just kept sitting and waiting, in a powerful state of nerves, talking non-stop, telling stories, laughing away; then I went in to the ladies. Half an hour later they started questioning the maids. Suspicion fell on the maid Darya. I showed great concern and sympathy; I remember, when Darya had gone to pieces altogether, I tried to persuade her to confess openly and in front of everyone, throwing herself on Maria Ivanovna's mercy. Everyone looked at me and I felt enormous pleasure just because I was preaching away with the note lying in my pocket. I drank the three roubles that very evening in a restaurant. I walked in and ordered a bottle of Lafitte; I'd never asked for a bottle by itself like that before; I just wanted to get rid of it quickly. My conscience didn't trouble me particularly, either then or later. I wouldn't have done it another time probably; you can believe that or not, as you like, I don't care. Well, gentlemen, that's it.'

'Except of course that it's not the worst thing you've ever done', said Darya Alexeyevna, disgusted.

'That's a psychological case-history, not an action', remarked Totsky.

'What about the maid?' asked Nastasya Filippovna, not trying to dissimulate a most fastidious distaste.

'The maid was dismissed the very next day, of course. It's a strict household.'

'And you let it happen?'

'Well that's marvellous! You don't mean I should have gone and accused myself?' Ferdischenko giggled, disconcerted nevertheless by the deeply unpleasant impression his story had made.

'What a filthy thing to do!' cried Nastasya Filippovna.

'Bah! You want to hear the vilest thing a man's done and you want him to be a hero at the same time! The vilest actions are always the filthiest, we'll hear Ptitsyn on that in a moment; and there's a lot that glitters on the outside and wants to seem virtuous because it has its own carriage. A lot of people have their own carriage ... How they got them of course ...'

In a word, Ferdischenko suddenly lost his temper and got completely carried away; he forgot himself and went too far; his whole face was contorted. Strange as it may seem, he might well have been expecting quite a different reception for his story. These 'errors' of taste and this 'exhibitionism', as Totsky had put it, happened very often with Ferdischenko and were very much in character.

Nastasya Filippovna was positively trembling with anger as she stared at Ferdischenko, who at once backed down and fell silent, almost cold with fear: he had gone too far.

'Shouldn't we call this off altogether?' asked Totsky slyly.

'It's my turn, but I claim my exemption and shan't speak', said Ptitsyn firmly.

'You don't want to?'

'I can't, Nastasya Filippovna; and anyway, I think a party-game like this is really impossible.'

'General, it seems you're next', Nastasya Filippovna turned to him. 'If you refuse as well you will throw us all out, and I shall be sorry because I was counting on telling something from my own life to finish off the game, only I wanted to go after you and Afanasy Ivanovich; I rely on you to give me courage', she added, laughing.

'Oh, if you promise as well', cried the general warmly, 'I'm willing to tell the story of my life if you like; but I admit that while I was waiting for my turn I did prepare a story of my own ...'

'And just from your excellency's face one may conclude that working up your little story has given you particular creative satisfaction ...' Ferdischenko nerved himself to observe, still somewhat flustered. His smile was venomous.

Nastasya Filippovna glanced fleetingly at the general and also smiled to herself. Her depression and irritation, however, were increasing all the time. Totsky was now doubly alarmed at her promise to tell a story of her own.

'Like everybody else, gentlemen, I have had occasion to perform actions during my life which weren't altogether pretty', the general began. 'The strangest thing of all though, is that I consider the tiny incident I'm about to tell you as the vilest action of my life. Incidentally, nearly thirty-five years have passed, but I can never recall it without a pang, so to speak. It was a very silly business: I was still an ensign at the time, working my way up in the army. Well, everyone knows a subaltern's existence: hot-blooded and tuppence in your pocket; I had a batman at the time, Nikifor, who was very conscientious about my welfare; he saved, sewed, scrubbed, and cleaned—he even stole anything he could lay his hands on, just so as to add to my possessions; he really was a most loyal and honest fellow. For my part, I was, naturally, firm but fair. It so happened that we were quartered in a little town for a time. I was billeted in a suburb with the widow of a retired sub-lieutenant. About 80 or near enough, the old girl was. Her little wooden house was ancient and dilapidated and she was too poor to have a maid, even. The main thing about her was that she had had a numerous family and relatives at one time; some had died, others gone away, some had forgotten about the old woman and her husband had been buried for about forty-five years. There had been a niece living with her for a few years before this, a humpbacked woman, wicked as a witch they said—even bit the old woman's finger once; still, even she died off so that the old woman had been existing all on her own for around three years. It was dull as could be for me, and she was so stupid you couldn't get anything out of her. Eventually she stole a cock from me. That business was never cleared up, but it couldn't have been anybody else. We quarrelled over it in real earnest, and it so happened that as soon as I applied, I was transferred to the other side of town, to a room in a house belonging to a merchant with a huge family—and an enormous beard, as I recall. Nikifor and I were glad to move and I left the old woman, still annoyed with her. Three days passed and I come back from drill and Nikifor announces, "we shouldn't have left the bowl at the old woman's, there's nothing to serve the soup in". I was astonished, of course: "What do you mean, how did we leave the bowl with the landlady?" Nikifor was surprised, and said that while we were moving the old woman had hung on to the bowl, saying it was in exchange for a pot of her own I had broken, and that I had made the offer myself. This meanness of hers naturally drove me wild; my blood boiled and I leapt to my feet and dashed round there. I get to the old woman's fairly beside myself, so to speak; I see her sitting in the passageway all on her ownsome in the corner, cheek resting on her hand, as if she was keeping out of the sun. I let out a flood of abuse straight away, "you so-and-so!" you know the sort of thing, Russian-style. As I look at her I feel there's something odd about her: she's sitting there staring at me, eyes popping and no word of reply, just staring, strange as can be, seeming to rock from side to side. I calmed down a bit in the end and looked closer, asking her something; no answer. I stood for a while hesitating; flies buzzed, the sun was going down, everything was quiet; at last I went out completely at a loss. I was summoned to see the major before I reached home, then I had to go to the squadron, so it was quite dark by the time I got back. Nikifor's first words were: "You know our old landlady's gone and died, your honour?" "When?" "Today, evening time, about an hour and a half ago." At the very time I'd been swearing at her, she'd been passing away. I was so shocked, I tell you, I couldn't get over it. I began brooding over it, you know, even dreaming about it. Of course I'm not superstitious, but I went to the funeral service on the third day. Well anyway, the longer time goes on, the more I think about it. I don't worry about it exactly, but I get to picturing it and it makes me feel uncomfortable. I've worked out what the main point is. Firstly she was a woman, a fellow creature, or human being as they put it nowadays; she'd lived, lived a long time, and finally reached her span. At one time she'd had children, a husband, household, relatives, all that bubbling around her, so to speak, all the laughter, so to speak, then all of a sudden, complete blank, everything vanished and her left alone, like . . . a kind of fly, bearing some immemorial curse. And so, at length, God brought her to her end. At sunset, a calm summer evening, my old woman flies away too—of course there's a moral lesson here; and then at the very moment, instead of tears of farewell, so to speak, some desperate young lieutenant, arms akimbo and full of himself, sees her off from the earth with a flood of Russian swear-words on account of a missing bowl! Of course I was guilty, and although I've long since looked on it as the action of another man, owing to the passage of time and changes in my own nature, I still regret what I did. So, I repeat, it really does seem strange to me, particularly since it wasn't entirely my fault: why did she take it into her head to die at that precise moment? Of course, there is one excuse; what I did was in a way psychological, but I couldn't rest easy all the same until about fifteen years ago, when I endowed two chronically ill old women in the almshouse, to soften the last days of their earthly existence by a decent provision. I intend leaving enough money in my will to make the provision permanent. Well, that's all there is to it, gentlemen. I repeat that maybe I've been guilty of a lot of things in my time, but this incident I honestly consider to be the very worst action of my entire life.'

'And instead of telling us the worst action of your life, your excellency, you've told us one of your good deeds; you've cheated Ferdischenko!' declared the latter.

'Indeed, general, I never imagined you had such a kind heart after all; I'm almost sorry', said Nastasya Filippovna casually.

'Sorry? Why on earth?' the general asked with a gracious laugh, drinking off his champagne, not without a touch of complacency.

Now it was the turn of Totsky, who had also prepared himself. They had all guessed that he wouldn't refuse as Ptitsyn had done, and for a number of reasons they awaited his story with particular interest, peering at Nastasya Filippovna the while. With an air of great dignity, totally in keeping with his noble bearing, Afanasy Ivanovich began one of his 'charming stories' in a low gentle voice. It should be pointed out that he was an imposing figure, tall, stately, balding with a touch of grey, and rather stout, with soft, florid, rather pendulous cheeks and false teeth. He wore elegant, loose-fitting clothes and exquisite linen. His plump white hands fairly drew the eye. On the index finger of his right hand there was a costly diamond ring. Throughout his story, Nastasya Filippovna gazed intently at the lace frill of her sleeve and kept pinching it with two fingers of her left hand; she did not once glance at the speaker.

'What eases my task above all else', began Afanasy Ivanovich, 'is the inescapable obligation to relate the very worst action of my entire life. In that case, of course, there can be no hesitation: conscience and the promptings of the heart immediately dictate exactly what one should say. I have to confess with a heavy heart that among the countless thoughtless and . . . wayward actions of my life, there is one which has left all-too painful an impression on my memory.

'It took place about twenty years ago; I had taken a trip into the country to see Platon Ordyntsev. He had just been elected marshal of nobility and was spending the winter holiday there with his young wife, Anfisa Alexeyevna. Her birthday coincided with this, so two dances had been arranged. At that time Dumas *fils'* charming novel, *La Dame aux Camélias*, was all the rage and had just created a sensation in high society. It is a poem, in my opinion, which is ageless and will never pass away. In the provinces all the ladies were in ecstasies over it, those who had read it at least. The charm of the book, the novelty of the treatment of the heroine, that seductive world so subtly dissected, and last but not least, all those enchanting details scattered about the book (for example about when to use alternate bouquets of red and white camellias), in short all these delightful touches, taken together, produced little short of a sensation. Camellias became the height of fashion. Everybody wanted camellias, everybody was looking for them. I ask you: how many camellias can you get hold of out in the provinces when they're in demand for every ball, few as those were? At the time, Petya Vorkhovskoi was languishing after Anfisa Alexeyevna, poor fellow. I honestly don't know if there was anything between them, that is, I mean whether he could have had any serious hope at all. The poor chap was going off his head trying to get hold of some camellias for Anfisa Alexeyevna on the night of the ball. It had become known that the Countess Sotskaya from Petersburg, the guest of the governor's wife, and Sophia Bespalova would be turning up with bouquets of white ones. Anfisa Alexeyevna wanted red, in order to produce her own effect. Poor Platon was almost driven mad of course, being the husband. He undertook to get hold of the flowers, and what do you think happened? The night before,

Katerina Alexandrovna Mytischeva had snapped them up. She was Anfisa Alexeyevna's deadly rival in all matters, and the two were at daggers drawn. Naturally there were hysterics and swooning. Platon was a failure. It goes without saying that if Petya could lay his hands on a bouquet somewhere at this interesting juncture, his cause would be greatly advanced. A woman's gratitude in such cases is limitless. He rushed about like a madman, but it was impossible, needless to say. I ran into him unexpectedly at eleven o'clock on the eve of the birthday ball at a neighbour of the Ordyntsevs, Maria Petrovna Zubkova. He fairly glowed. "What's happened?" "I've found them! Eureka!" "Well, friend, that is a surprise! Where? How?" "In Yekshaisk." This was a township about fifteen miles from there, in the next province. "Trepalov's in business there, big beard and big money, lives with his old woman and canaries instead of children. They're both mad on flowers and they've got camellias." "Good heavens, but you can't be sure, what if he won't give you them?" "I'll go down on my knees and grovel at his feet until he does, otherwise I won't leave!" "When are you going then?" "Tomorrow at crack of dawn, five o'clock." "Well, good luck!" So I was glad for him, you know; I got back to the Ordyntsevs'; past one o'clock, you know, it was still running through my mind. I was ready for bed when I had a brilliant idea! I went straight through to the kitchen and woke Saveli, the coachman, gave him fifteen roubles: "Have the horses ready in half an hour!" In that time the sleigh was at the gates; I was told Anfisa Alexeyevna had a migraine and was delirious in a fever. I got in and set off. I was in Yekshaisk before five and waited till dawn in the coach-house yard, not a moment more; before seven I was at Trepalov's. I tell him the tale. "Have you got any camellias? Father, dear sir, please help, save me, I'll get on my knees!" An old man before me, tall, grey, grim—a formidable old man. "No, no, not a hope. I refuse!" Down I flop at his feet! Full length! "My dear man, what are you doing, what are you doing?" he was positively alarmed. "There's a human life at stake!" I shout. "Go on take them, if that's the case, and God be with you." I cut my fill of red camellias! Marvellous, exquisite blooms; he had a small greenhouse full of them. The old man sighed. I pulled out a hundred roubles. "Now don't you go insulting me like that." "In that case", said I, "venerable sir, please accept the money for the local hospital to improve the food and maintenance." "Now that, dear sir", says he, "is another matter; that's a good and noble action and pleasing in the sight of the lord; I will present the money to the hospital as a gift in your name." I took a liking to him, you know, that Russian old man, a real Russky of the old school, *de la vraie souche*. Elated by my success I set off back, making a detour so as not to run into Petya. As soon as I arrived, I sent up the bouquet to Anfisa Alexeyevna for when she woke. You can imagine the joy, the gratitude, the tears of gratitude! Platon dead and done-for the day before, weeps on my chest. Alas! All husbands have been the same since the institution of . . . holy matrimony! I do not venture to add more, but Petya's chances were completely ruined after that episode. I thought he'd kill me when he found out, I even prepared myself to face him, but what actually happened I'd never have believed: he fainted away, delirium by evening and fever by morning; sobbing like a child, convulsions. A month later, barely convalesced, he volunteered for the Caucasus; quite a romantic tale! Finally he was killed in the Crimea. His brother, Stepan Vorkhovskoi, had made a name for himself at the time and commanded a regiment. I admit my conscience troubled me for many years afterwards: why, what reason had I for crushing him like that? It's not as though I was in love myself at the time. It was pure mischief, for the sake of a mere flirtation, no more. If I hadn't intercepted his bouquet, who knows, he might be alive now, happy and prosperous, with no thought of going out and fighting the Turks.'

Afanasy Ivanovich ceased speaking with the same weighty dignity with which he had commenced his story. It was noticeable that Nastasya Filippovna's eyes held a peculiar sparkle and her lips quivered when he had finished. Everyone beheld them both with curiosity.

'They've cheated Ferdischenko! They really have! No, but this is what I call cheating!' cried Ferdischenko plaintively, realizing that something might, indeed should, be said at this point.

'And whose fault is it you didn't catch on? You should learn from clever people!' Darya Alexeyevna cut him off almost triumphantly (she had long been an old and loyal friend and ally of Totsky).

'You're right, Afanasy Ivanovich, this is far too boring, better finish it off', said Nastasya Filippovna casually. 'I'll tell my own story as I promised, and let's play cards.'

'The promised story first though!' the general approved warmly.

'Prince', Nastasya Filippovna addressed him with abrupt asperity, 'here you see my old friends, the general and Afanasy Ivanovich, they keep wanting me to get married. Tell me what you think: shall I get married or not? Whatever you say, I'll do it.'

Afanasy Ivanovich went pale, the general stiffened. Everyone stared and craned their necks. Ganya froze on the spot.

'To . . . to whom?' asked the prince faintly.

'Gavrila Ardalionovich Ivolgin', Nastasya Filippovna continued, brusquely, firmly, and distinctly as before.

Some seconds of silence ensued; the prince appeared to be struggling to speak, but without success, as if some dreadful weight was pressing on his chest.

'N-no . . . don't!' he whispered at length, drawing his breath with an effort.

'Then let it be so! Gavrila Ardalionovich!' She addressed him imperiously and with a certain exultation. 'You have heard the prince's decision? Well, that is my answer; and let that be an end of the matter once and for all!'

'Nastasya Filippovna!' faltered Afanasy Ivanovich.

'Nastasya Filippovna!' the general brought out, his voice coaxing but alarmed.

There was a general stir of disquiet.

'What's the matter, gentlemen?' she pursued, regarding her guests with apparent surprise. 'Why so upset? And what faces you all have!'

'But . . . remember, Nastasya Filippovna', mumbled Totsky in a hesitant voice, 'you gave your promise . . . entirely of your own free will, you might have spared us some of this . . . I am at a loss . . . and embarrassed of course, but . . . well, now, at such a moment and . . . in front . . . in front of people, and it's all . . . to conclude such an important matter with a parlour-game like this, a matter of honour and feeling . . . on which depends . . .'

'I don't understand you, Afanasy Ivanovich; you really are confused. In the first place, what do you mean "in front of

people"? Aren't we in the excellent company of close friends?
And why "parlour-game"? I did really want to tell my story, well,
so I have; it's a good one surely? And why do you say "not
serious"? Surely it is serious? You heard me tell the prince:
"whatever you say, I'll do it"; if he'd said yes, I'd have given my
consent at once, but he said no, and I refused. My whole life was
hanging on a thread then; what could be more serious?'

'But the prince, what has the prince got to do with it? And who
is the prince when all's said and done?' muttered the general,
barely able to contain his exasperation that the prince should
have this mortifying measure of authority.

'What the prince has to do with it is that he is the first man I
have met in my whole life whom I can trust as a truly devoted
friend. He believed in me at first sight and I believe in him.'

'It only remains for me to thank Nastasya Filippovna for the
extraordinary tact with which she has . . . dealt with me', said
Ganya at length, pale, lips twisting and voice unsteady. 'Just how
it should have been . . . But the prince . . . The prince's part in
this . . .'

'Is to get his hands on the seventy-five thousand, you mean?'
Nastasya Filippovna interrupted suddenly. 'Is that what you
meant? Don't try to pretend; that's exactly what you meant to say!
Afanasy Ivanovich, I forgot to add: you take the seventy-five
thousand yourself and understand that I am giving you your
liberty for nothing. Enough is enough! You need to breathe freely
as well, after all! Nine years and three months! Tomorrow—a
new life, but today is my birthday and I'm my own mistress for
the first time in my entire life! General, you take your pearls too,
and give them to your wife, here they are; from tomorrow I'm
leaving this apartment for good. There will be no more soirées, ·
gentlemen.'

So saying, she suddenly rose as if intending to leave.

'Nastasya Filippovna! Nastasya Filippovna!' came from all
sides. Everyone was roused and stood up from their seats to
surround her, everyone was concerned at hearing these feverish,
jerky, frantic words; everyone felt a sense of something gone
wrong, no one could make sense of it or understand the situation.
At that moment there came a violent ringing of the bell, just like
at Ganya's apartment that afternoon.

'Aah-h! This is the denouement! At last! Half-past eleven!' cried Nastasya Filippovna. 'I beg you to sit down, ladies and gentlemen, this is the denouement!'

So saying, she took her seat. A strange laugh played about her lips. She sat silent, in a fever of expectation, and stared at the door.

'Rogozhin and his hundred thousand, for a certainty', muttered Ptitsyn under his breath.

15

THE maid Katya came in, considerably frightened.

'Heaven knows what's going on out there, Nastasya Filippovna; a dozen men have tumbled in, all drunk ma'am, they're asking to be shown in, they say it's Rogozhin and that you know all about it.'

'That's right, Katya, show them in at once.'

'Not . . . all of them, ma'am? They're in a disgraceful state. Terrible!'

'All of them, let them all in, Katya, don't be afraid, every last one, they'd come in anyway. Listen to the row they're making, just like this afternoon. Gentlemen, you may be offended', she addressed her guests, 'that I receive this sort of company in your presence. I'm very sorry and I apologize, but it has to be and I would very, very much like you to agree to be my witnesses at this denouement, though of course, that's up to you . . .'

The guests continued whispering and exchanging astonished glances, but it had become perfectly obvious that all this had been planned and arranged in advance and that Nastasya Filippovna, though clearly off her head, was determined to have her way. All of them were dying of curiosity. Besides, nobody present was likely to be too alarmed anyway. There were only two ladies: Darya Alexeyevna, a sprightly sort who had seen a lot in her time and would be difficult to fluster, and the beautiful, silent stranger. This silent stranger would hardly grasp what was going on: she was a visitor from Germany and didn't know any Russian; besides which she was apparently as stupid as she was beautiful.

She was a novelty, and it had become the thing to invite her to certain soirées, gorgeously attired and with her hair done up exhibition-style, and just sit her down like a beautiful picture to adorn the evening—just as other people borrow a picture, vase, statue, or screen on the occasion of their own party.

As for the men, Ptitsyn was a friend of Rogozhin's and Ferdischenko was in his element here; Ganya, still not recovered, had a vague but overmastering sense of the burning necessity of remaining in the pillory till the very end; the old schoolmaster, who had little notion of what was going on, was almost in tears and literally shook with fear as he observed this extraordinary agitation around him and in Nastasya Filippovna, whom he doted on like a grandchild; but he would sooner have died than desert her at such a moment. As for Totsky, he could not compromise himself with such goings-on of course, but he was far too interested in this affair, notwithstanding the crazy turn it had taken; besides, Nastasya Filippovna had let fall a few words for his benefit which made it impossible for him to leave before the business was finally cleared up. He resolved to sit it out to the end, saying nothing whatever, simply as a spectator, which indeed was appropriate to his dignity. Only General Yepanchin, deeply wounded as he had just been by the unceremonious and ridiculous return of his gift, might possibly be even more offended by all these freakish events or, for instance, by Rogozhin's appearance; besides, a man of his sort had already demeaned himself enough by agreeing to sit down alongside the likes of Ptitsyn and Ferdischenko; but whatever he might be led to do by the intensity of his passion, his feeling of what was due to him, his sense of duty, rank, and status, his own self-respect indeed, would prevail in the end, so that Rogozhin and company were unthinkable, at least in the presence of his excellency.

'Ach, general', Nastasya Filippovna at once cut him off as soon as he made to address her, 'I was forgetting! But rest assured I had anticipated your protest. If you feel very hurt I shan't insist on detaining you, though I would very much like to see you in particular close at hand. At all events, I thank you very much for your acquaintance and flattering attentions, but if you're afraid . . .'

'Good heavens, Nastasya Filippovna', cried the general in an access of chivalrous generosity, 'can it be me you're addressing? Now I'll stay by your side out of pure devotion and in case there should be any sort of danger . . . Besides which I have to confess I'm extremely curious. I only meant to say that they would spoil the carpets and maybe break something . . . and they shouldn't be let in at all in my opinion, Nastasya Filippovna!'

'Rogozhin in person!' announced Ferdischenko.

'What do you think, Afanasy Ivanovich', the general managed a quick whisper, 'hasn't she gone off her head? I don't mean metaphorically, I mean in the strict medical sense, eh?'

'I kept telling you she was always this way inclined', Afanasy Ivanovich whispered back, slyly.

'And feverish besides . . .'

Rogozhin's crew was made up much as it had been that afternoon; the only additions were a dissolute old wretch, the former editor of a disreputable paper specializing in exposés, who was rumoured to have pawned his gold teeth for drink, and a retired sub-lieutenant, a doughty rival and competitor in profession and calling of the afternoon gentleman with the fists; he was an utter stranger to the Rogozhin crowd, who had picked him up on the sunny side of Nevsky Prospect, where he was stopping passers-by and asking for alms in the high-flown language of Marlinsky,* under the crafty pretext that he himself 'used to give away fifteen roubles to beggars in his time'. The two rivals had taken against one another immediately. The afternoon gentleman with the fists considered himself positively affronted after the 'beggar' had been added to the party, and being taciturn by nature confined himself to growling occasionally, like a bear, and regarded with the utmost contempt the attempts of the 'beggar', who turned out to be a diplomat and man of the world, to ingratiate himself and curry favour. When it came to 'business', the sub-lieutenant looked likely to succeed more by skill and resource than main force, and besides he was quite a bit shorter than the man with the fists. Bragging fearfully, though without actually starting an argument, he had several times adroitly hinted at the superiority of English boxing—in short he was an out-and-out Westernizer. For his part, the gentleman with the fists merely smiled in annoyed contempt at the word 'boxing', and without deigning to contradict his rival openly, now and again silently displayed as if by accident, or more precisely moved into view, a wholly national object—a huge, sinewy, gnarled fist, covered in reddish down, and everyone realized that if this profoundly national object were to land flush on its target, it would reduce it to pulp.

Thanks to the efforts of Rogozhin himself, who had had his visit to Nastasya Filippovna very much in mind all day, none of them were really 'primed'. For his own part he had sobered up almost completely, but was practically dazed by all the events of that chaotic day, unlike any other in his entire life. One thing only he kept continuously in view, in mind and heart, every minute, every second. In pursuit of that one thing he had spent the whole time between five o'clock in the afternoon and eleven at night, in ceaseless anxiety and alarm, negotiating with sundry Kinders and Biskups who had almost gone crazy themselves, racing about like madmen on his behalf. All the same, they had contrived to raise that hundred thousand in cash of which Nastasya Filippovna had hinted so vaguely and mockingly in passing, at interest-rates Biskup himself was too ashamed to confide to Kinder above a whisper.

Just as earlier in the day, Rogozhin led the way; the others followed him, somewhat uneasy, fully conscious of their advantage, but slightly abashed for all that. Above all, they were afraid of Nastasya Filippovna, goodness knows why. Some of them even thought they were all going to be 'kicked downstairs' at once. One of that opinion was Zalyozhev, dandy and lady-killer. The rest, however, particularly the fist-man, cherished at heart a profound, if unspoken, contempt, even hatred, towards Nastasya Filippovna, and had come to her flat as if to lay siege. The magnificence of the first two rooms, however, objects they had never seen or heard of, rare furniture, pictures, the huge statue of Venus—it all aroused in them an overwhelming sense of respect, almost of fear. This, however, did not prevent them all from crowding little by little after Rogozhin into the drawing-room, insolently curious despite their apprehension; but once the fist-man, the 'beggar', and some of the others noticed General Yepanchin among those present, they were so disheartened for a moment that they even began retreating into the other room. Lebedev alone was bold and self-assured enough to step forward almost alongside Rogozhin, aware of the significance of one million four hundred thousand in cash, with one hundred thousand now, this minute, in their hands. It should be noted, however, that all of them, including the worldly-wise Lebedev, were somewhat uncertain as to the limits and extent of their powers; could they really do as they liked or not? There were moments when Lebedev was ready to swear that they could, but at others he felt uneasily impelled to recall several generally encouraging and reassuring civil-law articles, just in case.

The impression produced on Rogozhin himself by Nastasya Filippovna's drawing-room was the opposite of that made on all his companions. As soon as the door-curtain was raised and he caught sight of Nastasya Filippovna, all else ceased to exist for him, just as it had that afternoon, in fact more intensely than it had that afternoon. He turned pale and halted for an instant; it could be guessed that his heart was thumping wildly. He gazed fixedly at Nastasya Filippovna for several seconds, diffident and uncertain. Suddenly, as if taking leave of his senses entirely, he almost staggered up to the table, knocking against Ptitsyn's chair as he did so, and trod with his huge, filthy boots on the lace hem of the silent German beauty's magnificent blue dress; he didn't apologize, didn't even notice. On reaching the table, he placed upon it the strange object with which he had entered the room, bearing it before him in both hands. It was a large paper parcel, about six inches high and eight inches long, wrapped firmly and securely in a copy of the *Stock Exchange News* and tied very tightly all round and twice across with the kind of string they use on sugar-loaves. Then he stood up and without a word dropped his hands to his sides, as if awaiting sentence. He was wearing exactly what he had worn earlier in the day, except for a brand-new silk scarf round his neck, bright green and red, with an enormous diamond pin in the form of a beetle, and a massive diamond ring on a finger of his grimy right hand. Lebedev stopped short three paces from the table; the rest, as already mentioned, were gradually making their way into the room. Katya and Pasha, Nastasya Filippovna's maids, also came running to look through the door-curtain in utter amazement and fright.

'What is it?' asked Nastasya Filippovna, surveying Rogozhin with intent curiosity and indicating the 'object' with her eyes.

'A hundred thousand!' he replied almost in a whisper.

'So he kept his word, what a man! Please sit down, here, on this chair; I've got something to tell you later. Who've you got with you? All your afternoon crew? Well, let them come in and take a seat; there's room over there on the sofa, and another sofa there. Two armchairs there . . . don't they want to, or what?'

Indeed, some of them were positively embarrassed and retired to sit down in the other room, but others remained and disposed themselves as invited, though some way from the table, mostly in corners; some still wished to efface themselves, while distance quickly lent others a somewhat artificial courage. Rogozhin also sat down as indicated, but not for long; he soon got up again and remained on his feet thereafter. Gradually he began to make out the guests and survey them. On seeing Ganya, he smiled venomously and whispered to himself: 'There he is!' He glanced at the general and Afanasy Ivanovich without embarrassment, without any special curiosity even. When he noticed the prince, however, close by Nastasya Filippovna, he was extremely astonished and couldn't take his eyes off him for a long time, seemingly unable to come to terms with this encounter. He appeared at moments to be actually dazed. Besides the upheavals of the day, he had spent the whole of the previous night in a railway carriage and had not slept for almost forty-eight hours.

'This, gentlemen, is one hundred thousand', said Nastasya Filippovna addressing them all with a sort of feverishly eager defiance, 'here in this dirty package. Today he shouted like a madman that he would bring me a hundred thousand this evening and I've been waiting for him all this time. It was he who bargained for me: he started with eighteen thousand, then he jumped to forty, then finally this hundred. He kept his word after all! Lord how pale he is! . . . This all happened at Ganya's this afternoon: I went to pay his mama a visit, to my future family, and there his sister shouted at me to my face: "Won't they turn this shameless woman out?"—and spat in Ganechka's face, her own brother. A girl of spirit!'

'Nastasya Filippovna!' said the general reproachfully. He was beginning to comprehend the situation somewhat, after his own fashion.

'What's the matter, general? Unseemly, you mean? Let's stop

all this humbug, shall we? If I sat in a box at the French Theatre, like an image of unapproachable dress-circle virtue, and fled like a wild thing from all those who have been pursuing me for the last five years, looking a picture of proud innocence, it was only because my stupidity made me do it! And now he has come and put one hundred thousand on the table in front of you all, after five whole years of innocence—and their troikas are probably standing outside waiting for me. So, he valued me at a hundred thousand! Ganechka, I can see that you're still angry at me? Surely you didn't mean to bring me into your family, did you? Me, Rogozhin's woman! What did the prince tell you this afternoon?'

'I didn't say you were Rogozhin's woman, you aren't!' the prince brought out unsteadily.

'Nastasya Filippovna, that's enough now, my dear, that's enough, darling', Darya Alexeyevna could no longer contain herself. 'If they make you feel so wretched, why pay them any heed? And surely you don't intend going off with people like that, even for a hundred thousand? Of course a hundred thousand is quite something! You take it and chase him away, that's the way to deal with them; ah, in your place I'd see the lot of them . . . the very idea!'

Darya Alexeyevna had really got herself worked up into a temper. She was a soft-hearted creature and very apt to become emotional.

'Don't get upset, Darya Alexeyevna', Nastasya Filippovna smiled at her. 'I wasn't speaking to him in anger. Was I really reproaching him? I honestly can't understand how I could have been so foolish as to want to enter a respectable family. I saw his mother you know, and kissed her hand. As for that exhibition of mine at your place today, Ganya, it was because I quite deliberately wanted to see for the last time just how far you would go. Well, you really astonished me, I have to say. I was ready for a great deal, but not that! Surely you wouldn't have married me, knowing that the general had given me a string of pearls like that practically on the eve of your wedding and I had accepted them? And what about Rogozhin, then? After all, he had bid for me in front of your mother and sister in your own house, yet after that you came here to make a match, and nearly brought your sister!

Is it really true what Rogozhin said, that you'd crawl to Vasilevsky Island on your hands and knees for three roubles?'

'He certainly would', said Rogozhin quietly, but with an air of the utmost conviction.

'It would be all right if you were starving, but they say you get a good salary! And as well as the disgrace and everything else, just think of bringing a hated wife into your family—because you do hate me, I know that! No, now I can believe a man like that could murder for money! They're all of them so obsessed with greed, torn apart for money, they seem to have gone mad. A mere child and he's dying to be a money-lender! I can see him winding silk thread round his razor to make it firm,* then coming up quietly from behind and cutting his friend's throat, like a sheep, as I was reading just lately. Oh, what a shameless man you are! I'm shameless and you're worse. I say nothing about that bouquet-fancier there . . .'

'Is this you, is this really you, Nastasya Filippovna!' the general threw his arms up in genuine distress. 'You, so refined, such subtle ideas—and now! What language! What a way to talk!'

'I'm drunk, general', Nastasya Filippovna laughed suddenly. 'I want to have a good time! Today is my day, my high day and holiday, the one I've been waiting for long enough. Darya Alexeyevna, see that bouquet-fancier there, that *monsieur aux camélias*, sitting there laughing at us . . .'

'I'm not laughing, Nastasya Filippovna, I am merely listening with the utmost attention', Totsky parried with dignity.

'So then, why have I been tormenting him for all of five years and not let him go? Was he worth it? He's just the kind of man you would expect . . . What's more, he probably thinks I've treated him badly: he saw to my upbringing after all, kept me like a countess, and the money, the money he laid out! He found me a respectable husband back then—and now Ganechka; and what would you think? I haven't lived with him for the last five years, but I've been taking his money and thought I was in the right! That's how confused I was! Here you are saying, take the hundred thousand and chase them away if you're disgusted. It certainly is disgusting . . . I could have got married long ago, and not to Ganechka either, but that would have been disgusting enough too. And what have I got out of these five angry years of

mine? Believe me or not, about four years ago I used to think at
times: why don't I just go and marry my Afanasy Ivanovich? I
thought of that out of spite; there were lots of things going
through my head in those days; but I could have forced him to,
you know! He used to urge me to it himself, if you can believe it.
He didn't mean it of course, but he's very susceptible, he doesn't
know what self-restraint is. Later on though, thank the Lord, I
thought: is he worth all this anger! And I felt so disgusted at him
all of a sudden that if he had courted me himself, I wouldn't have
accepted. And five whole years I kept this up! No, better to be out
on the streets where I belong! Either have a fling with Rogozhin
or become a washerwoman tomorrow! Because I've got nothing
of my own; when I go, I'll leave everything of his, the very last
rag, and who will take me without anything, ask Ganya here,
would he? Even Ferdischenko wouldn't have me! . . .'

'Ferdischenko might not, Nastasya Filippovna, I'm frank about
it', interposed Ferdischenko, 'but the prince would! You sit here
complaining, but just look at the prince! I've had my eye on him
for a long while . . .'

Nastasya Filippovna turned to the prince, curious.

'Is that true?' she asked.

'Yes', whispered the prince.

'You'd take me as I am, with nothing?'

'Yes, Nastasya Filippovna . . .'

'Well here's another story!' muttered the general. 'Might have
known.'

The prince bent his sorrowful, stern, penetrating gaze on
Nastasya Filippovna, who continued to scrutinize him.

'Listen who's talking!' she said suddenly, addressing Darya
Alexeyevna again. 'It's pure goodness of heart, I know him. I've
found a benefactor! Still, it might be true what they say about
him, that . . . you know. What are you going to live on then, since
you're so much in love that you'll take Rogozhin's woman, prince
that you are? . . .'

'I take you as an honest woman, Nastasya Filippovna, not
Rogozhin's', said the prince.

'I'm an honest woman, you mean?'

'Yes.'

'Well that's . . . the sort of thing you read about in novels!

Prince, darling, that's all old-fashioned nonsense, the world has grown wiser nowadays. In any case, how can you get married, you'd need a nurse to look after you!'

The prince rose and, in a timid, quavering voice, but with an air of deep conviction, brought out:

'I know nothing of life, Nastasya Filippovna, I've seen nothing, you're right, but I . . . I believe that you would be doing me honour, not the other way about. I am nothing, but you have suffered and emerged from that hell pure, and that means a great deal. Why on earth do you feel shame and think of going off with Rogozhin? You're feverish . . . You've given Mister Totsky the seventy thousand back and you say that you'll give up everything there is here, everything, that's something no one here could do. I . . . Nastasya Filippovna . . . I love you. I would die for you, Nastasya Filippovna. I won't allow anyone to say a word against you. Nastasya Filippovna . . . if we're poor, I'll work, Nastasya Filippovna . . .'

At these last words Ferdischenko and Lebedev could be heard sniggering, and even the general grunted to himself in considerable displeasure. Ptitsyn and Totsky could not help smiling, but restrained themselves. The rest simply stood gaping in astonishment.

'. . . But perhaps we won't be poor, we'll be very rich, Nastasya Filippovna', the prince pursued in the same timid voice. 'I'm afraid I don't know for certain, and I'm sorry I haven't been able to find out about it all day, but in Switzerland I got a letter from Moscow from a Mister Salazkin, and he informs me that I may receive a very considerable legacy. Here's the letter . . .'

The prince did in fact draw a letter from his pocket.

'Well, is he raving or not?' muttered the general. 'This is an absolute madhouse!'

There followed a moment's silence.

'I believe you said the letter was from Salazkin?' said Ptitsyn. 'He's a well-known man in his circle; a well-known solicitor, and if it is really he who wrote to you, you may believe him implicitly. Luckily I know his handwriting, as I did some business with him recently . . . If you were to let me have a glance, perhaps I could tell you something.'

The prince wordlessly held it out to him with a trembling hand.

'Well what is it, what is it?' the general recovered himself, looking round at everyone, baffled. 'It's not really a legacy is it?'

All eyes were on Ptitsyn as he read the letter. The general curiosity had received a fresh and extraordinary impetus. Ferdischenko couldn't sit down; Rogozhin stared in bewilderment, shifting his gaze from Ptitsyn to the prince and back again in fearful anxiety. Darya Alexeyevna was on tenterhooks. Even Lebedev couldn't stand it; he emerged from his corner and craned his neck perilously to peer at the letter over Ptitsyn's shoulder, with the apprehensive air of a man about to be cuffed for his pains.

16

'IT's the genuine article', announced Ptitsyn, folding it up and returning it to the prince. 'You are to receive an extremely large sum, without any strings attached, through the incontestable will of your aunt.'

'Impossible!' exclaimed the general, like a pistol-shot.

All mouths gaped afresh.

Ptitsyn explained, addressing himself for the most part to the general, that the prince's aunt, whom he had never known personally, had died five months previously. She had been his mother's eldest sister and was the daughter of a Moscow merchant of the Third Guild,* by name Papushin, who had died bankrupt and poverty-stricken. The elder brother of this Papushin, however, who had also recently died, was a well-known and wealthy merchant. About a year ago, this man's only two sons had died almost within a month. This was such a shock to him that the old man himself took ill and died not long afterwards. He was a widower and had no heirs at all, apart from his niece, the prince's aunt, an extremely poor woman who was living with relatives. By the time she got the legacy this aunt was dying of the dropsy, but managed to make a will and at once instituted a search for the prince, entrusting the matter to Salazkin. Neither the prince nor the doctor with whom he was living in Switzerland had apparently cared to wait for official notification or make any enquiries, and the prince had decided to set off himself, with Salazkin's letter in his pocket . . .

'The one thing I can tell you', Ptitsyn concluded, turning to the prince, 'is that all this must be incontrovertible and correct, and everything Salazkin writes concerning the legality and incontestable nature of the case you may regard as so much ready money in your pocket. I congratulate you, Prince! Perhaps you'll get a million and a half too, or indeed even more. Papushin was a very rich man.'

'Three cheers for the last of the Myshkins!' whooped Ferdischenko.

'Hurrah!' croaked Lebedev in a drunken voice.

'And here was I lending him twenty-five roubles this morning, poor fellow, ha-ha-ha! It passes belief, indeed it does', said the general, almost dumbfounded. 'Well, congratulations, congratulations!' He rose and went up to the prince to embrace him. Behind him, others began to get up and make their way towards the prince. Even those who had withdrawn behind the door-curtain began appearing in the drawing-room. A hubbub arose, exclamations, even calls for champagne; all was jostling and bustle. For a moment they had even forgotten Nastasya Filippovna and the fact that it was still her soirée. Gradually, however, the idea dawned on all of them at once that the prince had just proposed to her. The affair consequently became three times as mad and extraordinary as before. Totsky shrugged his shoulders in profound amazement; he was almost alone in his chair, the rest were crowding round the table in disorder. Everyone affirmed later that Nastasya Filippovna became deranged from that very instant. She remained sitting and for some time surveyed everyone with an odd, astonished look, as if unable to take it all in and struggling to grasp the situation. Thereupon she turned to the prince and, with a menacing frown, stared hard at him; this, however, only lasted a second; perhaps it had occurred to her that all this was a joke or a show of mockery; the sight of the prince at once disabused her. She became lost in thought, then smiled again, as if not quite certain why . . .

'So I really am a princess!' she whispered to herself, as if it were a taunt, and as her glance fell by chance on Darya

Alexeyevna, she began to laugh. 'A surprise denouement...
I ... didn't expect this ... Come now, gentlemen, why are you
standing up? Be good enough to take your seats and congratulate
me and the prince! Someone asked for champagne I believe;
Ferdischenko, go and see to it. Katya, Pasha'—she caught sight
of her maids suddenly in the doorway—'Come here, I'm going to
be married, did you hear? To the prince, he's got a million and a
half, he's Prince Myshkin and he's marrying me!'

'God bless you dear, not before time! Don't go missing your
chance now!' cried Darya Alexeyevna, deeply moved by what had
happened.

'Come now, sit beside me, Prince', Nastasya Filippovna went
on. 'Like that, here comes the wine, congratulate us, gentlemen!'

'Hurrah!' shouted a great many voices. Lots of people crowded
round the wine, including almost all the Rogozhin party. But
though they were shouting, and very ready to do so, a good
number of them, despite the strangeness of the circumstances
and the surroundings, sensed that the situation had changed.
Others were bemused and waited about mistrustfully. Many
whispered among themselves that there was nothing in the least
extraordinary about it all, was there, princes went about marrying
all kinds, even gipsy girls from the camps. Meanwhile Rogozhin
stood looking, twisting his face into a fixed smile of incomprehension.

'Prince, dear fellow, bethink yourself!' hissed the general,
aghast, as he sidled up and tugged the prince's sleeve.

Nastasya Filippovna noticed this and began laughing.

'No, general! Now I'm a princess myself, you heard,—the
prince will stand up for me! Afanasy Ivanovich, you congratulate
me as well; now I'll sit next to your wife everywhere; what do you
think, is it a good thing to have a husband like that! A million and
a half, and a prince—and an idiot into the bargain, so they say,
what could be better? Now life is really beginning! You're too
late, Rogozhin! Take your parcel away, I'm marrying the prince
and I'm richer than you are!'

Rogozhin, however, had grasped the situation. Unspeakable
suffering was etched on his face. He flung up his arms as a groan
tore from his throat.

'Withdraw!' he shouted at the prince.

Laughter came from round about.

'Give him up for the likes of you, you mean?' Darya Alexeyevna retorted triumphantly. 'See him slap his money down on the table, peasant! The prince wants to marry her, but you've just come to make trouble.'

'I'll marry her too! Now, this minute! I'll give anything . . .'

'Look at him, a tavern drunkard, you should be thrown out!' repeated Darya Alexeyevna indignantly.

The laughter grew louder.

'You hear that, Prince', Nastasya Filippovna said. 'That peasant is bargaining for your fiancée.'

'He's drunk', said the prince. 'He loves you very much.'

'Won't you feel ashamed afterwards that your fiancée nearly went off with Rogozhin?'

'You were feverish; you're still feverish now, delirious almost.'

'And won't you feel ashamed when they tell you that your wife was Totsky's kept woman?'

'No, I shan't . . . You were with Totsky against your free will.'

'And you'll never reproach me with it?'

'No.'

'Be careful now, don't swear your whole life away!'

'Nastasya Filippovna', the prince said softly and with seeming compassion, 'I told you just now that I take your consent as an honour that you are doing me, not the other way about. You laughed at those words and I heard others laughing too. Perhaps I did express myself very comically, was comical myself, but I kept thinking that I . . . understand what honour is and I'm sure I spoke the truth. Just now you wanted to ruin yourself, irrevocably, because you'd never have forgiven yourself for it afterwards: and you're guilty of nothing. It can't be that your life is completely ruined already. What on earth does it matter that Rogozhin came to you or Gavrila Ardalionovich intended to deceive you? Why keep dwelling on that? Few people are capable of what you have done, I repeat, and as for wanting to go off with Rogozhin, you decided that in a feverish fit. You're still unwell and ought to go to bed. You wouldn't have stayed with Rogozhin, you'd have gone off to be a washerwoman tomorrow. You are a proud woman, Nastasya Filippovna, but perhaps you have reached such a pitch of wretchedness that you really do consider yourself guilty. You need a great deal of looking after, Nastasya Filippovna. I will look after you. I saw your portrait earlier today and at once recognized a familiar face. I immediately thought that you were somehow calling me ... I ... I will respect you all my life, Nastasya Filippovna', the prince concluded abruptly, as if recollecting himself all of a sudden, blushing and realizing who was listening to all this.

Ptitsyn virtuously inclined his head and looked at the floor. Totsky thought to himself: 'An idiot—still he knows that flattery will get you anywhere; it's a law of nature.' The prince also became aware of Ganya's flashing gaze from the corner, a look meant to incinerate him.

'There, the kindly soul!' pronounced Darya Alexeyevna, wholly melted.

'An intelligent fellow, but he's done for now!' murmured the general.

Totsky took his hat and made as if to rise and quietly slip away. He and the general exchanged glances, meaning to leave together.

'Thank you, Prince, no one has ever spoken to me like that before', said Nastasya Filippovna. 'Commercial transactions yes, but nobody decent has ever proposed to me. You hear, Afanasy Ivanich? What do you think of all the prince said? It's almost indecent, isn't it ... Rogozhin! Don't go just yet, now. But you weren't going to were you? Perhaps I will go with you after all. Where were you going to take me then?'

'Yekaterinhof,* reported Lebedev from his corner, as Rogozhin simply gave a start and stared wide-eyed, unable to credit what he was hearing. He was completely stunned, as if he had suffered a violent blow to the head.

'What do you mean dearie! You really are ill; have you gone mad, or what?' cried Darya Alexeyevna in alarm.

'And did you really think I'd ruin a babe-in-arms like that?' Nastasya Filippovna leapt up from the sofa, laughing. 'That's more in Afanasy Ivanovich's line: he's the child-fancier! Let's go, Rogozhin! Get your money ready. Never mind about getting married, but let's have your money all the same. Perhaps I won't marry you, anyway. You thought if you got married you could keep the parcel? Oh no! I'm a shameless hussy myself! I've been

Totsky's mistress ... Prince, you ought to marry Aglaya Yepanchina now, not Nastasya Filippovna, otherwise Ferdischenko will point the finger at you. You're not afraid, but I would be afraid of ruining you and being reproached by you later. As for saying that I'm doing you honour, Totsky knows all about that. But you've missed Aglaya Yepanchina, Ganya, you have; did you know that? If you hadn't bargained with her, she'd have married you like a shot! That goes for all of you, you have one choice—stick to either respectable or disreputable women! Otherwise you're bound to get into a tangle ... See the general there looking, with his mouth open ...'

'This is Sodom, Sodom!' the general repeated, shrugging his shoulders. He too had risen from the sofa; all were on their feet again. Nastasya was almost in a frenzy.

'Surely not!' groaned the prince, wringing his hands.

'You thought I wouldn't? Perhaps I have my own pride, shameless hussy or not! You said I was perfection a while ago; quite some perfection to head for the gutter just to be able to boast of trampling on a million and a title! Now then, what sort of a wife would I make you? Afanasy Ivanich, I really have tossed a million out of the window, haven't I? Now how could you imagine I would think myself lucky to marry Ganechka with your seventy-five thousand thrown in? You keep your seventy-five thousand, Afanasy Ivanich—you didn't make it a hundred, Rogozhin went one better! As for Ganya, I'll make it up to him, I've got an idea about that. And now I'm going to have a good time—I'm a woman of the streets after all! I've spent ten years in jail, now my time for happiness has come! What are you waiting for, Rogozhin? Get ready and let's go!'

'Let's go!' roared Rogozhin almost frantic with joy. 'Hey ... you there ... wine! Ach! ...'

'Stock up on the wine, I feel like drinking. Will there be music?'

'There will, there will! Don't come near her!' yelled Rogozhin in a frenzy, seeing Darya Alexeyevna approaching Nastasya Filippovna. 'She's mine! Everything's mine! A queen! It's all over!'

He was breathless with elation; he kept walking round Nastasya Filippovna, shouting at everybody: 'Keep well away!'

The whole company was by now crammed into the drawing-room. Some were drinking, others shouting and laughing, everyone was in a highly excited and uninhibited state. Ferdischenko was attempting to attach himself to them. The general and Totsky again made to slip out. Ganya also had his hat in his hand, but was standing mute as if still unable to drag himself away from the scene unfolding before him.

'Stand well away!' Rogozhin kept shouting.

'What's all the yelling for then?' laughed Nastasya Filippovna. 'I'm still the mistress here; if I want I can still turn you out. I haven't taken that money of yours yet, there it is lying there; give it here, the whole parcel! There's a hundred thousand here in this package? Ugh, disgusting! What's the matter, Darya Alexeyevna? You don't mean I should have ruined him, surely?' She indicated the prince. 'How can he get married, he still needs a nurse himself; the general there can be his nanny—look at the way he clings to him! Look, Prince, your fiancée's taken the money because she's a loose woman, and you wanted to marry her! Now what are you crying for? A bitter pill is it? You should laugh like I do', Nastasya Filippovna went on, though two large tears glistened on her own cheeks. 'Put your trust in time; it will all pass. Better to think twice now than later . . . But why are you all crying—there's Katya crying! Now what's the matter, Katya darling? I'm leaving you and Pasha a fair amount, I've already arranged it, but now it's goodbye! I've made a respectable girl like you look after me, a loose woman . . . It's better this way, Prince, really it is better, you would have despised me later and there'd have been no happiness for us. Don't swear, I don't believe you! And how silly it would have been, wouldn't it! . . . No, let's part as friends, after all I'm a dreamer myself and no good would have come of it. Haven't I dreamed about you? You're right I did, a long time ago, in his house in the country, five years living all by my little self; I would think and think, day-dream and day-dream, always imagining someone like you, kind, honest, and good and silly like you would suddenly arrive and say: "You're not to blame, Nastasya Filippovna, and I adore you!" You can go crazy, dreaming away like that . . . And then that man there would come, stay two months a year to disgrace, mortify, inflame, and debauch and then ride away, so that a thousand times I wanted to fling myself into the pond, but I was contemptible, I hadn't the courage, well, and now ... Rogozhin, ready?'

'Everything's ready! Stand clear!'

'Ready!' several voices cried out.

'The troikas are waiting with bells!'

Nastasya Filippovna snatched up the package.

'Ganka, I've had an idea: I want to reward you, because why should you lose everything after all? Rogozhin, would he crawl to Vasilyevsky Island for three roubles?'

'He would!'

'Well, listen then Ganya, I want to see what your soul is like for the last time; you tormented me yourself for three whole months; now it's my turn. You see this parcel, it's got a hundred thousand in it. I'm going to throw it into the fire, in front of everybody, all witnesses! As soon as the fire's got a good hold, crawl into the fireplace, without gloves though, bare hands, sleeves rolled back, and pull the parcel out of the fire. If you pull it out it's yours, all hundred thousand! You'll just burn your little fingers a bit—but it's a hundred thousand, just think! It won't take long to pull out now will it? And I will feast my eyes on your soul, seeing you crawl into the fire after my money. All are witnesses that the money will be yours. If you don't crawl in, it'll burn; I won't let anyone else do it. Get away! Everyone get away! My money! I took it for a night with Rogozhin. Isn't it my money, Rogozhin?'

'Yours, my joy! Yours, my queen!'

'Well now, everyone away, I can do what I like! Don't try and stop me! Ferdischenko, stoke up the fire!'

'Nastasya Filippovna, my hands won't move', replied Ferdischenko, stunned.

'E-ech!' shouted Nastasya Filippovna, seizing the fire-tongs and prodding at two smouldering logs. As soon as the fire flared up, she flung the package into it.

A general outcry followed; many people even crossed themselves.

'She's out of her mind, she's gone mad!' came shouts all around.

'Shouldn't we ... put her ... under restraint?' whispered the general to Ptitsyn, 'or send ... I mean she has gone mad, she has gone mad? Hasn't she?'

'N-no, it isn't quite madness, perhaps', hissed Ptitsyn, who was trembling and as white as a sheet, unable to drag his eyes away from the smouldering package.

'She's mad, isn't she? She is, isn't she?' the general persisted to Totsky.

'I kept telling you she was a colourful woman', murmured Afanasy Ivanovich, also rather pale.

'But, after all, a hundred thousand!'

'Good lord, good heavens!' was heard on all sides. Everybody crowded round the fireplace, all pressing forward, all exclaiming together . . . Some even jumped on chairs to see over the heads. Darya Alexeyevna scurried into the next room to whisper something fearfully to Katya and Pasha. The beautiful German lady had fled.

'Madame! Queen! All-powerful!' yelled Lebedev, crawling on all fours in front of Nastasya Filippovna, stretching his arms out towards the fireplace. 'A hundred thousand! A hundred thousand! I've seen them, they were wrapped up in my presence! Madame! Your grace! Order me into the fireplace: I'll get right in, I'll lay my whole head, my grey hairs in the fire! . . . A sick wife who can't walk, thirteen children—all orphans, I buried my father last week, just sat there starving, Nastasya Filippovna!!' After howling his fill, he made for the fireplace.

'Get away!' cried Nastasya Filippovna, pushing him back. 'Everybody spread out! Ganya, what on earth are you standing there for? Don't be shy! In you crawl! Your ship's come in!'

But Ganya had been through too much that day and evening and was unprepared for this final, unlooked-for ordeal. The crowd parted in front of them and he was left face-to-face with Nastasya Filippovna, about three paces from her. She was standing right by the fireplace, waiting, her burning, piercing stare fixed upon him. Ganya, in his dress clothes, hat and gloves in hand, stood mutely looking at the fire with his arms folded. A mad smile hovered over his face, white as a sheet. True, he couldn't take his eyes off the fire and the smouldering package, but it seemed that something new had entered his soul; it was as if he had sworn to withstand this torture; he did not move from the spot; after a few seconds it became clear to them all that he would not go for the parcel, that he had no wish to do so.

'Hey, they'll burn, you'll be a laughing stock', Nastasya Filippovna shouted at him, 'you'll hang yourself afterwards, I mean it!'

The fire which had flared up between the two smouldering logs had almost gone out when the parcel landed and bore down on it, but a small blue flame still clung on under one corner of the lower log. At length a long, thin tongue of fire licked at the parcel, took hold, and ran up round the corners of the paper wrapper, then suddenly the whole package flared up in the fireplace and a bright flame burst upwards. They all gasped.

'Madame!' Lebedev wailed again, struggling forward, but Rogozhin dragged him away and thrust him back again.

Rogozhin himself was motionless and all eyes. He could not tear himself away from Nastasya Filippovna, he was in a seventh heaven of intoxicated delight.

'Now that's like a queen!' he kept repeating by the minute to anyone around him. 'Now that's style!' he kept shouting, beside himself. 'Well which of you rogues would do a thing like that, eh?'

The prince looked on, sad and silent.

'I'd drag it out with my teeth for just a thousand!' Ferdischenko offered.

'With teeth I could do it as well!' gritted the gentleman with the fists from the very back, in an access of real despair. 'D-damnation! It's burning, it's burning up!' he shouted, seeing the flame.

'It's burning, it's burning!' came the unison shout, almost everyone surging towards the fireplace.

'Ganya, don't be pigheaded I'm telling you for the last time!'

'Crawl!' roared Ferdischenko, rushing towards Ganya in a positive frenzy and dragging at his sleeve, 'crawl, you show-off! It's burning! D-damn and blast you!'

Ganya knocked Ferdischenko away by main force, turned and walked towards the door; he had taken less than two steps when he swayed and clattered to the floor.

'He's fainted!' came the cry.

'Madam, it's burning!' wailed Lebedev.

'It's burning for nothing!' came the roar from all sides.

'Katya, Pasha, get him some water, spirits!' cried Nastasya

Filippovna, as she seized the fire-tongs and fished out the package.

All the outer layer of paper had burned away to ashes, but it was clear at once that the inside was untouched. The parcel had been wrapped in a triple layer of newspaper, and the money was safe. Everyone breathed more freely.

'There's only a miserable thousand damaged, the rest is all safe and sound', Lebedev said, much moved.

'It's all his! The whole parcel's his! You hear me gentlemen!' proclaimed Nastasya Filippovna, placing the package close to Ganya. 'He didn't do it, all the same, he stuck it out! His vanity must be even greater than his greed. It's all right, he'll come round! He'd have murdered me otherwise, probably ... See, he's coming to. General Ivan Petrovich, Darya Alexeyevna, Katya, Pasha, Rogozhin, you hear? The money is his, Ganya's. I'm presenting it to him to do as he likes with, as a compensation ... well, for whatever it might be! Tell him. Leave it lying next to him ... Rogozhin, march! Goodbye, Prince, for the first time I've seen a human being! Goodbye, Afanasy Ivanovich, *merci*!'

Amid thunderous noise and shouting, the whole Rogozhin crew made their way through the rooms to the front door after Rogozhin and Nastasya Filippovna. In the hall, she took her fur coat from the maids and, as the cook Martha ran in from the kitchen, she kissed them all again and again.

'Surely you're not going away and leaving us altogether, Madam? But where on earth will you go? And on your birthday, too, a day like this!' asked the weeping maids, kissing her hands.

'I'm going on the streets, Katya, you heard me say so—that's my place, or else be a washerwoman! Enough of Afanasy Ivanovich! Give him my regards, and don't think ill of me ...'

The prince rushed headlong for the main entrance, where everyone was getting into four troikas with bells. The general managed to overtake him on the staircase.

'For heaven's sake, Prince, come to your senses!' said he, seizing him by the arm. 'Forget her! You see what sort she is! I speak as a father ...'

The prince looked at him but tore himself free, and without a word ran downstairs.

By the main entrance from where the troikas had just moved off, the general saw the prince hail the first cabbie and shout for him to go to Yekaterinhof, after the troikas. Then the general's little grey trotter drew up and took him home, with new hopes and plans—and the pearls, which he had not forgotten to take with him. Amid his calculations the seductive image of Nastasya Filippovna flickered once or twice; the general sighed.

'A pity! A genuine pity! She's a lost woman! A mad woman! . . . Well it isn't Nastasya Filippovna the prince needs now . . .'

Two other guests of Nastasya Filippovna, who had decided to go for a little walk, uttered a number of edifying parting words in the same vein.

'You know, Afanasy Ivanovich, they say the Japanese do things this way', Ivan Petrovich Ptitsyn was saying. 'The man who's been insulted goes up to the offender and says to him: "You have insulted me, for that I have come to disembowel myself before your eyes." After he says that, he really does disembowel himself before the offender's eyes. He must feel a high degree of satisfaction, as if he had really taken his revenge. There are some strange characters in this world, Afanasy Ivanovich!'

'And you think there was something of that here too?' replied Totsky with a smile. 'Hmm, that's clever though . . . and that's an excellent analogy. However, you saw with your own eyes, my dear Ptitsyn, that I did everything I could; I couldn't do more, you must agree? But you have to agree also that there were some first-rate qualities in that woman . . . brilliant features. I even wanted to shout to her just now, if I could have permitted myself to do so in that bedlam, that she herself was my best justification against all her accusations. Tell me, who wouldn't have been so captivated sometimes by that woman that he would go against all reason and . . . all that? Take that peasant Rogozhin, slapping a hundred thousand down for her! What if everything that happened there tonight was just a passing fancy, romantic, unseemly, it was colourful and original all the same, you must agree. Heavens, what might have been made of a character like that, and such beauty! Still, in spite of all my efforts, and her education too—all gone! An uncut diamond—I've said so more than once . . .'

And Afanasy Ivanovich gave a profound sigh.

PART TWO

1

SOME two days after the strange goings-on at Nastasya Filippovna's soirée with which we concluded the first part of our narrative, Prince Myshkin made haste to leave for Moscow to settle the business of his unexpected legacy. There was talk at the time that there might be other reasons behind his hurried departure; about that, however, we can offer little information, nor about the prince's adventures in Moscow or during the time of his absence from Petersburg altogether. The prince was away for exactly six months, and even those who had some reason to be concerned about his fate could learn very little of him over this period. Rumours of one sort or another, albeit few and far between, did reach some people, but they too were, for the most part, strange and mutually contradictory. The greatest concern for the prince was evinced in the Yepanchin household, of course, as he had not even had time to say goodbye to them before he left. Actually, the general had seen him a time or two and they had conferred seriously about some matter. But if Yepanchin had met him, he did not apprise his family of the fact. In any case, at first, for almost a month, that is, after the prince's departure, it was not done to mention him in the Yepanchin household. Only the general's wife, Lizaveta Prokofievna, had spoken her mind right at the beginning that she 'had been cruelly mistaken in the prince'. Then, about two or three days later, she added, this time vaguely, without naming the prince, that 'the chief feature of her life was being mistaken about people'. Finally, some ten days later by now, she concluded the matter sententiously, annoyed at her daughters for some reason: 'Enough mistakes! There'll be no more of them from now on.' It has to be said at this point that a rather disagreeable atmosphere had existed in the house for quite some time. There was an oppressive sense of strain, an unspoken discord; everyone wore a frown. The general was busy day and night about his affairs; they had seldom seen him so active and busy—especially with official matters. The servants hardly got a glimpse of him. As for the Yepanchin girls, nothing was said by them aloud, of course. It may be that even when they were alone very little was said. They were proud girls, haughty and reserved even among themselves at times, though they did understand one another at first glance, not to mention first word, so that there was often no point in saying very much.

There was only one conclusion an outside observer could have drawn, had such a one chanced to be present, namely that, judging by all the facts so far mentioned, few though they are, the prince had nevertheless managed to create a considerable impression on the Yepanchin household, even though he had only appeared there once, and that fleetingly. It might just have been simple curiosity, inspired by some of the prince's eccentric doings, but whatever the reason the impression remained.

Little by little, even the rumours which had spread round the town became obscured by a pall of ignorance. True, there was talk of some simple-minded princeling (nobody could be sure of the right name) who had suddenly come into a vast fortune and got married to a visiting French lady, a celebrated can-can dancer from the Château des Fleurs in Paris. Others, however, had it that the legacy had gone to a certain general and the one who had married the visiting French can-can lady was a fabulously wealthy young Russian merchant who, drunk at his wedding, had burned in a candle no less than seven hundred thousand worth of current lottery tickets out of sheer bravado.

All these rumours subsided very quickly, however, greatly assisted by circumstance. For example, the whole of Rogozhin's entourage, many of whom might have had a tale to tell, had left for Moscow in a body in the wake of their chief, almost a week to the day after the fearful orgy at the Yekaterinhof pleasure gardens when Nastasya Filippovna had also been present. One or two people, the few who were interested, got to hear rumours that Nastasya Filippovna had run off the day after Yekaterinhof and disappeared, whereupon it was discovered that she had left for Moscow; as a consequence, Rogozhin's similar departure was felt to be more than coincidence.

There were rumours about Gavrila Ardalionovich Ivolgin too, as he was fairly notorious in his circle, but something happened in his case also which took the edge off all the malicious stories going round about him and later on put an end to them altogether: he fell seriously ill and was unable to go in to the office, let alone appear in society. He recovered after a month's sickness, but for some reason absolutely refused to work for the company, and his place was taken by another man. He failed to turn up at all at General Yepanchin's house, so that another official began work there too. Gavrila's enemies might have assumed that he was so embarrassed by all that had happened to him that he was ashamed to leave the house. He really did seem to be unwell, however: he became depressed, preoccupied, and irritable. That very winter Varvara married Ptitsyn; all who knew them at once ascribed this to the fact that Ganya was unwilling to go back to work, and had not only stopped supporting the household but himself needed help and looking after.

We will note in passing that Gavrila Ardalionovich too was not so much as mentioned in the Yepanchin household; it was as if he had never existed at all, let alone been in their house. None the less, all of them learned (and very speedily) one most remarkable circumstance, namely that on that most fateful of nights, after his disagreeable adventure at Nastasya Filippovna's, Ganya had not gone to bed after getting home. Instead, he had waited for the prince's return with feverish impatience. The prince had come back some time after five in the morning following his trip to Yekaterinhof, whereupon Ganya had gone to his room and placed on the table in front of him the charred parcel of money presented to him by Nastasya Filippovna as he lay unconscious. He earnestly begged the prince to return the gift to Nastasya Filippovna at the first opportunity. When Ganya had gone in to the prince he had been in a hostile, even desperate, frame of mind; but it seemed that certain words were exchanged between them, after which Ganya sat with the prince for two hours, weeping bitterly all the time. They parted on friendly terms.

This report, which reached all the Yepanchins, was subsequently confirmed to be no more than the truth. It was odd, of course, that news of this kind should have got out so quickly and become common knowledge; all that had taken place at Nastasya Filippovna's soirée was known in the Yepanchin household practically the next day, and in tolerable detail at that. As far as the information about Gavrila Ardalionovich was concerned, one might suppose it had been brought by Varvara, who had suddenly started calling on the Yepanchin girls and was very soon on terms of positive intimacy, greatly to Lizaveta Prokofievna's surprise. Varvara, however, though she thought fit for some reason to establish close relations with the Yepanchins, would certainly not have spoken of her brother to them. She was quite a proud woman in her own way, despite making friends with people who had virtually turned her brother out. Previously she had been acquainted with the Yepanchins but saw them rarely. Even now she scarcely showed herself in the drawing-room, just dropping in for a moment, as it were, from the rear staircase. Lizaveta Prokofievna had never cared for her previously and did not now, though she greatly respected Nina Alexandrovna, Varvara's mama. She was surprised and angry, putting this acquaintance with Varvara down to the wayward fancies of her headstrong daughters, who 'thought of nothing else but how to be contrary'; nevertheless, Varvara continued her visits both before and after her marriage.

However, a month after the prince's departure, Madame Yepanchina received a letter from old Princess Belokonskaya, who had left a fortnight before to stay with her eldest married daughter in Moscow. This letter produced a marked effect upon her. Although she revealed nothing of its contents either to her husband or her daughters, it became clear to the family from a number of indications that she had been much stirred, even excited, by it. She began talking in an oddly peculiar manner to her daughters, constantly bringing up the most unusual topics; clearly she wanted to get something off her mind, but kept holding back for some reason. On the day she got the letter she was very nice to them all, even kissing Aglaya and Adelaida, apologizing to them for something, though they were unable to make out exactly what. She even became indulgent towards her husband, whom she had kept in disgrace for a whole month. Naturally, next day she was terribly annoyed over her previous day's softness and contrived to quarrel with everyone before dinner, but towards evening the skies cleared again. At all events, she continued to be in a reasonably sunny humour for an entire week, which had not happened for ages.

A week later, however, another letter came from Princess Belokonskaya, and this time Madame Yepanchina resolved to speak out. She solemnly announced that 'old Belokonskaya' (she never called the princess anything else when speaking of her behind her back) had given her some very comforting news about that . . . 'queer fellow, that prince!' The old woman had traced him in Moscow, made inquiries about him, and heard nothing but good. The prince at length came to visit her himself and made a simply enormous impression on her. 'That's obvious, because she's invited him to call on her every day between one and two, and he trudges along there and hasn't worn his welcome out yet', concluded Madame Yepanchina, adding that through 'the old woman' the prince had begun to be received in two or three good houses. 'It's good he's not just sitting at home like a fool being shy.' The girls, to whom all this had been confided, at once noted that their mama had concealed a good part of her letter from them. Perhaps they found this out by way of Varvara, who might have, and of course did, know everything that Ptitsyn knew about the prince and his stay in Moscow. Indeed, Ptitsyn might well have been privy to more than anyone else. He was, however, an extremely reticent man so far as business was concerned, though naturally he kept Varya informed. Madame Yepanchina at once took against Varya even more on this account.

Whatever the facts of the matter, the ice had been broken and all of a sudden the prince could be mentioned aloud. Moreover, it again became clear what an extraordinary impression the prince had left on the Yepanchin household and the enormous interest he had aroused. Madame Yepanchina was positively astonished at the effect her news from Moscow had on her daughters. The girls in their turn were astonished to hear that their mama, who had solemnly announced that 'the chief thing in her life was constantly being mistaken in people', had at the same time been recommending the prince to the attention of the 'powerful' old Belokonskaya in Moscow; she must have begged on bended knee for it too, as the old lady was hard to rouse in such cases.

As soon as the ice was broken, however, and the wind had changed direction, the general was also quick to have his say. It turned out that he too had been taking a particular interest in the prince. He only spoke of 'the business side of the matter', however. It appeared that he had arranged for two reliable and, in their way, influential gentlemen in Moscow to keep an eye on the prince in his own interests, and especially on Salazkin, who had charge of his affairs. Everything that had been said about the legacy, 'about the fact of the legacy so to speak', had turned out to be correct, but the bequest itself in the end was not nearly as considerable as had been at first reported. The estate was to some extent encumbered; there were debts; various claimants had appeared; meanwhile the prince was conducting himself in a most unbusinesslike manner, notwithstanding all the advice he was given. 'God bless him of course': now that the ice of silence had been broken, the general was glad to announce this 'in all sincerity', since although 'the chap was a bit *you know*', he deserved his good fortune. Meanwhile, he had behaved foolishly all the same: for example, creditors of the late merchant had turned up with dubious or worthless documents; others, getting wind of the prince, had none at all—and what do you think? The prince had satisfied nearly all of them, despite his friends' protestations that all this riff-raff had absolutely no claim on him; his only reason for satisfying them all was that some actually had suffered loss.

To this, Madame Yepanchina responded that Belokonskaya had written to her in a similar vein, and that 'it was stupid, so stupid; once a fool, always a fool', she added brusquely, but her face betrayed how much she rejoiced at the 'fool's' actions. Eventually the general observed that his wife was as concerned for the prince as if he had been her own son, and that she had suddenly become very affectionate towards Aglaya; seeing this, Ivan Fedorovich adopted a highly businesslike air for some time.

But this pleasant state of affairs did not last long. Barely a fortnight passed before there came another sudden change; Madame Yepanchina fell to frowning, and after some shrugging of the shoulders the general resigned himself to 'the ice of silence' once more. The fact was, only two weeks previously he had received secret intelligence, brief and consequently unclear, but none the less reliable, that Nastasya Filippovna, who had at first disappeared in Moscow then been run to earth there by Rogozhin, and then again disappeared only to be found again, had finally almost promised to marry him. And now, only a fortnight later, his excellency had received a sudden report that Nastasya Filippovna had run away a third time, virtually from the altar, this time somewhere out of town—and meanwhile Prince Myshkin had likewise disappeared from Moscow, leaving all his affairs in the hands of Salazkin. 'With her or after her, we don't know, but something's afoot there', concluded the general. Lizaveta Prokofievna, for her part, had also been the recipient of disagreeable news. At all events, two months after the prince's departure all rumours about him had subsided in Petersburg, and the 'ice of silence' in the Yepanchin household remained unbroken. Varvara, however, continued to call on the girls.

To make an end of all these rumours and reports, we should add that by spring there had been considerable upheavals in the Yepanchin family, so that it was difficult not to forget the prince when he sent no news of himself and perhaps had no wish to do so. As winter proceeded they gradually came to the decision to go abroad for the summer, Lizaveta and her daughters, that is; the general, naturally, could not afford to waste time on 'frivolous amusements'. The decision came about as a result of extraordinary persistence on the part of the girls, who were absolutely convinced that the reason their parents did not wish to take them abroad was their constant preoccupation with finding husbands for them and marrying them off. Perhaps, too, the parents had finally been persuaded that husbands might also be found abroad, and one summer's trip would do no harm, indeed might even 'help things along'. It is pertinent here to mention that the projected marriage between Afanasy Ivanovich Totsky and the eldest Yepanchin daughter had come to grief without any formal proposal having been made. It had seemed to happen of itself, without any lengthy discussions or family strife. Since the prince's departure, it had all swiftly petered out on both sides. This too was a factor contributing to the oppressive atmosphere within the Yepanchin household, although Madame Yepanchina had declared at the time that she was so glad she could 'cross herself with both hands'. Despite being in disgrace, and aware that it was entirely his fault, the general sulked for a long time; he felt sorry for Afanasy Ivanovich: 'a fortune like that, and such a sharp fellow!' A little later, the general found out that Totsky had been captivated by a certain visiting French high-society lady, a marquise and a legitimist, and that they were going to be married and Totsky taken off to Paris, then somewhere in Brittany. 'Well, the Frenchwoman will be the ruin of him', decided the general.

So the Yepanchins prepared to set off before the summer. Then, suddenly, something happened which altered the whole situation and the trip was postponed once again, to the huge delight of the general and his wife. A certain Prince S came to Petersburg from Moscow, a man of some renown and noted for his most excellent qualities. He was one of those people, modern men of affairs one might say, honourable and modest, who genuinely and consciously want to be of service to the public, always working, and distinguished by the rare and happy quality of always being able to find work to do. Without courting publicity, and staying clear of the voluble bitterness of party controversy, the prince had a profound understanding of recent trends without regarding himself as a leading man. He had formerly been in the civil service and had afterwards taken part in the rural-council policy.* In addition, he was a constructive corresponding member of several Russian learned societies. Together with an engineer friend, he had amassed data and done research leading to an improved route for one of the most important of the newly planned railway lines. He would be about 35 years old. He belonged to 'the highest society', besides possessing a 'decent, solid, indisputable fortune', as the general put it, having encountered the prince in the course of important business at the office of his superior, the count. The prince took a particular interest in Russian 'practical men' and never missed a chance of meeting them. It so happened that the prince was also introduced to the general's family. Adelaida, the middle sister, impressed him considerably and he proposed to her before the spring. Adelaida was very much taken with him and so was Lizaveta Prokofievna. The general was very pleased. It goes without saying that the trip abroad was put off. The wedding was fixed for the spring.

The trip might still have taken place towards the middle or end of summer, if only as a kind of visit for a month or two for Lizaveta Prokofievna and her two remaining daughters to get over their sadness at Adelaida's leaving them. But once again something unlooked-for occurred: in late spring, Adelaida's wedding having run into delay and been deferred till midsummer, Prince S introduced a relative, distant but fairly well known to him, to the Yepanchin household. This was a certain Yevgeni Pavlovich Radomsky; he was still young, about 28, an aide-de-camp of the emperor, strikingly handsome, 'of good family', witty, dazzling, 'up-to-date', 'very well educated', and— possessed of quite unheard-of riches. As regards this last, the general was always wary. He made enquiries: 'That actually does seem to be the case—though, of course, it will have to be checked further.' This young aide-de-camp 'with a future' was highly recommended by old Princess Belokonskaya from Moscow. There was just one slightly delicate aspect of his reputation: it was strongly asserted that there had been certain liaisons and 'conquests' of unfortunate hearts. On glimpsing Aglaya, he became extremely assiduous in his visits to the Yepanchins. Certainly, nothing had so far been said, nothing even hinted at, but all the same, it seemed to the parents that there was no question of any trip abroad that summer. Aglaya herself, perhaps, had other ideas.

These events were taking place just before the second entry of our hero on to the stage of our narrative. By this time, to all appearances, Petersburg had contrived to forget about poor Prince Myshkin. If he were now to appear among those who knew him, it would be as if he had fallen from the skies. Meanwhile, we will report one more fact and with that conclude our introduction.

Kolya Ivolgin had at first carried on with his normal existence after the prince's departure. He went on going to school, visiting his friend Ippolit, seeing to the general, and helping Varvara round the house, always at her beck and call. The lodgers, however, quickly made themselves scarce: Ferdischenko moved away somewhere three days after the scenes at Nastasya Filippovna's and fairly soon disappeared from view; not a whisper was heard about him. It was said he was drinking hard somewhere, but this was unconfirmed. The prince had gone to

Moscow, so that was the end of the lodgers. Later on, after
Varvara got married, Nina Alexandrovna and Ganya went with
her to Ptitsyn's in the Izmailovsky Regiment quarter* of the city;
as for General Ivolgin, something completely unlooked-for
happened to him at just about the same time: he was imprisoned
for debt. He was sent there at the instance of his lady-friend, the
captain's widow, for failing to honour the IOUs he had given her
at various times, amounting to some two thousand roubles. All
this came as an absolute bombshell to the poor general, who was
'most decidedly the victim of his excessive faith in the generosity
of the human heart, broadly speaking'. Once having acquired the
soothing habit of signing IOUs and bills of exchange, it never
occurred to him that it could have any actual effect, even in the
future; he just thought it was all right. It turned out not to be all
right. 'Trust people after that, eh? Be noble and trusting!' he
exclaimed in sorrow, sitting among his new friends in the
sponging-house over a bottle of wine, regaling them with tales of
the siege of Kars and the resurrected soldier. Actually the life
suited him perfectly. Varya and Ptitsyn said it was just the place
for him and Ganya agreed entirely. Only poor Nina Alexandrovna wept bitterly on the quiet (somewhat to the surprise of
the household), and though always ailing, would drag herself
along to meet her husband as often as she could.

Since the 'general's mishap', as he put it, in fact since his
sister's marriage, Kolya had got altogether out of control and of
late barely spent a night at home. It was rumoured that he had
made a lot of new acquaintances and become rather well known
in the debtors' prison. Nina Alexandrovna couldn't do without
him there; at home they did not even trouble him with their
curiosity nowadays. Varya, so strict with him before, never
questioned his wanderings in the least now; Ganya, to the
considerable surprise of the family, spoke to him and at times
treated him in perfectly affectionate fashion, despite his own
depression, something that had never happened before, since the
27-year-old Ganya, naturally, had never paid his 15-year-old
brother the slightest friendly attention. Indeed, he had dealt
roughly with him, demanding that the family be strict with him
and continually threatening to take him by the ears, which used
to drive Kolya 'to the utmost limits of human endurance'. It

seemed almost as if Kolya was now becoming indispensable to Ganya at times. He had been greatly struck by Ganya's returning the money; for that he was prepared to forgive him a good deal.

Some three months had passed since the prince's departure, when the Ivolgins heard that Kolya had suddenly become acquainted with the Yepanchins and been warmly received by the young ladies. Varya soon found out about it; Kolya, however, had managed this 'on his own account' and not through Varya. Gradually the Yepanchins grew fond of him. Madame Yepanchina had taken strongly against him initially, but soon began making a fuss of him 'for his frankness and because he never indulged in flattery'. It was perfectly true that Kolya never flattered anyone; he contrived to be on a completely equal and independent footing with them, though he did read books and newspapers to Madame Yepanchina,—but then he had always been an obliging boy. He did, however, quarrel bitterly with her on a couple of occasions, declaring that she was a tyrant and he would no longer set foot in her house. The first quarrel had started over 'the woman question' and the second over what time of year was best for catching siskins. However incredible it might seem, on the second occasion she had sent a servant with a note for him, asking him to come immediately; Kolya made no difficulties, and at once put in an appearance. Aglaya alone was permanently set against him for some reason, and treated him disdainfully. It was she, however, who was destined to get quite a surprise because of him. One day—it was at Easter—Kolya took advantage of a moment when they were alone to hand her a letter, saying only that he had been told to deliver it to her personally. Aglaya gave the 'presumptuous little jackanapes' a thunderous look, but Kolya went out without waiting. She opened the note and read:

'Once you honoured me with your trust. Perhaps you have forgotten me altogether now. How is it that I am writing to you? I don't know; but I have an overwhelming urge to remind you of my existence, you and no one else. I have needed all three of you many times, but out of the three I saw only you. I need you, very much. I've nothing to write to you about and nothing to tell you. Nor did I want to; I want terribly that you should be happy. Are you happy? There, that's all I wanted to say to you.
Your brother Pr. L. Myshkin.'

Perusing this brief and rather incoherent missive, Aglaya suddenly flushed and became lost in thought. It would be hard for us to convey the train of her musings. Among other things, she asked herself whether she ought to show it to anybody. She felt shy about doing so, somehow. In the end, however, she flung the letter into her desk-drawer with an odd, derisive smile. The following day, she retrieved it and placed it in a thick, stoutly bound volume (she always did this with her papers, so as to find them quickly in case of need). It was only a week later that she happened to examine which book it was. It was *Don Quixote*. Aglaya burst out laughing for no apparent reason.

Nor is it known whether she showed her new acquisition to any of her sisters.

But when she read it through again, it suddenly occurred to her: surely the prince hadn't chosen this precocious, conceited puppy as his correspondent—for all she knew his only correspondent here? With an air of extreme casualness, she subjected Kolya to interrogation. The 'jackanapes', ever touchy, paid not the slightest attention to the casual air: very briefly and rather coldly he explained to Aglaya that although he had given the prince his permanent address, just in case, as he was leaving Petersburg, and offered his services at the same time, this was the first commission and letter he had received from him. As proof of his words, he showed her the letter he had got himself. Aglaya didn't scruple to read it. The prince had written:

'Dear Kolya, please give the enclosed sealed note to Aglaya Ivanovna. Keep well.

Your loving Pr. L. Myshkin.'

'All the same, it's silly to trust a little kid like you', said Aglaya, annoyed, as she returned the note and walked contemptuously by him.

This was more than Kolya could bear: he had begged to wear Ganya's brand new green scarf, without giving a reason, specially for this occasion. He was bitterly offended.

2

IT was the beginning of June, and the weather in Petersburg had been unusually fine for a whole week. The Yepanchins had their own luxurious country villa in Pavlovsk and Lizaveta Prokofievna suddenly got all excited, bestirred herself, and after less than two days' bustle off they went.

Two or three days after they had gone, Prince Lev Niko-layevich Myshkin arrived from Moscow by the morning train. No one met him at the station, but as he was getting out of the carriage the prince seemed to sense the strange, hot stare of eyes in the crowd besieging the new arrivals. A closer look revealed nothing more. Of course it was just his imagination; but it left a feeling of unease. Besides, he was sad and preoccupied as it was, and seemed worried about something.

The cabby took him to a hotel near Liteinaya. The place was not of the best. The prince took two small rooms, dark and poorly furnished, then washed, dressed, and without making any request, went out quickly as if afraid of wasting time or failing to catch someone at home.

If any of those who had known him when he first arrived in Petersburg six months before had seen him now, they might well have decided that outwardly he had altered considerably for the better. But that was hardly the case. Only his clothing was altogether different; all his garments were new and Moscow-cut by a good tailor, but even here there was something wrong: they were a shade too fashionable (as conscientious but not-too-talented tailors always make them) but beyond that, they were worn by a man totally uninterested in his appearance. Anyone inclined to see the funny side of things might well have found something to smile about, perhaps, but then people laugh at all sorts of things.

The prince took a cab to Peski, where he soon located a little wooden house in one of the Rozhdestvensky streets. To his surprise the cottage was clean and pretty, and kept neat and tidy, with flowers growing in the front garden. The windows to the street were open and from them came the sound of a continuous, hectoring voice, rising almost to a shout, as though someone were reading aloud or even making a speech; the voice was interrupted from time to time by a chorus of ringing laughter. The prince entered the yard, mounted the porch, and asked for Mister Lebedev.

'They're in there', answered the cook who had opened the door, sleeves rolled to the elbows, and jabbed a finger in the direction of the 'drawing-room'.

This drawing-room was papered in dark blue, and was neatly furnished with some pretension to elegance: it had a round table and a sofa, a bronze clock under a glass dome, a narrow looking-glass on the wall between the windows, and a small, extremely ancient chandelier with pendants, hanging on a bronze chain from the ceiling. Mister Lebedev himself was standing in the middle of the room with his back to the prince as he entered, wearing a waistcoat without the jacket, summer-fashion, thumping himself on the chest, and declaiming bitterly. His audience consisted of: a boy of about 15 with a cheery, intelligent sort of face, holding a book; a young girl of about 20 dressed in complete mourning, with a babe in arms; a girl of 13, also in mourning but laughing incontinently with mouth woefully agape, and lastly a very odd listener indeed. This was a 20-year-old young man lolling on the sofa, darkish, fairly good-looking, with long, thick hair, large, dark eyes, and with faint indications of beard and sideburns on his face. This spectator appeared to be a frequent interrupter of Lebedev's oratorical flow, the ensuing arguments no doubt prompting those present to laughter.

'Lukyan Timofeich, Lukyan Timofeich! You see! Look this way, won't you! . . . Well, be blowed to you then!'

And the cook went out, waving her arms, flushed with exasperation.

Lebedev turned round and, on seeing the prince, stood as if thunderstruck for a moment or two, then rushed towards him with an obsequious smile before seeming to freeze once again, saying:

'M-m-most illustrious Prince!'

Then suddenly, as if still unable to regain his self-possession, he turned, and for no reason at all rounded on the girl in mourning who was holding the infant, causing her to stagger backwards in surprise; then at once abandoning her, he turned on the 13-year-old standing in the doorway of the adjoining room, the traces of her recent laughter still on her lips. She could

not withstand his shouting and at once made a dash for the
kitchen; Lebedev even stamped his feet after her to frighten her
more, but catching the prince's bewildered eye, proceeded to
explain:

'To . . . show a bit of respect, heh-heh-heh!'

'You needn't go to these lengths . . .', the prince began.

'A moment, a moment, one moment only . . . like lightning!'

And Lebedev swiftly disappeared from the room. The prince
gazed in astonishment at the girl, the boy, and the sofa-recliner:
they were all laughing. The prince began to laugh as well.

'Gone to put his frock-coat on', said the boy.

'This is all very annoying', said the prince, 'and here was I
thinking . . . tell me, is he . . . ?'

'Drunk, you mean?' cried a voice from the sofa. 'Not a bit of it.
Three or four glasses, say five, well within bounds.'

The prince was turning to the voice from the sofa when the girl
spoke up, with the frankest of expressions on her winsome face:

'He never drinks much in the mornings; if you've come on some
business matter, go ahead. This is the time to catch him. He's
drunk only when he gets back of an evening; and even then he's
more liable to cry at night nowadays and read us something out of
the scriptures—it's five weeks since our mother died, you see.'

'That's why he ran off, it probably got too hard for him to
answer you', laughed the young man. 'I'll wager he's already
thinking out some way to cheat you.'

'Five weeks, that's all! Just five weeks!' said Lebedev,
returning in his frock-coat, blinking and pulling out his
handkerchief to wipe his eye. 'Orphans!'

'What have you put on your raggy old coat for?' said the girl.
'You've got a brand new coat hanging up behind your door,
didn't you see it or what?'

'Be quiet, busybody', Lebedev shouted at her. 'Ooh you!' He
made to stamp his foot at her. This time, however, she merely
burst out laughing.

'Who're you trying to frighten? I'm not Tanya, I'm not going to
run away. What you will do is wake little Liuba, give her
convulsions . . . all that shouting!'

'Sh-sh-sh! Never say such a thing.' Lebedev was terribly
alarmed all of a sudden and, rushing over to the child sleeping in

his daughter's arms, made the sign of the cross over it several times, his face a picture of dismay. 'Lord keep and preserve her! She's my own baby, my daughter Liuba', he turned to the prince, 'born in lawful wedlock of my lately deceased wife Yelena, died in childbirth. And this little peewit is my daughter Vera, dressed in mourning . . . And this, this, oh this . . .'

'Well, go on!' shouted the young man. 'Get on with it, don't be embarrassed.'

'Your excellency!' Lebedev burst out. 'Have you read about the Zhemarin family killing?'*

'Yes I have', said the prince, somewhat surprised.

'Well, that's the real, live murderer of that family, the very man!'

'What do you mean?' asked the prince.

'Speaking figuratively, of course. He's the future second murderer of the future second Zhemarin family, if there is one. He's getting ready for it . . .'

Everyone laughed. It occurred to the prince that perhaps Lebedev really was squirming and wriggling because he anticipated questions that he couldn't answer and was trying to gain time.

'Rebellion! Hatching plots!' cried Lebedev, as if unable to contain himself any longer. 'Now can I, is it right to look on a slanderer like him, a strumpet, so to speak, a monster, as a nephew of mine, the only son of my late sister Anisya?'

'Do give over, drunk as you are! Would you believe it Prince, he's gone and set up as a lawyer, goes round the law-courts making fancy speeches and keeps it up with his children at home. He spoke before the magistrates five days ago, and who do you think he was defending? Not the old lady who begged and prayed him, the one who'd been robbed by some rascal of a money-lender of five hundred roubles, all she had, oh no, it was the money-lender himself, Seidler, some Yid, and all because he promised him fifty roubles . . .'

'Fifty if I won, but only five if I lost', explained Lebedev suddenly, in quite a different tone of voice, just as if he hadn't been shouting at all.

'Well, it was a *faux pas* of course, things are different nowadays after all, and they just laughed their heads off at him. Still he was mighty pleased with himself; remember, impartial judges, says he, that this unhappy old man, lacking the use of his legs, earning an honest living, has been deprived of his last crust of bread; recall the wise words of the lawgiver: "Let mercy prevail in the courts." And if you can believe it, he's been going over the same speech to us here every morning, word for word as he did there; this is the fifth time today; he was reading it just before you arrived, he's so fond of it. He's in love with himself. And he's proposing to defend somebody else. You're Prince Myshkin, aren't you? Kolya told me about you; up till now he's never met anybody cleverer in the whole world . . .'

'Nor is there! Nor is there! Nobody cleverer!' Lebedev at once chimed in.

'Well, Uncle here is no doubt lying. Kolya likes you, but this one is just making up to you; I, meanwhile, haven't the least intention of flattering you, rest assured. You are no fool certainly; why not judge between me and him?' He addressed his uncle. 'How would you like the prince to judge between us, then? I'm rather glad you turned up, Prince.'

'By all means!' cried Lebedev stoutly, unable to resist glancing at the audience which had once more begun to draw nearer.

'Why, what is going on here then?' said the prince, frowning.

He really did have a headache; besides, he was becoming more and more convinced that Lebedev was evading him and glad to divert his attention.

'Exposition. I'm his nephew—he wasn't lying about that for once. I haven't finished my course at the university and that's what I want to do. I am insisting on it, because I'm a man of character. In the meantime, to keep myself, I'm taking a job on the railway for twenty-five roubles a month. I also admit that he's helped me two or three times already. I did have twenty roubles and gambled them away. Can you credit that, Prince, I was mean and base enough to lose them!'

'To a scoundrel, a scoundrel who shouldn't have been paid!' cried Lebedev.

'Yes, a scoundrel, but one who had to be paid', the young man went on. 'I can testify he's a scoundrel, and not just because he gave you a thrashing. He's a cashiered officer, Prince, a lieutenant who used to belong to Rogozhin's crowd, now teaches boxing. They're all on the loose now that Rogozhin's got rid of them. But the worst of it is that I knew he was a scoundrel, a blackguard, and a thief and yet I still sat down to play cards with him, and as I was in the process of losing my last rouble, I thought to myself: If I lose, I'll go along to Uncle Lukyan and ask him nicely, he won't refuse. That was a low thing to do! Really low! Bare-faced caddishness!'

'It certainly was bare-faced caddishness!'

'Well stop crowing, just wait a minute', cried his touchy nephew. 'He's only too pleased. I came here to see him, Prince, and confessed everything; I did the honourable thing, I didn't make excuses; I cursed myself solidly in front of him, everybody here can confirm it. I absolutely must have something to wear for the railway job, I'm going round in rags. Here, look at these boots! Otherwise I just can't turn up, and if I don't appear at the proper time someone else will get the job and I'll be in the doldrums again—and who knows when I'll get another chance. Now I'm only asking him for fifteen roubles and I promise never to ask him for money again; what's more, I promise to repay the whole amount to the last kopeck within three months. I'll keep my promise. I can live on bread and kvass, because I've got will-power. In three months I'll have earned seventy-five roubles. Counting what I lost, I'll owe him only thirty-five roubles, so I'll have enough to pay him back. He can fix what interest he likes, blast him! Doesn't he know me, or what? Ask him, Prince: when he helped me before, did I pay him back or didn't I? What does he want now? He's furious at me because I paid that lieutenant; that's the only reason! That's the sort of man he is, dog in the manger!'

'And he won't go away!' cried Lebedev. 'Just lies there and won't go away!'

'That's what I told you. I shan't go till you give it to me. You're smiling, Prince, you think I'm wrong?'

'I'm not smiling, but I do believe you're not quite right', the prince responded reluctantly.

'Say it straight out then, I'm totally in the wrong, don't beat about the bush; "not quite", I ask you!'

'If you prefer then, you're totally in the wrong.'

'If I prefer! That's good! You really think I don't know I'm on thin ice here. It's his money and his decision and I'm forcing him into it. But you, Prince . . . know very little of life. You get nowhere if you don't teach them a lesson. They have to be taught a lesson. After all, my conscience is clear; on my conscience, he won't lose a kopeck because of me. He'll get it back with interest. He's got moral satisfaction out of it as well: he's seen my humiliation. What more does he want then? What's he good for if he's no use to anyone? What does he do himself, for goodness' sake? Go on, ask him what he gets up to with other people, how he cheats them. How did he manage to get this house? I'll stake my life he's cheated you before and he's already thought up a way of doing it again! You're smiling, you don't believe me?'

'It seems to me all this isn't wholly relevant to the matter in hand', observed the prince.

'I've been lying here for three days now, and the things I've seen!' cried the young man, ignoring him. 'Can you imagine, he's suspicious of this angel, this motherless girl, my cousin, his own daughter, and searches her room for lovers every night! He steals in here looking for something under the sofa. He's off his head with his nerves; he sees burglars in every corner. Jumps up every minute of the night seeing if the windows are tight shut, or trying the doors, or looking in the oven, all this half-a-dozen times a night. He stands up for rogues in court, yet he gets up three times a night to say his prayers, here in the room, down on his knees banging his forehead on the floor for half an hour or more, and who does he not pray for, who does he not grieve over when he's had a few? He's prayed for the soul of the Countess Du Barry, I heard him with my own ears; Kolya heard him as well: he's clean off his head!'

'You see—you hear how he shows me up, Prince!' shouted Lebedev, flushed and genuinely furious. 'And what he doesn't know is that, however much of a drunken vagabond I may be, a swindler and a villain, all right, but one thing I can claim; I used to wrap that scoffer in his swaddling clothes when he was a baby and bathed him, and sat up nights on end without sleep with my widowed sister Anisya, when she was penniless and I as poor myself. I looked after them when they were sickly, stole firewood from the yard-sweeper downstairs, sang songs to him and cracked my fingers for him, me with an empty belly; that's what my nursing has come to—there he sits making game of me! Anyway, what business is it of yours if I did go and cross myself for the soul of Countess Du Barry? Prince, three days ago I read her life story for the first time in an encyclopaedia. Do you know the sort of woman she was, Du Barry? Tell me if you know or not.'

'So you're the only one who knows are you?' murmured the young man, summoning up a sneer.

'She was a countess who rose from a life of shame to reign in place of the queen; a great empress called her "*ma cousine*" in a letter she wrote to her in her own hand. A cardinal, a papal nuncio, offered to put silk stockings on her bare legs himself at a *levée du roi* (you know what a *levée du roi* was?)—and accounted it an honour to do so, a highly placed holy man like that! Do you know that? I can see by your face you don't! Well then, how did she meet her end? Answer if you know!'

'Oh go away! Pest.'

'After such honour, this former ruler of the land was dragged to the guillotine by Samson the executioner, innocent as she was, for the amusement of the Parisian fishwives, and she too terrified to know what was happening to her. She sees him bending her neck under the blade, kicking her forward—the crowd laughing—and starts shouting: "*Encore un moment, monsieur le bourreau, encore un moment!*" which means: "Wait just one more minute, mister executioner, just one!" And perhaps the Lord God will forgive her for that one moment, because a greater *misère* for a human soul than that is impossible to imagine. Do you know what the word *misère* means? Well, that's just what it means. When I read about that moment, the countess's cry, I felt pincers grip my heart. What business is it of yours, miserable worm, if I feel like mentioning a great sinner like that in my bedtime prayers. Maybe it was because most likely nobody has ever crossed himself for her sake, never even thought of it. I dare say she'll feel better in the next world because there's a sinner like her who prayed for her at least once here on earth. What are you laughing at? You're not a believer, atheist. But how do you know? Anyway you lied about overhearing me: I didn't just pray for Countess Du Barry alone; what I said was: "Grant rest, O Lord, to the soul of the great sinner Countess Du Barry and and all like her", and that's quite a different matter; there are many such great sinners and examples of the fickleness of fortune, who have had their share of suffering, and who are sorely afflicted yonder, groaning as they languish; and I prayed for you then, and people of your sort, impudent bullies like you, that's who I prayed for, if you really wanted to hear me saying my prayers . . .'

'Well all right, that's enough; pray for whoever you like, blast you, you've had your shout!' the exasperated nephew broke in. 'We've got a great reader on our hands, did you know that, Prince?' he went on, grinning rather uncomfortably. 'He's forever reading books and memoirs like that nowadays.'

'Still, your uncle's . . . not without a heart all the same', observed the prince reluctantly. This young man was becoming altogether repugnant to him.

'Now that's the sort of praise he loves to hear! See, he's already got his hand on his heart and puckered his lips up, he's got the taste for it. Maybe he's not heartless at that, but he's a rogue, that's the trouble; and a drunk besides, he's gone all to pieces like any man will after years on the bottle, that's why all his schemes are in such a bad way. Let's say he does love his children, and respected my late aunt . . . He's fond of me even, left me something in his will, honestly . . .'

'I'll leave you n-nothing!' shouted Lebedev, incensed.

'Listen Lebedev', said the prince firmly, turning from the young man. 'I know from experience that you're a man of business when you choose . . . I've got very little time just now, and if you . . . I'm sorry, what are your first names, I've forgotten?'

'Ti-Ti-Timofey.'

'And?'

'Lukyanovich.'

Everyone in the room burst out laughing.

'He's lying!' cried the nephew. 'He's even lying about that! He's not called Timofey Lukyanovich at all, Prince, he's Lukyan Timofeyevich! Now why did you lie, come on? Isn't it all the same to you whether you're Lukyan or Timofey, and what's it to the prince? He just lies out of habit, believe me.'

'That's not true is it?' asked the prince impatiently.

'It's really Lukyan Timofeyevich', Lebedev admitted in

discomfiture, humbly lowering his eyes and placing his hand on his heart again.

'But why on earth didn't you say that, for heaven's sake?'

'To humble myself', whispered Lebedev, lowering his head still more submissively.

'Ach, what's humble about that! Oh, if only I knew where to find Kolya!' said the prince, turning to leave.

'I'll tell you where Kolya is', offered the young man again.

'No-no-no!' Lebedev jerked his head up and started scurrying and bustling about.

'Kolya slept here last night, but he went off in the morning looking for his general, whom you bought out of jail, Prince, Lord knows why. The general had promised to spend the night here last night but he didn't arrive. Most likely he stayed at The Scales hotel, it's not far. Kolya must be there or with the Yepanchins in Pavlovsk. He had the money and intended going there yesterday. So it's either The Scales or Pavlovsk.'

'Pavlovsk, Pavlovsk! . . . And we'll go this way, this way, into the garden and . . . some coffee . . .'

So saying, Lebedev pulled the prince by the arm. They left the room, crossed a small yard, and went through a wicket-gate. Beyond it there really was a very small and charming little garden, in which all the trees were in leaf thanks to the fine weather. Lebedev sat the prince down on a green wooden bench in front of a green table fixed into the earth, and placed himself opposite. A minute later coffee really was served. The prince didn't say no. Lebedev went on peering into his eyes, eagerly and abjectly.

'I had no idea you had such a large establishment', said the prince, with the air of a man thinking of something else entirely.

'Or-orphans', began Lebedev, squirming, but stopped short: the prince was gazing absently in front of him, having forgotten his remark already of course. Another minute passed; Lebedev watched and waited.

'Well, then?' said the prince seemingly coming to. 'Ah yes! You're aware of course of what we have to discuss: it was because of your letter I came here. Say on.'

Lebedev was embarrassed, he wanted to say something but only managed a stutter: no words came out. The prince waited and smiled sadly.

'I believe I understand you very well, Lukyan Timofeyevich: you weren't expecting me most likely. You thought I wouldn't stir from my retreat at the first time of asking and you only wrote to keep your conscience clear. And now here I am. Well don't try and deceive me, enough of that. Enough of serving two masters. Rogozhin's been here three weeks, I know all about it. Have you managed to sell her to him like you did last time or not? The truth now.'

'The monster found out himself, on his own.'

'Don't call him names. He treated you badly of course . . .'

'Thrashed me, thrashed me!' Lebedev seized on this with frightful vehemence. 'He set his dog on me in Moscow. Right along the street with his borzoi bitch. Horrible bitch.'

'You take me for a child, Lebedev. Tell me, seriously, has she left him, in Moscow, I mean?'

'Honestly, honestly, in front of the altar again. He was counting the minutes while she was on her way to Petersburg and straight to me: "Save me, protect me, Lukyan, and don't tell the prince . . ." She's even more afraid of you than him, Prince. Herein lurks a mystery.'

And Lebedev slyly put a finger to his forehead.

'And now you've brought them together again?'

'Most illustrious Prince, how could I have prevented it?'

'Well, all right, I'll find it all out myself. Just tell me where she is now. With him?'

'Oh no! Not at all! She's on her own for the moment. "I'm a free woman", she says and—do you know, Prince, she really insists on it, "I'm still absolutely free"! She's still at my sister-in-law's on the Petersburg side of the river, as I wrote to you.'

'And she's there now?'

'Yes, if she's not in Pavlovsk, at Darya Alexeyevna's country cottage, what with the weather being so fine. I'm absolutely free, says she; she was boasting about her freedom to Kolya only yesterday—a bad sign that, sir!'

And Lebedev grinned.

'Does Kolya see her often?'

'He's thoughtless and hard to fathom, but not secretive.'

'Have you been there recently?'

'Every day, every day.'

'So you were there yesterday?'

'N-no; three days ago.'

'It's a pity you've had a few to drink, Lebedev! I was going to ask you something.'

'No-no-no, not a bit drunk.'

At this, Lebedev became all attention.

'Tell me then, how you left her?'

'S-searching . . .'

'Searching?'

'As if she was forever looking for something she'd lost. The very thought of her forthcoming marriage revolts her and she regards it as an insult. She thinks no more of *him* than she would of an orange-peel, well more than that, seeing as she's in fear and trembling. She forbids anyone to talk about it, and they only see one another if it's absolutely essential—and he takes it very much to heart! But there's no getting out of it, no sir! . . . Restless, sneering, deceitful, short-tempered . . .'

'Deceitful and short-tempered?'

'So she is; she nearly grabbed me by the hair last time because of something I said. I was rebuking her from Revelation.'

'What was that?' asked the prince, thinking he had misheard.

'Reading Revelation. A lady of vivid imagination, heh, heh! Besides, I've come to the opinion that she's very much inclined to serious topics, even if they are a bit out of the way. Oh she does like them, oh yes, even takes it for a particular mark of respect towards her. Yes, indeed. I'm good at interpreting Revelation, I've been doing it for fifteen years. She agreed with me that we're in the time of the third horse, the black one, the one that has the rider with scales in his hand, because in our age everything is weighed in the balance and settled by agreement, and all men seek only their own due: "one measure of wheat for one denarius and three measures of barley for one denarius" . . . as well as wanting to have freedom of spirit, a pure heart and a sound body, and all God's gifts added thereunto. But they cannot have these things by right alone, and the pale horse will follow and he whose name is Death, and after him, Hell . . . When we meet we discuss this and it has greatly affected her.'

'Do you believe that yourself?' asked the prince, surveying

Lebedev with an odd expression.

'I do, and interpret it accordingly. For I am poor and naked amid the vortex of humankind. Who respects Lebedev? Everybody makes game of him and practically kicks him on his way. Here in my interpretation I am equal to the mighty. What counts here is the mind! And a great man has trembled before me ... in his own armchair, as his mind grasped my message. Two years gone Easter, his most exalted excellency, Nil Alexeyevich, in whose department I was serving at the time, got to hear of me and sent Peter Zakharich specially to summon me to his office to question me in private: "Is it true that you're the expounder of Antichrist?" I didn't conceal the fact: "I am", I said, and I expounded and interpreted and laid it all before him without mitigating the horror—in fact I intensified it as I unfolded the allegorical scroll and calculated the figures. He was smiling, but at the figures and correspondences he started to tremble and begged me to close the book and leave. He promoted me at Easter and the week after rendered up his soul to God.'

'Really, Lebedev?'

'Indeed yes. He fell out of his carriage after a dinner ... hit his head on a stone and went off straight away like a little child, a little child. Seventy-three years old according to the service-list; reddish in the face, greyish hair, perfume sprinkled all over, and always smiling, smiling like a little child. Peter Zakharich remembered at the time: "It was you foretold it", said he.'

The prince began to rise. Lebedev was surprised, positively taken aback, that the prince should be getting up already.

'You've grown very blasé, heh-heh!' he ventured to remark obsequiously.

'Actually I don't feel too well, I've got a headache, from the journey probably', the prince responded, frowning.

'You need country air, sir', Lebedev suggested tentatively.

The prince stood, lost in thought.

'In three days' time I'm going myself, with all the family; it'll be good for the new-born babe and the house here can be put to rights in the meantime. To Pavlovsk as well.'

'You're going to Pavlovsk too?' the prince asked abruptly. 'What is all this, is everybody here going to Pavlovsk? You've got a villa of your own there, did you say?'

'Not everybody, sir, is going to Pavlovsk. Ivan Petrovich Ptitsyn has let me have one of the villas he got cheap. It's nice there, high up, plenty of greenery, not expensive; it's fashionable and musical, that's why everyone goes to Pavlovsk. Actually I'm staying in one wing, the house itself . . .'

'. . . is let?'

'N-n-no. Not . . . not quite.'

'Let it to me', the prince proposed suddenly.

This seemed to be just what Lebedev had been leading up to. The idea had occurred to him three minutes earlier. Actually he didn't need a tenant; he already had someone who had indicated he might take the house. Lebedev knew for a fact that it wasn't a question of 'might', the tenancy was assured. However, it had suddenly crossed his mind that a much more attractive notion, as he saw it, would be to let the cottage to the prince, taking advantage of the fact that the first tenant had not definitely committed himself. His imagination conjured up 'many meetings and a whole new turn of events'. He accepted the prince's offer with something approaching elation. In answer to the prince's direct query about terms, he simply waved his arms.

'Just as you like; I'll get by; you won't be the loser.'

They were both leaving the garden now.

'I could . . . I could . . . if you wished, I could let you know something extremely interesting, most worthy Prince, I could tell you something in connection with this very matter', murmured Lebedev, squirming with glee at the prince's side.

The prince halted.

'Darya Alexeyevna also has a villa at Pavlovsk, sir.'

'Well?'

'And a certain person is a friend of hers, and apparently intends to visit her often there. With a certain purpose in mind.'

'Well?'

'Aglaya Yepanchina . . .'

'Ach, that's enough, Lebedev!' The prince broke in, with the disagreeable sensation of having been touched on a sore spot. 'All that's . . . not what you're thinking. Just tell me when you're moving. The sooner the better as far as I'm concerned, I'm in a hotel . . .'

As they talked, they went out of the garden and crossed the

little yard to the gate without going into the house.

'What could be better, then?' it occurred to Lebedev at length. 'Move straight over to me from the hotel, this very day, and we'll all set off for Pavlovsk the day after tomorrow.'

'I'll see', said the prince, lost in thought as he passed through the gate.

Lebedev gazed after him. This abrupt reverie of the prince had disconcerted him. He had forgotten even to say goodbye as he left, not so much as a nod, which was out of keeping with what Lebedev knew to be the prince's courtesy and consideration.

3

By now it was after eleven. The prince knew that the general would be the only one he might find at home at the Yepanchin town-house, attending to his business affairs, though even that was unlikely. It struck him that the general might well carry him off to Pavlovsk at once, and he was very anxious to pay a certain call before that. At the risk of missing Yepanchin and putting off his trip to Pavlovsk until the next day, the prince resolved to seek out the house he so much wanted to visit.

This call was, in certain respects, a risky one for him, however. He was in two minds and hesitated. He knew the house was in Gorokhovaya Street, not far from Sadovaya, and decided to set off in that direction, hoping that once he had reached the spot he could make a final decision.

As he approached the intersection of the two streets he was surprised to find himself feeling intensely nervous; he had not expected his heart to pound so painfully. One house, no doubt because of its peculiar configuration, began to attract his attention while still some way off, and the prince recalled later saying to himself: 'That must be the house.' Profoundly curious, he went nearer to verify his surmise; he felt that it would be most disagreeable for some reason if he had guessed right. It was a large, gloomy, three-storied house, devoid of architectural pretension, and of a dirty-green colour. There are houses of this sort, put up at the end of the last century, which have survived unchanged in just such streets in Petersburg (where everything changes so swiftly), but they are few in number. They are solidly built, thick-walled, and have extraordinarily few windows; those on the ground floor frequently have bars. More often than not, the lower part of the building is occupied by a money-changer, a member of the castrate sect,* who lodges on the floor above. Outside and in, the place looks cold and forbidding, as if everything was concealing itself and hiding away somehow, though why such an impression should be created merely by the external look of a house would be hard to explain. The combined effect of architectural lines has its own secret of course. These houses are inhabited almost exclusively by tradespeople. Approaching the gate and glancing at the notice, the prince read: 'The House of Hereditary Honoured Citizen Rogozhin.'

Without further hesitation he opened the glass door, which slammed noisily shut behind him, and began making his way up the main staircase to the first floor. The stone staircase was dark and of rough workmanship; the walls had been painted a red colour. He knew that the entire first floor of this dreary dwelling was occupied by Rogozhin, together with his mother and brother. The servant who opened the door admitted the prince without announcing his arrival, and led him along for quite a while; they passed through a large reception room which had walls of imitation marble, an oak parquet floor, and twenties' furniture, coarse and ponderous; they also passed through some tiny rooms, twisting and zigzagging, mounting two or three steps and then descending as many before knocking eventually on one particular door. It was opened by Parfion Semyonich in person; seeing the prince, he went so pale as he stood rooted to the spot, that for a moment he looked like some stone idol with a fixed and terrified gaze, his mouth twisted into a kind of smile of utter bewilderment—as if he found something unthinkable and almost miraculous in this visit of the prince's. Though the prince had expected something of the kind, he could not help being astonished.

'Parfion, perhaps I've come at the wrong time, I can go away, you know', he brought out at length, embarrassed.

'It's all right! It's all right!' Parfion recovered himself at last. 'By all means, come in!'

They talked in the manner of old friends. In Moscow, chance had thrown them together frequently and for long periods; there had even been moments during their meetings which had indelibly impressed themselves on each of their hearts. Now, however, it had been over three months since they had set eyes on one another.

Rogozhin's face still retained its pallor and a tiny flickering twitch. Although he had invited his visitor inside, his intense embarrassment persisted. While he was showing the prince over to the armchairs and seating him at the table, the latter chanced to turn towards him and halted, struck by his strange and grim expression. Something seemed to transfix the prince, and at the same time he recalled something recent, sombre and painful. Without sitting down, he remained motionless for a while, looking Rogozhin straight in the eyes; at first, they seemed to glitter even more intensely. At length Rogozhin smiled, though rather disconcerted and seemingly at a loss.

'What are you staring like that for?' he muttered. 'Sit down!'

The prince sat down.

'Parfion', he said, 'tell me frankly, did you know I was coming to Petersburg or not?'

'I thought you would come, and as you see, I was right', he added, smiling sardonically: 'But how was I to know you'd be coming today?'

A certain harsh abruptness and the odd irritability of the question which comprised the answer, surprised the prince even more.

'Well even if you had known I'd come *today*, why be so cross about it?' said the prince softly, bemused.

'Why do you ask that then?'

'This morning, when I was getting off the train, I saw a pair of eyes looking just as you did a moment ago behind me.'

'You don't say so! And whose eyes were they then?' muttered Rogozhin suspiciously. The prince thought he gave a start.

'I don't know; I even thought I'd imagined it in the crowd; I'm beginning to imagine quite a lot of things. I feel almost like I did five years ago when I used to have my fits, Parfion, my friend.'

'Well, maybe you did imagine it. I don't know . . .', muttered Parfion.

The affectionate smile on his face at that moment did not ring true; it was as if something in it had broken and he did not have the strength to stick it back together again, no matter how hard he tried.

'So then, off abroad again is it?' he asked, suddenly adding: 'Remember how we travelled in the same carriage from Pskov last autumn, me on my way here and you . . . in that cloak, remember, those gaiters?'

And Rogozhin abruptly burst out laughing, this time with undisguised malice, glad of the chance, it seemed, to find some vent for it.

'You've settled down here for good?' asked the prince, surveying the study.

'Yes, this is home. Where else should I be then?'

'We've not met for a long time. I've heard such things about you, not like you at all.'

'People will say anything', observed Rogozhin coldly.

'But you've got rid of all your gang; you're living in your father's house and behaving yourself. Well, that's all to the good. Is the house yours then or do you own it jointly?'

'It's mother's. She's across the corridor.'

'And where does your brother live?'

'Semyon Semyonich lives in one wing.'

'Is he a family man?'

'A widower. Why do you want to know?'

The prince looked at him without replying; he was suddenly lost in thought and appeared not to have heard the question. Rogozhin waited without pressing the point. Both were silent for a while.

'On my way here I picked out your house a hundred yards away', the prince said.

'How so?'

'I've no idea. Your house looks like all your family, and your whole Rogozhin existence, and if you asked me why I came to that decision, I simply couldn't tell you. Sheer imagination of course. It frightens me that it should bother me so much. It would never have occurred to me that you lived in a house like this, but as soon as I set eyes on it it struck me at once: "Why that's just the sort of house he was bound to have." '

'There you are then!' Rogozhin smiled vaguely, not quite following the prince's obscure train of thought. 'This house was built by my grandfather', he remarked. 'Castrates always lived here, the Khludyakovs, and they still rent it from us.'

'It's so dark in here. You're living in darkness', said the prince, glancing round the study.

It was a sizeable room, lofty and rather gloomy, and cluttered with furniture of all kinds—office desks for the most part, bureaux and cupboards, holding business records and papers. The broad red morocco sofa clearly served Rogozhin as a bed. The prince noted two or three books on the table where Rogozhin had seated him; one of them, Solovyov's *History*, was open and had a bookmark in it. A number of oil paintings in tarnished gilt frames adorned the walls. They were sombre and smoke-begrimed, and it was hard to make out anything of them. One full-length portrait attracted the prince's attention: it depicted a man of about 50 wearing a frock-coat of German cut, but long skirted; he had two medals round his neck. His beard was very sparse and short and he had a furrowed, sallow face and mistrustful, secretive, melancholy eyes.

'That wouldn't be your father, would it?'

'That's just who it is', replied Rogozhin with an unpleasant grin, as if prepared for some instant jocular familiarity at the expense of his late parent.

'He wasn't an Old Believer* was he?'

'No, he went to church, but he did use to say that the old faith was closer to the truth. He had great respect for the castrates too. This used to be his office. Why did you ask if he was an Old Believer?'

'The wedding; you'll be having it here?'

'Y-yes', Rogozhin replied, startled almost by the unexpectedness of the question.

'Will it be soon?'

'Doesn't depend on me, you know very well.'

'Parfion, I'm not your enemy and I've got no intention of interfering with you in any way. I'm repeating now what I've said before, once on a very similar occasion. When your wedding was going forward in Moscow I didn't interfere, as you know. The first time *she* came running to me, practically from the altar, begging me to "save" her from you. I'm repeating her own words. Afterwards she ran away from me too, you sought her out and brought her to the church, and now she's fled here from you again, so they say. Is that true? Lebedev wrote to me about it, that's why I came. That you've made it up again I only heard for the first time on the train yesterday, from one of your former friends—Zalyozhev, if you want to know. I travelled here with an end in view: I wanted to persuade her to go abroad for her health; she's very distressed in body and mind, especially mentally, and in my opinion she needs properly looking after. I didn't want to take her abroad myself, I wanted to arrange it all without my being personally involved. I'm telling you the honest truth. If it's really true that everything's all right between you again she won't get a glimpse of me, and I'll never come here any more either. You know very well that I'm not deceiving you, I've always been open with you. I've never concealed from you what I thought about all this, I always said that marrying you would be certain disaster for her. And for you too . . . perhaps worse than for her. If you were to part again, I would be very pleased, but I don't intend to upset or sow division between you myself. Rest assured of that and trust me. Anyway, you know very well whether I was ever your *real* rival, even when she ran away to me. You laughed just there; I know what made you smile. Yes, we lived apart there, in different towns, and you know all that for a fact. I explained to you before, didn't I, that I loved her "out of compassion, not love". I think that was an accurate definition. You said you understood my words then; was that so? Did you? There, what a hateful look you've got! I came to reassure you because you are dear to me also. I love you greatly, Parfion. And now I'm going and I will never come back. Goodbye.'

The prince rose.

'Sit with me for a while', said Parfion softly, remaining where he was, chin resting in his right palm. 'I haven't seen you for a long time.'

The prince sat down. Both fell silent again.

'When you're not in front of me I start hating you at once, Lev Nikolayevich. Over these three months when I haven't seen you I've hated you every minute, honest to God. I felt like poisoning you. That's how it was. Now you haven't been with me a quarter of an hour and all my anger passes off, you're as dear to me as ever you were. Sit with me for a while . . .'

'When I'm with you, you trust me and when I'm not you stop trusting me at once and start suspecting things. You're just like your father!' the prince replied, smiling in friendly fashion in order to conceal his emotion.

'I trust your voice when I'm with you. I'm very well aware we can't be regarded as equals, you and I . . .'

'Why did you have to add that? And now you're cross again', said the prince, marvelling at Rogozhin.

'Well as regards that, friend, nobody asks our opinion, they decide that without us. And we love in different ways too, we're different in everything', he went on softly, then paused. 'You say you love her out of compassion. There's no such compassion in me towards her. And she hates me more than anything. I dream about her every night: always her with another man, laughing at me. That's the way it is, friend. She's going to marry me and she never gives me a thought, it's as though she were changing her shoes. Believe it or not, I haven't seen her for five days because I daren't show my face: "Why have you come?" she'll ask. Not to mention her shaming me . . .'

'Shaming you? What do you mean?'

'As if you didn't know! Wasn't it you she ran away with from the altar, you said so yourself just now.'

'But you don't believe yourself that she . . .'

'Didn't she shame me with that officer in Moscow, Zem-tiuzhnikov? I know for a fact she did', declared Rogozhin with conviction. 'And that was after she'd fixed the wedding-day herself. She's not that kind, you think? Don't try and tell me she isn't, friend. That's all nonsense. Perhaps she isn't when she's with you, I dare say she'd be horrified at the idea, but that's just how she is with me. She treats me like dirt. I know for a fact she pretended to have an affair with Keller, that officer, the boxer fellow, just to make me look a fool . . . Oh, you don't know half the tricks she played on me in Moscow! And the money, the money I've laid out . . .'

'But . . . how on earth can you get married now? . . . How will you go on afterwards?' asked the prince, horrified.

Rogozhin gave the prince a grim and terrible look and made no reply.

'I haven't been to see her for five days', he went on, after a moment's pause. 'I keep worrying she'll send me packing. "I'm still my own mistress", says she; "if I want to I'll chase you away altogether and go off abroad." She's already told me that, about going abroad', he remarked, as if in parenthesis, with a meaning look into the prince's eyes. 'It's true, sometimes she's only trying to scare me, she finds everything I do funny. Other times, she scowls and frowns and never says a word; that's what really frightens me. The other day I thought: I'll make sure I never come with empty hands—that only made her laugh and later on she lost her temper even. She gave her maid Katka a shawl I'd brought her; she'd probably never seen the like, even if she did live in the lap of luxury before. As for the wedding-day, I can't even mention it. I ask you, what sort of fiancé is it who's simply too afraid to see her? So here I sit, and when I can't bear it any more, I sneak up and down her street on the sly, or hide myself round the corner. The other day I was patrolling near her gate till dawn practically—I had the idea something was going on at the time. Anyway, she looked out of the window: "What would you have done with me", says she, "if you'd seen me being unfaithful?" I couldn't stop myself saying: "You know very well." '

'And what does she know?'

'Well how should I know?' Rogozhin gave an angry laugh. 'In Moscow that time I couldn't catch her with anybody, though it wasn't for want of trying. Once I took hold of her and said: "You've promised to marry me and enter an honourable family, and do you know what you are now? You're one of that sort!" '

'You told her that?'

'I did.'

'And then?'

' "I'd think twice about taking you on as a servant", says she, "never mind be your wife." "Then I'm not leaving", says I, "it's all the same to me." "Well, I'll get Keller and tell him to throw you out", says she. So I flung myself at her and beat her black and blue.'

'Never!' cried the prince.

'I'm telling you: it happened', Rogozhin confirmed quietly,

though his eyes were flashing. 'For a day and a half I didn't eat, drink, or sleep. I never left her room, I was on my knees before her: "I'll die", I said, "I won't go until you forgive me and if you order me to be put out, I'll drown myself because—what would I be without you now?" She was like a madwoman all that day, weeping, then trying to knife me, then cursing me. She sent for Zalyozhev, Keller, and Zemtiuzhnikov, everybody, and made a show of me, putting me to shame. "Let's all go to the theatre tonight, gentlemen", says she. "Let him stay here if he doesn't want to leave. I'm not tied to him. They'll serve you tea without me, Parfion Semyonich, you must be starving after today." She came back on her own: "They're all cowardly wretches", says she, "they're all scared of you, and tried to make me the same: said you wouldn't ever go—and probably cut my throat. Well I'm going off to my bedroom and I'm not locking the door: that's how much I'm afraid of you! I want you to know and see that! Did you have your tea?" "No", says I, "and I'm not going to." "If your honour was involved, I could understand it, but this doesn't become you at all." And she kept her word, she didn't lock her room. In the morning she came out laughing: "Have you gone mad, or what?" says she. "You'll die of hunger like that, you know." "Forgive me", says I. "I don't want to, I'm not going to marry you, I've told you. You haven't been sitting in that chair all night, have you? No sleep?" "No", I say. "Well, that's clever! And no lunch or dinner today either?" "I told you no—forgive me!" "This really doesn't become you at all, if you only knew, it's like a saddle on a cow. You don't mean to frighten me, do you? What do I care if you sit there starving; that's really frightening, I must say!" She was angry, but not for long, then she started nagging at me again. I wondered at her not being really angry at me. She's vindictive, you know; if anyone does her wrong she holds it against them for a long time! Then it crossed my mind that she thought so little of me that she couldn't even be angry for long. And that's true. "Do you know", she says, "who the pope is?" "I've heard of him", I said. "You, Parfion Semyonich, have never studied world history", says she. "I've never studied anything", I said. "Very well", says she, "I'm giving you this to read: there was a pope once and he was angry at a certain emperor, who knelt for three days barefoot in the snow in front of the palace, with nothing to eat or drink, before the pope forgave him. What do you think that emperor meditated about during those three days, on his knees too, what vows did he make? . . . Wait a moment, I'll read it to you myself!" She jumped up and fetched a book: "It's poetry", she says, and started reading me a poem about how the emperor spent the three days vowing to be revenged on the pope. "Surely that takes your fancy, Parfion Semyonich?" "It's all true", said I, "what you read." "Aha, so you say yourself it's true, that means maybe you're vowing that when she marries me, I'll remind her of all this and then I'll have some fun with her!" "Well I don't know", I said, "maybe that is the way I'm thinking about it." "What do you mean, you don't know?" "Just that, I don't know, there's other things to think about." "What are you thinking about now, then?" "That you're going to get up and pass by me, and I'll watch you and follow you with my eyes; your dress will rustle, as my heart sinks, and when you leave the room I'll remember every little word you said, the tone of voice, and what you were talking about; this last night I thought of nothing, just kept listening to the sound of your breathing as you slept and turned over once or twice . . ." She laughed. "As for beating me though, you don't think or remember?" "Maybe I do", I say, "I don't know." "And what if I don't forgive you and don't marry you?" "I told you, I'll drown myself." "You'll murder me first, perhaps . . ." She said that and fell to thinking. Then she got irritated and went out. An hour later she comes out to me looking very dark. "I'll marry you, Parfion Semyonich", she says, "and not because I'm frightened of you, but because I'm done for in any case. What better way than this? Sit down", she says. "They'll bring you something to eat directly. And if I marry you, I'll be a faithful wife, rest assured and never doubt that." She was quiet for a moment, then said: "At least you're not a lackey; I used to think before that you were a real lackey, through and through." Then she named the day for the wedding, but a week later she ran away from me to Lebedev here. When I got here, she says to me: "I'm not turning you down altogether; it's just that I want to wait a while longer, as long as I feel like it, since I'm still my own mistress. You can wait too, if you like." That's how it is between us now . . . What do you make of it all, Lev Nikolayevich?'

'What are your own thoughts?' countered the prince, gazing

sadly at Rogozhin.

'I'm not capable of thinking, am I!' he burst out. He would have added something else, but stopped short in hopeless misery.

The prince got up and once again made to leave.

'I shan't hinder you all the same', he said softly, almost pensively, as if in answer to some secret inner thought of his own.

'You know what', cried Rogozhin in sudden animation, eyes kindling. 'I can't understand why you're giving in to me like this. Or have you stopped loving her altogether? Before, you were really miserable—I could see that. So why on earth do you come galloping over here hell for leather? Compassion is it? Heh-heh!' (At this his face twisted into an angry grimace.)

'You think I'm deceiving you?' enquired the prince.

'No, I believe you, it's just that I don't understand the business at all. Most likely your compassion is stronger than my love!'

Something savage burned in his face, clamouring for an outlet.

'It would be hard to distinguish your love from hate', smiled the prince, 'and when it passes, the situation may be even worse. Friend Parfion, I say to you now . . .'

'That I'll kill her?'

The prince shuddered.

'You'll hate her for this present love of yours and all the torment you're accepting at the moment. What amazes me most of all is how she can be going to marry you again. I could hardly credit what I heard yesterday, I felt miserable. After all, she's twice rejected you and fled from the altar, that must mean she has misgivings! What can she want from you now, anyway? Not your money, surely? That's nonsense. You've got rid of a fair amount of that in any case, I've no doubt. And surely not just to find a husband. She can find somebody else besides you, of that I'm sure. Anybody except you would be better, because you really are liable to go ahead and kill her and perhaps she's only too well aware of that now. Why do you have to love her so intensely? Though it's true . . . I've heard tell there are people who seek for just that kind of love . . . only . . .'

The prince paused, sunk in thought.

'Why are you smiling at father's portrait again?' asked Rogozhin, intent on noting the least change in the prince's expression, however fleeting.

'Why was I smiling? Oh, it simply occurred to me that if this misfortune hadn't befallen you, if this love hadn't happened, you would really have turned out the image of your father and in short order too. You'd have settled down on your own in this house, with your obedient and silent wife, a man of a few stern words, trusting nobody and having no need to, just making money in dreary silence. At most, you'd have praised the old books now and again and taken an interest in crossing yourself with two fingers, and then only in your old age . . .'

'Be as sarcastic as you like. She was saying exactly the same thing recently when she was looking at that portrait! Amazing how you think alike about everything nowadays . . .'

'She hasn't been to see you has she?' asked the prince, curious.

'She has. She spent a long time looking at that picture, asking me about the old man. "You'd have been exactly like him", she smiled at me towards the end. "You're a man of violent passions, Parfion Semyonich, so violent you'd have been on your way to Siberia with them, the convicts, if you hadn't had a head on your shoulders. Because you have got a good mind", she says. That's what she said, do you believe me or not? It's the first time I've ever heard her say such a thing! "You'd have soon dropped all this foolery. Since you're totally uneducated, you'd start piling up money and you'd have settled down in this house like your father, along with your castrates; in fact you'd have gone over to their religion in the end and you'd become so fond of your money, you'd make ten million, not two, and die of starvation sitting on your money-bags, because for you passion is everything, and you make everything into a passion." That's exactly what she said, practically word for word. She's never spoken to me in that way before! She usually talks nonsense or scoffs at me; even this time she started by laughing, but later on she turned gloomy; she walked all over the house, inspecting everything; she seemed frightened of it. "I'll change everything", I said, "have it all redecorated, or maybe buy another house before the wedding." "On no account", says she. "Don't change anything here, this is how we're going to live. I want to live beside your mother, when I become your wife." I took her to see my mother and she was as respectful as if she had been her own daughter. My mother hasn't been altogether in her right mind for the last two years (she's an invalid), but after my father's death she got to be just like a baby, never utters a word: she can't walk and just bows from her chair to everyone she sees; it would take her three days to realize she hadn't been fed, I do believe. I took mother's right hand and folded it: "Bless her, mother, she's going to marry me"; so she kissed my mother's hand with emotion and said, "Your mother's had to bear much sorrow, hasn't she?" She caught sight of this book here: "Why've you started reading *Russian History*?" (It was she who told me herself once in Moscow: "You should try and educate yourself somehow, read Solovyov's *Russian History* at least; you really know nothing at all.") "That's good, carry on reading that", she says. "I'll write you out a list of what books you should read first of all—if you want me to, that is." She'd never ever spoken to me like that before, I was amazed; I breathed like a human being for the first time.'

'I'm very pleased about that, Parfion', said the prince, genuinely touched, 'very pleased. Who knows, perhaps God will bring you together after all.'

'That will never happen!' cried Rogozhin vehemently.

'Listen to me, Parfion, if you love her so much, surely you want to earn her respect? And if you want to do that, surely you must hope for a happy outcome? I said just now that it was a rare puzzle to me why she wanted to marry you. But even if I can't understand it, I'm certain there must be a sufficient rational reason for it. She's convinced of your love and she must be convinced of some of your good qualities too. It could hardly be otherwise! What you said just now confirmed it. You say yourself she found herself able to talk to you in quite a different way from her previous way of behaving and speaking. You're mistrustful and jealous, that's why you exaggerate everything bad you notice. Of course she can't possibly think so badly of you as you say. That would mean that she was deliberately risking drowning or stabbing by marrying you. How can that be? Who would deliberately court drowning or stabbing?'

Rogozhin listened to the prince's fervent words with a bitter smile.

'How grimly you're looking at me now, Parfion!' the prince burst out, painfully.

'Drowning or stabbing!' Rogozhin brought out at length. 'Ha!

That's the very reason she's marrying me, because the knife's surely waiting for her! Surely you've realized before now what all this is about?'

'I don't understand you.'

'Well, maybe you don't at that, heh-heh! They say you're . . . *that way*. She loves someone else—get that into your head! Just as I love her now, she loves another man now. And you know who that other is? It's you! Don't tell me you didn't know?'

'Me!'

'You. She's been in love with you ever since that party back then. It's just that she thinks she can't marry you because she'd bring shame on you and ruin your whole life. "Everybody knows what I am", says she. She keeps on saying that. She's kept telling me so straight to my face. She's afraid of shaming and destroying you, but it's all right with me, she can marry me—that's how much she thinks of me, remember that as well!'

'But then how could she run away from you to me and . . . from me . . .'

'And from you to me! Ha! Who knows what idea she'll take into her head all of a sudden! It's as if she were in a fever these days. First she's shouting at me: "I'll marry you and make an end of myself. Be quick and fix the wedding!" She's in a hurry to name the day, and as soon as the time draws near—she takes fright, or gets some other notion into her head—God knows, you've seen it yourself, haven't you: crying, laughing, shaking feverishly. It's hardly surprising she ran away from you, is it? She ran away from you before because she realized how much she loved you. She couldn't bear it after a while. You said just now that I sought her out in Moscow that time; it's not true—she ran away from you to me of her own accord: "Name the day", she says, "I'm ready! Let's have champagne! Let's away to the gypsies! . . ." she shouts. If it wasn't for me she'd have drowned herself long ago; I'm telling you the truth. The reason she hasn't thrown herself in is that I'm probably even worse than the water. She's marrying me out of spite . . . If she does, I'm telling you, it'll be *out of spite*.'

'But then how can you possibly . . . how can you . . .' the prince cried, unable to finish the sentence. He stared at Rogozhin in horror.

'Why don't you say it?' said Rogozhin, grinning. 'If you like I'll tell you what you're thinking to yourself this very minute: "Well, how on earth can she marry him now? How can I let her do it?" It's obvious what you're thinking . . .'

'I didn't come here because of that, Parfion, I tell you, it wasn't what I had in mind at all . . .'

'Maybe it wasn't what you came for or what you had in mind, but that's what it is now, heh-heh! Anyway, enough of this, why are you so upset? Didn't you really know? You amaze me!'

'All this is jealousy, Parfion, it's morbid, you're exaggerating it out of all proportion', murmured the prince, thoroughly agitated. 'What's the matter?'

'Leave that now', said Parfion, and quickly seized the small knife the prince had taken from the table next to the book and returned it to its former place.

'It was as if I knew when I was coming into Petersburg, as though I had a premonition . . .' the prince went on. 'I didn't want to come back here! I wanted to forget everything here, tear it out of my heart! Well then, goodbye . . . What's the matter now?'

As he spoke, the prince had absently picked up the knife again and once more Rogozhin took it from his hand and threw it on the table. It was a plain-looking knife, with a horn handle and fixed blade, some seven inches long and broad in proportion.

Seeing that the prince was taking particular note of the knife being snatched from his hand twice over, Rogozhin seized it with ill-tempered annoyance, placed it in the book, and flung the book on to another table.

'You cut pages with it, do you?' asked the prince, but somehow abstractedly, seemingly still sunk in profound meditation.

'Yes, the pages . . .'

'It's a garden knife, isn't it?'

'Yes it is. Can't I use a garden knife to cut pages with?'

'But it's . . . brand-new.'

'Well, what if it is? Surely I can buy a new knife now?' Rogozhin was shouting in a kind of frenzy, more exasperated with every word.

The prince started, and shot an intent glance at Rogozhin.

'Lord, listen to us!' he laughed suddenly, recollecting himself

completely. 'Forgive me, friend. When my head aches so and this
illness of mine . . . I get really absent-minded and silly. It wasn't
this I was going to ask you about at all . . . Can't recall what it
was. Goodbye . . .'

'Not that way', said Rogozhin.

'I've forgotten!'

'This way, this way, come, I'll show you.'

4

THEY passed through the same rooms the prince had already
traversed once, Rogozhin walking a little in front and the prince
following. They entered the great hall. Here there were several
pictures on the walls, all portraits of bishops or landscapes, of
which it was impossible to make anything out. Over the doorway
into the next room hung an oddly-shaped picture, some five feet
wide and no more than ten inches high. It depicted the Saviour,
just taken down from the cross. The prince gave it a cursory
glance as if it reminded him of something, but made to pass into
the next room without pausing. He felt very depressed and was
anxious to get out of this house as soon as possible. Rogozhin,
however, suddenly halted in front of the painting.

'All these pictures here', he said, 'were bought by my old dad
for a rouble or two in auctions. He was fond of them. An expert
looked them all over once: rubbish, he called them, but this—this
one over the door, wasn't rubbish, he said, though it cost two
roubles as well. The old man was offered three hundred and fifty
for it and the merchant Savelev, Ivan Dmitrich—he's keen on
art—went as high as four hundred. Last week he offered my
brother, Semyon Semyonich, five hundred. But I've kept it for
myself.'

'Yes it's . . . a copy of a Holbein', said the prince, having
managed to examine the painting. 'And though I'm no great
expert, it looks an excellent copy to me. I saw that picture abroad
and I can't forget it. But . . . what's the matter? . . .'

Rogozhin had suddenly lost interest in the painting and
resumed his former progress. Of course, his peremptory

behaviour could well be accounted for by preoccupation and the oddly irritable mood which had so suddenly manifested itself in him; all the same, it puzzled the prince somewhat that a conversation which he had not begun should have been so abruptly broken off, and that Rogozhin had not even answered him.

'Tell me, Lev Nikolayevich, I've been meaning to ask you for a long time, do you believe in God or not?' Rogozhin all of a sudden spoke again after walking on a few paces.

'That's an odd question . . . and your face! . . .' the prince couldn't help observing.

'I do love looking at that picture', muttered Rogozhin after a pause, having forgotten his question it seemed.

'That picture!' cried the prince, struck by a sudden thought. 'That picture! A man could lose his faith looking at that picture!'

'Yes, that's another thing going', Rogozhin confirmed surprisingly. By now they had reached the front door.

'What?' the prince halted at once. 'What do you mean? I was really just joking, but you're so serious! And why did you ask me whether I believed in God or not?'

'Oh, nothing, no reason. I've wanted to ask you before now. There are lots of unbelievers these days. Tell me, is it true (you've lived abroad after all) what a drunk chap told me, that in Russia there's more unbelievers than in other countries? He said it was easier for us than for them because we've gone further than they have . . .'

Rogozhin smiled sardonically; having posed his question, he swiftly opened the door and grasped the handle, waiting for the prince to go out. The prince, taken by surprise, did so. Rogozhin followed him on to the landing and closed the door behind him. They stood facing one another, looking as if they had both forgotten where they were and what they were supposed to do next.

'Goodbye, then', said the prince, holding out his hand.

'Goodbye', said Rogozhin, pressing the proffered hand firmly, but purely automatically.

The prince descended a step, then turned round.

'About faith', he said, smiling, clearly not wishing to leave Rogozhin in this fashion, brightening up, moreover, as a sudden recollection struck him. 'As regards faith, I had four separate encounters in two days last week. One morning I was travelling on one of the new railways and talked for four hours with somebody called S in the same carriage. We struck up an acquaintance on the spot. I'd heard a lot about him prior to that, including the fact that he was an atheist. He really is a very learned man and and I was glad to talk to a genuine scholar. Besides, he's extremely well-bred and talked to me as if I were his complete equal in knowledge and comprehension. He doesn't believe in God. One thing did strike me, though: the whole time, he didn't seem to be talking about that at all, and it struck me particularly because whenever I've met an unbeliever before and read their books, they invariably seemed to be talking and writing about something else, while appearing to stick to the issue at hand. That's what I told him at the time, but most likely didn't make myself clear or express myself properly, because he didn't understand at all . . . That evening I stayed the night in a country hotel where a murder had been committed the previous night, and everybody was talking about it when I arrived. Two elderly peasants, not drunk, who were friends and had known each other for years, had had their tea and proposed sleeping in the same room. One of them had noticed over the preceding two days that the other was wearing a silver watch on a yellow bead chain, which he had not seen on him before, apparently. This man was not a thief, in fact he was notably honest, and by peasant standards by no means poor. He was so taken by this watch, however, so tempted by it, that at length he couldn't control himself: he drew out his knife and, when his friend turned his back on him, came up warily behind him, took aim, and rolling his eyes up to heaven, crossed himself, saying a bitter prayer under his breath: "Lord forgive me for Christ's sake!" and cut his friend's throat with one stroke, like a sheep, and took his watch from him.'*

Rogozhin went off into peals of laughter. He was in paroxysms. It was strange indeed to see him laughing after his recent morose humour.

'Now that I like! No, but that beats everything', he cried convulsively, gasping for breath. 'One doesn't believe in God at all, and the other's so devout he cuts people's throats with a prayer . . . No, friend Prince, truth is stranger than fiction! Ha-ha-ha! No, that beats everything.'

'In the morning I went for a wander round the town', the prince went on as soon as Rogozhin had stopped laughing, though his lips still quivered spasmodically and convulsively. 'I saw a drunken soldier there, staggering about on the wooden pavement, looking totally confused. He came up to me: "Won't you buy this silver cross, sir? I'll let you have it for twenty kopecks. It's silver!" I saw he had a cross in his hand, on a worn blue ribbon, he must have just taken it off. You could see at a glance it was really tin, a sizeable, eight-pointed cross, the complete Byzantine pattern. I took out a twenty-kopeck piece and gave it to him and put the cross round my neck at once—I could see by his face how pleased he was to have cheated the foolish gentleman as he set off to drink the proceeds—that was certain. At that time, friend, I was quite carried away by all the impressions that had burst upon me in Russia. I had comprehended nothing of Russia before, as if I'd grown up speechless and had fantasies for memories during the five years I spent abroad. So I walked on, thinking no, I won't be too hasty in condemning this Christ-seller. Only God knows what is concealed in those weak and drunken hearts. An hour later, on my way back to the hotel, I chanced upon a peasant woman with a new-born baby. The woman was still young and the baby would be about six weeks. And the child smiled at her, for the first time since it was born, going by her expression. As I watched, she suddenly crossed herself as devoutly as could be. "What are you doing, my dear?" said I (I was always asking questions at that time). "Well, sir", she said, "just as a mother rejoices when she notices her baby smile for the first time, so does God rejoice every time he beholds from on high a sinner kneeling before him, praying with all his heart." This was what a simple peasant woman told me, in practically those words—a thought so profound, so subtle, so truly religious, comprehending the whole essence of Christianity, that is, the whole concept of God as our Father and of God rejoicing in man, like a father rejoicing in his child—the fundamental idea of Christ! An ordinary peasant woman! True, she was a mother . . . who knows, perhaps the wife of that soldier. Listen, Parfion, a few moments ago you asked me a question, and this is my answer: the essence of religious feeling has nothing to do with reasoning, or transgressions, or crimes, or atheism; it is something quite different and always will be, it is something our atheists will always gloss over and avoid discussing. The important thing, though, is that you will find it most quickly and clearly in a Russian heart, that's my conclusion! This is one of the chief convictions I've acquired in this Russia of ours. There are things to be done, Parfion! Believe me, there's work to be done in our Russian world! Remember how we used to get together in Moscow at one time . . . And, I certainly didn't want to come back here now! And I most certainly didn't dream of meeting you like this! . . . Well, there it is . . . Goodbye, *au revoir*! God be with you!'

He turned and went on down the stairs.

'Lev Nikolayevich!' cried Parfion from above, when the prince had reached the first half-landing. 'That cross, the one you bought from the soldier, have you got it on you?'

'Yes I have.'

And the prince halted again.

'Come up and show it to me.'

More odd behaviour! He thought for a moment, then walked upstairs and showed him the cross, without taking it from his neck.

'Give it to me', said Rogozhin.

'Why? Surely you're not . . .'

The prince was unwilling to part with the cross.

'I'll wear it and take mine off for you to wear.'

'You want to exchange crosses? By all means, Parfion, if that's what you wish I'm delighted. We'll be brothers!'

The prince took off his tin cross and Parfion his gold one and they exchanged them. Parfion was silent. The prince noticed with dismayed surprise that the old mistrust, the old bitter, almost sneering, smile still lingered on the face of the man he had called brother, or at least revealed itself intensely at moments. At length Rogozhin silently took the prince's arm and stood for a while, seemingly irresolute, then suddenly drew him after him, saying almost inaudibly: 'Come along!' They crossed the hall and rang the bell of the door opposite the one they had just left. It was speedily opened. A little old woman, all bent and dressed in black, with a kerchief on her head, bowed low to Rogozhin without speaking; he asked her something quickly and, without waiting for an answer, led the prince on through more rooms. Dark rooms succeeded one another, all of a singular, chill cleanliness and furnished with ancient furniture under clean white covers. Without being announced, Rogozhin conducted the prince straight into a small room, rather like a drawing-room, divided by a polished mahogany partition with a door at each end, behind which, doubtless, lay the bedroom. In the corner of the drawing-room, by the stove, a little old woman was sitting in an armchair, actually not looking as old as all that, with her rather healthy, round, pleasant face, but her hair was quite white and it could be seen at a glance that she had lapsed into her second childhood. She wore a black woollen dress with a large black kerchief round her neck, and had a clean white cap on with black ribbons. Her feet were resting on a footstool. Close by her was another clean old lady, no doubt some poor relation, a little older than her, also dressed in mourning and a white cap, who was silently knitting a stocking. Both of them were habitually silent, no doubt. The first old lady, catching sight of Rogozhin and the prince, smiled at them and inclined her head affectionately several times to indicate pleasure.

'Mother', said Rogozhin, kissing her hand, 'this is my great friend, Prince Lev Nikolayevich Myshkin; we've exchanged crosses; he was like my own brother to me in Moscow at one time, and did a lot for me. Bless him mother, as if he were your own son. Wait old lady, that's it, let me put your fingers right . . .'

But before Parfion could take hold of her, the old lady put three fingers together and devoutly crossed the prince three times. Then she nodded to him in tender affection.

'Well then, let's go, Lev Nikolayevich', said Parfion. 'I only brought you here for that . . .'

When they were out on the stairway again, he added:

'She doesn't understand anything people say you know, and didn't realize what I said, but she blessed you all the same, which means she wanted to . . . Well, goodbye then, time for both of us to part.'

And he opened his own door.

'Well, let me embrace you at least for heaven's sake before I go, you strange creature!' the prince cried, looking at him in affectionate reproach as he made to embrace him. But no sooner had Parfion raised his arms than he let them fall again. He could not bring himself to do it; he turned away so as not to look at the prince. He didn't want to embrace him.

'Don't worry! I may have taken your cross but I won't cut your throat for your watch!' he muttered thickly, unaccountably breaking into an odd abrupt laugh. Then, all of a sudden, his face became transformed: he went terribly pale, his lips trembled, and his eyes blazed. He raised his arms, warmly clasped the prince, and spoke breathlessly:

'Well take her then if that's how it is to be! She's yours! I give way! . . . Remember Rogozhin!'

And abandoning the prince, he hurried in and slammed the door behind him.

5

I⊤ was already late, almost half-past two, and the prince failed to catch General Yepanchin at home. Leaving his card, he resolved to go to The Scales hotel and ask for Kolya—and leave him a note if he wasn't there. At the hotel he was told that Nikolai Ardalionovich had 'gone out this morning, sir, but on his departure had let it be known that should anyone come asking for him, he would perhaps be back by three o'clock, sir. If he were not here by half-past three, it would mean he had taken the train to Pavlovsk and Madame Yepanchina's villa, sir, and would be eating there, sir.' The prince sat down to wait, and as he was there, ordered lunch.

Kolya had still not appeared by half-past three or even four o'clock. The prince went out and set off automatically, following his nose. In Petersburg in early summer there can be delightful days sometimes—still, bright, and very warm. As luck would have it, this particular day was one of those. The prince wandered aimlessly about for some time. He was not very familiar with the city. He would halt occasionally at street intersections, in front of houses, or in the squares or on bridges; once he dropped into a confectioner's to have a rest. Sometimes he would fall to studying the passers-by with considerable curiosity, but for the most part he took no notice either of them or of where he was going. He was in an agony of tension and anxiety, and at the same time he felt a profound craving for solitude. He wanted to be alone and surrender quite passively to this agonizing sense of strain, without seeking the smallest abatement. He loathed the idea of trying to resolve the questions that flooded his mind and heart. 'All this isn't my fault, is it?' he kept muttering to himself, almost unaware of what he was saying.

By six o'clock he found himself on the platform of the Tsarskoye Selo station. Solitude had soon become intolerable to him; a fresh impulse of warmth had seized his heart, and for an instant the darkness in which his soul was languishing became brightly lit. He bought a ticket to Pavlovsk and was impatient to be off, but of course he was being followed, and it was reality, not the fantasy he had perhaps been inclined to think it. Almost in the act of boarding the train, he abruptly threw the ticket he had just purchased on to the ground and walked out of the station, bemused and deep in thought. A little while later, in the street, he suddenly seemed to recall something, suddenly become aware of a very odd circumstance which had long been troubling him. He caught himself in an action he had been repeating for a considerable time, but which he had not noticed till that moment: for several hours now, even in The Scales, or before that even, he would abruptly start looking every now and then for something in his vicinity. He would forget about it for long intervals, half an hour or more, then suddenly look about him again, anxiously searching.

No sooner had he become aware of this morbid, and hitherto quite unconscious, movement which had possessed him for so long, than he was suddenly struck by another recollection, one he found intensely intriguing: it came to him that at the very moment when he became aware that he was searching for something in his vicinity, he had been standing on the pavement in front of a shop-window, inspecting the goods on sale with eager curiosity. He now felt he had to find out for certain whether he really had been standing in front of that shop-window, perhaps a matter of five minutes ago, or whether he had imagined it or got it mixed up with something else. Did the shop and its contents even exist? After all, he did feel particularly unwell today, almost as he used to feel when an attack of his old illness was coming on. He knew that in this preliminary stage he could be extremely absent-minded, and often mixed up things and people if he didn't pay them particularly close attention. But there was also a particular reason why he was suddenly so bent on verifying whether he had stood in front of the shop: among the items on display there was one which he had looked at and even estimated at sixty silver kopecks—he remembered it, notwithstanding all his anxiety and vacancy of mind. It followed that if the shop really existed and the object was actually on display, it was because of that object he had stopped. That meant the thing held such an overwhelming interest for him that it had attracted his attention at the very time when he had been in such a wretched state of confusion after just emerging from the railway station. He walked back, glancing to his right, almost in anguish, his heart pounding in nervous impatience. But here was the shop, he'd found it at last! He had been a quarter of a mile away when the thought of returning had occurred to him. And there was the sixty-kopeck object; 'sixty kopecks of course, couldn't be more!' he confirmed, and began to laugh. It was a hysterical laugh, however; he felt extremely wretched. He now clearly recalled that it was on this very spot, standing in front of this window, that he had turned round, as he had earlier that day when he had caught Rogozhin's eyes upon him. Convinced now that he had not been mistaken (actually he had been quite sure, even before checking) he left the shop and made haste to get away from it. All this certainly needed thinking over; it was clear now that he hadn't been imagining things at the station either—something assuredly linked to all the disquiet he had been feeling really had happened. And yet a kind of overwhelming inner revulsion once more overcame him: he had no desire to think the matter through, and he didn't; he fell to thinking about something else entirely.

He pondered, among other things, the fact that there was a stage in his epileptic condition just before the fit itself (if it occurred during waking hours) when all of a sudden, amid the sadness, spiritual darkness, and oppression, there were moments when his brain seemed to flare up momentarily and all his vital forces tense themselves at once in an extraordinary surge. The sensation of being alive and self-aware increased almost tenfold in those lightning-quick moments. His mind and heart were bathed in an extraordinary illumination. All his agitation, all his doubts and anxieties, seemed to be instantly reconciled and resolved into a lofty serenity, filled with pure, harmonious gladness and hope, filled too with the consciousness of the ultimate cause of all things. But these moments, these flashes, were merely the prelude to that final second (never more than a second) which marked the onset of the actual fit. That second was, of course, unendurable. Reflecting on that moment afterwards when he had recovered, he often used to tell himself that all these gleams and lightning-flashes of heightened self-awareness, and hence also of 'higher existence', were nothing more than the illness itself, violating the normal state of things as it did, and thus it was not a higher mode of existence at all—on the contrary, it should be regarded as the lowest. And yet he arrived at length at a paradoxical conclusion: 'What if it is the illness then?' he decided finally. 'What does it matter if it is some abnormal tension, if the end-result, the instant of apprehension, recalled and analysed during recovery, turns out to be the highest pitch of harmony and beauty, conferring a sense of some hitherto-unknown and unguessed completeness, proportion, reconciliation, an ecstatic, prayerful fusion with the supreme synthesis of life?' These nebulous expressions seemed perfectly comprehensible to him, though still inadequate. But that it really was 'beauty and prayer', that it really was 'the supreme synthesis of life', this he could not doubt, or even admit the possibility of doubt. These were no weird figments brought on by hashish, opium, or wine, degrading the intellect and distorting the soul. He could judge that soberly once the fit was over. These moments were purely and simply an intense heightening of self-awareness, if he had to express his state in a word, self-awareness and, at the same time, the most direct sense of one's own existence taken to the highest degree. If in that second, in the final conscious moment before the attack, he could have managed to tell himself clearly and deliberately: 'Yes, for this moment one could give one's whole life!' then of course, that moment on its own would be worth one's whole life. He did not insist on the dialectical part of his argument, however: stupor, spiritual darkness, and idiocy stood before him as the plain consequence of those 'supreme moments'. He would not have argued the point seriously. There was doubtless some flaw in his conclusion, that is, in his assessment of the moment, but the reality of the sensation troubled him, all the same. What could one do with this reality then? After all, the thing had happened before, he had managed to tell himself in that second that for the profound experience of infinite happiness, it might be worth his whole life. 'At that moment', as he had once told Rogozhin in the course of their Moscow encounters, 'at that moment I seem to understand the strange phrase, "there should be time no longer". Most likely', he added with a smile, 'it was the same second in which the epileptic Mahomet's overturned water-jug failed to spill a drop, while he contrived to behold all the mansions of Allah.' Yes, in Moscow he had met Rogozhin frequently and they had talked of much else besides this. 'Rogozhin said this morning that I had been a brother to him then; today was the first time he ever said that', mused the prince.

He was thinking about that while sitting on a bench under a tree in the Summer Gardens. It was about seven o'clock. The gardens were deserted; a darkness obscured the setting sun for a moment. It was sultry; it looked as if a thunderstorm was brewing somewhere in the distance. His present mood of contemplation held a certain charm for him. His mind and memory clung to every external object and gave him pleasure: he kept longing to forget something, the present, the actual, but a glance round him recalled his bleak thoughts to him again at once, the thoughts he wanted so much to escape. He remembered talking at lunch to the waiter at the inn about an extraordinarily strange murder which had taken place recently and caused a sensation and given rise to a great deal of talk. But no sooner had he recalled this when once again something peculiar happened to him.

A sudden intense, overwhelming desire seized his will, a temptation almost. He got up from his bench and went out of the gardens, heading straight for the Petersburg Side.* A short time before he had asked a passer-by on the Neva Embankment to point out the Petersburg Side to him across the river. He had done so but the prince had not gone there. In any case there was no point in doing so today; he knew that. He had known the address long enough; he could easily have found the house of Lebedev's kinswoman, but he knew almost for a certainty that he wouldn't find her at home. 'She's surely gone to Pavlovsk, or Kolya would have left a message at The Scales as arranged.' So if he was going there now it was not because he expected to see her, of course. It was a different dark, tormenting curiosity that was luring him on now. A new thought had struck him all of a sudden . . .

But for him it was more than sufficient to have set off and to know where he was going: a minute later he was walking along once more, almost oblivious to his surroundings. To consider his 'sudden thought' any further seemed at once utterly revolting and virtually unthinkable. He stared at everything that chanced to meet his eye in an agony of strained attention; he looked at the sky and at the Neva. He spoke to a small child he encountered. Perhaps the epileptic state was becoming more and more acute. The storm really did seem slowly to be drawing slowly closer. Distant thunder could be heard. It was getting very oppressive . . .

For some obscure reason he kept remembering Lebedev's nephew, the one he had seen that morning, just as sometimes one can't get some persistent and stupidly tiresome snatch of music out of one's head. It was odd that he should keep remembering him in the guise of the murderer that Lebedev himself had mentioned when introducing him. Yes, he had read about that murderer just lately. He had read and heard a lot about such cases since his return to Russia; he followed all that sort of thing with keen interest. He'd got rather carried away in his chat with the waiter about this very Zhemarin murder. The waiter had agreed with him, he remembered that. He recalled the waiter too; he was a grave and discreet lad, not lacking in intelligence. Still, 'Lord alone knows what he's like really, it's hard to make out new people in a new country.' He was beginning to believe passionately in the Russian soul, however. Oh, how much, how very much had he been through in these six months that to him was totally new and unexpected, previously unheard of and unguessed! But a stranger's soul is a dark mystery, the Russian soul is a dark mystery—a mystery to many. He had long been friends with Rogozhin for instance, close friends, 'brothers'—but did he know Rogozhin? Anyway, what a hideous, chaotic muddle it all was at times! And what a revoltingly complacent pimple that nephew of Lebedev's was! Still, what am I saying? The prince went on musing, he didn't kill those creatures, those six people, did he? I'm getting things mixed up . . . very strange! I feel rather dizzy . . . and what a dear, sweet face Lebedev's elder daughter has, the one standing up with the baby, so innocent, her childlike expression and laughter! Odd that he'd almost forgotten that face and only now brought it to mind. Lebedev probably adored them all as he stamped his foot at them. What was as certain as two plus two, was that Lebedev adored his nephew as well!

In any case, who on earth was he to weigh them in the balance and pronounce sentence, he who had just arrived that morning? Lebedev had set him a problem today and no mistake: had he expected a Lebedev like that? He hadn't known a Lebedev like this before, had he? Lebedev and Du Barry, good heavens! Anyway, if Rogozhin committed murder he wouldn't make such a mess of it. None of this chaos about it. Murder weapon made to order and six people butchered in a frenzy! Rogozhin didn't have a specially ordered weapon, did he? . . . He had . . . but . . . was it certain Rogozhin would kill?! The prince gave a sudden start. 'Isn't it criminal and base of me to assume such a thing with such open cynicism!' he exclaimed, and his face at once flooded with colour from very shame. He was astonished and stood transfixed on the road. He at once recalled the Pavlovsk and Nikolayevsky stations and his blunt question to Rogozhin about the eyes, and Rogozhin's cross, which he was wearing now, and his mother's blessing, which Rogozhin had arranged himself, and his last convulsive embrace and final renunciation just now on the stairs—and after all that to catch himself perpetually on the look-out for something, and that shop and the item in the window . . . how sordid it was! And after all that, here he was walking along with his 'special purpose' and this particular 'sudden idea' of his! Despair and grief seized his soul. He wanted to turn back to the hotel at once; he actually did turn back and start walking, but he halted after a minute, reflected, and resumed his former direction.

After all, he was already on the Petersburg Side, close to the house; and he wasn't going there with his former purpose, not his 'sudden idea'! How could that be? Yes, his illness was coming back, there could be no doubt about it; he might have a fit this very day. It was the fit that was bringing on all these dark imaginings, the 'idea'! Now the darkness was dissipated, the demon banished; doubt did not exist, there was gladness in his heart! And—he hadn't seen her for so long, he had to see her, and . . . yes, he would have liked to meet Rogozhin now, he would take his hand and they would go together . . . His heart was pure; how could he be Rogozhin's rival? Tomorrow he would go to Rogozhin himself and tell him he had seen her; after all, hadn't he flown here that day, as Rogozhin had said that morning, for the sole purpose of seeing her! Perhaps he would even find her at home—it wasn't certain that she was in Pavlovsk, was it?

Yes, everything had to be brought into the open now, so that everyone could read one another's thoughts clearly, no more of these gloomy, emotional renunciations like Rogozhin's, let it all come about freely and . . . in the light. Rogozhin could stand the light, couldn't he? He had said he didn't love her that way, that he had no pity, 'no compassion of that sort'. True, he had added that 'your compassion may be stronger than my love', but he wasn't being fair to himself. Hmm, Rogozhin at his book—wasn't this 'compassion', the beginnings of 'compassion?' Didn't the very presence of that book demonstrate that he was fully aware of his attitude to her? And his story that afternoon? That was much deeper than mere infatuation. Did her face inspire only infatuation? Could even that face inspire passion now? It inspired suffering, it overwhelmed your soul, it . . . a searing, agonizing recollection passed through the prince's heart.

Agonizing, yes. He remembered the recent agony he had gone through when he had first begun to notice the marks of madness in her. He had almost been in despair. How could he have abandoned her when she fled from him to Rogozhin? He should have pursued her, not waited for news of her. But . . . surely Rogozhin had noticed the signs of insanity in her by now? Hmm . . . Rogozhin saw different reasons for everything, passionate reasons! And such insane jealousy! What did he mean by his offer that morning? (The prince blushed all of a sudden and his heart seemed to tremble within him.)

Why bring that up anyway? There was madness on both sides. For him, the prince, to love that woman passionately was virtually unthinkable. It would be almost tantamount to cruelty, inhumanity. Yes, yes! Rogozhin had not been fair to himself; he had a great heart, capable of suffering and compassion. When he learnt the whole truth and when he was convinced what a pitiful creature that broken, half-demented woman was, wouldn't he forgive her all that had passed, all the torment he had suffered? Would he not become her servant, brother, friend, guardian angel? Compassion would instruct even Rogozhin and lend purpose to his existence. Compassion was the most important, perhaps the sole law of human existence. Oh, how he had wronged Rogozhin, it was ignoble and unpardonable! No, it was not the Russian soul that was a dark mystery—the darkness was in his own soul, if he was capable of imagining such horror. For a few fervent and heartfelt words in Moscow, Rogozhin was calling him brother and he . . . But this was illness, raving! It would all be resolved! . . . How grimly Rogozhin had spoken that morning about 'losing his faith'. That man must be suffering terribly. He said he 'liked looking at that picture'; it wasn't that he liked it, he sensed a need to look at it. Rogozhin wasn't just a passionate soul, he was a warrior; he wanted to bring back his lost faith by force. He felt an agonizing need for it now . . . Yes! To believe in something! In someone! How strange that Holbein picture was though . . . Ah, this is the street! That must be the house—yes, number 16, 'house of collegiate secretary Filisova'. Here we are! The prince rang and asked for Nastasya Filippovna.

The lady of the house told him herself that Nastasya Filippovna had left for Darya Alexeyevna's in Pavlovsk that morning, 'and it might even be, sir, that she would stay there for several days' . . . Filisova was a small, fortyish woman, sharp-eyed and sharp-featured, with a keen and crafty look. To her request for his name—a request to which she deliberately imparted an air of mystery—the prince initially declined to reply, but at once returned and earnestly besought her to give his name to Nastasya Filippovna. Filisova responded to this earnestness with redoubled attention and an air of deep secrecy by which she clearly meant to convey: 'Don't worry, I understand, sir.' The prince's name had obviously created the most tremendous impression. He looked absently at her, then turned round and walked back towards his hotel. He left, however, with a different expression from when he had rung the bell. Once again an extraordinary change had come over him, almost instantly: once again he looked pale, debilitated, grief-stricken and overwrought; his knees shook and a vague, forlorn smile played about his blueish lips: his 'sudden idea' had all at once been confirmed and justified—and he believed in his demon again!

But had it been confirmed? Had it been justified? Why this trembling again, this cold sweat, this spiritual darkness and chill? Was it because he had seen those eyes again just now? But he had walked out of the Summer Gardens with the sole intention of seeing them! That was the essence of his 'sudden idea', after all. He had been extremely anxious to see those 'eyes of this morning' so as to be convinced, once and for all, that he would certainly encounter them there at the house. That had been his shuddering desire, so why on earth was he so crushed and amazed at having actually seen them? As if he hadn't expected it! Yes, they were the same eyes (that they *were* the same there could no longer be the slightest doubt), which had glittered at him in the crowd that morning when he had got off the Moscow train at the Nikolayevsky station; they were the same (definitely the same!) he had sensed behind his shoulders when he was sitting down at Rogozhin's that morning. Rogozhin had denied it: he had enquired, with his chilling, lopsided smile: 'Whose eyes were they then?' And just a while ago, when he had been catching the Pavlovsk train at Tsarskoye Selo station to go and see Aglaya and had suddenly glimpsed those eyes again, for the third time that day, the prince had felt a strong urge to go up to Rogozhin and say to him 'whose eyes were they then?' But he had fled from the station and recovered himself only when he was standing in front of the cutler's shop and pricing a certain item with a hartshorn handle at sixty kopecks. The strange and horrible demon had seized upon him for good and did not mean to leave him. This demon had whispered to him in the Summer Gardens, as he sat oblivious under the lime-tree, that if Rogozhin had been so intent on keeping him under observation and dogging his steps since early morning, then, when he found out that the prince had not gone to Pavlovsk (which would have been fateful news for Rogozhin) he would most certainly go to that house on the Petersburg Side and lie in wait for him there, for the prince who had given his word only that morning that he 'would not see her' and 'that was not the reason he had come to Petersburg'. And here was the prince rushing off avidly to that very house, and what if he really did encounter Rogozhin there? He had seen only an unhappy man, whose state of mind was gloomy but perfectly comprehensible. This unhappy man wasn't even hiding himself now. Yes, that morning Rogozhin had denied it and told a lie, but he had been standing at the station practically without concealment. It was more the case that it was he, the prince, who had been hiding himself rather than Rogozhin. And now, at the house, he was standing on the pavement across the street, barely fifty yards away, with his arms folded, waiting. There he was in full view and deliberately so, it seemed. He was standing like an accuser, a judge, not like . . . not like what?

And why on earth hadn't he, the prince, gone up to him just now, of his own accord, and then turned aside as if noticing nothing, although their eyes would have met? (Yes, their eyes met—and they looked at one another!) Hadn't he just now wanted to take his arm and go there with him? Hadn't he wanted to go and see him next day and tell him he had been with her? Hadn't he renounced his demon half-way there, when his soul had suddenly filled with joy? Or was there really something in Rogozhin, that is in the whole aspect of the man that day, in the sum of his words, movements, actions, which might justify the prince's dreadful forebodings and the outrageous whisperings of his demon? Something that was obvious, but hard to analyse and articulate, impossible to justify by sufficient reasoning, but which, however difficult or impossible, created a completely overwhelming impression, leading inevitably to total conviction? . . .

Conviction of what? (Oh, how the monstrous 'humiliation' of this conviction, 'this vile foreboding', tormented the prince, and how he blamed himself for it!) 'Tell me, if you dare, of what?' he asked himself incessantly, challenging and reproachful— 'Formulate it, dare to express all you think, clearly, precisely, without hesitation! Oh, how dishonourable I am!'—he kept repeating indignantly, his colour rising. 'After this, how can I look this man in the face for the rest of my life! Oh, what a day! God, what a nightmare!'

There was a moment at the end of that long and tormenting walk back from the Petersburg Side, when the prince was suddenly seized by an irresistible urge—to go to Rogozhin's house that very minute, wait for him, embrace him with tears and remorse, tell him everything, and put an immediate end to all this. But he was already standing in front of his hotel . . . How he had disliked the place this morning, these corridors, the whole building, his room, from the very first moment; several times that day the thought of having to come back here had filled him with a peculiar revulsion . . . 'Why on earth do I believe in all sorts of premonitions today, like some sick woman?' he thought, grimacing irritably as he halted in the gateway. A new, unbearable wave of shame, verging on despair, froze him to the spot at the very entrance. He stopped for a moment. It happens to people sometimes: unbearable sudden recollections, especially if shame is involved, usually halt them for a moment on the spot. 'Yes, I'm a man without a heart, and a coward!' he repeated cheerlessly, and moved jerkily forward only to stop dead again.

The gateway, dark at any time, was particularly so at that moment: the looming thunder-cloud had engulfed the evening light and opened up just as the prince was approaching the building: the rain fairly poured down. As he jerked forward after his momentary pause, he had been just inside the gates where they opened on to the street. All of a sudden he glimpsed a man in the semi-darkness within the gates, just by the steps. The man seemed to be waiting for something, but quickly flitted from view and disappeared. The prince hadn't been able to get a good look at him, and of course couldn't say for certain who he was. Besides, any number of people could have passed through the gates; it was a hotel and there was lots of coming and going into the corridors and back. Nevertheless, he had a sudden total and overwhelming conviction that he had recognized the man and that it was certainly Rogozhin. An instant later, the prince rushed after him up the steps. His heart stood still. 'It will all be decided now!' he said to himself, with an odd certainty.

The steps up which the prince ran from the gateway led to the corridors on the ground and first floors, along which lay the hotel rooms. The staircase, as in all old buildings, was of stone. Dark and narrow, it spiralled round a thick stone pillar. On the first half-landing there was a niche-like recess in this pillar, no more than a pace wide and half that deep. There was room for a man in there, however. In spite of the darkness, the prince, as he ran up on to the landing, at once made out someone hiding there in the recess for some reason. The prince had a sudden impulse to go on past without glancing to his right. He took one step but then couldn't help turning round.

The two eyes of that morning—the selfsame eyes—suddenly encountered his own. The man hiding in the recess was also able to take a step outside. They stood facing one another for a second, almost touching. Then the prince abruptly seized him by the shoulder and turned him back towards the staircase, nearer to the light: he wanted a closer look at the face.

Rogozhin's eyes glittered and a manic smile distorted his features. His right hand rose and something flashed in it; the prince did not think of stopping him. All he remembered was apparently shouting:

'Parfion, I don't believe it!'

Then all at once everything seemed to open up before him: an extraordinary inner light flooded his soul. That instant lasted, perhaps, half a second, yet he clearly and consciously remembered the beginning, the first sound of a dreadful scream which burst from his chest of its own accord and which no effort of his could have suppressed. Then consciousness was extinguished instantly and total darkness came upon him.

He had suffered an epileptic fit, the first for a very long time. As is well known, attacks of epilepsy, the notorious falling sickness, occur instantaneously. In that one instant the face suddenly becomes horribly contorted, especially the eyes. Spasms and convulsions rack the entire body and all the facial features. A frightful, unimaginable scream, quite unlike anything else, bursts from the chest; it seems as if everything human is annihilated in that scream, and it is quite impossible, or at least very difficult, for the observer to imagine or concede that it is the man himself who is screaming. One even gets the impression that it is someone else screaming inside the body of the man. At least that is how many people have described their impressions; the sight of a man in an epileptic paroxysm fills many another with a positive and unbearable horror, having something of the mystical about it. It must be presumed that it was this impression of sudden horror, accompanied as it was by all the other terrible emotions of that moment, which paralysed Rogozhin, so saving the prince from the inescapable blow of the knife which was descending upon him. Then, before he had time to realize that it was a fit, seeing that the prince had reeled away from him and suddenly fallen backwards down the stairs, striking his head violently against a stone step, Rogozhin rushed headlong past the prostrate body and fled from the hotel, scarcely aware of what he was doing.

Thrashing and writhing in spasmodic convulsions, the body of the stricken man slithered down the steps, no more than fifteen, to the foot of the staircase. Very soon, within about five minutes, someone noticed him lying there and a crowd gathered. A whole pool of blood near his head caused puzzlement: had the man hurt himself, or had there been 'foul play'? Soon, however, some of them recognized the signs of epilepsy; one of the hotel guests identified the prince as a recent arrival. The general dismay was most happily resolved at length by a fortunate circumstance.

Kolya Ivolgin, who had promised to be back at The Scales by four o'clock, but had instead gone to Pavlovsk, had on a sudden impulse declined lunch at Madame Yepanchina's, returned to Petersburg, and hurried back to The Scales where he arrived at around seven o'clock. Learning from the prince's note that he was in Petersburg, he made his way quickly to the address given. On being informed at the hotel that the prince had gone out, he went down to the dining-room to wait for him there, having tea and listening to the organ. Overhearing by chance that someone had had a fit, a well-founded presentiment made him rush to the spot, where he recognized the prince. The necessary measures were taken at once. The prince was carried to his room; though he had regained consciousness, he did not fully come to himself for a long time. A doctor summoned to examine his head injury prescribed a lotion and declared that there was not the smallest danger to life. When, an hour later, the prince finally began to be aware of what was going on around him to a large extent, Kolya took him from the hotel to Lebedev, who received him with extraordinary warmth and much bowing. For the prince's sake he brought forward his journey to the country, and three days later they were all in Pavlovsk.

6

LEBEDEV'S villa was not large, but it was comfortable and even pretty. The part to be let had been specially embellished. On the rather spacious veranda by the street entrance, a number of orange, lemon, and jasmine trees had been placed in large, green, wooden tubs, which in Lebedev's opinion gave the house a most seductive appearance. Some of these trees had been acquired along with the villa, and he was so taken by the effect they produced on the veranda that he resolved to take the opportunity of purchasing some more in an auction. When all the shrubs had at length been brought to the villa and placed in position, Lebedev ran down the veranda steps into the street several times to admire his property from there, each time mentally increasing the sum he proposed to ask from his future tenant. Enfeebled, despondent, and exhausted though he was, the prince liked the villa very much. Actually, on the day he arrived in Pavlovsk, the third day, that is, after his attack, the prince to all appearances was almost well again, though inwardly he still felt far from recovered. Over those three days he had been glad to see everyone around him—Kolya, who hardly quitted his side, the Lebedev family (without the nephew, who had disappeared somewhere), and Lebedev himself: he had even been pleased to receive a visit from General Ivolgin while he was still in Petersburg. On the very day of his arrival, towards evening, quite a number of visitors collected round him on the veranda: Ganya was the first to arrive, though the prince barely recognized him, so much had he altered and grown thinner. Then Varya and Ptitsyn turned up, being Pavlovsk villa-residents themselves. General Ivolgin, for his part, was practically a permanent guest of Lebedev, apparently even travelling with him to Pavlovsk. Lebedev was trying to confine him to his own quarters and not allow him access to the prince, though he was on friendly terms with him and they had evidently known one another for some long time. The prince noticed that over the three days they would occasionally hold long discussions, quite often shouting and arguing, even about intellectual topics, and that this afforded Lebedev a good deal of pleasure. It almost seemed as if he couldn't do without the general. Ever since their arrival in Pavlovsk, Lebedev had observed the same precautions with regard to his own family, however, as he did with the general; on the pretext of not disturbing the prince, he would not allow anyone to see him, stamping his feet, rushing at his daughters, and chasing after them. Even Vera and the baby were not excepted, if there was the least suspicion that they were heading for the prince's terrace—this despite all the latter's requests that no one was to be sent away.

'In the first place, it would lead to a total lack of respect if they were allowed to do as they liked, and secondly, it would be positively unseemly for them . . .' Lebedev explained in answer to the prince's blunt question.

'But why on earth not?' the prince appealed to him. 'Really, you're only worrying me with all this supervision and watching over me. I get bored on my own, I've told you that several times, and your waving your arms about and going round on tiptoe depresses me even more.'

The prince was hinting that, despite chasing everyone else in the house away on the pretext that the patient had to be left in peace and quiet, Lebedev himself had been coming in practically every minute for the last three days, each time opening the door, poking his head round, and surveying the room as if to make sure the prince was still there and hadn't run away. Then, slow and stealthy, he would tiptoe over to the armchair, sometimes unwittingly startling his tenant. He kept enquiring whether he needed anything, and when the prince began at length to point out that he wanted to be left in peace, he would turn round submissively and make his silent way to the door on tiptoe, waving his arms all the time as he walked, as if to say he had just looked in, wouldn't say a word, had gone out, look, and wouldn't be back. And yet ten minutes later, or quarter of an hour at most, he would turn up again. Kolya's free access to the prince pained

Lebedev most profoundly, prompting him to aggrieved resentment. Kolya noticed that Lebedev listened at the door to what
they were saying for half an hour at a time, and of course he
informed the prince of it.

'You're acting as if I belonged to you, keeping me under lock
and key like this', protested the prince. 'I want things to be
different, at least while I'm in the country; let me assure you that
I will receive whomever I like and go wherever I like.'

'Without the slightest shadow of doubt', Lebedev waved his
arms.

The prince looked him up and down keenly.

'Well now, Lukyan Timofeyevich, have you brought that little
safe of yours with you to Pavlovsk, the one that used to hang over
your bed?'

'No, I haven't.'

'You haven't left it there have you?'

'I couldn't fetch it. I would have had to wrench it out of the
wall . . . solidly fixed, solid.'

'But you've likely got another one here just like it?'

'Even better, even better, that's why I bought this villa.'

'Aha. And who was it you didn't let in to see me earlier on? An
hour ago?'

'That . . . that was the general, sir. It's true I kept him out. He
shouldn't come. I hold the man in high regard, Prince; he's . . . a
great man, sir; you don't believe me? Well, you'll see, but still . . .
it would be best if you didn't receive him, sir, most illustrious
Prince.'

'And why not, pray? And why is it, Lebedev, that you're
standing on tiptoe at this moment and always come up to me as if
you had some secret to whisper in my ear?'

'I'm vile, vile, I feel it', responded Lebedev unexpectedly,
thumping his chest in emotion, 'but wouldn't the general be too
munificent for you, sir?'

'Too munificent?'

'Yes, sir. In the first place he proposes to come and live with
me; that's nothing, sir, but he's so impetuous he wants to be part
of the family straight away. We've worked out the family tree
several times and it turns out we're related. It seems you're also
some sort of nephew of his on your mother's side. If you are his

nephew, then it follows that you and I are related, most illustrious Prince. It doesn't signify at all, sir, a trifling weakness of his, but he was assuring me just now that every day since he was an ensign, up to the eleventh of June last year, he never had fewer than two hundred sitting down to dine every day. It got so that they never rose from the table, which means that they had lunch and dinner and drank tea for fifteen hours out of the twenty-four for thirty years on end without the slightest break, except for changing the tablecloth. As one would get up and leave, another would arrive, and on holidays and royal birthdays the numbers rose to three hundred. At the Russian millennial celebrations, he counted seven hundred. That's frightful, sir, isn't it? Stories like that are a very bad indication, sir; even letting such open-handed folk in the house makes one nervous and I thought, wouldn't he be too hospitable for you and me?'

'But you seem to be on such good terms with him.'

'Like brothers, but I treat it all as a joke; if we are kinfolk, so much the more honour for me. I can see he's a most remarkable man, despite those two hundred persons at dinner and the Russian millennium. I really mean it, sir. You spoke of secrets just now, Prince—that is, I come up to you as if I had a secret to impart; and as a matter of fact I have: a certain lady has just let me know that she would like to meet you in secret.'

'Why on earth secret? By no means. I'll go and see her myself, today even.'

'Oh by no means, by no means', Lebedev waved his arms, 'and she isn't afraid of what you're thinking either. By the way, that monster comes round every single day asking after your health, do you know that?'

'You call him a monster a little too often. It makes me very suspicious.'

'There's no need to harbour any suspicions at all, sir, none at all', Lebedev hastened to head this off. 'I was simply trying to explain that the certain lady was not afraid of him, but of something else, something else entirely.'

'Afraid of what then, go on, tell me', demanded the prince impatiently, watching Lebedev's mysterious grimacings.

'That's the secret.'

And Lebedev grinned.

'Whose secret?'

'Yours. You forbade me yourself, most illustrious Prince, to mention it in your presence . . .', murmured Lebedev, thoroughly enjoying the process of arousing his listener's curiosity to an agony of impatience before abruptly concluding: She's afraid of Aglaya Ivanovna.'

The prince frowned and was silent for a moment.

'Really, Lebedev, I shall give up this villa of yours', he said abruptly. 'Where are Gavrila Ardalionovich and the Ptitsyns? Are they with you? Have you lured them away as well?'

'They're coming, sir, they're coming. Even the general. I'll open all the doors and call my daughters in too—everybody, everybody, at once, at once', Lebedev whispered in alarm, waving his arms about and rushing from one door to another.

At that moment, Kolya turned up on the veranda, coming in from the street, and announced that visitors were following him, Madame Yepanchina and her three daughters.

'Shall I let the Ptitsyns and Gavrila Ardalionovich in or not? Let the general in or not?' Lebedev came hurrying up, stunned by this news.

'Why ever not? Everybody who wants to! I do assure you, Lebedev, that you've rather misunderstood my position from the very beginning; you keep making this mistake. I haven't the smallest reason for hiding or concealing myself from anybody', the prince laughed.

Looking at him, Lebedev felt it his duty to laugh too. Despite his extreme nervousness, Lebedev was also apparently extremely pleased.

Kolya had spoken no more than the truth; he had come only a few steps ahead of the Yepanchins in order to announce them, so that visitors suddenly arrived from both sides: the Yepanchins from the terrace and the Ptitsyns, Ganya, and General Ivolgin from the house.

The Yepanchins had only just learned from Kolya that the prince was ill and was in Pavlovsk. Up till then Madame Yepanchina had been in a state of considerable bewilderment. Two days earlier, General Yepanchin had shown the prince's card to the family and this had firmly convinced Lizaveta Prokofievna that the prince himself would certainly be arriving in

Pavlovsk to call on them in the wake of the card. Her daughters vainly assured her that a man who had not written for six months was hardly likely to be in such a hurry now, and perhaps he had a great many things to concern him in Petersburg besides themselves—what did they know of his business affairs? Madame Yepanchina grew decidedly cross at these remarks and was ready to wager that the prince would turn up next day at the latest, though 'that will be too late'. Next day she waited all morning, then till lunch and through till evening; when it was quite dusk, Lizaveta Prokofievna lost her temper over everything and fell out with everybody, without, of course, mentioning the prince as the reason for these squabbles. Not a word was said about him the whole of the third day either. When Aglaya inadvertently blurted out at dinner that *maman* was annoyed because the prince hadn't come—to which the general at once rejoined that 'it wasn't *his* fault was it?'—Lizaveta Prokofievna rose and angrily left the table. At length, Kolya appeared towards evening with all the news and all the prince's adventures, so far as he knew them. As a result, Madame Yepanchina was triumphant, but Kolya got a good scolding in any case. 'He hangs around here for days on end and there's no getting rid of him, he might at least have let us know if he didn't think of paying us a visit himself.' Kolya was on the point of losing his temper for that 'can't get rid of him', but he postponed this till another time. If the words hadn't been so offensive, then indeed he might have excused them altogether, so pleased was he to see Lizaveta Prokofievna's anxiety and agitation on hearing of the prince's illness. For a long time she kept insisting that a medical celebrity of the first magnitude should be specially sent for from Petersburg and rushed here by the first train. Her daughters dissuaded her; they did not, however, wish to lag behind *maman* when she got herself ready at once to visit the sick man.

'He's on his deathbed', said Lizaveta Prokofievna as she bustled about, 'and we aren't going to bother about the social niceties, are we? Is he a friend of the family or not?'

'Still, we shouldn't butt in before we know how things stand', Aglaya pointed out.

'Very well, don't come then, and a good thing too. Mr Radomsky will be here and nobody to receive him.'

At these words Aglaya, it goes without saying, at once set off after them as she had intended doing all along. Prince S, who was sitting with Adelaida, immediately agreed to escort the ladies, at her request. Even before this, at the beginning of his acquaintance with the Yepanchins, he had been most intrigued by what he had heard when they told him about the prince. It turned out that he knew him, they had met somewhere quite recently and spent a fortnight together in some small town. That had been about three months ago. Prince S had indeed a great deal to say about the prince and spoke very warmly of him altogether, so that it gave him genuine pleasure to call on an old acquaintance. General Yepanchin was not at home on this occasion. Yevgeni Pavlovich Radomsky had not arrived yet either.

It was only a few hundred yards from the Yepanchins to Lebedev's villa. Lizaveta Prokofievna's first disagreeable impression when she got there was to find a whole throng of visitors around the prince, not to mention that among them were one or two personages she positively detested; the second was to see a laughing young man, fashionably dressed and to all appearances perfectly healthy, advancing to meet her, rather than one expiring on his deathbed as she had expected. She even stopped short in bewilderment, to the intense delight of Kolya, who of course could very easily have explained to her before she set off that nobody had a mind to die and there was certainly no deathbed. He had not explained, however, artfully anticipating her comic wrath when she, as he calculated, would surely bristle at finding her dear friend the prince in good health. Kolya was even tactless enough to mention this aloud and so cause Lizaveta Prokofievna to lose her temper altogether. He was constantly sparring with her, sometimes extremely acrimoniously, in spite of their mutual affection.

'Not so fast, sweet child, don't rush things and spoil your triumph!' replied Lizaveta Prokofievna, settling herself in the chair the prince had provided.

Lebedev, Ptitsyn, and General Ivolgin ran to get chairs for the young ladies. Lebedev also provided a seat for Prince S, contriving to demonstrate a profound respect in the very bend of his back. Varya greeted the young ladies with ecstatic whispering, as usual.

'I really did think I'd find you practically in bed, Prince. I exaggerated everything so much in my fright, without a word of a lie, I felt terribly put out when I saw your cheerful face just now, but I swear it was only for a moment till I had time to think. I always talk and act more sensibly when I have time to think; I expect you do as well. In actual fact, I might have been less pleased if a son of my own had recovered; if you don't believe me, so much the worse for you. This spiteful boy here plays much worse tricks on me. He's a protégé of yours I believe; so I'm giving you fair warning that one fine morning, believe me, I shall deny myself the pleasure of enjoying the honour of his further acquaintance.'

'But what have I done now?' cried Kolya. 'However much I assured you that the prince was almost well again, you wouldn't have wanted to believe me because it was a lot more interesting to picture him on his deathbed.'

'Shall you be staying long?' Lizaveta Prokofievna addressed the prince.

'All summer, perhaps longer.'

'You're alone though? Not married?'

'No, not married', the prince smiled at the naivety of the thrust.

'Nothing to smile at: it does happen. I was talking about the villa: why didn't you come to us? We've got a whole wing empty; still, as you like. Is it him you're renting from? This fellow?' she added in an undertone, nodding towards Lebedev. 'Why's he cringing all the time?'

At that moment, Vera emerged on to the veranda with the child in her arms as usual. Lebedev, fidgeting about by the chairs at a complete loss over what to do with himself, but desperately unwilling to leave, pounced on Vera, waving his arms to drive her off the veranda, and even so far forgetting himself as to start stamping his feet.

'Is he a madman?' added Madame Yepanchina suddenly.

'No, he's . . .'

'Drunk is it? Nice company you keep', she snapped, her glance comprehending the rest of the visitors. 'Still, what a sweet girl, who is she?'

'Vera Lukyanova, daughter of Lebedev there.'

'Ah! . . . Very sweet. I would like to be introduced.'

Lebedev, however, overhearing the praises of Lizaveta Prokofievna, had already dragged his daughter forward to be introduced.

'Orphans, orphans!' he wailed as he approached. 'And this child in her arms is an orphan too, her sister, my little daughter Liubov, born in the most lawful of wedlock to my dear wife Yelena, died about six weeks ago in childbirth, by the will of God . . . yes, ma'am . . . she's been a mother, though she's only a sister and no more . . . no more than that, no more . . .'

'And you, sir', snapped Lizaveta Prokofievna in considerable indignation, 'are no more than a fool, I'm sorry to say. Well, enough of that, you know it yourself, I imagine.'

'Perfectly true, ma'am!' Lebedev bowed low and respectfully.

'Listen, Mister Lebedev, is it true what they say that you can interpret Revelation?' asked Aglaya.

'Perfectly true . . . fifteen years now.'

'I've heard of you. You've been in the papers haven't you?'

'No, that was another interpreter, someone else, miss. He's dead now, and I'm left to carry on', said Lebedev, beside himself with joy.

'Be good enough to interpret it for me one of these days, as we are neighbours. I know nothing about Revelation at all.'

'I cannot refrain from warning you, Aglaya Ivanovna, that all this is pure charlatanry on his part', came a swift intervention from General Ivolgin, who was on tenterhooks in his desperate eagerness to start a conversation somehow; he settled himself next to Aglaya. 'Of course, things are different on holiday', he went on, 'different rules and pleasures, and your inviting this ridiculous amateur to interpret the Apocalypse is a pastime like any other, and a remarkably intelligent one, but I . . . You seem to regard me with surprise? General Ivolgin, permit me to introduce myself, I used to carry you in my arms, Aglaya Ivanovna.'

'Very pleased to meet you. I know your wife and daughter', mumbled Aglaya, doing her very best not to burst out laughing.

Lizaveta Prokofievna flared up at this. Something long pent up in her heart all of a sudden demanded an outlet. She could not abide General Ivolgin, whom she had known at one time, many years before.

'You're lying, sir, as usual, you never carried her in your arms', she snapped indignantly.

'You've forgotten, *maman*, honestly he did, in Tver', Aglaya suddenly confirmed. 'We were living in Tver then. I was 6 years old then, I remember. He made me a bow and arrow and taught me to shoot and I killed a pigeon. Remember we killed a pigeon, you and I?'

'And he brought me a cardboard helmet and a wooden sword', cried Adelaida. 'I remember it as well!'

'And I remember it too', affirmed Alexandra. 'You had fallen out over the wounded pigeon and were made to stand in the corner. Adelaida stood there in her helmet and sword.'

When the general had told Aglaya that he had carried her in his arms, he just said it because he was keen to start a conversation, and because he practically always began a conversation with young people in that way, if he wanted to make their acquaintance. This time, however, as luck would have it, he spoke no more than the truth, and, as luck would have it, he had forgotten it himself. When Aglaya suddenly confirmed that they had shot a pigeon together, his memory came back in a flash and he recalled everything to the last detail, as quite often happens with old people recalling events of long ago. It is difficult to say what there was in that memory to produce so powerful an impression on the poor general, who was, as usual, somewhat tipsy; however, he was suddenly deeply moved.

'I remember, I remember it all!' he cried. 'I was a junior captain at the time. You were a little dear, so pretty. Nina . . . Ganya . . . I was welcome in your house then. General Yepanchin . . .'

'And now look at you!' Madame Yepanchina cut in. 'So you haven't drunk away your finer feelings, after all, seeing it affects you like this! You've worn your wife out. There's children to look after while you're in a debtors' prison! Go away, sir, stand in some corner behind the door and shed tears as you remember your lost innocence, and perhaps God will forgive you. Go on, go along, I mean it. Nothing helps a person to amend more than remembering the past with contrition.'

To repeat that she was in earnest, however, was unnecessary: the general, like all confirmed drunkards, was very sensitive, and

like all drunkards who have come down in the world, could not
bear to be reminded of his happier past. He rose and headed
meekly for the door, causing Lizaveta Prokofievna to feel sorry
for him at once.

'Ardalion Alexandrich, dear man!' she called after him, 'wait
a moment; we are all sinners; when you feel your conscience
pricking you a little bit less, come and see me and we'll sit and
talk about the past. I'm probably fifty times more a sinner than
you; well, goodbye, go along, there's nothing for you here ...'
she added, suddenly afraid he might return.

'You'd better not go after him for the moment', the prince
stopped Kolya as he was about to run after his father. 'Otherwise
he'll start feeling annoyed in a minute and all this will be for
nothing.'

'That's true, leave him alone; go in half an hour', decided
Lizaveta Prokofievna.

'That's what comes of telling the truth for once in a lifetime',
Lebedev ventured to add. 'It reduced him to tears!'

'Well you're a fine one to talk, sir, if what I've heard is true',
Lizaveta Prokofievna cut him short at once.

The reciprocal relationships of the various visitors gathered
about the prince gradually defined themselves. The prince, of
course, was in a position to appreciate to the full the sympathy
shown to him by Madame Yepanchina and her daughters, and
indeed did so. He told them sincerely that, before their arrival, he
had certainly intended calling on them himself—that very day,
his illness and the late hour notwithstanding. Lizaveta
Prokofievna, glancing at his visitors, responded that he could do
so even now. The polite and tactful Ptitsyn very soon rose and
betook himself to Lebedev's rooms and was most anxious to take
Lebedev away with him. The latter promised to come soon;
meanwhile, Varya was chatting to the girls and remained behind.
She and Ganya were extremely relieved at the departure of the
general; Ganya himself soon followed Ptitsyn. For the few
minutes that he had remained on the terrace with the
Yepanchins, he had behaved with unassuming dignity, and was
not in the least put out by the stares of Lizaveta Prokofievna who
twice surveyed him from top to toe. Really, anyone who had
known him before would have thought him greatly altered.

Aglaya was much pleased by this.

'That really was Gavrila Ardalionovich just going out?' she asked suddenly, as she liked to do sometimes, breaking into other people's conversation with a loud, abrupt question of her own addressed to no one in particular.

'Yes', answered the prince.

'I hardly recognized him. He's changed a lot . . . and greatly for the better.'

'I'm very glad for his sake', said the prince.

'He's been very ill', added Varya with glad commiseration.

'How has he changed for the better?' asked Lizaveta Prokofievna in angry incomprehension, almost frightened. 'How do you mean? Nothing's any better. What do you think's got better then?'

'There's nothing better than the "poor knight"', proclaimed Kolya, who had been standing by Lizaveta Prokofievna's chair all this while.

'I think so too', said Prince S, and laughed.

'I am of precisely the same opinion', declared Adelaida solemnly.

'What "poor knight?" ' asked Madame Yepanchina, gazing round at the speakers in bewildered exasperation, but on seeing Aglaya's blushes she added wrathfully: 'Some nonsense, I'll be bound! What "poor knight" is this?'

'It's not the first time that favourite of yours, that urchin there, has twisted other people's words!' answered Aglaya in haughty indignation.

In any angry outburst of Aglaya's (and she was very often angry), there peeped out virtually every time, despite her obvious implacable seriousness, something so childlike and impatiently schoolgirlish, so poorly disguised, that it was impossible not to laugh at her sometimes as you looked at her, greatly to Aglaya's annoyance be it said, who couldn't understand what people were laughing at—'How could they, how dare they laugh?'

Her sisters and Prince S laughed now, and even Prince Lev Nikolayevich smiled, though he too had coloured for some reason. Kolya roared with laughter at his triumph. Aglaya got angry in real earnest and became twice as pretty. Her embarrassment greatly became her, as indeed did her vexation at herself for being embarrassed.

'He's twisted your words often enough', she added.

'I'm going by what you said yourself!' cried Kolya. 'A month ago, you were looking through *Don Quixote* and you exclaimed those very words—that there was nothing better than the "poor knight". I don't know who you were talking about just then: Don Quixote or Yevgeni Pavlich, or a certain other person, but it was about somebody and it was a long conversation . . .'

'I see you're letting yourself go a little too far with those guesses of yours, young man', Lizaveta Prokofievna checked him, annoyed.

'Am I the only one?' Kolya persisted. 'Everybody said so at the time, just as they are now; Prince S there, and Adelaida Ivanovna, and everyone said that they were for the "poor knight", so that means there must be a "poor knight". He certainly exists, and I think that if it wasn't for Adelaida Ivanovna, we would have known who the "poor knight" was long ago.'

'Why is it my fault then?' laughed Adelaida.

'You wouldn't draw his portrait, that's why it's your fault! Aglaya Ivanovna asked you to draw the "poor knight" 's portrait and even made up the entire subject of the picture for you—you remember that subject? You didn't want to . . .'

'But how on earth could I have drawn it—and whom? According to the subject, the "poor knight"

> No man or woman ever saw
> The visor lifted from his face.

What face could I have drawn, then? What was I to draw: a visor? An unknown individual?'

'I don't understand any of this—what do you mean, visor?' said Madame Yepanchina testily, beginning to have a very shrewd idea as to who was meant by the 'poor knight' (a name probably agreed on long before). But what really infuriated her was that Prince Lev Nikolayevich was also embarrassed to the point of sheepishness, like some 10-year-old boy. 'Well then, can we have an end to this silliness? Will someone explain this "poor knight" or not? Is it some terrible secret beyond anyone's comprehension?'

But everyone just carried on laughing.

'It's simply that there's a certain strange Russian poem', Prince S at last intervened, obviously anxious to drop this and quickly change the subject, 'about a "poor knight", it's a fragment, with no beginning or end. About a month since, everybody was laughing after dinner and as usual trying to find a subject for Adelaida Ivanovna to paint. As you know, it's a family occupation finding subjects for Adelaida's pictures. Then we hit on the "poor knight", I don't recall who first suggested it . . .'

'Aglaya Ivanovna!' cried Kolya.

'Perhaps it was, I dare say, I've just forgotten', Prince S went on. 'Some of us laughed at a subject like that, others declared there could be nothing more elevated, but to depict the "poor knight" he had to have a face; we began to go over the faces of everyone we knew, but none of them would do, so there we left it; that's all there is to tell; I don't understand why Kolya thought fit to remember it all and bring it up. It was amusing and relevant at the time but really quite uninteresting now.'

'Because some new silliness is meant by it, something ill-natured and offensive.'

'No silliness, just the profoundest esteem', Aglaya suddenly brought out, quite unexpectedly, in a deep, grave voice: she had completely recovered herself and mastered her previous embarrassment. Nor was this all; from certain signs one might have thought to look at her that she was delighted at the joke going so far, and this turn in her feelings coincided with the moment when the prince's increasing embarrassment had reached the point of being only too obvious to everyone.

'First they're cackling like mad things, then it's profoundest esteem all of a sudden! They've run wild! Why esteem? Just tell me why for no reason at all you're suddenly talking about profoundest esteem?'

'Profoundest esteem', Aglaya went on, gravely solemn as before, in response to her mother's almost rancorous question, 'because the poem depicts a man who is capable of an ideal, and secondly, once having set up his ideal, capable of believing in it, and in that belief capable of devoting his whole life blindly to it. That doesn't always happen in this age of ours. The poem doesn't say exactly what the "poor knight"'s ideal actually was, but it's clear that it was some bright vision, "a vision of pure beauty", and the lovesick knight has even wound a rosary round his neck in place of a scarf. It's true there is some sort of obscure unexplained device he inscribed on his shield, the letters A.N.B. . . .'

'A.N.D.', corrected Kolya.

'And I say A.N.B. and that's what I meant to say', Aglaya cut him short in annoyance. 'Whichever it was, it's clear the "poor knight" didn't care what his lady was or did. It was enough that he had chosen her and believed in her "true beauty" and did her homage for ever after; that was the merit of it, that even if she were to become, say, a thief later on, he would be bound to believe in her and break a lance for the sake of her pure beauty. The poet seems to have wanted to unite in one striking image the whole grand concept of medieval knightly platonic love as embodied in one pure and high-minded knight; of course, all that is the ideal. In the "poor knight" it has reached its final stage—asceticism; one has to admit that to be capable of such feeling means a good deal, and such feelings in themselves leave a profound mark behind them—most laudable from one point of view, not to mention Don Quixote. The "poor knight" is Don Quixote, but serious, not comic. At first I didn't realize and I laughed, but now I love the "poor knight", but more than that, I applaud his exploits.'

Thus Aglaya concluded, and looking at her it was hard to tell whether she was in earnest or laughing.

'Well, he's a fool of some sort, him and his exploits!' declared Madame Yepanchina. 'And you, madam, have been talking a deal of nonsense, a regular lecture; it doesn't become you, if you ask me. In any case it's insufferable. What poem is this? Recite it, seeing you know it! I must know what this poem is like. I never could stand poetry, I must have had a premonition. For heaven's sake put up with it, Prince, it seems you and I have to put up with this together', she addressed Prince Lev Nikolayevich. She was thoroughly vexed.

Prince Lev Nikolayevich was on the point of saying something, but his continuing embarrassment prevented him from speaking. Aglaya alone was not in the least discomfited, seemed glad indeed, despite having overstepped the mark in her 'lecture'. She got up at once, still grave and solemn as before, with an air of having been prepared for this and only waiting to be asked. She walked out into the middle of the veranda and stood in front of the prince, who remained seated in his armchair. Everyone stared at her in some surprise, and virtually all of them, Prince S, her sisters, her mother, regarded this new foolery in the making with the disagreeable sensation that it had gone rather too far as it was. It was obvious, however, that it was this very ceremonious affectation over starting her reading that Aglaya enjoyed. Lizaveta Prokofievna was about to send her back to her place, but at the very moment when Aglaya began declaiming the well-known ballad, two new visitors, talking loudly, walked on to the veranda from the street. They were General Ivan Fedorovich Yepanchin and, behind him, a certain young man. This occasioned some stir.

7

THE young man who accompanied the general was about 28, tall and slim, with a fine, intelligent face; his large dark eyes flashed with wit and irony. Aglaya did not even turn round to look at him, but went on with her recitation, affectedly continuing to gaze at the prince alone and addressing herself exclusively to him. It had become obvious to the prince that she had some ulterior motive in doing all this. The new arrivals at least made his position a little less awkward. Seeing them, he half rose, nodded courteously to the general from a distance, signalled to them not to interrupt the recitation, and himself contrived to retreat behind his chair from where he could lean his elbow on the back and carry on listening to the ballad in a more comfortable and less ridiculous position, as it were, than when he had been seated. For her part, Lizaveta Prokofievna twice motioned peremptorily for the newcomers to stand where they were. The prince, by the way, was very interested in this new visitor accompanying the general; he correctly surmised that this was Yevgeni Pavlovich Radomsky, of whom he had heard a good deal and thought about more than once. He was puzzled by his wearing civilian dress though; he had heard that Yevgeni Pavlovich was a military man. A mocking smile played round the lips of the new arrival all through the recital, as if he had already heard something about the 'poor knight'.

'Perhaps it was he who first thought of it', mused the prince to himself.

But it was quite different with Aglaya. All the initial affectation and pomposity of her reading was now overlaid with such earnestness, such insight into the meaning and spirit of the poetic work, enunciating each word with such understanding, speaking the lines with such supreme simplicity, that by the end of the reading she had not only gripped the attention of all present, but by her rendering of the lofty spirit of the ballad, she seemed in part to justify the overdone affected gravity with which she had so solemnly stepped into the middle of the veranda. In that gravity might now be discerned only her boundless, even naive, regard for the poem she had undertaken to render. Her eyes shone and a faint, barely perceptible shudder of inspiration and ecstasy passed over her beautiful features. She read:

> A poor and simple knight was there.
> Who spoke but little, plain, austere;
> Though seeming pale and full of care,
> His spirit would admit no fear.
>
> A single vision he possessed,
> Beyond the power of human art
> To guess the mystery impressed
> And deeply graven on his heart
>
> Thenceforth, his soul consumed with fire,
> On womankind he cast no look,
> To speak with them had no desire;
> His silence to the grave he took.
>
> Around his neck no scarf he wore,
> A rosary hung in its place;
> No man or woman ever saw
> The visor lifted from his face.
>
> In token of a love so chaste,
> True to his radiant vision sealed,
> Three letters in his blood he traced,

And N.F.B* glowed on his shield.

In Palestine when on crusade,
As into battle, hearts aflame,
The paladins rushed unafraid,
Each calling on his lady's name,

Light of heaven, sacred Rose!
That was his cry, as fierce and grim,
He fell like thunder on his foes;
The saracen shrank back from him

Returning to his distant fief,
He lived his life out, pent inside,
Still silent, still a prey to grief,
Like a madman, thus he died.

Recalling all this subsequently, the prince was for long greatly perplexed and exercised by one unresolved problem: how could such genuinely noble feeling be coupled with such openly malicious mockery? That it was mockery he had no doubt; he realized that clearly and had grounds for doing so: during her recitation Aglaya had taken the liberty of changing the letters A.N.D. to N.F.B. He could not doubt that this was deliberate and that he had not misheard (this was later confirmed). At all events, Aglaya's prank—a joke of course, though too barbed and thoughtless—was premeditated. Everyone had been talking (and 'laughing') over the 'poor knight' a month before. And yet, as far as the prince could remember, Aglaya had pronounced those letters in perfect seriousness, without a hint of a smile or any undue stress on the letters to bring out their hidden significance; on the contrary, her unchanging gravity, taken together with her innocent, naive simplicity, might have led one to believe that the letters were really part of the ballad as printed in the book. The prince experienced a distinctly disagreeable pang. Lizaveta Prokofievna, of course, had been oblivious to this and noticed neither the letter-substitution nor the hint. All General Yepanchin understood was that poetry was being recited. Many of the other listeners understood and were surprised, both at the audacity of the prank and its intention, but they remained silent and tried not to show it. Yevgeni Pavlovich, however, the prince was willing to wager, not only understood but was attempting to show that he did: his smile was too ironic.

'How lovely!' cried Madame Yepanchina in genuine rapture as soon as the reading finished. 'Who wrote it?'

'Pushkin, *maman*, don't show us up, you should be ashamed!' cried Adelaida.

'I could be a lot worse with daughters like you!' retorted Lizaveta Prokofievna bitterly. 'Ashamed! Let me have this poem of Pushkin's the minute we get home.'

'But I don't think we've got a Pushkin at all.'

'We've had two tattered volumes lying about the house since I don't know when', Alexandra put in.

'Send Fedor or Alexey by the first train to town and buy one, Alexey would be best. Aglaya, come here! Kiss me, you read beautifully but—if you meant what you read—she added almost whispering, then I'm sorry for you; if you read it to make fun of him, I can't approve of your feelings, so in any case it would have been better not to read it at all. You understand me? Go along, madam, I shall speak to you another time, we've sat too long here.'

Meanwhile, the prince had welcomed General Yepanchin and the general introduced Yevgeni Pavlovich Radomsky to him.

'I collected him on the way, he'd just got off the train; he found out I was coming here and all the family were here . . .'

'I found out you were here too', Yevgeni Pavlovich broke in, 'and since I made up my mind long ago to seek your friendship as well as your acquaintance, I didn't want to lose any time. You aren't well? I've just learned . . .'

'Quite well and very pleased to meet you, I've heard a good deal about you and spoken about you to Prince S', answered Lev Nikolayevich extending a hand.

Mutual courtesies were exchanged, both shook hands and looked keenly into one another's eyes. In an instant the conversation became general. The prince noticed (he was noticing everything now, swiftly and avidly, even including, perhaps, things which were not there at all), that Yevgeni Pavlovich's civilian dress was creating general and quite considerable surprise, so much so that everything else was for a time forgotten and set aside. One might have supposed that there was something enormously significant in this change of attire.

Adelaida and Alexandra were questioning Yevgeni Pavlovich in puzzlement. Prince S, his kinsman, glanced at him with considerable disquiet, while the general was talking with something approaching agitation. Aglaya alone cast a curious but entirely unperturbed glance at Yevgeni Pavlovich for a moment, as if merely wondering whether military or civilian dress suited him best, but after a moment turned away and looked at him no more. Lizaveta Prokofievna too asked no questions, though she may also have been a little concerned. It struck the prince that Yevgeni Pavlovich was not in her good graces.

'Surprised, bowled over!' General Yepanchin kept repeating in answer to all questioning. 'I couldn't believe it when I met him earlier on in Petersburg. And why so sudden? That's what puzzles me. He's the first to say one shouldn't go at things like a bull at a gate.'

It emerged during the conversation that Yevgeni Pavlovich had announced his forthcoming retirement from the army well in advance; each time, however, he had treated the matter so lightly that it had been impossible to believe him. Indeed, he always talked of serious things in such a jocular fashion that it was hard to make him out, especially if that was his intention.

'After all, it's only temporary, a few months—a year at most', laughed Radomsky.

'But there's no need for it at all, at least from what I know of your affairs', the general persisted with some heat.

'What about doing the round of my estates? You advised that yourself; besides, I want to travel abroad too . . .'

The conversation, however, soon turned elsewhere, though it was evident that a most curious unease persisted, excessively so in the view of the watching prince; there was some peculiar reason behind it all no doubt.

'So, the "poor knight" is back on stage?' Yevgeni Pavlovich began as he approached Aglaya.

To the prince's astonishment, she gave him a look of bewildered interrogation as though she wanted to indicate that they could never have spoken of any 'poor knight' and that she didn't even understand the question.

'But it's late, it's too late to send to town for a Pushkin, it's too late!' Kolya was arguing with Lizaveta Prokofievna with all his might. 'For the thousandth time, it's too late!'

'Yes, it really is too late to send to town now', Radomsky intervened at this point, after hastily leaving Aglaya. 'I imagine the Petersburg shops will be closed, it's after eight', he confirmed, taking out his watch.

'You've done without it long enough, you can wait till tomorrow', put in Adelaida.

'Anyway, it's not proper for high-society folk to be too interested in literature', added Kolya. 'Ask Yevgeni Pavlovich. It's much more the thing to have a yellow carriage with red wheels.'

'Out of a book again, Kolya', observed Adelaida.

'Oh, everything he says is out of books', said Yevgeni Pavlovich. 'He quotes whole sentences out of critical journals. I have long had the pleasure of Master Nikolai's conversation, but this time he isn't quoting a book. He's obviously hinting at my yellow carriage with its red wheels. Only I've already changed it, you're too late.'

The prince listened carefully to what Radomsky was saying. He was struck by his excellent manners, unassuming and genial; he particularly liked the way he spoke amiably, as man to man, to the provoking Kolya.

'What's this?' asked Lizaveta Prokofievna, addressing Lebedev's daughter Vera, who was standing before her with a number of large, beautifully bound books, in almost mint condition.

'Pushkin', said Vera. 'Our Pushkin. Daddy asked me to bring them for you.'

'How's this? Is that true?' Lizaveta Prokofievna was astonished.

'Not as a gift! Not as a gift! I wouldn't presume to do that!' Lebedev sprang out from behind his daughter's back. 'At cost price, madame! This is our very own family Pushkin, Annenkov's edition, you can't get hold of it these days, cost price madame! I present it with reverence, madame, desiring to sell it and so satisfy the noble impatience of the most noble literary sensibilities of your excellency.'

'If you're selling, then thank you. I dare say you won't lose by it; but do stop cringing, sir. I've heard about you, I'm told you're very well-read. We must have a talk sometime; will you bring me the books yourself, or what?'

'With reverence, madame, and . . . respect!' Lebedev cringed, vastly pleased, seizing the books from his daughter.

'Well, as long as you don't lose them, bring them without respect if you like, but on one condition', she added looking at him keenly, 'you'll get no further than the doorway, and I don't intend to see you today. You could send your daughter now if you like, I've really taken to her.'

'Why on earth don't you tell him about those people?' Vera said impatiently to her father. 'If not, they'll come in here of their own accord, won't they? They've started making a row. Lev Nikolayevich', she addressed the prince, who had already picked up his hat, 'some people came to see you a good while ago, four men, they're waiting out there complaining but daddy won't let them in here.'

'Who are they?' asked the prince.

'They say they're here on business, but they're in the mood to stop you on the street if they're not allowed in. You'd better see them, Lev Nikolayevich, and get them off your back. Gavrila Ardalionovich and Ptitsyn are arguing with them but they won't listen.'

'Pavlischev's son! Pavlischev's son! Don't do it, don't do it!' Lebedev milled his arms about. 'It's not worth the bother, sir; to trouble yourself on their account, illustrious Prince, would be improper. No, sir. Not worth it . . .'

'Pavlischev's son! Good lord!' cried the prince, greatly disconcerted. 'I know . . . but surely I . . . I asked Gavrila Ardalionovich to see about that. He told me just now . . .'

But Gavrila Ardalionovich had already come out on to the veranda; Ptitsyn was following him. In the nearest room a commotion could be heard, and General Ivolgin's loud voice, apparently trying to shout others down. Kolya ran off at once in that direction.

'This is most interesting!' observed Radomsky aloud.

'So he knows about it!' thought the prince.

'What "Pavlischev's son" is this? What son can Pavlischev have? . . .' enquired General Yepanchin, bewildered, to find as he surveyed the faces of all present that he was the only one who knew nothing of this novel turn of events.

The stir of expectancy was indeed general. The prince was profoundly surprised that such a completely private affair had already excited their interest so much.

'It would be a very good thing', said Aglaya coming up to the prince with a particularly grave air, 'if you were to put an end to this business *personally*, and allow us all to be your witnesses. They want to heap dirt on you, Prince; you must vindicate yourself triumphantly, and I'm terribly glad for you in advance.'

'And I want a stop put to this disgraceful claim once and for all', cried Madame Yepanchina. 'No mercy, Prince, no holding back! My ears have been buzzing with this business and I've been worried to death on your account. Besides, I'm curious to see them. Call them in and we'll sit down. Aglaya was right. You've heard something of this, Prince?' she added, turning to Prince S.

'Of course I have, in your house. But I'm particularly anxious to have a look at these young people', replied Prince S.

'These are the so-called nihilists, are they?'

'No, ma'am, they're not exactly nihilists', Lebedev stepped forward, almost shaking with excitement. 'These are different, ma'am, special. My nephew says they have gone further than the nihilists, ma'am. You are mistaken if you think they will be put out by your presence, your excellency; they won't be, ma'am. Nihilists are sometimes well-informed sorts of people, even scholarly, but these have gone beyond that because, first and foremost, they're men of action, ma'am. It is really a kind of development of nihilism, not straightforwardly, more indirectly, through hearsay. They don't express themselves through news-paper articles, they act directly, ma'am; it's not a question of the pointlessness of Pushkin or anything like that, or the need to break Russia up into fragments; no, ma'am, nowadays it's regarded as an absolute right that, if anybody wants something badly, all barriers should be disregarded, even if half-a-dozen people have to be rubbed out in the process. All the same, Prince, I would not advise you . . .'

But the prince was already moving to open the door for the visitors.

'You slander them, Lebedev', he said, smiling. 'You're too much aggrieved against your nephew. Don't believe him, Lizaveta Prokofievna. I assure you, Gorskys and Danilovs* are merely exceptions. These people are just . . . in error . . . But I would prefer it not to be here in front of everybody. I'm sorry, Lizaveta Prokofievna, once they come in I'll show them to you then I'll take them away. Come in, gentlemen!'

What exercised him more was a tormenting notion of a different sort. He wondered whether or not someone had arranged the business beforehand for this time, this hour, before these particular witnesses and perhaps in anticipation of his mortification rather than his triumph? But he was greatly despondent at the thought of his 'monstrous and wicked suspicions'. He felt that he would have died if anyone knew he had such an idea in his head, and at the moment his visitors walked in, he was genuinely ready to believe that he was morally beneath the lowest around him.

Five persons came in, the four newcomers and General Ivolgin behind them, impassioned, agitated, and in full spate of eloquence. 'There's one on my side for certain!' thought the prince with a smile. Kolya slipped in along with them; he was talking fervently to Ippolit who was one of the visitors; Ippolit was listening and grinning.

The prince sat his visitors down. They all looked so young, hardly grown-up at all in fact, that one might well wonder both at the occasion and the fuss being made of it. General Yepanchin, for example, knowing and understanding nothing of this 'new affair', was quite indignant at the sight of their youthfulness, and would no doubt have registered some kind of protest had not he been inhibited by his wife's puzzlingly zealous championship of the prince's personal interests. He remained, however, partly out of curiosity, and partly out of goodness of heart, hoping he might assist or that his authority, at any rate, might be of use; but General Ivolgin's distant bow to him as he entered fired his indignation again, and he made up his mind to be resolutely silent.

Among the four young visitors, however, one was about 30 years old, the 'retired lieutenant' of Rogozhin's crowd, the boxer, who in his time had 'given fifteen roubles each to beggars'. It was a fair guess that he had come along to bolster the others, in the role of loyal friend and, should need arise, to lend support. Of the rest, the first and most prominent place was taken by the one who went by the name of 'Pavlischev's son', though he introduced himself as Antip Burdovsky. He was poorly and slovenly dressed, and the sleeves of his stained coat had a mirror-like sheen; his greasy waistcoat was buttoned up to the neck and there was no sign of a shirt; he wore an impossibly dirty silk scarf twisted into a rope. His hands were unwashed and his face was generously pimpled. He was fair-haired and had, if one can use the phrase, an innocently insolent expression. He was fairly tall, lean, and about 22 years old. His face displayed not the faintest hint of irony or self-questioning; on the contrary, it expressed nothing but a total, stolid complacency as to his own rights, and at the same time something approaching a curious and ceaseless craving to be, and to feel, permanently aggrieved. He spoke emotionally, hurriedly, and with a stammer, as if unable to finish his words, being tongue-tied or even a foreigner, although he actually was a Russian born and bred.

He was accompanied firstly by Lebedev's nephew, already familiar to readers, and secondly by Ippolit. Ippolit was a very young man, about 17 or perhaps 18, with an intelligent, though permanently petulant expression on his face. This face bore the terrible marks of disease. He was pale yellow and as thin as a skeleton; his eyes glittered and two red spots burned in his cheeks. He coughed incessantly; every word, almost every breath, was accompanied by hoarse wheezing. It was clearly tuberculosis at a very advanced stage. It looked as if he had only two or three weeks to live. He was very tired and was the first to subside on to a chair. The rest of them fussed about as they came in and were almost embarrassed, but looked gravely about them, obviously fearing to lose their dignity in some way, which sorted oddly with their reputation as spurners of all useless social forms, prejudices, indeed virtually everything in the world apart from their own interests.

'Antip Burdovsky', stammered 'Pavlischev's son' announcing himself.

'Vladimir Doktorenko', Lebedev's nephew introduced himself.

'Keller!' mumbled the retired lieutenant.

'Ippolit Terentyev', squeaked the last one in an unexpectedly shrill voice. At length all of them arranged themselves in a row on chairs facing the prince, and, having introduced themselves, at once scowled and transferred their caps from one hand to another to keep their spirits up. All of them made as if to speak, yet stayed silent, waiting for something with an air of defiance which seemed to say: 'No, friend, you're wrong, you won't catch us like that.' It could be sensed that once somebody uttered the first word, all of them would start talking together, interrupting and running ahead of one another.

8

'GENTLEMEN, I did not expect to see any of you', the prince began. 'I've been unwell up till today and I entrusted your case (he was speaking to Antip Burdovsky) to Gavrila Ardalionovich Ivolgin at least a month ago, as I informed you at that time. However, I'm not trying to avoid a personal explanation, though you will agree that now is hardly ... I suggest we go to another room, if this won't take long ... My friends are here at the moment, and believe me ...'

'Friends ... the more the merrier, but look here sir', Lebedev's nephew interrupted suddenly in a highly sententious tone, though without raising his voice unduly, 'may we point out in turn that you could have shown us more consideration than to keep us waiting in your servants' hall for two hours ...'

'And of course ... and I ... that's princely behaviour for you! And this ... you must be a general! And I'm not your servant! And I, I ...', Antip Burdovsky suddenly began mumbling in acute agitation; his lips trembled, and there was an intensely aggrieved quaver in his voice as the spittle flew from his mouth. It was as if he had burst, or erupted, but he was in so much of a hurry all of a sudden that after the tenth word it was impossible to understand what he was saying.

'It was princely behaviour!' Ippolit shouted in his shrill, cracked voice.

'If it had happened to me', growled the boxer, 'I mean if I had been directly involved as a man of honour, in Burdovsky's place ... I'd ...'

'Gentlemen, I only heard of your presence a minute ago, really', the prince repeated again.

'We are not afraid of your friends, Prince, whoever they may be, because we are within our rights', declared Lebedev's nephew once more.

'But what right did you have, pray', Ippolit squeaked again, by now greatly wrought-up, 'to submit Burdovsky's case to the judgement of your friends? Maybe we don't want a court of your friends; it's very obvious what that would lead to! . . .'

'But if you don't want to talk here, Mr Burdovsky', the prince managed to get in a word at length, considerably taken aback by this beginning, 'as I say, let's go to another room at once, I repeat I only heard about you all just this minute . . .'

'But you have no right, no right, no right! . . . your friends . . . So! . . .' Burdovsky suddenly started babbling again, looking wildly and apprehensively about him, increasingly impassioned as his shyness and suspicion grew. 'You have no right!' Having got this out, he halted abruptly as if cut short, silently fixing his myopic, bulging, bloodshot eyes on the prince; he stared questioningly at him, his whole body hunched forward. This time the prince was so surprised that he lapsed into silence himself and looked at him wide-eyed in return, without saying a word.

'Lev Nikolayevich!' called out Lizaveta Prokofievna all of a sudden, 'read this at once, this very minute, it's directly concerned with your business.'

She hastily held out to him a certain weekly humorous paper and pointed out an article. While the visitors were coming in Lebedev had sidled up to Lizaveta Prokofievna, with whom he was trying to ingratiate himself, wordlessly pulled this paper out of his pocket, and placed it before her eyes, indicating a marked passage. What Lizaveta Prokofievna had managed to read had shaken and upset her considerably.

'Perhaps better not to read it aloud?' faltered the prince, highly embarrassed. 'I could read it by myself . . . later on . . .'

He had barely had time to touch it before Lizaveta Prokofievna impatiently snatched the paper from his hand and turned to Kolya. 'In that case you'd better read it, read it now, out loud! So everybody can hear.'

Lizaveta Prokofievna was an ardent and impulsive lady, so that sometimes, with barely a thought, she weighed anchor all of a sudden and put out to sea regardless of the weather. General Yepanchin stirred uneasily. But while they all stopped involuntarily in that first moment and waited in bafflement, Kolya unfolded the paper and began reading aloud from the place Lebedev sprang over to indicate.

'"*Proletarians and Scions of Nobility, an Episode of Daylight and Everyday Robbery! Progress! Reform! Justice!*

"Strange things take place in our so-called Holy Russia, in our age of reforms and private enterprise, an age of national movements and hundreds of millions exported annually, an age of encouragement of industry and paralysis of working human hands and so on and so forth, the list is endless, gentlemen, so let us to business. A strange incident occurred to a sprig of our defunct landed gentry (*de profundis!*), one of those sprigs, however, whose grandfathers lost all their money at the roulette-wheel, whose fathers were compelled to serve as cadets and junior officers in the army and died, as a rule, while being tried for some innocent mistake in the calculation of public moneys, and whose children, like the hero of our tale, either grow up to be idiots or get involved in criminal activity, of which, incidentally, they are acquitted by our juries, supposedly for their edification and reform; or at length they get involved in one of those incidents which astound the public and sully these already disgraceful times of ours. During the winter, about six months ago, our noble scion, wearing gaiters, foreign-fashion, and shivering in his unlined bit of cloak returned to Russia from Switzerland where he had been treated for idiocy (*sic!*). It must be admitted he was fortunate at that, because as well as that interesting malady he was treated for in Switzerland (now, can anyone be treated for idiocy, just imagine it?!!) he could well prove the truth of the Russian saying: some folk have all the luck! Judge for yourselves: left a babe in arms on the death of his father, who, they say, was a lieutenant who died while on trial for the sudden disappearance of the company funds during a game of cards and possibly also for the award of an excessive number of strokes of the birch to one under his command (you recall the days of old, gentlemen!), our baron was brought up thanks to the charity of a certain very rich Russian landowner. This landowner—let us call him P—was the owner in that former golden age, of four thousand serf souls (serf souls! Do you understand an expression like that, gentlemen? I do not. I will have to look in a dictionary: "the legend is fresh, but hard to credit"), and was seemingly one of those Russian idlers and parasites who spend all their lazy lives abroad, at the spas in summer and in winter at the Paris Château des Fleurs where they have left vast sums in their time. It could be said with certainty that at least one-third of the rent paid during the serf-owning period went into the pockets of the proprietor of the Château des Fleurs (lucky fellow that he was!). However that may be, the happy-go-lucky P brought up our nobleman's orphaned child like a prince, engaged tutors and governesses for him (pretty ones no doubt) whom, incidentally, he brought over from Paris himself. But this last scion of a noble line was an idiot. The Château des Fleurs governesses couldn't help, and till he was 20, their young charge hadn't learned to speak any language, including Russian. This last was excusable, however. At length a fantastic notion came into P's feudal head—that the idiot might be taught sense in Switzerland. It was a logical fantasy at that: a parasite and propertied man would naturally suppose he could buy even intelligence for money in the market-place, particularly in Switzerland. Five years passed while he was treated by some celebrated professor in Switzerland, and thousands were spent on it: the idiot, it goes without saying, did not become intelligent, but they say he did grow to resemble a human being nevertheless, let's not argue the point. Then P ups and dies suddenly. There was no will of course, his affairs were in a mess as usual and there were crowds of greedy heirs who couldn't have cared less about any last scions of the line being treated for idiocy out of charity in Switzerland. The said scion, idiot though he was, tried to cheat his professor and, so they say, managed to get treatment for two years free of charge by concealing the death of his benefactor. But the professor was no mean charlatan himself; alarmed at last by his patient's lack of money, and still more at the appetite of this 25-year-old parasite, he dressed him in his old gaiters, gave him his worn-out old cloak, and sent him off at his own expense third class *nach Russland*, to get rid of him. It seemed that fortune had turned her back on our hero. Not a bit of it, gentlemen: fortune which wipes out whole provinces with famine, pours out all her gifts at once upon this little aristocrat, like Krylov's Cloud* which passed over the parched fields and discharged itself over the ocean. At the very moment he turned up in Petersburg from Switzerland, a relative of his mother's (who was of the merchant class herself of course) dies in Moscow, a childless old soul, merchant, bearded Old Believer, who leaves a few million in his will, incontestable, cool hard cash (would it had been you and I, dear reader) all to our sprig, all this to our baron, who had been treated for idiocy in Switzerland! Well now, the boot was on the other foot. Suddenly a whole crowd of friends and acquaintances gathered round our gaitered baron, who was throwing himself at a certain celebrated beauty, a kept woman. Even relatives turned up and a whole clutch of noble ladies besides, desperate for holy matrimony— and what could be better: an aristocrat, a millionaire, an idiot—all qualities at once, not something you can find with a lantern in daylight or have made to order!..."'

'This... I don't understand this at all!' cried General Yepanchin at the very pitch of indignation.

'Do stop, Kolya!' cried the prince pleading with his eyes. Exclamations came from all sides.

'Read on! Read on! Whatever you do!' cut in Lizaveta Prokofievna, obviously restraining herself with an immense effort. 'Prince, if the reading stops we shall quarrel.'

There was nothing for it. Kolya, flushed and excited, went on reading in an agitated voice.

'"But while our new-fledged millionaire was in seventh heaven so to speak, something altogether unlooked-for occurred. One fine morning a visitor came to see him, composed and stern of countenance, soberly and elegantly dressed, courteously dignified and measured of speech and with an obvious leaning towards progressive views. He briefly explained the reason for his visit: he was a well-known lawyer and he had been instructed by a certain young man to act in his interest. This young man was none other than the son of the late P, though he used a different name. The lascivious P had, in his youth, seduced a girl who was poor but honest, one of his house-serfs, who had been brought up European-fashion—doubtless he was taking advantage of one of the seigneurial rights he enjoyed under the old serf system.

Noticing the inevitable and imminent consequence of this
liaison, he hurriedly gave her in marriage to a man of excellent
character who worked in the civil service and who had long been
in love with the girl. To begin with he helped the newly-weds,
but very soon the husband's upright character saw to it that his
assistance was declined. Time passed and little by little P
managed to forget the girl and the son she had borne him, and
later, as we know, he died without settling his affairs. His son,
meanwhile, born in lawful wedlock, grew up under another
name, having been adopted by his mother's upright husband.
The latter nevertheless died in due season, and the son was left
to fend for himself in one of our remote provinces with an ailing
mother who had lost the use of her legs. He himself earned a
living in the capital by honest toil every day, giving lessons in
merchants' houses, and so kept himself first at school then later
on while he was attending external university lectures, which he
hoped would be useful to him in his subsequent career. Still, how
much can you earn from a Russian merchant for lessons at ten
kopecks an hour, especially with an ailing, crippled mother whose
eventual death in her remote province barely lightened his load?
The question is now: how should our noble sprig have decided in
all fairness to act? Of course, dear reader, you think he told
himself: 'All my life I have made use of P's gifts; on my
education, my governesses, tens of thousands went to Switzerland on my treatment for idiocy and here I am now with millions
at my disposal, while the noble character of P's son, in no way to
blame for the actions of his light-minded father who forgot about
him, is being worn down giving lessons. Everything that was
spent on me should by rights have gone to him. These huge sums
spent on me are not really mine. It was simply a blind error of
fortune; they should have gone to P's son. They should have
been employed to his benefit not mine, as happened through the
fantastic whim of the light-minded and forgetful P. If I were truly
noble, considerate, and just, I ought to give his son half my
inheritance, but as I am first and foremost a prudent man and am
well aware that this matter lies outside the law, I shall not give
him half my millions. But it would at any rate be too mean and
shameful on my part' (the noble scion forgot that it would not be
prudent either), 'if I do not return to P's son the tens of

thousands spent by P on my idiocy. That would be only right and fair. What would have become of me if P had not brought me up and had taken care of his son instead of me?'

"But no, gentlemen! Our noble scions don't think in that way. Despite the pleading of the young man's lawyer, who had undertaken almost against his will to act for him solely from motives of friendship—no matter how he pointed out the obligations of honour, generosity, justice, and even self-interest, the Swiss ward remained unswayed; and what of it? All that would be nothing, but what was really unforgivable and could not be excused by any interesting illness was that this millionaire, scarcely emerged from his professor's gaiters, could not grasp that the noble disposition of the young man, killing himself giving lessons, was not begging for assistance or asking for alms; he was asking for his rights and for what was due to him, outside the law as it might be; not even asking indeed, his friends were merely interceding on his behalf. With a lordly air and revelling in his newly acquired power to grind people's faces in the dirt with impunity, because of his millions, our sprig takes out a fifty-rouble note and sends it to the young man as a form of arrogant charity. You don't believe me, gentlemen? You are outraged, you are affronted, you are racked by cries of indignation; but nevertheless that is what he did! Naturally the money was returned to him at once, hurled back in his face, so to speak. How then is this matter to be settled? It isn't a legal matter, public opinion is all that remains. We therefore place this story before the public, vouching for its accuracy. We learn that one of our most celebrated humorists has concocted an admirable epigram on the subject, which deserves a place in metropolitan sketches of manners, let alone provincial:

> For five long years young Liova[1] played
> Secure in Schneider's[2] cloak
> And passed the time so blithe and gay
> With childish game and joke.
>
> Then he came home in gaiters tight,

[1] Diminutive of the noble scion's name.
[2] The name of the Swiss professor.

Enormous wealth to find,
And prays to heaven day and night,
While robbing students blind." '

When Kolya had finished he quickly handed the paper to the prince and, without saying a word, rushed off and hid in a corner, covering his face with his hands. He felt intolerably ashamed and his childish sensitivity, not yet inured to filth, was outraged, perhaps even excessively so. He felt that something extraordinary had happened to cast a blight over everything, and that he was practically the cause of it by the very fact of having read it aloud.

But it appeared that everyone had sensed something of the kind as well.

The girls felt very awkward and ashamed. Lizaveta Prokofievna was keeping her intense anger in check as well as perhaps bitterly regretting her involvement in the affair; for the moment she said nothing. The prince was experiencing what very shy people often do in like circumstances: he was so ashamed at the conduct of other people, so ashamed for his visitors, that initially he was afraid even to look at them. Ptitsyn, Varya, Ganya, even Lebedev—all of them looked rather embarrassed. Strangest of all, Ippolit and 'Pavlischev's son' were also apparently taken aback; Lebedev's nephew was also clearly displeased. Only the boxer sat perfectly at ease, gravely twirling his moustaches; his eyes were lowered but not from embarrassment, on the contrary, out of dignified modesty it seemed, and only-too-obvious triumph. He gave every sign of enjoying the article very much indeed.

'This is beyond everything', General Yepanchin growled under his breath. 'Fifty lackeys must have put their heads together to compose that.'

'Pa-armit me to inquire, dear sir, how you can make such insulting suppositions?' Ippolit demanded, all a-tremble.

'This, this, this for a man of honour . . . you must agree, general, if a man of honour . . . it's nothing less than an insult!' growled the boxer, also suddenly rousing himself for some reason, twirling his moustaches and twitching his shoulders and body.

'In the first place, I'm not your "dear sir", and secondly, I have no intention of offering you any explanations', came General

Yepanchin's brusque reply. By now in a thoroughly bad temper, he rose and, without a word, walked to the exit from the veranda, where he stood with his back to the company, highly annoyed at Liza Prokofievna who had no thoughts of quitting her seat even now.

'Gentlemen, gentlemen, do let me say something at least', cried the prince in despairing agitation, 'and please let us talk so that we understand one another. I don't care about the article, gentlemen, let it go, but it's all untrue, you know, what's been printed; I'm saying that because you know it yourselves; it's shameful really. So I would be truly surprised if any one of you had written it.'

'Up till this minute, I didn't know anything about the article', declared Ippolit. 'I don't approve of it.'

'Although I knew it had been written', added Lebedev's nephew, 'I . . . also would not have advised its publication, because it's premature.'

'I knew, but I have the right . . . I . . .', muttered 'Pavlischev's son'.

'What! You wrote all that yourself?' asked the prince, with a searching look at Burdovsky. 'I simply don't believe it!'

'One might, however, refuse to recognize your right to ask such questions', interposed Lebedev's nephew.

'I was only surprised that Mr Burdovsky managed to . . . but . . . I mean to say that if you've already put the matter before the public, why did you get so annoyed just now, when I began talking about it in front of my friends?'

'At last, and about time', murmured Lizaveta Prokofievna indignantly.

'And Prince, you are pleased to forget', Lebedev couldn't resist saying as he squeezed through between the chairs, almost in a fever, 'you are pleased to forget, sir, that it is only your good will and unexampled kindness of heart which made you receive them and hear them out, which they had no right to demand, especially since you had already entrusted the matter to Gavrila Ardalionovich, and that too you did because of your excessive kindliness, and that now, most illustrious Prince, amid your chosen friends, you cannot sacrifice their company for the sake of these gentlemen, sir, and could see all these gentlemen off the veranda, sir, so to speak, so that I as master of the house with the greatest of pleasure, sir . . .'

'Quite right too!' rumbled General Ivolgin suddenly from the back of the room.

'Enough, Lebedev, that's enough now . . .', began the prince, but an explosion of indignation drowned his words.

'No, I'm sorry, Prince, I'm sorry, now it is certainly not enough!' Lebedev's nephew virtually shouted them all down. 'Now this business has to be set out clearly and firmly, since people obviously don't understand it. Now legal quibbles have been brought in and on that basis comes a threat to throw us off the veranda! Surely, Prince, you don't take us for such fools that we don't realize that our case is outside the law, and if it is dealt with legalistically, we haven't the right to demand a single rouble from you? But what we certainly do realize is that if the letter of the law does not apply here, there is such a thing as human, natural right, the law of reason and the voice of conscience; no matter if this law of ours is not written down in some rotten human code of laws, a decent and honest man, a right-thinking man in other words, is bound to remain a decent and honest man even when it isn't written down in codes of law. That is the reason we came here, not afraid we might be thrown off the veranda (as you threatened just now), because we do not *ask*—we *demand*, and as for the impropriety of our visit at such a late hour (although we did not arrive late, it was you who kept us waiting in the servants' hall), that, I say, is why we came without fear, because we supposed you to be a right-thinking man, a man of honour and conscience. Yes, it's true, we didn't come cap in hand, we haven't come as poor relations or parasites, but with our heads held high, like free men, without any intention of pleading, but with a free and proud demand (you hear, not to beg, to demand, make careful note of that!). We put a question to you directly and with dignity: do you consider yourself in the right in the case of Burdovsky or not? Do you admit that you were Pavlischev's beneficiary, even saved from death by him? If you do (as you must), do you, after receiving millions, intend or consider that it squares with your conscience to recompense the son of Pavlischev in his need, even if he does bear the name of Burdovsky? Yes or no? If yes, that is, in other words, if you have what you call in your language honour and conscience and what we designate more precisely common sense, then give us satisfaction and the matter is closed. Satisfaction without conditions and without gratitude from our side, don't expect that, because you're not doing it for our sake but for the sake of justice. If you don't intend to give us satisfaction, however, that is, if your answer is no, then we will leave at once and the matter is at an end; we will say this to your face, in front of all your witnesses, that you are a man of coarse mind and undeveloped sensibility; that henceforth you have no right and will not dare to call yourself a man of honour and conscience—you wish to purchase that right too cheaply. That is all. I have put the question. Turn us out if you dare. You can do that, there are more of you. But remember, we demand, not beg. Demand, not beg!'

Lebedev's nephew stopped, by now thoroughly impassioned.

'Demand, demand, demand, not beg . . . !' stammered Burdovsky, going lobster-red.

These words of Lebedev's nephew created a certain general stir, a murmur of protest even, though obviously no one of the company was eager to get involved in the business with the possible exception of Lebedev, who was in a positive fever of excitement. (It was odd: Lebedev, palpably on the side of the prince, seemed now to feel a certain pleasurable family pride after his nephew's speech; at all events he glanced round the whole gathering with an air of marked satisfaction.)

'In my opinion', the prince began quite softly, 'in my opinion, Mister Doktorenko, you are perfectly correct in half of what you've just said, I would even agree with the greater part; I should have been in total agreement with you if you had not left something out of your speech. What you omitted, I am in no condition to explain exactly, but for it to be completely fair, something is missing of course from what you said. But let us to business, gentlemen, tell me, why did you print that article? There isn't a word in it that isn't libellous; in my opinion, therefore, gentlemen, you have acted shabbily.'

'Look here! . . .'

'My dear sir! . . .'

'This is . . . this is . . . this . . .', came all at once from the excited visitors.

'As regards the article', Ippolit seized shrilly on the point, 'as regards this article, I've already told you that neither I nor the others approve of it! It was he who wrote it (he indicated the boxer sitting next to him), it was wretchedly written, illiterate and in retired-serviceman style, that much I admit. He's stupid and an opportunist too, I agree, I tell him that to his face every day, but he was half-right all the same: free expression of opinion is the right of every man, including Burdovsky therefore. He can answer for his own absurdities. As for my protest on behalf of us all just now about the presence of your friends, I feel I should explain, ladies and gentlemen, that I protested solely in order to assert our rights, but that in fact we really do want to have witnesses and all four of us agreed on that shortly before we came here. Whoever your witnesses may be, your friends if you like, they cannot but acknowledge Burdovsky's claim (since it is obviously a matter of mathematical proof). It's even better that the witnesses should be your friends; the truth will be the plainer.'

'It's true, we did so agree', confirmed Lebedev's nephew.

'Then why did you begin by raising such a clamour and fuss about it just now, if that's what you wanted?' the prince asked in surprise.

'But about the article, Prince', the boxer broke in, desperately keen to have his say and agreeably excited (it might have been suspected that the presence of the ladies was having a powerful and visible influence on him)—about the article, well, I admit that I was the author, though my sick friend, for whom I usually make allowances on account of his condition, has just now criticized it so severely. But I wrote it and published it in the magazine of a sincere friend of mine in the form of a letter to the editor. It's just the poem that isn't really mine, it actually belongs to the pen of a well-known humorist. I only read it to Burdovsky, and not all of it at that; I got his permission to publish it at once, but after all I could have published it without permission. Freedom of expression is a universal right, noble and salutary. I hope that you yourself, Prince, are progressive enough not to deny that . . .'

'I'm not going to deny anything, but you must admit that in your article . . .'

'I was harsh, you're going to say? But there's the matter of the public interest here, so to speak, you have to admit that, and in any case a scandal like this can't be overlooked can it? The public interest must be served, and so much the worse for the guilty. As for certain inexactitudes, hyperboles as it were, you also have to agree that the initiative is what is most important, the aim and intention; the salutary example is important, individual cases can be gone into later; lastly there's the question of style, the humorous form of the thing—and anyway, everybody writes like that, you have to admit! Ha-ha!'

'You were on the wrong track altogether! I assure you, gentlemen', cried the prince. 'You published the article on the assumption that I would in no way agree to satisfy Mister Burdovsky, so you would get back at me somehow by frightening me. But how could you know? Perhaps I had decided to satisfy Mister Burdovsky. I now declare to you plainly, in front of everyone, that I will do so . . .'

'Now at last we have wise and generous words from a wise and most generous man!' proclaimed the boxer.

'Heavens!' blurted Lizaveta Prokofievna.

'This is intolerable!' muttered the general.

'Please, ladies and gentlemen, please', begged the prince. 'I will explain the matter. Five weeks ago, Chebarov—your authorized representative, Mr Burdovsky—came to see me in Z. You have flattered him rather in your article, Mr Keller', the prince turned to the boxer with an abrupt laugh, 'but I didn't take to him at all. I realized at once that this Chebarov was at the bottom of it all, and that perhaps it was he who had taken advantage of your simplicity, Mr Burdovsky, to induce you to initiate the whole business, if I am to speak plainly.'

'You've no right . . . I . . . am not simple . . . this is . . .', babbled Burdovsky nervously.

'You have no right at all to make any such assumptions', Lebedev's nephew interposed sententiously.

'It is in the highest degree offensive!' squeaked Ippolit. 'That assumption is offensive, false, and irrelevant!'

'I'm sorry, gentlemen, I'm sorry', the prince hastened to apologize. 'Please forgive me; it was because I thought it might be better for us to be absolutely frank with one another, but as you wish, it's up to you. I told Chebarov that as I wasn't in Petersburg, I would immediately authorize a friend to deal with the matter and that I would advise you in that regard, Mr Burdovsky. I tell you frankly, gentlemen, that the whole thing seemed to me a complete swindle, for the sole reason that Chebarov was involved . . . Oh, don't be offended, gentlemen! For heaven's sake don't be offended!' the prince exclaimed in alarm, seeing once again Burdovsky's outraged perturbation and the agitated protest of his friends. 'It couldn't relate to you personally, if I said I regarded the thing as a swindle! I knew none of you personally at that time, did I? I didn't even know your names; I was just going by Chebarov; I was speaking in a general sense because . . . if you only knew how dreadfully I've been cheated since I received my legacy!'

'Prince, you are terribly naive', remarked Lebedev's nephew sardonically.

'Nevertheless—a prince and millionaire! You may possibly have a genuinely kind and simple heart, but of course that doesn't mean you can evade the general law', declared Ippolit.

'Possibly, very possibly, gentlemen', the prince said hurriedly, 'though I don't understand what general law you're referring to. Still, I'll go on, as long as you don't take offence for no reason; I swear I haven't the slightest intention of offending you. And really, gentlemen: can't one say a single candid word without you immediately taking offence? Anyway, to start with I was amazed that a son of Pavlischev existed, and in such an appalling situation as Chebarov described. Pavlischev was my benefactor and a friend of my father. (Ah, why did you write such lies about my father in your article, Mr Keller? There was no misappropriation of company funds and no abuse of subordinates—I am absolutely convinced of that—how could your hand bring itself to write such a calumny?) As for what you wrote about Pavlischev, that is altogether intolerable: you call that most noble of men lascivious and frivolous with such boldness and assurance, as if you were really telling the truth, whereas of all men on earth he was the most virtuous! He was a remarkable scholar too; he corresponded with many respected and learned persons and devoted a good deal of money to scholarly projects. As for his kindliness and his good works, oh of course you were correct in writing that I was almost an idiot at that time and understood nothing (though I could speak and understand Russian), but now I can appreciate everything which I can remember now . . .'

'Please', squeaked Ippolit, 'isn't this getting rather too sentimental? We're not children. You wanted to come straight to the point and it's after nine, remember.'

'Certainly, by all means, gentlemen', the prince at once assented. 'After my initial scepticism, I decided that I might be wrong and that Pavlischev might indeed have had a son. But I was most astonished when that son was so blithely, I mean so publicly ready to betray the secret of his birth and, above all, disgrace his mother. Because Chebarov was already threatening me with public exposure at the time . . .'

'That's stupid!' cried Lebedev's nephew.

'You have no right . . . no right!' shouted Burdovsky.

'The son is not responsible for the father's immorality and the mother is innocent', squealed Ippolit vehemently.

'The more reason there was to spare her, surely . . .', said the prince timidly.

'Prince, you are not merely naive, you've gone some way beyond that, perhaps', Lebedev's nephew grinned malevolently.

'And what right had you?' squealed Ippolit in a most unnatural voice.

'None at all, none at all!' the prince hastily put in. You're right about that, I admit, but I couldn't help it and I immediately told myself at the time that my personal feelings ought not to influence me in the matter, for if I acknowledged that I was obliged to satisfy Mr Burdovsky's demands because of my regard for Mr Pavlischev, then I was bound to satisfy them come what may, that is, whether I respected Mr Burdovsky or not. I only brought this up, gentlemen, because it seemed unnatural all the same, that a son should betray his mother's secret so publicly . . . In short, that was what chiefly convinced me that Chebarov was a scoundrel and must have duped Mr Burdovsky and put him up to the swindle himself.'

'Well, that really is intolerable!' came the cry from his visitors, some of whom even leapt up from their seats.

'Gentlemen! But that's just why I came to the conclusion that poor Mr Burdovsky must be a simple, defenceless man, an easy prey to swindlers, therefore the more reason for me to help him as 'Pavlischev's son'—in the first place by thwarting Mr Chebarov, secondly by advising him in a conscientious and friendly manner, and thirdly by giving him ten thousand roubles, which is all that Pavlischev could have spent on me, according to my calculations . . .'

'What? Only ten thousand!' cried Ippolit.

'Well, Prince, your arithmetic's rather weak, or maybe a sight too strong, though you make yourself out to be a simpleton!' exclaimed Lebedev's nephew.

'I won't accept ten thousand', said Burdovsky.

'Antip! Accept it!' prompted the boxer in a swift and audible whisper, bending over Ippolit's chair from behind. 'Accept, and later on we'll see!'

'Lo-ok here, Mr Myshkin', squeaked Ippolit, 'please understand that we're not fools, not common fools—as no doubt all your guests and these ladies are thinking as they sneer so indignantly at us, and especially that fine gentleman' (he indicated Radomsky), 'whom I have not of course the honour of knowing, though I believe I have heard something about him . . .'

'Please, please, gentlemen, you misunderstand me again!' the prince addressed them nervously. 'In the first place, you, Mr Keller, estimated my fortune very inaccurately in your article. I never inherited any millions at all: I might have an eighth or tenth part of what you suppose; secondly, no tens of thousands were spent on me in Switzerland: Schneider used to get six hundred a year, and that was only for the first three years. Pavlischev never went to Paris for pretty governesses; more calumny. In my opinion, the total spent on me altogether comes to much less than ten thousand, but I decided on ten thousand and you will agree that in paying the debt I could not possibly offer Mr Burdovsky more, even if I were terribly fond of him: I could not do that, if only out of tact, just because I was paying a debt, not handing out charity. I fail to see why you don't understand that, gentlemen! But I intended to make all that up to him afterwards through my friendship and a practical interest in the future of this poor Mr Burdovsky, so plainly the victim of deception, because without being duped he certainly could not have agreed to anything as shabby as this disclosure about his mother, for instance, in Mr Keller's article ... But why on earth all the excitement again, gentlemen? We shall never understand one another at this rate, shall we? I was right about it, wasn't I? I can see now with my own eyes that my guess was correct', the prince urged excitedly, thinking to allay their agitation and failing to notice that he was only increasing it.

'What? Right about what?' they demanded, almost frenzied.

'Well for goodness' sake, in the first place I've had time to study Mr Burdovsky myself, I can see now the sort of man he is ... He's an innocent person being deceived by everyone! A defenceless man ... and that's precisely why I must show him mercy. Secondly, Gavrila Ardalionovich, to whom the matter was entrusted and from whom I have heard nothing for a long time, as I was travelling and then taken ill for three days in Petersburg, told me when we met an hour ago that he had got to the bottom of all Chebarov's schemes and has proof that Chebarov is exactly the person I thought him to be. I know, gentlemen, that many people do regard me as an idiot. Chebarov counted on my reputation as one easily parted from his money and thought he could cheat me with ease by playing on my feelings towards Pavlischev. What matters, though—now gentlemen, please hear me out, hear me out!—what matters is that it now turns out that Mr Burdovsky is not Pavlischev's son at all! Gavrila Ardalionovich has just informed me of this and assures me that he has positive proof. Well, what do you think of that? It's incredible after all that's been done! And positive proof, mind you! I still can't believe it, myself, I assure you; I still can't believe it, because Gavrila Ardalionovich hasn't had time to inform me of all the details yet, but there's not the slightest doubt now that Chebarov is a rogue! He has duped Mr Burdovsky and all of you gentlemen who have come here so nobly in support of your friend, a support he badly needs, as I understand only too well! He has duped you all and involved you all in a case of fraud, because that's what it amounts to, essentially, obtaining money by false pretences!'

'Fraud? ... Not Pavlischev's son? ... How can that be? ...', the exclamations came from all sides. The entire Burdovsky group was utterly dismayed.

'But of course it's fraud! If Mr Burdovsky turns out not to be
Pavlischev's son, his demands must constitute plain fraud, if he
knew the truth of course, that is! But that's the whole point, isn't
it? He's been imposed upon, that's why I am insisting his name
be cleared; that's why I repeat that he deserves sympathy for his
naivety and must not be left without support, otherwise he will
also be implicated as a swindler in this affair. You know, I'm
already convinced he doesn't understand a thing! I was in the
same state before I went to Switzerland, babbling incoherent
words, trying to get something out and not being able to . . . I
understand that; I can sympathize intensely, because I'm virtually
the same myself, I am entitled to pronounce on that! Anyway,
although there's no such person as Pavlischev's son and the
whole thing is nothing but a hoax, nevertheless I am not altering
my decision. I am prepared to return the ten thousand in memory
of Pavlischev. Before Mr Burdovsky, I had wanted to use the ten
thousand on a school in memory of Pavlischev, but it will be the
same either way, because if Mr Burdovsky isn't Pavlischev's son,
he's almost 'Pavlischev's son': he has been wickedly deceived
himself and he genuinely thought he was Pavlischev's son! Do
listen to what Gavrila Ardalionovich has to say and we can put an
end to all this, don't be angry, don't excite yourselves, just sit
down! Gavrila Ardalionovich will now tell us all about it, and I
admit that I'm extremely keen to hear all the details myself. He
tells me, Mr Burdovsky, that he even travelled to Pskov to see
your mother, who is far from being dead as you were made to
write in the article . . . Sit down, gentlemen, do sit down!'

The prince seated himself and once more managed to get Mr
Burdovsky's company to do the same after they had started from
their places. For the last ten or twenty minutes he had been
talking loudly and fervently, rattling along impatiently, carried
away indeed, trying to talk or shout everyone down. Afterwards,
of course, he was bound to regret some of the words and phrases
he had blurted out. If he hadn't been roused and his patience
tried almost beyond bearing, he wouldn't have permitted himself
to utter certain of his conjectures so flatly and hastily or indulge
in needless plain-speaking. But one poignant pang of regret
pierced his heart as soon as he had sat down. Apart from having
'offended' Burdovsky, of course, by so openly suggesting he had

the same illness from which he himself had been cured in Switzerland—apart from that, his offer of ten thousand instead of the school had been made crudely and tactlessly in his opinion, as if it had been charity, particularly in view of it having been spoken aloud in front of other people. 'I should have waited and made the offer tomorrow when we were alone', thought the prince at once, 'but there's no help for it now! Yes, I'm an idiot, a real idiot!' he decided to himself in an access of shame and distress.

Meanwhile Gavrila Ardalionovich, up to now stubbornly silent and aloof, moved forward at the prince's invitation and, standing by his side, began giving a calm and lucid account of the affair entrusted to him by the prince. All conversation ceased at once. Everyone listened with rapt curiosity, especially Burdovsky's company.

9

'You will not deny, of course', began Gavrila Ardalionovich, addressing himself directly to Burdovsky, who was all attention, eyes staring in astonishment and plainly utterly dismayed, 'you will not, nor would you, of course, wish seriously to dispute that you were born precisely two years after the marriage of your respected mother to collegiate secretary Burdovsky, your father. The time of your birth is very easy to prove by documentary evidence, so the distortion of fact in Mr Keller's article, so offensive to you and your mother, can only be explained by Mr Keller's own flight of fantasy, thinking, no doubt, to strengthen your claim and so promote your interests. Mr Keller says that he read the article to you beforehand, though not all of it . . . there can be no doubt he didn't read up to that part . . .'

'No, I didn't, that's true', the boxer broke in, 'but all the facts were given to me by a competent person, and I . . .'

'Excuse me Mr Keller', Gavrila Ardalionovich stopped him. 'Allow me to speak. I assure you that we will come to your article at the proper time and you can give your explanations then, but for the moment we had better take things in order. By pure chance, with the help of my sister, I have obtained from an intimate friend of hers, Vera Alexeyevna Zubkova, a widowed landowner, a letter written to her from abroad twenty-four years ago by the late Mr Pavlischev. After making the acquaintance of Madame Zubkova, I applied, at her direction, to a distant relative of hers, Timofey Fedorovich Viazovkin, a retired colonel and one-time great friend of Mr Pavlischev's. I managed to obtain another two letters from Mr Pavlischev, also written abroad. From these three letters and their dates, and from the facts they mention, it can be mathematically demonstrated, without the slightest possibility of refutation or even doubt, that Mr Pavlischev went abroad (where he remained three years together), precisely eighteen months before you were born, Mr Burdovsky. Your mother, as you are aware, never left Russia . . . I won't read the letters at this moment. It's late; I am only stating the facts. But if you wish to fix an appointment with me, tomorrow morning if you like, and bring any number of witnesses and handwriting experts, then I am certain you will not fail to be convinced of the plain truth of the facts I have stated. If that is the case, then the whole business falls to the ground and that's the end of it.'

Once more there was a general stir and great excitement. Suddenly Burdovsky himself rose from his chair.

'If that's so, then I've been deceived, deceived, but not by Chebarov—long before that; I don't want experts, I don't want a meeting, I believe you, I refuse . . . I can't take the ten thousand . . . goodbye . . .'

He took his cap and pushed back his chair to leave.

'If you can, Mr Burdovsky', Ganya stopped him, speaking softly and sweetly, 'then stay for five minutes at least. There are a few more extremely important facts that have turned up in this matter, especially as regards yourself, extremely curious at all events. In my opinion, you really should hear what they are, and it may be that you will feel better yourself, once the whole business is cleared up . . .'

Burdovsky sat down in silence, lowering his head slightly, apparently deep in thought. Lebedev's nephew, who had risen to accompany him, also resumed his seat; though he had retained his composure and self-assurance, he too seemed considerably perplexed. Ippolit was scowling and dejected, apparently greatly astonished. At that moment, however, he began coughing so violently that his handkerchief was stained with blood. The boxer seemed almost afraid.

'Ech, Antip!' he cried bitterly. 'Didn't I tell you at the time . . . the day before yesterday, you might not really be Pavlischev's son!'

There was restrained laughter, two or three louder than the rest.

'The fact you have just stated, Mr Keller', said Ganya, seizing on this, 'is most valuable. Nevertheless, I am fully entitled to state, on the basis of the most accurate information, that although Mr Burdovsky was perfectly well aware of his date of birth of course, he had no notion at all of Pavlischev's residence abroad, where he passed the greater part of his life, returning to Russia for only brief periods. Besides which, the mere fact of Pavlischev's trip at that time is hardly so remarkable in itself that people would remember it after twenty years or more, even those who knew Pavlischev well, let alone Mr Burdovsky, who wasn't even born then. Of course it was not impossible to undertake inquiries, but I have to confess that the information I obtained came to me quite by chance and might very well not have done so; for Mr Burdovsky, and even Chebarov, therefore, such inquiries were really almost impossible, even if it had occurred to them to conduct them. But it might not have occurred to them at that . . .'

'Please, Mr Ivolgin', Ippolit suddenly interrupted crossly, 'what is the point of all this rigmarole, if you'll excuse the expression? The case has been explained now, we have agreed to accept the principal fact, so why drag out this painful and humiliating business any further? Perhaps you want praise for your skilful investigations, to show the prince and us what a good inquiry agent, what a fine detective you are? Or do you mean to excuse and justify Burdovsky on the grounds that he got involved in the matter through ignorance? That is insolence, my dear sir! Burdovsky doesn't need your excuses and justification, if you wish to know! He feels hurt now, he feels wretched over the whole business as it is, he's in an awkward position, you should have realized that and understood . . .'

'All right, Mr Terentyev, all right', Ganya managed to

interpose, 'do calm down, there's no need to excite yourself; you are very unwell aren't you? I sympathize with you. In which case, if you so wish it, I have finished, that is, I will be forced to give a brief account of those facts which, I am convinced, really should be known in detail', he added, noticing a general stir of something like impatience. 'I wish only to say, adducing proof, for the information of everyone concerned in this matter, that your mother, Mr Burdovsky, was the recipient of so much attention and solicitude from Pavlischev because she was the sister of that serf-girl he had loved so deeply in the early days of his youth. He would certainly have married her, if she had not died suddenly. I possess proof that this intimate fact, which is perfectly true and accurate, is very little known, indeed almost forgotten. I might inform you, moreover, that when she was only 10 years old, your mother was taken by Mr Pavlischev to be brought up in place of her sister, that a considerable dowry was set aside for her, and that all this gave rise to most alarming rumours among Pavlischev's numerous relations; they even thought he would wed this ward of his, but it ended, when she was 20 years of age, with her marrying Mr Burdovsky, a land-survey official; it was a love-match—that I can prove most precisely. I have here a number of incontestable facts demonstrating that your father, Mr Burdovsky, who had no head for business at all, threw up his job as soon as he got your mother's fifteen thousand dowry and went into commercial dealings; he was cheated, lost his capital, and started drinking to drown his sorrows. He fell ill as a result and died prematurely, eight years after marrying your mother. Subsequently, according to your mother's own testimony, she was left in poverty and would have perished altogether without Pavlischev's constant and generous help. He made her an allowance of up to six hundred a year. Furthermore, there is a very great deal of evidence that he was extremely fond of you as a child. According to this evidence, again confirmed by your mother, it transpires that his fondness was chiefly because, when you were young, you seemed to be tongue-tied, a cripple, a pitiful, miserable sort of child (and Pavlischev, as I elicited on unimpeachable evidence, had a peculiar kind of tender affection for all who were afflicted and ill-favoured by nature, a fact of crucial importance in this case, in my opinion). Lastly, I can pride myself on some meticulous investigation concerning the vital point—how this exceptional fondness of Pavlischev's towards you (it was due to his efforts that you went to secondary school and had special tuition) engendered at length, little by little, the notion among Pavlischev's relatives and household that you were his son and that your real father had been simply a deceived husband. But the point to remember is that this notion only solidified into a firm and generally held conviction during the last years of Pavlischev's life, when everybody began getting worried about the will, and the original facts had been forgotten and inquiries were impossible. No doubt the idea reached you also, Mr Burdovsky, and took complete possession of you. Your mother, whose acquaintance I had the honour to make, knew about all these rumours, though to this day she does not know that you, her son, had also been taken in by the fascination of the story (I did not enlighten her either). I found your dear mother, Mr Burdovsky, in Pskov, ill and in the extreme poverty into which she fell after Pavlischev's death. She told me with tears of gratitude that it was only through you and your support that she was still alive; she expects a good deal of you in the future and fervently believes in your future success . . .'

'Well this is really intolerable!' Lebedev's nephew declared loudly and impatiently. 'What has all this romantic tale got to do with it?'

'It's disgusting, indecent!' Ippolit jerked sharply in his chair. Burdovsky, however, noticed nothing and did not even stir.

'To do with it? The reason?' Gavrila Ardalionovich expressed arch surprise as he venomously prepared his conclusion. 'Well in the first place, Mr Burdovsky can now be perfectly sure that Mr Pavlischev loved him out of magnanimity, not as a son. He needed to know that one fact, having confirmed and approved Mr Keller's action just now, after the article was read. I say this because I regard you as an honourable man, Mr Burdovsky. Secondly, it turns out that there was not the slightest hint of thievery or fraud involved, even on Chebarov's part; that's an important point for me also, because the prince in his excitement just now implied that I shared his opinion as regards the fraud aspect of this unhappy affair. On the contrary, everyone involved has acted in good faith, and though Chebarov may indeed be a great rogue, he comes out of this affair as no more than a sharp lawyer with an eye for an opportunity. He hoped to make a considerable amount as the legal figure in the affair, and his calculations were not only subtle and skilful, they were perfectly well-founded: he based them on the prince's open-handedness and his grateful veneration towards the late Pavlischev; most importantly, he based them on the prince's known chivalrous views touching the obligations of honour and conscience. As for Mr Burdovsky himself, one could say that, owing to certain convictions of his own, he was so worked upon by Chebarov and the company he kept that he embarked on the affair in a virtually disinterested fashion, almost as a service to truth, progress, and humanity. Now that the facts have been made known, it must be clear to everybody that Mr Burdovsky is without taint, appearances notwithstanding, and the prince can the-more speedily and readily offer him both his friendly co-operation and the practical assistance he mentioned just now when he was speaking of schools and Pavlischev.'

'Stop, Gavrila Ardalionovich, stop!' shouted the prince, genuinely dismayed, but it was too late.

'I told you, I've said it three times', cried Burdovsky in exasperation, 'that I don't want money! I won't take it . . . why . . . I don't want . . . I'm off! . . .'

And he almost ran from the veranda. Lebedev's nephew, however, caught him by the sleeve and whispered something to him. At this, he swiftly came back and, taking a large, unsealed envelope from his pocket, threw it on to the table by the prince.

'There's your money! . . . How dare you . . . dare you! Money! . . .'

'The two hundred and fifty roubles you presumed to send him through Chebarov as charity', explained Doktorenko.

'It says fifty in the article!' shouted Kolya.

'It's my fault!' said the prince, approaching Burdovsky. 'I'm greatly to blame as regards you, Burdovsky, but I didn't send it as charity, believe me. I am to blame now as . . . I was just now.' The prince was very distressed; he looked tired and frail and his words were incoherent. 'I talked about fraud, but I didn't mean you, I was mistaken. I said you . . . were ill like me. But you're not the same as me, you . . . give lessons, you support your mother. I said you had defamed your mother, but you love her; she says so herself . . . I didn't know . . . Gavrila Ardalionovich didn't have time to tell me just now . . . it's my fault. I presumed to offer you ten thousand, but I was wrong, I shouldn't have done it like that, and now . . . I can't because you despise me . . .'

'This is a madhouse!' cried Lizaveta Prokofievna.

'Of course, that's just what it is!' exclaimed Aglaya with asperity, unable to contain herself. Her words, however, were lost in the general hubbub; everyone was talking loudly by now, discussing, quarrelling, laughing. General Ivan Fedorovich Yepanchin was incensed as he waited for Lizaveta Prokofievna with an air of wounded dignity. Lebedev's nephew got in the last word:

'Yes, Prince, give you your due, you certainly know how to make use of your . . . well, illness, to put it politely. You've managed to offer your money and your friendship in such an artful way, that now it's impossible for any honourable man to accept them at all. It's either a little too innocent or a little too cunning . . . only you know which.'

'Excuse me, gentlemen', exclaimed Ganya, who had opened the envelope meanwhile, 'there are only a hundred roubles here, not two hundred and fifty at all. I point this out, Prince, so as to avoid any misunderstandings.'

'Never mind, never mind', the prince waved a hand towards him.

'No, no "never minds"!' Lebedev's nephew seized on this at once. 'Your "never mind" is an insult, Prince. We aren't concealing anything, we declare openly: yes, there are only a hundred roubles there, not the whole amount, but it makes no difference does it? . . .'

'Y-yes, it does', Ganya contrived to break in, with an air of innocent puzzlement.

'Don't interrupt me; we're not the fools you take us for, mister lawyer', cried Lebedev's nephew in savage irritation. 'Of course, one hundred roubles isn't the same as two hundred and fifty, and it does make a difference, but it's the principle that matters; the initiative is what's important here, and the fact that a hundred and fifty roubles are missing is a mere detail. What matters is that

Burdovsky does not accept your charity, your highness, he throws it in your face, so in that sense it's all the same whether it's one hundred or two hundred and fifty roubles. Burdovsky hasn't accepted the ten thousand: you saw that; he wouldn't even have brought back the hundred if he'd been dishonest! The hundred and fifty went on Chebarov's trip to see the prince. Laugh at our awkwardness if you like and our lack of skill in this affair; as it is you've done your best to make us look ridiculous, but don't dare to say that we're dishonest. We shall give the hundred and fifty roubles, with interest, dear sir, back to the prince between us, even if it's a rouble at a time. Burdovsky is a poor man, he has no millions, but Chebarov presented his bill after his journey. We hoped we would win . . . Who wouldn't have done the same in his place?'

'Who indeed!' Prince S exclaimed.

'I shall go mad here!' cried Lizaveta Prokofievna.

'This reminds me', laughed Radomsky, who had been standing watching all this time, 'of the celebrated defence lawyer who recently pleaded the poverty of his client as an excuse for murdering six people in one fell swoop, in order to rob them.* He suddenly ended his speech like this: "It's only natural", says he, "that my client in his poverty should have thought of murdering the six people; who on earth in his position wouldn't have thought of it?" Something like that, most amusing though.'

'Enough!' declared Lizaveta Prokofievna abruptly, fairly shaking with anger. 'Time to put an end to this nonsense!'

She was most dreadfully aroused; she tossed her head menacingly as she stared round at the whole company with flashing eyes, barely distinguishing friend from foe at that moment in the impatience of her fierce and haughty defiance. This was the point when long-suppressed anger at length explodes, and the urge to give battle at once, to attack someone immediately, becomes the overmastering impulse. Those who knew Lizaveta Prokofievna sensed immediately that something exceptional had happened to her. Ivan Fedorovich actually said to Prince S the following day—'she is like that sometimes, but even with her it rarely gets to the pitch it did yesterday, once in three years perhaps, no more than that ever! No more than that!' he added earnestly.

'That's enough, Ivan Fedorovich! Leave me alone!' exclaimed Lizaveta Prokofievna. 'Why offer me your arm now? You couldn't take me away before, could you? You're the husband, you're the head of the family, you should have taken me out by the ear, fool that I am, if I didn't obey and go with you. You might have considered your daughters at least! So now we'll find our way by ourselves, shame enough to last a year . . . Wait, I've still got to thank the prince! . . . Thank you Prince, for the entertainment! To think it was me who sat on to hear what the young people had to say . . . It's vile, vile! It's chaos, an outrage, you wouldn't see this in your wildest dreams! Are there really many like them? . . . Be quiet Aglaya! Be quiet Alexandra! This is none of your business! . . . Don't keep fussing around me, Yevgeni Pavlich, you're getting on my nerves! . . . So you are asking their forgiveness, dear, are you?' she resumed, addressing the prince. ' "I'm sorry", he says, "for presuming to offer you lots of cash", and what are you laughing at, Mister Swagger?' she turned on Lebedev's nephew all of a sudden. ' "We reject your money", he says, "we demand, not beg!" As if he didn't know that this idiot will call on them tomorrow, offering his friendship and cash! You will, won't you? Yes or no?'

'Yes', said the prince, his voice gentle and meek.

'You heard that! It's exactly what you're counting on, isn't it?' She turned to Doktorenko again. 'The money is as good as in your pocket, and all your swagger is just to pull the wool over our eyes . . . No, darling, find some other fool, I can see right through you . . . right through your little game!'

'Lizaveta Prokofievna!' cried the prince.

'Let's go, Lizaveta Prokofievna, it's high time; we can take the prince with us', smiled Prince S as coolly as he was able.

The girls stood apart, almost in dismay, while the general was dismayed in good earnest; general astonishment reigned. Those standing furthest away were grinning surreptitiously and whispering among themselves; Lebedev's face was a picture of utter rapture.

'You'll find chaos and outrage everywhere, madame', said Lebedev's nephew weightily, a good deal disconcerted all the same.

'But nothing like this! Not like what you're doing, sir, nothing like this!' Lizaveta Prokofievna caught him up gleefully, seemingly hysterical. 'Leave me alone, will you', she shouted at those urging her away. 'Oh no, if, as you said yourself just now, Yevgeni Pavlovich, that even a defence counsel stated in court that there was nothing more natural for a man than to do away with six people on account of his poverty, then it's the end of the world and that's all about it. I've never heard the like. Now it all makes sense! This tongue-tied one here (she indicated Burdovsky, who was regarding her with utter bewilderment), wouldn't he commit murder? I'll wager he would! He won't take your money, perhaps, the ten thousand, because it's against his conscience, perhaps, but he'd come in the night to cut your throat and steal it from your cash-box. That would be according to conscience! That would be an honourable course for him! That would be "an impulse of noble despair", "a protest", or goodness only knows what... Tcha! Everything's backside-foremost with them, upside-down. A girl grows up in a house, then all of a sudden she jumps into a droshky in the street: "Mummy, I got married to some Karlich or Ivanich the other day, goodbye!"* That's a proper way to behave, you think? Natural, to be applauded? The woman question? This boy here (she indicated Kolya), even he was arguing the other day that this is what the 'woman question' amounts to. Even if the mother's a fool, you should still treat her as a human being!... What was the idea of coming in here with your noses in the air, "don't dare come near us, here we come. Give us every right, but not a squeak out of you. Show us every mark of respect, unprecedented respect, but we'll treat you worse than the lowest servant!" They seek the truth and stand on their rights, but they slandered him right and left in their article like heathens: "We do not beg we demand, and you'll hear no gratitude from us, because you're doing it to satisfy your own conscience!" What a morality! After all, if you're not going to show any gratitude, the prince can answer you the same way—by saying that he doesn't feel any gratitude towards Pavlischev, because he too was only doing good to salve his conscience. Yet it's that gratitude of his towards Pavlischev that you were counting on, weren't you? He didn't borrow any money from you, did he? He doesn't owe you anything, so what were you counting on if not on his gratitude?

How can you repudiate it yourself then? You're mad! They regard society as savage and inhumane because it despises a seduced girl. But if you regard society as inhumane, you have to admit that the girl suffers from society's attitude; if that's the case, how can you expose her before that same society in the newspapers and expect her not to suffer? It's madness! Presumption! They don't believe in God, they don't believe in Christ! You're so eaten up with pride and vanity, you'll end up devouring each other, I prophesy that for you. And isn't that utter nonsense, isn't it confusion, isn't it an outrage? And after all that, this shameful man has to crawl to them and ask forgiveness! Are there many like you, then? What are you laughing at? That I've lowered myself talking to you? So I have, and there's nothing I can do about that! . . . And you can stop grinning, scarecrow!' she flung suddenly at Ippolit. 'He can hardly breathe himself, but corrupts other people. You've corrupted this lad here', she again pointed to Kolya. 'All he can do is rave about you, you teach him atheism, you don't believe in God, but you're not too old to be whipped, sir, oh, to blazes with you! . . . Well are you going to them tomorrow, Prince Lev Nikolayevich?' she asked the prince once more, almost out of breath.

'Yes.'

'Then I don't wish to know you after this!' She turned quickly to go, but abruptly came back. 'You're going to see this atheist too?' she indicated Ippolit. 'What on earth are you grinning at me for?' she shouted, rushing towards Ippolit, unable to stand his sarcastic smirking.

'Lizaveta Prokofievna! Lizaveta Prokofievna!' came in unison from all sides.

'*Maman*, this is shameful!' shouted Aglaya.

'Don't worry, Aglaya Ivanovna', replied Ippolit calmly, though Lizaveta Prokofievna had unaccountably seized him by the arm and was gripping it tightly; she was standing in front of him, her frenzied stare boring into him. 'Don't worry, your *maman* will soon see that she shouldn't attack a dying man . . . I'm perfectly willing to explain why I was laughing . . . I'd be very grateful for your permission . . .'

At this he suddenly had a terrible bout of coughing, which lasted a whole minute before he could control it.

'Here he's dying and still speechifying!' exclaimed Lizaveta Prokofievna, releasing his arm and watching him wipe the blood from his lips with something approaching horror. 'You oughtn't to be talking! You should just go and lie down . . .'

'That's what I'll do', Ippolit replied in a low, husky voice, almost a whisper. 'I'll lie down as soon as I get home today . . . In two weeks' time I'm going to die, I know that, Dr Botkin himself told me last week . . . So, if you will allow me, I should like to say a few last words.'

'Have you lost your senses, or what? Nonsense! You should be having treatment and no buts! Be off, be off to your bed! . . .', cried Lizaveta Prokofievna in alarm.

'If I go to bed now, I shan't get up again before I die', smiled Ippolit. 'I wanted to take to my bed yesterday and not get up again, but I decided to put it off till the day after tomorrow, while my legs could still carry me . . . so I could come here with them today . . . only I'm so very tired . . .'

'Sit down, sit down, what are you standing for? Here's a chair', Lizaveta Prokofievna cried and placed a chair for him herself.

'I thank you', Ippolit went on softly, 'and you sit opposite and we'll have a talk . . . we must do that, Lizaveta Prokofievna, I insist.' He again smiled at her. 'Just think, today is the last time I shall be out in the open air, among people, and in two weeks' time I shall be under the earth for certain. So this is a kind of farewell to people and to nature. Although I'm not very sentimental, actually I'm very glad that it's happened in Pavlovsk: at least I can see a tree in leaf.'

'What do you mean, talk!' Lizaveta Prokofievna was becoming more and more alarmed. 'You're all feverish. All squeals and squeaks a minute ago and now you're out of breath, you're panting!'

'I shall be all right presently. Why do you want to refuse my last wish? . . . You know I've wanted to meet you for a long time, Lizaveta Prokofievna; I've heard a lot about you . . . from Kolya; he's practically the only one not to desert me . . . You're an unusual woman, an unpredictable woman, I've seen that now for myself . . . You know I was even rather fond of you?'

'Good lord, and I was really going to hit him.'

'Aglaya Ivanovna held you back; I'm not mistaken, am I? It is your daughter, Aglaya Ivanovna? She's so pretty, I guessed who she was at once, though I've never seen her. At least let me look at a beautiful woman for the last time', Ippolit's smile was twisted and awkward. 'The prince is here, and your husband, and the whole company. Why won't you let me have my last wish?'

'A chair!' shouted Lizaveta Prokofievna, but seized one herself and sat down opposite Ippolit. 'Kolya', she commanded, 'you go with him at once, see him home, and tomorrow I'll certainly . . .'

'If you please, I'd like to ask the prince for a cup of tea . . . I'm very tired. You know, Lizaveta Prokofievna, you wanted to invite the prince back to your villa to drink tea, I believe; why not stay and we'll pass the time here, and the prince will give us all tea, no doubt. I'm sorry to be giving all the orders . . . But I do know you as a kind-hearted person, the prince as well . . . we're all absurdly kind-hearted folk . . .'

The prince bestirred himself. Lebedev rushed out at full speed, with Vera after him.

'True enough', decided Madame Yepanchina crisply, 'talk if you must, but keep your voice down and don't get carried away. You've made me feel sorry for you . . . Prince! You don't deserve that I should take tea with you, but so be it, I'll stay, but I'm not apologizing to anyone! Anyone! Nonsense! . . . Still, if I did scold you Prince, I beg your pardon—however, just as you like. I'm not detaining anyone, though.' She addressed her husband and daughters abruptly, with an expression of considerable anger, as if they were greatly to blame for something in her eyes. 'I can get home by myself . . .'

She was not allowed to finish. Everybody came up and surrounded her readily. The prince at once began pressing them all to stay for tea and apologized for not thinking of it before. Even the general was gracious enough to murmur something reassuring, and asked Lizaveta Prokofievna whether it was not too cool for her out on the veranda. He nearly asked Ippolit how long he had been at university, but forbore. Radomsky and Prince S suddenly became extremely affable and cheerful, the faces of Adelaida and Alexandra registered pleasure even through their lingering astonishment; in a word, everyone was clearly glad that the crisis with Lizaveta Prokofievna had passed. Aglaya alone was frowning as she sat down away from the others in silence. The rest of the company stayed on as well; no one wanted to leave, not even General Ivolgin, despite Lebedev whispering something to him in passing which was probably not over-pleasant and caused him to efface himself at once in a corner. The prince also approached Burdovsky and his group with his invitation, missing out nobody. They mumbled stiffly that they would wait for Ippolit, and at once betook themselves to the furthest corner of the veranda, where they again seated themselves all in a row. Doubtless Lebedev had made the tea for himself long ago, as it appeared instantly. Eleven o'clock struck.

10

IPPOLIT moistened his lips a little with the cup of tea Vera Lebedeva handed him, set it down on the table, and then suddenly looked about him in bemusement, almost as if he were embarrassed.

'Look, Lizaveta Prokofievna, these cups', he began speaking with an odd haste, 'they're porcelain and excellent porcelain at that, I think. Lebedev always keeps them locked up in the display cabinet. They're never brought out and used . . . that's how it is; they were part of his wife's dowry . . . that's how it usually is . . . and here he's handing them out, in your honour, of course, that's how pleased he is . . .'

He was about to add something more, but failed to find words.

'He's feeling self-conscious, I knew he would!' Radomsky whispered in the prince's ear. 'That's dangerous, don't you think? It's a sure sign he'll come out with something so eccentric, just out of spite, that even Lizaveta Prokofievna, I fear, won't tolerate it.'

The prince looked at him questioningly.

'You're not concerned if it happens?' asked Radomsky. 'Nor am I really, I rather hope it does; all I want is for dear Lizaveta Prokofievna to get her deserts, tonight, this minute; till that happens I don't want to leave. You're looking feverish.'

'Later; don't bother me. Yes, I am feeling unwell', responded the prince absently, with a touch of impatience. He had caught his name, Ippolit was talking about him.

'You don't believe it?' Ippolit was laughing hysterically. 'Naturally, but the prince will believe it straight away and he won't turn a hair.'

'You hear, Prince?' Lizaveta Prokofievna turned towards him, 'you hear?'

There was laughter round about. Lebedev kept pushing himself forward fussily, bustling about in front of Lizaveta Prokofievna.

'He says that this cringing fellow, this landlord of yours, corrected that gentleman's article, the one that was read against you just now.'

The prince looked at Lebedev in astonishment.

'Why don't you say something?' Lizaveta Prokofievna even stamped her foot.

'Well', the prince murmured, still staring at Lebedev, 'I can see now he did correct it.'

'Is it true?' Lizaveta Prokofievna turned swiftly to Lebedev.

'Perfectly true, your highness!' Lebedev replied firmly and unhesitatingly, placing his hand on his heart.

'You'd think he was proud of it!' she almost leapt from her chair.

'I'm vile, vile!' mumbled Lebedev, beginning to beat his breast and incline his head lower and lower.

'What's it to me whether you're vile or not? He thinks if he says "vile" he can wriggle out of it. Aren't you ashamed, Prince, having to do with such wretched people? That's again I'm asking you. I'll never forgive you!'

'The prince will forgive me!' Lebedev said with affectionate conviction.

'Strictly from honourable motives', said Keller in a loud, ringing voice as he addressed Lizaveta Prokofievna directly, 'strictly from honourable motives, madam, and so as not to betray a compromised friend, I kept quiet about the corrections just now, despite his offering to kick us down the stairs, as you heard yourself, madam. To put the matter right, I admit that I did have recourse to him as a competent person, for six roubles, but not at all for the style; it was to find out facts which were for the most part unknown to me. About the gaiters, his appetite at the Swiss professor's, the fifty roubles instead of two hundred and fifty—all that sequence of events is his responsibility, for six roubles, but he didn't correct my style.'

'I must point out', Lebedev interrupted in a fever of impatience, his voice near to grovelling, as the laughter continued to swell, 'that I corrected only the first half of the article, but as we disagreed and fell out over a certain idea, I didn't correct the second half, ma'am, so anything illiterate there (and there certainly is!) is nothing to do with me, ma'am . . .'

'That's all that concerns him!' cried Lizaveta Prokofievna.

'Allow me to enquire', Radomsky asked Keller, 'when the article was corrected?'

'Yesterday morning', replied Keller, 'we had a meeting, and swore to keep it secret on both sides.'

'That was when he was crawling to you and assuring you of his devotion! What wretches! I don't want your Pushkin, and I don't want your daughter to come to me!'

Madame Yepanchina was on the point of rising when she turned abruptly to the laughing Ippolit:

'Did you mean to make me a laughing-stock, dear, or what?'

'God forbid', Ippolit smiled wryly. 'But what strikes me most of all is your amazing eccentricity, Lizaveta Prokofievna; I confess, I deliberately gave Lebedev away, I knew the effect it would have on you, only on you, because the prince will certainly forgive him, doubtless already has . . . perhaps even thought up an excuse for him, that's so isn't it, Prince?'

He was panting, his strange agitation increasing with every word.

'Well? . . .' said Lizaveta Prokofievna angrily, astonished at his tone. 'Well?'

'I've heard a good deal about you, in the same vein . . . with much gladness . . . and learned to respect you very much', Ippolit went on.

He was saying one thing, but the words seemed to be implying something else entirely. He spoke with a hint of a sneer, at the same time with an incongruous agitation, gazing suspiciously about him, obviously muddled and faltering at every word; all this, taken together with his consumptive appearance and the strange, glittering, almost frenzied look in his eyes, could not help but keep him the object of attention.

'I would have been surprised, however, knowing hardly anything of the world (that I admit), at your staying here in the company of my friends—hardly fitting for you—but that you also allowed these ... young ladies to hear the details of this scandalous affair, even if they've read all about such things in novels. Perhaps, still, I don't know ... because I get confused, but at all events, who besides you could stay behind ... at the request of a boy (yes, a boy, I admit that too) and spend the evening with him and get so utterly involved ... so that next day you'd be ashamed of yourself ... (I realize I'm not expressing myself properly), all that I greatly appreciate and respect profoundly, although I can see from his excellency your husband's face alone, how disagreeable he finds all this ... He-he!' he giggled, losing the thread completely, before coughing so much that he was unable to resume for about two minutes.

'Gone and choked himself!' said Lizaveta Prokofievna, cold and brusque, regarding him with grim curiosity. 'Well, dear lad, I've had enough of you. Time to go!'

'And may I point out to you for my part, dear sir', General Yepanchin spoke up crossly all of a sudden, having finally lost patience altogether, 'that my wife is here as the guest of Prince Lev Nikolayevich, our mutual friend and neighbour, and in any case it is not for you, young man, to sit in judgement on what Lizaveta Prokofievna does, nor to mention aloud and in my presence what is written on my face. Yes indeed. And if my wife stayed behind here', he went on, getting more irritable with every word, 'it was more from astonishment, sirrah, and the wholly understandable modern interest in such odd young people. I stayed myself, just as I stop in the street sometimes when I see something worth a glance as a ... as ... as ...'

'A curiosity', suggested Radomsky.

'Excellently put and quite right', the general rejoiced, having got his comparisons somewhat tangled, 'as a curiosity indeed. But in any case, what I find most astonishing and even aggrieving, if it is grammatical to put it that way, is that you, young man, couldn't comprehend that Lizaveta Prokofievna has stayed with you now because you're ill—if you really are dying, that is—out of compassion, so to speak, because of your piteous words, sirrah, and that no mud can attach itself to her name, character, and social standing in any way ... Lizaveta Prokofievna!' concluded the general, red in the face, 'if you wish to go, let us take leave of the good prince and ...'

'Thank you for the lesson, general', Ippolit gravely broke in, gazing thoughtfully at him.

'Let's be off, *maman*, how long is this to go on! ...', Aglaya brought out, angrily impatient as she rose from her chair.

'Two minutes more, dear Ivan Fedorovich, if you will.' Lizaveta Prokofievna turned to her husband with a dignified air: 'I think he's altogether feverish and this is just raving; I'm sure of that from his eyes; he can't be left like this. Lev Nikolayevich, could he stay the night here, so he doesn't have to drag himself to Petersburg today? *Cher* Prince, are you getting bored?' she suddenly addressed Prince S for some reason. 'Come here, Alexandra, tidy your hair up, my dear.'

She tidied her hair, which was perfectly tidy already, then kissed her; she'd only called her over for that.

'I thought you capable of developing ...', Ippolit spoke up again, emerging from his meditation. 'Yes! That's what I wanted to say.' He seemed pleased at the sudden recollection. 'So Burdovsky really wants to protect his mother, doesn't he? But it turns out that it's he who has shamed her. Now the prince wants to assist Burdovsky and from the goodness of his heart offers him his tender friendship and large amounts of money and is, perhaps, the only one of you who doesn't feel revulsion towards him, and here they are standing face to face like sworn enemies ... Ha-ha-ha! You all detest Burdovsky because, in your opinion, his behaviour towards his mother is unbecoming and in poor taste, isn't that so? You all do love the beauty and elegance of outward appearances, it's what you live for isn't it? It is, isn't it? I've long suspected it was only for that! Well, you should know that probably not one of you has loved his mother like Burdovsky does! I know that you, Prince, have sent money secretly to Burdovsky's mother by way of Ganya, and I'll bet you anything—he-he-he!' he laughed hysterically—'I'll wager that Burdovsky will now accuse you of want of tact and disrespect towards his mother, he really will, ha-ha-ha!'

Here he choked again and began coughing.

'Well, is that all of it? Have you got everything out now?' Lizaveta Prokofievna interrupted impatiently, keeping her anxious gaze fixed on him. 'Well then, off you go and lie down, you're feverish. Oh Lord, he's still talking!'

'You're laughing, are you? Why do you keep laughing at me? I've noticed you keep on laughing at me!' Restless and irritable, he abruptly addressed Radomsky who actually was laughing.

'I only wanted to ask you, Mister . . . Ippolit . . . I'm sorry, I've forgotten your surname.'

'Mister Terentyev', said the prince.

'Yes, Terentyev, thank you, Prince, it was mentioned just now but it slipped my mind . . . I wanted to ask you, Mister Terentyev, whether what I've heard is true—you consider that you would only have to speak out of the window to the common people for quarter of an hour, for them to agree with you at once about everything and follow you immediately?'

'I may very well have said that . . .', replied Ippolit, seeming to recall something. 'Yes, I certainly did!' he added suddenly, brightening up again and looking hard at Radomsky. 'What of it, then?'

'Nothing at all; I just wanted to know, to complete the picture.'

Radomsky fell silent, but Ippolit kept on looking at him in expectant impatience.

'Well then, have you finished, or what?' Lizaveta Prokofievna asked Radomsky. 'Hurry up and finish, sir, it's time he was in bed. Or don't you know how?' She was extremely annoyed.

'Indeed', resumed Radomsky with a smile, 'I'm very much tempted to add that everything I've heard from your comrades, Mister Terentyev, and everything you've expounded in so accomplished a fashion just now, boils down, in my opinion, to a theory of the triumph of right—before and apart from all else, to the exclusion of all else indeed, even before analysing exactly what that right is. Perhaps I'm mistaken?'

'Of course you are. I don't even understand what you mean . . . What else?'

Sounds of protest came from the corner. Lebedev's nephew muttered something in an undertone.

'Very little else', Radomsky went on. 'I merely wished to point out that it's easy to jump straight from that position to the idea of might is right, that is, the right of the individual clenched fist and personal will, as it very often has been, incidentally, in world affairs. Proudhon himself maintained that might was right. In the American Civil War, many of the most advanced liberals declared for the plantation-owners, on the ground that negroes were negroes, inferior to the whites, and therefore the whites' power over them was right . . .'

'Well?'

'You mean you don't repudiate might is right?'

'Go on.'

'You're consistent anyway; I merely wanted to observe that from might is right, it's not a great step to the right of tigers and crocodiles, even Danilov and Gorsky.'

'I don't know: what else?'

Ippolit was hardly listening to Yevgeni Pavlovich. If he kept saying 'Well?' or 'What else', it appeared to be more an old conversational habit he had acquired, rather than from any attention or curiosity.

'Er, nothing else . . . that's it.'

'Anyway I'm not angry with you', Ippolit concluded quite unexpectedly, even holding out his hand with a smile, barely conscious of what he was doing. Radomsky was at first surprised, but touched the proffered hand gravely, as if receiving forgiveness.

'I can't help adding', he said in the same ambiguously respectful tone, 'my gratitude to you for your courtesy in permitting me to speak, because from my numerous observations, your liberal is incapable of allowing anyone to have their own point of view without immediately swearing at their opponent, or worse . . .'

'You're absolutely right there', put in General Yepanchin, and folding his hands behind his back, he retreated with an air of utter boredom to the veranda steps, where he yawned in vexation.

'Now that's enough from you, sir', Lizaveta Prokofievna suddenly announced to Radomsky. 'I'm sick and tired of you all . . .'

'Time to go!' Ippolit suddenly got up anxiously, almost in dismay, and gazed about him in bewilderment. 'I've detained you; I wanted to tell you everything . . . I thought you all . . . for the last time . . . it was a delusion . . .'

It was clear that he was emerging sporadically from virtual delirium for a sudden few seconds, recalling and speaking with full awareness, for the most part in disconnected phrases, perhaps pondered and worked out during the long, dreary hours of his illness, in bed, in sleepless solitude.

'Well, goodbye!' he said with curt abruptness. 'You think it's easy for me to say "goodbye" to you? Ha-ha!' he laughed wryly at his own *awkward* question, then suddenly, as if angry with himself for failing to say everything he had wanted to, spoke loudly and angrily: 'Your excellency! I have the honour to request your attendance at my interment, if you will do me such an honour that is, and . . . all of you ladies and gentlemen, after the general! . . .'

He started laughing again, but now it was the laugh of a madman. Lizaveta Prokofievna moved anxiously towards him and seized him by the arm. He regarded her intently, the laugh now cut short and seemingly frozen on his face.

'Do you know I came here to see the trees? These here . . .' he indicated the trees in the park. 'That's not silly is it? There's nothing silly in that, is there?' he asked Lizaveta Prokofievna earnestly, whereupon he became lost in thought. After a second, he raised his head and began eagerly surveying the crowd. He was looking for Radomsky, who was standing not far away to his right, as before, but he had forgotten this by now as his eyes roved. 'Ah, there you are, you're still there!' he found him at length. 'You kept laughing just now about me wanting to speak from a window for fifteen minutes . . . But do you know, I'm not 18 yet: I've lain so long on that pillow and stared so long out of that window, and pondered so much . . . about everybody . . . that . . . A dead man has no age, you realize. I thought of that only last week, when I woke up in the night . . . And do you know what your greatest fear is? You fear our sincerity above all else, even though you despise us! I thought of that too, as I was lying on my pillow one night . . . You thought I wanted to make fun of you a little while ago, Lizaveta Prokofievna? No, I wasn't making fun of you, I simply wanted to praise you . . . Kolya was saying that the prince called you a child . . . that's nice . . . Yes, what was it I . . . something else I wanted . . .'

He buried his face in his hands and became plunged in thought.

'Ah, yes: when we were saying goodbye just now, I thought: here are these people and they will never be there again, never! The trees as well—there'll just be the brick wall, red, Meyer's house . . . opposite my window . . . well, tell them about all that . . . just try and tell them: here's a beautiful girl . . . but you're dead . . . introduce yourself as a dead man, say "a dead man can say anything" . . . and that Princess Maria Alexevna won't scold,* ha-ha! You're not laughing?' His eyes surveyed them all mistrustfully. 'You know, lots of ideas used to come to me on that pillow . . . I've decided, you know, that nature is very ironic . . . you said just now I was an atheist, but nature you know . . . why are you laughing again? You're terribly cruel!' he suddenly brought out with sad indignation, looking round at them all. 'I have not been corrupting Kolya', he concluded in quite a different tone, with earnest conviction, as if just remembering that also.

'Nobody here's laughing at you, nobody, do calm down!' Lizaveta Prokofievna was almost anguished. 'There's a new doctor coming tomorrow; that one of yours was mistaken; sit down, do! You can barely stand up! You're raving . . . Oh, what are we to do with him now?' she fussed about, seating him in his chair. A tear glistened on her cheek.

Ippolit stopped short, almost overcome, and lifting his hand, reached out gingerly and touched the tear-drop. He smiled a sort of childlike smile.

'I . . . you . . .', he said joyously, 'you don't know how I . . . how he, Kolya there, always spoke of you with such enthusiasm. I loved that enthusiasm of his. I have not been corrupting him! He's the only one I'm leaving . . . I wanted to leave them all, all of them, but there was no one, no one . . . I wanted to be a public figure, I had the right . . . Oh, all the things I wanted! I don't want anything now, I don't want to want anything, I vowed not to want anything any more; let them seek the truth without me, let them! Yes, nature is ironic! Why does she create the best of beings', he suddenly enlarged on this fervently, 'only to make a mockery of them afterwards? It is her doing that the only human being acknowledged on earth as perfect . . . her doing that having shown him to men, she destined him to say things which have caused so much blood to be spilt, that had it been spilt at once people would have drowned in it most likely! Oh, it's a good thing I'm dying! Perhaps I too would have uttered some frightful lie, betrayed by nature in the same way!... I haven't corrupted anyone... I wanted to live for the happiness of all men, to discover and proclaim the truth... I used to look out of the window at Meyer's wall and think of speaking for just fifteen minutes and convincing everybody, everybody, and now, for once in my life I've met you, if not the people, and what has come of it? Nothing! What's come of it is that you despise me! So I'm useless, so I'm a fool, so it's time to go! And I haven't managed to leave a single memory of me behind! No sound, no trace, not a single thing accomplished, not one of my convictions spread abroad! Don't laugh at a fool! Forget him! Forget everything... forget it please, don't be so cruel! Do you realize that if this consumption hadn't come along, I'd have killed myself...'

It seemed he had a good deal more to say, but he did not finish; throwing himself into his chair he buried his face in his hands and wept like a little child.

'Well, what are we going to do with him now?' cried Lizaveta Prokofievna, as she rushed over to him, seized his head, and pressed it as hard as could be to her bosom. He sobbed convulsively. 'There, there, there, don't cry now, there that'll do, you're a good boy, God will forgive you your ignorance; that's enough now, be a man ... besides, you'll be ashamed of yourself...'

'At home', said Ippolit, striving to raise his head, 'I have a brother and sisters, little children, poor, innocent... she will corrupt them! You are a saint, you... are a child yourself—save them! Tear them away from that woman... she... shame... Oh, help them, help them, God will repay you a hundredfold, for God's sake, for Christ's sake!'

'Well, tell me what's to be done now, Ivan Fedorovich!' cried Lizaveta Prokofievna, exasperated—'Be good enough to break your regal silence! If you don't decide, I should tell you that I'm staying the night here myself; you've lorded it over me long enough!'

Lizaveta Prokofievna posed the question with considerable

spirit and anger, expecting an immediate answer. In these circumstances, however, people tend for the most part to respond with silence and a passive, non-committal interest, no matter how large the company, and give vent to their thoughts much later. Among those present were some who were quite prepared to stay there till morning if need be, without uttering a word, Varvara Ardalionovna, for example, who had been sitting a little apart the whole evening, silently listening with intense interest, having perhaps her own reasons for so doing.

'My opinion, my dear', declared the general, 'is that what is needed now, so to speak, is a sick-nurse, rather than all our commotion, and perhaps a sober, reliable person for the night. At all events, we should ask the prince and . . . give him some peace and quiet at once. Tomorrow we can take up the matter again.'

'It's twelve o'clock now, we're going. Is he coming with us or staying with you?' Doktorenko addressed the prince in angry exasperation.

'If you wish—stay here with him as well', said the prince, 'there's room enough.'

'Your excellency', Mr Keller unexpectedly and rapturously skipped up to the general, 'if you want a competent man for the night, I'm prepared to make the sacrifice for a friend . . . what a soul! I've long regarded him as a great man, your excellency! I've neglected my own education, of course, but when he criticizes me, it's just pearls, pearls scattering, your excellency! . . .'

The general turned away in despair.

'I'll be very glad if he stays, of course, he'll have trouble getting back', announced the prince in answer to Lizaveta Prokofievna's irritable questioning.

'Are you asleep or what? If you don't want him, sir, I can take him home with me! Heavens, he can hardly stand upright! Are you feeling ill, or what?'

Having failed to find the prince on his deathbed that evening, Lizaveta Prokofievna really had overestimated his state of health, but his recent illness and the painful recollections associated with it, the fatigue of this strenuous evening, the incident with 'Pavlischev's son', and this present incident with Ippolit—it had all exacerbated the prince's morbid sensitivity almost to the point of actual fever. Moreover, his eyes now expressed a new anxiety, almost a fear; he was looking at Ippolit in trepidation, apparently in expectation of something more from him.

All of a sudden Ippolit stood up, fearfully pale, with an expression of terrible shame verging on despair contorting his features. This was expressed chiefly in the fearful and hateful way he looked at the gathering and in the forlorn, wryly ironic smile spreading across his trembling lips. He dropped his eyes at once and made his way unsteadily, still with the same smile, towards Burdovsky and Doktorenko, who were standing by the veranda steps: he was going with them.

'That's just what I was afraid of!' cried the prince. 'It was bound to happen!'

Ippolit swiftly rounded on him in the most savage frenzy, his every facial feature seeming to quiver and speak out.

'Ah, that's what you were afraid of! "It was bound to happen", you think? Then let me tell you, that if I hate anybody here', he yelled hoarsely, shrieking and spluttering, '—I hate you all, all of you!—it's you, you jesuitical, syrupy little soul, idiot, millionaire-benefactor, you more than anyone and anything in the world! I understood and hated you long ago, when I first heard of you I hated you with all the hatred in my soul . . . You're responsible for all this! It's you who've brought on my attack! You've made a dying man ashamed of himself, you're to blame, you, you, you for my contemptible cowardice! If I had any time left to live, I'd kill you! I don't need your good works, I won't take anything from anybody, anybody, you hear? I was delirious, so don't dare to crow! . . . Damn every one of you, once and for all!'

At this point he choked completely.

'Ashamed of his tears!' hissed Lebedev to Lizaveta Prokofievna, ' "it was bound to happen!" Bravo Prince! Saw right through him . . .'

But Lizaveta Prokofievna did not deign to glance at him. She was standing proudly erect, head thrown back, surveying 'those wretched people' with contemptuous curiosity. When Ippolit had finished, the general made to shrug his shoulders; she looked him up and down angrily, as if to ask him to account for his gesture, and turned at once to the prince.

'Thank you Prince, eccentric friend of our family, for the agreeable evening you have provided for us all. No doubt your heart must be glad that you managed to involve us with your fooleries ... Let's have no more of it, dear friend of the household, and thank you for letting us get a good insight into what you are at least.'

She began adjusting her cloak indignantly, waiting for 'them' to go. A droshky, for which Doktorenko had sent Lebedev's schoolboy son a quarter of an hour earlier, now rolled up for 'them'. The general had his say too, immediately after his wife.

'Really Prince, I didn't expect ... after all ... after all our friendly relations ... and there's my wife ...'

'How can you, how can you, father!' exclaimed Adelaida, quickly moving to the prince and giving him her hand.

The prince smiled forlornly at her. Suddenly a hot, rapid whisper seemed to scorch his ear.

'If you don't get rid of these loathsome people this minute, I shall hate you all my life, all my life!' hissed Aglaya; she seemed to be in a kind of frenzy, but she had turned away before the prince was able to look at her. In any case, there was nothing and nobody for him to get rid of: the ailing Ippolit had somehow been bestowed in the cab by this time and the droshky had driven off.

'Well then, how long is this to go on, Ivan Fedorovich? What do you think? How long do I have to put up with these spiteful urchins?'

'Why, my dear, I ... am ready of course and ... the prince ...'

The general, however, did offer to shake hands with the prince, but had no time to do so before fleeing in the wake of Lizaveta Prokofievna, who was descending noisily and angrily from the veranda. Adelaida, her fiancé, and Alexandra took their leave of the prince with sincere affection. Radomsky did likewise, the only man there in high spirits.

'It turned out as I expected! I'm only sorry that you had to suffer as well, poor chap', he whispered with the sweetest of smiles.

Aglaya left without saying goodbye.

But the adventures of the evening were not yet over; Lizaveta Prokofievna had perforce to endure one more quite unexpected encounter.

She had not had time to descend the steps to the road which

went round the park, when all of a sudden a splendid open carriage, drawn by two white horses, galloped past the prince's villa. Two gorgeous ladies were sitting in it. But after driving no more than ten yards past, the carriage came to an abrupt halt; one of the ladies turned round swiftly, as though she had caught sight of a friend she needed to see.

'Yevgeni Pavlich! Is that you?' a beautiful, ringing voice cried out, making the prince start, and perhaps one other besides him. 'Well, I am glad I've run you to ground at last! I sent a messenger to you in town; no, two! They've been searching for you all day!'

Radomsky was standing thunderstruck on the veranda steps. Lizaveta Prokofievna also stood still, but not in horrified stupefaction like Yevgeni Pavlovich: she regarded the impudent woman with the same proud, cold contempt as she had looked at the 'wretched people' five minutes before, and at once turned her steady gaze on Yevgeni Pavlovich.

'Good news!' the ringing voice went on. 'Don't worry about Kupfer's promissory notes; Rogozhin's bought them up for thirty. I persuaded him. You can stop worrying for another three months at least. And we'll probably come to a friendly arrangement with Biskup and all that crowd. So there you are, everything's all right, you see. Don't worry. Till tomorrow!'

The carriage moved off and quickly disappeared.

'She's mad!' cried Yevgeni Pavlovich at length, red with indignation and looking about him in bewilderment. 'I haven't an idea what she was talking about! What promissory notes? Who is she?'

Lizaveta Prokofievna went on looking at him for two seconds more; finally she set off towards her villa at a brisk walk. The others followed. A minute later, Yevgeni Pavlovich appeared before the prince again on the veranda, greatly agitated.

'Prince, tell me the truth, you don't know what this means?'

'I know nothing about it', replied the prince, himself in a state of extreme morbid tension.

'No?'

'No.'

'Nor do I', Yevgeni Pavlovich began to laugh suddenly. 'Honestly, I've had nothing to do with those notes, believe me, word of honour! . . . Why, what's the matter, are you going to faint?'

'Oh, no, no, I assure you, no . . .'

11

It was three days before the Yepanchins relented. Although the prince blamed himself a great deal as usual, and quite sincerely expected chastisement, inwardly he had been fully convinced all the same that Lizaveta Prokofievna could not be seriously angry with him, and was really more angry with herself. Such a long period of disfavour, therefore, had plunged him by the third day into a state of unrelieved gloom. There were other circumstances contributing to this—one in particular. Over the three days, it had grown and developed within the prince's morbidly sensitive imagination—and of late the prince had been blaming himself for two extremes of behaviour; for his remarkably 'senseless and tiresome' credulity and at the same time for his 'mean and gloomy suspiciousness'. At all events, by the end of the third day, the incident of the eccentric lady who had spoken to Yevgeni Pavlovich from her carriage had assumed mysterious and terrifying proportions in his mind. For the prince, the heart of the mystery, leaving aside other aspects of the matter, rested in the painful question: was he also responsible for this new 'enormity', or was it only . . . But he did not say who else it might be. As to the letters N.F.B., that was simply an innocent prank in his view, the most childish of pranks, so that it would be shameful, indeed in one respect almost dishonourable, to brood over it.

However, on the day after the outrageous 'party', for whose disorders he had been so prominent a 'cause', the prince had the pleasure of a morning visit from Prince S and Adelaida: they had come *chiefly*, they said, to enquire about his health and had dropped in while out for a walk together. Adelaida had just noticed a particular tree in the park, a wonderful, wide-spreading old tree, with long, gnarled branches, covered with young foliage; it was hollow and had a cleft in it; she had resolved to draw it without fail, she simply must! She talked of almost nothing else for the entire half-hour of her visit. Prince S was gracious and agreeable as usual, asking the prince about times past and recalling the circumstances of their first meeting, so that almost nothing was said of the previous night's events. At length, Adelaida couldn't contain herself and laughingly confessed that they had come incognito, but that was as far as her confession went, although it could be deduced from the incognito that her parents, chiefly, that is, Lizaveta Prokofievna, were particularly ill-disposed towards him. However, during their visit Adelaida and Prince S did not utter a single word about her, or Aglaya, or even about the general. When they left to resume their walk, they did not invite the prince to accompany them. There was no hint of asking him to visit them; in that regard, Adelaida let fall a very characteristic remark: speaking of a water-colour she had done, she suddenly felt very much like showing it to him. 'How can that be arranged quickly? Wait! I can either send it to you with Kolya today, if he calls, or bring it myself tomorrow again, when I go walking with the prince', she had got over her difficulty at length, pleased to have solved the problem so neatly and so conveniently for everybody concerned.

At length, almost on the point of departure, Prince S suddenly appeared to remember:

'Oh, yes', he asked, 'you don't happen to know, dear Lev Nikolayevich, who that lady was who called to Yevgeni Pavlich from the carriage?'

'It was Nastasya Filippovna', said the prince, 'surely you've found that out before now? I don't know who was with her.'

'I know, I'd heard!' Prince S pursued. 'But what did her shouting mean? I'm really mystified, I confess . . . and others too.'

Prince S clearly spoke in considerable puzzlement.

'She talked of some promissory notes of Yevgeni Pavlovich', replied the prince very simply, 'that Rogozhin had got hold of from some money-lender, at her request, and that Rogozhin would wait till Yevgeni Pavlich could redeem them.'

'I heard that, I heard that, my dear Prince, but that simply couldn't possibly be true! Yevgeni Pavlich couldn't have given any promissory notes! With a fortune like his . . . True, he has done so on occasion in the past, due to carelessness, I've helped him out myself . . . but with a fortune like his, to be giving

promissory notes to money-lenders and worrying about them—
it's just impossible. And he can't be on such terms of friendly
familiarity with Nastasya Filippovna either, that's the really
puzzling part. He swears he knows nothing about it and I fully
believe him. However, the thing I wanted to ask you, dear Prince,
is whether you knew anything yourself? I mean, have any
rumours reached you in some miraculous fashion?'

'No, I know nothing, and I do assure you that I was not in any
way involved.'

'Ach, what a mood you're in, Prince! I just don't recognize you
today. Could I really have supposed that you were involved in any
such business as that? . . . Well, of course, you're upset today.'

He embraced and kissed him.

'Involved in what "business" like that? I don't see any
"business" at all.'

'There's no doubt that this lady wanted to thwart Yevgeni
Pavlich in some way, by making him appear in the eyes of
witnesses to be something he is not and could not possibly be',
answered Prince S rather coldly.

Prince Lev Nikolayevich was embarrassed, but still kept his
intent and questioning look on Prince S; the latter however did
not go on.

'Not just promissory notes then?' the prince murmured at
length, in some impatience. 'Was she not just speaking literally
yesterday?'

'Well that's what I'm telling you, judge for yourself—what
could there be in common between Yevgeni Pavlich and . . . her,
not to mention Rogozhin? I repeat, he's enormously rich, I know
it for a fact; then there's another fortune expected from his uncle.
Nastasya Filippovna simply . . .'

Prince S abruptly fell silent, evidently not wishing to talk
further to the prince about Nastasya Filippovna.

'But he must know her at all events?' asked Prince Lev
Nikolayevich, after a moment's silence.

'There was something of the sort; he's a harum-scarum chap!
But if there was, it was a very long time ago, the dim and distant
past, I mean two or three years ago. After all, he used to know
Totsky. There can't be anything like that now, and they could
never have been on that sort of familiar footing. She hasn't been

here all this time, you know that yourself; not been anywhere. A lot of people still don't know she's turned up again. I've noticed the carriage for about three days, no more.'

'It's a magnificent carriage!' said Adelaida.

'Yes, the carriage is magnificent.'

They both departed on the most amicable, one might say the most fraternal of terms with Prince Lev Nikolayevich.

For our hero, meanwhile, this visit had been of crucial significance. Doubtless he had suspected a good deal himself since the previous night (and perhaps even earlier), but until this visit of theirs he could not bring himself to justify his misgivings altogether. Now it was becoming clear: Prince S, of course, had interpreted the matter incorrectly, but all the same he had wandered close to the truth, he had realized there was an intrigue afoot. ('Perhaps he does understand it all really', thought the prince, 'it's just that he doesn't want to say anything, so he's deliberately getting it wrong.') It was as clear as could be that they had called on him (especially Prince S) in the hope of discovering something; if that was the case, it was plain they thought him to be involved in the intrigue. Moreover, if all that was so and it really did have any significance, then she must have some dreadful purpose in mind—what could it possibly be? This was terrible! And how could anyone stop her? There was no way of stopping her when she was set on gaining her ends! The prince already knew that from experience. 'She's mad. Mad.'

But that morning there were far too many other insoluble matters all arising at once and all demanding immediate solution, so that the prince was much dispirited. He was somewhat diverted by Vera Lebedeva, who came to see him with little Liuba and laughingly retailed some lengthy story. She was followed by her sister, with her open mouth, and after them came Lebedev's schoolboy son, who assured him that 'the star Wormwood' in Revelation which fell to earth upon the sources of the waters was, according to his father's interpretation, the network of railways which had spread across Europe. The prince did not believe that this was Lebedev's interpretation, and it was resolved that he be asked about it on the first convenient occasion. From Vera Lebedeva, the prince learned that Keller had settled in with them the day before and all the signs were that he intended a long stay;

there was company there for him and he had struck up a friendship with General Ivolgin. He had announced, however, that he was staying with them solely to complete his education. On the whole, the prince had begun to like Lebedev's children more and more as time went by. Kolya had not been there all day: he had set off for Petersburg very early that morning. (Lebedev had also gone at first light to see to some little affairs of his own.) But the prince was waiting impatiently for Gavrila Ardalionovich, who was supposed to drop by that day without fail.

He arrived towards seven in the evening, immediately after dinner. One glance at him made the prince think that this gentleman at least must know every detail of the affair—after all how could he fail, with two such helpers as Varya and her husband? The prince's relations with Ganya, however, were still somewhat peculiar. He had, for example, entrusted Ganya with managing the Burdovsky affair and asked him particularly to do so, but despite this, as well as something else of the sort previously, it was as if it had been agreed not to mention certain subjects. It sometimes occurred to the prince that Ganya, for his part, actually did want a relationship of completely open and amicable sincerity; now, for instance, as soon as he came in, the prince felt at once that Ganya was utterly convinced the time had arrived to break the ice between them once and for all. (Gavrila Ardalionovich was in haste however; his sister was waiting for him at Lebedev's and they were both in a hurry to be about their business.)

But if Ganya really was expecting a flood of impatient questioning, compulsive volunteering of information, or friendly confidences, he was, of course, very much mistaken. For the duration of the twenty minutes of his visit the prince was pensive, almost preoccupied. There could be no thought of the questions, or rather the one main question, which Ganya was expecting. At this point Ganya too resolved to speak with considerable reserve. He went on talking incessantly for the whole of the twenty minutes, laughing and carrying on the lightest of swift and engaging chatter, without touching on the paramount issue at all.

Ganya told him, among other things, that Nastasya Filippovna had been in Pavlovsk only a matter of four days and was already attracting general notice. She was living with Darya Alexeyevna in a cramped little house on Matrosskaya Street somewhere, though her carriage was one of the finest in Pavlovsk. A whole crowd of suitors, old and young, had already gathered around her; mounted riders occasionally escorted her equipage. Nastasya Filippovna, just as before, was very fastidious and only received those of her choice. And yet a whole company had formed round her, on whom she could rely in case of need. One young man, already formally betrothed, had fallen out with his fiancée on her account; one old general had all but cursed his own son. She often took a distant relative of Darya Alexeyevna out driving with her, a most charming young girl, just turned 16; this girl was an accomplished singer, so that of an evening their little house attracted general notice. Nastasya Filippovna, however, conducted herself with the utmost propriety, dressing modestly but with impeccable taste, and all the ladies were 'envious of her taste, her beauty, and her carriage'.

'Yesterday's eccentric incident', Ganya went on, 'was of course premeditated, and shouldn't be taken into account. To find any fault with her, one would have to make a special effort or slander her—which will happen in any case', Ganya concluded, expecting the prince would be sure to ask why he had called yesterday's incident premeditated, and why slander would not be slow to follow. The prince, however, did not enquire.

On the subject of Radomsky, Ganya expatiated of his own accord, without need of question, which was very odd, since he had introduced the topic without any reason at all. In Ganya's opinion, Yevgeni Pavlovich had not known Nastasya Filippovna and even now knew her very slightly, and that only because he had been introduced to her some four days previously while out walking; he was hardly likely to have been at her house in the company of others even once. As for the promissory notes, there might be something in that (Ganya knew this for certain); Radomsky's fortune was, of course, a large one, but 'certain matters to do with his estate really were in some disorder'. At this interesting juncture, Ganya abruptly broke off. About Nastasya Filippovna's prank of the previous night, he said not a single word, apart from the passing reference already mentioned.

At length, Varya arrived to fetch her brother. She stayed for a moment, announcing (again without prompting) that Radomsky would be in Petersburg that day and the next, that her husband, Ivan Petrovich Ptitsyn, was also in Petersburg and also about Radomsky's business, most likely, and there really did seem to be developments on that score. As she was going out, she added that Lizaveta Prokofievna was in an infernal temper that day, but most puzzling of all was that Aglaya had fallen out completely with the whole family, not just her father and mother but both her sisters as well, and this 'was altogether a bad sign'. After conveying this last item of news as if in passing, despite its being of crucial significance for the prince, brother and sister departed.

The prince was very glad to be left alone at last; he descended from the veranda, crossed the road, and went into the park; he wanted to reflect and decide on his next step. That step, however, was not the sort that is brooded over; it was precisely the sort that is not brooded over, but simply resolved upon. He had a sudden, terrible urge to leave all this behind and go back where he had come from, somewhere far away, somewhere remote, to leave at once, without bidding anyone goodbye. He foresaw that if he remained here even for a few days, he would be drawn irrevocably into this world, a world which would henceforth be his. He did not ponder the matter ten minutes, however, before deciding that to run away was 'impossible', it would be tantamount to cowardice, that faced with such problems he had positively no right not to resolve them or at least not to do all he could to that end. So reflecting, he returned to the house after barely fifteen minutes' walk. He felt totally wretched at that moment.

Lebedev was still not at home, so that towards evening Keller managed to burst his way in, not drunk but in a confidential and confessional mood. He announced bluntly that he had come to tell the prince the story of his life and that was why he had stayed behind in Pavlovsk. There wasn't the smallest chance of getting rid of him: he wouldn't have gone for anything in the world. Keller had prepared himself for a lengthy and disjointed recital, but all of a sudden he skipped virtually from his first words to his conclusion and declared that he had so lost 'any ghost of morality' (solely out of disbelief in the Almighty), that he had stooped to thieving. 'Can you imagine that?'

'Listen, Keller, if I were you I wouldn't confess that unless I had to', the prince began, 'but perhaps you're deliberately slandering yourself, aren't you?'

'I'm telling you, just you, for the sole purpose of assisting my spiritual development! Nobody else; I'll die and bear my secret under my shroud! But Prince, if you knew, if you only knew, how hard it is to get hold of money these days! Where can you get it, I ask you? There's only one answer: fetch us your gold and diamonds and we'll advance you money against them, that is exactly what I haven't got, can you imagine that? In the end I lost my temper waiting and waiting. "Do you take emeralds as security as well?" "I do", says he. "Well, that's fine", say I and I put on my hat and walked out; to hell with you, swine that you are! So I did!'

'You didn't really have any emeralds did you?'

'Of course I didn't! Oh Prince, you look on life with shining innocence, positively pastoral you might say!'

The prince at length felt not so much sorry for him as conscience-stricken. A thought even crossed his mind: 'Mightn't it be possible to make something out of this man through someone's good influence?' His own influence he considered to be utterly unsuitable, for a number of reasons—not out of any self-depreciation, but because of his peculiar way of looking at things. Little by little they got to talking, and were eventually reluctant to part. Keller was extraordinarily eager to confess things it was impossible to imagine anyone talking about. As he began each tale he would earnestly assure the prince that he repented and was inwardly 'filled with tears', meanwhile relating it as if he were proud of his action, so amusingly at times that both he and the prince ended up laughing like madmen.

'The main thing is that there is a kind of childlike trustfulness about you, and an extraordinary truthfulness', the prince said at length. 'I wonder if you know how much you redeem yourself by that alone?'

'Noble, noble, I'm chivalrously noble!' confirmed Keller, touched by this. 'Still, Prince, you know it's all just day-dreaming, bravado so to speak, in actual fact nothing ever comes of it. And why's that? I just can't understand it.'

'Don't give up hope. Now we can definitely say that you have shown me all your secrets; at least I imagine it's impossible to add anything more to what you've told me, isn't that so?'

'Impossible?' exclaimed Keller with a kind of pity. 'Ah Prince, how Swiss your view of human nature still is, so to speak.'

'There can't be more, surely?' said the prince in timid surprise. 'Then what on earth did you expect from me, Keller, please tell me, and why did you come to me with your confession?'

'From you? What did I expect? Firstly it's a pleasure just to see unaffected good nature like yours; it's nice to sit and talk with you; at least I know I'm dealing with a most virtuous person; and secondly . . . secondly . . .'

He faltered.

'Perhaps you wanted to borrow some money?' prompted the prince with grave simplicity, with a touch almost of diffidence.

Keller gave a violent start; with the same look of astonishment he shot a swift glance at the prince's eyes and banged his fist on the table.

'Well, that's how you throw a man completely! Heavens, Prince, innocence and simplicity like that were unheard of in the golden age, yet at the same time you go straight through a fellow like an arrow, with the deepest pychological insight. Now forgive me, Prince, but this demands some explanation, because I'm . . . I'm just amazed! Of course I did intend to ask you for a loan eventually, but you asked about money as if you found nothing reprehensible in it, as though it were just a matter of course.'

'Well . . . from you it was.'

'And you're not annoyed?'

'Well . . . why should I be?'

'Listen Prince, I stayed on here after yesterday evening, firstly out of special respect for the French Archbishop Bourdaloue* (we were opening bottles at Lebedev's till three), but secondly and chiefly (and I swear by all the crosses there are, I'm telling you nothing but the truth), I stayed behind because I wanted to promote my spiritual development by making a complete and heartfelt confession to you; I fell asleep at four with that in my head, soaked in tears. Do you believe the word of a most honourable man? At the very moment I was dropping off, genuinely filled with tears inside and out, so to speak—because I was sobbing in the end, that I do remember—a devilish thought occurred to me: "Why not ask him for a loan afterwards, after the confession I mean?" So I prepared the confession, so to speak, like a sort of "*fines herbes* garnished with tears", using those tears to smooth the way, so that you would melt and hand over a hundred and fifty. Contemptible, don't you think?'

'Oh that can't be true, can it? The two things just got mixed. Two ideas coincided; that very often happens. It's always happening to me. I don't think it's a good thing, in fact, and you know Keller, I chiefly blame myself. You might have been talking about me just now. It's crossed my mind sometimes', the prince went on, very earnestly, genuinely and deeply interested in this, 'that everybody's like that, so that I even started thinking well of myself because it's terribly hard to fight against these double thoughts; I've had experience. Lord knows how they come to one or what gives rise to them. But here you are bluntly calling it contemptible! Now I shall be afraid of thoughts like that again. At all events, I'm not your judge. Still, in my opinion, one can't just call it contemptible, what do you think? You descended to trickery to coax money out of me with your weeping, but you swear yourself, don't you, that your confession had another purpose too, noble not just mercenary; as regards the money, you want it to go drinking with, don't you? But after a confession like that, it would be a sign of weakness. Still, how can someone give up drinking at a minute's notice? It's impossible, isn't it? What's to be done then? The best thing is to leave it to your conscience, what do you think?'

The prince looked at Keller with considerable interest. This double-thought problem had obviously been exercising his mind for some long time.

'Well, after that I can't imagine why they call you an idiot!' exclaimed Keller.

The prince reddened somewhat.

'The preacher Bourdaloue, now, he wouldn't have spared a man, but that's what you've done—and you've judged me compassionately! To punish myself and show how touched I am, I won't ask for a hundred and fifty roubles, give me twenty-five and leave it at that. That's all I need, at least for a fortnight. Before then I shan't come asking for money. I wanted to give Agatha a treat but she doesn't deserve it . . . Oh, sweet Prince, may God bless you!'

Lebedev came in, having just returned home, and frowned on noticing the twenty-five in Keller's hand. The latter, however, finding himself once more in funds, was in haste to leave and at once made himself scarce. Lebedev immediately began speaking ill of him.

'You're being unfair, he really was genuinely contrite', the prince remarked at length.

'What's there in that? It's exactly like me yesterday: "I'm vile, vile", but it's only words, sir!'

'So it was only words with you? And I was thinking . . .'

'Well all right, I'll tell you the truth, just you, because you see through a man: words and deeds, truth and falsehood—they all exist side by side in me and all absolutely sincere. Truth and actions are part of my genuine repentance, believe me or not, I swear it's so—and lies and mere words make up these fiendish (and ever-present) thoughts I have about how I can gain an advantage even in this situation and get the better of a man even through my tears of repentance! That's the honest truth! I wouldn't tell anyone else, they'd just laugh or ignore me, but you, Prince, will judge me compassionately.'

'There you are, that's exactly what he was saying to me just now', exclaimed the prince, 'and you both seem to take pride in it! You positively astonish me, but he's more sincere than you are and you've turned it into a regular way of life. Come, that'll do, stop frowning, Lebedev, and putting your hand on your heart. Haven't you got anything to tell me? You wouldn't come in for nothing . . .'

Lebedev began to pull faces and cringe.

'I've been waiting all day to ask you one question; answer with the truth for once in your life, the whole truth: were you or were you not involved in any way with that business of the carriage yesterday?'

Lebedev squirmed again, began giggling, rubbing his hands, even sneezing repeatedly in the end, but still could not bring himself to say anything.

'I can see you did have a hand in it.'

'But indirectly, only indirectly! I'm telling the honest truth. The only way I was involved was in letting a certain lady know beforehand that a certain company had gathered at my house and that certain persons were present.'

'I know you sent your son *there*; he told me about it a little while ago, but what on earth is all this plotting!' cried the prince impatiently.

'It's not my plot, not mine', Lebedev waved this away. 'It's other people, other people, and more of a fantasy, so to speak, than a plot.'

'Well what's it all about then, do explain for God's sake! Surely you realize it directly concerns me? Radomsky's character is being blackened, isn't it?'

'Prince, most illustrious Prince!' Lebedev began his posturing once again, 'you won't allow me to tell you the whole truth; I've already tried to tell you the truth of the matter more than once; you didn't let me go on ...'

The prince was silent for a moment, thinking.

'Well, all right, the truth then', he said heavily, plainly after a considerable inner struggle.

'Aglaya Ivanovna ...', Lebedev began at once.

'Be quiet, be quiet!' cried the prince furiously, flushed with indignation, and perhaps shame. 'That's impossible, it's nonsense! You've made it all up yourself, or people as mad as you have. And don't let me hear about it from you ever again.'

Late that evening, after ten, Kolya appeared with a whole budget of news. The news was of two kinds, relating to Petersburg and Pavlovsk. He swiftly related the more important Petersburg developments (chiefly to do with Ippolit and the previous day's events), meaning to return to them later, then quickly went on to the Pavlovsk news. He had returned from Petersburg three hours before and gone straight to the Yepanchins without calling in on the prince. 'They're in a terrible state there!' Naturally the carriage business took pride of place, but something else of that sort must have happened, something the prince and he knew nothing of. 'Naturally, I didn't pry and I didn't want to question anyone about it; still, I was well received, much better than I expected, but about you Prince, not a word.' What was most important and interesting was that Aglaya had quarrelled with the family that day over Ganya. He did not know the details, but it was over Ganya—'Can you imagine!'—and it was a furious quarrel, so it must have been important. The general had arrived home late, arrived frowning, arrived in the company of Radomsky, who was welcomed with open arms; Radomsky himself was surprisingly agreeable and cheerful. The most significant news of all was that Lizaveta Prokofievna had summoned Varya, who was sitting with the girls, and without more ado turned her out of the house once and for all—this in the most polite fashion, however. 'I heard it from Varya herself.' But when Varya had left Lizaveta Prokofievna and said farewell to the girls, they did not even know she had been forbidden the house altogether and that she was saying goodbye to them for the last time.

'But Varvara Ardalionovna was here with me at seven o'clock', said the astonished prince.

'She was turned out at eight, after seven anyway. I'm very sorry for Varya, sorry for Ganya . . . They're always up to something, certainly, they can't exist without that. I could never find out what they were up to and I don't want to. But I can assure you, dear kind Prince of mine, that Ganya does have a heart. He's a failure in many ways, of course, but in many ways he has good points which are worth discovering and I'll never forgive myself for not understanding him before . . . I don't know whether I should go on visiting the Yepanchins after the business with Varya. Of course, I did take up a totally separate and independent stance right from the start, still, it needs thinking over.'

'You needn't feel too sorry for your brother', the prince observed. 'If things have gone this far, then Lizaveta Prokofievna must think him dangerous, and certain hopes he entertains must be confirmed.'

'What? What hopes?' exclaimed Kolya in wonderment. 'You don't think that Aglaya . . . that's impossible!'

The prince said nothing.

'You're a terrible sceptic, Prince', added Kolya after a minute or two. 'I've noticed that recently you've become a great sceptic; you're starting to believe nothing and imagine everything . . . was I right to use "sceptic" in this context?'

'I think so, though really I'm not too sure myself.'

'Well I'll drop "sceptic", I've found another explanation', Kolya suddenly shouted out. 'You're not a sceptic, you're jealous! You're infernally jealous of Ganya over a certain proud miss!'

At this, Kolya jumped to his feet, laughing uproariously in a way he had perhaps never laughed before. Seeing that the prince had blushed deeply, Kolya laughed even more; he was terribly tickled by the notion that the prince was jealous over Aglaya, but stopped short at once on noticing that the prince was genuinely distressed. They then talked on, earnest and concerned, for another hour or more.

Next day, the prince spent the whole morning in Petersburg on some urgent business. Returning after four in the afternoon, he fell in with General Yepanchin at the railway station. The general caught him by the arm and, after a fearful look round, pulled the prince after him into a first-class carriage, so that they could travel together. He was burning with impatience to discuss something important.

'In the first place, dear Prince, don't be angry with me, and if there's been anything on my side, forget it. I would have called on you myself yesterday, but I wasn't sure how Lizaveta Prokofievna would feel about that ... At home it's ... just hell, some inscrutable sphinx has taken up residence and I walk about without an idea of what's going on. As far as you're concerned, I believe you're less to blame than any of us, though of course a lot happened because of you. You see, Prince, it's nice to be a philanthropist, but not as nice as all that. You've already tasted the fruit yourself, perhaps. Of course I love good works and respect Lizaveta Prokofievna, but ...'

The general went on for a long time in this vein, but his words were remarkably incoherent. He was obviously shaken and bemused by something utterly beyond his comprehension.

'Speaking for myself, there can be no doubt that you had nothing to do with all this', he brought out more clearly at length, 'but best not to visit us for a while, I ask you as a friend, till there's a change in the weather. As regards Radomsky', he cried with unusual heat, 'it's all a senseless slander, the worst slander there could be! It's a plot; there's an intrigue here, some urge to destroy everything and set us at odds. You see, Prince, between you and me: not a single word has passed between Radomsky and me so far, you understand? We're not linked in any way—but that word may well be spoken, and soon, perhaps very soon! All this to spoil things! And why, for what reason, I don't understand. She's an amazing, unpredictable woman, I'm so afraid of her I barely sleep at night. And what a carriage—white stallions, that's the height of fashion, that's really what the French call *chic*! Who gave her those? Honest to God, I was sinful enough to think it was Radomsky the other day. But it turns out it couldn't have been, and if that's the case why is she trying to cause trouble? That's the question! Is it to make sure of keeping hold of Radomsky? But I tell you again, on my oath, he doesn't know her and those promissory notes are pure invention! And to be so brazen, shouting across the street at him in that familiar way! It's clearly a plot! The obvious thing to do is dismiss it with contempt and redouble our regard for Radomsky. That's just what I told Lizaveta Prokofievna. Now I'll let you into what I think deep down; I'm absolutely convinced she did it to revenge herself on me personally, remember, for what happened before, though I never did her any wrong. I blush to think of it. Now here she's turned up again, just when I thought she'd disappeared for good. Where's that Rogozhin got himself to, answer me that? I'd thought she was Mrs Rogozhin long before now . . .'

In short, the man was completely at sea. He had been talking for almost the whole hour of the journey, posing questions and answering them himself, pressing the prince's hand, and at least convincing him by that alone that he had not the faintest suspicion of him. That was important for the prince. He concluded with a story about Radomsky's uncle, who was the head of some department in Petersburg: 'Highly important position, 70 years old, bon viveur, gourmet, altogether a susceptible old reprobate . . . ha-ha! I know he'd heard about Nastasya Filippovna, in fact he was fishing there himself. I dropped in on him recently. He wasn't receiving, he was unwell, but rich, he's rich, a man of consequence and . . . may he be spared for many more years, but there again everything comes to Radomsky . . . Yes, yes . . . but I'm afraid all the same! I don't know why, but I'm afraid . . . It's as if there was something in the air, like a bat—there's trouble brewing and I'm afraid, I'm afraid! . . .'

And at length, three days later, as we mentioned before, came the formal reconciliation between the Yepanchins and Prince Lev Nikolayevich.

12

IT was seven o'clock in the evening and the prince was thinking of going for a walk in the park. All of a sudden, Lizaveta Prokofievna came on to the veranda unaccompanied.

'*First of all*, don't you dare imagine I've come to apologize', she began. 'Nonsense! You're to blame for everything.'

The prince made no reply.

'Well, are you or not?'

'Just as much as you are. But neither of us were guilty of anything intentionally. Two days ago I thought I was to blame, but I've now decided that's not so.'

'So that's what you think is it? Well all right; just listen then and sit down because I don't intend to stand.'

They both sat down.

'*In the second place*, not a word about those spiteful urchins. I'm going to sit and talk to you for ten minutes; I came to find out something, whatever you might have thought, and if you utter one squeak about those impudent young whelps, I'll get up and leave and break with you altogether.'

'Very well', replied the prince.

'And now, may I ask, did you about two or two and a half months ago around Easter send a letter to Aglaya?'

'I d-did.'

'Whatever for? What was in the letter? Show it to me!' Lizaveta Prokofievna's eyes were blazing, she was fairly trembling with impatience.

'I haven't got the letter.' The prince was surprised and became horribly shy. 'If it still exists, then Aglaya Ivanovna has it.'

'Don't try and wriggle out of it! What did you write about?'

'I'm not wriggling and I'm not afraid of anything. I see no reason why I shouldn't write . . .'

'Be quiet! You can have your say afterwards. What was in the letter? Why are you blushing?'

The prince thought for a moment.

'I don't know what's in your mind, Lizaveta Prokofievna. What I can see is that you're upset over this letter. You will agree that I could refuse to answer a question like that, but to show you that I'm not afraid of anything to do with the letter and don't regret writing it, and that I'm certainly not blushing because of that (here the prince blushed twice as deeply as before), I'll read you the letter, as I believe I can remember it by heart.'

So saying, the prince repeated the letter almost word for word.

'What a rigmarole! What is this nonsense supposed to mean?' enquired Lizaveta Prokofievna bluntly, after listening to the letter with close attention.

'I don't really know myself, altogether: I know my feelings were sincere. I did have moments of intense existence and soaring hopes there.'

'What sort of hopes?'

'It's hard to explain, but they weren't the kind you're perhaps thinking of. Hopes . . . well, in a word hopes for the future and joy, hopes that *there* I wasn't a foreigner, an alien being. I was suddenly very pleased to be back in my native land. So one sunny morning I picked up a pen and wrote her a letter; why to her, I don't know. Sometimes one feels like having a friend close by; that must have been how it was with me . . .', added the prince, after a pause.

'You're in love, then?'

'N-no. I . . . I wrote to her like a sister; I did sign as a brother.'

'H-mm; on purpose; I understand.'

'I'm finding it very hard to answer all these questions of yours, Lizaveta Prokofievna.'

'I know it's hard, but it doesn't matter at all to me how hard it is. Listen to me and tell me the truth before God: are you lying to me or not?'

'I'm not lying.'

'It's true you're not in love.'

'Perfectly true, I think.'

'Listen to him, "I think"! The young pup delivered it?'

'I asked Nikolai Ardalionovich . . .'

'The young pup! the young pup!' Lizaveta Prokofievna broke in vehemently. 'I don't know who this Nikolai Ardalionovich is! The young pup!'

'Nikolai Ardalionovich . . .'

'The young pup, I tell you!'

'No, not a young pup, he's Nikolai Ardalionovich', the prince replied at length, firmly, though quietly.

'Well all right, dear man, have it your own way. I'll remember this.'

For a few moments she strove to control her emotions and recover herself.

'And what's the "poor knight"?'

'I've no idea at all; I wasn't involved; a joke of some sort.'

'Well it's nice to know that all of a sudden! But surely she couldn't have been interested in you? She called you a "little freak" and an "idiot" herself.'

'You needn't have told me that', said the prince reproachfully, his voice close to a whisper.

'Don't be angry. She's a headstrong lass, spoiled and giddy—if she takes a fancy to somebody, she's sure to scold him and call him names to his face; I used to be the same myself. Don't start crowing, please, dear man, she's not yours; I can't believe that and it'll never happen! I'm telling you so that you can take steps this minute. And listen, swear you're not married to *that woman*.'

'Good heavens, Lizaveta Prokofievna, what are you saying?' The prince almost leapt to his feet in astonishment.

'You almost married her didn't you?'

'I almost married her', whispered the prince, and hung his head.

'What then, it's her you're in love with, is that it? You're here because of *her*? *That woman*?'

'I didn't come here to get married', responded the prince.

'Is there anything you hold sacred in this world?'

'There is.'

'Swear that it wasn't to marry her.'

'I swear by whatever you like.'

'I believe you; kiss me. At last I can breathe freely, but remember; Aglaya doesn't love you, take steps, she won't be yours as long as I live! You hear?'

'I hear.'

The prince was blushing so much he couldn't look directly at Lizaveta Prokofievna.

'Don't you forget it then. I've been waiting for you like a gift from providence (you weren't worth it!), I've soaked my pillow in tears of a night—not on your account, my dear, don't worry yourself, I have a different sorrow of my own, one that is unchanging and never leaves me. But this is why I waited for you with such impatience: I keep on believing that God himself sent you to be a friend and brother to me. I've got no one apart from old Belokonskaya and she's gone away, besides she's got as silly as a sheep in her old age. Now answer a simple yes or no: do you know why that woman shouted out from her carriage the other day?'

'I give you my word I was not involved and know nothing about it!'

'All right, I believe you. Now I've changed my mind, but yesterday morning I still thought Yevgeni Pavlich was the reason for it all. Yesterday morning and the whole of the day before. Now I can't help agreeing with the others: it's obvious some sort of trick was played on him to make him look a fool for some reason, some purpose (which is suspicious in itself, and most unseemly!)—but Aglaya's not marrying him, I tell you! He may be a good enough man, but that's how it's going to be. I hesitated before, but my mind's made up: "Lay me in my coffin first and bury me in the earth—then you can marry off my daughter", that's what I told my husband today. You can see I trust you, can't you?'

'I see and understand.'

Lizaveta Prokofievna gave the prince a piercing stare, anxious, perhaps, to see what effect the news about Yevgeni Pavlich had produced.

'Do you know anything about Gavrila Ivolgin?'

'You mean . . . I know a good deal about him.'

'Did you know he was keeping in touch with Aglaya?'

'I certainly did not.' The prince was surprised, even startled. 'You say he's in touch with Aglaya Ivanovna? Impossible!'

'Just recently, yes. His sister's been smoothing the way for him there all winter. Working away like a rat.'

'I don't believe it', repeated the prince firmly, after an agitated pause for reflection. 'If that had been going on I'd surely have known.'

'He'd hardly come to confess and weep on your bosom! What a ninny you are, a ninny! Everybody deceives you like . . . like . . . Aren't you ashamed to trust him? Can't you see he's cheated you right and left?'

'I know very well that he deceives me sometimes', the prince brought out reluctantly in a low voice, 'and he knows I know . . .', he added, and broke off.

'You know and still trust him? Now I've heard it all! Still, it's to be expected from you, I don't know why I'm surprised. Heavens, has there ever been a man like you? Ach! And do you know that this Ganka or Varya have put her in touch with Nastasya Filippovna?'

'Whom?'

'Aglaya.'

'I don't believe it! That's impossible! What's the point of that?' He leaped up from his chair.

'I don't believe it either, though the evidence is there. She's a headstrong lass, a crazy, fantastical girl! She's wicked, wicked, wicked. I'll keep saying that for a thousand years. She's wicked. They're all like that now with me, even that wet hen Alexandra, but this one's unmanageable. But I don't believe it either! Maybe because I don't want to', she added, as if to herself. 'Why haven't you been to see me?' She turned to the prince again. 'Why haven't you been for the last three days?' she shouted impatiently at him again.

The prince began telling her his reasons, but she again interrupted.

'Everybody deceives you and thinks you're a fool! You went to town yesterday; I'll wager you went down on your knees to ask that rascal to accept your ten thousand!'

'Not at all, it never crossed my mind. I never even saw him, and besides he isn't a rascal. I've had a letter from him.'

'Show me it!'

The prince took a note from his briefcase and handed it to Lizaveta Prokofievna. It ran as follows:

'Dear Sir,

In the eyes of others I haven't the smallest right to possess any pride. In their opinion I'm too insignificant for that. But that's in the eyes of others, not yours. I am perfectly convinced that you, dear sir, are perhaps better than other men. I part company with Doktorenko in disagreeing with him on that point. I shall never take a kopeck from you, but you helped my mother, and for that I am obliged to be grateful, if only out of weakness. At all events I look upon you differently now and felt that I

should inform you of that. Having done so, I assume there cannot be any
further communication of any sort between us.

                                                    Antip Burdovsky.
P.S. The remaining two hundred roubles will be repaid without fail in
due course.'

'What nonsense!' Lizaveta Prokofievna decided, throwing the
note back. 'Not worth the trouble of reading. What are you
grinning at?'

'Admit it, you thought it was nice too.'

'What! This rigmarole, eaten up with vanity! Can't you see
they're all off their heads with vanity and pride?'

'Yes, but still he has admitted he was wrong and broken with
Doktorenko, and the vainer he is the more that must have cost his
vanity. What a little child you are, Lizaveta Prokofievna!'

'Do you want me to slap your face, is that it?'

'No, I certainly don't. Because you're pleased about the note
and are just hiding it. Why be ashamed of your emotions? You're
like that in everything, aren't you?'

'Don't dare come a step towards my house now!' Lizaveta
Prokofievna sprang from her chair, pale with anger. 'Not hide
nor hair of you ever again from now on!'

'And in three days you'll come here yourself and invite me . . .
For shame! These are your finest feelings, why be ashamed of
them? You're just torturing yourself, aren't you?'

'I'll die before I invite you ever again! I'll forget your name!
I've forgotten it now!!'

She flounced out.

'I've already been forbidden to visit!' the prince shouted after
her.

'Wha-at? Who's forbidden you?'

She turned in a flash as if jabbed with a needle. The prince
hesitated before answering, realizing he had unwittingly said a
good deal too much.

'Who forbade you?' shouted Lizaveta Prokofievna furiously.

'Aglaya Ivanovna.'

'When? Come on, out with it then!!'

'She sent this morning to tell me not to dare to call on you.'

Lizaveta Prokofievna stood as if petrified, but she had her wits
about her.

'What did she send? Who did she send? That puppy was it? By word of mouth?' she exclaimed suddenly.

'I got a note', said the prince.

'Where? Hand it over! Now!'

The prince considered for a moment, but finally pulled a crumpled bit of paper from his waistcoat pocket. It bore the words:

'Prince Lev Nikolayevich! If, after all that has happened, you intend to surprise me by visiting our villa, you will not, let me assure you, find me among those pleased to see you.

Aglaya Ivanovna.'

Lizaveta Prokofievna pondered for a moment, then suddenly rushed towards the prince, seized him by the arm, and pulled him after her.

'Now! Come on! This minute, to spite them!' she cried in an extraordinary access of eager excitement.

'But aren't you exposing me to . . .'

'To what? The innocent ninny! Just as if he wasn't a man at all! Well now I shall see it all with my own eyes . . .'

'At least let me get my hat . . .'

'Here's your wretched little hat, come on! Can't even choose a fashionable hat properly! . . . She did it . . . after what had happened . . . heat of the moment', muttered Lizaveta Prokofievna, towing the prince in her wake and not letting go of his arm for a moment. 'I stuck up for you this morning, I said out loud you were a fool for not coming . . . otherwise she wouldn't have written a stupid note like that! It's unseemly, it's not right for a well-bred, well-brought up, clever, clever girl! . . . Hmm', she went on, 'she was annoyed you didn't come and she didn't realize that you can't write to an idiot in that fashion, because he'll take it literally, and that's how it's turned out. What are you listening in for?' she cried, realizing she had said too much. 'She needs a clown like you, she hasn't seen one for long enough, that's why she's asking for you! And I'm glad, glad she'll put you through it! It's what you deserve. And she knows how to do that, oh, she certainly does! . . .'

PART THREE

1

You hear complaints all the time that we lack practical people; there are plenty of politicians for instance; plenty of generals too; nowadays directors of all sorts can be found in any quantity you like—but there are no practical people. At least that's the complaint. It's even said that on some railways you can't find decent staff; the story goes that it's impossible for some steamship line to recruit passable administrative personnel. One day you hear of trains colliding or bridges collapsing on some newly-opened line; the next they're writing about a train practically stuck in a snow-drift for the winter; it travelled a few hours and stood in the snow for five days. In one place they tell you there are hundreds of tons of produce rotting while they wait for dispatch, in another you hear (though it's hard to credit) that a railway administrator, some inspector that is, has administered a punch on the nose to some merchant's clerk who was pestering him about the dispatch of his goods, explaining his administrative action on the grounds that he had 'got a little heated'. It's terrifying to think how many civil servants there apparently are; everyone's been in the civil service, or is in it now, or intends to be—how can it come about that a decent administrative staff for a steamship line can't be put together out of this kind of material?

The answer sometimes given to this question is a very simple one, so simple it's hard to credit. It's true, say they, that everyone in the country is, or has been, in the service and that this has been going on for two hundred years, on the best German pattern, from grandfather to grandson; the trouble is that civil servants are the least practical folk you can find, and things have got to the stage where abstract knowledge, divorced from practice, has been, until quite recently, regarded even by civil servants themselves as virtually the supreme virtue and recommendation. However, we should not be discussing civil servants, we really wanted to talk about practical men. There is no doubt here that timidity and a complete lack of personal initiative have always been regarded among us as the principal and best indicators of the practical man—and are still so regarded. But why blame only ourselves, if we take this opinion to be an accusation? Everywhere, throughout the world, lack of originality has always been looked on since time immemorial as the outstanding quality and highest recommendation of a sensible, businesslike, and practical man, and ninety-nine per cent of men (at the very least) have always held this opinion, with only one per cent regarding the matter differently, then as now.

At the outset of their careers, inventors and geniuses have almost always been looked on in society as no better than fools (and very often at the end too)—that's a banal observation, everybody knows that. For instance, if everyone put their money for scores of years into loan banks, ending up with millions in there at four per cent, then it stands to reason that when the loan banks ceased to exist and everyone had to act on their own initiative, then the greater part of these millions must certainly be lost in the stock-market panic or pass into the hands of swindlers; indeed, that was strictly in accordance with the demands of decency and decorum. Yes, decorum; if by general consent a decorous timidity and a decent lack of originality have been considered among us to be the essential qualities of the sensible and decent man, it would be most indecorous, indecent even, to make changes all of a sudden. What loving mother, for example, would not be dismayed and sick with fright if her son or daughter should deviate a fraction from the rails: 'No, better if he's happy and has a comfortable life, and no originality', is what every mother thinks as she rocks her infant. And from time immemorial, our nurses croon and sing as they rock their children: 'You'll be dressed in gold I see, a general is what you'll be!' So, even our nurses have regarded the rank of general as the zenith of Russian happiness, and it has become, therefore, the most popular national ideal of serene and perfect bliss. And indeed, who among us after getting a fair mark in the examination and serving thirty-five years in the public service, could not end up as a general with a large bank account? Thus it is that a Russian attains almost effortlessly the designation of a sensible and practical man. In actual fact, the only person among us who could not become a general is the original man, in other words the restless man. There may be a certain misunderstanding here, but generally speaking it seems to be true enough, and our society has been perfectly correct in its definition of the ideal practical man. All the same, we have digressed too much; we actually wanted to say a few explanatory words touching the Yepanchin household we have come to know. Practically all the members of this household, or at least the more thoughtful of them, suffered continually from a certain family tendency, diametrically opposed to the virtues we have just been discussing. Without fully realizing this (it is indeed hard to do so), they nevertheless suspected on occasion that all did not go in their family as it did in others. With others things ran smoothly, with them the opposite; everyone else kept to the rails, they were always coming off them; everyone else was always decorously diffident, they were not. Lizaveta Prokofievna, it's true, was rather too apprehensive; still that was not the decorous, worldly diffidence for which they longed. Perhaps, however, it was only Lizaveta Prokofievna who was anxious: the girls, despite being shrewd and ironic creatures, were still young, and the general, though he did grasp things (albeit not without a struggle), would simply say 'H-mm' in difficult situations, and ended up by placing all his reliance on his wife. The responsibility, in consequence, rested entirely upon her. It wasn't that the family was, for instance, remarkable for any personal initiative or jumped off the rails through any conscious craving for originality, which would have been most unseemly. Indeed, no! There was really nothing of that kind, that is, no consciously defined purpose, and yet the end-result was that the Yepanchin household, though highly respected, was all the same, somehow, not quite what every respectable family generally ought to be. Of late Lizaveta Prokofievna had begun to blame herself and her 'wretched' character for everything, which merely served to intensify her sufferings. She constantly called herself 'a stupid, eccentric, ill-bred old woman', and tormented herself with her imaginings; she was continually flustered and at a loss how to resolve the most ordinary contingencies, and always exaggerated every misfortune.

At the very beginning of our narrative we mentioned that the Yepanchins enjoyed the genuine respect of everyone. Even General Ivan Fedorovich, though of obscure origin, was received everywhere and accorded respect. Indeed, he deserved respect, in the first place as a man of wealth and status, and secondly as a thorough gentleman, though not over-bright. Still, a certain dullness of mind seems to be an almost essential qualification, if not for every public servant, then at least for anyone seriously intent on making money. Finally, the general had good manners, he was unassuming, and knew how to hold his tongue without being taken advantage of—and all this not just because of his rank, but because he was also an honest and honourable man. Most important of all was that he enjoyed powerful patronage. As for Lizaveta Prokofievna, as explained previously, she was of good family, though we think little of that unless there are the necessary connections to go with it. But she eventually acquired these too; she was respected and in the end loved by people of such eminence that everyone naturally had to follow their example in respecting and receiving her. Clearly her anxieties over her family were groundless, mere trifles absurdly exaggerated; but if somebody has a wart on their nose, or forehead, it does really seem as if the only thing anyone has to do is look at your wart, make fun, and despise you for it, even if you have discovered America. Nor can it be doubted that Lizaveta Prokofievna really was considered 'odd' in society, but she was held in genuine esteem; in the end, she began to doubt this regard—and that was the whole trouble. Looking at her daughters, she was constantly racked by the suspicion that she was for ever damaging their prospects, that she was ridiculous, ill-bred, and insupportable—for which, of course, she was perpetually accusing her own daughters and Ivan Fedorovich and quarrelling with them for days, at the same time loving them to distraction, almost passionately.

What worried her most was the suspicion that her daughters were becoming as 'odd' as she, that there were no girls in society like them, nor ought there to be. 'They're growing up into nihilists, definitely', she would tell herself constantly. Over the past year, and especially of late, this gloomy notion had become ever-more firmly established in her mind. 'To start with, why don't they get married?' she kept asking herself. 'Just to torment their mother, that's their one aim in life, and it's all because of these new ideas, this damned woman question! Didn't Aglaya take it into her head six months past to cut off her marvellous hair? Lord, even I never had hair like that when I was young! Weren't the scissors in her hand and didn't I go down on my knees to make her change her mind?! . . . Well, I suppose she did it out of spite, to torment her mother; she's a wicked girl, headstrong, spoiled, but above all wicked, wicked, wicked! But didn't that fat Alexandra compete with her in cutting off her plaits as well, and not out of spite either, not being wayward, just straightforwardly like a fool, because Aglaya had convinced her that she would sleep better without her hair and her headaches would go? And the suitors they'd had—how many in the last five years, how many had there been? And there had been some really nice fellows, splendid-looking fellows among them! What were they waiting for, not marrying? Just to provoke their mother—no other reason but that! None! None whatever!'

At last the sun had risen for the maternal heart also; at least one daughter, at least Adelaida, would finally be settled. 'One off our hands at least', Lizaveta Prokofievna would say, whenever she had to speak aloud on the subject (privately she expressed herself much more tenderly). And how well, how suitably the whole thing had been managed; it was spoken of in respectful terms even in society. A man of repute, a prince, a good man, with a fortune—what could be better? But she had always been less concerned about Adelaida than her other daughters, though her artistic inclinations sometimes troubled Lizaveta Prokofievna's ever-fearful heart. 'She has a cheerful nature and plenty of common sense to go with it—she'll be all right, that one.' Thus she comforted herself at length. Aglaya caused her the greatest anxiety. Incidentally, she didn't know what to think about the eldest, Alexandra: should she be worried on her account or not? Sometimes it seemed to her that the girl was a hopeless case; 25 years old—bound to be an old maid. 'And with her looks! . . .' Lizaveta Prokofievna even wept for her at nights, while Alexandra Ivanovna slept as peacefully as might be through those selfsame nights. 'Well what on earth is she then—a nihilist or just plain silly?' That she was no fool, Lizaveta Prokofievna had no doubt at all: she valued Alexandra's opinion and was fond of asking her advice. But that she was a 'wet hen' could not be doubted either: 'So placid, you can't make her out! Anyway, wet hens weren't placid either, oh dear, they've got me all muddled up!' Lizaveta Prokofievna had a kind of inexplicable compassionate sympathy for Alexandra, more even than for Aglaya, whom she idolized. Her bitter outbursts (which were the chief expressions of her maternal solicitude and sympathy), her teasing and names like 'wet hen', only made Alexandra laugh. It sometimes got to the point where the slightest thing would enrage Lizaveta Prokofievna terribly and cause her to lose her temper. For example, Alexandra liked to sleep late and dreamed a good deal as a rule; these dreams of hers were always remarkable for being extraordinarily uneventful and innocent, like a child of 7 might have; so it was the very innocence of her dreams that began to irritate her mama for some reason. On one occasion Alexandra dreamed of nine hens, and a regular quarrel blew up out of that between her and her mother—why? It was hard to explain. Once, and only once, she managed to dream something out of the ordinary, it seemed—she dreamed of a monk in a sort of dark room which she was afraid to enter. This dream was at once relayed triumphantly to Lizaveta Prokofievna by her two laughing sisters, but their mama lost her temper again and called all three of them fools. 'Hmm! Placid as a fool and a wet hen, no making her out, yet she's sad, she looks really sad sometimes. What is she unhappy about? What can it be?' Occasionally she would put this question to Ivan Fedorovich, formidably hysterical, expecting an immediate answer after her usual manner. The general would hum and haw, frown, shrug his shoulders, and pronounce at length, hands spread wide:

'A husband is what she wants!'

'Well God forbid he's anything like you, Ivan Fedorovich,' she would explode at last like a bomb, 'not like you in what he thinks and comes out with, Ivan Fedorovich; not such a boorish boor as you, Ivan Fedorovich . . .'

Ivan Fedorovich would promptly make his escape, and Lizaveta Prokofievna would calm down after her 'explosion'. It goes without saying that towards evening she would invariably become particularly attentive, quietly affectionate and respectful towards Ivan Fedorovich, her 'boorish boor' Ivan Fedorovich, her dear sweet Ivan Fedorovich, adored by everyone, whom she had loved all her life—was even now in love with her Ivan Fedorovich, who was in turn perfectly aware of the fact and profoundly esteemed his Lizaveta Prokofievna for it.

But Aglaya was her chief and constant anxiety.

'Exactly like me, exactly, the very picture of me in every way', Lizaveta Prokofievna would say to herself, 'headstrong, horrid little imp! Nihilist, eccentric, crazy, wicked, wicked, wicked! Oh Lord, how wretched she's going to be!'

But as we have said already, the risen sun had seemingly softened and illuminated everything for the moment. For almost a month, Lizaveta Prokofievna had been able to put her worries to one side. Adelaida's forthcoming wedding had caused society talk about Aglaya too, and among it all Aglaya had comported herself so beautifully everywhere, so calmly, so intelligently, so imperiously, a trifle on the haughty side—but didn't that become her so well! For a whole month she'd been so affectionate and friendly towards her mother! ('Of course, a very close eye needs to be kept on that Yevgeni Pavlovich, he needs getting to the bottom of, and Aglaya doesn't seem to favour him above the others either!') Still, what a wonderful girl she'd turned into all of a sudden—and so pretty, Lord how pretty she was, more so every day! And now . . .

And now this wretched little princeling had turned up, this miserable little idiot, and everything was in turmoil again and everything in the house turned upside down!

What had really happened though?

Others would probably not have regarded anything as having occurred, but what made Lizaveta Prokofievna different was that, because of her ingrained anxiety, she always contrived to discover something in the mix and muddle of the most ordinary events that at times made her sick with apprehension, inspiring the most inexplicable imaginings and terrors, which were consequently the hardest thing of all to bear. What must she have felt now all of a sudden when through all this turmoil of absurd and groundless fears, something really significant seemed to be taking shape, something which really did seem to justify her alarms, doubts, and suspicions?

'And how dared they, how dared they send me that accursed anonymous letter about that creature, saying she was in touch with Aglaya?' thought Lizaveta Prokofievna all the way home, as she dragged the prince after her, and then at home, when she had sat him down at the circular table round which the whole household had assembled, 'how dared they think of such a thing? I would die of very shame if I believed a syllable of it or if I'd shown Aglaya that letter! Jeering at us Yepanchins like that! And it's all because of you, Ivan Fedorovich, all because of you! Oh why didn't we go to Yelagin: I said we should go to Yelagin, didn't I? It might be Varya that's written this letter, I know, or perhaps . . . it's all your fault, Ivan Fedorovich, all of it! That *creature* has played this trick on him to remind him of their former association, to make him look a fool, just as she used to laugh at him, fool that he was, and lead him by the nose when he was taking her those pearls too . . . And the upshot is we're all involved whether we like it or not, your daughters are involved, Ivan Fedorovich, grown girls, young ladies, young ladies of the best society, marriageable girls; they were present, they were standing there, they heard it all, and they're involved in the business of those urchins, I hope you're pleased. They were there and heard it all as well! I'll never forgive him, never forgive this wretched little prince, never! And why has Aglaya been hysterical for three days, why has she practically fallen out with her sisters, even Alexandra? She used to kiss her hands out of pure respect, just as she might her mother. Why has she been so hard to fathom these three days? What has Gavrila Ivolgin to do with it? Why has she been singing his praises yesterday and today, and bursting into tears? Why is that blasted "poor knight" mentioned in the anonymous letter, when she has never shown the prince's letter even to her sisters? And why . . . why did I run off to him like a scalded cat and drag him here myself? Lord, I must have been mad to do that! Talking to a young man about my daughter's secrets and . . . and about secrets that are practically to do with him! Heavens, it's a good thing he's an idiot and . . . and . . . a friend of the family! But surely Aglaya couldn't have been attracted by that little freak! Lord, what nonsense I'm talking! Dear me, we're all odd specimens, we should all be put on show under glass, me first of all, at ten kopecks a peep. I shan't forgive you for that, Ivan Fedorovich! And why doesn't she make game of him now—she said she would! Look at her, look, staring at him, all eyes, says nothing, doesn't go out, just stands there, and she asked him not to come herself . . . He sits there all pale. And that blasted, blasted chatterbox Yevgeni Pavlovich monopolizes the conversation! Look at him, going on and on, you can't get a word in edgeways. I could have found out everything straight away, if I could have brought the topic up . . .'

The prince was indeed sitting at the round table, rather pale, and seemed to be at one and the same time in considerable apprehension and, at moments, possessed by an unaccountable rapture. Ah, how he feared to glance in that direction, that corner whence two familiar dark eyes were regarding him steadfastly, and how at the same time his heart melted with joy at the fact that he was sitting there among them again, and would hear the familiar voice—after what she had written to him. 'Lord, she's going to say something!' He for his part had not uttered a single word and was listening intently to Yevgeni Pavlovich 'going on and on'. The latter had seldom been in such a happy and animated mood as he was this evening. The prince listened to him and for a long time understood hardly a word. Everyone had assembled, with the exception of Ivan Fedorovich, who had not yet returned from Petersburg. Prince S was also present. It seemed they had intended, in a little while, to go and listen to the band before tea. The present conversation had apparently got under way before the prince's arrival. Soon Kolya appeared from somewhere and slid on to the veranda. 'He must be back on the old footing', the prince thought to himself.

The Yepanchin villa was luxuriously furnished after the manner of a Swiss chalet and was elegantly set about on all sides with flowers and greenery. It was also surrounded on every side by a small but beautifully maintained flower-garden. Everyone sat out on the veranda, just as at the prince's; this terrace, however, was more spacious and smartly appointed.

The topic of conversation was not to the liking of many of those present. As might have been expected, it had arisen out of a heated argument, and everyone of course was keen to change the subject, but Yevgeni Pavlovich was apparently persisting all-the-more obstinately, oblivious of the impression he was creating; the arrival of the prince seemed to stimulate him even more. Lizaveta Prokofievna was frowning, though she didn't quite follow his argument. Aglaya, who was sitting apart from the others, practically in one corner, did not leave the room; she continued to listen, maintaining an obdurate silence.

'I'm sorry', Yevgeni Pavlovich was protesting heatedly, 'I'm not saying anything against liberalism at all. Liberalism isn't a sin; it's a necessary part of the whole, which would fall apart or decay without it; liberalism has as much right to exist as the most right-thinking conservatism; it is Russian liberalism that I'm attacking, and I must repeat again, the reason I am attacking it in fact is that the Russian liberal is not a *Russian* liberal, he's an *un-Russian* liberal. Show me a Russian liberal and I'll kiss him in front of you all this minute.'

'If he's willing to let you, that is', said Alexandra, who was in a state of unusual excitement. Even her cheeks were redder than usual.

'There she is, does nothing but eat and sleep, and you can't make her out', thought Lizaveta Prokofievna to herself, 'then once a year, all of a sudden she ups and says something that leaves you speechless.'

The prince noticed fleetingly that Alexandra did not like Yevgeni Pavlovich talking so flippantly about a serious matter and appearing so vehement while seeming to be joking.

'I was maintaining just a moment ago, just before you came in, Prince', Radomsky went on, 'that up to now our liberals have come from only two levels of society, the old landowning class, now a thing of the past, and the clergy. And as these two classes eventually turned into out-and-out castes, something entirely set apart from the nation, and have become more and more so with every generation, then it follows that everything they have done and are doing is altogether non-national . . .'

'What? You mean everything that has been accomplished, all of that is un-Russian?' protested Prince S.

'Not national; Russian perhaps, but not national; and our liberals aren't Russian and the conservatives aren't Russian, none . . .'

'Well I like that!' Prince S retorted hotly. 'How can you maintain such a paradox, if you're being serious, that is? I can't allow aspersions like that against the Russian landowners; you're one yourself.'

'I'm really not talking about Russian landowners in the sense you take it, you know. It is an honourable class, if only because I belong to it; especially now it has ceased to exist . . .'

'Surely you're not saying there's been nothing national in our literature?' Alexandra broke in.

'I'm no literary expert, but there's nothing Russian in Russian literature either, as I see it, apart from Lomonosov, Pushkin, and Gogol.'

'In the first place that's quite a lot, and secondly one was from the common people and two were landowners', Alexandra laughed.

'Perfectly right, but don't crow. Since of all the Russian writers up till now, only those three managed to say something to everyone that was really theirs, really their own, not borrowed from anyone else, the three have accordingly become national writers. Any Russian who says, writes, or does anything of his own, something that is his by right, not borrowed, inevitably becomes national, even if he speaks Russian badly. That's my yardstick. But we weren't discussing literature, we were talking about socialists and we got on to it through them; well that's my contention, that we haven't got a single Russian socialist; not now or ever, because all our socialists come from the landowners and clerics as well. All our professed, much-trumpeted socialists, here and abroad, are nothing more than liberals of the landowner class in the days of serfdom. Why do you laugh? Show me their books, their teaching, their memoirs, and though I'm no literary critic I will undertake to write you the most convincing treatise, in which I shall prove as clearly as daylight that every page of their books, pamphlets, and memoirs has been written by a former Russian landowner. Their rancour and malicious wit are typical, even typically pre-Famusov!* Their ecstasies, their tears may be real, perhaps genuine tears, but—landowners'! Landowners' or seminarists' . . . You're laughing again—you too, Prince? Don't you agree either?'

Indeed, they were all laughing, and the prince smiled too.

'I can't tell you, just like that, whether I agree or not', said the prince, cutting short his smile and giving a start like a schoolboy called upon in class, 'but I assure you I am listening with the greatest of pleasure . . .'

As he spoke, he was almost gasping for breath and cold sweat stood out upon his brow. These were the first words he had spoken since he had sat down. He made as if to look about him, but his nerve failed; Radomsky caught the movement and smiled.

'I will state a fact, ladies and gentlemen', he resumed in the same tone of voice, that is, with great vehemence and heat, but at the same time seeming almost to laugh at his own words, 'a fact, an observation, a discovery even, which I have the honour of ascribing to myself, I might say to myself alone; at least nothing has ever been said or written down anywhere on the point. This fact expresses the essential nature of Russian liberalism of the kind I'm discussing. To begin with, what is liberalism really, speaking in general, if not an assault (reasonable or erroneous is not the point) on the existing order of things? That's so, isn't it? Well then, my fact is that Russian liberalism is not an assault on the existing order of things, it is an attack on the very essence of the things we have, the things themselves, not just on their ordering, not on the Russian system but on Russia herself. My liberal has reached the stage of denying Russia itself—that is, he hates and beats his own mother. Every evidence of the wretchedness and failure of Russia prompts him to laughter, delight even. He detests folk customs, Russian history, everything. If there is any excuse for him, it's only that he doesn't realize what he's doing and takes his hatred for Russia for the most fruitful kind of liberalism—oh, you often come across a liberal here who is applauded by the others and who may well be in actual fact the most absurd, obtuse, and dangerous conservative, and doesn't know it himself! Not too long ago, some of our liberals used to regard this hatred of Russia as being almost equivalent to a genuine love of country—and were praised because they perceived what that love of country was better than others could; nowadays they've become more outspoken, and even the words "love of country" make them feel ashamed; they've even banished and dismissed the very concept as something pernicious and of little account. This is an actual fact, I insist, and . . . after all the whole truth has to be spoken sometimes, plainly and candidly; but at the same time, this fact has never existed in the case of any people anywhere since time immemorial, so it must be fortuitous and could cease to exist, I would agree. There cannot be a liberal anywhere who would hate his own country. How can we explain it with us then? By what I said before, the Russian liberal is for the moment an un-Russian liberal; there's no other way, it seems to me.'

'I take everything you have said as a joke, Yevgeni Pavlich,' Prince S demurred gravely.

'I haven't seen every liberal and can't undertake to judge', said Alexandra, 'but I have listened to your idea with great resentment: you've taken a particular case and erected it into a general rule, that can't be fair.'

'A particular case? Aha! The word has been spoken.' Radomsky seized on this. 'Prince, what think you, a particular case or not?'

'I too have to say that I have seen little and had little to do with . . . liberals', said the prince, 'but it seems to me that you may be partly right and the Russian liberalism you were speaking of really is somewhat inclined to hate Russia itself, not just the established order. Of course, only somewhat . . . of course, it can't possibly be true of all liberals . . .'

He faltered and stopped short. Despite all his nervousness, he had been extremely engrossed by the conversation. One of the prince's peculiar traits was the extraordinarily naive attention with which he always listened to anything that interested him and the naive replies he gave when he was asked a question. His face and even his posture expressed this naivety, this trust, unsuspecting of derision or humour. But although Yevgeni Pavlovich had addressed him for some time with a peculiar sort of smirk, this reply made him contemplate him rather gravely, as if he had never expected an answer like that from him.

'I see . . . that's rather odd of you', he said. 'Was that a serious answer, Prince? Tell me the truth.'

'Wasn't it a serious question then?' the prince responded, surprised.

Everyone laughed.

'Trust him!' said Adelaida. 'Yevgeni Pavlich is always making a fool of people! If you did but know the things he says sometimes with the straightest of faces!'

'I think this is a tedious subject that shouldn't have been started', said Alexandra bluntly. 'We did want to go for a walk . . .'

'So let's go then, it's a marvellous evening!' cried Radomsky. 'But to prove to you that I was speaking perfectly seriously this time, and above all to prove that to the prince—you, Prince, have intrigued me considerably and I swear I'm not yet such a frivolous fellow as I must certainly seem, though I'm frivolous right enough! And . . . if you will allow me, ladies and gentlemen, I will ask the prince one last question, to satisfy my own curiosity, and make that the conclusion. This question occurred to me, as luck would have it, a couple of hours ago (you see Prince, I too sometimes reflect on serious matters!); I thought of an answer, but let us see what the prince has to say. Just now "particular case" was mentioned. It's a very significant phrase nowadays and you often hear it. Not long ago, everyone was talking and writing about that frightful murder of six people by this . . . young man and the strange speech of the defence counsel saying that in his poverty-stricken condition, it must *naturally* have occurred to the accused to do away with these six people. Those weren't the exact words, but that was the sense or near enough. In my own personal opinion, the lawyer, when he put forward such a strange notion, was utterly convinced that he was voicing the most liberal, the most humane, and progressive thought that could be expressed in our time. Well, what do you think: this perversion of thought and conviction, the very possibility of such a wrong-headed and extraordinary point of view—is it a particular case or a typical attitude?'

They all burst out laughing.

'Particular, of course, particular', laughed Alexandra and Adelaida.

'And may I remind you again, Yevgeni Pavlich', added Prince S, 'that your joke is wearing very thin.'

'What do you think, Prince?' said Radomsky, ignoring this last, and sensing Prince Lev Nikolayevich's gravely curious gaze upon him. 'What do you think, is this a particular instance or is it typical? I admit I thought of this question specially for you.'

'No, it's not a particular instance', said the prince, quietly but firmly.

'For heaven's sake, Lev Nikolayevich', cried Prince S with some exasperation, 'don't you see he's trying to catch you out? He really is joking and has picked on you to have his fun with.'

'I thought that Yevgeni Pavlich was being serious', the prince reddened and dropped his eyes.

'My dear Prince', went on Prince S, 'don't you recall what we spoke of once, two or three months ago? We actually talked about the number of fine, talented defence lawyers already to be found in our newly-instituted law courts! And how many splendid jury verdicts there had been? How glad you were and how glad I was to see it . . . we said it was something to be proud of . . . Whereas this contorted defence, this weird argument, is a chance thing of course, one among thousands.'

Prince Lev Nikolayevich thought for a while, but with an air of profound conviction, though he spoke softly and even timidly, he replied:

'I only wanted to say that one very often does come across the perversion of ideas and convictions, as Yevgeni Pavlich put it, it's unhappily a good deal more the general rule than an individual instance. If that were not the case, such impossible crimes as these would not take place . . .'

'Impossible crimes? But I can certainly assure you that exactly the same sort of crime, worse perhaps, took place in the past, always has done, not just in this country but everywhere, and I imagine will continue to take place for a long time to come. The only difference is that in the past they didn't receive so much publicity, whereas nowadays people have begun to talk openly and even write about them, that's why it seems such criminals have only just appeared. That's where you make your mistake Prince, and a very naive mistake it is, Prince, I assure you', said Prince S with a smile of derision.

'I do know that there have been a great many crimes in the past too, and just as appalling; I have visited prisons recently and managed to get to know a number of accused persons and criminals. There are even worse felons than this one, people who have murdered ten victims without the slightest remorse. But there was one thing I did notice: the most hardened and unrepentant criminal is all the same aware that he is a *criminal*, that is, his conscience tells him that he has acted wrongly, however impenitent he might be. They are all like that; but these people that Yevgeni Pavlich was talking about don't even want to acknowledge themselves criminals. They think to themselves that they had a right to do it, and even . . . that they did the right thing, it almost comes to that. That's where the terrible difference lies, I think. And bear in mind that they are all young, that is the very age when they can most easily and helplessly succumb to the perversion of ideas.'

Prince S had ceased laughing by now and heard the prince out with some bewilderment. Alexandra, who had been wanting for ages to make some remark, kept quiet, as if struck by a thought. Yevgeni Pavlovich, for his part, stared at the prince in positive astonishment, this time without a hint of a smirk.

'And why are you so surprised at him, my dear sir?' interposed Lizaveta Prokofievna unexpectedly. 'Did you think he's not as clever as you and couldn't argue on your level, is that it?'

'No, ma'am, it wasn't that', said Yevgeni Pavlovich, 'but how on earth was it, Prince (excuse the question), if you can see and observe the matter so well, how on earth (again excuse me) during that odd business . . . the other day . . . with Burdovsky, wasn't that the name? . . . How could you fail to notice that very same perversion of ideas and moral convictions? It's exactly the same thing, isn't it! I thought then that you just didn't see it.'

'Whereas we saw it all dear sir', Lizaveta Prokofievna said angrily. 'Here we are sitting showing off in front of him, and he's got a letter today from one of them, the leader of them, the pimply one, remember Alexandra? He apologizes, after his own fashion, and announces he's dropped that mate of his, the one who put him up to the business beforehand—remember, Alexandra?—and that he trusts the prince more now. Well we haven't received any such letter yet, so we're in no position to turn up our noses here at him.'

'And Ippolit has moved into our villa as well!' cried Kolya.

'What? He's here already?' The prince was alarmed.

'He arrived just after you left with Lizaveta Prokofievna. I brought him from town!'

'Well, I'll wager anything you like', Lizaveta Prokofievna flared up suddenly, quite forgetting that she had just been praising the prince, 'I'll wager he went over to his garret yesterday and asked his forgiveness on bended knee to get the spiteful little monster to deign to come here. Did you go there yesterday? You confessed as much earlier on. Well did you or not? Did you go down on your knees or didn't you?'

'Of course he didn't', cried Kolya, 'just the opposite: Ippolit seized the prince's hand yesterday and kissed it twice, I saw it myself. That's all there was to it, except that the prince just said that he'd feel better in the country and Ippolit agreed to come at once, as soon as he felt better.'

'You shouldn't, Kolya . . .', muttered the prince, getting up and retrieving his hat. 'Why are you telling them, I . . .'

'Where are you off to?' Lizaveta Prokofievna stopped him.

'It's all right, Prince', Kolya went on, by now highly agitated, 'don't go and disturb him, he's asleep after the journey; he's very happy and you know, Prince, in my opinion it would be much better if you two don't meet for the moment. Put it off till tomorrow even, otherwise he'll get embarrassed again. He told me yesterday morning that he hadn't felt as well and strong as this for six months; he even coughs far less than he used to.'

The prince noticed that Aglaya had suddenly left her place and come up to the table. He did not dare look at her, but he sensed with the whole of his being that she was looking at him at that instant, perhaps grimly, that her face was flushed and that there was certainly indignation in her dark eyes.

'Well, I think you've done the wrong thing in fetching him here, Nikolai Ardalionovich, if it's the same consumptive boy who wept the other night and invited us to his funeral', remarked Yevgeni Pavlovich. 'He spoke so eloquently about his neighbour's wall, he's bound to feel homesick for it, take my word for it.'

'That's the truth: he'll pick a quarrel, have a fight with you and go away, that's all there is to it!'

And Lizaveta Prokofievna drew her sewing-basket towards her in dignified fashion, forgetting that everybody had risen to go for a walk.

'I recall him being very proud of that wall', Radomsky pursued. 'He won't be able to die eloquently without it, and he very much wants to die eloquently.'

'What of it, then?' muttered the prince. 'If you don't want to forgive him, he'll die without . . . He's come now because of the trees.'

'Oh, for my part I forgive him everything; you can pass that on to him.'

'That's not the point', the prince responded quietly and with apparent reluctance, still keeping his eyes lowered and fixed on one spot on the floor. 'It has to be that you agree to accept his forgiveness also.'

'What on earth have I to do with it? How have I wronged him?'

'If you don't realize, well . . . but you do realize don't you? He wanted . . . to bless you all and receive your blessing in turn, that's all . . .'

'Dear Prince', interposed Prince S somewhat apprehensively, after exchanging glances with several of those present, 'it is not easy to establish paradise on earth, and you do seem to count on that a little; paradise is a difficult business, Prince, a great deal more difficult than it seems to your splendid heart. I think it better if we drop the subject, otherwise we shall indeed all get embarrassed again, and then . . .'

'Let's go and listen to the band', said Lizaveta Prokofievna abruptly, as she rose angrily from her seat.

Everyone else followed suit.

2

THE prince suddenly went up to Radomsky.

'Yevgeni Pavlich', he said with an odd intensity, seizing him by the arm, 'I assure you I regard you as the noblest and best of persons, despite everything; you may be sure of that . . .'

Radomsky actually stepped back a pace from sheer astonishment. For a moment he had to restrain an irresistible urge to laugh, but on looking closer he saw that the prince was apparently not himself, or at least was in a peculiar state of mind.

'I wouldn't mind betting', he cried, 'that wasn't at all what you meant to say, Prince, and perhaps not to me at all . . . But what's the matter? Are you feeling unwell?'

'Possibly, very possibly, that was a very shrewd remark, that perhaps it wasn't you I wanted to speak to!'

As he said this he gave an odd, even foolish smile, then suddenly, almost impassioned, exclaimed:

'Don't remind me of the way I acted three days ago! I've been very ashamed of it ever since . . . I know it was my fault . . .'

'Yes . . . but what did you do that was so awful?'

'I can see that you more than anyone are ashamed of me, Yevgeni Pavlovich. You're blushing, that's the sign of a good heart. I'm going now, I assure you!'

'What on earth's he talking about? Is that the way his fits start?' Lizaveta Prokofievna asked Kolya, alarmed.

'Ignore it, Lizaveta Prokofievna, I'm not having a fit; I'm going now. I know that I . . . am afflicted. I was ill for twenty-four years, till I was 24 years old. So accept what I say now as the words of an invalid. I'm going presently, presently, don't worry. I'm not blushing—because it would really be strange to blush over a thing like that, wouldn't it? But in society, I am out of place . . . I'm not saying that out of pride . . . I've been thinking it over these past three days and decided that I must let you know frankly and honourably at the first opportunity. There are ideas, lofty ideas, of which I must not begin to speak, because I would certainly make everyone laugh; Prince S reminded me of this just now . . . I have no graceful gestures, I have no sense of proportion; my words are inappropriate to my ideas, which devalues those ideas. So therefore I have no right . . . then again I'm over-sensitive, I'm . . . sure that no one could hurt me in this house, where I am loved more than I deserve, but I know (in fact I'm certain) that after twenty years of illness, something is bound to remain so that people can't help laughing at me . . . sometimes . . . isn't that so?'

He seemed to be waiting for a reply, some sort of confirmation, as he gazed around. They all stood profoundly bemused by this unexpected, morbid, and in any case gratuitous outburst. The outburst, however, gave rise to a curious incident.

'Why are you saying this here?' Aglaya cried out suddenly. 'Why are you saying this to *them*? Them! Them!'

She seemed to be furiously indignant: her eyes blazed. The prince stood mute and speechless in front of her before abruptly turning pale.

'There's not one person here worthy of such words!' Aglaya burst out. 'None of them here, none of them is worth your little finger, nor your mind, nor your heart! You're more honest than any of them, nobler, better, kinder, cleverer! There are some here not worthy of bending down and picking up the handkerchief you've just dropped ... Why are you abasing yourself, setting yourself lower than them? Why have you got everything twisted up inside, why is there no pride in you?'

'Lord, who would have thought it?' Lizaveta Prokofievna clasped her hands.

'The poor knight! Hurrah!' shouted Kolya ecstatically.

'Be quiet! ... How dare people insult me here in your house!' she flung suddenly at Lizaveta Prokofievna, by now in that state of hysteria when the normal rules of behaviour are set aside and all inhibitions ignored. 'Why is everyone, without exception, tormenting me? Why have they been pestering me for three days on end because of you, Prince? I shan't marry you for anything! Never and not for anything, I'll have you know! Understand that! How could anyone marry a ridiculous person like you? Take a look at yourself in the mirror, the way you're standing now! ... Why do they tease me about marrying you. Why? You ought to know! You're in the plot with them!'

'Nobody's ever teased you!' murmured an alarmed Adelaida.

'No one ever thought of such a thing and no one said a word about it!' cried Alexandra.

'Who's been teasing her? When? Who could have said that to her? Is she making it up?'

'Everybody's been talking, everybody, three days on end! I'll never marry him, never!'

With this cry, Aglaya burst into bitter sobbing, buried her face in her handkerchief, and fell into a chair.

'But he hasn't asked you yet ...'

'I haven't asked you, Aglaya Ivanovna', the prince suddenly blurted.

'Wh-at?' Lizaveta Prokofievna brought out in astonishment, indignation, and horror. 'What was tha-at?'

She couldn't believe her ears.

'I meant ... I meant', faltered the prince, 'I only wanted to make it clear to Aglaya Ivanovna ... have the honour to explain that I hadn't the least intention . . . have the honour to ask for her hand . . . at any time . . . I had nothing to do with it, honestly I hadn't, Aglaya Ivanovna! I never wanted to, I never entertained it, and I never will, you'll see: rest assured of that! Some wicked person must have slandered me to you! Please don't worry!'

So saying, he approached Aglaya. She took away the hand-kerchief which covered her face, shot a swift glance at him and his panic-stricken countenance, and realizing the import of his words suddenly burst out laughing in his face. Her laughter was so gay and unforced, so humorous and mocking that Adelaida was the first to follow suit, especially when she also took a glance at the prince. She rushed over to her sister, embraced her, and began laughing in the same unrestrained, gay, schoolgirl fashion. As he looked at them, the prince too suddenly began to smile and repeat with a glad and happy expression:

'Well, thank God, thank God!'

Now Alexandra could no longer contain herself and broke into hearty laughter. It seemed as if all three would never stop.

'The mad things!' muttered Lizaveta Prokofievna. 'First they frighten you to death, then . . .'

But Prince S was also laughing by now, as was Radomsky; Kolya couldn't stop, and the prince too, looking at them all, joined in.

'Let's go for a walk, let's go for a walk!' cried Adelaida. 'All of us together, and the prince simply must come; there's no need for you to leave, you dear man! What a dear he is, Aglaya! Isn't he, mama? Besides I must, I just have to kiss and hug him for . . . for clearing things up with Aglaya. Mama, dear, may I kiss him? Aglaya, do let me kiss *your* prince!' she cried mischievously, and suiting the action to the word she sprang over to the prince and planted a kiss on his forehead. He seized her hands and held them so tightly that she almost cried out, as he gazed at her with infinite gladness and suddenly brought her hand to his lips and kissed it three times.

'Do come along!' Aglaya called. 'Prince, you will escort me. May he, *maman*? A suitor who has refused me? You have rejected me for good haven't you now, Prince? Now that's not the way to offer your arm to a lady, don't you know how to take a lady's arm? That's it, now let's go, we'll go in front of the others; do you want us to go on ahead tête-à-tête?'

She talked away without a pause, still laughing intermittently.

'Thank God, thank God!' affirmed Lizaveta Prokofievna, not knowing herself what she was so glad about.

'What very odd people!' thought Prince S, for perhaps the hundredth time since he had fallen in with them, but . . . he liked these odd people. As for the prince, perhaps he wasn't too sure that he really liked him; Prince S was somewhat downcast and preoccupied as they all set off on their walk.

Yevgeni Pavlovich seemed in the best of spirits as he amused Alexandra and Adelaida all the way to the pleasure-gardens. They seemed a little too ready to laugh at his jokes, so much so that he had the fleeting suspicion they were not listening to him at all. This thought prompted him to roar with perfectly genuine laughter all of a sudden, giving no reason (such was the nature of the man!). The sisters, who were in a most festive mood, kept glancing at Aglaya and the prince as they walked in front; the younger sister had clearly set them a major puzzle. Prince S kept trying to discuss extraneous subjects with Lizaveta Prokofievna, perhaps to divert her, and succeeded in boring her to distraction. She seemed not to be mistress of her thoughts and answered at random—occasionally not at all. But Aglaya Ivanovna had by no means finished with her mystifications that evening. The final one fell to the lot of the prince alone. When they had gone about a hundred yards from the house, Aglaya spoke to her steadfastly silent escort:

'Look over to the right.'

The prince looked.

'Look closer. Do you see that bench in the park, over there by the three big trees . . . a green bench?'

The prince replied that he did.

'Don't you think it's a lovely spot? I sometimes come here on my own to sit, early in the morning, about seven, when everybody's still asleep.'

The prince mumbled that it was indeed a beautiful spot.

'And now go away, I don't want to walk arm-in-arm with you. Or better, keep your arm there, but don't say a word to me. I want to think . . .'

The warning was needless in any case: the prince would not

have uttered a word the whole way without being told to. His heart had begun pounding violently when he heard about the bench. A minute later he thought better of it and dismissed his absurd idea, much ashamed.

On weekdays, the public which foregathers in the Pavlovsk pleasure-gardens is, as everyone knows, or at least maintains, more 'select' than on Sundays and public holidays, when 'all sorts of people' arrive from the city. The ladies' dresses are elegant rather than festive. It is the done thing to meet by the bandstand. The orchestra is perhaps the best of our park ensembles and plays the latest things. The utmost propriety and decorum rule, despite a generally homely, even intimate, atmosphere. Acquaintances, all summer residents, come together to look one another over. Many of them derive genuine pleasure from it and only come for that; but there are also those who come just for the music. Unpleasant scenes are extremely rare, though they do occur, even on weekdays. But after all, such things are unavoidable.

On this occasion, the evening was beautiful and there were a good many people about. All the places by the orchestra were taken. Our company seated themselves to one side, near the left-hand exit from the gardens. The crowds and the music enlivened Lizaveta Prokofievna a little and distracted the young ladies; they contrived to exchange glances with some of their acquaintance and nod graciously to others from afar; they scrutinized the dresses, noted some discordant details, and discussed them with sarcastic smiles. Yevgeni Pavlovich also bowed frequently to friends. Aglaya and the prince, who were still together, had already attracted a certain amount of attention. Soon, several young men of their acquaintance came up to the young ladies and their mama; two or three stayed to converse; they were all friends of Yevgeni Pavlovich. Among them was a very handsome young army officer, very gay, very talkative; he hastened to strike up a conversation with Aglaya and strove with all his might to engage her interest. Aglaya was very gracious towards him and in high good humour. Yevgeni Pavlovich asked the prince's permission to introduce his friend to him; the prince was barely aware of what was required of him, but the introduction took place and they both bowed and shook one another's hand. Yevgeni

Pavlovich's friend asked the prince some question, but the prince appeared not to reply, or mumbled something under his breath in so odd a fashion that the officer eyed him narrowly before a glance at Yevgeni Pavlovich made him realize why the latter had contrived the introduction. He smiled faintly and turned once more to Aglaya. Yevgeni Pavlovich was the only one to notice that Aglaya suddenly flushed at this.

The prince was not even aware that others were talking and paying their attentions to Aglaya; at times he almost forgot he was sitting next to her himself. Sometimes he felt like going off somewhere, just disappearing on the spot; he wouldn't have minded some gloomy, deserted place, just so long as he could be alone with his thoughts and no one know where he was. Or be back at home at least, on the veranda, but no one else to be there, not Lebedev nor the children; to fling himself on to the sofa, bury his face in a cushion, and just lie there for a day and a night, then another day. There were moments when he dreamed of the mountains, and one familiar spot in the mountains, a place he liked to recall, where he had loved to go while he was still living there, from whence he could look down on the village, on the faint white thread of the waterfall, the white clouds, the ancient castle ruins. Oh, how he wished he was there now, thinking of but one thing—oh, all his life only of that—a thousand years would not be too long! And here let him, oh let him be forgotten completely. That was what really should happen, far better if they had not known him at all and it had all been just a vision seen in a dream. But was it not all the same, dreaming or waking? Sometimes he would start gazing at Aglaya and keep his eyes fixed on her face for five minutes at a time, but his look was very strange: it was as if he were seeing her as an object a mile away from where he was, or looking at her portrait rather than herself.

'Why are you looking at me like that, Prince?' she asked suddenly, interrupting her gay conversation and laughter with those around her. 'You frighten me; I keep feeling you want to reach out and touch my face with your finger. He does look like that, doesn't he, Yevgeni Pavlovich?'

The prince listened, apparently surprised at being addressed, realized it was so, though perhaps not fully understanding what had been said, and made no reply. Seeing that she and the others were laughing, however, he opened his mouth all of a sudden and began laughing himself. The laughter around him intensified; the officer, evidently a humorous individual, was fairly spluttering.

'The idiot!' Aglaya suddenly whispered angrily to herself.

'Heavens! Surely she can't . . . a man like that . . . surely she hasn't gone off her head altogether?' Lizaveta Prokofievna gritted to herself.

'It's a joke. The same joke as with the "poor knight" that time', Alexandra whispered firmly in her ear, 'that's all it is! She's just making fun of him again in her usual way. The joke's gone too far though; we'll have to put a stop to it, *maman*! Earlier on she was pulling faces like an actress and frightening us out of sheer devilment . . .'

'It's a good thing she's picking on an idiot like him', whispered Lizaveta Prokofievna in return. Her daughter's remark had eased her mind, all the same.

The prince, however, had overheard them calling him an idiot and gave a start, but not because of that. He forgot the 'idiot' at once. He had glimpsed among the crowd, somewhere to one side—he could not have put his finger on exactly where or at what point—but not far from where he sat, a certain face, pale, with dark curly hair and a familiar, very familiar, smile and glance. It flickered and was gone. He had very possibly imagined it; all he remembered was the wry smile, the eyes, and the dressy light-green necktie which the elusive gentleman had been wearing. Nor was the prince able to determine whether the man had disappeared among the crowd or slipped through into the gardens.

A moment later, however, he began to look about him swiftly and uneasily: this first apparition might foreshadow and herald a second. That would almost certainly be the case. Had he really overlooked the possibility of an encounter when they were setting out for the gardens? True, on his way to the gardens he had no idea, it seemed, that he was actually going there—such had been his state of mind. Had he been capable of being more alert, he might have noticed a quarter of an hour before that Aglaya was also glancing uneasily about her from time to time, as though she too were looking for someone in the vicinity. Now that his own

disquiet had become very noticeable, Aglaya's own nervous
perturbation also increased; as soon as he looked over his
shoulder, she followed suit almost at once. The reason for their
alarm quickly became apparent.

From the side entrance to the gardens, near where the prince
and the whole Yepanchin company were sitting, there appeared,
all of a sudden, a whole crowd of people, ten at least. In front of
this throng were three women; two of them were astonishingly
pretty, and it was hardly surprising that there should be such a
crowd of admirers in their train. But there was something
peculiar about both the women and their admirers, something
quite unlike the rest of the public who had come to hear the
music. Virtually everyone noticed them at once, but for the most
part they pretended not to have seen them at all, apart from a few
young persons who smiled at them as they said something to one
another in an undertone. Not to see them at all was impossible:
they were clearly flaunting themselves, talking loudly and
laughing. It might have been supposed that a good many among
them were drunk, though some looked to be dressed in
fashionable and elegant clothes; among their number, however,
were some most odd-looking folk, oddly dressed and with oddly
flushed faces; there were military types present; some were far
from young; some were comfortably dressed in wide, well-
tailored garments, wearing rings and cuff-links, sporting magnificent pitch-black wigs and side-whiskers together with a
peculiarly impressive, though somewhat fastidious expression on
their face—the kind of people, however, who are shunned like
the plague in society. In our resort gatherings of course, there are
those who are notable for their attachment to decorum and who
enjoy a particularly good reputation; nevertheless, the most
circumspect individual cannot always be on his guard against a
brick falling off a neighbour's house. Such a brick was now
getting ready to fall on that decorous company which had
assembled by the bandstand.

In passing through from the gardens to the bandstand, there
were three steps to be negotiated. The crowd came to a halt at
these steps; they hesitated to come down, but one of the women
moved forward; only two of her train ventured to follow. One was
a middle-aged man of rather modest appearance, perfectly

respectable to look at, but clearly an outsiderish sort of fellow, the sort of man nobody ever knows and who knows nobody. The other who clove to his lady was an out-and-out tramp of a most dubious aspect. No one else followed the eccentric lady, but as she went down the steps she didn't look back; it was as if she didn't give a fig whether anyone was coming after her or not. She laughed and talked loudly as before; she was richly and elegantly dressed, though a shade more opulently than was fitting. She walked past the musicians to the other side of the bandstand, where a carriage was awaiting somebody by the side of the road.

The prince had not seen *her* for three months or more. Ever since his arrival in Petersburg he had intended to go and see her, but some kind of mysterious premonition had stopped him. At all events, he was quite unable to gauge how he would feel when he met her, though he did sometimes try fearfully to imagine it. One thing was clear to him—the encounter would be painful. Several times over the last six months he had recalled the initial impression that woman's face had made on him, when he had only seen it in her portrait; even in that, there had been too much that was painful, as he remembered it. That month in the provinces when he had seen her practically every day had had a terrible effect on him, so much so that he sometimes tried to drive the very recollection of it from his mind, recent as it was. There had always been something that tormented him in the very face of that woman; in his conversations with Rogozhin, the prince had attempted to explain this feeling as an infinite sense of compassion, and that was the truth; even in the portrait, that face had aroused in his heart a veritable anguish of pity; the sense of compassion and even suffering for this creature never left his heart and had not left it now. Indeed not, it was stronger now than ever. Yet the prince remained dissatisfied with what he had said to Rogozhin; it was only now, at this moment of her sudden reappearance, that he realized, intuitively perhaps, what had been lacking in his words to Rogozhin. He had not found words to express his horror—yes, horror! Now, at this moment, he sensed it to the full; he was sure, totally convinced according to his own peculiar reasoning, that the woman was deranged. If, loving a woman more than anything in the world or anticipating the possibility of such a love, one were suddenly to see her chained up, behind iron bars, under a warder's truncheon, the feeling would be something like what the prince was enduring now.

'What's the matter with you?' Aglaya whispered swiftly, looking round at him and naively tugging at his arm.

He turned his head towards her and looked at her, gazing into those dark eyes, which were unaccountably sparkling at that moment; he tried to smile at her, but all at once, as if he had instantly forgotten her, he turned his eyes to the right again and once more began to follow his extraordinary vision. Nastasya Filippovna at that moment was walking right past the ladies' chairs. Yevgeni Pavlovich went on saying something doubtless very amusing and interesting to Alexandra. The prince remembered that Aglaya suddenly said in a half-whisper: 'What a . . .'

A vague and unfinished phrase; she instantly checked herself and added no more, but that was sufficient in itself. As she passed by, apparently unaware of anything out of the ordinary, Nastasya Filippovna abruptly wheeled in their direction, as if only now noticing Yevgeni Pavlovich.

'Well! So here he is!' she exclaimed, suddenly coming to a halt. 'No messenger can find him and here he is sitting where you'd never expect as if on purpose . . . I thought you'd be, you know . . . at uncle's!'

Radomsky bristled and threw a furious look at Nastasya Filippovna, before abruptly turning away from her again.

'What! Surely you've heard? He doesn't know yet, fancy that! Shot himself! This morning your uncle shot himself! I was told today at two o'clock; half the town knows by now. Some say three hundred and fifty thousand are missing from the public accounts, others say five hundred thousand. And here was I counting on him leaving you a fortune; he's blown the lot. The naughty, naughty old man . . . Well, goodbye and good luck! But aren't you going over there? You certainly picked the right time to resign your commission, cunning devil! What am I saying, you knew, you knew in advance: maybe yesterday you knew . . .'

Although, in the brazen way she was pestering him and the way she flaunted their acquaintance and a non-existent intimacy, there was assuredly some ulterior purpose that was beyond all doubt by now, Yevgeni Pavlovich's initial thought was to get away somehow and at all costs ignore his tormentor. But Nastasya

Filippovna's words had struck him like a thunderbolt; hearing of his uncle's death, he went as white as a sheet and turned towards his informant. At that moment, Lizaveta Prokofievna rose quickly from her chair and, getting everyone else up after her, almost ran from the place. Only the prince remained where he was for a second, seeming to hesitate, while Radomsky still stood there dumbfounded. But the Yepanchins had not moved twenty paces before a frightful scene took place.

Radomsky's officer friend, who had been talking to Aglaya, was in the highest degree affronted.

'What's needed is a horsewhip, otherwise there's no dealing with a creature like that!' he said quite loudly. He appeared to have been Radomsky's confidant previously.

Nastasya Filippovna whirled upon him at once. Her eyes flashed; she rushed up to the young man standing two paces from her, a total stranger, seized the thin, plaited riding-crop he was holding, and struck the offender across the face with all her strength. It all happened in a flash . . . The officer, beside himself with rage, flew at her; Nastaya Filippovna's followers were no longer in evidence: the respectable middle-aged man had already contrived to make himself scarce, while the tipsy gentleman stood to one side, laughing for all he was worth. A minute later the police would have arrived, of course, but that minute would have cost Nastasya Filippovna dear, had not aid arrived from an unexpected quarter: the prince, who had also stopped a pace or two away, managed to grasp the officer's arm from behind. In wresting his arm free, the officer gave him a violent shove in the chest; the prince was flung a few paces backwards and collapsed into a chair. Nastasya Filippovna had two more defenders by now, however. Confronting the officer's attack stood the boxer, author of the article familiar to the reader, and regular member of Rogozhin's former entourage.

'Keller! Retired lieutenant', he introduced himself with a flourish. 'If you want it hand to hand, captain, I will take the place of the weaker sex, at your service; I'm an expert at boxing English-style. Don't push, captain; I sympathize over the deadly insult, but I can't permit you to raise your fist against a lady in public. If, however, as becomes a most hon-our-able person, you prefer some other method, then naturally, you take my meaning, captain . . .'

But the captain had already recovered himself and was not listening to him. At that moment, Rogozhin emerged from the crowd and swiftly took Nastasya Filippovna's arm to lead her away. Rogozhin himself seemed horribly shaken; he was pale and trembling. As he led Nastasya Filippovna away he managed a vicious laugh in the officer's face, and said in the tone of a triumphant shopkeeper:

'Phew! You really caught it! Got your ugly mug bloodied, haven't you! Phew!'

Fully recovered now, and well aware of whom he had to do with, the officer, covering his face with a handkerchief, politely addressed the prince who had risen from his chair:

'Prince Myshkin? To whom I had the pleasure of being introduced?'

'She's mad! Deranged! I assure you!' responded the prince in a tremulous voice, extending his shaking arms towards him for some reason.

'I, of course, cannot pretend to such information, but I must know your name.'

He nodded and walked off. The police arrived precisely five seconds after the last participants had disappeared. In any case, the scene had lasted no more than two minutes at the outside. Several of the public got up from their places and left, some simply exchanged their seats for others; some had enjoyed the scandalous scene immensely, while others were much intrigued and began eagerly discussing the affair. In short, the matter came to an end in the usual fashion. The band struck up again. The prince went off after the Yepanchins. If he had thought to glance to his left when he was sitting in the chair after being pushed, he would have seen Aglaya, who had stayed to watch the scandal, some twenty yards from him, disregarding the summons of her mother and sisters as they walked on. Prince S ran up to her and finally persuaded her to leave quickly. Lizaveta Prokofievna recalled that, when Aglaya had caught them up, she was in such a state of agitation that she had probably never heard their calls. Two minutes later, however, just as they re-entered the park, she spoke up in her usual careless and petulant tone of voice:

'I just felt like seeing how the farce would end.'

3

THE pleasure-garden incident horrified both mother and girls. In her alarm and agitation, Lizaveta Prokofievna had literally almost run all the way home with her daughters. In her view and understanding, so much had happened and come to light as a result that, despite all the tumult and alarms, certain ideas were now taking definite shape in her mind. But really, everyone realized that something exceptional had taken place, and perhaps it was all to the good that some kind of extraordinary mystery was beginning to be revealed. Notwithstanding Prince S's previous assurances and explanations, Yevgeni Pavlovich had now been 'exposed', unmasked, shown up, and 'formally found out in his relations with that creature'. So thought Lizaveta Prokofievna— and her two eldest daughters. The upshot of this conclusion was that even more mysteries had been generated. Although the girls were privately rather annoyed at their mother's exaggerated alarm and conspicuous flight, they were reluctant to worry her with questions during the initial period of upset. Besides which, they rather had the feeling that their little sister Aglaya knew more of this affair than both of them and their *maman* put together. Prince S too looked as black as night and was also greatly preoccupied. Lizaveta Prokofievna did not exchange a word with him the whole way, but he seemed oblivious of the fact. Adelaida attempted to ask him: 'What uncle were they talking about just now, and what exactly happened in Petersburg?' With the longest of faces he muttered something very vague in reply, about inquiries and the whole thing being utterly absurd of course. 'That's certainly true!' responded Adelaida, and asked no more questions. For her part, Aglaya had become unusually serene, remarking only that they were going too fast. Once, she turned and saw the prince trying to catch up. Noticing his efforts to overtake them, she gave a mocking smile and looked round no more.

At length, almost at the villa itself, they encountered General Yepanchin coming to meet them; he had just returned from Petersburg. His first words were to enquire after Yevgeni Pavlovich, but his wife walked grimly past, without answering or even glancing at him. From the eyes of his daughters and

Prince S he at once divined that a domestic storm was brewing. Quite apart from this, his own countenance mirrored a certain unusual perturbation. He took Prince S by the arm and stopped him by the door to exchange a few words with him in a near-whisper. Judging by the troubled expressions of both as they later emerged on to the veranda and made towards Lizaveta Prokofievna, one might have thought they had both heard some momentous piece of news. Gradually everybody assembled in Lizaveta Prokofievna's room upstairs, leaving only the prince alone on the veranda. He sat in a corner as if expecting something, though not knowing why; it did not enter his head to leave on seeing the commotion in the household; he seemed oblivious of the whole universe, and prepared to sit it out for two years on end wherever he might be put. From up above he occasionally caught snippets of anxious conversation. He couldn't have said himself how long he had been sitting there. It was getting late, and the light was fading fast. Suddenly Aglaya came out on to the veranda; outwardly she was quite calm, though rather pale. On catching sight of the prince, whom she 'had obviously not expected' to see here sitting in his chair, Aglaya smiled in apparent puzzlement.

'What are you doing here?' She went up to him.

The prince muttered something, embarrassed, and leapt up from his chair. Aglaya, however, at once sat down next to him, and he too resumed his seat. She shot a sudden intent glance at him, then looked out of the window, apparently aimlessly, then again at him. 'Perhaps she feels like laughing', it occurred to the prince, 'but no, in that case she would have laughed, wouldn't she?'

'Perhaps you'd like some tea, I'll see to it', she said after a pause.

'N-no . . . I don't know . . .'

'Well how can one not know that! Ah yes, listen: if someone challenged you to a duel, what would you do? I meant to ask you earlier.'

'But . . . who on earth . . . no one would challenge me to a duel.'

'But if they did? Would you be very afraid?'

'I think I would be very . . . afraid.'

'Really? So you're a coward?'

'N-no; perhaps not that. A coward is someone who is afraid and runs away; someone who is afraid and doesn't run away isn't a coward', smiled the prince after some reflection.

'And you wouldn't run away?'

'Perhaps I wouldn't at that', he laughed at length at Aglaya's questioning.

'I may be a woman, but I wouldn't run away for anything', she observed, almost petulantly. 'Anyway you're making fun of me and being evasive as usual to make yourself more interesting; tell me, do they usually fire from twelve paces? And some at ten? Is it from ten now? That must mean getting killed or wounded surely?'

'They can't hit one another very often in duels.'

'What do you mean? Pushkin was killed, wasn't he?'

'That might have been by mistake.'

'It certainly wasn't; it was a duel to the death so he was killed.'

'The bullet hit so low that d'Anthès* was probably aiming somewhere higher, the chest or the head; nobody aims where that bullet hit, that means it probably hit Pushkin by chance, a fluke. I've been told that by people who know.'

'A soldier I was talking to once told me that it's laid down in regulations, when they fan out, to aim half-way up the body; that's how they put it—"half-man". So it can't be at the chest or the head, they have to fire deliberately half-way up. I asked an officer afterwards, and he said that it was perfectly true.'

'That's true, because they fire from long distance.'

'Can you shoot?'

'I've never fired a gun.'

'Surely you can load a pistol?'

'No, I can't. That is, I understand how it's done, but I've never loaded one myself.'

'Well then, that means you can't, because you have to have practice. Do listen and remember it: to begin with, buy good powder, not damp (very dry they say, not damp), the fine stuff, not the sort they use to fire big guns. They say you have to cast the bullet yourself somehow. Have you got any pistols?'

'No, and I don't want any', the prince laughed suddenly.

'Oh, what nonsense! Buy one immediately, a good one, French or English, they say they're the best. Then take a pinch of powder or perhaps two pinches and sprinkle it in. Better put plenty in. Ram it in with felt (they say it has to be felt for some reason), you can get that somewhere, a mattress, or doors are covered with felt sometimes. Then when you've inserted the felt, lay the bullet in—listen now, the bullet afterwards and the powder before, otherwise it won't go off. What are you laughing at? I want you to shoot several times a day and learn how to hit the target for certain. Will you do that?'

The prince laughed and Aglaya stamped her foot in annoyance. Her serious air during a conversation of this sort somewhat surprised the prince. He rather had the feeling that there was something he ought to find out about, enquire about, something rather more important than how to charge a pistol. But all that had flown out of his head, apart from the one fact that she was sitting before him, that he was looking at her, and whatever she was saying to him at that moment hardly mattered.

At length General Yepanchin himself came out on to the veranda from upstairs; he was heading somewhere with an anxious look of scowling determination.

'Ah, Lev Nikolaich, you . . . Where are you off to?' he asked, disregarding the fact that the prince had no thought of moving from his seat. 'Let's go, I'd like a word.'

'*Au revoir*', said Aglaya, extending her hand to the prince.

It was quite dark by now on the veranda and the prince was unable to make out her face very clearly at that moment. A minute later, as he and the general were leaving the villa, he suddenly flushed terribly and clenched his right hand tightly.

It turned out that the general was going his way; despite the lateness of the hour, Ivan Fedorovich was hurrying to a discussion with someone. Meanwhile he abruptly began talking to the prince, rapidly, anxiously, rather incoherently, with frequent allusions to Lizaveta Prokofievna. If the prince had paid more attention, he might have divined that Ivan Fedorovich, among other things, wanted to find something out from him too, or rather to put a plain and direct question to him, but couldn't bring himself to touch on the main point at issue. To his shame, the prince was so dreamily preoccupied that he heard nothing at all to begin with, and when the general halted in front of him with some fervent question, he was compelled to admit that he had taken nothing in.

The general shrugged his shoulders.

'You're all getting to be a queer lot, in every way', he launched into speech again. 'I tell you, I just can't understand Lizaveta Prokofievna's notions and fears. She's in hysterics, crying and saying we've been shamed and disgraced. How? Who by? When and why? I admit I'm to blame, I'm ready to admit that, very much to blame, but that bothersome woman's persecutions (and her outrageous behaviour into the bargain) could, if the worst came to the worst be prevented by the police and I intend seeing someone today to put a word in. It can all be dealt with quietly, nice and gently, unofficially—certainly without scandal. I also admit that the future is pregnant with possibilities and there's a great deal left unexplained; there's an intrigue going on too; but if nothing is known here, they can't explain anything there; if I haven't heard, you haven't heard, he hasn't heard, and the other fellow hasn't heard, who, I ask you has heard? How is one to explain it, do you think, except that half of it's imagination, non-existent, like for example, moonshine . . . or other apparitions.'

'*She* is mad', muttered the prince, suddenly recalling painfully all that had passed recently.

'That's it in a nutshell, if it's her you mean. The same idea has occurred to me now and again and I've dropped off to sleep like a lamb. But now I see that the others here are more probably correct and I don't believe in the madness idea. She's an absurd woman, granted, but at the same time not only is she not mad she's a shrewd one. That sally of hers about Kapiton Alexeich today demonstrates that beyond doubt. There's some trickery involved on her part, or at least jesuit-cunning, for purposes of her own.'

'What Kapiton Alexeich is this?'

'Oh, good heavens, Lev Nikolayevich, you're not listening to a word. That's what I started with, telling you about Kapiton Alexeich; it was such a shock I'm still shaking all over . . . That's what kept me in town today. Kapiton Alexeich Radomsky, Yevgeni Pavlovich's uncle . . .'

'Ah!' exclaimed the prince.

'Shot himself this morning, at dawn, seven o'clock. Well-respected old man, 70 years old, bon viveur—and just like she said, public money, a great deal of public money!'

'How on earth could she . . .'

'Have found out? Ha-ha! As soon as she turned up, a whole regiment formed up around her, didn't it? You know the kind of people who call on her nowadays and seek "the honour of her acquaintance". Naturally she could have heard something earlier today from her visitors, since all Petersburg knows about it and half Pavlovsk, or perhaps all Pavlovsk by now. But that was a shrewd remark of hers about his uniform, as I was told it, about Yevgeni Pavlovich resigning his commission just at the right time! What a fiendish insinuation! No, that's no sign of madness. Of course, I refuse to believe that Yevgeni Pavlovich could have known about the calamity in advance, I mean that at seven o'clock on such-and-such a date and so forth. But he could have sensed what was coming. And here am I, all of us and Prince S expecting old Radomsky to leave him his fortune! Terrible, terrible! Not that I'm accusing Yevgeni Pavlovich of anything, you understand, I must make that clear, but all the same, it is a bit suspicious. Prince S is greatly shocked. It's all very queer.'

'But what on earth is suspicious in what Yevgeni Pavlovich has done?'

'Nothing! He's behaved in the most honourable fashion. I wasn't hinting at anything at all. His own fortune, I believe, is not involved. Lizaveta Prokofievna, of course, won't listen to a word . . . But the main thing is all these family crises, or rather squabbles, one hardly knows what to call them . . . You, Lev Nikolayevich, are a friend of the family in the true sense. Just imagine, it now turns out, though it's not certain mind you, that Yevgeni Pavlovich proposed to Aglaya over a month ago and was apparently formally turned down.'

'That's impossible!' cried the prince with some heat.

'Why, you don't know anything about it, do you?' the general was surprised and taken aback, halting as if transfixed. 'Look, my dear fellow, perhaps it was wrong and improper of me to let that out, but it was because you . . . because you . . . are that sort of person, one might say. Perhaps you do know something about it?'

'I know nothing . . . about Yevgeni Pavlovich', muttered the prince.

'No more do I! And yet, friend, people are determined on

digging a hole in the ground and burying me; they don't want to consider how hard it is for a man, and that I won't be able to stand it. There was such a scene just now, frightful! I'm talking to you like my own son. The worst thing is that Aglaya is more or less laughing at her mother. That business about her turning down Radomsky a month ago and there being a fairly formal proposal comes from her sisters, it's a guess . . . still, a well-founded one. But then she's such a self-willed and fanciful creature, words fail me. Every noble and brilliant quality of heart and mind, she has them all if you like, but along with that she's so flighty and teasing—really an imp of mischief and full of fancies as well. Just now she laughed in her mother's face, and at her sisters and Prince S; as for me, she hardly ever stops laughing at me, but I, well, I love her you know, I love her even when she's laughing at me and I do believe the little devil loves me for that in particular, more than all the others, I mean. I'll wager she's had her fun with you too by now, over something or other. I found you two talking after today's storm upstairs; she was sitting with you as if nothing had happened.'

The prince flushed deeply and clenched his right hand, but said nothing.

'My dear, good Lev Nikolayevich', said the general suddenly with heartfelt warmth, 'I . . . and Lizaveta Prokofievna even (who, incidentally has started abusing you again, and me too on your account, lord knows why), we love you all the same, we genuinely love and respect you in spite of everything, I mean in spite of all appearances. You have to admit though, my dear chap, you have to admit yourself how exasperating and puzzling it was to hear that little imp as cool as you please (because she stood in front of her mother with such an air of profound contempt for our questions, mine especially, because I was stupid enough, dammit, to imagine I could play the heavy father—well, I made a mistake); this imp, cool as you please, all of a sudden ups and announces with a grin that this "deranged woman" (that's what she said, and I thought it odd she should use the same word as you: "surely you might have guessed before now", says she), "this deranged woman has taken it into her head to get me married off to Prince Lev Nikolayevich, and that's why she's driving Yevgeni Pavlovich out of our house." That's all she said; no more explanation than

that, laughs away while we were gaping, then slams the door and
goes out. After that, I was told about the scene between the two
of you this afternoon and . . . and . . . look here, my dear Prince,
you're not a touchy fellow and you're pretty sensible, I've noticed
that about you, but . . . don't take offence, I swear she's just
making game of you. Like a child does, so don't be angry with
her, but that's definitely how it is. Don't go thinking anything—she's just making fun of you and all of us for lack of
anything better to do. Well, goodbye then, you know how we feel
about you? How we really feel about you? That won't change,
never, under any circumstances . . . but . . . I go this way, *au
revoir*. I've not often been at sixes and sevens to this extent (isn't
that what they say?) . . . Holiday in the country, I ask you!'

Left alone at the crossroads, the prince looked about him, then
swiftly crossed the street and went up to the lighted window of a
villa before unfolding a tiny scrap of paper, which he had been
clutching tightly in his right hand during the whole of his
conversation with Ivan Fedorovich. He read it by the feeble beam
of light.

'Tomorrow at seven o'clock in the morning I shall be on the green
bench in the park waiting for you. I have made up my mind to talk with
you about an extremely important matter, which affects you directly.

P.S. I hope you won't show this note to anyone. Although I'm
ashamed to give you instructions like this, I decided you needed to be
told and so I wrote it—blushing with shame for your absurd character.

P.P.S. It's the same green bench I showed you this morning. For
shame! I had to add this too.'

The note had been written in haste and roughly folded, most
likely before Aglaya had come out on to the veranda. In a state of
inexpressible excitement bordering on fear, the prince clenched
the piece of paper once again in his hand and leapt swiftly away
from the window and the light, like some startled thief; as he did
so, however, he collided heavily with a gentleman who was
standing directly behind him.

'I have been following you, Prince', the gentleman said.

'Is it you, Keller?' cried the prince, astonished.

'I've been looking for you, Prince. I waited around for you at
the Yepanchin place—naturally I couldn't go in. I came after you
while you were walking with the general. I am at your service,

Prince, Keller is at your disposal. I am ready for any sacrifice, even to die if necessary.'

'But . . . why?'

'Well, a challenge is bound to follow. This Lieutenant Molovtsov, I know him; I don't mean personally . . . He doesn't tolerate insults. He's inclined to regard the ordinary man, me and Rogozhin I mean, as riff-raff, perhaps rightly—so you're the only one who has to answer. You have to foot the bill, Prince. He's made inquiries about you, so I've heard, and his friend is sure to call on you tomorrow, or maybe he's waiting for you now. If you honour me by making me your second, I'm ready to be reduced to the ranks. That's why I was looking for you, Prince.'

'So you're talking about a duel as well!' the prince suddenly broke into a laugh, to Keller's utter astonishment. He fairly roared with laughter. Keller, who really had been on tenterhooks until he had satisfied himself by offering to be a second, was almost offended at seeing the prince's hilarity.

'Well, you did grab his arms today in public. It's hard for a man of honour to pass that over.'

'And he pushed me in the chest!' cried the prince, still laughing. 'There's nothing for us to fight about! I'll apologize, and that will be the end of it. But if he wants to fight, we will! Let him take a shot at me; I look forward to it! Ha-ha! I know how to load a pistol now! Do you know, I've just been taught to load a pistol! You know how to do it, Keller? First of all you have to buy powder, pistol-powder, not damp and not the coarse stuff they use in big guns; after that you put the powder in first, get some felt from the door or somewhere, then roll the bullet in, but not the bullet before the powder, otherwise it won't fire. Ha-ha! Isn't that the most marvellous reason, friend Keller? Ah, Keller, I'll hug and kiss you in a minute. Ha-ha-ha! How did you suddenly turn up in front of him today? Come along to my place as soon as you can and drink some champagne. We'll all drink ourselves silly! Do you know I've got a dozen bottles of champagne in Lebedev's cellar? He "happened to have them" and he sold them to me the other day, the day after I moved in; I bought the lot! I'll get everybody together! So then, are you going to sleep tonight?'

'Like every other, Prince.'

'Well then, pleasant dreams! Ha-ha!'

The prince crossed the road and vanished into the park, leaving the somewhat disconcerted Keller to reflect. He had never seen the prince in such a strange mood before, nor could he have imagined such a thing up till now.

'A fever, perhaps, he's a highly-strung chap and all this has affected him, but of course he won't back down. That sort don't, no sir!' Keller mused to himself. 'Champagne, eh! Interesting news, that. Twelve bottles, a nice round dozen; not bad, a decent garrison. I'll bet Lebedev took that champagne as security from somebody. Hmm . . . he is rather nice, this prince of ours; he's the sort I like; still, no sense in wasting time . . . if there's champagne going, this is just the right time for it . . .'

That the prince was acting as if he were feverish was, of course, no more than the truth.

He wandered about in the darkness of the park and at length 'found himself' walking along an avenue. He had some recollection of passing through that avenue before, thirty or forty times back and forth, from the bench to a certain old tree, tall and conspicuous, about a hundred yards off. Even if he had wanted to, he would have been quite unable to remember what he had been thinking about during the hour at least he had been in the park. He did catch himself in one thought, however, which set him rocking with laughter all of a sudden; not that there was anything to laugh about, he just kept feeling he had to. It occurred to him that the notion of a duel might not have arisen in Keller's head only, and therefore this business of how to charge a pistol might not have been fortuitous . . . 'Bah!' He halted suddenly, as another thought dawned on him. 'She came down on to the veranda today when I was sitting in the corner and was terribly surprised to find me there and—how she laughed . . . started talking about tea; and yet she already had that paper in her hand all the time, so she must surely have known I was sitting on the veranda, so why on earth was she surprised? Ha-ha-ha!'

He snatched the note from his pocket and kissed it, then at once stopped and fell to thinking.

'How curious it is! How curious!' he said a moment later, even a touch wistfully: at moments of intense joy he always felt sad—why, he did not know himself. He stared keenly about him, surprised he had come to this place. He felt weary, and went over to the bench and sat down. All around lay a profound stillness. The music in the pleasure-gardens was over. There was probably not a soul in the park; of course it was at least half-past eleven. The night was still, warm, and clear—a Petersburg night in early June, but in the dense, shadow-laden park, in the walk where he was sitting, it was almost completely dark.

If anyone had told him at that moment that he had fallen in love, passionately in love, he would have rejected such a notion in astonishment, perhaps even indignation. And if anyone had added that Aglaya's note was a love-letter, appointing a tryst, he would have burned with shame for the man and perhaps challenged him to a duel. All this was perfectly sincere and he never had the least doubt of it or permitted the slightest 'ambivalent' thought of the possibility of this girl loving him, or even of him loving this girl. The possibility of love in the case of a 'man like him' he would have regarded as monstrous. He imagined it was simply a bit of devilment on her part, if there was actually anything in it at all; but by this time he had become indifferent towards devilment and thought it perfectly understandable. It was something quite different which preoccupied and worried him. He fully believed what the general had let slip just now in his excitement, about her laughing at everyone and him, the prince, in particular. He did not feel in the least offended by it; as he saw it, that was as it should be. What was of paramount importance for him, was that he would see her again tomorrow, would be sitting next to her on the green bench early in the morning, gazing at her as he listened to instructions on how to load a pistol. He wished for nothing more. What it was she intended to tell him and what the important matter was that affected him directly—this was a question which had flitted through his mind once or twice. Nor did he doubt for a moment the actual existence of this 'important matter' on whose account he had been summoned, but he hardly gave it a thought now. In fact, he felt not the slightest urge to think about it.

The scrape of quiet footsteps on the sandy path made him look up. A man whose face was hard to distinguish in the darkness approached the bench and sat down next to him. The prince swiftly moved nearer, almost touching him, and made out Rogozhin's pale face.

'I knew you'd be wandering about here somewhere, it didn't take long to find you', muttered Rogozhin through his teeth. It was the first time they had met since their encounter in the hotel corridor. Stunned by Rogozhin's sudden appearance, the prince was unable to gather his wits for some while and an agonizing sensation rose again in his heart. Rogozhin apparently realized the effect he was creating, but although he too was disconcerted at first, he spoke with rather an air of studied familiarity; the prince soon realized that there was nothing studied about it, however, and no particular embarrassment either: if there was a certain awkwardness in his conversation and gestures, it was only on the surface, in his heart this man could never change.

'How did you ... find me here?' asked the prince, for something to say.

'Keller told me (I called on you), he said you'd gone into the park; well, thinks I, so that's it.'

'What do you mean, "that's it"?' the prince anxiously picked up the careless phrase.

Rogozhin grinned but gave no explanation.

'I got your letter, Lev Nikolaich; you're wasting your time ... why bother? ... But I've come to you from *her*: she wants you to come at once; she wants to tell you something urgently. Wants to see you tonight.'

'I'll come tomorrow. I'm going home now; will you ... come with me?'

'Why? I've told you all there is; goodbye.'

'Are you sure you won't come?' the prince asked softly.

'You're a strange fellow, Lev Nikolaich, a proper wonder.' Rogozhin smiled sardonically.

'Why? Why are you so angry towards me now?' pursued the prince with wistful vehemence. 'After all, you know now that all those things you imagined are not true. Still, I thought that your malevolence towards me had not abated, you know why? Because you tried to kill me, that's why your anger doesn't pass away. I tell you, the only Parfion Rogozhin I know is the one I exchanged crosses with that day in brotherhood; I wrote that to you in my letter yesterday so that you might forget all that raving and not start talking to me about it again. Why do you keep away from

me? Why hide your hand from me? I tell you I consider
everything that took place then as just a kind of frenzy: I now
know what you went through that day in every detail, as if it had
been myself. What you were imagining didn't and couldn't exist.
Why should there still be hatred between us?'

'As though you could feel anger!' laughed Rogozhin again in
response to this sudden fervent speech by the prince. He had
actually turned away from him, having retreated a pace or two,
his hands hidden from view.

'It's not right for me to come and see you at all now, Lev
Nikolaich', he added slowly and sententiously by way of
conclusion.

'You hate me as much as that, do you?'

'I don't like you, Lev Nikolaich, so why should I come to your
house? Ah, Prince, you're just like a child, when you want a toy,
you must have it at once, but that's not the way things are. What
you're saying is just what you wrote in your letter—do you think I
don't believe you? I believe your every word and I know that
you've never deceived me yet and never will; all the same, I don't
like you. You see, you write that you've forgotten everything and
remember only your sworn brother Rogozhin, not the one who
raised a knife against you that time. How do you know how I feel,
then?' (Rogozhin smiled again.) 'Perhaps I haven't once repented
since then, and here you are sending me your brotherly
forgiveness. Perhaps I was thinking of something quite different
by that evening, but about that . . .'

'You forgot to think!' finished the prince. 'Of course! I'll wager
you went straight off to the train, and rushed away to Pavlovsk, to
the bandstand, to follow her and watch her in the crowd just as
you did today. That's no surprise! Why, if you hadn't been in
such a state that you could only think of one thing, perhaps you
wouldn't have raised your knife against me. I had a sense of
foreboding from the morning of that day, looking at you; do you
know what you looked like then? Perhaps I had a vague notion of
it while we were exchanging crosses. Why did you take me to the
old woman that day? Did you think that would stay your hand? Ah
no, you couldn't have thought that, just felt it, the way I did . . .
We two felt exactly the same. If you hadn't raised your hand
against me (which God averted), what would I seem to you now?

After all, I did suspect your intentions, didn't I? It's a sin we share, equally. (Don't scowl, though! Well, why are you laughing, then?) "Didn't repent"! Why, even if you wanted to, perhaps you couldn't have repented, because in addition to all that, you don't like me. And even if I were as innocent in your eyes as an angel, you still wouldn't be able to tolerate me as long as you think she loves me and not you. That must be what jealousy is. But this is what I've thought about this week, Parfion, I'll tell you: do you realize, she probably loves you now perhaps more than anyone, so that the more she torments you, the more she loves you. She won't tell you that, but you have to have eyes to see it. After all, what is she marrying you for? She'll tell you some day. Some women want to be loved that way, and she's one of that sort! Your love and your character must overwhelm her! You know, a woman can torture a man with her cruelty and mockery without feeling the slightest twinge of conscience, because every time she looks at you she thinks to herself: "Now I'm going to torment him to death, but I will make it up to him later with my love . . ."'

Rogozhin broke into a laugh, after listening to this.

'Well now, Prince, haven't you managed to get into that situation yourself? If what I've heard about you is true.'

'What, what could you have heard?' The prince gave a sudden start and broke off in great embarrassment.

Rogozhin went on laughing. He had listened to the prince not without interest, and perhaps not without pleasure; the prince's eager and joyful enthusiasm had greatly impressed and heartened him.

'Well, even if I hadn't heard, now I can see for myself it's true', he went on. 'I mean, when did you ever talk like this before? It's as if someone else was speaking. If I hadn't heard it about you, I wouldn't have come here; especially in the park at midnight.'

'I don't understand you at all, Parfion Semyonich.'

'Why, she told me all about you long ago, and now I've seen it myself this afternoon, you sitting with that girl by the band. She swore to me, yesterday and today she swore that you were head over heels in love with Aglaya Yepanchina. I don't care, Prince, and it's not my affair either; if you're no longer in love with her, she's still in love with you. You know very well that she wants you to marry that girl, she's set her mind to it, heh-heh! She says to me: "Till that happens, I'm not marrying you, once they go to the church, so do we." What's behind it I have no idea, I've never understood it: either she loves you beyond all measure, or . . . but if she loves you, why does she want you to marry someone else? Says she: "I want to see him happy", so she must love you.'

'I've told you and written to you, that she's . . . not in her right mind', said the prince, listening to all this in anguish.

'Lord only knows! Perhaps you're the one who's wrong about that. She did name the day though, after I brought her back from the gardens: three weeks from now—maybe before, prob-ably—says she, we'll be married; she swore to it, took down an icon and kissed it. So now, Prince, it's up to you, heh-heh!'

'That's madness! What you've just said about me will never happen, never! I'll come to see you both tomorrow . . .'

'How can she be mad?' Rogozhin remarked. 'How can she be sane for everybody else, and deranged just for you? How could she write letters to her? If she'd been mad, they'd have noticed it in the letters.'

'What letters?' asked the prince, startled.

'She writes letters there, to *her*, and they are read. Didn't you know? Well, you'll find out; she'll probably show them to you herself.'

'I refuse to believe it!' exclaimed the prince.

'Oh dear! it's well seen you've only walked a little way along that path, Lev Nikolaich, you're just setting out. Just you wait; you'll have your own private police force, you'll be on patrol yourself day and night, you'll know every step taken, if only . . .'

'Stop it, and don't say that to me ever again!' cried the prince. 'Listen, Parfion, I was walking here just now before you came and started laughing all of a sudden, I don't know why, the only reason was that I remembered my birthday was tomorrow, as if on cue. It's almost twelve o'clock now. Let's go and celebrate the day! I've got some wine, let's drink, wish for me what I don't know what to wish for myself; it's you in particular I want to wish it for me, and I'll wish complete happiness for you. If not, give me back the cross! You didn't send it back to me next day, did you? You're still wearing it? You're wearing it now?'

'Yes', said Rogozhin.

'Well, let's go then. I don't want to celebrate my new life

without you—because my new life has begun! You didn't know,
Parfion, that my new life has begun today?'

'Now I can see very well that it has; I'll tell *her* so. You're not
yourself at all, Lev Nikolaich!'

4

As he approached his villa with Rogozhin, the prince was greatly
surprised to observe that a numerous and noisy company had
assembled on his brightly lit veranda. They were all in high
spirits, laughing and shouting, even conducting arguments at the
top of their voices; at first glance, one might have supposed them
to be having a famously good time. Indeed, when he had climbed
on to the veranda, he saw that they were all drinking—drinking
champagne what's more, and for some considerable time at that,
enabling a good many of the revellers to become very agreeably
animated. The guests were all known to the prince, but it was
odd how they had all assembled at once, as if they had been
invited, though the prince had invited nobody and had only
remembered his birthday just now by mere chance.

'You must have told somebody you were providing champagne, so they came running', muttered Rogozhin, mounting the
veranda after the prince. 'We know all about that; you've only got
to whistle for them . . .', he added, almost savagely, remembering
of course his own recent past.

Everyone surrounded the prince, calling out greetings and
good wishes. Some were very noisy while others were much more
sedate, but they all hastened to congratulate him, having heard
about his birthday, and everyone waited their turn. The prince
was intrigued by the presence of certain individuals, Burdovsky,
for example; but the most astonishing thing of all was the sudden
appearance of Radomsky amid the throng; the prince could
scarcely believe his eyes, and felt a pang of alarm on catching
sight of him.

Lebedev meanwhile, flushed and almost rapturous, came
trotting up with explanations; he was fairly well *primed*. It
emerged from his babbling that everyone had assembled quite

naturally, indeed by chance. Ippolit had been the first to arrive, towards evening, and since he was feeling a great deal better, had asked to wait for the prince on the veranda. He settled himself on the sofa; after that Lebedev came down to join him, followed by the entire household, including his daughters and General Ivolgin. Burdovsky had arrived as escort with Ippolit. Ganya and Ptitsyn had dropped in not long before as they were passing (their appearance coincided with the incident at the pleasure-garden); then Keller had turned up, announced the birthday, and demanded champagne. Radomsky had arrived only some half-hour before. Kolya too had most strenuously insisted on a party with champagne, and Lebedev had promptly produced it.

'It's my own though, my own!' he stammered to the prince. 'At my own expense, to celebrate and congratulate you, and there will be refreshments, my daughter is seeing to the snacks; but Prince, did you but know what they are discussing. You remember Hamlet: "To be or not to be?" A contemporary theme, sir, very contemporary! Questions and answers . . . And Mister Terentyev is in the highest . . . won't go to bed! He's just had a sip of champagne, just a sip, won't hurt him . . . Come closer Prince, and you decide it! Everybody's been waiting for you, everybody's been waiting for your pleasant wit . . .'

The prince observed Vera Lebedeva's sweet, affectionate glance, as she hastened to push through the crowd towards him. He stretched out a hand to her first, past all the others; she flushed with pleasure and wished him 'a happy life *from this day forward*'. She then bolted off to the kitchen to see to the refreshments; but even before the prince's arrival, as soon as she could spare a moment from her labours, she had been visiting the veranda, all ears among the heated arguments which raged among the tipsy guests on matters which seemed most abstract and curious to her. Her younger sister, she of the open mouth, had fallen asleep on the chest in the next room, but the boy, Lebedev's son, was standing close to Kolya and Ippolit, and the look on his excited face was enough to show that he was ready to stand there for another ten hours at a stretch, listening and enjoying.

'I've really been waiting for you, I'm awfully glad you've come in such a good mood', said Ippolit as the prince came up to shake his hand immediately after Vera.

'But how do you know I'm in "such a good mood"?'

'I can tell by your face. Say hello to the gentlemen and hurry up and come and sit here next to us. I've been waiting for you specially', he added, laying significant stress on the fact of his waiting. In answer to the prince's query whether it wasn't bad for him to be sitting up so late, he replied that he was surprised himself that three days before he had wanted to die, and that he'd never felt better than this evening.

Burdovsky sprang to his feet and muttered that he just happened to be there, that he'd 'escorted' Ippolit, and that he too was glad; he'd 'written rubbish' in the letter and was now 'just glad . . .' He shook the prince's hand firmly and sat down without finishing his sentence.

Last of all, the prince went up to Yevgeni Pavlovich, who immediately took his arm.

'I just want to say a word or two', he whispered under his breath, 'on an extremely important matter; let's go somewhere for a moment.'

'A word or two', whispered another voice in the prince's other ear, as another hand took his other arm. The prince observed with astonishment a wildly rumpled red-faced figure, laughing and winking; he at once recognized Ferdischenko, who had turned up from Lord knows where.

'You remember Ferdischenko?' asked the figure.

'Where did you spring from?' exclaimed the prince.

'He's sorry!' shouted Keller, trotting up. 'He hid himself and wouldn't come out to see you, hid himself away in a corner; he's sorry, Prince, and feels guilty.'

'What about, for goodness' sake? What about?'

'It was I who came across him, Prince, I met him just now and brought him along: he's a rare friend of mine, but he's sorry.'

'Very pleased to see you, gentlemen; go ahead and mingle with the company, I'll be back in a minute', the prince freed himself at length, anxious to hear what Radomsky had to say.

'It's most entertaining here', the latter remarked. 'I've enjoyed the half-hour waiting for you. The point is, dearest Lev Nikolayevich, I've sorted out that business with Kurmishev and called in to put your mind at rest; you've nothing to worry about.

He's taken an extremely sensible view of the matter, particularly as, in my opinion, he was the more at fault.'

'What Kurmishev is this?'

'Why, the one whose arms you grabbed today . . . He was so infuriated he wanted to send to you for satisfaction tomorrow.'

'Never! How ridiculous!'

'Of course it is, and ridiculous is how the end would have been, most likely; but we do have these people . . .'

'Perhaps you had another reason for coming, Yevgeni Pavlovich?'

'Oh, naturally, there's another reason.' Radomsky burst out laughing. 'Dear Prince, tomorrow at first light I'm going to Petersburg about this wretched business (over my uncle I mean); just imagine: it's all true and everybody knew about it but me. I was so stunned I haven't been able to go and see them, the Yepanchins; I shan't be able to tomorrow either, as I'll be in town, you follow me? I may be away a day or two—the fact is my affairs are in something of a mess. Although it's not vastly important, I decided that I needed to speak frankly and openly, without delay—before I leave, that is. I'll sit and wait for a while, if you'll allow me, until the company breaks up; besides, I've nowhere else to go: I'm so upset I couldn't go to bed. At all events, although it's shameful and indecent to hound a man so, I'll tell you plainly: I have come to seek your friendship, my dear Prince; you're an absolutely incomparable person, I mean you don't tell lies at every turn, or perhaps at all, and I need a friend and counsellor in a certain matter because I am now definitely to be numbered among the wretched . . .'

He laughed once again.

'The trouble is', the prince considered for a moment, 'you want to wait till the party breaks up, but God knows when that will be. Wouldn't it be better if we went off into the park; really, they can wait; I'll make my excuses.'

'No, not that. I have my reasons for not wanting them to suspect us of discussing anything special. There are people here who are very interested in our relationship—didn't you know that, Prince? It would be much better if they saw us on terms that were very friendly but no more than that—you follow me? They'll go in an hour or two; I'll take up twenty minutes of your time, well—half an hour . . .'

'Oh, by all means, please do; I'm very glad to have you without explanations; and thank you very much for your kind words about friendly relations. You must excuse me for being rather preoccupied today; you see, I just can't keep my mind on things at the moment.'

'I can see that, I can see that', murmured Radomsky, with a slight, ironic smile. He was in a most humorous mood that evening.

'What do you see?' The prince gave a start.

'And have you no suspicion, dear Prince', went on Yevgeni Pavlovich, still smiling but without replying to the direct question, 'have you no suspicion that I've come simply to deceive you and find something out from you in the process, eh?'

'There's no doubt you have come to find out something', the prince laughed at last, 'and even resolved on deceiving me a little as well, perhaps. But what of it, really? I'm not afraid of you; besides, I don't really care somehow, do you believe me? And . . . and . . . and since I am convinced above all that you are an excellent fellow, we really shall end up by becoming friends. I've taken a great liking to you, Yevgeni Pavlovich, you're a . . . very, very decent fellow in my opinion!'

'Well it's a delight to have dealings with you at any rate, whatever they might be', Radomsky declared. 'Come, I'll drink a glass to your health; I'm really pleased I imposed myself on you. Ah!' he stopped suddenly. 'Has this Mr Ippolit moved into your house?'

'Yes.'

'He isn't liable to die at any minute, then?'

'Why?'

'Oh nothing, no reason; I've just spent half an hour with him . . .'

Ippolit had been waiting for the prince all this time, constantly glancing at him and Yevgeni Pavlovich while they talked apart from the others. He brightened up feverishly as they approached the table. He was nervous and excited; sweat stood out on his forehead. Besides a constant roving unease, his glittering eyes also registered a kind of vague impatience; his gaze wandered aimlessly from object to object, one face to the next. Although he had taken a considerable part in the hubbub of conversation up till then, his animation was hectic; actually he paid little attention to the actual conversation; his arguing was incoherent, scoffing, and carelessly paradoxical; he would fail to finish his sentences, and abandon topics he had brought up himself with heated vehemence one minute before. The prince was surprised and grieved to find that Ippolit had been allowed to drink two whole glasses of champagne that evening without hindrance, and that the half-empty glass in front of him was already the third. It was only later that he found this out, however; at the present moment he was not being very observant.

'You know, I'm terribly glad that today of all days is your birthday!' Ippolit cried out.

'Why?'

'You'll see; hurry up and sit down; in the first place because all your . . . people have got together. That's what I expected, there'd be a crowd; for the first time in my life I guessed right! A pity I didn't know it was your birthday though, otherwise I'd have brought a present . . . Ha-ha! Well perhaps I have brought one! Is it long till daylight?'

'Less than two hours till dawn', put in Ptitsyn, glancing at his watch.

'What's the point of dawn when you can read outside without it?' someone remarked.

'The point is that I want to see the rim of the sun. Is it in order to drink to the sun's health, Prince, what do you think?'

Ippolit was putting his questions brusquely, addressing everyone in an uncivil manner, almost peremptory; he seemed however to be unaware of this.

'Let's drink, by all means; but wouldn't it be better to calm down a little, Ippolit, eh?'

'You're always going on about sleep; Prince, you are my nanny! As soon as the sun rises and "resounds" in the sky (who was it wrote "in the sky the sun resounded"? It makes no sense but it's grand!)—then I'll go to sleep. Lebedev, the sun's the source of life, isn't it? What does "sources of life" mean in Revelation? You've heard of the "star Wormwood",* Prince?'

'I've heard that Lebedev interprets that "star Wormwood" as the network of railways all over Europe.'

'No, sir, permit me sir, that's not allowed, sir!' cried Lebedev, leaping up and waving his arms about, seemingly attempting to quell the tide of general laughter that was starting up. 'Permit me, sir. With these gentlemen . . . All these gentlemen', he turned towards the prince suddenly, 'you see, the fact of the matter is, in certain respects, sir . . .', and here dispensing with formalities, he thumped the table twice, which intensified the laughter still more.

Though Lebedev was in his usual 'evening' condition, on this occasion he was over-excited and exasperated by the preceding lengthy 'learned' argument, and in such circumstances he tended to treat his opponents with boundless and frankly undisguised contempt.

'That is not so, sir! Half an hour ago, Prince, we made it a rule not to interrupt; not to laugh while somebody was speaking, to let him say freely all he had to say, and then let the atheists raise their objections if they wished; we installed the general as chairman, so we did, sir! Otherwise what would we get, sir? That way anybody could lose track, expounding some lofty idea, sir, some profound idea, sir . . .'

'Well get on with it, get on with it: nobody's interrupting you!' cried several voices.

'Get on with it, but stick to the point.'

'What is this "star Wormwood"?' queried someone.

'I've no idea!' responded General Ivolgin with an air of consequence, in his new capacity as chairman.

'I really love these arguments and people getting in a temper, Prince, intellectual ones of course', muttered Keller meanwhile, as he wriggled in his chair in a positive ecstasy of eagerness. 'Intellectual and political', he turned abruptly and unexpectedly to Yevgeni Pavlovich sitting practically next to him. 'You know, I really love reading about the English parliament in the papers, I don't mean what they're discussing (you know I'm no politician), it's how they address each other, how they behave as politicians, so to speak: "the noble viscount sitting opposite", "the noble count who shares my opinion", "my noble opponent, who has astonished Europe with his proposal", I mean all these nice expressions, all this parliamentarism of a free people—that's what's attractive to folk like me! I'm enchanted, Prince. I've always been an artist at bottom, honestly Yevgeni Pavlovich.'

'So what does it mean then after all that', cried Ganya with some heat from another corner of the room. 'Does it mean you think railways are accursed, the ruination of mankind, an evil come down to earth to pollute "the springs of life"?'

Gavrila Ardalionovich was in a particularly excitable mood that evening, a mood of gaiety verging on exaltation, as it seemed to the prince. He was making fun of Lebedev of course, provoking him, but he soon grew impassioned himself.

'Not the railways, no sir!' protested Lebedev, losing his temper and enjoying himself enormously at one and the same time. 'The railways won't pollute the springs of life, but the whole thing, sir, altogether accursed, the entire spirit of these last centuries, in its scientific and practical totality, is perhaps really accursed, sir.'

'Cursed for certain or just possibly?' enquired Yevgeni Pavlovich. 'The distinction is rather important in this case.'

'Cursed, cursed, certainly accursed!' affirmed Lebedev recklessly.

'Don't overdo it, Lebedev, you're much better-natured of a morning', remarked Ptitsyn, smiling.

'But much franker of an evening, much more sincere and frank', Lebedev turned to him heatedly, 'more direct and straightforward, more honest and honourable, and though I may leave myself open to your thrusts, I don't care a jot, sir; I challenge you all now, all you atheists: how are you going to save the world and where have you found the right road for it to travel—you, men of science, industry, co-operation, wage-levels and so forth. How? Credit? What is credit? Where will credit lead you?'

'My, what a curiosity you have!' remarked Yevgeni Pavlovich.

'Well, I consider that anyone who isn't interested in such questions is just a high-society idler, sir!'

'Still, it does lead to a common solidarity and a balancing of interests', Ptitsyn pointed out.

'And that's all it does, that's all! Without adopting any moral stance aside from selfishness and material necessity! Universal peace, universal happiness—out of necessity! Is that how I am to understand you my dear sir, if I may venture to enquire?'

'Well, the universal necessity of living, drinking, and eating and the utter, indeed scientific, conviction that only universal co-operation and solidarity of interests will satisfy that necessity, is, I think, a sound enough notion to serve as a foundation and "spring of life" for the future of mankind', Ganya pointed out, now aroused in good earnest.

'The need to drink and eat, you mean just the instinct of self-preservation . . .'

'Is the instinct of self-preservation such a little matter then? Surely the sense of self-preservation is the normal law of humankind?'

'Who told you that?' shouted Yevgeni Pavlovich. 'It is of course a law, but no more normal than the law of destruction or self-destruction. Surely the whole normal law of mankind doesn't consist in self-preservation?'

'Aha!' cried Ippolit, turning swiftly to Yevgeni Pavlovich and staring at him in wild curiosity; seeing him laughing, however, he did likewise, nudging Kolya who was standing beside him and asking him again what time it was, even pulling Kolya's silver watch towards him and staring avidly at the hands. Then, seemingly oblivious to all else, he stretched out on the sofa, placed his hands behind his head, and began staring at the ceiling; thirty seconds later he was again at the table, sitting up straight and giving ear to the chattering of Lebedev, who was by now thoroughly wrought-up.

'That's an insidious idea, scoffing and shrewd', Lebedev seized avidly on Yevgeni Pavlovich's paradox, 'aimed at provoking your opponents to a fight, but it's so true! Because you're a sneering man-about-town, a cavalry officer (though not without abilities!), you don't realize yourself the profundity of your idea, its truth! Yes, sir. The law of self-destruction and the law of self-preservation are equally powerful in humankind! The devil rules over mankind equally until a time that is not revealed to us. You're laughing? You don't believe in the devil? Disbelief in the devil is a French notion, a frivolous idea. Do you know who the devil is? Do you know what his name is? Without knowing his name even, you laugh at his form, as Voltaire does, the hoofs and tail and horns you invented yourselves; for the unclean spirit is a great and dread spirit, not with the hoofs and horns you have invented for him. But he is not under discussion at this moment! . . .'

'How do you know he's not under discussion at this moment?' shouted Ippolit all of a sudden, and burst into paroxysms of laughter.

'A shrewd and suggestive thought!' Lebedev approved. 'But again, that's not the point. Our question is whether the "springs of life" have not become enfeebled with the growth of . . .'

'The railways?' cried Kolya.

'Not railway communications, my young and reckless stripling, but the whole tendency for which railways may serve, so to speak, as an illustration, an artistic expression. They race along, they rumble, they clatter as they hurry by for the good of humanity, so they tell us! "Too much noise and industry has got into humanity, there is little spiritual peace", complains one thinker who has sought seclusion. "That may be so", comes the triumphant reply from another thinker who is always travelling about, "but the clatter of carts bringing bread to a starving humanity is perhaps better than spiritual peace", and he walks off in his vanity. But I don't believe in those carts bringing bread to a starving humanity, vile Lebedev that I am! Because those carts bringing bread to all mankind without a moral basis for their action, could in absolute cold blood debar a significant part of humanity from the enjoyment of that which they bring, which has indeed happened before now . . .'

'These carts can cold-bloodedly disbar people?' someone pursued.

'It has happened before', confirmed Lebedev, without condescending to notice the question. 'There has already been Malthus, the friend of humanity. But a friend of humanity with an unsteady moral basis is a devourer of mankind, not to speak of his vanity; you only have to wound the vanity of any one of these numberless friends of humanity and he's ready at once to set fire to the world and its four corners out of petty revenge—just like any one of us, in fact, being honest, like me as well, the vilest of all, because I might well be the first to fetch the firewood and then run off. But again that's not the point!'

'What is the point then, for heaven's sake?'

'What a bore!'

'The point lies in the following story from times gone by,

because I feel I must tell a story from times gone by. In our times, in our country, which, I trust, you love as dearly as I do, gentlemen, because I for my part am willing to shed every drop of blood . . .'

'Get on! Do get on with it!'

'In our country, as in Europe, mankind is visited by terrible universal famines, as far as can be calculated and, as I remember, not more than once every quarter of a century, in other words once every twenty-five years. I won't argue over the exact figure but it's extremely rare, comparatively speaking.'

'Comparatively with what?'

'With the twelfth century and those to either side of it. Because then, as the scribes affirm, universal famine used to occur every two years, or three anyway, so in those circumstances mankind even resorted to cannibalism, though they kept it secret. One of these cannibals, as he was approaching old age, announced of his own accord, without any compulsion, that in the course of a long life of deprivation he had killed and eaten personally, in deadly secret, sixty monks and several lay infants, about six, no more—that is, very few compared to the number of clerics he had consumed. He had never laid a finger on any lay adults with this purpose in mind.'

'That is impossible!' cried the chairman himself, the general, sounding almost affronted. 'I often discuss and argue with him gentlemen, and always about ideas of this sort; but he usually comes out with such nonsense, your ears get tired, not a grain of truth in it!'

'General! Remember the siege of Kars, and let me tell you, gentlemen, that my story is the unadorned truth. For my part I will observe that almost every genuine fact, though it has its own immutable laws, is almost always incredible and unlikely. In fact the more real it is, the less probable it sometimes is.'

'Surely he couldn't have eaten sixty monks?' There was general laughter.

'It's obvious he didn't eat them all at once, but perhaps over fifteen or twenty years, it's perfectly understandable and natural . . .'

'Natural?'

'And natural!' Lebedev ground out with pedantic insistence.

'And besides, a Catholic monk by his very temperament is inquisitive and easily led, it would be all too easy to lure him into the forest or some secluded spot and deal with him in the aforesaid manner, but I don't deny that the number of persons devoured seems excessive to the point of self-indulgence.'

'Perhaps it really is true, gentlemen', remarked the prince suddenly.

Up till then he had been listening to the disputants in silence without getting involved in the conversation; often he had laughed heartily after the bursts of general laughter. He was obviously delighted at the noise and gaiety, even the fact that they were drinking so much. Perhaps he mightn't have said a word the whole evening, but it suddenly came into his head to speak. He spoke with such gravity that everybody at once turned towards him in curiosity.

'What I really mean to say, gentlemen, is that famine was a frequent occurrence in those days. Even I have heard about that, although I don't know history well. But I think it must have been so. When I found myself in the Swiss mountains, I was most astonished to see the ruins of old feudal castles built on the mountain-slopes, on steep crags at least half-a-mile straight up (which means several miles by mountain paths). Everyone knows what a castle is; it is a whole mountain of stones. Fearful work, impossible! And of course it was built by all the poor people, the vassals. In addition they had to pay all kinds of taxes and support the clergy. In those circumstances how could they maintain themselves and till the land? There weren't many of them then and a great number must have been dying of starvation, with perhaps literally nothing to eat. I sometimes used to wonder how it was that this people had not died out altogether or something else happened to them; how could they survive and endure? Lebedev is certainly correct in saying that there were cannibals, perhaps a great many; what I don't understand is why he brought the monks into it and what he means by that.'

'Probably because in the twelfth century monks were the only thing you could eat, because they were the only ones who were fat', observed Ganya.

'Perfectly brilliant and perfectly correct!' cried Lebedev. 'Because he never laid a finger on lay persons. Not one among sixty clerics, it's a fearful thought, a historical thought, a statistical thought, and it is from such ideas that history is made up, for those who know; it follows with numerical precision that in those days the ecclesiastics lived at least sixty times as happily and comfortably as the rest of mankind at that time. And were perhaps sixty times fatter than the rest of humanity . . .'

'Exaggeration, exaggeration, Lebedev!' The hilarity was loud around him.

'I agree it is a historical thought but what are you leading up to?' the prince pursued his line of questioning. (He spoke so seriously, without a trace of humour or mockery directed towards Lebedev, who was the target of the company's mirth, that his tone in the context of that company could not fail to sound comic; a little more and they would have started laughing at him too, but he was unaware of this.)

'Can't you see he's deranged, Prince?' Yevgeni Pavlovich leaned towards him. 'I was told earlier on that he's obsessed with being a lawyer and making court speeches, and he wants to sit the examination. I'm waiting for a marvellous parody.'

'I am leading up to a tremendous conclusion', thundered Lebedev meanwhile. 'But let us analyse first of all the psychological and legal position of the accused. We see that the accused or so to speak, my client, despite the impossibility of finding any other sustenance, has several times during the course of his curious career, detected a desire in himself to repent and keep clear of the clergy. We can see this clearly from the facts: it is written that he did consume five or six infants, a comparatively insignificant figure, but nevertheless remarkable from another point of view. It is plain that, tormented by agonizing pangs of remorse (for my client is religious and a man of conscience, as I shall prove), and to abate his sin as far as possible, he changed his diet six times by way of experiment, from monkish to secular. That it was experimental is again beyond doubt, because if it had been done purely for reasons of gastronomical variety, six would have been too insignificant: why only six and not thirty? (I'm taking it half and half.) But if it was only an experiment, from sheer despair and fear of blasphemy and offending the church, then the figure of six becomes very understandable; six attempts are quite sufficient to allay the pangs of conscience, since the attempts could not have been successful, after all. In my opinion, an infant is too little, I mean, not of large size, so that over a given period of time the number of lay infants would have had to be three or five times as great as the clergy, so that if the sin was diminished on one side, it would in the end have increased on the other, in quantity if not in quality. In reasoning this way, gentlemen, I am of course seeing it through the eyes of a twelfth-century criminal. For my part, as a man of the nineteenth century, I might well reason differently, I might inform you, so you needn't grin at me gentlemen—in your case, general, it would be quite unseemly. In the second place, an infant is not at all nutritious, in my personal opinion, rather over-sweet and sickly, so that it leaves behind the gripes of conscience without satisfying the appetite. Now the conclusion, the finale, gentlemen, the finale which contains the solution of one of the greatest problems of that age and ours! The criminal ends up by going and denouncing himself to the clergy and giving himself up to the government. One may ask what torments awaited him in those days, the wheel, the stake, the fire? Who was it then who prompted him to denounce himself? Why not just stop at sixty, keeping the secret till his dying breath? Why not simply swear off the monks and live in penance as a hermit? Why not, indeed, become a monk himself? Therein lies the solution! There must have been something stronger than the stake, the fire, even the habit of twenty years! There must have been an idea more powerful than any disaster, famine, torture, plague, leprosy, and all that hell which mankind could not have borne without that one binding idea which directed men's minds and fertilized the springs of life! Show me anything resembling that power in our age of depravity and railways ... I meant to say our age of steamships and railways, but I say: depravity and railways, because I'm drunk but I tell the truth! Show me a force which binds today's humanity together with half the power it possessed in those centuries. And now dare to tell me that the springs of life have not been weakened and tainted under this "star", this net which ensnares the people. And don't try to browbeat me with your prosperity, your riches, the rarity of famine and the speed of communications! The riches are greater but the force is less; there is no more a binding principle; everything has grown soft, everything and everyone grown flabby! We've all grown flabby, all, all of us! . . . But that's enough, that's not the point now; the point now, most worthy Prince, is shouldn't we be seeing about the refreshments prepared for the guests?'

Lebedev, who had provoked some of his audience to the verge of genuine indignation (it should be noted that bottles were being opened ceaselessly all this time), disarmed all his adversaries at a stroke by this abrupt conclusion to his speech. His own word for such a conclusion was 'a neat lawyer's twist'. Gay laughter arose once more and the guests brightened up; everyone got up from their tables to stretch their legs and take a turn along the veranda. Keller was the only one still disgruntled at Lebedev's speech, and was at a pitch of excitement.

'He attacks enlightenment and preaches twelfth-century fanaticism, posturing away there—and not because he's naive either: how did he get the money for this house then, may I ask?' He spoke aloud, stopping each and everyone he met.

'I've seen a real Apocalypse interpreter', the general was saying to another audience in another corner, among them Ptitsyn, whom he had buttonholed, 'the late Grigory Semyonovich Burmistrov: now there was one to make your hair stand on end, so to speak. To begin with, he would put his spectacles on and open up a great ancient tome bound in black leather, then there was his grey beard and his two medals for charity work. He would start off so stern and severe, generals used to bow down before him and ladies fainted, well—and this fellow ends up with refreshments! It's unheard-of!'

Ptitsyn smiled as he listened to the general and seemed about to pick up his hat, but apparently couldn't bring himself to do so, or kept forgetting his intention. Even before everyone got up, Ganya had stopped drinking and pushed the glass away from him; a bleak expression passed across his face. When the company rose, he went over to Rogozhin and sat down next to him. One might have thought they were on the friendliest of terms. Rogozhin, who, to begin with, had also been on the point of leaving quietly several times, was now sitting motionless, head bowed, as if he too had forgotten that he meant to go. He had not touched a drop of wine all evening and was plunged in thought; only occasionally did he raise his eyes and survey one and all. It seemed as though he was now waiting for something of great significance for him to happen here, and had resolved not to leave till then.

The prince had drunk only two or three glasses in all and was simply in good spirits. Half-rising from the table, he caught Radomsky's eye and, recalling their impending talk, gave him a friendly smile. Yevgeni Pavlovich nodded and suddenly indicated Ippolit, at whom he had been staring. Ippolit was asleep, stretched out on the sofa.

'Just tell me, will you, why that urchin has forced himself on you, Prince?' he said all of a sudden, with such evident exasperation, venom even, that the prince was surprised. 'I'll wager he's up to no good!'

'I've noticed', said the prince, 'you've been taking a great interest in him tonight, Yevgeni Pavlovich, or so it seemed; am I right?'

'You can add that I've got enough of my own to think about in my present situation, so I'm surprised myself at not being able to keep my eyes off that repulsive countenance all evening.'

'He's got a nice face . . .'

'There, there, look!' cried Yevgeni Pavlovich, tugging at the prince's arm. 'Now! . . .'

The prince again regarded Radomsky with surprise.

5

IPPOLIT, who had dropped off to sleep on the sofa towards the end of Lebedev's oration, now suddenly awoke as if somebody had nudged him in the ribs; he shivered, half-raised himself, looked about him, and went pale; he gazed around half-fearfully, but his face registered something approaching horror when everything came back to him.

'What, are they going? Is it all over? Has the sun come up yet?' he kept asking anxiously, grabbing at the prince's arm. 'What's the time? For God's sake, the time? I've overslept. Have I been asleep long?' he added with an air of despair, as if he had missed something on which his entire fate depended, at the very least.

'You've been asleep seven or eight minutes', replied Radomsky.

Ippolit glanced eagerly at him and pondered for a few moments.

'Ah . . . that's all! So then I . . .'

Here he greedily took a long deep breath, as if ridding himself of some great burden. He realized at length that nothing was 'over', that it was not yet dawn, and that the guests had merely got up from the tables to have a bite to eat. The only thing that was over was Lebedev's babbling. He smiled, and a hectic flush in the form of two bright patches began to play across his cheeks.

'So you were even counting the minutes while I slept, Yevgeni Pavlich', he jibed. 'You've been staring at me all evening, I've noticed you . . . Ah, Rogozhin! I was dreaming about him just now', he whispered to the prince, frowning and nodding towards Rogozhin as he sat at the table. 'Ah, yes', he suddenly changed direction again, 'where's the orator, then? Where's Lebedev, then? Lebedev must have finished, mustn't he? What was he talking about? Is it right, Prince, that you once said the world would be saved by "beauty"? Gentlemen', he suddenly shouted loudly to all and sundry, 'the prince says the world will be saved by beauty! And I say he has playful notions like that because he's in love. Gentlemen, the prince is in love; just now, as soon as he came in, I was convinced of it. No blushing Prince, or I shall feel sorry for you. What beauty is going to save the world? Kolya told me what you said . . . Are you a devout Christian? Kolya says you call yourself a Christian.'

The prince regarded him keenly and made no reply.

'You're not going to answer? You think I'm very fond of you, perhaps?' Ippolit asked abruptly, almost blurting the words.

'No, I don't think so. I know you don't like me.'

'What! Even after what happened yesterday? Wasn't I frank with you yesterday?'

'I knew yesterday you didn't like me.'

'That's because I'm jealous of you, is that it, jealous? You've always thought that and you're thinking it now, but . . . but why am I telling you about it? I want some more champagne; give me another glass, Keller.'

'You shouldn't have any more, Ippolit, I shan't give you any . . .'

And the prince pushed the glass away from him.

'You're right . . .', he acquiesced at once, on apparent reflection. 'People may say . . . well what the devil do I care what they say! Isn't that right, isn't that right? Let them talk afterwards, eh Prince? What does it matter to any of us what happens *afterwards*! . . . Actually I'm still half-asleep. What an awful dream I had, I remember now . . . I wouldn't wish dreams like that on you, Prince, even if perhaps I don't care for you really. Anyway, even if you don't like a fellow, why wish him harm, eh? Why do I keep asking questions, always asking questions? Give me your hand, I'll give it a good squeeze, like so . . . You have reached out your hand though, so you must know I am pressing it in good faith? . . . Indeed, I shan't have any more to drink. What's the time? Come to that, there's no need, I know what time it is. The hour is at hand! Now is the time. What are they doing in that corner—setting out the refreshments? So this table is free? Excellent! Gentlemen I . . . not all of them are listening . . . I intend reading out a certain article, Prince; the snacks are more interesting of course, but . . .'

Then suddenly, quite unexpectedly, he pulled out of his left breast pocket a large, official-size package, stamped with a big red seal. He placed it on the table in front of him.

This surprise had its effect on the company, which was not primed for it, or rather was *primed* but not for that. Radomsky actually jumped in his chair; Ganya quickly moved closer to the table; Rogozhin did the same, but with a kind of fastidious irritation, as though realizing what was afoot. Lebedev, who chanced to be close by, came up and looked at the package with curious little eyes, trying to guess what was coming.

'What have you got there?' the prince asked, uneasily.

'As soon as the rim of the sun comes up, I'll lie down, I told you that; I honestly will: you'll see!' cried Ippolit. 'But . . . but . . . do you really think I'm not capable of breaking open that package?' he added, surveying them all with a kind of defiance, apparently indifferent as to whom he addressed. The prince saw that he was trembling all over.

'Nobody here thinks any such thing', replied the prince for them all. 'Why do you suppose anyone should have that idea and what . . . what is this strange notion you have of reading? What have you got there, Ippolit?'

'What's he got there? What's happened to him now?' came the questions on all sides. Everyone came over, some of them still eating; the package with the red seal drew them all like a magnet.

'I wrote it myself yesterday, directly after I promised to come and live with you, Prince. I was writing it all day yesterday, then all night. I finished it this morning; last night, towards morning I had a dream . . .'

'Would it not be better tomorrow?' put in the prince timidly.

'Tomorrow "there shall be time no longer"!' laughed Ippolit hysterically. 'Still, don't worry, I'll get through it in forty minutes, well an hour . . . And you see how interested everybody is; they've all gathered round; they're all looking at my seal. If I hadn't sealed the article up in a packet there'd have been no effect! Ha-ha! That's mystery for you! Unseal it or not, gentlemen?' he shouted, his eyes glittering as he laughed his strange laugh. 'Mystery! Mystery! And do you remember, Prince, who proclaimed that "there shall be time no longer"? It was proclaimed by the great and mighty angel in the Apocalypse.'

'Better not read it!' Radomsky suddenly exclaimed, but with such an air of concern that many thought it strange.

'Don't read it!' the prince cried out also, laying his hand on the package.

'What's this about reading? It's eating-time', someone remarked.

'An article? For a magazine is it?' enquired another.

'Maybe it's boring', added a third.

'What's going on then?' asked the rest. The prince's fearful gesture had apparently alarmed Ippolit himself.

'So . . . I shouldn't read it?' he whispered to him timidly, a wry smile on his bluish lips. 'Not read it?' he muttered, surveying the entire company, all the eyes and faces, seeming to use his effusiveness as a weapon.

'You're . . . afraid?' he turned again to the prince.

'Of what?' asked the latter, his expression steadily altering.

'Has anybody got a twenty-kopeck piece?' Ippolit suddenly leapt from his chair as if he'd been pulled to his feet. 'Any kind of coin?'

'Here!' Lebedev produced it at once; the idea flashed through his mind that the invalid had gone mad.

'Vera Lukyanovna!' Ippolit swiftly invited, 'here, toss it on to the table, heads or tails? Heads—I read it!'

Vera stared timorously at the coin, then at Ippolit, then at her father, and rather awkwardly, with her head tilted back as if convinced that she mustn't see the coin herself, tossed it on to the table. It came up heads.

'I read it!' hissed Ippolit, seemingly overwhelmed by fate's decision; he could not have gone paler if he had received a death sentence. 'What's happened, though?' he started suddenly after a half-minute silence. 'Did I really toss a coin just now?' He looked round at them all with that same aggressive sincerity. 'But really, that's an astonishing psychological phenomenon!' he exclaimed suddenly, addressing the prince in genuine amazement. 'It's . . . it's an incredible phenomenon, Prince!' he repeated, becoming more animated as he seemed to recollect himself. 'You make a note of it, Prince, remember it, I believe you're collecting information on capital punishment . . . so they tell me, ha-ha! Oh God, what ludicrous absurdity.' He sat down on the sofa and, putting both elbows on the table, clutched at his head. 'It's shameful even, isn't it? . . . Well, what the devil do I care whether it's shameful.' He raised his head almost immediately. 'Gentlemen! Gentlemen, I am breaking the seal', he proclaimed with a kind of abrupt resolution. 'I . . . I, still I'm not forcing anyone to listen! . . .'

With hands trembling in excitement, he unsealed the packet and drew out several closely written sheets of notepaper. He placed these in front of him and began shuffling them.

'What's happening? What on earth's going on? What's he going to read?' muttered a number of people gloomily; others were silent. All of them seated themselves, however, and watched inquisitively. Perhaps they really were waiting for something extraordinary to happen. Vera caught hold of her father's chair, almost crying with fright; Kolya was in virtually the same state of apprehension. Lebedev, who had already taken his seat, suddenly rose, picked up the candles, and moved them nearer to Ippolit to give him a better light to read by.

'Gentlemen, this . . . you'll see presently what this is', Ippolit added for some reason, then abruptly started reading: ' "A Necessary Explanation!" Epigraph: "*Après moi le déluge*" . . . Oh, hell!' he cried, as if he had burnt himself. 'Could I really have put such a stupid epigraph? . . . Listen, gentlemen! . . . I assure you that all this may turn out to be the most awful rubbish! It's just a few of my ideas . . . If you think there's . . . anything mysterious in it . . . or forbidden . . . I mean . . .'

'You might miss out the prologue', Ganya interrupted.

'Wriggling out of it', added another.

'Too much talk', said Rogozhin, who had said nothing up till then.

Ippolit suddenly looked at him, and when their eyes met Rogozhin grinned bitterly and savagely at him before slowly uttering a strange remark:

'This isn't the way to go about the thing, lad, not this way . . .'

Nobody knew what Rogozhin meant of course, but his words made rather an odd impression on them all: a certain common idea fleetingly touched each and every one of them. The words produced a frightful effect on Ippolit, however: he began shaking so violently that the prince stretched out his hand to support him. He would probably have cried out, if his voice had not failed him. For a whole minute he was unable to utter a word as he stared at Rogozhin, breathing heavily. At length, still gasping, he brought out with a supreme effort:

'So it was you . . . you were . . . you?'

'Was what? What did I do?' replied the baffled Rogozhin, but Ippolit, flaring up as sudden fury gripped him, cried out with harsh vehemence:

'*You* were in my room last week, after one in the morning, on the day I'd been to see you, *you*!! Admit it was you!'

'Last week, in the middle of the night? Are you sure you haven't gone off your head, lad?'

The 'lad' once more said nothing for a minute, index finger propping his forehead, as if plunged in thought; but through his pale smile, still twisted in fear, there suddenly flickered something crafty, even gleeful.

'It was you!' he repeated at length, almost in a whisper, but with utter conviction. '*You* came to my room and sat for a whole hour in the chair by the window without saying anything; more than an hour; between one and three in the morning; you got up and left after two . . . It was you, you! Why you tried to frighten me, why you came to torment me, I don't understand, but it was you!'

Despite the fearful trembling which still persisted, a look of infinite hatred suddenly flashed in his eyes.

'Presently, gentlemen, you will know all about this . . . I . . . I . . . listen . . .'

Once again he snatched up his papers in desperate haste; they had scattered and got out of order. He strove to put them together as they fluttered in his shaking hands, but it was a long time before he had got them settled.

The reading at last commenced. For about the first five minutes, the author of this unexpected article still kept gasping for breath and read jerkily and incoherently; after that his voice grew firmer and began to convey the meaning of what he read perfectly adequately; it took the occasional fit of coughing to stem the flow. He grew extremely hoarse by half-way, but the extraordinary fire which animated him more and more as the reading proceeded, reached its supreme pitch towards the end, as did the painful effect on his listeners. Here is the whole of this 'article':

' "My Necessary Explanation
Après moi le déluge!

"Yesterday morning the prince came to see me; among other things, he tried to persuade me to come and live at his villa. I knew very well he would be sure to insist and I was certain he would come straight out with it, and say that at the villa it would be 'easier for me to die among people and trees', as he puts it. Today, however, he didn't say *die*, he said 'it'll be easier to live' instead, which is, after all, practically the same thing for me in my situation. I asked him what he meant by these never-ending 'trees' of his and why he kept harping on about them to me, and I was astonished to learn from him that apparently I had said, that evening, that I had come to Pavlovsk to look at trees for the last time. When I pointed out to him that it was all the same whether one died under trees or looking through the window at my bricks, and there was no need to make such a fuss over a matter of a couple of weeks, he agreed at once; in his opinion though, the greenery and fresh air would surely bring about some physical change in me, and my nerves and *my dreams* would be relieved. I again pointed out, laughing, that he was talking like a materialist. He replied with that smile of his that he had always been a materialist. As he never lies, these words must have some sort of significance. He has a nice smile; I've studied him carefully of late. I don't know whether I like him now or not; I've no time for such considerations now. My five-month hatred of him, I have to say, has begun to ebb away completely over this last month. Who knows, perhaps the chief reason I came to Pavlovsk was to see him. But . . . why did I leave my room then? A condemned man should not leave his corner; and if I hadn't made a definite decision at this point, but on the contrary delayed until the last moment, then of course I wouldn't have left my room and would certainly not have accepted the suggestion that I should move in with him 'to die' in Pavlovsk.

"I must hurry up and be sure to finish off all this 'explanation' by tomorrow. That means I won't have time to read it over and make corrections; I'll read it through tomorrow to the prince and the two or three witnesses I expect to find with him. As there won't be a word of a lie in it, nothing but the final and solemn truth, I'm curious to see what impression it makes on me personally at the time, the minute I begin to read it. I shouldn't have written 'final and solemn truth'; for two weeks there would be no point in lying anyway, come to that, because it isn't worth living for two weeks. This is the soundest guarantee that I shall write nothing but the truth. (NB Not to forget the idea: am I mad at this moment, these moments, that is? I was told positively that consumptives sometimes lose their minds for a time in the final stages. Verify this tomorrow from the audience's impression during the reading. This question has to be settled definitely, with complete certainty, otherwise I can't set about anything.)

"I have the feeling that I have just written something dreadfully stupid; but I have no time to correct it, as I said; besides, I have promised myself, deliberately, not to correct a single sentence in this manuscript, even if I notice that I am contradicting myself every few lines. What I want to do during tomorrow's reading is to determine whether the logical flow of my ideas is correct; whether I can detect my own mistakes, and therefore whether everything I have brooded over in this room over the past six months is true or no more than mere raving.

"If I had had to quit my room and say farewell to Meyer's wall two months ago, as I am doing now, I'm sure I would have felt sad. Now, however, I feel nothing, and yet I'm leaving both room and wall *for ever*! My conviction that for two weeks it's not worth feeling regret, or giving oneself over to sensation at all, must have mastered my nature and is now perhaps controlling my every feeling. But is that true? Is it true that my nature has now been taken over completely? If I were to be tortured at this moment, wouldn't I cry out—and not say it wasn't worth feeling pain as I only had two weeks left to live?

"But is it true that I have only two weeks to live and no more? I was lying that time in Pavlovsk: Botkin had told me nothing and had never seen me; but about a week ago, a student, Kislorodov, was brought to see me. He's a materialist, an atheist and nihilist as far as his convictions go—that's exactly why I called him in: I needed a man who would finally tell me the naked truth, without sugaring the pill or any beating about the bush. And that he did, very readily and dispensing with the niceties—with evident pleasure, what's more (which I thought was going a bit too far). He came straight out and said I had about a month left, perhaps a little longer under decent conditions; but then again I might die a lot sooner than that. In his opinion, I might die suddenly, tomorrow for instance: such things have happened. Not above three days before, in Kolomna, a consumptive young girl in a similar condition to mine was just getting ready to go to market for groceries when she suddenly felt ill, lay down on the sofa, gave a sigh, and died. Kislorodov informed me of all this with a certain flaunting of his lack of feeling and tact, as if he were paying me the compliment of regarding me too as an all-denying, superior being like himself, to whom dying of course is a mere nothing. At all events, the fact is attested: a month and no more! I am quite certain he was not mistaken.

"I was very much surprised at the prince guessing the other day that I was having 'bad dreams'; he said literally that in Pavlovsk 'my nerves and *my dreams*' would be changed for the better. And why dreams? Either he's a doctor or else a man of extraordinary mind who can divine a great many things. (But

there cannot be the slightest doubt that in the final analysis he is
an 'idiot'.) As luck would have it, I was having a nice little dream
just before he arrived (I have hundreds like that nowadays,
incidentally). I fell asleep—I think an hour before he came—and
found myself in a room (not my own). It was larger and loftier
than mine, better furnished, light and airy; there was a cupboard,
a chest of drawers, a sofa, and my bed, big and wide and covered
with a green silk eiderdown. In this room, however, I saw a
frightful creature, a sort of monster. It was something like a
scorpion but not a scorpion, it was more loathsome and much
more horrible, in that there are no such animals in nature and it
had appeared *specially* to me, and there was a kind of mystery
about that. I had a very close look at it: it was brown and had a
carapace, a reptile about eight inches long, two fingers thick at
the head, gradually tapering off towards the tail so that the tip of
the tail was no more than a fifth of an inch broad. About two
inches from the head, two claws about four inches in length stuck
out at an angle of forty-five degrees, one on each side, so that the
whole creature seen from above had the form of a trident. I didn't
notice a head, but I did see two feelers, not long, looking like two
strong needles, also brown. There were two similar feelers at the
end of the tail and on each claw, making eight in all. The creature
was running very swiftly around the room, supported on its claws
and tail; as it ran, its abdomen and claws wriggled like little
snakes, with astonishing speed, despite the carapace, and it was
most loathsome to watch. I was dreadfully afraid it would sting
me; I had been told it was poisonous, but what tormented me
most was—who had sent it to my room, what was their purpose
with me, and what lay behind it all? It kept hiding underneath the
chest of drawers or the cupboard, and crawling off into corners. I
got up on a chair and tucked my legs under me. It swiftly ran the
length of the room and disappeared somewhere near my chair. I
peered around fearfully, but as I was sitting with my legs drawn
up, I hoped it would not crawl up on to the chair. Suddenly I
heard a kind of crackling rustle behind me, close to my head; I
turned round and saw the reptile was crawling up the wall and
was already level with my head; it was even touching my hair with
its tail, which was twirling and wriggling with amazing speed. I
leapt up and the creature vanished. I was afraid to lie down on

the bed in case it had crawled under my pillow. My mother and a friend of hers came into the room and tried to catch the foul thing, but they were calmer than I was and weren't even afraid. But they didn't realize the situation. All of a sudden the reptile crawled out again; it was crawling, very quietly this time, once more across the room towards the door, purposefully it seemed, squirming with a slowness that was even more hideous. At this point, my mother opened the door and summoned our dog Norma—a huge, shaggy, black Newfoundland; she died five years ago. She rushed into the room and stopped dead over the vile thing. The creature halted too, but continued squirming and clicking the ends of its claws and tail on the floor. If I'm not mistaken, animals are incapable of sensing supernatural terror; but at that moment I felt that in Norma's fear there was something very strange, almost something correspondingly supernatural, and that she must also be sensing, as I did, that there was something fateful and mysterious about the beast. She backed away slowly from the reptile as it crawled slowly and cautiously towards her; it was intent, it seemed, on darting forward and stinging her. Despite her intense fear, Norma looked horribly savage, trembling as she was in every limb. Suddenly she began to bare her fearful teeth, opened wide her huge red maw, then set herself, chose her moment, and suddenly seized the reptile in her teeth. The creature must have jerked itself powerfully free and tried to squirm away, because Norma caught it again, this time in the air, and twice more took it whole into her jaws, as if swallowing it. The carapace began cracking under her teeth; the creature's tail and claws thrashed horribly as they dangled from her mouth. All of a sudden, Norma gave a piteous whine: the foul creature had managed to sting her tongue after all. She opened her mouth in pain, whining and howling, and I saw the mangled creature was still wriggling across the width of her jaws, emitting large quantities of white fluid from its half-crushed body on to her tongue, like when a cockroach is squashed . . . That's when I woke up, and the prince came in." '

'Gentlemen', cried Ippolit, abruptly looking up from his reading, almost ashamed, 'I haven't read this through, but I really think I have put in a lot of irrelevant material. This dream . . .'

'Is a case in point', Ganya was swift to put in.

'There is too much of a personal nature, I agree, I mean about me in particular . . .'

As he said this, Ippolit looked weary and enfeebled, and he wiped the sweat from his brow with a handkerchief.

'Yes, sir, rather too much interested in yourself', hissed Lebedev.

'Gentlemen, I am not forcing anyone, I repeat; anyone not interested may leave.'

'Turning people out . . . of someone else's house', muttered Rogozhin, barely audible.

'And what if we all upped and left?' said Ferdischenko suddenly. He had not ventured to speak up till now, incidentally.

Ippolit all at once lowered his eyes and clutched his manuscript; but at the same instant raised his head again and, with eyes flashing and two red spots in his cheeks, looked straight at Ferdischenko and spoke.

'You don't like me at all!'

Laughter broke out, though the majority did not join in. Ippolit flushed horribly.

'Ippolit', said the prince, 'close your manuscript and give it to me, then go to bed here, in my room. We'll have a talk before you go to sleep and again in the morning. On condition you never unfold those pages again. Would you like to do that?'

'How can I?' Ippolit threw him a look of positive astonishment. 'Gentlemen!' he cried out once more, feverishly excited. 'That was stupid, I didn't know how to take it. I won't interrupt my reading again. Anyone who wants to listen can do so . . .'

He took a swift gulp of water from the glass, quickly set his elbows on the table so as to shield himself from their eyes, and forged on with his reading. His feelings of shame soon passed off, however . . .

' "The idea" (he continued reading) "that it was not worth living for just a few weeks started to take hold of me in real earnest, I believe, about a month ago, when I had four weeks left to live. It got the better of me completely however, only three days ago when I got back from Pavlovsk that evening. The first moment that the notion possessed me absolutely was on the prince's veranda, at the very moment when I had decided to make one final trial of life, and wanted to see people and trees (let's suppose I did say that myself), when I got into a passion over Burdovsky's rights—'my neighbour'—and longed for them all to spread their arms wide and embrace me and ask my forgiveness for something, as I would them; in a word I ended up looking like a stupid fool. It was in those hours that my 'last conviction' flared up in me. Now I can only stand astonished that I could have existed for six whole months without that 'conviction'! I knew for a fact that I had consumption and was incurable. I didn't deceive myself and I understood the position clearly. But the clearer it became to me, the more feverishly I longed to live; I clung to life and wanted to live, come what may. I admit that I might have been bitter at the dark, deaf, and blind fate which had decreed that I should be crushed like a fly, without knowing why of course; but why on earth didn't I stop at that? Why did I actually *begin* to live, knowing that I must not do such a thing? Try, knowing that by now there was nothing for me to try? Meanwhile I couldn't even read a book, and stopped reading altogether: what was the point of learning anything for the sake of six months? That thought made me give up a book more than once.

"Yes, that wall of Meyer's could tell many a tale! I've written a lot on it. There wasn't a stain on that filthy wall I don't know by heart. Damned wall! And yet it is dearer to me than all the trees in Pavlovsk, or it would be dearer than all the trees in Pavlovsk if I cared one way or the other now.

"I can recall now the avid interest I began to take in *their* lives; I had had no such interest before. I sometimes used to wait for Kolya with scolding impatience, when he was so ill himself he couldn't stir from his room. I pried so much into every trivial detail, and was so interested in every rumour that I do believe I became a regular gossip. I couldn't comprehend, for example, why these people with so much life at their disposal were incapable of getting rich (that's something I still don't understand, incidentally). I knew one poor man who died of starvation later on, as I was informed, and I recall being infuriated: had it been possible to bring that poor man back to life, I believe I should have murdered him. Sometimes I would feel better for weeks at a time and I was able to go out; but the street made me so angry at length that I would deliberately spend whole days locked in my room, though I could have gone out like everybody else. I couldn't bear those people bustling and peeping about, eternally anxious, glum, and fearful, scurrying about me on the pavements. Why their everlasting misery, why the eternal anxiety and bustle; their everlasting glum nastiness (because they are nasty, nasty and spiteful)? Whose fault is it if they are unhappy and incapable of living, though they each have sixty years of life ahead of them? Why did Zarnitsyn permit himself to die of starvation, when he had sixty years ahead of him? And every one of them shows you the rags he wears, his toil-worn hands, and shouts angrily: 'I work like a horse, I toil all day, I'm poor and hungry as a dog! Others don't have to work and wear themselves out, yet they're rich!' (The eternal refrain!) By their side, running and bustling about from morn till night, there's some wretched, shrivelled-up creature 'of noble birth', Ivan Fomich Surikov—he lives in our block, on the floor above—always out at elbows, buttons missing, running errands for various people, again from morning till night. If you talk to him it's: 'I'm poor, a miserable pauper, my wife's died, I couldn't afford medicine, my child froze to death in the winter; my eldest daughter's a kept woman . . .', he's always snivelling and complaining! Oh, I never had any pity for those fools, never, nor have I now—I say it with pride! Why isn't he a Rothschild himself? Whose fault is it that he hasn't got Rothschild's millions? That he hasn't got a mountain of gold imperials and napoleons, a mountain as high as a helter-skelter at a Shrovetide fair? If he's alive, everything must be within his power! Whose fault is it that he doesn't understand that?

"Oh, now it's all the same to me, I haven't the time to be angry, but then, then, I repeat, I used to bite my pillow at nights and tore my sheet out of sheer rage. Oh, how I used to dream then, how I longed, deliberately longed to be turned out into the street, 18 years old, hardly clothed, hardly covered, and left completely on my own, with nowhere to live, no work, not a crust of bread, no relations, not a single acquaintance in the vast city, hungry, ill-treated (so much the better!) but healthy—then I would have shown them . . .

"Shown them what?

"Ah, you surely don't suppose I don't know how I have humiliated myself as it is by this 'Explanation' of mine! Well, who is there among you who doesn't think me a puny little wretch, ignorant of life, forgetting I am no longer 18, forgetting that to live as I have over the last six months is equivalent to reaching a ripe old age! Still, let them laugh and say all these things are mere fairy-tales. I have filled nights on end with them; I can remember them all now.

"But do I have to tell them all over again, when the time for fairy-tales has passed for me? And tell whom? I used to amuse myself with them when I saw clearly that even studying Greek grammar was barred to me, as I once had a fancy to do: 'I shall die before I reach the syntax', I thought on page one, and threw the book under the table. It's lying there yet; I've forbidden Matryona to pick it up.

"Let anyone who comes across my 'Explanation' and who has the patience to read it through, take me for a madman or a schoolboy even, or, most likely, a man under sentence of death, who naturally considers that everyone apart from himself takes life far too lightly, and is inclined to waste it too cheaply, employ it too lazily, too unscrupulously, and therefore not one of them is worthy of it! Well, what of that? I declare that my reader is mistaken and that my conviction has nothing whatever to do with my death sentence. Ask them, just ask them all, what it is they all, every one of them, understand by happiness. Ah, rest assured that Columbus was happy, not when he had discovered America but while he was discovering it; you may be sure that the climax of his happiness was, perhaps, exactly three days before the discovery of the New World, when his mutinous crew almost turned the ship towards Europe and sailed back! It wasn't the New World that mattered, it might not have existed. Columbus died virtually without having glimpsed it, and not really knowing what he had discovered. What matters is life, life alone, the continuous and infinite process of discovering it, not the discovery itself! What's the use of talking! I suspect that everything I am saying now is so platitudinous that I shall most probably be set down as a junior schoolboy presenting his composition on 'the sunrise', or people will say that perhaps I had something to say, but no matter how hard I tried I couldn't manage to make myself clear. I would add, however, that in every human idea that possesses genius or originality, or in any serious human idea at all that arises in someone's mind, there is always something that can't be conveyed to others by any means whatever, even if whole tomes were written about it and thirty-five years were spent explaining it; something always remains that doesn't want to leave your head for anything, and stays with you for ever; you'll die without ever having passed on the crucial point of your idea to anyone. But if I too have been incapable of conveying all that has been tormenting me for six months, then at least they will realize that, having attained my 'ultimate conviction', I have paid very dearly for it; this, for certain private reasons, is what I considered essential to set out in my 'Explanation'.

6

"I HAVE no wish to lie: reality has been seeking to snag even me on its hook this last six months and sometimes I have been distracted enough to forget my own death sentence, or rather, I didn't wish to think about it; I even occupied myself in various activities. When I became really ill, about eight months ago, I put an end to all my relationships and dropped all my former companions. As I'd always been a rather morose individual, my friends had no trouble in forgetting me; of course they'd have forgotten me in any case. My domestic circumstances at home, 'within the household' I mean, were those of a recluse. About five months ago I locked myself away for good and all and cut myself off from the family quarters. My wishes were always respected and no one ventured to enter my room, except at a certain fixed time to tidy up and fetch me my dinner. My mother tremblingly obeyed my orders, and dared not so much as whimper in my presence if I decided to let her come in occasionally. She was always hitting the children to stop them making a noise or disturbing me; I did my share of complaining about their noise too; they must really love me now! I also tormented 'faithful Kolya', as I nicknamed him, pretty thoroughly. Latterly he tormented me in turn: it was natural enough, that's what people are created for, to torment one another. I noticed, however, that he put up with my irritability, as if he had promised himself beforehand that he would humour the patient. Naturally that got on my nerves; but apparently he had taken it into his head to imitate the prince in 'Christian humility', which was really rather laughable. He's an impetuous young boy and will copy anybody, of course, but I did sometimes think it was time he started having a mind of his own as well. I'm extremely fond of him. I tormented Surikov too, the one who lives above us and runs errands for people from morning till night; I kept trying to prove to him that his poverty was his own fault, so that at length he took fright and stopped coming to see me. He's a very meek sort of person, the meekest creature imaginable (NB They say meekness is a mighty force; I'll have to ask the prince about that, it's one of his own remarks.) But when last March I went upstairs to see how they had 'frozen the baby to death' as he put it, and inadvertently smiled at the corpse of his infant, because I had started to explain to Surikov that it was 'his fault', the wretch's lips began to quiver and, grabbing my shoulder with one hand, he showed me the door with the other and said softly, almost whispered I mean: 'Get out, sir!' I went, and I was very pleased at that; I was pleased at the time, at the very moment he was showing me out; but later on his words, whenever I recalled them, made a deep impression on me, an odd sort of contemptuous pity for him, which I had no desire to feel at all. Even at the moment of an insult like that (I am aware, after all, that I had insulted him, though without intending it), even at a moment such as that, the man was incapable of losing his temper. His lips had not begun to quiver from anger at all, I'll swear to that: he grabbed me by the arm and uttered his magnificent 'Get out, sir' without a hint of anger. Dignity there was, a great deal of it, enough to be incongruous (so that there was a lot that was comical in all this, to tell the truth), but there was no anger. Perhaps he simply began to despise me all of a sudden. Since then, when I've run into him once or twice on the stairs, he's started taking his hat off to me—something he never used to do before; he didn't stop as he had done previously, though; he ran past me in embarrassment. If he really did despise me, then it was in his own peculiar fashion: he *meekly* despised me. Or perhaps he took his hat off out of sheer dread at seeing the son of his creditor, because he always owed my mother money and could never extricate himself from his debts. Come to think of it, that is the most likely explanation. I was on the point of having it out with him and I'm perfectly sure he would have started apologizing inside ten minutes, but I decided it was better to leave him alone.

"Just at that time, I mean the time when Surikov 'froze' his baby, around the middle of March, I suddenly felt much better for some reason, and that lasted for about two weeks. I began going out of the house, mostly at dusk. I used to love the March twilight, when it was just getting chilly and the gas-lamps were lit; I walked for miles sometimes. One evening I was overtaken in the dark on Shestilavochnaya Street by a down-at-heel 'gentleman'. I couldn't make him out too well; he was wearing a wretched apology for an overcoat which was much too tight and short for him, as well as being too light for the time of year. He was carrying a paper parcel. When he drew level with a street-lamp about ten yards ahead of me, I noticed something drop out of his pocket. I hurried to pick it up—just in time, because someone in a long kaftan suddenly appeared on the scene, but seeing what I had in my hand he didn't stop to argue, he just glanced quickly at my hands and slid off again. It was a large, old-fashioned, morocco pouch, well-stuffed; somehow, though, I guessed immediately that whatever it might contain, it wasn't money. The owner of the wallet was walking on about forty yards ahead and was soon lost to view in the crowd. I started to run and shout after him, but as the only thing I could shout was 'Hey!', he didn't turn round. All of a sudden, he darted into the gateway of a house. When I ran in through the gates, where it was very dark, there was no one in sight. The house was of immense size, one of those monster blocks of small apartments put up by speculators; some of them can have up to a hundred rooms. When I had run through the gates I thought I saw a man walking along in the far right-hand corner of the vast courtyard, though I could scarcely make him out in the darkness. When I reached the corner, I noticed the entrance to a flight of stairs; the staircase was narrow, extremely dirty, and entirely unlit; up above, though, I could still hear a man running up the steps, so I set off after him, thinking to catch him up while someone opened the door for him. And so I did. The flights of steps were very short but they were numberless, so that I became horribly out of breath; a door opened and closed again—on the fifth level, I guessed from three floors lower down. Several minutes passed while I ran up and got my breath back on the landing, then looked for the bell. At length the door was opened by a peasant woman, who was stoking up the samovar in the tiny kitchen; she listened to my questions in silence, without taking in a word of course, before opening a door into the next room, also very small and horribly low-ceilinged, poorly furnished with the bare essentials and with an enormous, wide, curtained bed, on which lay 'Terentych' (as the woman called out to him). I took him to be drunk. On the table a candle-end was guttering in its iron holder, and there was a bottle, almost empty. Terentych mumbled something to me as he lay and waved towards another door. The woman had gone out, so there was nothing for it but to open that door. I did so and went into the next room.

"This room was even more narrow and cramped than the previous one; I didn't know where to turn round; a narrow single bed in the corner took up an awful lot of space; the rest of the furniture consisted of just three plain chairs, piled high with rags of all sorts, and the plainest of wooden kitchen tables standing in front of an ancient settee covered in oilcloth. It was next to impossible to get between the settee and the table. There was a lighted tallow candle in the same sort of holder as in the other room, while on the bed squalled a tiny baby, not more than three weeks old possibly, judging by its crying; he was being 'changed', I mean swaddled, by a pale, sickly looking woman, apparently young and wearing very little; possibly just starting to get up after her confinement; the child kept on crying in expectation of the emaciated breast. Another child was asleep on the settee, a 3-year-old girl, apparently covered by a tailcoat. By the table stood a gentleman in a very shabby frock-coat (he'd already shed his overcoat and it was lying on the bed). He was unwrapping some blue paper containing about two pounds of white bread and two small sausages. The table held, besides this, a pot of tea and some fragments of black bread lying about. An open trunk stuck out from under the bed, along with two bundles of rags.

"In short, the place was in a terrible mess. I got the impression from the first that both the gentleman and the lady were decent people, reduced by poverty to that humiliating condition where disorder at length overwhelms every effort to cope with it, and even compels people to the bitter necessity of finding in the disorder itself, as it daily increases, a kind of bitter and, as it were, vengeful feeling of pleasure.

"When I entered, the gentleman, who had just got in before me and was undoing his provisions, was talking rapidly and excitedly to his wife; the latter, though she had not finished the swaddling, had already started her whimpering; the news must have been routinely wretched. The gentleman was about 28 to look at, and his dark, lean face, framed in its black sideburns above a chin glossily close-shaven, struck me as quite pleasant, even attractive; it was a morose face and bore a morose expression, along with a certain hint of over-defensive pride, all-too-easily wounded. When I entered, a strange scene took place.

"There are people who derive considerable pleasure from their irritable touchiness, especially when it reaches an extreme pitch (which always happens very quickly); at such moments, they feel it is even more enjoyable being offended than not. These touchy folk are always tormented by remorse afterwards, if they are intelligent enough to realize, of course, that they were ten times as angry as they ought to have been. This gentleman stared at me for some time, as amazed as his wife was alarmed, as if it were something terribly bizarre that anyone should enter their room; suddenly he fell on me with something like frenzy. I had no time to mutter more than a word or two, but he, especially on perceiving that I was decently dressed, must have considered himself fearfully affronted by my daring to peer into his nook so unceremoniously and see the squalid circumstances of which he was so ashamed. Of course he was delighted at the chance to vent on someone else the bitterness he felt at all his failures. For a moment it even occurred to me that he was going to start a fight; he had turned ashen, like a woman in hysterics, and alarmed his wife dreadfully.

" 'How dare you come in like that? Out of here!' he shouted, trembling and having real difficulty in getting his words out. Then suddenly he saw his wallet in my hands.

" 'I believe you dropped this', said I, as coolly and calmly as I was able. (That was the right procedure, incidentally.)

"He stood before me in absolute consternation, and for some time seemed incapable of taking anything in; then he quickly clutched at his side-pocket, gaped in dismay, and clapped his hand to his brow.

" 'Heavens! Where did you find that? How did it happen?'

"I explained in the briefest fashion, and even more coldly, had that been possible, how I had picked up the wallet, called out and run after him, and how at length, by guesswork and dint of groping, had pursued him up the stairs.

" 'Oh, good lord!' he cried, turning to his wife. 'All our papers are in it, the last of my instruments and everything . . . Oh, my dear sir, do you know what you've done for me? I should have been lost!'

"I had taken hold of the door-handle meanwhile, intending to leave without replying; but I was short of breath myself, and suddenly my emotions found vent in such a violent paroxysm of coughing that I could barely stand up. I saw the gentleman rushing about in all directions trying to find me somewhere to sit down, before clutching at the rags on one of the chairs and hurling them to the floor. He hastened to offer me the chair and sat me down carefully. My cough lasted without remission for another three minutes or so. When I recovered myself he was sitting on another chair close by, also no doubt cleared by throwing rags to the floor; he was examining me closely.

" 'Are you . . . ill?' he spoke in the tones doctors usually employ when talking to patients. 'I'm a medical man myself' (he didn't say 'doctor'); so saying, he indicated the room for some reason, as if in protest at his present situation. 'I see you . . .'

" 'I've got consumption', I said as shortly as I could, and rose to my feet.

"He too jumped up at once.

" 'Perhaps you're overstating the case and . . . if measures were taken . . .'

"He was greatly disconcerted and seemed incapable of recovering his composure; the wallet was still stuck in his left hand.

" 'Oh, don't distress yourself', I cut him short again, grasping the door-handle, 'I was examined by Botkin last week' (I've brought Botkin in here again), 'and the diagnosis is certain. I'm sorry . . .'

"I made to open the door once more and leave my doctor, as he was embarrassed, grateful, and crushingly ashamed, but my accursed coughing seized me again. At this point the doctor insisted that I sit down again and rest myself. He turned to his wife and she, without quitting her place, said a few kind and grateful words to me. This greatly embarrassed her and prompted a flush to suffuse her thin, sallow cheeks. I stayed on, but with a steady air of demonstrating that I greatly feared to trespass on their privacy (as was only proper). My doctor's remorse had begun to torment him, that was clear to see.

" 'If I . . .', he began, only to break off instantly and change the subject. 'I'm so obliged to you and feel so guilty . . . I . . . you see . . .', he indicated the room again, 'at the present moment I'm in such a situation . . .'

" 'Oh', I said, 'it doesn't take any seeing; it's common enough; you've lost your employment no doubt, and you've come to Petersburg to explain the position and find another post.'

" 'How . . . did you find out?' he asked in astonishment.

" 'I could see at once.' I couldn't help the sneer in my voice as I answered. 'Lots of folk come here from the provinces, full of hopes; they run about hither and yon and live just like this.'

"He abruptly began to speak with emotion, his lips unsteady; he began his plaintive tale and it did hold my interest, I must confess; I sat there with him for nearly an hour. He told me his story, one common enough, incidentally. He had been a provincial doctor, a government post, but then various intrigues had started and even his wife became involved. His pride was touched and he lost his temper rather; then came changes in the provincial government which favoured his enemies; his position was undermined and complaints were lodged; he lost his job, and used the last of his means to get to Petersburg and explain matters. Naturally, in Petersburg he couldn't get a hearing for a long time, then the answer was negative, then they lulled him with promises; after that came harsh words; he was ordered to write something in explanation, then they refused to accept what he had written; he was instructed to file a petition. In short, he had been chasing about for five months and had run through all his savings; his wife's last rags had been pawned, and now a child had come along and, and . . . 'today came the final rejection of the petition, and I've almost no bread left, there's nothing left, my wife's had a baby. I, I . . .'

"He jumped up from his chair and turned away. His wife was weeping in the corner and the child had started squalling again. I took out my notebook and began writing in it. When I had finished and got up, he was standing before me, watching with timid curiosity.

" 'I've noted your name', I told him, 'well, and all the rest of it: place of work, the name of your governor, dates, months. I have an old school-friend, Bakhmutov, and his uncle Peter Matveyevich Bakhmutov, councillor of state and director . . .'

" 'Peter Matveyevich Bakhmutov!' my medical man cried, almost shaking. 'But it's on him that practically everything depends!'

"Really, in this story of my medic and its happy ending, which I chanced to help bring about, everything came together and fitted in as if it had been deliberately planned, exactly like in a novel. I told these poor people that they should try not to repose any hope in me, that I was a poor schoolboy (I deliberately exaggerated my insignificance; I had finished my course long ago and was no schoolboy), and there was no point in them knowing my name, but that I would go straight to my friend Bakhmutov on Vasilyevsky Island, and since I knew for a fact that his uncle, the councillor of state, was a childless bachelor who worshipped his nephew and doted on him exceedingly as the last sprig of the family, 'perhaps my friend will be able to do something for you and for me, of course, through his uncle . . .'

" 'All I need is an opportunity to explain matters to his excellency! If only I might be accorded the honour of addressing him in person!' he exclaimed. His eyes glittered as he trembled feverishly. He actually said '*be accorded*'. Repeating once more that the business would probably be a flop and it would all be a waste of time, I added that if I didn't come to see them next morning, it would mean that it was all over and there was no point in cherishing any expectations. They saw me out with bows, almost beside themselves. I shall never forget the expressions on their faces. I took a cab and set off at once for Vasilyevsky Island.

"There had been no love lost between this Bakhmutov and me

for several years at school. We regarded him as an aristocrat, at least that was what I called him: he used to dress superbly and come to school in his own carriage. He didn't put on airs at all and was an excellent comrade, always exceptionally cheerful and even witty on occasion, though far from being bright, despite his being always top of the class; I was never first in anything, as it happens. All the boys liked him except me. He did make overtures to me a number of times in those years, but each time I rejected him in sullen irritation. I hadn't seen him for a year now; he was at the university. When I went in to him, some time after eight (amid considerable formality: I was announced), he greeted me with initial surprise, quite stiffly in fact, but he cheered up and suddenly burst out laughing as he looked at me.

" 'But what put it into your head to come and see me, Terentyev?' he exclaimed with that invariably good-natured familiarity, sometimes impudent, but never wounding, that I so liked in him and so detested him for. 'But what's this?' he cried in alarm. 'You look so ill!'

"My coughing had returned to torment me and I collapsed into a chair, barely able to get my breath.

" 'It's all right, I've got consumption', I said. 'I've come to ask a favour.'

"He sat down, astonished, and I immediately recounted the doctor's story, explaining that as he had immense influence over his uncle he might be able to do something.

" 'I will, I certainly will, and tomorrow I'll get to work on my uncle; I'm very pleased at the lucid way you put it . . . But really, how did it occur to you to come and see me, Terentyev?'

" 'A great deal depends on your uncle in this affair; besides, you and I, Bakhmutov, have always been enemies, and as you're a man of honour, I just thought you would not refuse an enemy', I added ironically.

" 'Like Napoleon appealing to England!' he exclaimed, laughing. 'I'll do it! I'll do it at once! I'll go now if possible', he added hastily, seeing that I was grave and unsmiling as I rose from my chair.

"And in fact the business was settled between us in this most unexpected fashion, to everyone's complete satisfaction. In six weeks our medico had got a post in a different province, together with travelling expenses and even some cash besides. I suspect that Bakhmutov, who had got into the fixed habit of visiting the doctor (while I deliberately refrained from doing so and received him almost coldly whenever he dropped in on me)—Bakhmutov, I suspect, had even pressed the doctor into accepting a loan from him. I saw Bakhmutov about three times over these six weeks, the third time being when we were celebrating the doctor's departure. The send-off had been organized by Bakhmutov at his house and took the form of a champagne dinner, which the doctor's wife also attended, though she very soon left to see to the baby. It was a fine evening in early May, and the huge disc of the sun was sinking down into the bay. Bakhmutov was seeing me home; we went by way of the Nikolayevsky Bridge, both of us a little drunk. Bakhmutov was talking about his delight at the happy ending to the story, thanked me for something, then explained how happy he felt now after this good deed and that I deserved all the credit. He kept assuring me that those people were wrong who taught and preached that individual acts of charity were unimportant. I was also desperately keen to say something.

" 'Anyone who slights an individual act of charity', I began, 'is attacking the nature of man and despises his personal dignity. The organization of public charity, however, and the question of personal freedom, are two different questions and are not mutually exclusive. Individual good deeds will always exist because the personality needs it to be so, the vital need of one personality to act upon another. There used to be an old man living in Moscow, a "general"—I mean a councillor of state, who had a German name; he had spent his whole life dragging round prisons talking to the inmates; every party of convicts on their way to Siberia knew beforehand that the "little old general" would visit them at Sparrow Hills. He took the business with the most devout seriousness; he would arrive and walk along the ranks of prisoners surrounding him, and halt in front of each man, asking him what he needed. He hardly ever lectured anyone and called them all his "dears". He would hand out money and send them various necessities—foot-rags, undergarments, cloth; sometimes he brought religious tracts and distributed them among the literate, in the full conviction that they would read them on the journey, and that the literate would in turn read to the illiterate.

He rarely asked about their crimes, but he would listen if a prisoner brought up the subject himself. All the convicts were treated alike, no distinctions made. He used to talk to them like brothers, but they began to look on him as a father towards the end. If he noticed a woman convict with a babe-in-arms, he would come up and fondle the child and snap his fingers to make it laugh. This went on for many years, right up to his death; it got so that he was known all over Russia and Siberia too, by all the convicts that is. A man who had been in Siberia told me he had personally witnessed how the most hardened of criminals remembered the general, who, by the way, was seldom able to give out more than twenty kopecks per man on his visits. True, their recollection of him was not all that warm or particularly solemn. One of the "unfortunates", who had murdered a score of people or slaughtered six children, just for the fun of it (there are such people, so they say), would suddenly for no reason, perhaps only once in his entire twenty years, give a sigh and say: "What about the little old general, I wonder if he's still alive?" He might even smile as he said it—and that would be that. How can you know what seed may have been dropped into his soul for ever by the "little old general" he still hadn't forgotten after twenty years? How can you know, Bakhmutov, what significance this contact between one personality and another can have in the destiny of that other? . . . We have here a man's entire life and the countless ramifications which are hidden from us. The best chess-player in the world, the sharpest of them, can only calculate a few moves in advance; it was written about almost as a miracle when one French player could see ten moves ahead. How many moves have we to do with here, and how much is beyond our ken? Scattering your seed, in offering charity, in performing your good deed in whatever fashion it may be, you give away part of your personality and take in part of another's; there is a mutual communion, and with a little more attention you will be rewarded by knowledge, the most unexpected discoveries. At length you will assuredly begin to look on your work as a science; it will lay hold of your entire life and may fill it too . . . On the other hand, all your thoughts, all the seeds you have broadcast, perhaps already forgotten, will take root and flourish; he who received it from you will pass it on to another. And how do you know what part you will play in the resolution of the destinies of mankind? If this knowledge and a whole life of such work at length raises you to such heights that you are able to sow some mighty seed and bequeath some great idea to the world, then . . .', and so on, I talked a good deal.

" 'And to think that a man such as you is to be denied life!' cried Bakhmutov, railing vehemently against someone.

"We were standing on the bridge at that moment, leaning on the balustrade, and gazing down at the Neva.

" 'Do you know what's just occurred to me', I said, leaning still further over the balustrade.

" 'Not to throw yourself into the water?' cried Bakhmutov, almost in a panic. Perhaps he had read the thought in my face.

" 'No; for the moment it's just this thought I have: I've got about two or three months to live, perhaps four; but if, for example when I have only two months left, and if I should be terribly eager to do one good deed which would demand a lot of work, running about, and fuss, something like this business of our doctor, then in that case I would have to turn it down, wouldn't I, for lack of time, and hunt up some other "good deed" on a smaller scale and within my *means* (if I should be as keen as all that on good deeds). It's an amusing thought, you must admit!'

"Poor Bakhmutov was very anxious about me. He saw me right to my door and was tactful enough to refrain from commiseration altogether; he said nothing practically the whole way. As he made his farewells, he pressed my hand warmly and asked my permission to visit me. I replied that if he were to come to me as a 'comforter' (because even if he didn't say a word, he would still have come as comforter, I explained that to him), he was bound to remind me of death still more every time he came. He shrugged his shoulders, but he agreed with me; we parted quite civilly, which I hadn't altogether expected.

"But that evening and night was sown the first seed of my 'last conviction'. I seized avidly on this *new* idea, and just as avidly considered all its implications and aspects (I didn't sleep a wink) and the deeper I brooded on it and the more I entertained it, the more fearful I became. A terrible panic gripped me at length and remained with me over the subsequent days. Sometimes, thinking of this continual panic of mine, I would suddenly go cold as a new terror struck me: might I not conclude from my state of mind that my 'last conviction' had taken too firm a grip on me and was bound to lead to its logical conclusion? I lacked the resolution for such a conclusion. Three weeks later it was all over and resolution came to me, but as the result of an utterly strange circumstance.

"Here in my explanation, I note down all these numbers and dates. It will be all the same to me of course, but *now* (and perhaps only at this moment), I want those who will judge my action to be able to see clearly the logical sequence of reasoning which has led up to my 'last conviction'. I wrote just now that the final resolution that was lacking to carry out my 'last conviction' came to me, I believe, not through any logical process, but through a kind of strange shock, a certain odd circumstance, perhaps quite unconnected with what had gone before. About ten days ago, Rogozhin came to see me on a certain matter which is pointless to go into now. I had never seen him before, but I'd heard a good deal about him. I gave him all the information he needed and he soon left, and since information was all he had come for, matters between us might well have ended there. He intrigued me a great deal, however, and all that day I was a prey to strange thoughts; I nerved myself to go and see him myself next day, to return the visit. Rogozhin was clearly none-too pleased at seeing me, and even hinted 'tactfully' that there was no point in our further acquaintance; nevertheless, I spent a most curious hour there, as, no doubt, did he. There was such a contrast between us that neither of us could have been oblivious to it, especially me: I was a man already counting his days, while he was living his life to the full, head-on, living for the present, with no thought of 'final' conclusions, figures, or anything else which was not relevant to what . . . to what . . . well to what he was mad about; I trust Mr Rogozhin will forgive my using that expression, if only because I am a poor author, unable to express my thoughts. Despite all his lack of courtesy, he struck me as a man of intelligence, capable of deep understanding, though he took little interest in matters which did not concern him personally. I gave him no hint of my 'last conviction', but I felt that he guessed what it was as he listened to me. He said nothing, he's terribly reticent. As I left, I hinted to him that, despite all the differences and contrasts between us—*les extrémités se touchent** (I interpreted that to him in Russian), so that perhaps he himself isn't as far from my 'last conviction' as it might appear. He gave me a very sour and sullen grimace by way of reply, then he got up and fetched me my cap himself, pretending I was going of my own choice, and showed me out of his gloomy house just like that, on the pretext of seeing me off out of politeness. His house astonished me; it's like a graveyard, but he seems to like it; still, that's understandable; the full and spontaneous life he leads is too full in itself to need a setting.

"This visit to Rogozhin tired me exceedingly. Besides, I had been feeling poorly since morning; towards evening I felt very weak and lay down on the bed; at times I felt extremely hot and there were moments of actual delirium. Kolya stayed with me till eleven. However, I do remember everything he talked about, in fact what both of us talked about. But when my eyes closed at times I kept on picturing Surikov apparently receiving millions in money. He just didn't know where to put it all; he fairly racked his brains over it, trembling in case someone should steal it, and at length apparently decided to bury it in the ground. In the end I advised him that instead of wastefully burying a heap of gold like that in the earth, he should melt the whole pile down into a little coffin for the 'frozen baby' and exhume the baby for the purpose. Surikov seemed to accept my scoffing with tears of gratitude and at once set about effecting the plan. I saw myself spit and walk away from him. Kolya assured me, when I had fully recovered consciousness, that I hadn't slept at all, I had been talking to him about Surikov the whole time. At times I was in the depths of despondency and distress, and Kolya was anxious when he left me. When I got up to lock the door after him, I suddenly recalled the picture I had seen that day at Rogozhin's, above the doorway in one of the gloomiest rooms in his house. He had shown it to me himself in passing; I believe I stood in front of it for about five minutes. There was nothing in it of artistic merit, but it aroused a strange feeling of disquiet in me.

"The picture shows Christ, just taken down from the cross. I believe artists usually depict Christ, whether on the cross or taken down from it, as still retaining a trace of extraordinary beauty in the face; they seek to preserve this beauty in him, even during the most terrible agonies. There was no hint of beauty in Rogozhin's picture; it is an out-and-out depiction of the body of a man who has endured endless torments even before the crucifixion—wounds, torture, beatings from the guards, blows from the populace when he was carrying the cross and fell beneath it, and finally the agony of the cross, lasting six hours (according to my calculations at least). Of course it is the face of a man *just taken down* from the cross, that is, it preserves a great deal of the warmth of life; nothing has had time to stiffen, so that suffering still lingers on the face of the dead as though it were still being experienced (this is very well caught by the artist); still, the face has not been spared in the slightest; this is nature unadorned, truly how a corpse must look, whoever it may be, after such agonies. I know that the Christian Church laid it down in the first centuries that Christ's passion was not symbolic but actual, and that his body must have been wholly and entirely subject to the laws of nature on the cross. In the picture, the face is terribly mangled by blows, swollen, with terrible, swollen, bloody bruises, the eyes open and unfocused; the whites wide open, gleaming with a kind of deathly, glazed lustre. But it's odd; as you look at this corpse of a tortured man a most curious question comes to mind: if a corpse like that (and it must certainly have been exactly like that) was seen by all his disciples, his future chief apostles, and seen by the women who followed him and stood by the cross, by all in fact who believed in and worshipped him, how could they have believed, looking at such a corpse, that the martyr would rise again? The compulsion would be to think that if death was so dreadful, and nature's laws so powerful, how could they possibly be overcome? How could they be overcome when even he had failed, he who had vanquished even nature during his lifetime, he whom nature obeyed, who said '*Talitha cumi!*'* and the girl arose, who cried 'Lazarus come forth!' and the dead man came forth? Looking at that picture, one has the impression of nature as some enormous, implacable, dumb beast, or more precisely, much more precisely, strange as it may seem—in the guise of a vast modern machine which has pointlessly seized, dismembered, and devoured, in its blind and insensible fashion, a great and priceless being, a being worth all of nature and all her laws, worth the entire earth—which indeed was perhaps created solely to prepare for the advent of that being! The picture is, as it were, the medium through which this notion of some dark, insolent, senselessly infinite force to which everything is subordinated is unwittingly conveyed. The people who surrounded the dead man, not one of whom is shown in the picture, must have felt a terrible anguish and confusion on that evening, which had shattered all their hopes and almost their entire belief at one fell blow. They must have dispersed in a state of dreadful fear, though each of them also carried away within him one mighty thought which could never now be wrested from them. And if the master himself, on the eve of his execution, could have seen this image, would he have mounted the cross as he did, and died as he did? This question too is bound to come to mind as you look at the picture.

"All of this swam fitfully through my mind, perhaps in actual delirium, sometimes even in concrete images, for a whole hour and a half after Kolya had gone. Can something which has no image appear in the form of an image? But at times I did seem to see, in a kind of strange and impossible form, that infinite force, that blind, dark, dumb creature. I remember somebody with a candle in his hand, apparently leading me by the arm and showing me a sort of huge and repulsive tarantula, assuring me that it was that same dark, blind, all-powerful creature and laughing at my indignation. There is always a little lamp burning at night in my room in front of the icon, a dim and feeble light, yet you can see everything and even read under the lamp itself. I think it was some time after twelve; I hadn't slept a wink and was lying with my eyes open; suddenly the door of my room opened and in came Rogozhin.

"He came in, closed the door, looked silently at me, and softly went over to the table in the corner, which stands practically under the lamp. I was most surprised, and watched him expectantly. Rogozhin leaned his elbows on the table and began to stare at me in silence. Two or three minutes passed, and I remember that his silence greatly annoyed and exasperated me. Why on earth didn't he speak? It seemed odd to me that he'd come so late, but I remember that I wasn't tremendously surprised about it. Rather the contrary: though I hadn't expressed my idea clearly enough that morning, I knew that he understood it and it was the sort of idea which might prompt one to come and talk it over, however late it might be. I naturally thought that's what he had come for. We had parted that morning on somewhat hostile terms, and I distinctly recalled him giving me one or two sarcastic looks. It was the same derision I read in his look now, and it was that which annoyed me. That it actually was Rogozhin, and not some apparition, not delirium, I had no doubt whatever from the beginning. The thought never crossed my mind.

"Meanwhile he went on sitting and staring at me with that same smirk. I angrily turned over in bed, leaned my elbow on the pillow, and resolved in turn not to say a word, even if we sat there all the time like that. For some reason I was absolutely determined that he should be the first to speak. I think about twenty minutes went by. Suddenly a thought came to me: what if it was a hallucination and not Rogozhin at all?

"Neither during the course of my illness nor before it have I ever once seen an apparition; but I have always felt, as a boy and even now, that should I see a ghost just once I should die on the spot—and that despite my not believing in ghosts at all. But when the thought occurred to me that this was not Rogozhin, but a mere apparition, I don't remember being frightened in the least. Not only that, I was positively resentful. Another odd thing was that the question of whether it was an apparition or Rogozhin himself didn't concern or alarm me at all as much as it perhaps should have done; I believe I was thinking about something else at the time. I was a great deal more interested, for instance, in why Rogozhin, who had been wearing morning dress and slippers that day, was now in a white waistcoat, white tie, and tails. Another thought flashed through my mind: if it was a phantom and I wasn't afraid of it, why on earth shouldn't I get up, go over to it, and reassure myself. Perhaps I was afraid after all and didn't dare. But as soon as I thought of being afraid, I felt as if ice coursed through my whole body; I felt a chill down my spine and my knees trembled. At that very instant, as if guessing I was afraid, Rogozhin moved the arm he had been leaning on, straightened up, and started to open his mouth, seemingly about to laugh; he was staring straight at me. I was seized with such a fury that I longed to rush at him, but as I had sworn to myself that

I would not be the first to speak, I stayed on the bed, particularly as I was still uncertain whether it actually was Rogozhin or not.

"I don't remember exactly how long this went on; nor can I recall whether I lost consciousness at times or not. All I know is that Rogozhin got up at last and surveyed me as slowly and intently as when he had come in, though he had stopped grinning; softly, almost on tiptoe, he went to the door, opened it, and went out, closing it behind him. I didn't get up; I don't remember how long I lay with open eyes, thinking and thinking; God knows what I was thinking about; I don't remember dropping off to sleep either. I was woken next morning by a knock at the door after nine. I've made it a rule that if I don't open the door myself by nine, or shout for tea, then Matryona has to knock. When I opened the door for her, I thought at once: how could he have got in when the door was locked? I made enquiries and became convinced that it was impossible for the real Rogozhin to have got in, because all our doors are locked at night.

"It was this peculiar incident, which I have described in such detail, that was the reason for my definite 'resolve'. It was not logic, therefore, no logical conviction which assisted me in coming to my final decision; it was disgust. I can't go on participating in a life which assumes such bizarre and outrageous forms. That apparition humiliated me. I cannot bring myself to submit to a dark force that takes the form of a tarantula. It was only at dusk, when at last I sensed the final moment of total resolve, that I felt better. That was only the first stage; for the second I travelled to Pavlovsk, but that has been explained sufficiently already.

7

"I HAD a small pocket pistol; I got it when I was a boy, at that silly age when when one suddenly develops a fancy for stories of duels and bandit hold-ups; or I'd be challenged to a duel and stand nobly facing the barrel. A month ago I examined it and prepared it for use. I hunted out two bullets in the drawer where it was lying, and enough powder in the horn for three charges. The pistol is no good, it aims off to one side and its range is only fifteen paces; but of course it can blow your head off if you put it close to your temple.

"My intention was to die in Pavlovsk, in the park at sunrise, so as not to disturb anyone in the house. My 'Explanation' would make everything clear to the police. Those who are keen on psychology, and anyone else who pleases, can draw what conclusions they like from it. However, I wouldn't want my manuscript to be published. I would like the prince to keep one copy for himself and let Aglaya Ivanovna Yepanchina have another. Such is my wish. I leave my skeleton to the Medical Academy for scientific purposes.

"I do not recognize any jurisdiction over me and I know that I am beyond the reach of any judicial power. Quite recently I had an amusing thought: what if I suddenly took it into my head to kill anyone I liked, ten people at once even, or perpetrate something frightful, something regarded as the worst possible thing in the world, the court would be at a loss how to deal with me, having two or three weeks to live, now that torture has been abolished. I would die in comfort in their hospital, nice and warm, with a doctor in close attendance, perhaps a good deal warmer and more comfortable than at home. I can't understand why the same idea doesn't occur to people in my position, not even as a joke. Perhaps it does at that; there are plenty of cheery fellows, even among us.

"But even if I don't recognize any judicial power over me, I know all the same that I shall be judged when I am a deaf and voiceless defendant. I don't wish to go without leaving a word in my defence—a voluntary defence, not enforced, not as a justification, oh no! I don't have to apologize to anyone for anything—but simply because I feel like it.

"Now to begin with, there is this curious consideration: by what right, with what motive, would anyone think to dispute my right to these two or three weeks I have left? What business is it of any court of law? Who actually wants me not only to be condemned, but to behave nicely while I endure the term of my sentence? Surely no one really wants that? For morality's sake? I could understand that if I was a picture of health, and attempted my life when it 'might be of use to my neighbour' and so forth, then morality might reproach me in the old-fashioned way for disposing of my life without asking permission, or some such reason. But now, now when my sentence has already been read out to me? What sort of morality is it which not only demands your life but your last gasp too, as you yield up the final atom of your being, listening to the prince's consolation? He will certainly use his Christian proofs to reach the happy conclusion that actually it's better that you should be dying. (Christians like him always get round to that idea: it's their pet hobby-horse.) And what are they after with their ridiculous 'Pavlovsk trees'? Trying to sweeten the last hours of my life? Can't they realize that the more I forget myself, the more I surrender to this last illusion of life and love, with which they try to screen off Meyer's wall and everything that is frankly and openly written on it, the unhappier they make me? What do I want with your nature, your Pavlovsk park, your dawns and sunsets, your blue skies and your smug faces, when all this feast that has no end has begun by excluding me alone? What is there for me in all this beauty, when I am forced to be aware every minute, every second, that even this tiny fly buzzing in the sunbeam near me, even that is a participant in all this festival and chorus, knows its place, loves it, and is happy, while I am the sole outcast, and only my cowardice has prevented me from wanting to face it before now! Oh, I know very well how the prince and the rest of them would have liked to make me sing for the sake of decency and triumphant morality that celebrated classic stanza of Millevoix's:

'O, puissent voir votre beauté sacrée
Tant d'amis sourds à mes adieux!
Qu'ils meurent pleins de jours, que leur mort soit pleurée,
Qu'un ami leur ferme les yeux!'*

—instead of all these 'mischievous and wicked' speeches. But believe me, believe me, my dear innocents, that even in these edifying lines, in this academic benediction on the world in French verse, there is embedded so much concealed bitterness, so much irreconcilable, self-deluding, rhymed malice, that even the poet himself may have fallen into the trap and taken that malice for tears of affection, and so died, God rest him! Let me tell you that there is a limit to the shame inherent in the realization of one's own insignificance and weakness, beyond which a man cannot go, and at which he begins to take an immense satisfaction in this very shame of his ... Well, of course, humility is a mighty force in that sense, I admit that—but not in the sense in which religion accepts humility as a force.

"Religion! I admit the existence of eternal life, perhaps I always have. Suppose that consciousness, kindled by the will of a higher power, suppose it looked round at the world and said: 'I am!'—and suppose that it has been commanded by that higher force to annihilate itself, for some sufficient reason, even without any explanation—it had to be; all that granted, I admit all that, but again comes the eternal question: what point is there in my humility in all this? Why couldn't I just be devoured without demanding that I praise what is devouring me? Will somebody up there really be offended that I don't want to wait out my two weeks? I can't believe that; it would be a much more likely supposition that my paltry life, the life of an atom, was needed to complete some universal harmony, some plus-or-minus equation, or some contrast etc. etc., just as the lives of countless creatures are required as a daily sacrifice, without whose death the rest of the world cannot go on (though I must say that is not a very exalted idea in itself). But let it be so! I agree that otherwise, without this ceaseless devouring of one by another, it would have been totally impossible to organize the world; I am even prepared to admit that I comprehend nothing of that organization; but there is one thing I do know beyond all doubt: once I had been endowed with the consciousness that 'I am', what is it to do with me if the world has been created with errors and that otherwise it can't continue to exist? Who then can judge me after that—and on what charge? Say what you like, but it's all insufferable and unjust.

"At the same time, no matter how hard I tried, I could never imagine that there was no future life or providence. Most probably it all does exist, but we understand nothing of that future life, nor anything of the laws that govern it. But if it is so difficult, even absolutely impossible, to comprehend, how could I be held responsible for failing to make sense of the incomprehensible? Of course they tell me, and the prince along with them, naturally, that this is just where obedience comes in, one must obey without question, out of pure decorum, and for this meekness of mine I will certainly be rewarded in the next world. We greatly demean providence if we ascribe our conceptions to it out of pique that we can't understand its workings. But there again, if it's impossible to understand, then I repeat, it is hard if we have to answer for what man is not equipped to comprehend. And if so, how can I be judged for not being able to understand the true will and laws of providence? No, best leave religion out of this.

"Enough of this anyway. When I reach these lines, the sun will probably rise and begin to 'resound in the sky', and its mighty immeasurable power will pour forth on all below. So be it! I shall die, looking directly at the source of power and life, and I shall not want this life! If I had had the power not to be born, I would certainly not have accepted existence on these absurd terms. But I still have the power to die, though the days I render back are numbered. No great power, and no great revolt either.

"A final explanation: I'm not dying because I haven't the strength to endure these three weeks; oh, I should have had strength enough, and had I so wished, I should have been sufficiently consoled by my very awareness of the wrong being done to me; but I'm no French poet and I don't want consolations of that sort. Finally, there's the temptation: nature has so limited my actions by its three-week sentence, that perhaps suicide is the only action I can start and finish by my own free will. Well, perhaps I want to make use of my last opportunity to *act*? A protest is sometimes no small thing . . ."'

The 'Explanation' was over; Ippolit had finished at last.

There occurs, in extreme cases, that final stage of cynical candour, when a highly strung person, exasperated and goaded beyond endurance, is no longer afraid of anything and is prepared for any sort of unseemly incident, indeed glad of it; he flings himself at people with the vague but firm intention of hurling himself from a belfry a minute later, by so doing resolving all misunderstandings, if any such exist. The imminent exhaustion of physical strength is often the herald of such a state of mind. The extraordinary, almost unnatural, tension which had been supporting Ippolit up to this point had reached its final pitch. In himself, this 18-year-old boy, worn out by illness, seemed as weak as a fluttering leaf plucked from a tree, but as soon as he surveyed his audience—for the first time in the last hour—his air and smile expressed the most imperious, contemptuous, and offensive disgust. His gesture of defiance had been swift, but his hearers too were highly indignant. Everyone was getting up from the table in noisy irritation. Tiredness, wine, and nervous strain increased the general disorder and the nastiness of their impressions, if one may put it that way.

Suddenly Ippolit sprang from his chair as though he had been hauled upright.

'The sun has risen!' he shouted, as he glimpsed the gleaming tree-tops and pointed them out to the prince as something miraculous. 'It has risen!'

'Did you think it wouldn't or something?' remarked Ferdischenko.

'Blazing hot again all day', murmured Ganya with casual irritation, holding his hat as he stretched and yawned. 'What'll we do if this drought lasts a month? . . . Are we going or not, Ptitsyn?'

Ippolit listened with an incredulity that bordered on stupefaction; all of a sudden he turned very pale and began to shake bodily.

'You're trying to insult me with that very poor attempt at feigned indifference', he said to Ganya, staring him straight in the eye. 'You're a swine!'

'Well, if that doesn't beat all', yelled Ferdischenko. 'Letting go like that. How utterly feeble!'

'He's just a fool', said Ganya.

Ippolit got hold of himself somewhat.

'I realize, gentlemen', he began, still shaking, and faltering at every word, 'that I may have deserved your retaliation and . . . I'm sorry to have bored you with my ravings' (he indicated his manuscript), 'or rather, not to have bored you altogether . . .' (he gave a silly smile), 'have I bored you, Yevgeni Pavlich?' he suddenly fired the question at him. 'Have I or not? Tell me!'

'A bit long-drawn-out, still . . .'

'Say it all! Don't lie for once in your life!' Ippolit commanded, trembling.

'Oh, I really don't care! Be good enough to leave me alone', Radomsky turned fastidiously away.

'Good night, Prince', Ptitsyn came up.

'But he's going to shoot himself any moment! Look at him!' cried Vera, dashing over to Ippolit in great alarm, even seizing his arms. 'Why, he said he'd shoot himself at sunrise, what on earth are you thinking of?'

'He won't shoot himself!' several voices muttered maliciously, Ganya's among them.

'Gentlemen, be careful!' shouted Kolya, also grabbing at Ippolit's arm. 'Just look at him! Prince! Prince! Do something!'

Vera, Kolya, Keller, and Burdovsky crowded round Ippolit; all four of them imprisoned his arms.

'He has the right, he has the right! . . .', muttered Burdovsky, though he too looked totally bewildered.

'Excuse me, Prince, but what are to be the arrangements?' asked Lebedev, as he came up, drunk and angered to the point of insolence.

'What arrangements?'

'No, sir; I'm sorry, sir; I am the master of the house, sir, though I don't wish to be lacking in respect towards you . . . Let's say you are the master as well, but I don't want this, in my own house . . . That's it, sir.'

'He won't shoot himself; the wretched boy's just playing the fool', shouted General Ivolgin unexpectedly, with indignant self-assurance.

'That's the spirit, general!' Ferdischenko responded.

'I know he won't shoot himself, General, highly respected general, but all the same . . . I am the master of the house, you see.'

'Listen to me, Mr Terentyev', said Ptitsyn suddenly, having said goodbye to the prince and holding out his hand to Ippolit, 'I think in your manuscript you mentioned your skeleton and about leaving it to the Academy? Were you talking about your own skeleton, your very own I mean, bequeathing your own bones?'

'Yes, my bones . . .'

'Just so. Otherwise mistakes can be made; they say it did happen once.'

'What are you teasing him for?' cried the prince suddenly.

'You've made him cry', added Ferdischenko.

But Ippolit was certainly not crying. He made to stir from his chair, but the four persons who stood round him suddenly grabbed his arms as one man. Laughter broke out.

'That's what he was leading up to, that's why he read his story', remarked Rogozhin, 'so people would hold his arms. Farewell, Prince. Ech, we've been sitting for ages, my bones are aching.'

'If you really meant to shoot yourself, Terentyev', laughed Radomsky, 'then in your shoes I'd deliberately not do it, just to spite them after compliments like that.'

'They're dying to see me shoot myself', Ippolit rounded on him belligerently.

'They're annoyed they're not going to.'

'So you don't think they'll see it?'

'I'm not trying to provoke you; on the contrary, I think it's very likely you will shoot yourself. The main thing is not to lose your temper . . .', drawled Radomsky in a patronizing tone.

'I can see now I made a terrible mistake reading them this manuscript!' said Ippolit, suddenly giving him an appealing look, as though asking a confidant for some friendly advice.

'It's an absurd situation, but . . . really I don't know what to advise', replied Yevgeni Pavlovich, smiling.

Ippolit kept his eyes fixed sternly and silently upon him. At moments he might have been miles away.

'No, sir, I'm sorry, what a way to talk about such things, sir', said Lebedev, ' "I'll shoot myself in the park", he says, "so I don't disturb anybody!" He thinks he won't disturb anybody if he walks downstairs and a couple of yards into the park.'

'Gentlemen . . .', the prince began.

'No, sir, I'm sorry, sir, highly respected Prince', Lebedev broke in furiously, 'since you can see the man's serious, and since at least half of your guests take the same view and are sure that after what has been said he is in honour bound to shoot himself, I, sir, as master of this house, declare before witnesses that I invite your assistance!'

'But what are we to do, Lebedev? I'm ready to assist you!'

'Just this, sir: firstly he must this minute surrender the pistol he was bragging about, along with all its accessories. If he does that, I would be agreeable to him spending the night in this

house, bearing in mind his state of health—under my supervision
of course. But tomorrow he absolutely must go—where is up to
him; I'm sorry, Prince! If he won't give up the gun, I shall at once
seize his arms, I'll take one arm, the general the other, and I shall
immediately send for the police; then it will be a police matter,
sir. Mister Ferdischenko, as a friend, will fetch them, sir.'

A hubbub ensued; Lebedev was working himself up beyond all
reason; Ferdischenko was preparing to go for the police; Ganya
kept insisting that nobody was going to shoot himself. Yevgeni
Pavlovich said nothing.

'Prince, have you ever jumped off a belfry?' Ippolit whispered
to him suddenly.

'N-no . . .', the prince replied innocently.

'You surely don't think I hadn't anticipated all this hostility!'
hissed Ippolit again, staring at the prince with his glittering eyes,
as though actually expecting an answer from him. 'Enough of
this!' He shouted abruptly to all present. 'It's my fault . . . more
than anyone else's! Lebedev, here's the key' (he took out his
purse and produced a steel ring with three or four little keys),
'here, it's this one, last but one . . . Kolya will show you . . .
Kolya! Where's Kolya?' he shouted, looking at Kolya without
seeing him. 'Yes . . . there, he'll show you. He helped me to pack
my bag. Take him, Kolya; in the prince's study, under the
table . . . my bag . . . with this key, underneath, in a little case . . .
my pistol and powder-horn. He packed them himself, Mister
Lebedev, he'll show you; but on condition that early in the
morning, when I go back to Petersburg, you return my pistol.
You hear? I'm doing this for the prince, not you.'

'Now that's better!' Lebedev grabbed for the key and ran into
the next room, grinning malevolently.

Kolya stopped and made as if to say something, but Lebedev
dragged him off after him.

Ippolit looked at the laughing guests. The prince noticed that
his teeth were chattering, as if he were chilled to the bone.

'What swine they all are!' again he hissed frenziedly to the
prince. Each time he spoke to the prince, he leaned over and
whispered.

'Forget them; you're very weak . . .'

'Presently. Presently . . . I'll go presently.'

Suddenly he embraced the prince.

'You're thinking perhaps I'm mad?' He looked at him, with a queer laugh.

'No, but you . . .'

'In a minute, in a minute, be quiet; don't say anything; just stand there . . . I want to look in your eyes . . . Stand like that and I'll just look. I shall bid farewell to a Man.'

He stood motionless, silently looking at the prince, very pale, his temples damp with perspiration, and clutching rather oddly at him as though fearful of letting go.

'Ippolit, Ippolit, what's the matter?' exclaimed the prince.

'In a minute . . . all right . . . I'll lie down. I'll drink one toast to the sun . . . I want to, I want to, leave me alone!'

He swiftly seized a glass from the table, leapt from his chair, and was by the veranda steps in an instant. The prince ran after him, but just at that very moment Radomsky happened to hold out his hand in farewell. A second passed and then came a general outcry from the veranda. There then ensued a moment of extraordinary confusion.

What had happened was this:

When he reached the top of the steps, Ippolit had stopped with his glass in his left hand, and his right resting in his coat-pocket. Keller swore later that Ippolit had been keeping his hand in that pocket earlier when he had been talking to the prince, and had used his left hand to grip his shoulder and collar; it was this right hand in the pocket business which, avowed Keller, had aroused his initial suspicion. At all events, a certain uneasiness had prompted him to run after Ippolit. Even he had been too late, however. All he saw was something glinting in Ippolit's right hand and a small pocket pistol instantly appear against his temple. Keller had darted forward to grab the pistol but Ippolit had immediately pulled the trigger. There followed a sharp, dry, snap, but no report. When Keller had enveloped him, he fell into his arms as if unconscious, perhaps actually imagining he was already dead. Keller had taken possession of the pistol. Ippolit was borne up and a chair placed under him, as everyone crowded round with exclamations and questions. They had all heard the click of the trigger and seen the man still alive, without so much as a scratch. Ippolit himself was sitting, uncomprehending of what was going on, gazing round at them all with a meaningless expression on his face. Lebedev and Kolya rushed in at this moment.

'A misfire?' some were asking.

'Perhaps it wasn't loaded?' hazarded others.

'It was loaded!' proclaimed Keller, as he examined the pistol. 'But . . .'

'Did it really misfire?'

'There was no percussion cap at all', announced Keller.

It is difficult to describe the ensuing pitiful scene. The initial general alarm was quickly replaced by laughter; some actually guffawed, finding a malicious pleasure in it all. Ippolit was weeping hysterically, wringing his hands and rushing at everyone, even Ferdischenko, seizing him with both hands and swearing to him that he had forgotten to insert the percussion cap 'by sheer chance, it wasn't deliberate', that 'the caps are all here, in my waistcoat pocket, a good dozen' (he showed them round to everyone), that he hadn't inserted one beforehand out of fear that the gun might go off in his pocket by accident, and that he had always reckoned he would have time to put it in when the time came; then he just forgot. He rushed up to the prince, then Radomsky, and implored Keller to return his pistol and he would show them all that 'his honour, honour . . .' that now he would be 'dishonoured for ever'.

He really did fall insensible at last. He was carried into the prince's study and Lebedev, by now completely sober, sent for the doctor at once, while he himself, along with his son and daughter, General Ivolgin, and Burdovsky, remained by the bedside of the sick man. When the unconscious Ippolit had been carried out, Keller stood in the middle of the room and announced in a voice loud enough for all to hear, articulating and emphasizing every word, in positively inspired fashion.

'Gentlemen, if any one of you expresses doubts in my hearing that the percussion cap was forgotten deliberately and tries to assert that the unhappy young man was just putting on an act, then he'll have me to deal with.'

But no one answered him. The guests at length dispersed, all in one crowd and in some haste. Ptitsyn, Ganya, and Rogozhin went off together.

The prince was greatly surprised to find that Radomsky had changed his mind and was leaving without discussing matters with him.

'You did want to speak to me when everyone had gone, didn't you?' he asked him.

'So I did', responded Yevgeni Pavlovich, abruptly sitting down and seating the prince beside him, 'but I've changed my mind for the moment. I must admit I'm rather bemused, and so are you. My mind's in a whirl; besides, what I want to talk about is extremely important to me, and you too. You see, Prince, for once in my life I want to do something completely honourable, I mean without any ulterior motive, well, I don't think I'm capable of a completely chivalrous action at the moment, and nor are you, perhaps, so . . . well . . . we'll talk it over later on. Perhaps there'll be a gain in clarity if we both wait two or three days, which I shall now spend in Petersburg.'

At this point he got up again, which made it seem odd that he had sat down in the first place. It occurred to the prince that Radomsky was irritated and annoyed about something and had a hostile look in his eyes, quite different from what had been there before.

'By the way, are you going to the patient now?'

'Yes . . . I'm worried', said the prince.

'Don't be; he'll live another six weeks yet, most likely, and he might even recover here. But you'd best get rid of him tomorrow.'

'Perhaps I really did provoke him by . . . not saying anything; perhaps he thought I too doubted he would shoot himself. What do you think, Yevgeni Pavlovich?'

'No such thing. It's too good-natured of you to be still worrying about that. I've heard tell of someone shooting himself to gain applause or out of chagrin because he didn't get it, but I've never actually seen it happen. Above all, I wouldn't have credited such a frank admission of feebleness! Still, you turn him out tomorrow.'

'Do you think he'll shoot himself again?'

'No, he won't do it now. But beware of these home-grown Lacenaires of ours!* I tell you again, crime is too common a recourse for these talentless, greedy, impatient nobodies.'

'Surely he's not a Lacenaire?'

'The essence is the same, though their occupations may be different. You'll see whether this gentleman isn't capable of despatching a dozen souls, to amuse himself as he mentioned just now in his "Explanation". Those words of his will stop me sleeping now.'

'Perhaps you're worrying over-much.'

'You're amazing, Prince; you don't think he has it in him to kill a dozen individuals *now*?'

'I'm afraid to answer that; it's all very strange, but . . .'

'Well, as you please, as you please!' concluded Yevgeni Pavlovich crossly. 'And you're such a courageous individual; just don't be one of the dozen yourself.'

'He won't kill anybody, most likely', said the prince, eyeing Radomsky thoughtfully. The latter gave a grim laugh.

'Goodbye, it's time I went! Did you notice though, he willed a copy of his confession to Aglaya Ivanovna?'

'Yes, I did notice and . . . I'm giving it some thought.'

'Just so, in case of that "dozen" I mentioned.' Yevgeni Pavlovich laughed again and went off.

An hour later, some time after three, the prince went down into the park. He had made an effort to sleep but had been prevented by the violent pounding of his heart. In the house, however, things had been set to rights, and calm had been restored, so far as that was possible; the patient had gone off to sleep and the doctor had announced that he was in no special danger. Lebedev, Kolya, and Burdovsky had bedded down in the patient's room, taking it in turns to be on duty; there was, consequently, nothing to worry about.

The prince's disquiet, however, was growing by the minute. He wandered through the park, gazing absently round him before halting in surprise as he reached the bandstand in the pleasure-garden and saw the row of empty benches and the music-stands for the orchestra. He was shaken by the place, which seemed hideous to him for some reason. He turned back and followed the precise path along which he had walked the day before with the Yepanchins, until he reached the green bench where the assignation was to take place, seated himself upon it, then all of a sudden burst into loud laughter, which at once made him very cross with himself. His despondency persisted; he yearned to go away somewhere . . . He did not know where. A bird was singing above him in the tree and he began looking for it among the leaves; all at once the bird took wing, and he was reminded for some reason of the 'tiny fly' in the hot 'sunbeam' that Ippolit had written about, that it 'knew its place, and was a participant in the general chorus, while he alone was the outcast'. This sentence had struck him poignantly yesterday, and he recalled it now. A long-forgotten memory stirred within him and suddenly took on clarity of form.

It had been in Switzerland, during the first year of his treatment, the first months in fact. He had been a complete idiot at that time, hardly capable of speaking properly, sometimes unable to comprehend what was being asked of him. One bright, sunny day he had gone into the mountains, tormented by a thought that simply refused to take shape. In front of him was the brilliant sky, with the lake below and the bright and limitless horizon all around him, seeming to go on for ever. He gazed for a long time, tormented by his emotions. He now remembered stretching his arms out to that bright, endless blue, and weeping. What was tormenting him was that he was completely alien to all this. What was this feast, what was this permanent grand festival, which had no end, to which he had for long been drawn, always—ever since childhood, but could not join. Every morning the same bright sun came up; every morning there was a rainbow on the waterfall; every evening the highest snow-capped mountain, far off at the sky's rim, glowed with purple flame; every 'tiny fly' buzzing near him in the hot sunlight was a participant in that chorus: it knew its place, loved it, and was happy; every blade of grass grew and was happy! Everything had its own path and everything knew its own path, and went forth with a song and returned with a song; he alone knew nothing and comprehended nothing, not people, not sounds, he was alien to everything, an outcast. Oh, of course, he hadn't been able to say that in so many words at the time or utter his question; he suffered in mute incomprehension; but it now seemed to him that he had said all those things then also, all the selfsame words, and that Ippolit had taken the 'tiny fly' from him, from his words and tears of that time. He was certain of it, and the thought set his heart pounding . . .

He had fallen asleep on the bench, but his anxiety remained with him. Just before he dozed off he remembered that Ippolit was going to murder a dozen people, and smiled at the absurdity of supposing any such thing. A beautiful, clear stillness lay all about him; only the leaves rustled, which seemed to make everything around even more silent and secluded. He had a great many dreams, all troubled enough to make him start every minute. At length a woman came to him; he knew her, tormentingly well; he could always name her and point her out, but it was odd, she seemed to have quite a different face from the one he had always known, and he was agonizingly reluctant to acknowledge her as the same woman. There was so much remorse and horror in that face, that she seemed to be a fearful criminal and had just committed some horrible crime. A tear trembled on her pale cheek; she beckoned to him and placed her finger to her lips, as if warning him to follow her quietly. His heart stood still; he was reluctant to admit that she was a criminal for anything, anything in the world, but he sensed that something frightful was on the point of happening, something that would affect his whole life. She wanted to show him something apparently, not far off, here in the park. He got up to follow her, when suddenly there came the sound of bright, clear laughter; someone's hand turned up in his own; he seized the hand, pressed it hard, and woke up. Before him, laughing loudly, stood Aglaya.

8

SHE was laughing, but she was annoyed too.

'Asleep! You were asleep!' she exclaimed in scornful surprise.

'It's you!' mumbled the prince, recognizing her with astonishment, still not fully awake. 'Ah yes! The meeting . . . I was asleep here.'

'So I saw.'

'Were you the only one who woke me? Was there no one else here apart from you? I thought there was . . . another woman here . . .'

'There was another woman here?!'

At last he was quite awake.

'It was only a dream', he said pensively, 'strange, a dream like that at such a moment . . . Sit down.'

He took her hand and seated her on the bench, then sat down beside her and became lost in thought. Aglaya did not initiate a conversation; she merely surveyed her companion steadily. He also glanced at her, but only occasionally, as if not seeing her there at all. She began to blush.

'Ah, yes', the prince started. 'Ippolit shot himself!'

'When? In your house?' she asked without any great astonishment. 'But he was still alive yesterday evening, wasn't he? How on earth could you sleep there after all that?' she exclaimed, suddenly becoming more animated.

'Oh, but he isn't dead, the pistol didn't go off.'

At Aglaya's insistence, the prince was forced to recount at once and in great detail the whole story of what had taken place the previous night. She kept urging him along, while herself continually interrupting him with questions, almost all of them irrelevant. She was greatly interested in what Radomsky had said, however, and indeed asked him to repeat it several times.

'Well, that'll do, we must make haste', she announced, having heard everything. 'We can only stay here an hour, till eight, because I must be in the house at eight o'clock before they find out I've been sitting here—and I have something to discuss; I have a lot to tell you. Only you've put me off completely. As for Ippolit, I think his pistol was bound not to fire, that would be just like him. But you're convinced he really wanted to kill himself and there was no deception involved?'

'No deception.'

'That's more likely. He did write that you were to bring me his confession? Why haven't you brought it then?'

'But he isn't dead, is he? I'll ask him for it.'

'Be sure to bring me it, and there's no need to ask. He'll probably be very pleased, because perhaps that's the very reason he tried to kill himself, so that I would read his confession afterwards. Please, I beg you not to laugh at what I say, Lev Nikolaich, it could very likely be the case.'

'I'm not laughing, because I'm as sure as you are that it could very likely be true in part.'

'You're sure? You don't really think that too?' Aglaya was hugely amazed.

She put her questions quickly and spoke rapidly, but seemed to lose the thread at times and often didn't finish her sentences; she was constantly in a hurry to warn him about something; all in all, she was in a state of considerable anxiety and probably quailing a little too, notwithstanding her bold and faintly defiant air. She was wearing a simple, everyday dress which suited her extremely well. She was sitting on the edge of the bench, blushing and starting at frequent intervals. The prince's confirmation that Ippolit had shot himself so that she could read his confession had taken her completely aback.

'Of course', explained the prince, 'he wanted us all to approve of him, besides yourself . . .'

'What do you mean, approve?'

'I mean . . . how shall I put it? It's very hard to put in words. It's just that he probably wanted people to crowd round and tell him how fond they were of him, and how much they respected him, and for them all to implore him to go on living. It's very likely he had you in mind most of all, because he mentioned you at such a moment . . . though perhaps he didn't know himself that he had you in mind.'

'That I completely fail to understand: he had me in mind and didn't know what he had in mind. Still, I think I do understand: do you know, I must have thought of poisoning myself thirty times or more, even when I was 13 years old, then writing it all down in a letter to my parents; I also thought of how I would lie in my coffin and everyone would weep over me and blame themselves for being so cruel to me . . . Why are you smiling again?' she added swiftly, knitting her brows. 'What do you think of when you're day-dreaming by yourself? Perhaps you imagine you're a field marshal defeating Napoleon?'

'Well now, honestly, I do think that, especially when I'm going to sleep', laughed the prince, 'only it isn't Napoleon, it's always the Austrians I'm defeating.'

'I don't feel at all like joking with you, Lev Nikolaich. I'll see Ippolit myself; please let him know. I think it's all very horrid of you, because it's very ill-bred just to look on and pronounce judgement on a man's soul, as you judge Ippolit. You have no tenderness in you; only truth—and that's not justice.'

The prince considered.

'It seems to me that you're being unfair to me', he said. 'After all, I don't find anything wrong in him thinking as he did, because everybody tends to think that way; besides, he might not have been thinking at all, just wanting . . . he wanted to meet people for the last time and earn their esteem and affection; those indeed are very laudable feelings, it's just that it didn't turn out that way somehow; his illness is involved and something else besides! Then again, for some people things always turn out well, while for others it's an unmitigated disaster.'

'You put that last bit in about yourself, no doubt?' observed Aglaya.

'Yes, I meant myself', the prince responded, unconscious of any malice in the question.

'All the same, if I'd been you I should never have dropped off to sleep; it seems as if you go to sleep wherever you happen to be; that's not very nice of you.'

'But I haven't slept all night, then I went out walking, walking, then to the music . . .'

'What music?'

'Where they were playing yesterday; after that I came here, sat down, got to thinking, and fell asleep.'

'Ah, that was the way of it? That alters things in your favour . . . But why did you go to the music?'

'I don't know, I just did . . .'

'All right, all right, for the moment; you keep interrupting me, what's it to me if you went to the music? What woman were you dreaming about?'

'It was . . . about . . . you've seen her.'

'I understand, I understand very well. You're very much . . . how was she in the dream, what did she look like? I don't want to know anyway', she broke off in sudden vexation. 'Stop interrupting me . . .'

She paused briefly, as if nerving herself or trying to banish her annoyance.

'This is the reason I asked you to come here: I want to request

you to be my friend. Why suddenly stare at me like that?' she
added almost angrily.

The prince really was regarding her very keenly at that
moment, noting that she had started to blush again. Whenever
that happened, the more she blushed, the more she seemed to
get annoyed with herself, a fact plainly demonstrated in her
flashing eyes; a minute later, as a rule, she would have
transferred her anger on to the person she was talking to,
whether it was his fault or not, and started quarrelling with him.
Aware of this, and sensing her awkwardness and shyness, she
rarely started a conversation and was more reticent than her
sisters, at times too much so. Whenever she was absolutely
compelled to say something, especially in ticklish situations like
this, she would initiate the conversation with a most haughty air
and, it seemed, a kind of defiance. She invariably sensed
beforehand when she was starting to blush, or was on the point of
doing so.

'Perhaps you don't wish to accept my proposal?' she glanced
haughtily at the prince.

'Oh no, I do, but it wasn't at all necessary . . . I mean I never
thought proposals like that needed to be made.' The prince was
embarrassed.

'What on earth did you think, then? Why do you suppose I
asked you to come here in that case? What's in your mind?
Though I expect you take me for a little fool, like they all do at
home.'

'I didn't know they took you for a fool, I . . . I don't.'

'You don't? That's very intelligent of you. And particularly well
put.'

'I think you're perhaps very intelligent sometimes', the prince
went on. 'You said something very clever all of a sudden just now.
You were referring to my doubts about Ippolit: "only truth and
that's not justice." I'll remember that and think it over.'

Aglaya suddenly flushed with pleasure. All these fluctuations
in mood took place without the slightest dissimulation and with
remarkable swiftness. The prince too was delighted, and laughed
from sheer pleasure as he looked at her.

'Now listen', she resumed, 'I've been waiting a long time to tell
you all this—ever since the time you wrote me that letter, earlier

even . . . You've already heard half of it from me yesterday: I regard you as an extremely honest and truthful man, more honest and truthful than anyone else, and if anybody says about you that your mind . . . I mean you are mentally ill sometimes, then that's unjust; I've decided that it's so and I've been arguing about it, because although you actually do suffer from mental illness (you mustn't be angry, I'm taking the overall view), the essential part of your mind is superior to all of theirs, it's the sort of mind they've never even dreamed of, because there's two kinds of brain, the main one and the secondary one. That's so, isn't it? Isn't it?'

'Perhaps it is', the prince could barely bring out the words; his heart was fluttering and knocking violently.

'I knew you'd understand', she went on solemnly. 'Prince S and Yevgeni Pavlich don't understand a thing about the two minds. Neither does Alexandra, but just imagine, *maman* did.'

'You're very like Lizaveta Prokofievna.'

'What? Really?' Aglaya was astonished.

'Indeed you are.'

'Thank you', she said after a moment's thought, 'I'm very glad I'm like *maman*. You must hold her in high regard then?' she added, wholly oblivious of the artlessness of the question.

'Very much, very much so, and I'm pleased you realized it at once.'

'I'm glad too, because I've noticed how people . . . laugh at her sometimes. But listen, this is the main thing: I've thought it over for a long time and finally chosen you . . . I don't want to be a laughing-stock at home, I don't want to be looked on as a little fool; I don't want to be teased . . . I've realized it all at once and turned Yevgeni Pavlovich down flat, because I don't want this continual matchmaking. I want . . . I want . . . well, I want to run away from home, and I've chosen you to help me.'

'Run away from home!' exclaimed the prince.

'Yes, yes, yes, run away from home!' she cried suddenly, her anger flaring up intensely. 'I don't want . . . just don't want to be made to blush there all the time. I don't want to blush in front of them, nor in front of Prince S, nor Yevgeni Pavlich, nor anybody else, and so I've chosen you. With you I want to talk about everything, even the most important things, whenever I like; and you, on your side, mustn't hide anything from me. I want to be able to talk about everything with one person at least, just as I do with myself. They suddenly started saying I was waiting for you, and that I love you. That was before you came back even, and I hadn't shown them your letter; now everybody's talking about it. I want to be brave and be afraid of nothing. I don't want to do the round of their dances, I want to be of some use in the world. I've wanted to go away for ever-so long. I've been bottled up with them for twenty years—with them always trying to marry me off. I wanted to run away when I was 14, fool that I was. Now I've got it all worked out and I've been waiting for you so that I can ask you questions about abroad. I've never seen a single Gothic cathedral. I want to go to Rome, I want to look round all the learned institutions, I want to study in Paris; all this last year I've been preparing myself and studying and I've read lots of books, and all the forbidden ones. Alexandra and Adelaida can read all the books they like, they're allowed, but I don't have all of them given to me, I'm supervised. I don't want to quarrel with my sisters, but I informed my father and mother long ago that I wanted to change my social status entirely. I decided to take up teaching and I've been counting on you, because you said you loved children. Can we not take up teaching together, if not now, then later on? Together we'll be of some use to the world in the future; I don't want to be a general's daughter . . . Tell me, are you a very learned person?'

'Oh no, not at all.'

'That's a pity, and I thought . . . how did I come to think that then? But you'll be my guide all the same, because I've chosen you.'

'That's absurd, Aglaya Ivanovna.'

'I want to, I want to run away from home!' she cried. Her eyes began flashing once again. 'If you won't agree, then I'll marry Ganya. I don't want them to regard me as a vile woman at home, accusing me of goodness knows what.'

'Are you mad?' the prince almost leapt from his seat. 'What are they accusing you of? Who is accusing you?'

'At home they all do—mother, sisters, father, Prince S, even your nasty Kolya! If they don't say it directly, they think it. I told them so to their faces, both mother and father. *Maman* was unwell the whole day; and the next day Alexandra and Papa told me I didn't understand the foolishness I was talking, or the words I was using. And I told them straight out that I understood everything, all the words, and that I wasn't a little girl any more, and that two years before I had deliberately read two novels by Paul de Kock,* to find everything out. *Maman* nearly fainted when she heard that.'

A curious thought suddenly crossed the prince's mind. He gave Aglaya a searching glance and smiled.

He could hardly believe that sitting next to him was the same haughty girl who had once so proudly and disdainfully read Ganya's letter to him. He couldn't understand how, in such a disdainful, stern beauty, there could exist such a child who perhaps even now didn't *understand all the words*.

'Have you always lived at home, Aglaya Ivanovna?' he asked. 'I mean, have you never been anywhere, a school of some sort, not studied anywhere?'

'I've never been anywhere; just stayed at home, corked up in a bottle, and I'm to be married straight out of the bottle. Why are you smirking again? I've noticed that you seem to laugh at me as well and take their side', she added, frowning menacingly. 'Don't make me angry; I don't know what's the matter with me as it is . . . I'm sure you came here today absolutely certain I was in love with you, and this was a lover's tryst', she snapped irritably.

'I really was afraid of that yesterday', the prince blurted artlessly (he was most embarrassed), 'but today I'm sure that you . . .'

'So!' cried Aglaya, her lower lip beginning to quiver, 'you were afraid that I . . . you dared to think that I . . . good lord! You suspected perhaps that I had brought you here as a trap so that they could catch us and compel you to marry me . . .'

'Aglaya Ivanovna! For shame! How could such a sordid idea come to your pure, innocent heart? I'll wager you don't believe a single word you've said and . . . you don't know what you're saying yourself!'

Aglaya sat staring doggedly at the ground, as though herself alarmed at what she had said.

'I'm not at all ashamed', she muttered. 'How do you know my heart's innocent? How dared you send me a love letter that time?'

'Love letter? My letter—a love letter? It was a most respectful letter, it came straight from my heart at the worst moment of my life! I thought of you then as a source of light . . . I . . .'

'Well, all right, all right', she broke in abruptly, in quite a different tone of voice, filled with remorse verging on trepidation, still striving not to look directly at him. She made to touch his shoulder, to reinforce her appeal for him not to get angry. 'All right', she added in an agony of shame, 'I see that I used a very stupid expression. I just did it . . . to test you. Treat it as if it was never said. If I've offended you, then forgive me. Don't stare at me like that, please, look away. You said it was a very sordid thought; I said it deliberately to hurt you. Sometimes I'm afraid of what I feel like saying myself, then I just come out with it. You said just now that you wrote that letter at the worst moment of your life . . . I know what moment that was', she said softly, staring at the ground again.

'Ah, if you could know the whole of it!'

'I do know the whole of it!' she cried in a new access of emotion. 'You had been living for a whole month in the same apartment with that vile woman you ran away with . . .'

As she uttered this, she turned pale rather than blushing and rose to her feet apparently automatically but, bethinking herself, at once sat down; her lip continued to quiver for a long time. The silence lasted a whole minute. The prince had been terribly taken aback by the abruptness of her outburst and did not know how to account for it.

'I don't love you at all', she said suddenly, almost snapping out the words. The prince made no reply; another minute's silence ensued.

'I love Gavrila Ardalionovich', she said in a rapid undertone, her head still lower.

'That's not true', said the prince, almost whispering in his turn.

'You mean I'm lying? It is true; I gave him my word three days ago on this very bench.'

The prince was startled.

'It's not true', he repeated resolutely. 'You've made all that up.'

'How amazingly polite you are! I'd have you know he's reformed; he loves me more than his life. He burned his hand in front of me just to show that he loved me more than his life.'

'Burned his hand?'

'His hand, yes. I don't care if you believe it or not.'

The prince once more fell silent. There had been nothing playful about Aglaya's words. She was angry.

'You mean he brought a candle with him, if this is where it happened? Otherwise I don't see . . .'

'Yes he brought a candle. What's so incredible about that?'

'A whole one or in a candlestick?'

'Well yes . . . no . . . half a candle . . . a candle-end . . . a whole candle, what does it matter, stop badgering me! . . . And matches too, if you want to know. He lit the candle and held his finger over it for half an hour; do you think that's impossible?'

'I saw him yesterday; his fingers are all right.'

Aglaya suddenly burst out laughing just like a child.

'Do you know why I lied just now?' She abruptly turned to the prince with childlike confidence, the laughter still quivering on her lips. 'It was because if, when you're telling a lie, you neatly insert something rather unusual, something bizarre, you know, something that very seldom or never happens, the lie becomes much more plausible. I've noticed that. Only it didn't work with me, because I couldn't do it properly . . .'

She abruptly frowned again, seeming to recollect herself.

'If', she said, turning to the prince with a grave, even mournful, expression, 'if, when I recited the "poor knight" to you that day, I wanted to . . . praise you in one way, I also wanted at the same time to stigmatize your behaviour and show you that I knew everything . . .'

'You're very unfair to me . . . to that unhappy woman of whom you spoke in such dreadful terms just now, Aglaya.'

'Because I know everything, everything, that's why I spoke in that way! I know that six months ago you offered to marry her in front of everybody. Don't interrupt, you see I mention it without comment. After that she ran off with Rogozhin; later on you lived with her in some village or town and she left you for someone else.' (Aglaya blushed furiously.) 'Then she came back again to Rogozhin, who loves her like . . . a madman. Then you, another very intelligent person, came galloping after her, the moment you heard she'd returned to Petersburg. Yesterday evening you

rushed to her defence, and now you're dreaming about her . . .
You see, I know everything; you did come here because of her,
didn't you? It was because of her?'

'Yes, it was', answered the prince softly, inclining his head in
sad meditation, unaware of Aglaya's blazing expression fixed
upon him, 'it was because of her, only to find out . . . I don't
believe she'll be happy with Rogozhin, although . . . in short, I
don't know what I could have done for her here, or how I could
have helped her, but I came.'

He gave a start and glanced at Aglaya, who was listening to him
with hatred.

'If you came without knowing why, that means you must love
her a lot.'

'No', the prince replied, 'no, I don't love her. Ah, if you only
knew the horror I feel when I recall the time I spent with her!'

At these words, a pronounced shudder passed through his
whole body.

'Tell me everything', said Aglaya.

'There's nothing involved that you ought not to hear. I don't
know why I wanted to tell the whole story just to you; perhaps it
was because I was very fond of you. That unhappy woman is
profoundly convinced that she is the lowest, most vicious
creature in the world. Oh, don't hold her up to scorn, don't cast
the stone. She has suffered enough already from the consciousness of her undeserved shame! And God in heaven, what is her
fault? Oh, she keeps crying frenziedly every minute that she does
not acknowledge any guilt, that she's a victim of other people, the
victim of a libertine and a villain. But whatever she says to you, I
want you to know that she is the first to disbelieve it; on the
contrary, she believes with all her conscience that she herself is to
blame. Whenever I tried to dispel that darkness, it caused her
such intense misery that my heart will always ache when I recall
that dreadful time. It seems my heart was pierced once and for
all. She ran away from me—you know why? Precisely to
demonstrate to me that she was a vile woman. But the worst thing
of all was that she herself, perhaps, was unaware that I was the
only one she wanted to prove that to; she may have run off
because of some irresistible inner urge to do something
disgraceful, so as to be able to say to herself at once: "There,

you've done something shameful again, so you must be a vile creature!" Oh, perhaps you won't understand this Aglaya! Do you know that this perpetual awareness of shame perhaps contains for her a sort of horrible, perverse pleasure, as if it were a revenge on someone. At times, I did manage to get her to the point of seeing the light around her again, so to speak; but she would immediately work herself up again and reach a stage where she bitterly accused me of setting myself up high above her (when that had never entered my thoughts). Eventually, when I proposed marriage, she bluntly declared that she did not ask for anyone's condescending sympathy, nor any help; nor did she want to be "raised to anyone's level". You saw her yesterday; you surely don't imagine she's happy in that crowd, or that that's her kind of society? You don't know how cultivated she is, the grasp of her mind! She used to positively astonish me at times!'

'Did you preach ... sermons like that to her too?'

'Oh no', the prince went on pensively, oblivious of the tone of the question, 'I hardly opened my mouth. I often wanted to talk, but I honestly didn't know what to say. You know, there are some situations where it's better to say nothing. Oh, I loved her; loved her very much ... but later ... later she guessed.'

'Guessed what?'

'That I felt only pity for her, and that I ... didn't love her.'

'How do you know she didn't really fall in love with that ... landowner she went away with?'

'No, I know all about it; she was just having fun with him.'

'And she never did that to you?'

'No, it was out of bitterness that she laughed at me; oh, she would reproach me dreadfully, in her anger—and suffer agonies herself! But ... afterwards ... oh don't remind me, don't remind me of it!'

He hid his face in his hands.

'And did you know she writes me letters every day?'

'So it's true!' cried the startled prince. 'I'd heard but I still didn't want to believe it.'

'Heard it from whom?' Aglaya started apprehensively.

'Rogozhin told me yesterday, but not in so many words.'

'Yesterday? Yesterday morning? When yesterday? Before the music or after?'

'After; in the evening, after eleven.'

'Aha, well if it was Rogozhin . . . And do you know what she writes to me about in these letters?'

'Nothing would surprise me; she's mad.'

'These are the letters.' Aglaya took out three letters in separate envelopes and threw them in front of the prince. 'She's been imploring, persuading, flattering me into marrying you. She's . . . well yes, she's clever even if she is mad, and you're right to say she's a good deal cleverer than I am . . . she writes that she's fallen in love with me and every day looks for an opportunity to catch sight of me, if only from a distance. She writes that you love me, that she knows it and has been aware of it for a long time, and that you talked with her about me. She wants to see you happy; she's quite sure that only I can be that happiness . . . She writes so outlandishly . . . it's strange . . . I haven't shown the letters to anyone, I've been waiting for you; you know what this means? Can't you guess?'

'It's madness; it proves she's demented', said the prince, his lips beginning to quiver.

'You're not crying are you?'

'No, Aglaya, no, I'm not crying', the prince regarded her.

'What on earth am I to do about it? What do you advise me? I can't go on receiving such letters!'

'Oh, let her be, I implore you!' cried the prince. 'What can you do in this murky business? I'll make every effort to stop her writing you any more letters.'

'If you do, you're a man with no heart!' cried Aglaya. 'Surely you can see that it's not me she's in love with, it's you, it's you alone she loves! Surely you can't have found out everything about her and failed to notice that? You know what this means, what these letters signify? It's more than jealousy! She . . . do you think she's really going to marry Rogozhin, as she writes in her letters? She'd do away with herself the day after our wedding!'

The prince gave a start; his heart stood still. Yet he gazed in astonishment at Aglaya: it felt strange to acknowledge that this child had become a woman long ago.

'God knows, Aglaya, I would give my life to restore her peace of mind and make her happy, but . . . I can't love her now and she knows that!'

'Sacrifice yourself then, it's your vocation! You're the great
benefactor aren't you? And don't call me "Aglaya" . . . You called
me simply "Aglaya" just now as well . . . You must, you have to
restore her to life, you must go away with her again, to calm and
pacify her heart. After all, you do love her really, don't you!'

'I can't sacrifice myself like that, though I did want to once
and . . . perhaps I do now. But I know *for certain* that with me she
would be ruined, that's why I am abandoning her. I was supposed
to see her today at seven o'clock; I might well not go now. Her
pride won't allow her to forgive me for my love—and we shall
both come to grief. It's perverse, but there's nothing natural
about the whole situation. You say she loves me, but how can it
be love? Can there be such love after what I have endured
already? No, it may be something else but not love!'

'How pale you are!' Aglaya was suddenly alarmed.

'It's all right; I didn't get much sleep; I feel weak, I . . . we
really did talk about you then, Aglaya . . .'

'So it's true! You really *could talk to her about me* and . . . and
how could you be fond of me when you had only seen me once?'

'I don't know. In the darkness I was in at the time I fancied . . .
I dreamed perhaps of a new dawn. I don't know how it was that I
thought of you first . . . I wrote you the truth at the time, that I
didn't know. It was all a dream of escape from the horror I was
in . . . After that I began to study. I wasn't going to come back
here for three years . . .'

'So you've come back because of her?'

Aglaya's voice was beginning to quiver.

'Yes, because of her.'

Two minutes of gloomy silence passed. Aglaya rose to her feet.

'If you're saying', she began unsteadily, 'if you yourself believe
that this . . . your woman . . . is mad, then of course I can have
nothing to do with her deranged fantasies . . . Kindly take these
three letters, Lev Nikolayevich, and throw them back at her from
me! And if she', Aglaya suddenly raised her voice, 'if she dares to
send me one more line, then tell her that I shall complain to
father and she'll be put away in an asylum . . .'

'The prince jumped up in alarm as he saw Aglaya's sudden
fury; then it was as if a mist descended before him . . .

'You can't feel like that . . . it can't be true!' he mumbled.

'It is! It is true!' shouted Aglaya, almost beside herself.

'What is? What is true?' came a startled voice from close by. Before them stood Lizaveta Prokofievna.

'What's true is that I'm going to marry Gavrila Ardalionovich! That I love Gavrila Ardalionovich and I'm going to elope with him tomorrow!' Aglaya flung at her. 'Do you hear? Does that satisfy your curiosity? Are you satisfied now?'

And she ran off to the house.

'No, dear sir, don't you go away now', Lizaveta Prokofievna stopped the prince. 'Be good enough to come home with me and tell me all about it . . . The things I have to suffer, and I didn't sleep a wink either . . .'

The prince followed her.

9

ON arriving at her villa, Lizaveta Prokofievna halted in the first room; she could go no further and subsided on to a settee, completely worn out, even omitting to invite the prince to sit down. It was a fairly large drawing-room, with a circular table in the middle; there was a stove, and a multitude of flowers on the chiffoniers by the windows; a french window in the far wall led into the garden. Alexandra and Adelaida came in at once, puzzled, and looked questioningly at the prince and their mother.

In the country, the girls usually got up at nine o'clock. Aglaya, however, had taken to rising somewhat earlier over the last two or three days and going for a walk in the garden, though this was at eight or even later, certainly not at seven o'clock. Lizaveta Prokofievna, who really hadn't slept all night as a result of her various worries, had risen at about eight with the deliberate intent of encountering Aglaya in the garden, assuming that she was already up; she had not found her, however, either in the bedroom or the garden. At this, she had become extremely alarmed and roused her daughters. They learned from the maid that Aglaya Ivanovna had gone out into the park before seven. The girls smiled over this new whim of their wayward little sister, and pointed out to mama that Aglaya might well be angry with her if she went to seek her out in the park, and that she was probably sitting with a book on the green bench she had been talking about three days before; she had almost fallen out with Prince S about it, after the latter had failed to notice anything special about its location. Having stumbled across the meeting, and overheard her daughter's strange words, Lizaveta Prokofievna had been dreadfully dismayed for a number of reasons, but now, having brought the prince back with her, she was sorry at having made anything of it: 'Why on earth shouldn't Aglaya meet the prince in the park and talk to him, even if it had been arranged beforehand?'

'Don't be thinking, my dear Prince', she braced herself to say, 'that I've dragged you in here to cross-examine you . . . After yesterday evening's events, dear, I might well not have wished to see you for a long time . . .'

She faltered.

'But still, you'd very much like to know how Aglaya Ivanovna and I came to meet this morning?' the prince finished, with the utmost composure.

'Well what if I do!' Lizaveta Prokofievna flared up. 'I won't mince words. I'm not offending anyone and had no intention of doing so.'

'Dear me, no offence taken; naturally you wish to know; you are her mother. Aglaya Ivanovna and I met this morning by the green bench at precisely seven o'clock as a result of her invitation of yesterday. She sent me a note yesterday evening, informing me that she needed to see me to discuss something of importance. We met and talked for a whole hour about matters solely concerning Aglaya Ivanovna; that is all.'

'Of course that's all, my dear Prince, I have absolutely no doubt of that', Lizaveta Prokofievna declared with dignity.

'Excellent, Prince', said Aglaya, suddenly entering the room. 'Thank you with all my heart, for considering me incapable of demeaning myself here by lying. That's enough, *maman*, unless you wish to interrogate him further?'

'You know that up till now I have never had occasion to blush before you for anything . . . though I dare say you would have been glad if I had', responded Lizaveta Prokofievna sententiously. 'Goodbye, Prince. Forgive me for inconveniencing you. I trust you will remain assured of my unfailing regard.'

The prince at once bowed to both sides and left silently. Alexandra and Adelaida grinned and whispered to each other. Lizaveta Prokofievna regarded them severely.

'It was only because the prince bowed so beautifully, *maman*', laughed Adelaida. 'Sometimes he's so lumpish, now suddenly he's like . . . like . . . Yevgeni Pavlich.'

'Refinement and dignity are taught by the heart, not the dancing-master', declared Lizaveta Prokofievna, and proceeded upstairs to her room without bestowing so much as a glance on Aglaya.

When the prince got home, by now about nine o'clock, he found Vera and the maid on the veranda. They were sweeping up and tidying away after the previous night's disorders.

'Thank goodness we managed to finish before you arrived!' said Vera joyously.

'Good morning; I'm feeling a little dizzy, I didn't sleep well; I wouldn't mind having a nap.'

'Here on the veranda like yesterday? All right. I'll tell everyone not to wake you. Papa's gone out somewhere.'

The maid went out and Vera followed her, but came back and approached the prince solicitously.

'Prince, have pity on that . . . unhappy boy; don't send him away today.'

'I wouldn't do that for anything; it's up to him.'

'He won't do anything now . . . and don't be hard on him.'

'Certainly not, why should I?'

'And . . . and don't laugh at him; that's the main thing.'

'Oh, by no means!'

'I'm silly to talk about such things to a man like you', said Vera, colouring. 'And even though you're tired', she laughed as she turned to go, 'your eyes look really nice . . . happy.'

'Happy? Really?' the prince asked eagerly and burst into elated laughter.

Vera, however, artless and direct as a a boy might be, was suddenly embarrassed, blushed still more, and hastily left the room, still laughing.

'What a . . . splendid girl she is . . .', thought the prince and instantly forgot about her. He went over to a corner of the veranda, where there was a settee with a little table in front of it. He sat down, buried his face in his hands, and remained sitting like that for some ten minutes; suddenly he put his hand hastily and apprehensively in his pocket and took out the three letters.

But the door opened again and in came Kolya. The prince seemed relieved at having to replace the letters in his pocket and put off the evil moment.

'Well, such goings-on!' said Kolya, seating himself on the settee and broaching the subject directly, as such boys do. 'What do you think of Ippolit now? He's gone right down in your estimation?'

'Why on earth . . . but Kolya, I'm tired . . . and anyway it's too upsetting to start on that again . . . How is he, though?'

'He's asleep and will be for another two hours. I understand; you didn't sleep at home, out walking in the park . . . the excitement of course . . . I should just think so!'

'How did you know I was walking in the park and didn't sleep at home?'

'Vera told me just now. Tried to talk me out of coming in; but I had to, just for a minute. I've been at the bedside for the last two hours; I've got Kostya Lebedev doing his shift now. Burdovsky's left. So lie down, Prince; good night . . . I mean good day! You know, I'm really overwhelmed!'

'Naturally . . . all this . . .'

'No, Prince, not that; it's the confession that shook me. Mainly the part about providence and the life to come. There's a gigant-ic idea there!'

The prince looked fondly at Kolya, who had dropped in precisely in order to have a chat about the gigantic idea as soon as might be.

'But the main thing isn't the idea itself, it's the whole background. If Voltaire, Rousseau, or Proudhon had written it, I'd have read and remembered it but I wouldn't have been struck to the same extent. But a man who knows for certain he has only ten minutes left and talks like that—that's pride for you! That's the supreme assertion of personal dignity for you, it's pure defiance, that's what it is . . . No, it's just gigantic strength of will! And after all that, to allege that he deliberately left the cap out of the pistol—that's just vile, unbelievable! Yet you know, he hoodwinked us last night: I had never helped him pack his bag, and I had never seen any pistol; he did all his packing himself, so that took me off guard. Vera says you're letting him stay here; I swear there won't be any danger, especially as we are always with him.'

'Who was with him last night?'

'Kostya Lebedev, Burdovsky, and myself; Keller stayed a while then went away to sleep in Lebedev's room, because we didn't have anywhere for him to lie down. Ferdischenko also slept with Lebedev and left at seven. The general always sleeps there; now he's gone too ... Lebedev might be coming to see you presently; he was looking for you, for some reason; he twice asked where you were. Do you want to let him in or not, if you're going to sleep? I'm going off to bed as well. Oh yes, I should have mentioned one thing; the general surprised me just now: Burdovsky woke me after six, just on six in fact, to take my turn on duty; I went out for a minute and ran into the general who was still so drunk he didn't recognize me: stands in front of me like a post; then he flew at me as soon as it dawned on him: "What about the patient? I was on my way to enquire about the patient ..." I made my report, so and so. "That's all right then", says he, "but what I was coming about, what I really got up for, was to warn you; I have reasons for believing that one shouldn't talk freely in Ferdischenko's presence, one should ... refrain." Do you understand that, Prince?'

'Really? Still ... it doesn't concern us.'

'No, of course it doesn't, we're not freemasons! That's why I was so surprised at the general's coming specially to wake me up at night to warn me.'

'Ferdischenko's gone, you say?'

'At seven; he dropped by as he was going out—I was on duty. He said he was going to have his sleep out at Vilkin's—that's a drinking-partner of his. Well, I'm off! And here's Lukyan Timofeich ... The prince wants to sleep, Lukyan Timofeich; about turn!'

'Just for one minute, highly esteemed Prince, about a certain matter which I regard as important', said Lebedev in an undertone, as he entered with a solemn bow; his tone was stiff and heavily significant. He had not been to his rooms, having only just returned to the house, and thus was still holding his hat. His face was grave and held a most unusual hint of dignity. The prince invited him to be seated.

'You were enquiring for me twice? Perhaps you're still upset over yesterday's . . .'

'Over the boy yesterday, you mean, Prince? Oh no, sir; yesterday my thoughts were in a whirl . . . but today I don't propose to countermand your intentions in any way whatever.'

'Counter . . . what did you say?'

'I said countermand; the word is French, like many other words which have entered the make-up of the Russian language; but I don't particularly defend it.'

'How comes it you are so formal and ceremonious this morning, Lebedev, and talking like a dictionary?' smiled the prince.

'Nikolai Ardalionovich!' Lebedev addressed Kolya with something approaching affection. 'As I have to inform the prince of a certain matter, touching upon . . .'

'Of course, naturally it's none of my business! *Au revoir*, Prince!'

'I like that child for his quick understanding', Lebedev announced, gazing after him. 'He's a sharp lad, though he does get in the way. I have had a most unfortunate experience, my dear Prince, yesterday evening or early this morning—I still hesitate to signify the precise time.'

'What happened?'

'The loss of four hundred roubles from my pocket, my dear Prince; I've been robbed', added Lebedev with a sour smile.

'You've lost four hundred roubles? What a shame.'

'Especially to a poor man, living by his own honest toil.'

'Of course, of course; how did it happen?'

'On account of the wine, sir. I have come to you as my saviour, my dear Prince. I had received the sum of four hundred silver roubles from one of my debtors at five o'clock yesterday afternoon and came back here on the train. I had my wallet in my pocket. When I changed out of my uniform into my indoor coat, I transferred the money at the same time, so as to keep it by me and lend it that evening to meet a request . . . expecting an agent of mine.'

'Incidentally, Lukyan Timofeich, is it true you advertise in the papers that you lend money on the security of gold and silver items?'

'Through an agent; my own name does not appear, nor my address. With next to no capital and in view of the augmentation of my family, you must agree that a fair rate of interest . . .'

'Of course, of course; I was only asking; I'm sorry I interrupted you.'

'The agent didn't come. Meanwhile, they brought that unhappy boy in; I was already in an exalted condition after dinner; the guests arrived, we drank . . . tea . . . and I . . . got rather merry, to my undoing. When that fellow Keller finally put in an appearance and announced your special day and your instructions concerning the champagne, then I, dear and most esteemed Prince, possessing a heart (which no doubt you've already noticed, no more than I deserve), possessing a heart, I won't say tender, but at least grateful, a fact I take pride in—to show greater respect for the festive occasion, and in the expectation of congratulating you personally, took it into my head to exchange my old rags and tatters for the civil-service uniform I had taken off when I came in—which I did, as you no doubt observed, Prince, seeing me in uniform all evening. When I was changing, I forgot about the wallet in the coat . . . Verily, when God desires to chastise a man, he first of all deprives him of reason. And it was only this morning, at half-past seven, when I woke up and leapt out of bed like a madman and the first thing I did was to grab my coat—the pocket was empty! There wasn't a sign of the wallet!'

'Oh dear, how unpleasant!'

'Unpleasant is the word; with your unfailing delicacy you have put your finger on it', Lebedev added, a touch slyly.

'Well, you know . . .', the prince pondered, uneasily, 'this is really a serious matter.'

'Serious is the word—another word you've found, Prince, to signify . . .'

'Oh, that's enough, Lukyan Timofeich, there's nothing in that. Words are not the point . . . Do you suppose you might have dropped it out of your pocket when you were in a drunken state?'

'I might have. Anything's possible when you're in a drunken

state, as you have so candidly expressed it, dear Prince! But please consider, sir: if I had shaken out the wallet from my pocket when I was changing my coat, the shaken object should be lying there on the floor. Where is that object, sir?'

'You didn't put it away anywhere, a drawer in your desk, perhaps?'

'I've searched and rummaged everywhere, though I never put it away and I distinctly remember that I opened no drawers.'

'Have you looked in the safe?'

'First thing I did, sir, several times this morning already . . . But how could I have put it away in the safe, truly esteemed Prince?'

'I must confess, Lebedev, this thing worries me. Someone must have found it on the floor, then?'

'Or stolen it from my pocket! Two alternatives, sir.'

'That worries me a lot, because who precisely . . . That's the question!'

'No shadow of a doubt, that is the crucial question; it's amazing how you find words and ideas that hit the nail on the head, most excellent Prince!'

'Ah, Lukyan Timofeich, no sarcasm please, this is . . .'

'Sarcasm!' exclaimed Lebedev, throwing up his hands.

'All right, all right, don't worry, I'm not angry; it's something else . . . it's the people I'm afraid for. Whom do you suspect?'

'That's a very difficult question to answer and . . . most complicated! I can't suspect the maid: she was in her kitchen all the time. Nor my own children . . .'

'I should think not.'

'So it must have been one of the guests, sir.'

'Is that possible?'

'Absolutely and utterly not, but it can only have been that. I will admit, however, in fact I'm convinced, that if it was theft, it was not committed in the evening when everybody was together, but during the night or even towards morning by one of those who spent the night here.'

'Oh, good lord!'

'Naturally I exclude Burdovsky and Kolya; they didn't even enter my room, sir.'

'I should think not, even if they had gone in! Who did spend the night in your room?'

'Counting me, there were four of us in two adjoining rooms: the general, Keller, Mister Ferdischenko, and I. It must have been one of us four, sir!'

'One of three, you mean; but who?'

'I counted myself in to be fair and accurate; but you will agree, Prince, that I couldn't have robbed myself, though there have been cases . . .'

'Oh, Lebedev, how tedious this is!' the prince cried impatiently. 'Come to the point, why drag things out?'

'There are three, therefore, sir; first of all, Mister Keller, an irregular person, a drinker and in some respects a liberal, in relation to the pocket I mean, sir; for the rest he has chivalrous leanings, so to speak, rather than liberal. He started off sleeping in the invalid's room and only moved in with us during the night, under the pretext that the bare floor was hard for him to sleep on.'

'You suspect him?'

'I did, sir. When I jumped out of bed like a madman towards eight and clapped my hand to my head, I at once woke the general, who was sleeping the sleep of the just. Bearing in mind the strange disappearance of Ferdischenko, which was enough in itself to arouse our suspicions, we immediately decided to search Keller, who was sleeping . . . like . . . like, almost like a top, sir. We searched him thoroughly: not a penny in his pockets, and we couldn't find a single pocket without a hole in it. There was a blue-check cotton handkerchief, in an unseemly state, sir. In addition, there was a love-note from a housemaid, demanding money with threats, together with pieces of the article you already know of, sir. The general concluded that he was innocent. To complete our investigation we woke him up, which took a good deal of poking; he could hardly understand what was going on; his jaw gaped, drunken appearance, facial expression foolish and innocent, even stupid—it wasn't him, sir!'

'Well, I'm very glad!' The prince sighed pleasurably. 'I was so afraid for him!'

'Afraid? You had some grounds for suspicion there then?' Lebedev narrowed his eyes.

'Oh no, just a manner of speaking', the prince faltered. 'It was frightfully stupid of me to say I was afraid. Please Lebedev, don't tell anyone . . .'

'Prince, Prince! Your words are locked in my heart . . . deep in my heart! As in the grave, sir! . . .', said Lebedev ecstatically, pressing his hat to his heart.

'All right, all right! . . . So it's Ferdischenko? That is, I mean you suspect Ferdischenko?'

'Who else is there?' said Lebedev softly, staring fixedly at the prince.

'Well of course, stands to reason . . . who else indeed . . . all the same though, I mean what evidence is there?'

'Evidence we have, sir. In the first place his vanishing at seven o'clock or even before.'

'I know, Kolya told me he'd called in on him and said he was going to have his sleep out at . . . I've forgotten where, a friend of his.'

'Vilkin it is, sir. So Kolya has already spoken to you?'

'He didn't say anything about any theft.'

'Because he doesn't know, I'm keeping the matter a secret for the moment. So he goes off to Vilkin's; a sensible course, one might think, for one drunk man to go off to another like himself, even if it was before dawn and with no reason, sir. But this is where the trail begins: on his way out he leaves an address . . . Now note the question, Prince: why did he leave an address? . . . Why did he deliberately go out of his way to see Kolya and tell him that he was going to have his sleep out at Vilkin's? Who cared about him leaving, and particularly that he was going to Vilkin's? What was the point of announcing it? No, what we have here is cunning, sir, a thief's cunning! It was meant to say: "See, I am deliberately not concealing my tracks, how can I be a thief after that? Surely a thief wouldn't tell you where he was going?" Too anxious to avert suspicion and obliterate his footprints in the sand, so to speak . . . You follow my meaning, my dear Prince?'

'I do, I do indeed, but that's not sufficient is it?'

'The second clue, sir: the trail turns out to be a false one, the address in question is incorrect. An hour later, that is at eight o'clock, I was already knocking at Vilkin's door; he lives here on Fifth Street, I know him in fact, sir. There was no sign of Ferdischenko. I did manage to get from the maid, who is as deaf as a post, sir, that about an hour earlier someone actually had been knocking, and fairly loudly too, and he'd broken the bell-pull. The maid hadn't opened up, not wanting to wake Mister Vilkin, or perhaps she didn't want to get out of bed herself. That does happen, sir.'

'And that is the sum total of your evidence? It's not much.'

'But, Prince, who else can I suspect, sir, consider?' Lebedev declared affectingly, and there was something crafty in his smirk.

'You ought to search your rooms and all the drawers again!' the prince said in a worried tone, after a reflective pause.

'I have, sir!' sighed Lebedev, even more affectingly.

'Hm! . . . And why, why did you have to go and change that coat!' cried the prince, banging the table in annoyance.

'A question out of an old comedy, sir. But most kindly Prince! You are taking my misfortune too much to heart. I'm not worth it. I mean I alone am not worth it; but you are concerned for the criminal too . . . the worthless Mister Ferdischenko?'

'Oh yes, yes, you really have worried me', the prince absently interrupted, displeased. 'And so, what do you intend doing . . . if you're so confident it is Ferdischenko?'

'Prince, dear Prince, who else could it be, sir?' Lebedev squirmed ever-more pathetically. 'The absence of any other we might think of, and, as it were, the utter impossibility of suspecting anyone other than Mister Ferdischenko constitutes, after all, yet another piece of evidence, the third against Mister Ferdischenko! Because again, who else is there? I can't very well suspect Mister Burdovsky, now can I, heh-heh-heh!'

'There you are, what nonsense!'

'Nor the general, could I now, heh-heh-heh!'

'What rubbish!' the prince said, almost angrily, fidgeting impatiently in his seat.

'I should think it is rubbish! Heh-heh-heh! That man really made me laugh, the general I mean, sir! There we are hot on the trail to Vilkin's—and I should tell you that the general was even more shaken than I was when I woke him up as soon as I had discovered the loss. So much so, in fact, that he went red in the face, then pale, and eventually reached a pitch of righteous indignation I never expected of him. A most honourable man! He's always telling lies, that's his weakness, but he's a man of the noblest feelings, not a great intellect, sir, but his innocence inspires profound trust. I've already told you, dear Prince, that I have a fondness for him, even love, sir. Suddenly he comes to a halt in the middle of the road, throws open his coat, and bares his chest: "Search me", he says. "You searched Keller, then why don't you search me? Justice demands it!" says he. His arms and legs were all of a tremble, white as a sheet, a grim sight. I laughed and said: "Listen", I said, "General, if somebody else said that about you, I'd take my head off with my own hands, put it on a big dish, and carry it to anyone who doubted you. Do you see this head? I'd say, well, I'm prepared to vouch for him with this head, and I'd go through fire for him. That's how much I'm ready to vouch for you!" Well, he flung himself into my arms, right there in the middle of the road, sir, burst into tears, still shaking, and clutched me so tightly to his chest that I could scarcely get my breath: "You're my one friend", he says, "left to me in my misfortunes!" A man of feeling, sir! Well, of course, he immediately told me an appropriate tale on the way about how as a young man he had been suspected of stealing half a million roubles, and how the following day he had rushed into a burning house and dragged from the flames both the count who had suspected him and his own wife, Nina Alexandrovna, still a spinster at the time. The count embraced him and that's how his marriage to Nina Alexandrovna came about; and the day after that they found the box with the missing money among the charred ruins; it was iron, English-made, with a secret lock, and had somehow fallen under the floor-boards without anyone noticing; it was only discovered owing to the blaze. All lies, sir. But when he began talking about Nina Alexandrovna, he positively whimpered. A most noble person, Nina Alexandrovna, even if she is angry with me.'

'You aren't acquainted with her?'

'Hardly at all, sir, but I would like to be, with all my heart, if only to be able to defend myself to her. Nina Alexandrovna has a grudge against me, because I'm supposed to be leading her husband astray by encouraging his drinking. Not only is that not the case, I'm actually breaking the habit; I may well be keeping him away from the most pernicious company. Besides, he's a friend, sir, and I swear to you that I never leave him nowadays, sir: where he goes, I go, because one can only influence him that way, through his emotions. He never visits his captain's widow at all nowadays, though he secretly longs to do so, and sometimes groans for her, especially in the morning when he's getting up and putting his boots on—why at that particular time I don't know. He's got no money, sir, and he can't possibly turn up without that, sir. He hasn't asked you for money has he, dear Prince?'

'No, he hasn't.'

'He's ashamed to do that. He wanted to: he even admitted to me that he wanted to pester you, but he's shy, sir, as you lent him some not long ago; besides, he thinks you wouldn't give him any. He blurted it all out to me as his friend.'

'And you don't give him any?'

'Prince! My dear Prince! Never mind money, I'd give my life for him . . . no, still I don't want to exaggerate—not life, but if it was a fever, let's say, a boil, or a cough even, I'd put up with it, if it were absolutely necessary of course. I regard him as a great man, if ruined! There, sir; never mind money, sir!'

'So you do give him money?'

'N-no, sir; I've never given him money, sir, and he knows very well that I won't, sir, but it's only as a means of restraining and reforming him. Now he's insisting on going to Petersburg with me; I'm going to Petersburg, you see, to catch Mister Ferd-ischenko before the trail goes cold, because I know for a fact he's there by now, sir. My general is very keen, sir; but I suspect he'll give me the slip in Petersburg and go off to his widow. I confess I shall deliberately let him go, as we have already arranged to split up as soon as we reach Petersburg, the better to catch Mister Ferdischenko. So I'll let him go and then all of a sudden, like a bolt from the blue, I'll pounce on him at the widow's—just to put him to shame as a family man, and indeed a human being.'

'Don't make a scene though, Lebedev, for goodness' sake, don't make a scene', said the prince in an undertone, much perturbed.

'Oh no, sir, it's only to shame him and see the look on his face; you can learn a lot from that, dear Prince, particularly in a man like him! Ah, Prince! Though my own misfortune is great, I can't help thinking even now about reforming him morally. I have a great favour to ask of you, dear Prince; to be honest, it's really why I've come: you know the general's household, you even lived there, sir; if, most benevolent Prince, you could bring yourself to assist me in this matter, really just for the general's sake and his happiness . . .'

Lebedev even put his hands together, as if in prayer.

'In what way, though? How on earth can I assist you? I assure you I'm very anxious to understand you properly, Lebedev.'

'It was only in that conviction that I came to you, sir! It might be done through Nina Alexandrovna; keeping a constant eye on his excellency and watching over him in the bosom of his family, as it were. Unfortunately I don't know her, sir . . . then again there's Kolya, who worships you, so to speak, from the bottom of his youthful soul, he might help . . .'

'N-no . . . Nina Alexandrovna mixed up in this . . . God forbid! Or Kolya . . . Perhaps I'm still failing to understand you properly, Lebedev.'

'There's absolutely nothing to understand about it!' Lebedev fairly rose from his chair. 'Just sympathy, sympathy and kindness—that's the only medicine for our patient. You will permit me, Prince, to think of him as a sick man?'

'That merely demonstrates your tact and intelligence.'

'I will explain it to you with an example taken from actual practice, to make it the clearer. You see what sort of man he is, sir: nowadays he has the one weakness, his fondness for this widow, and he cannot present himself there without money, and it is there that I intend to catch him, for his own good, sir; but let us suppose that it was not just the widow, but that he'd actually committed a crime, well, some extremely dishonourable action (although he's totally incapable of that), even in that case, I say that the only way to reach him is through tender generosity, because he is the most sensitive of men, sir! Believe me, he wouldn't hold out five days, he'd blurt it out himself, burst into tears and confess everything—especially if we act skilfully and honourably through your own and his family's supervision over his every movement . . . Oh most benevolent Prince!' Lebedev leapt to his feet in a kind of exaltation. 'I am not saying that he will for certain . . . I am ready, so to speak, to shed my last drop of blood for him this very minute, though you will agree that his lack of self-control, his intemperance, and the widow woman—all that taken together, could lead him into anything.'

'Of course, I am always ready to assist in a matter like this', the prince said, getting to his feet, 'but I must confess, Lebedev, I'm terribly worried; tell me, you really are still . . . I mean, you say yourself that you suspect Mister Ferdischenko.'

'Well who else is there? Who else is there, most open-hearted Prince?' Lebedev again placed his hands together affectingly, smiling gently.

The prince frowned and stood up.

'You see, Lukyan Timofeich, it would be an awful thing to make a mistake here. This Ferdischenko . . . I wouldn't like to say anything bad about him . . . but this Ferdischenko . . . I mean, who knows, perhaps it is him! What I'm trying to say is that perhaps he really is more capable of it than . . . than anyone else.'

Lebedev's eyes and ears were alert.

'You see', the prince's frown deepened as he got into a muddle, pacing the room while striving not to glance at Lebedev, 'I was informed . . . I was told that Mister Ferdischenko, apart from being the sort of man in whose company you should be careful not to say . . . too much, you follow me? What I'm leading up to is that he might actually be more capable than another . . . so that there's no mistake, that's the main thing, you understand?'

'And who told you that about Mister Ferdischenko?' Lebedev caught him up on this.

'Just a whisper; still I don't believe it myself . . . I'm terribly annoyed that I've had to tell you this, I assure you, I don't believe it myself . . . such nonsense . . . Dear me, how stupid of me to mention it!'

'You see, Prince', Lebedev was fairly quivering at this point, 'it is important, very important now, I don't mean this about Mister Ferdischenko, but how the information reached you.' (As he said this, Lebedev trotted back and forth after the prince, trying to match his stride.) 'I also have something to say, Prince: this morning, when we were on our way to Vilkin's house, the general was seething with anger, naturally, and suddenly started hinting at the same thing about Mister Ferdischenko, but in such a vague and incoherent fashion that I just had to put a number of questions to him; as a consequence, I came to the firm conclusion that the whole thing was merely one of his excellency's inspirations ... With the best of intentions, as it were. The reason he tells lies is that he can't restrain his generous impulses. Do see sir, that now, if he lied, and I'm sure he did, how could you have come to hear of it? You realize, Prince, that with him it was just on the spur of the moment—so therefore who on earth told you? It's important, sir, it's ... it's very important, sir, and ... as it were ...'

'Kolya told me just now, and he was told by his father earlier when he met him in the passage at six, or just after, when he had gone out for some reason.'

And the prince told him everything in detail.

'Now then, sir, that's what I call evidence, sir', Lebedev laughed soundlessly, rubbing his hands. 'Just what I thought, sir! This means that his excellency deliberately interrupted his sleep of innocence before six, to go and wake his beloved son and warn him of the great danger of associating with Mister Ferdischenko! What a dangerous man Mister Ferdischenko must be after that, and how acute his excellency's parental unease must have been, heh-heh-heh!'

'Look here, Lebedev', the prince was now utterly bemused. 'Look here, do it quietly! Don't make a scene! Please, Lebedev, I implore you ... If you do, I swear I'll assist you, but no one must know about it; no one must know!'

'Rest assured, most benevolent, sincere, and noble Prince', cried Lebedev in positive rapture, 'rest assured, that all this business will be locked away in this most honourable heart of mine! Gently does it, sir, together! Gently does it, sir, together! I'd give the last drop of blood ... Most illustrious Prince, I am vile in soul and spirit, but ask anyone, a scoundrel even, who he would rather have dealings with—a scoundrel like himself, or a most noble person such as you, most sincere Prince. He will answer—the latter, and therein lies the triumph of virtue! *Au revoir*, dear Prince! Gently does it, sir ... gently does it and ... together, sir.'

10

THE prince eventually realized why he went cold whenever he touched the three letters, and had kept putting off the evil moment of reading them till the evening. When he had fallen into a heavy slumber on the couch, still unable to nerve himself to open any of the three envelopes, he again experienced an oppressive dream and the same 'sinful' woman came to him once more. Once more she gazed at him with tears glistening on her long lashes, once more summoned him to follow, and once more he woke up, as before, with the agonized recollection of her face. He wanted to go to *her* at once, but could not; at length, almost in despair, he opened the letters and began to read.

The letters also had much in common with dreams. Sometimes you have fearful dreams, impossible, bizarre; when you wake up, you remember them clearly and marvel at an odd fact: first of all, you recall that your reason never deserted you all through the dream; you even recall that you behaved extremely shrewdly and logically throughout all that long, long time when you were surrounded by murderers, who tried to deceive you, concealing their intentions, treating you in friendly fashion, while they had their weapons ready and were only waiting for a signal; you recall how cleverly you hoodwinked them eventually, and hid from them; then you guessed that they were perfectly well aware of your trick and were just pretending not to know your hiding-place; but again you outwitted and cheated them, all this you remember clearly. But why was it that your reason was able to reconcile itself to the obvious absurdities and impossibilities with which your dream was crammed? One of your killers turned into a woman before your very eyes, then from a woman into a sly and hideous little dwarf—and you accepted it at once as an established fact, with barely a hesitation, and this at the very moment when your reason, on the other hand, was at a pitch of intensity and demonstrating extraordinary power, shrewdness, perception, and logic? Why is it also that when you have woken up and completely recovered your sense of reality, you feel each time, sometimes with great intensity, that you have left behind something personally unresolved along with your dream? You laugh at the absurdity of your dream, yet at the same time sense that there is a sort of idea inherent in the interweaving of these absurdities, but that this idea is actual and has to do with your real life, something existing in your heart now, as it has always done; something new, prophetic, and yet expected, has been told you by your dream; the impression is vivid; it may be joyful or agonizing, but what it was or what has been said to you—all this you are unable either to comprehend or recall.

Almost the same thing happened after these letters. But even before opening them, the prince felt that the very fact that they existed and could exist was in itself like a nightmare. How could *she* have brought herself to write to *her*, he kept asking himself, as he wandered about alone that evening (sometimes unaware himself of where he was walking). How could she have written *about that*, and how could an insane project like that have taken root in her brain? And yet that dream had already come into being, and for him the most astonishing thing was that, as he read those letters, he himself almost came to believe in the feasibility, even the justification, of that dream. Yes, of course, it was a dream, a nightmare, sheer madness; and yet there was something in it too, something poignantly real and agonizingly right, which justified the dream, the nightmare and the madness. For several hours on end he seemed to be haunted by what he had read, recalling fragments of it, brooding over them and thinking them through. Sometimes he felt like telling himself that he had foreseen all this and guessed it all along; it even seemed to him that he had read it all before, long long ago, and all the heartache he had suffered since then, his torment and fear—all that was contained in these letters he had read long ago.

'When you unfold this letter' (the first missive began), 'the first thing you do will be to glance at the signature. That signature will tell you everything and explain everything, so I have no need to justify myself or explain anything to you. If I were in any way your equal, you might well be affronted at such insolence; but who am I and who are you? We are such opposites, and I am so far beneath you that I could not possibly offend you, even if I wished to.'

Elsewhere she had written:

'Don't take my words for the morbid raptures of a sick mind, but for me—you are perfection! I have seen you, I see you every day. I'm not trying to appraise you at all, it is not through reason that I arrived at my estimate of your perfection; I've simply come to believe in it. But I am guilty of one thing: I love you. One shouldn't love perfection, should one? One should look on perfection simply as perfection, isn't that so? Nevertheless I am in love with you. Though love is a great leveller, do not be afraid; I have never considered myself your equal, not even in my most secret thoughts. I have written "do not be afraid"; could you possibly be afraid? . . . If it were possible, I would kiss the ground you walk upon. Oh, I don't consider myself your equal . . . Look at the signature, quick, look at the signature!'

'However, I do notice' (she wrote in another letter), 'that I am linking you with him without having asked you once yet whether you love him. He fell in love with you after seeing you just once. He remembered you as "a light"; those were the actual words I heard him use. But I had realized, without need for words, that for him you were the light. I lived with him for a whole month and realized that you too loved him; to me, you and he are one.'

'What is this' (she wrote further on), 'yesterday I walked past you and you seemed to blush. It can't have happened, I must have been mistaken. If you were taken to the filthiest thieves' kitchen and shown vice in all its nakedness, you ought not to blush: you ought never to resent an affront. You can hate everyone who is low and vile, not on your own account, but for the sake of the others, those whom they injure. But no one can wrong you. You know, I can't help feeling that you even ought to love me. For me you are the same as for him, a bright spirit; an angel cannot hate, it cannot help loving. Is it possible to love everyone, all people, all one's neighbours? I've often put that question to myself. Of course not, it's unnatural even. The abstract love of humanity almost always comes down to loving oneself alone. But for us that's impossible, and you are a different matter: how could you not love anyone when you cannot compare yourself to anyone and when you are above any affront, above any personal resentment? You alone can love without selfishness, you alone are capable of loving not for yourself, but for the one you love. Oh, how bitter it would be for me to learn that you feel shame or anger on my account! That would be your ruin; you would at once become my equal . . .

'Yesterday, after I had encountered you, I came home and thought of a picture. Artists always depict Christ according to the gospel stories; I would paint him differently: I would show him alone—his disciples did leave him alone sometimes, after all. I would leave him alone with just one little child. The child would be playing near him, perhaps telling him something in his childish prattle. Christ would be listening to him, but presently fall to thinking; his hand would rest unconsciously on the child's little fair head. He looks towards the distant horizon; a thought as great as the whole world dwells in his look; his face is sad. The child has fallen silent and leans his elbow against his knees and, cheek on hand, raises his head and stares intently at him, wondering as children sometimes do. The sun is setting . . . That's my picture! You are innocent and all your perfection is in your innocence. Ah, remember only that! Why should you care about my passion for you? You are now all mine, I will be close to you all my life . . . I shall soon be dead.'

Finally, in the last letter:

'For God's sake don't concern yourself about me; don't think I'm abasing myself by writing like this to you either, or that I am the sort of creature who enjoys humiliating herself, even out of a perverse sense of pride. No, I have my own consolations, but I find it difficult to explain that to you. It would be hard for me to say it clearly to myself even, though I agonize about it. But I do know that I cannot humiliate myself even out of some access of pride—and I am incapable of the self-abasement that stems from purity of heart. It follows then that I am not humiliating myself at all.

'Why do I want to bring the two of you together: for your sake or my own? For my own, of course; it would solve all my problems, I've told myself that long ago . . . I have heard that your sister, Adelaida, said once of my portrait, that with beauty like that one could turn the world upside down. But I have renounced the world; does that amuse you, coming from me with my diamonds and lace, in the company of drunkards and rogues? Pay no attention to that, I have almost ceased to exist and I know it; heaven alone knows what is living within me instead. I read it every day in two frightful eyes constantly fixed on me, even when they are not present. Those eyes are *silent* at the moment (they always are), but I know their secret. His house is dark and dreary and it has a secret. I am sure he has a razor wrapped in silk, tucked away in a drawer, like that Moscow murderer;* he too lived with his mother and kept a razor wrapped in silk to cut one throat with. All the time I was in their house, I kept thinking that there was a corpse hidden under the floor-boards, by his father perhaps, wrapped in oilcloth, just like that Moscow man, with bottles of Zhdanov fluid put round it; I could show you the very corner. He never says anything, but I know he loves me so much he can't possibly help hating me. Your wedding and mine— together: that's how he and I have arranged it. I have no secrets from him. I would kill him out of fear ... but he will kill me first ... he laughed just now and said I was raving; he knows I am writing to you.'

And there was much much more of the same wild ramblings throughout the letters. One of them, the second, was written in a tiny hand on two large sheets of paper.

The prince at length emerged from the darkened park, where he had wandered for a long time, just as he had on the previous day. The bright, clear night seemed to him even lighter than usual; 'can it still be so early?' he thought. He had forgotten to bring his watch with him. He caught the sound of what seemed like distant music; 'it must be in the pleasure-gardens', he thought again, 'of course they haven't gone there again today'. With this realization, he found himself standing before their villa; he had known very well that he would be certain to end up here eventually, as with faltering heart he stepped on to the veranda. No one came to meet him and the veranda was deserted. He waited for a moment before opening the door into the drawing-room. 'They never keep this door locked', flashed through his mind, but the room too was empty; it was almost totally dark. He stood in the middle of the room, perplexed. Suddenly a door opened and Alexandra came in with a candle in her hand. She was surprised to see the prince and halted questioningly in front of him. Evidently, she was merely passing through the room, from one door to another, without the least expectation of finding anyone there.

'How did you get here?' she enquired at length.

'I ... dropped by ...'

'*Maman* is rather unwell, so is Aglaya. Adelaida is going to bed and so am I. We've spent the whole evening at home on our own.

Papa and Prince S are in Petersburg.'

'I came . . . I came here . . . now . . .'

'You know what time it is?'

'N-no . . .'

'Half-past twelve. We always go to bed at one.'

'Ah, I thought it was . . . half-past nine.'

'Never mind!' she laughed. 'Why didn't you come earlier? You might have been expected.'

'I . . . thought . . .', he babbled as he went out.

'Good night! Tomorrow I'll give them all a laugh.'

He went off along the road skirting the park towards his own villa. His heart was pounding and his mind was in turmoil; everything around him seemed dream-like. And then suddenly, just as he had wakened twice before at the same apparition in his dream, the very same apparition again appeared to him. The same woman emerged from the park and stood before him, as if she had been waiting for him here. He gave a start and halted; she seized his hand and squeezed it hard. 'No, this was no phantom!'

And so, at last, she was standing face to face with him for the first time since they had parted; she was saying something to him, but he stared silently at her; his heart was overflowing and ached with anguish. Oh, he could never afterwards forget that meeting with her, and always the remembrance was accompanied by the same anguish. She sank to her knees before him, there in the roadway, like one demented; he stepped back in alarm as she tried to catch his hand and kiss it, and exactly as in his dream of that day, tears glistened on her long lashes.

'Get up! Get up!' he said in a startled whisper, trying to raise her to her feet. 'Get up at once!'

'Are you happy? Happy?' she was asking. 'Just say one word, are you happy now? Today, now? With her? What did she say?'

She did not get up as he asked; she was questioning him hastily and spoke hurriedly, as if she were being pursued.

'I'm going tomorrow, as you told me to. I won't . . . I am seeing you for the last time, the last time! It really is the very last time!'

'Do calm yourself, get up!' he said in despair.

She gazed at him hungrily, clutching at his hands.

'Goodbye!' she said at last, then rose and walked swiftly away, almost breaking into a run. The prince saw Rogozhin suddenly appear at her side, take her by the arm, and lead her away.

'Wait, Prince', shouted Rogozhin, 'I'll be back in five minutes.'

He actually did come back in five minutes; the prince was waiting for him on the selfsame spot.

'I've put her in the carriage', he said. 'There's been a carriage waiting on the corner since ten o'clock. She knew you'd be spending the whole evening with that other one. I told her exactly what you wrote to me in your letter today. She won't be writing to that other one again. She has promised, and she'll be leaving tomorrow, according to your wishes. She wanted to see you for the last time, though you refused to see her; we've been waiting for you over on that bench there, to catch you on your way home.'

'She brought you with her of her own accord?'

'What if she did?' Rogozhin grinned. 'I saw what I already knew. No doubt you've read the letters?'

'Have you really read them, though?' asked the prince, shocked by this idea.

'I should think I have; she showed me every letter herself. Remember about the razor, heh-heh!'

'She's mad!' cried the prince, wringing his hands.

'Who knows about that, perhaps she isn't', said Rogozhin softly, as if to himself.

The prince made no reply.

'Well, goodbye', said Rogozhin, 'I'm going tomorrow too; don't think badly of me! By the way, friend', he added, turning abruptly, 'why didn't you give her an answer? "Are you happy or not?" '

'No, no, no!' exclaimed the prince, in unspeakable misery.

'As if you would say "yes"!' Rogozhin gave a sardonic laugh and went off without a backward glance.

PART FOUR

1

ABOUT a week had gone by since the meeting of two characters in our story on the green bench. One fine morning, at about half-past ten, Varvara Ardalionovna Ptitsyna, who had been out visiting friends, returned home, immersed in melancholy reflection.

There are people who are hard to describe in a phrase which will present them in one stroke at their most typical and characteristic; they are the people usually dubbed 'ordinary' or 'the majority', and who actually do make up the huge majority of any society. In their novels and stories, writers for the most part try to take certain social types and present them vividly and skilfully—types who are very rarely encountered in real life precisely as they are drawn, but who are nevertheless almost more real than reality itself. Podkolyosin* as a type may well be an exaggeration, but he is by no means a figment of the imagination. How many intelligent people, learning of Podkolyosin through Gogol, immediately began to discover that scores, nay hundreds of their close acquaintances and friends were awfully like Podkolyosin? They knew before Gogol wrote that these friends resembled Podkolyosin, but what they didn't yet know was that that was their name. In real life, bridegrooms very rarely leap out of windows before their wedding, because apart from anything else, it is an awkward form of exit; yet all the same, how many bridegrooms, even intelligent and worthy men, have been ready to confess before their wedding that, in the bottom of their heart, they were Podkolyosins. Nor does every husband exclaim at every turn: *'Tu l'as voulu, George Dandin!'** But heavens, how many millions and billions of times has this cry from the heart been repeated by husbands all over the world after their honeymoon, or, who knows, perhaps on the day after their wedding?

And so, without entering any more deeply into the question, we will merely say that in real life the typical characteristics of people seem to get diluted, and all these George Dandins and Podkolyosins do actually exist, darting and rushing about us every day, though somehow in a rather attenuated form. Conceding then, for the sake of strict accuracy, that George Dandin may also be encountered in our everyday existence entirely as Molière created him—however seldom that might be—we will now conclude our disquisition, which is beginning to sound like a magazine review. Yet still the question remains: what is a novelist to do with people who are commonplace, absolutely 'ordinary', and how are they to be presented to the reader so as to make them in the least interesting? To avoid them altogether in the narrative is out of the question, since ordinary folk at every turn form the main and vital link in the chain of human affairs; to leave them out would be to transgress against plausibility. Filling novels with human types only, or simply with odd and fantastic people, would be implausible, indeed uninteresting. In our view, a writer should try to seek out interesting and instructive nuances even among commonplace elements. When, for example, the very nature of certain commonplace characters consists in their perpetual and invariable ordinariness, or still better, when, notwithstanding all their strenuous efforts to get out of the rut of commonplace routine at whatever cost, they still end up by remaining permanently and unchangeably ordinary and commonplace, then such characters take on a kind of typicalness of their own, an ordinariness which steadfastly refuses to accept what it is, and desperately desires to become original and independent, without possessing the least capacity for independence.

Certain characters in our story also belong to this category of 'ordinary' or 'commonplace' people; up till now (I admit) they have been insufficiently explained to the reader. Among them are Varvara Ardalionovich Ptitsyna, her husband Mister Ptitsyn, and her brother Gavrila Ardalionovich.

In actual fact there is nothing more annoying than to be, say, rich, of good family, presentable appearance, reasonably well educated, quite bright, even kind-hearted, and at the same time to possess no talent at all, no outstanding quality, no bee in your bonnet even, not a single idea of your own, to be positively 'the same as everybody else'. Wealth yes, but not on the Rothschild scale; an honourable family, but one never distinguished in any way; a pleasing appearance, but largely inexpressive; a decent education, but not knowing how to apply it; intelligence, but no *ideas of one's own*; a heart, but lacking generosity, and so on and so forth in every respect. There are an enormous multitude of such people in the world, far more indeed than might appear; like all people, they may be divided into two main categories—those of limited intelligence and those who are 'much cleverer'. The first are happier. For a limited 'ordinary' person, there is nothing easier, for instance, than imagining himself to be an extra-ordinary and original one and enjoying the fact without any misgivings. Some of our young ladies have only to crop their hair, don blue spectacles, and call themselves nihilists to persuade themselves at once that, in putting on their spectacles, they had started to have their own 'convictions'. Some people have only to sense a glimmer of kindly and humanitarian emotion in their hearts to become convinced on the spot that no one could feel as they do, and that they are in the vanguard of social progress. Another has but to accept on hearsay some notion or other, or read half a page from the middle of a book, to believe at once that it is 'his own idea' and was conceived in his own brain. This innocent arrogance, if one may use the expression, can go to astonishing lengths; it all sounds incredible, but one is constantly encountering it. This innocent arrogance, this total confidence the stupid have in themselves and their abilities, was wonderfully depicted by Gogol in his remarkable Lieutenant Pirogov.* Pirogov hasn't the slightest doubt that he is a genius, indeed superior to any genius; so confident is he that he never once questions the fact, indeed questions do not exist for him. The great writer was constrained to give him a thrashing in order to appease the outraged moral sensibilities of his reader, but seeing that the great man merely shook himself and ate a cream cake to recoup his strength after his punishment, he just threw up his hands in amazement and thus abandoned his readers. I have always been sorry that Gogol conferred such a junior rank on the great Pirogov, because Pirogov is so self-satisfied that nothing could have been easier for him to imagine, as his epaulettes grew thicker and more twisted with seniority and promotion, that he was a great commander, or rather not imagine it—simply to have no doubt of it: if he had been a general, he was bound to have been a great commander! And how many of those have made terrible blunders on the battlefield afterwards! And how many Pirogovs have there been among our writers, scholars, and publicists? I say 'have been', but they exist now of course . . .

One of the dramatis personae of our narrative, Gavrila Ardalionovich Ivolgin, belonged to the second, 'much cleverer', category, though fired from top to toe with the desire for originality. This category, however, as we have noted earlier, is far less happy than the first. The point is that the 'clever' commonplace man, even if he occasionally (and perhaps throughout his life) imagines himself to be a man of great originality and genius, nevertheless nurtures a worm of doubt in his heart which sometimes has the effect of driving this clever man to utter despair; if he does actually resign himself, it is only when he has been wholly poisoned by vanity driven inwards. Still, that would be an extreme case: with the vast majority of people in the *clever* category, matters take a much less tragic turn; liver complaints in old age, more or less, and that's the sum of it. And yet, before giving in and resigning themselves, these people go on playing the fool for an extraordinarily long time, from their youth up to the age of submission, all of it stemming from the desire to be original. Some odd instances of this may be encountered: occasionally an honest man will be prepared to stoop to some base action, just to be original; it may even happen that some unhappy man is not only honest but positively good, the prop of his household, sustaining and feeding by his toil not only his own family but others too—but what happens? For the duration of his life he can never rest! The reflection that he has carried out his human obligations so assiduously is no comfort or consolation to him; on the contrary, it is this thought that exasperates him: 'So this', he says, 'is what I've frittered away my whole life on, this is what has tied me hand and foot, this is what has prevented me inventing gunpowder! If it hadn't been for that I'd certainly have discovered either gunpowder or America—I'm not sure which, but I'd surely have discovered it!' What is most typical of these gentlemen is that over a lifetime they can never be certain exactly what it is they have to discover, or what they have been on the point of discovering all their lives: gunpowder or America? But their sufferings and yearning for discovery would certainly have sufficed for Columbus or Galileo.

Gavrila Ardalionovich was starting out in this very direction, but was still just starting. He had long years of playing the fool before him. A profound and constant awareness of his own mediocrity, and a concomitant overwhelming desire to convince himself that he was a man of supremely independent mind, had rankled in his soul ever since he was a boy. He was a young man of envious and impulsive desires, apparently born with over-wrought nerves. The impulsive nature of his desires he took to be their strength. In his passionate desire to excel, he was sometimes prepared to take the most reckless plunge; but as soon as matters got as far as that reckless plunge, our hero invariably turned out to be too prudent to take it. This mortified him. Perhaps he might even have nerved himself, had occasion offered, to commit some really vile action, just as long as he could achieve something of what he wanted, but as ill-luck would have it, as soon as the moment of decision arrived he always turned out to be too honest for anything really vile. (He had always been agreeable to minor acts of baseness.) He regarded the poverty and decline of his household with hatred and revulsion. He even treated his mother with haughty disdain, despite being very well aware that her character and reputation were, for the moment, the main prop of his own career. On starting work with General Yepanchin, he had at once told himself: 'If I am to act like a villain, I might as well do it properly, so long as I profit by it', and practically never did do it properly. In any case, why did he imagine he had to act like a rogue? He had simply been afraid of Aglaya, but he didn't break off with her; he kept spinning things out, just in case, although he never seriously believed she would ever stoop to him. Later on, during the business with Nastasya Filippovna, he suddenly imagined that money was the means to *every* end. 'As well be hung for a sheep as a lamb', he used to repeat complacently to himself every day, though with a certain apprehension; 'if I'm going to be a swine, I might as well go all the way', he would continually reassure himself. 'This is where your ordinary man loses his nerve, but we shan't do that!' After losing Aglaya and being crushed by circumstances, he totally lost heart and actually gave back to the prince the money which the mad woman had hurled at him, money she had been given, in her turn, by a madman. Afterwards he had regretted returning this money a thousand times, despite constantly bragging about his action. He actually wept for three days while the prince was in Petersburg, though he also contrived over the same three days to conceive a hatred towards the prince for regarding him with too much compassion, despite his having returned a sum of money 'that not everyone could have brought themselves to do'. However, the honest admission to himself that all his anguish boiled down to the continual mortification of his vanity tormented him horribly. It was only a long time later that he reviewed the situation and realized how seriously things might have turned out with a strange and innocent creature like Aglaya. He was eaten up with remorse; he gave up his position and abandoned himself to gloom and despondency. He was living with his father and mother at Ptitsyn's house, at the latter's expense, and openly despised him, though he heeded his advice and was sensible enough almost always to ask him for it. For instance, Ganya was annoyed with Ptitsyn because his brother-in-law did not set out to become a Rothschild. 'If you're a money-lender, go all the way, squeeze people, coin money out of them, be a man of mark, be a King of the Jews!' Ptitsyn was a modest, quiet man; he would only smile, but on one occasion he deemed it necessary to have a serious talk with Ganya, and did so with a certain dignity. He demonstrated that he was doing nothing dishonest and that Ganya ought not to call him a Jew; he was not to blame if borrowing was expensive; he operated fairly and honestly, and was in actual fact only an agent in these affairs, and that, last but not least, thanks to his scrupulous conduct of business he had earned a first-class reputation among the very best people and his business was expanding. 'I shall never be a Rothschild, that's not the reason I do it', he added, laughing, 'but I'll have a house on Liteinaya, perhaps even two, and stop at that.' 'And who knows, perhaps three!' he thought to himself, but he never went as far as this aloud, and kept his dream to himself. Nature loves and cherishes such people: she will reward Ptitsyn not with three but four houses, most likely, just because he had known since childhood that he would never be a Rothschild. However, beyond four nature will certainly never go, and Ptitsyn will get no further than that.

Ganya's sister was quite a different sort of person. She also possessed strong desires, but they were persistent rather than impulsive. She had a great deal of common sense when matters came to a head, nor was it lacking at other times. True, she too belonged to the category of 'ordinary' people who dreamed of originality, but on the other hand she had very quickly come to realize that she had not a scrap of any particular originality in her, and had not let that worry her too much—who knows, out of an odd sort of pride? She had taken her first practical step with the utmost resolution—by marrying Mister Ptitsyn; in marrying him, however, she did not think of saying to herself: 'If I'm to act like a villain, I might as well do it properly, as long as I get what I want', as Ganya would not have omitted to say if similarly placed (and indeed practically said as much in her presence when, as her elder brother, he was expressing approval of her decision). Quite the contrary in fact: Varya married after having made absolutely sure that her future husband was a modest, agreeable, and almost cultivated man, who would never on any account do anything really discreditable. Varya did not trouble herself about mean actions of a minor nature, looking upon them as trifles; that sort of thing was everywhere. She wasn't after the ideal man, after all! Besides, she knew that in marrying, she was providing a roof for her mother, father, and brothers. Seeing her brother so wretched, she was inclined to help him, despite their former domestic misunderstandings.

Ptitsyn sometimes used to urge Ganya, in a friendly way of course, to enter the civil service. 'Here you are despising the generals and the high-ups', he would sometimes say jokingly, 'but you wait, all of "them" will end up as generals in their turn; just you wait and see.' 'Where do they get the idea I despise generals and the high-ups?' Ganya thought sarcastically to himself. In order to assist her brother, Varya made up her mind to extend her circle of activity: her childhood memories were of considerable help in ingratiating herself with the Yepanchins; both she and her brother had played with them as children. We will note here that, if Varya had been pursuing some unusual fancy in visiting the Yepanchins, she might at once have left the category of people she had voluntarily joined; she was pursuing no such fancy; what she had in mind was a rather sound calculation on her part: it was based on the nature of the family. She had studied Aglaya's character indefatigably and had set herself the task of bringing her brother and Aglaya together again. Perhaps she actually did achieve something; perhaps she also made a number of errors, counting too much on her brother, for example, and expecting from him what he could never have provided under any circumstances. At all events she had conducted herself rather skilfully at the Yepanchins: she made no mention of her brother for weeks: she was always extremely frank and honest and behaved with simple dignity. As to the depths of her conscience, she was never afraid to look into them and did not reproach herself in the least. This is what gave her strength. One thing she did notice about herself was that she lost her temper too easily, perhaps, that she had a good deal of pride, and even wounded vanity too; she noticed this at certain times particularly, for example, almost every time she left the Yepanchins.

And now, as we have already said, she was returning home from their house in melancholy, rueful reflection. There was a hint of bitter mockery in her dejection too. Ptitsyn lived in an unattractive but spacious wooden house on a dusty street in Pavlovsk. It was shortly to become his own property, so he was already engaged in selling it in turn to someone else. As she mounted the porch, Varya could hear an extraordinary noise coming from aloft and made out the shouting voices of her brother and papa. Entering the drawing-room, she caught sight of Ganya pacing up and down, white with fury and almost tearing his hair; she frowned and sank on to a sofa with an air of exhaustion, keeping her hat on. Very well aware that if she kept silent another minute and failed to ask her brother why he was pacing the room, he would certainly lose his temper, Varya at length hastened to speak up in the form of a question:

'Same as before?'

'Same as before indeed!' cried Ganya. 'The same—no, lord knows what's going on now, but it's not the same! The old man's working himself into a frenzy . . . mother's bawling. Honestly,

Varya, say what you like, but I'm going to turn him out of the house or . . . or I'll leave myself', he added, doubtless recollecting that he couldn't very well turn people out of someone else's house.

'One must make allowances', Varya murmured.

'Allowances for what? Who for?' Ganya flared up. 'For his vile doings? No, you can say what you like, but this is impossible, impossible, impossible! And the way he behaves: he's the one to blame and yet he still goes throwing his weight about. "The gate's not big enough for me, take the fence down! . . ." What are you sitting there like that for? Are you not well?'

'I'm all right', responded Varya, irritated.

Ganya looked at her more closely.

'Have you been over there?'

'Yes.'

'Wait, they're at their shouting again! It's a disgrace, especially at a time like this!'

'What time is that? There's nothing special about it.'

'Found out anything?' he asked.

'Nothing unexpected at least. I've found out it's all true. My husband was closer to the truth than either of us; it's turned out as he forecast all along. Where is he?'

'He's out. What's happened?'

'The prince is the official fiancé, that's settled. The elder sisters told me. Aglaya has consented; they've even stopped pretending (there's been so much secretiveness up till now). Adelaida's wedding has been postponed again so both weddings can take place together on the same day—romantic isn't it! Just like a poem. And you'd be better employed composing a wedding poem than pacing up and down for nothing. Princess Belokonskaya is going to be there this evening; she's come just at the right time; there'll be company. He'll be presented to Belokonskaya, although he's met her already; then they'll announce it, I believe. The only thing they're worried about is in case he drops or smashes something when he comes into the room, or flops over himself; that would be just like him.'

Ganya heard her out with great attention, but to his sister's surprise, this stunning news seemed to have no corresponding effect on him at all.

'Well, well, that was the way things were going', he said after a reflective pause. 'That's the end, then!' he added with an odd sort of grin, glancing slyly at his sister's face as he went on pacing back and forth, but much more slowly now.

'It's a good thing you can take it philosophically at least; I must say I'm glad', said Varya.

'Yes, it's a weight off the shoulders; yours at least.'

'I believe I've worked for your interests in good faith, without arguing or bothering you; I've never asked you what sort of happiness you were looking for with Aglaya.'

'It wasn't . . . happiness I was looking for, was it?'

'Well, please don't start analysing it! Of course it was. Of course for us it's all over: we've got the worst of it. I must confess I've never been able to take the business seriously; I only took it on "just in case", counting on those funny ways of hers, but mainly to please you; it was ten-to-one against it coming off. I don't even know yet just what it was you were after.'

'Now you and your husband will start pushing me into the civil service, reading me lectures on perseverance and will-power, taking care of the pennies and so forth, I know it off by heart', Ganya gave a loud laugh.

'He's got some new scheme in mind!' thought Varya.

'How are they taking it—are they pleased—the parents, I mean?' Ganya asked suddenly.

'N-no, I don't think so. Still, you know yourself; the general is pleased; the mother is worried; even before, she always loathed the idea of him as a fiancé; that's well known.'

'I didn't mean that; he's impossible as a prospective husband, unthinkable, that's obvious. I'm asking about now, what's going on there now? Has formal consent been given?'

'She hasn't said no so far—that's about it, but you can't expect anything else from her. You know how ridiculously shy and bashful she is: when she was a child she used to hide in cupboards to avoid meeting visitors and not come out for two and three hours at a time; she's grown up to be a great hulking girl but she's just the same now. You know, I have an odd feeling it's really serious, even on her side. They say she makes awful fun of the prince morning till night, just to cover things up, but no doubt she manages to say something to him on the quiet every

day, because he looks as if he's walking on air, he just glows . . .
He's terribly droll, they tell me. They told me that themselves. I
also got the feeling they were laughing at me to my face, the older
girls, I mean.'

Ganya started scowling eventually; Varya might have been
enlarging on this theme deliberately, so as to find out what he was
really thinking. But once more there came shouting from above.

'I'll kick him out!' barked Ganya, as if glad to vent his
exasperation on something.

'And then he'll go disgracing us everywhere like he did
yesterday.'

'What . . . what do you mean, yesterday? What's like yesterday?
Surely he didn't? . . .' All of a sudden, Ganya was horribly
alarmed.

'Oh lord, don't you know?' Varya recovered herself.

'What . . . it surely can't be that he was there?' exclaimed
Ganya, fairly exploding with shame and fury. 'Good God, but
you've just come from there! Did you find out anything? Was the
old man there? Yes or no?'

And Ganya made a rush for the door; Varya flung herself at
him and clutched him with both hands.

'What are you doing? Where are you off to?' she said. 'Let him
out now and he'll do something a lot worse, he'll go round to
everybody!'

'What did he do there? What did he say?'

'Oh, they couldn't tell me themselves; they couldn't under-
stand him. He just frightened them all. He went to see General
Yepanchin but he was out; then he demanded to see Lizaveta
Prokofievna. First of all, he asked her for a job, to work for her.
Then he started complaining about us, me and my husband, and
especially you . . . he said all sorts of things.'

'Couldn't you find out?' Ganya trembled, on the verge of
hysterics.

'How could I? He could barely understand himself what he
was saying, and perhaps they didn't tell me everything.'

Ganya clutched his head and ran to the window; Varya sat
down by the other window.

'Aglaya's a funny girl', she remarked suddenly. 'Stops me and
says: "Please pass on my special personal regards to your parents;

I shall probably find an opportunity to see your papa in the near future." She said it so seriously, awfully strange . . .'

'She wasn't being sarcastic, was she?'

'That's the point, she wasn't; that's the odd thing about it.'

'Does she know about the old man or not, what do you think?'

'I haven't the least doubt that they know nothing in the house; but you've given me an idea: perhaps Aglaya does know. She's the only one who does, because her sisters were as surprised as I was when she passed on her regards to father so seriously. And why just to him? If she knows, the prince must have told her.'

'It's not hard to find out who told her! A thief! That's the last straw. A thief in the family, "the head of the family".'

'Oh, what rubbish!' shouted Varya, losing her temper completely. 'A drunken prank, no more than that. And who invented it all? Lebedev, the prince . . . they're no better themselves; giants of intellect!'

'The old man is a thief and a drunkard', Ganya pursued bitterly, 'I'm a pauper, my sister's husband's a money-lender—Aglaya must have been really impressed! Very nice, I must say!'

'That sister's husband who is a money-lender . . .'

'Feeds me, is that it? Please, don't mince words.'

'Why are you in such a temper?' Varya recovered herself. 'You don't understand the situation, you're like a schoolboy. You think all those things might have damaged you in Aglaya's eyes? You don't know the sort she is; she would reject the most eligible fiancé and be delighted to run off and starve in a garret with some student—that's her dream! You could never comprehend how intriguing she would find you if you were capable of enduring our circumstances with pride and fortitude. The prince hooked her, firstly because he wasn't trying, and secondly because everybody regards him as an idiot. It's the very fact that she's set her family by the ears over him that she really enjoys. Ah-h, how little you understand!'

'Well now, we'll see whether I do or not', muttered Ganya enigmatically. 'Still I wouldn't like her to know about the old man. I thought the prince would hold back from telling her. He did keep Lebedev quiet; he didn't want to tell me everything either, when I insisted . . .'

'So you can see for yourself, everybody knows in any case. So what do you want now? What are you hoping to achieve? Even if there was any hope left, this would only make her look on you as a martyr.'

'Oh, she'd be scared of a public scandal too, never mind her romantic ideas. Thus far and no further, everyone draws the line somewhere; you're all like that.'

'You say Aglaya would be scared?' Varya burst out, giving her brother a contemptuous look. 'What a nasty little soul you've got! None of you deserve to get a thing. Suppose she is absurd and has her little ways, she's still a thousand times better than any of us.'

'Well all right, all right, don't get upset', murmured Ganya complacently.

'It's mother I'm sorry for', Varya went on. 'I'm worried in case she gets to hear about this business of father's, oh dear, I am afraid!'

'No doubt she has now', remarked Ganya.

Varya got up to go upstairs to Nina Alexandrovna, but stopped and looked closely at her brother.

'Who on earth could have told her?'

'It must have been Ippolit. It would have been a treat for him to report it to mother as soon as he moved here.'

'But how did he come to know, tell me if you please. The prince and Lebedev resolved not to tell anyone. Even Kolya doesn't know about it.'

'Ippolit? He found out himself. You have no idea what a cunning little beast he is; the kind of scandalmonger he is and what a nose he has for sniffing out anything unpleasant, anything scandalous. Believe me or not, but I'm sure he has Aglaya eating out of his hand! And if he hasn't, he will. Rogozhin has some connection with him as well. How can the prince fail to notice it? And how he'd love to catch me out now! He regards me as his personal enemy; I realized that long ago, but why this, what he hopes to gain is beyond me, he's dying, after all! But I'll get the better of him; you'll see, he won't catch me out, it'll be the other way round.'

'Why did you get him to come here if you hate him so much? And is he worth getting the better of?'

'You were the one who advised bringing him here.'

'I thought he would be useful; did you know he's fallen in love with Aglaya himself now and been writing to her? They were asking me about it . . . he was on the point of writing to Lizaveta Prokofievna.'

'He's not a danger in that sense', said Ganya, with a venomous laugh. 'Still, there's something afoot. It's quite likely he is in love, he's a boy! But . . . he wouldn't write anonymous letters to the old woman. He's such a spiteful, worthless, conceited nobody . . . I'm convinced, I know for certain he's made me out to be an intriguer to her—that was the first step. I have to admit, fool that I was, I said rather too much to him. I thought he'd be on my side, if only to get even with the prince; he's such a cunning little beast! Oh I can see right through him now. He heard about the theft from his mother, the captain's widow. If the old man did nerve himself to do it, it was on account of the widow. All of a sudden, right out of the blue, he informs me that "the general" has promised his mother four hundred roubles, just like that, straight out, no beating about the bush. I saw it all, of course. And the way he peered into my eyes with a kind of gloating; no doubt he told mama as well, just for the pleasure of breaking her heart. And why isn't he dying, tell me that! He promised to die in three weeks, and here he is putting on weight! He's stopped coughing; yesterday evening he said himself he hadn't coughed up blood for two days.'

'Get rid of him.'

'I don't hate him, I despise him', announced Ganya proudly. 'Well all right, all right, suppose I hate him, suppose I do!' he cried suddenly, absolutely furious. 'And I'll tell him so to his face, even when he's dying on his bed! If you'd read his confession—lord, what naive insolence! It's Lieutenant Pirogov all over again, or Nozdrev* in a tragedy, a wretched urchin too! Oh, I'd have loved to give him a thrashing, just to give him a shock! Now he's getting his own back on everybody because he didn't manage to do it that other time . . . What's that? More noise up there! What is going on anyway? I'm not standing for it, and that's flat. Ptitsyn!' he shouted at his brother-in-law, who had just come in. 'What is all this, is there to be no end of it? It's . . . it's . . .'

But the din was rapidly approaching. The door was suddenly

flung wide and old Ivolgin, shaking, purple in the face, and beside himself with rage, also pounced on Ptitsyn. Behind the old man came Nina Alexandrovna, Kolya, and, bringing up the rear, Ippolit.

2

FIVE days had passed since Ippolit had moved into Ptitsyn's house. It happened naturally somehow, without too many words or any disagreement between him and the prince; not only had they not quarrelled, but to all appearances they had parted friends. Gavrila Ardalionovich, so hostile towards Ippolit the other evening, came to see him, of his own accord, on the third day after the event, most likely prompted by some sudden idea. Rogozhin too, for some reason, began to visit the invalid. At first, the prince thought it might well be for the best if the 'poor boy' were to move out of his house. During the course of the move, however, Ippolit spoke of moving to Ptitsyn, 'who is kind enough to give me a place of my own', and as if deliberately, not once saying that he was moving to Ganya's, although it was Ganya who had insisted on him being accepted in the house. Ganya noticed this at the time and it rankled within him.

He had been correct in saying to his sister that the invalid was on the mend. A glance was enough to see that Ippolit really did feel somewhat better than before. He came unhurriedly into the room behind the rest, wearing a sardonic and ill-natured grin. Nina Alexandrovna entered in a state of considerable alarm. She had altered a great deal over the last six months and had lost weight; having married off her daughter and moved into her house, she had virtually ceased to interfere overtly in her childrens' affairs. Kolya was worried and looked bemused; there was a lot he hadn't understood in the 'general's madness' as he termed it, since of course he did not know the principal reasons for this latest domestic upheaval. But he could see that his father was constantly picking quarrels everywhere to such an extent, and had altered so greatly all of a sudden, that he seemed not to be the same man. It also disturbed him that the old man had practically stopped drinking for the past three days. He knew his father had fallen out with Lebedev and the prince, even quarrelled with them. Kolya had just got back to the house with a half-bottle of vodka, bought with his own money.

'Honestly, mama', he had assured Nina Alexandrovna upstairs, 'honestly, it's better if he has a drink. He hasn't touched a drop for three days now; he must be miserable. Really, it's better; I used to bring him drink in prison . . .'

The general flung the door open and stood on the threshold, fairly quivering with indignation.

'My dear sir!' he thundered at Ptitsyn. 'If you have really decided to sacrifice a venerable old man to a milksop and an atheist, your own father sir, at least your wife's father, a man who has served his sovereign, I shall never set foot inside your house again from this moment on. Make your choice, sirrah, choose at once: me or this—screw here! Yes, screw! I said it without thinking, but he is a screw! Because he bores into my heart like a screw, and shows not the least respect . . . like a screw!'

'Don't you mean a corkscrew?' Ippolit put in.

'No, not a corkscrew, for you see a general before you, not a bottle. I have decorations, medals . . . and you, sir, have damn all! It's either him or me! Decide, sirrah, this minute, this very minute!' he shouted at Ptitsyn again in his rage. Kolya at this point placed a chair for him, and he subsided on to it, practically exhausted.

'Really, it would be better if you had a lie-down sir', muttered Ptitsyn, aghast.

'He's still got nerve enough to make threats!' said Ganya to his sister in an undertone.

'Lie down?' shouted the general. 'You are insulting me, my dear sir; I'm not drunk. I can see', he pursued, getting to his feet again, 'that everything here is against me. Everything and everybody. Very well! I'm going . . . but let me tell you, dear sir, let me tell you . . .'

He was not permitted to finish, and they sat him down again; they began imploring him to calm himself. Ganya went off in a fury into a corner. Nina Alexandrovna was trembling and weeping.

'But what did I do to him? What's he complaining about?' cried Ippolit, grinning hugely.

'Haven't you done anything then?' Nina Alexandrovna put in suddenly. 'You especially should be ashamed and . . . tormenting an old man in that inhuman way . . . especially in your position . . .'

'In the first place, just what is my position, madam? I hold you in high regard, madam, you in particular, personally, but . . .'

'He's a screw!' shouted the general. 'He's boring into my heart and soul! He wants me to believe in atheism! Listen to me, milksop, I was showered with honours before you were born; you're just an envious worm, cut in half, with a cough . . . dying of spite and unbelief . . . And why did Ganya bring you here? Everyone's against me, from strangers to my own son!'

'Oh stop it, do, playing the ham!' shouted Ganya. 'You'd do better not to disgrace us all over town!'

'What, me shame you, milksop! You? I could only do you honour, not bring you disgrace!'

This time they couldn't restrain him from leaping to his feet; but Ganya too had evidently thrown restraint to the winds.

'Get away with you, talking about honour!' he cried savagely.

'What did you say?' thundered the general, going pale as he advanced a step towards him.

'That I only have to open my mouth for . . .', Ganya cried suddenly, but stopped short. Both of them stood facing each other, deeply shaken, especially Ganya.

'Ganya, stop it!' cried Nina Alexandrovna, darting forward to restrain her son.

'What nonsense, all of you!' Varya snapped indignantly. 'That's enough, mama', she said, taking hold of her.

'I'm only sparing him for mother's sake', Ganya declared tragically.

'Speak!' roared the general in a veritable frenzy. 'Speak, on pain of a father's curse . . . speak!'

'Your curse! Now I'm really frightened! And whose fault is it that you've been behaving like a mad thing for eight days? Eight days, sir, you see I've been keeping count . . . Just see you don't drive me too far: I'll tell them everything . . . Why did you haul yourself over to the Yepanchins yesterday? And you call yourself an old man, grey hairs, the head of a family! You're a fine one, I must say!'

'Shut up, Ganka!' shouted Kolya. 'Shut up, you fool!'

'But what about me, how have I offended him?' Ippolit pursued, in the same sneering tone of voice. 'Why does he call me a screw, you heard him? It was him who pestered me; he came along just now and started talking about some Captain Yeropegov. I don't desire your company in the least, General; I avoided it before, as you know very well. Captain Yeropegov's affairs are nothing to do with me, are they? I didn't come here on account of Captain Yeropegov. I merely expressed my opinion aloud that perhaps this Captain Yeropegov never existed. He went and raised the roof.'

'He most certainly never existed!' snapped Ganya.

The general, however, stood dumbfounded, gazing round blankly. The extreme bluntness of his son's words had stunned him. For an initial instant he was unable to find a word to say. Only after Ippolit had laughed uproariously at Ganya's response, with a shout of: 'There you are, you heard him, your own son says it too—there never was a Captain Yeropegov', did the bewildered old man finally mumble something:

'Kapiton Yeropegov, not captain . . . Kapiton . . . lieutenant-colonel, retired, Yeropegov . . . Kapiton.'

'There was no Kapiton either!' Ganya was wholly incensed by now.

'Why . . . why wasn't there?' mumbled the general, as the colour flooded his cheeks.

'That's enough, now!' Ptitsyn and Varya tried to halt matters.

'Do shut up, Ganya!' Kolya shouted again.

Their intervention, however, seemed to jog the general's memory.

'What do you mean wasn't't? How did he not exist?' he flung menacingly at his son.

'Because he just didn't. He didn't and that's all about it, and he couldn't have existed! So there! And stand away from me, I tell you.'

'And this is my son . . . my own flesh and blood, whom I . . . oh God! Yeropegov, Yeroshka Yeropegov never existed!'

'There you are, one minute it's Yeroshka, then it's

Kapitoshka!' Ippolit turned the screw.

'Kapitoshka, sirrah, Kapitoshka, not Yeroshka! Kapiton, Kapitan Alekseyevich, I mean Kapiton . . . lieutenant-colonel . . . retired . . . married Maria . . . Maria Petrovna Su . . . Su . . . friend and comrade . . . Sutugova . . . knew him from cadet college. I shed my blood for him . . . shielded him . . . killed. There was no Kapitoshka Yeropegov! Didn't exist!'

The general was shouting recklessly, but in a way that suggested it was unconnected with the matter in hand. Certainly, on another occasion he would have endured things a good deal more wounding than the news of the total non-existence of Kapiton Yeropegov. He would have done some shouting, created a scene, lost his temper, but in the end he would have gone upstairs to his room to have a lie-down. Now, however, such are the extraordinary ways of the human heart, it turned out that an insult such as this scepticism about Yeropegov was the last straw. The old man went purple, raised his arms, and shouted out:

'That's enough! My curse . . . out of this house! Kolya, fetch my bag, I'm going . . . away!'

He hurried out in a towering rage. Nina Alexandrovna, Kolya, and Ptitsyn rushed after him.

'Now what have you done!' said Varya to her brother. 'He'll take himself off over there again. The disgrace, the disgrace of it!'

'Then he shouldn't go round thieving!' shouted Ganya, almost choking with anger. Suddenly his eyes lit on Ippolit; Ganya fairly shook. 'And as for you, dear sir', he cried, 'you would do well to remember that you're in someone else's house after all, and . . . enjoying hospitality, and you shouldn't be teasing an old man, who has obviously gone out of his mind.'

Ippolit also seemed to wince, but instantly recovered himself.

'I can't wholly agree with you that your papa has gone out of his mind', he replied placidly. 'On the contrary, it appears to me that he's been improving of late, honestly; you don't believe me? He's so cautious and suspicious, sounds everything out and weighs his every word . . . He had an ulterior motive in starting on about this Kapitoshka; imagine, he wanted to lead me on to . . .'

'Oh, what do I damn well care what he wanted to lead you on

to! Kindly don't try any of your tricks with me and stop prevaricating, sir!' yelled Ganya. 'If you know the real reason for the old man's state of mind (and you've been spying away on me these five days, so you probably do know), then you certainly oughtn't to be tormenting the . . . unfortunate man, and torturing my mother by exaggerating the affair, because the whole thing's just nonsense, a drunken escapade, no more than that, not even proven. I don't give that much for it . . . but you have to taunt him with it and pry, because you . . . you are . . .'

'A screw', Ippolit grinned.

'Because you're trash, tormenting people for half an hour, trying to frighten them by threatening to shoot yourself with your unloaded pistol, with which you made such a disgraceful spectacle of yourself, you failed suicide, you walking bag of gall. I afforded you hospitality, you put on weight, stopped coughing, and you repay me . . .'

'Just two words, if you please, sir; I'm staying with Varvara Ardalionovna, not you, and I rather fancy that you're enjoying Mister Ptitsyn's hospitality yourself. Four days ago, I asked my mother to find me a flat in Pavlovsk and come over herself, because I really do feel better here, though I haven't put on weight and I still cough. My mother informed me yesterday evening that the apartment is ready, and for my part, I hasten to advise you that after thanking your dear mother and sister, I shall be moving there this very day, a decision I made yesterday evening. Forgive me, I interrupted you; you had a good deal more to say, I think.'

'Oh, in that case . . .', Ganya had begun to shake.

'In that case, allow me to sit down', Ippolit went on, supremely composed, seating himself on the chair the general had occupied. 'I am ill, after all; well, now I'm ready to listen to you, especially since it's our last conversation and may even be our last meeting.'

Ganya suddenly felt ashamed of himself.

'Rest assured, I shan't demean myself by settling accounts with you', he said, 'and if you . . .'

'There's no need for you to be so high and mighty', Ippolit cut him short. 'As for me, the first day I came here I vowed to myself that I would not forego the pleasure of giving you a piece of my mind, as thoroughly and candidly as I could, when we were parting. I intend to fulfil that vow—after you have finished of course.'

'And I'm asking you to leave the room.'

'Talking would be better. You'll regret not having had your say.'

'Don't, Ippolit; all this is terribly embarrassing; please be good enough to stop it', said Varya.

'Just to please a lady', Ippolit laughed heartily as he got up. 'By all means, Varvara Ardalionovna, I'm willing to cut it short for your sake, but that's all I can do because some clarification of matters between me and your brother has become an absolute necessity, and I am resolved not to go before clearing up any misunderstandings.'

'You're nothing but a scandalmonger', cried Ganya. 'That's why you can't bear to go before spreading some more tales.'

'There you are', observed Ippolit coolly, 'you can't keep it in. Really, you'll regret it if you don't say all you have to say. I'll yield the floor to you. I'll wait.'

Gavrila Ardalionovich looked scornfully at him and said nothing.

'You won't. You want to show your firmness of character—please yourself. As for me, I'll be as brief as possible. Two or three times today I've been twitted on the score of hospitality; that's unfair. By inviting me to your house, you were trying to ensnare me yourselves; you counted on me wanting to avenge myself on the prince. You had also heard that Aglaya Ivanovna had shown sympathy for me and read my confession. Reckoning, for some reason, that I would devote myself to your interests just like that, you hoped to find an ally in me. I am sparing the details! I am not asking for any admissions or confirmation on your part either; I'm content to leave you with your conscience, now that we thoroughly understand one another.'

'But you're making a mountain out of a molehill!' Varya cried.

'I told you: a puppy and scandalmonger', said Ganya.

'With your permission, Varvara Ardalionovna, I will go on. The prince, of course, I can neither love nor esteem; but he is a truly good man, although . . . absurd as well. But there would have been no reason at all for my hating him. I didn't let on while your brother was trying to incite me against the prince; I just looked forward to something of a laugh when it all came out. I knew your brother would blurt it all out to me and make a complete mess of it all. And so it turned out . . . I'm willing to have mercy on him now, but solely out of my regard for you, Varvara Ardalionovna. But having made it clear to you that I'm not as easily taken in as all that, I'll also explain why I was so strongly disposed to hold your brother up to ridicule. I want you to know that I did it out of hatred, I candidly admit that. Before dying (because I am dying even if I am putting on weight, as you assure me), before dying, I felt I would depart for paradise vastly easier in my mind if I managed to make a fool of at least one representative out of that numberless category of people who have persecuted me all my life, whom I have hated all my life, and of whom your highly esteemed brother is such a glaring example. I detest you, Gavrila Ardalionovich, for the sole reason—and you may find this surprising—*for the sole reason* that you are the embodiment, the personification, the incarnation and acme of all that is most brazen, smug, vulgar, and nauseatingly commonplace! You are pompously commonplace, a commonplace full of self-assurance and Olympian calm; you are the most ordinary of the ordinary! Not the smallest hint of an original idea is ever destined to take shape either in your heart or your mind. But your envy knows no bounds; you are firmly convinced that you are a supreme genius, but doubt does visit you sometimes all the same, in your darker moments, and you are filled with resentment and envy. Oh, there are still dark clouds on your horizon; they will pass when you become completely stupid, which won't be long; still, you have a long and chequered road ahead of you, I won't say a bright one, I'm glad to say. To begin with, I prophesy that you will never gain a certain lady . . .'

'Well, this is intolerable!' cried Varya. 'Will you stop, you nasty, spiteful creature?'

Ganya turned pale, trembled, and said nothing. Ippolit stopped, bestowed an intent and gloating look on him, then transferred his gaze to Varya, grinned, bowed, and went out without adding a single word.

Ganya might justifiably have complained at his fate and lack of success. For some time, Varya could not bring herself to speak to him, and didn't even glance at him when he passed by her with his long strides; at length he went over to the window and stood with his back to her. Varya was thinking of the Russian saying: 'It cuts both ways.' Once again, uproar could be heard from upstairs.

'Are you going?' Ganya had abruptly turned to her, as he heard her getting up. 'Wait a moment; just take a look at this.'

He came over to her and tossed on to the chair a piece of paper, folded into the shape of a little note.

'Heavens!' cried Varya, clasping her hands.

The note contained exactly seven lines.

'Gavrila Ardalionovich! Convinced of your kindly feelings towards me, I am venturing to ask your advice in a certain matter of great importance to me. I would like to meet you tomorrow at precisely seven o'clock, on the green bench. It is not far from our villa. Varvara Ardalionovna, who *must* accompany you, knows the place very well.

A. Y.'

'Well really, what is one to make of her after this?' Varya gestured helplessly.

However little Ganya felt like boasting at that moment, he could not help flaunting his triumph, especially after Ippolit's humiliating predictions. A self-satisfied smile lit up his face, and Varya herself fairly beamed with joy.

'And this on the very day when they are announcing the engagement. Really, what is one to make of her after this?'

'What do you think she wants to talk about tomorrow?' Ganya asked.

'That doesn't matter, the main thing is she wants to meet you for the first time in six months. Now listen to me, Ganya: whatever's going on and however it turns out, bear in mind it's *important*! It's of the utmost importance. Don't start bragging again, and don't miss your chance again, but watch you aren't too timid either. She's bound to have realized why I've been trailing over there for the last six months. And just imagine: she never said so much as a word to me today, not a hint. I actually had to smuggle myself in there; the old woman didn't know I was there, or she'd have turned me out most likely. I took the risk for your sake, to find out at all costs . . .'

Again there came noise and shouting from up above; several people were coming down the stairs.

'We mustn't let it happen now for anything!' cried Varya in a flurry of alarm. 'There mustn't be a hint of scandal! Go and apologize!'

But the head of the family was already outside: Kolya was lugging a bag in his wake. Nina Alexandrovna stood weeping on the porch; she was trying to run after him but Ptitsyn was restraining her.

'You're only making it worse doing that', he was telling her. 'He's got nowhere to go, he'll be fetched back in half an hour. I've already had a word with Kolya about it; let him have his fun.'

'Why the heroics, where are you going then?' shouted Ganya from the window. 'You've got nowhere to go, have you?'

'Come back, papa!' shouted Varya. 'The neighbours can hear.'

The general halted, turned round, flung out his arm, and cried:

'My curse be upon this house!'

'He would ham it up of course', muttered Ganya, banging the window shut.

The neighbours actually were listening. Varya ran out of the room.

When she had gone, Ganya picked the note up from the table, kissed it, clicked his tongue, and pirouetted in the air.

3

THE commotion over the general would have come to nothing at any other time. There had been similar stupid incidents in the past, though not very often; as a rule he was a very meek person with genuinely virtuous inclinations. A hundred times, perhaps, he had taken up arms against the disorderly habits which had overwhelmed him in recent years. He would suddenly recall that he was a 'head of a family', make it up with his wife, and weep genuine tears. He esteemed Nina Alexandrovna to the point of adoration because she had silently forgiven him so many times and went on loving him, even in his clownish and humiliating moods. The noble struggle against muddle and laxity did not last long as a rule; the general was, in his own way, too much the man of spasmodic impulse; he was simply unable to stand the idle life of a penitent in his own household, and ended up by rebelling; he would indulge in reckless behaviour while, at the same time, reproaching himself for so doing, but he couldn't stop himself: he would start a quarrel, his speech would become high-flown and eloquent, he would demand that boundless and impossible veneration be accorded him; eventually he would vanish from the house, sometimes for long periods. Over the last two years he had had only a vague idea of his family's doings, apart from hearsay; he had ceased to be involved in the details, and felt not the slightest inclination to act otherwise.

This time, however, there was something unusual in 'the commotion over the general': everyone seemed to know something and everyone seemed afraid to talk about it. The general had 'formally' appeared to his family, that is, returned to Nina Alexandrovna only a matter of three days previously, but somehow not at all peaceable or remorseful as he had invariably been on his previous appearances—quite the contrary; he displayed marked irritability. He was voluble and agitated, talking heatedly to everyone he came across, falling upon them, as it were, but always on subjects so wildly diverse as to render it wholly impossible to find out what was really worrying him. At times he was jovial, but more often than not he would be lost in thought—though about what exactly, he didn't know himself. He would abruptly raise some topic—to do with the Yepanchins, the prince, or Lebedev—then he would break off all of a sudden and stop altogether, responding to all further questioning with a blank smile, unaware that he had been asked a question or even that he was smiling. He had passed the previous night moaning and groaning and had fairly worn Nina Alexandrovna out. She had been up all night preparing hot poultices for him; towards morning he had suddenly dropped off to sleep for four hours, before waking up with an intensely agitated fit of morbid depression, which had culminated in the quarrel with Ippolit and his 'curse upon this house'. It was also noticeable that over the three days he had been constantly subject to vainglorious moods and was, in consequence, extremely quick to take offence. For his part, Kolya kept on reassuring his mother that all this was a result of the general's craving for drink, and perhaps for

Lebedev, with whom he had become extraordinarily friendly of late. Three days before, however, he had suddenly quarrelled with Lebedev and broken with him in a towering rage; there was even some sort of scene with the prince. Kolya had requested an explanation from the prince, but eventually began to suspect there was something that even he appeared unwilling to tell him. If, as Ganya had assumed with perfectly good grounds, there actually had been some specific talk between Ippolit and Nina Alexandrovna, it was strange that the ill-disposed gentleman, whom Ganya had so bluntly dubbed a scandalmonger, had not taken pleasure in enlightening Kolya in the same fashion. It was very possible that he was not such a spiteful 'puppy' as Ganya had depicted him when talking to his sister, but was malicious after some other fashion; nor was he likely to have passed on his observations to Nina Alexandrovna solely with a view to 'breaking her heart'. We should not forget that the springs of human action are usually infinitely more complex and various than we constantly make them out to be afterwards, and can rarely be defined clearly. Sometimes the best thing the narrator can do is restrict himself to a straightforward recital of events. That is what we shall do for the rest of this account of the contretemps involving the general; try as we may, we are compelled to allot somewhat more attention and space to this secondary character in our story than we had originally planned.

Events had succeeded one another in the following order:

When Lebedev returned later on in the day, after his trip to Petersburg with the general in search of Ferdischenko, he said nothing in particular to the prince. Had not the prince been extremely distracted and occupied with other important personal considerations, he would soon have noticed that, so far from volunteering any information over the following two days, Lebedev seemed unaccountably intent on avoiding him. When at length this did strike him, the prince was surprised to note that, if they chanced to run across one another during those two days, he never found Lebedev otherwise than in a most blissful state of mind, and almost invariably accompanied by the general. The two friends were never apart for a moment. The prince occasionally overheard the sound of loud and lively conversation drifting down from upstairs, laughter and good-natured argument; once even, very late at night, he suddenly caught the unexpected strains of a bacchanalian barrack-room song and at once recognized the general's throaty bass. The song, however, did not last long before breaking off abruptly. There ensued almost an hour of extremely animated and apparently drunken conversation. It might have been guessed that the friends who had been having such a good time upstairs were now embracing, and one of them at length burst into tears. Then followed a sudden violent quarrel, also rapidly subsiding soon after. All this time, Kolya had been in an oddly anxious frame of mind. For the most part, the prince was out of the house and would sometimes get home very late; he was always told that Kolya had been looking and asking for him all day. When they did meet, however, Kolya was unable to tell him anything in particular, other than that he wasn't happy about the general and his present mode of behaviour: 'They trail about getting drunk in a tavern not far from here, hug each other and quarrel in the street, egging each other on; there's no separating them.' When the prince pointed out to him that the same thing had gone on practically every day previously, Kolya was at a loss how to reply or explain the precise nature of his present uneasiness.

The morning after the bacchanalian song and quarrel, as the prince was leaving the house at around eleven, he was confronted by the general, who was extremely excited about something, almost distraught.

'I've been seeking the honour and opportunity of meeting you for ages, my dear Lev Nikolayevich, a long time, a very long time', he mumbled, squeezing the prince's hand extremely hard, almost painfully, 'a long, long time.'

The prince asked him to be seated.

'No, I won't sit down, and in any case I'm detaining you, I . . . some other time. Still, it seems I may offer felicitations on . . . the fulfilment . . . of your heart's desire.'

'What heart's desire?'

The prince was embarrassed. He had been under the impression, like many another in his situation, that absolutely no one had seen, or guessed, or realized anything at all.

'Don't distress yourself, don't distress yourself! I shan't intrude on the intimate feelings. I've been through it myself and I know how it is when someone else's . . . nose . . . as the saying goes, pokes itself where it's not wanted. I go through that every morning. I've come about another matter, an important matter. A most important matter, Prince.'

The prince again asked him to sit down and did so himself.

'It's just for one second . . . I've come for some advice. Of course, I am living without any practical concerns, but out of self-respect and . . . business efficiency, in which Russians are so lacking, as a rule . . . I wish to place myself, my wife, and my children in a position . . . in a nutshell, Prince, I'm seeking advice.'

The prince warmly praised his intention.

'Well, that's all nonsense', the general was quick to break in, 'that's not the main thing I wanted to talk about, it's something else, something most important. I made up my mind to explain matters to you in particular, Lev Nikolayevich, being a man in whose sincerity of approach and nobility of feeling I have the utmost confidence as . . . as . . . you're not surprised at my words, Prince?'

The prince was watching his visitor with the keenest attention and curiosity, if not with any special surprise. The old man was rather pale, his lips quivered faintly at times, and his hands couldn't seem to find anywhere to put themselves. He had been sitting only a few minutes, yet he had contrived more than once to rise abruptly from his chair and sit down again just as abruptly, obviously not paying the slightest attention to his movements. There were some books on the table and he picked one up, still talking, glanced at the opened page, then closed it and replaced it at once before picking up another without opening it, and went on holding it in his right hand thereafter, constantly waving it about in the air.

'Enough!' he cried suddenly. 'I can see that I've been a great nuisance.'

'Not in the least, good heavens, do go on; on the contrary, I'm listening most carefully and trying to guess . . .'

'Prince! I wish to place myself in a position of respect . . . I want to respect myself and . . . my rights.'

'A man with such a desire is worthy of respect on that account alone.'

The prince brought out the hackneyed phrase in the certainty that it would have an excellent effect. He sensed instinctively that some such high-sounding but agreeable sentence, spoken at the appropriate moment, might well disarm and soothe the soul of a man like the general, especially in the situation he was in. At all events, a visitor like this had to be sent away with a heart made light, and this was his aim.

The phrase flattered, touched, and greatly pleased the general: he was suddenly profoundly moved, altered his tone instantly, and plunged into lengthy and rapturous explanations. But however much effort he made to listen, the prince literally could not comprehend a word of it. The general spoke for ten minutes, vehemently and rapidly, as though hard put to it to express his milling thoughts; towards the end, indeed, tears began glistening in his eyes, but for all that, it was only sentences without beginning or end, unexpected words and unexpected thoughts, bursting forth unexpectedly and tumbling over one another.

'Enough! You have understood me and I am content', he concluded, getting to his feet. 'A heart such as yours cannot fail to understand one who suffers. Prince, you are the ideal of nobility! What are others beside you? But you are young and I bless you. What I really came to ask you was to fix an hour for an important conversation, and that is my chief hope. I seek only friendship and sympathy, Prince; I could never cope with the yearnings of my heart.'

'But why can't it be now? I'm ready to listen . . .'

'No, Prince, no!' the general broke in hotly. 'Not now! Now is but a dream. It is too, too important, too important! That hour of talk will be the hour of irrevocable destiny. That hour will be *mine* and I would not wish us to be interrupted at such a sacred moment by someone coming in, or some brazen fellow, and there are many such', here he bent down towards the prince, whispering in an odd and secretive manner, 'a brazen fellow not worth the heel . . . of your shoe, beloved Prince! Oh, I don't say my shoe! Note particularly that I didn't mention my shoe; because I have too much self-respect to say that bluntly; it is merely that you alone are capable of understanding that, in dismissing my own heel in this case, I may actually be demonstrating an enormous pride in my own dignity. No one else would understand apart from yourself, *he* least of all. *He* understands nothing, Prince; he is totally, totally incapable of understanding! One must have a heart in order to understand!'

Eventually the prince became quite alarmed and fixed a meeting with the general for the same time the following day. The latter departed in high spirits, greatly comforted and almost at peace with himself. That evening at seven, the prince sent to ask Lebedev to come and see him for a moment.

Lebedev appeared with great alacrity, 'esteeming it as an honour', as he at once began on the threshold; there was no hint that he had hidden himself away for three days and obviously avoided encountering the prince. He perched on the edge of the chair, grimacing and smiling, his little laughing eyes peering out; he was rubbing his hands with an intensely naive air of expectation—of hearing something, something tremendously significant, long awaited and guessed by one and all. This jarred on the prince; he was beginning to realize that everyone had suddenly started expecting things from him; they were all giving him glances, as though wanting to congratulate him for something, with their hints, smiles, and winking. Keller had already dropped by for a moment more than once, clearly wanting to offer his felicitations: he had begun rapturously and incoherently, but failed to complete a sentence and swiftly vanished. (He had been drinking very heavily somewhere these last few days, and was notorious in a certain billiard-saloon.) Even Kolya, despite his dejection, had also started up a vague conversation with the prince on a couple of occasions.

The prince asked Lebedev bluntly and rather irritably what he thought of the general's present state and why he was so agitated. He briefly recounted that morning's scene to him.

'Everyone has his troubles, Prince, and . . . especially in our strange and turbulent age, sir; yes indeed, sir', Lebedev replied rather stiffly, and lapsed into an offended silence, with the air of a man grievously disappointed in his expectations.

'What a philosophy!' the prince smiled ironically.

'Philosophy's essential, sir, most essential in an age like ours, sir, in its practical application, but it is neglected, sir, that's the trouble, sir. For my part, dear Prince, though I have been honoured at being entrusted with your confidence in a certain matter you know of, sir, it was only up to a certain point and not a step further than the circumstances relating to that point alone . . . That I understand and am not complaining in the least . . .'

'Lebedev, you're not angry about something, are you?'

'Not at all, not in the least, my dear and most radiant Prince, not in the least!' Lebedev cried blissfully, laying his hand on his heart. 'On the contrary, I have realized at once that neither through my worldly status, nor my qualities of mind and heart, nor my personal wealth, nor my former conduct, let alone knowledge, am I worthy of the honour of your trust, so far exceeding any hopes of mine, and that if I am able to serve you it is as a slave or a hireling, not otherwise . . . I speak in sorrow, not anger, sir.'

'Lukyan Timofeich, please!'

'Not otherwise! So it is now, in the present instance! Meeting you and watching over you with heart and mind, I said to myself that I was not worthy of friendly communication, but in my capacity as landlord, I might receive, at the appropriate moment, before the anticipated event, a warning as it were, or at least an intimation in view of certain impending and anticipated changes . . .'

As he enunciated this, Lebedev, still nurturing hopes of satisfying his curiosity, fixed his sharp little eyes on the prince who was staring at him in astonishment.

'I understand absolutely nothing of all that', cried the prince, almost angry, 'and . . . you are a dreadful schemer!' He suddenly broke into loud genuine laughter.

Lebedev instantly did the same, and his beaming countenance showed that his expectations had been rekindled and even redoubled.

'And do you know what I'm going to tell you, Lukyan Timofeich? Don't take it amiss, but I'm surprised at your simplicity—and not only yours! In your simplicity you're expecting to hear something from me now, this very minute, so that I feel positively conscience-stricken and ashamed that I have nothing with which to satisfy you. I swear that there is absolutely nothing, believe me or believe me not!'

The prince laughed once more.

Lebedev stood on his dignity. It was true that he could be very naive and tiresome in his curiosity; but at the same time he was quite an artful and slippery individual, and on certain occasions he could be rather too crafty-silent; by constantly rebuffing him, the prince had almost made an enemy of him. The prince did not rebuff him, however, because he despised him, but because the object of his curiosity was a delicate one. Even as recently as a few days before, the prince had regarded certain dreams of his own as a crime, whereas Lebedev took the prince's rejection simply as evidence of a physical aversion and mistrust and would go away cut to the heart—jealous not only of Kolya and Keller, but even of his own daughter, Vera Lukyanovna. At this very moment even, he might perhaps have genuinely wished to tell the prince something of surpassing interest to him, but instead he lapsed into a sullen silence and said nothing.

'How then can I be of service to you, dear Prince, since you . . . called me all the same just now?' he said at length, after an interval of silence.

'Oh, it was really about the general', the prince said with a start, also roused from a moment's reflection, 'and . . . about that theft of yours, the one you told me about . . .'

'About what, sir?'

'Why it's as if you don't understand me now! Oh heavens, Lukyan Timofeich, why are you always acting some part! The money, the money, the four hundred roubles you lost that time, in your wallet, that you came here to tell me about, the morning when you were on your way to Petersburg—do you understand me now?'

'Ah, you mean that four hundred roubles!' drawled Lebedev, as if it had just dawned on him. 'Thank you, Prince, for your sincere interest; you flatter me too much, but I found it, sir, long ago!'

'Found it! Ah, thank God!'

'A most generous exclamation on your part, since four hundred roubles is no small matter to a poor man toiling to make a living, with a numerous family of motherless children to bring up . . .'

'That's not what I meant! Of course I'm glad you found it as well', the prince hastily corrected himself, 'but . . . how on earth did you find it?'

'Very easily, sir, I found it under the chair where I had hung my coat, so the wallet obviously must have slipped out of the pocket on to the floor.'

'Under the chair? How can that be—you told me you'd searched in every nook and cranny, didn't you? How on earth did you overlook the most obvious place?'

'That's just it, I did look, sir! I do remember looking, only too well! I crawled about on hands and knees, feeling with my hands, shifting the chair back; I couldn't believe my eyes, but I could see there was nothing there, just a smooth, empty space like the palm of my hand here, sir, but I still kept on feeling around. A person always goes through that faint-hearted feeling when he's very anxious to find ... when there has been an important and grievous loss, sir; he can see there's nothing there, the place is empty, but he still looks there a dozen times.'

'Yes, I dare say; but how could it have happened all the same? ... I still don't understand it', muttered the prince in bewilderment. 'Before, you said it wasn't there and you had searched the place, and now it's suddenly turned up?'

'It's suddenly turned up, sir.'

The prince gave Lebedev a curious look.

'And the general?' he asked abruptly.

'What exactly do you mean, sir—the general, sir?' Lebedev was again at a loss.

'Oh, great heavens! I'm asking you what the general said when you found the wallet under the chair? After all, you'd been looking for it together earlier, hadn't you?'

'Earlier we did, together, sir. But this time I have to admit that I kept quiet, sir, preferring not to inform him that I had found the wallet on my own.'

'But ... what on earth for? Was all the money there?'

'I opened the wallet and the money was all there, to the last rouble, sir.'

'You might have come and told me at least', remarked the prince thoughtfully.

'I was rather afraid to bother you personally, Prince, with your own, perhaps, extremely important, so to speak, considerations to think about; besides I pretended that I hadn't found anything. I opened the wallet, examined it, then closed it and put it back under the chair.'

'But whatever for?'

'Oh n-nothing; curious to see what would happen, sir.' Lebedev giggled all of a sudden and rubbed his hands.

'So it's still lying there after three days?'

'Oh no, sir, it lay there only a day. You see, sir, I half wanted the general to find it, sir. If I'd found it eventually, then why shouldn't the general notice something sticking out from under the chair, staring him in the face, so to speak? I lifted the chair up a number of times and moved it around, so that the wallet was in clear sight, but the general never noticed it, and so it went on for a whole day. He's very abstracted these days, it's hard to make him out; he talks, tells stories, laughs, roars with laughter, and then all of a sudden he flies off the handle with me, I've no idea why, sir. We were going out of the room eventually and I deliberately left the door open; he hesitated and wanted to say something, probably anxious about a wallet with so much money in it, but he got terribly angry all of a sudden and didn't say anything, sir; we hadn't gone two steps down the street when he left me and went off in the other direction. We only got together again in the evening in the tavern.'

'But still, you did pick the wallet up from under the chair in the end?'

'No, sir; that very night it went missing from under the chair, sir.'

'So where on earth is it now, then?'

'Why here, sir', Lebedev laughed suddenly, rising to his full height from the chair and regarding the prince pleasantly, 'it turned up in the skirt of my very own coat. Here, won't you look, have a feel of it, sir.'

Sure enough, there was a sort of pouch-shape in the left-hand flap of the coat, conspicuously protruding; one touch was enough to establish that it was a leather wallet, fallen down through a hole in the pocket.

'I took it out and had a look; it's all there, sir. So I put it back and I've been walking since yesterday morning with it in my coat-lining. It even knocks against my legs, sir.'

'And you don't take any notice of it?'

'And I don't take any notice of it, sir, heh-heh! And just think, dear Prince, though it's not a thing worthy of your special notice, my pockets are always in good repair, and now all of a sudden a hole like that in one night! I've taken a close look and it's as if it had been done with a penknife; incredible, isn't it, sir?'

'And ... the general?'

'He's been angry with me the whole day, yesterday and today; dreadfully peevish, sir; one minute he's on top of the world and quite flatteringly expansive, the next he's weeping sentimental tears, then he'll suddenly lose his temper altogether and really frighten me, sir, honestly he does, sir; after all, I'm not a military man, sir. Yesterday we were sitting in the tavern, and my coat-flap was open right in front of him, as large as life; he glances sideways at it, getting annoyed. He hasn't looked me straight in the eye for a long time now, apart from when he's been very drunk or sentimental; but yesterday he did it twice and a cold shiver ran down my spine. I intend to discover the wallet tomorrow, by the way, but I'll be spending a pleasant evening with him before then.'

'Why are you tormenting him like that?' cried the prince.

'I'm not, Prince, I'm not', Lebedev took him up on this vehemently. 'I really do love him, sir and ... respect him, sir; and now, believe me or believe me not, he's become still dearer to me; I've grown to value him even more, sir!'

Lebedev said all this with such seriousness and sincerity that the prince grew positively indignant.

'You love him and torment him like that! For pity's sake, the very fact that he put the wallet back under the chair in full view and into the coat, by that very fact he's plainly showing you that he doesn't want to deceive you and is genuinely asking your forgiveness. You hear: he's asking your forgiveness! It means he's relying on the delicacy of your feelings; in other words, he believes in your friendship towards him. And you inflict such humiliation on such a ... transparently honourable man!'

'Extremely honourable, Prince, extremely honourable, Prince!' Lebedev rejoined, eyes sparkling. 'And you alone, most noble Prince, could have spoken such a true word! For that alone I am devoted to you to the point of adoration, even, though I'm rotten through and through with vices of all kinds! It is decided! I'll find

the wallet now, sir, and not tomorrow; there, I'm taking it out
before your eyes, sir; that's it, and the money plain to see; there,
take it, most noble Prince, and keep it till tomorrow. Tomorrow
or the next day I'll fetch it, sir; and do you know, Prince, the
money must have been lying out in the garden somewhere, under
a stone, that first night it was missing; what do you think?'

'Be careful not to tell him straight out that you've found the
wallet. Just let him see there's nothing in your coat-lining any
more. He'll understand.'

'Really, sir? Wouldn't it be better to tell him, sir, and pretend I
hadn't guessed till now?'

'N-no', the prince considered, 'n-no, it's too late now; it's
more dangerous; really, better to say nothing! And make a fuss of
him, but . . . don't show it too much . . . and . . . you know . . .'

'I know, Prince, I know, that is, I know I'll probably not be able
to do it, because one must have a heart like yours in this affair.
Besides, he's quick-tempered himself and apt to get carried
away. He's started treating me much too haughtily sometimes;
one minute he's snivelling and embracing me, then suddenly he
starts humiliating me and sneering contemptuously at me; well,
I'll just go and show him my coat-lining deliberately, heh-heh!
Au revoir, Prince, I can see I'm detaining you and intruding on
your most interesting emotions, so to speak.'

'But, for heaven's sake, keep it quiet, like before!'

'Gently does it, sir, gently does it, sir!'

But though the matter was settled, the prince was, if anything,
even more anxious than before. He could hardly wait for his
interview with the general the following day.

4

THE appointed hour was eleven, but the prince was, quite
unexpectedly, late. On his return home he found the general
waiting for him. He could see at once that he was none too
pleased, perhaps indeed because he had had to wait. Making his
apologies, the prince hurriedly seated himself, but felt oddly
diffident, as though his visitor was made of porcelain and he

constantly feared to break him. Previously he had never felt shy
with the general, nor had the idea ever occurred to him. The
prince quickly realized that here was quite a different person
from the day before: instead of confusion and vagueness there
was a remarkable control; one might have thought that this was a
man firm in his resolve. His composure, however, was more
apparent than real. At all events, the visitor was graciously at
ease, while still preserving a dignified restraint; in fact he began
by treating the prince with a certain air of condescension—a trait
occasionally met with in proud people, who are graciously at ease
despite having been gratuitously insulted. His voice was gentle,
though not without an aggrieved note in the intonation.

'Your book I borrowed yesterday', he pointedly indicated the
book he had brought, which was lying on the table. 'Thank you.'

'Ah yes; did you read the story, General? How did you like it?
It's interesting, isn't it?' The prince rejoiced at the opportunity of
initiating the conversation indirectly.

'Interesting, perhaps, but crudely written and of course
absurd. Probably a lie in every line.'

The general spoke with aplomb and even a hint of a drawl.

'Ah, it's such an unaffected story; an old soldier's eyewitness
account of the French in Moscow; some parts are wonderful.
Besides, any eyewitness account is valuable, whoever writes it.
Don't you think?'

'If I'd been the editor, I wouldn't have printed it; as for
eyewitnesses in general, people will believe a crude liar, as long
as he's amusing, sooner than a man of worth and merit. I know
some accounts of 1812 that . . . I have decided, Prince, to leave
this house—Mr Lebedev's house.'

The general shot a significant glance at the prince.

'You have your own accommodation in Pavlovsk . . . at . . .
at . . . your daughter's . . .', said the prince, not knowing how to
respond to this. He recalled that the general had come for advice
on a matter of crucial importance, something on which his fate
depended.

'At my wife's; in other words at home in my daughter's house.'

'I'm sorry, I . . .'

'I am leaving Lebedev's house, because, dear Prince, because I
have broken with that fellow; I broke with him last night, and I'm

sorry it wasn't sooner. I demand respect, Prince, and expect to
get it even from those to whom I give my heart, so to speak.
Prince, I often give my heart to people and I'm almost always
deceived. That man was unworthy of my gift.'

'He's rather a muddled person', the prince observed carefully,
'and some aspects of his . . . but amongst it all, one can perceive
he has a heart and a shrewd and sometimes amusing mind.'

The refined expression and respectful tone evidently flattered
the general, although he kept glancing at the prince now and then
with sudden mistrust. But the prince's tone was so natural and
sincere that doubt was out of the question.

'That he also has good qualities', the general continued, 'I was
the first to proclaim when I was on the point of bestowing my
friendship on that individual. I have no need of his house or his
hospitality, since I have a household of my own. I am not trying to
justify my own shortcomings; I'm intemperate; I've drunk wine
with him and perhaps now I regret that. But it wasn't for drink
alone that I took up with him, was it? Forgive me, Prince, for the
rough candour of an exasperated man. It was his qualities, as you
say, which attracted me. But if he has the impudence to tell me to
my face that he lost his left leg as a child in 1812, and buried it in
the Vagankov Cemetery in Moscow, that's going too far; it shows
disrespect and effrontery . . .'

'Perhaps it was just a joke, for the sake of a good laugh.'

'I understand that, sir. An innocent untruth for a good laugh,
even a coarse one, does not offend the human heart. A man may
indeed lie out of pure friendship, if you like, just to give his
companion pleasure; but if there's a hint of disrespect, if by this
sort of disrespect, your friend wishes to show that the bonds of
friendship are chafing, then a man of honour has only one
recourse—to turn away and break off the connection, consigning
the offender to his proper place.'

The general fairly reddened as he spoke.

'But Lebedev couldn't even have been in Moscow in 1812;
he's too young, it's ridiculous.'

'There's that, to begin with; but supposing he could have been
born then, how can he assert to my face that a French chasseur
pointed his gun at him and shot his leg off for fun; that then he
picked up the leg and took it home and later buried it in the

Vagankov Cemetery, and says he erected a memorial over it with an inscription on one side: "Here lies the leg of Collegiate Secretary Lebedev", and on the other: "Rest in peace, beloved ashes, till resurrection's joyous dawn", and that finally he has a service read over it every year (which is blasphemy in any case) and travels to Moscow every year for that purpose. To prove it, he asks me to go to Moscow with him, to show me the grave and the selfsame captured French cannon in the Kremlin; he assures me it's number eleven from the gates, an old-fashioned French falconet.'

'And meanwhile, he's got two healthy legs for all to see!' laughed the prince. 'I assure you it's a harmless joke; you shouldn't be angry.'

'Allow me my own view as to that, sir; as for seeing his legs, it may not be as incredible as all that; he alleges that it's one of Chornosvitov's . . .'*

'Ah yes, they say you can dance with a Chornosvitov leg.'

'I know it for a fact, sir; after he had invented his leg, the first thing Chornosvitov did was run and show it to me. But the Chornosvitov leg was invented later, much later . . . And he also says that throughout their entire married life, his late wife did not know that he, her own husband, had a wooden leg. "If you were Napoleon's page in 1812", says he, when I pointed out all these absurdities, "then allow me to bury my leg in Vagankov Cemetery." '

'Surely you weren't . . .', the prince began, then stopped in embarrassment.

The general looked at the prince in utter disdain, almost sneering.

'Do go on, Prince', the drawl was especially suave, 'do go on. I'll make allowances, say it: admit you find laughable the mere idea that you see before you a man in his present humiliation and . . . uselessness, yet hear at the same time that this man was an eyewitness of . . . great events. *He* hasn't managed to pass on any tittle-tattle about me yet has he?'

'No, I've heard nothing from Lebedev—if it's Lebedev you're talking about . . .'

'Hmm, I thought differently. Actually our conversation yesterday all got started because of that . . . strange piece in the

*Archive.** I remarked on its absurdity, and since I was an eyewitness myself . . . you smile, Prince, you're looking at my face?'

'N-no, I . . .'

'I'm young-looking', the general dwelt on his words, 'but I'm rather older than I seem. In 1812 I was 10 or 11. I'm rather hazy about my age. In the army list it's less; it's been a weakness of mine to pretend to be younger all my life.'

'I assure you, general, I don't find it strange at all that you were in Moscow in 1812, and . . . you can tell the story . . . as well as anyone who was there. One of our writers begins his autobiography by saying that French soldiers fed him with bread when he was a babe in arms in Moscow in 1812.'

'There you are, you see', the general approved indulgently. 'My own case, of course, is out of the usual run, but there's nothing extraordinary about it. Very often the truth does seem impossible. A page! It does sound strange, of course. But a 10-year-old boy's escapade can perhaps be put down to his age. It couldn't have happened to a 15-year-old, because at that age I wouldn't have run away from our wooden house on Old Basmannaya Street on the day Napoleon entered Moscow, or left my mother, who was shaking with fear because she'd been too late to get out of the city. At 15 I'd have been afraid, but being 10- I feared nothing and squeezed through the crowd right up to the steps of the palace where Napoleon was dismounting from his horse.'

'That's really an excellent observation of yours, that it's at 10-years old we fear nothing', the prince assented, tortured by the thought that he would blush at any moment.

'Certainly, and everything happened as simply and naturally as can only happen in real life; if a novelist had the handling of it, he'd have thought up something unheard-of and incredible.'

'Oh, how true that is!' cried the prince. 'The same idea struck me only recently. I know of a genuine case of murder for the sake of a watch, it's in the papers now.* If some writer had made it up, the critics and social observers would immediately have raised the cry that it was incredible; and yet if you read it in the papers as a fact, you sense that Russian actuality is made up of just such facts. You have put your finger right on it, General!' the prince concluded warmly, terribly pleased at being able to cover his blushes.

'That's right, isn't it? Isn't it?' cried the general, his eyes also sparkling with pleasure. 'A boy, a child, not realizing the danger, pushes his way through the crowd to see the glitter, the uniforms, the retinue, and at last, the great man himself, whose name has been shouted at him so much. At that time, everybody had done nothing else but shout about him for years on end. The world rang with that name and I took it in with my mother's milk, so to speak. I chanced to catch the eye of Napoleon, passing by a couple of yards away; I was dressed as a gentleman's son, I was always dressed well. I was the only one like that in the whole crowd. You have to admit . . .'

'Certainly, it must have astonished him and proved to him that not everyone had fled from Moscow, there were still some noblemen left with their children.'

'Exactly, exactly! He wanted to win over the boyars! When his eagle eye lighted on me, my eyes must have sparkled in response. *'Voilà un garçon bien éveillé! Qui est ton père?'** I replied at once, almost breathless with excitement: 'A general who died on the field of the fatherland.' *'Le fils d'un boyard et d'un brave par-dessus le marché! J'aime les boyards. M'aimes tu, petit?'** To this swift question I replied just as swiftly: 'A Russian heart is capable of recognizing a great man even in his country's foe!' I mean, actually I can't remember whether I said that in so many words . . . I was a child . . . but that certainly was the gist! Napoleon was amazed; he thought for a moment and said to his suite: 'I like the spirit of this boy! But if all the Russians think the way this child does, then . . .' He went into the palace without finishing. I immediately mingled with the retinue and ran in after him. The courtiers were already making way for me, regarding me as a favourite. But that was over in a flash . . . All I remember is that, when the emperor entered the first hall, he halted in front of a portrait of the Empress Catherine and gazed at it for a long time, lost in thought, before saying at length: 'That was a great woman!' and walking on. Two days later, everyone in the palace and the Kremlin knew me and called me *'le petit boyard'*. I only went home to sleep. At home they were almost out of their minds. Two days after that, Napoleon's page, Baron de

Bazancourt, died from the rigours of the campaign. Napoleon remembered me, and I was brought to the palace without any explanation; they tried on me the uniform of the dead page, a boy of 12 or so, and when they brought me in my uniform before the emperor and he inclined his head, I was told that I had found favour and been appointed a page to his majesty. I was glad, because I really had felt strongly drawn to him for a long time . . . besides, you must admit, there was the splendid uniform, which means a lot to a child . . . I used to go about in a dark-green coat with long, narrow tails; gold buttons, scarlet piping on the sleeves, embroidered with gold braid, a high, stiff, open collar—also gold-embroidered—and embroidery on the lapels; close-fitting white buckskin breeches, a white silk waistcoat, silk stockings and buckled shoes . . . and when the emperor went riding and I was one of his retinue, I wore high boots. Though the situation of the French was far from brilliant, and great disasters were already being anticipated, etiquette was maintained as far as possible, indeed the greater the sense of impending calamity grew, the more punctilious its observance became.'

'Yes, of course', murmured the prince, with an air almost of desperation. 'Your memoirs would be . . . extremely interesting.'

The general, of course, was merely going over what he had been telling Lebedev the previous day, and it was, in consequence, a fluent recital; at this point, however, he again stole a mistrustful glance at the prince.

'My memoirs', he declared with redoubled pride. 'Write my memoirs? That has never tempted me, Prince! If you wish to know, my memoirs have already been written but . . . are lying in my desk. When my eyes are sprinkled with earth, let them be published then, and without doubt they will be translated into other languages, not on account of their literary worth, no, but for the significance of the tremendous facts to which I was an eyewitness, even though a child; the more so, in fact; being a child, I penetrated the innermost sanctum, the bedroom of the 'great man'! I heard the nocturnal groans of that 'titan in misfortune', he could not be ashamed of groaning and weeping in front of a child, though I had already realized that the reason for his sufferings was the silence of the Emperor Alexander.'

'He did write letters . . . with peace proposals', the prince timidly assented.

'In actual fact, we do not know what kind of proposals he made, but he did write every day, every hour, letter after letter! He was terribly agitated. One night when we were alone together, I rushed to him with tears in my eyes (how I loved him!): "Beg, oh beg the Emperor Alexander's forgiveness!" I cried. I should have said: "Make peace with the Emperor Alexander" but, childlike, I blurted out everything I was thinking in a naive way. "Oh, my child!" he answered. He paced back and forth across the room. "Oh, my child!" It was as if he had ceased to notice that I was 10 years old and was actually fond of talking to me. "Oh, my child, I am willing to kiss the feet of the Emperor Alexander, but for the King of Prussia and the Emperor of Austria, oh, for them nothing but everlasting hatred and . . . after all . . . you know nothing of politics!" He seemed to recollect to whom he was speaking and lapsed into silence, but his eyes went on flashing for long after that. Well, if I described all these facts, and I was a witness of tremendous events—if I were to publish them now, all these critics, all these literary vanities, all these jealousies, coteries, and . . . no, sir, your humble servant, sir!'

'You're right as regards coteries, of course, and I quite agree with you', the prince replied softly, after the briefest of pauses. 'I read Charasse's book* on the Waterloo campaign just recently. It is obviously a serious work, and according to the experts it is written with a profound knowledge of the subject. But his joy at Napoleon's humiliation is apparent on every page, and if it had been possible to deny Napoleon the slightest mark of talent in his other campaigns too, it seems Charasse would have been extremely glad to do so; that's a bad thing in a serious work of this nature, because it betrays an axe to grind. Were your duties with . . . the emperor onerous?'

The general was overjoyed. The earnestness and simplicity of the prince's remarks swept away the last remnants of his mistrust.

'Charasse! Oh I was so angry myself! I wrote to him at once, but . . . really I can't remember now . . . You ask if my service was onerous? Oh no! I had the title of page, but I didn't take it seriously even then. In any case, Napoleon very soon lost any hope of winning the Russians over, and of course he would have forgotten about me as well, having appointed me as a matter of policy, if . . . if he hadn't taken a fancy to me personally, I can say that boldly now. As for me, my heart went out to him. I had no duties: I had to appear at the palace occasionally and . . . accompany the emperor on his walks, but that was all. I could ride decently. He used to go riding before dinner, usually accompanied by Davoust, myself, and the Mameluke Rustan . . .'

'Constant', the prince suddenly blurted.

'N-no, Constant wasn't there then; he was on his way with a letter to . . . the Empress Josephine; but his place was taken by two orderlies and some Polish uhlans . . . well that made up the whole suite, apart from the generals of course, and the marshals Napoleon took with him for consultation and to survey the terrain and the troop dispositions, and . . . Davoust was there more often than anyone, as I recall: an enormous, stout, phlegmatic man in glasses, with a strange look in his eyes. He was the one the emperor consulted most often. He valued his ideas. I recall them talking things over for days on end; Davoust used to come morning and evening, they even quarrelled frequently; eventually Napoleon seemed to agree with him. There were just the two of them in the study, apart from me as the third, unnoticed by them. Suddenly Napoleon's eye chanced to light on me and an odd thought was reflected in his eyes. "Child", he said to me suddenly, "what do you think: if I were to adopt the Orthodox faith and free your serfs, would the Russians come over to me or not?" "Never!" I shouted indignantly. Napoleon was astounded. "In that child's eyes, blazing with patriotism", he said, "I have read the opinion of the entire Russian people. Enough, Davoust! It's all a fantasy! Present your other plan."'

'Yes, but that first plan contained a grand conception!' said the prince, obviously interested. 'So you ascribe that idea to Davoust?'

'They discussed it together at least. Of course, the idea was Napoleonic, an eagle of an idea, but the other plan had its points too . . . This was the celebrated *"Conseil du lion"*,* as Napoleon himself dubbed Davoust's plan. The idea was that they would shut themselves up in the Kremlin along with all the troops, construct barracks, dig fortifications, and site their artillery; then they would slaughter as many horses as possible and salt down the carcasses. They would get hold of or pillage as much grain as they could and then sit out the winter. In the spring, they would break through the Russian lines. Napoleon was greatly taken with this project. We used to ride round the Kremlin walls every day, with him pointing out where the walls should be demolished, where they should be reinforced, where to put up lunettes, ravelins, or a row of blockhouses—glance, decision, drive! At last it was all settled; Davoust pressed for a final decision. Again they were alone together, with me as the third. Once more Napoleon paced the room, arms folded. I couldn't take my eyes off his face, my heart was pounding. "I'm going", said Davoust. "Where to?" asked Napoleon. "To salt down the horses", said Davoust. Napoleon gave a shudder; his destiny was in the balance. "Child", he said to me abruptly, "what do you think of our intention?" Of course, he was asking me the way a man of great intellect will sometimes turn to the toss of a coin at the last moment. I addressed Davoust rather than Napoleon, and spoke as if inspired: "Get yourself back home, general!" The plan was in ruins. Davoust shrugged his shoulders and muttered as he went out: *"Bah! Il devient superstitieux!"** The retreat was ordered the following day.'

'All this is extremely interesting', the prince brought out very quietly indeed, 'if it all happened like that . . . that is, I mean . . .' He hastened to correct himself.

'Oh, Prince!' cried the general, so carried away by his narration that he was unable to stop at the most imprudent statements. 'You say: "If it happened!" But there was more, believe me, much more! All that is just bare bones, political facts. But I repeat, I was witness to the nocturnal tears and groans of that great man; that no one saw but me! True, towards the end he no longer wept, there were no tears, just groaning sometimes; but his face seemed to grow more and more overcast. It was as though eternity was hovering over him with her sombre wing. Sometimes at night we spent hours on end together in silence—Rustan the Mameluke would be snoring in the adjoining room; he was a terribly sound sleeper, that man. "Still, he is loyal to me and my dynasty", Napoleon used to say of him. Once I felt it all terribly painfully and he suddenly noticed the tears in my eyes; he looked affectionately at me: "You're sorry for me!"

he cried. "You, a child, and perhaps another child will be sorry for me—my son, *le roi de Rome*; all the others hate me, all of them, and my brothers will be the first to betray me in my misfortune!" I burst into sobs and ran to him; at this he broke down too; we embraced and our tears mingled. "Write a letter to the Empress Josephine!" I sobbed to him. Napoleon gave a start, thought for a moment, and said to me: "You have reminded me of another heart which loves me; thank you, my friend!" He sat down at once and wrote the letter that Constant went off with the following day.'

'You did splendidly', said the prince. 'In the midst of his grim thoughts, you led him on to feelings of kindness.'

'Exactly, Prince, and how beautifully you explain it, only to be expected from a man with a heart like yours!' cried the general rapturously, and oddly enough, real tears began to glisten in his eyes. 'Yes, Prince, yes, it was a wonderful sight. And you know, I almost went away to Paris with him, and I would have shared his exile of course on the "sultry prison isle", but alas, our destinies diverged! We parted company: he to his sultry island where, perhaps, he recalled at least once the tears of the poor little boy who embraced and forgave him in Moscow; I was sent off to the Cadet Corps, where I found nothing but drilling, rough comrades, and . . . Alas! All had turned to dust and ashes! "I do not wish to deprive your mother and take you with me!" he told me on the day of the retreat. "But I'd like to do something for you." He was already mounting his horse. "Write me something in my sister's album as a souvenir", I managed to say timidly, as he was gloomy and greatly distraught. He turned back, asked for a pen, and took the album. "How old is your sister?" he asked, pen in hand. "Three years old", I replied. *"Petite fille, alors."** And he scratched in the album:

> *"Ne mentez jamais!**
> Napoléon, votre ami sincère."*

What advice at a moment like that, eh, Prince?'

'Yes, that was remarkable.'

'That page, under glass in a gold frame, hung in the most prominent place in my sister's bedroom till the day of her death—she died in childbirth; where it is now . . . I don't know ... but ... good lord, it's two o'clock already! How I've kept you, Prince! It's unforgivable.'

The general rose from his chair.

'Oh, on the contrary!' mumbled the prince. 'I've been so engrossed and ... anyway ... it was most interesting; I'm so grateful to you!'

'Prince!' said the general, once again squeezing his hand painfully and looking intently at him with glittering eyes, as though recollecting himself all of a sudden and startled by some sudden thought. 'Prince! You are so good, so simple-hearted, that I feel positively sorry for you sometimes. I am moved to look at you; oh, may God bless you! May your life begin and flourish ... in love. My life is finished! Ah, forgive me, forgive me!'

He went out swiftly, his face in his hands. The prince could not doubt the sincerity of his emotion. He was also aware that the old man had departed in elation at his success. All the same, the prince felt a misgiving—that he belonged to that category of liars who, despite deriving sensual pleasure verging on intoxication from their lies, nevertheless suspect at the very height of their elation that they are not believed and cannot possibly be believed. In his present situation, the old man might easily recover himself, be overcome with shame, suspect the prince of pitying him too much, and take offence. 'Might I have done better not to let him be carried away to that extent?' the prince wondered uneasily, then could hold out no longer and roared with laughter for about ten minutes. He was about to reproach himself for laughing, but realized at once that he had nothing to reproach himself for, because he felt an infinite pity for the general.

His misgivings were borne out. That very evening he received a strange note, brief but firm. The general informed him that he was parting from him for ever, that he held him in esteem and was grateful to him, but even from him he could not accept 'marks of compassion, insulting to the dignity of one already unhappy enough'. When the prince heard that the old man had moved back to his wife, he felt almost at ease on his account. But we have already seen that the general had caused some sort of trouble at the Yepanchins too. We cannot go into details here, only pausing to remark that the upshot of the encounter was that the general had frightened Lizaveta Prokofievna and his bitter insinuations against Ganya had aroused her indignation. He had been ignominiously turned out. That was why he had passed such a night and such a morning, and run almost dementedly into the street.

Kolya was still largely in the dark as to what was wrong, and was even sanguine that a show of severity might bring him round.

'Well, where do you think we can trail off to now, General?' he said. 'You don't want to go to the prince, you've quarrelled with Lebedev, you've got no money and I never have any: here we are, on our uppers out in the street.'

'It's nicer sitting with your betters than standing on your uppers', muttered the general. 'I used to raise the roof with that ... pun in the officers' mess ... in forty-four ... Eighteen ... forty-four, yes! ... I don't remember ... Oh, don't remind me, don't remind me! "Where is my youth, where is my freshness?" Like ... who said that Kolya?'

'It's in Gogol, *Dead Souls*, papa', answered Kolya, stealing a timid glance at his father.

'Dead souls! Oh yes, dead! Kolya, when I'm buried, write on the tombstone: "Here lies a dead soul!" "Disgrace pursues me!" Who said that, Kolya?'

'I don't know, papa.'

'Yeropegov didn't exist! Yeroshka Yeropegov! ...', he shouted, stopping short in the street in an access of rage. 'And that was my son, my own flesh and blood! Yeropegov, who was a brother to me for eleven months, the man I fought a duel for ... Prince Vygoretsky, our captain, said to him over a bottle: "Grisha, where did you get your St Anne's cross, tell me that?" "On the field of the fatherland, that's where I got it!" I shouts: "Bravo, Grisha!" Well, there was a duel over it, then he married ... Maria Petrovna Su ... Sutugina and got killed on the field ... A bullet ricocheted off the cross on my chest and straight through his forehead. "I shall never forget!" he shouted, and fell on the spot. I ... I served with honour, Kolya; I served nobly, but disgrace—"disgrace pursues me!" You and Nina come to my tombstone ... "Poor Nina!" That's what I used to call her back then, Kolya, long ago, at the beginning, she loved me so ... Nina, Nina! What have I done with your life! How can you love me, soul of patience! Your mother has the soul of an angel, Kolya, you hear me? An angel!'

'I know that, papa. Dear papa, let's go back home to mama! She was running after us! Why have you stopped? As if you didn't realize . . . Now why are you crying?'

Kolya was crying himself as he kissed his father's hands.

'You're kissing my hands, mine!'

'Yes, yes, yours! What's so surprising about that? Why go bawling in the middle of the road? Call yourself a general, a military man? Come along, let's go!'

'May God bless you, dear boy, for being respectful to a disgraceful—yes! A disgraceful old fellow, your own father . . . I hope you have just such a boy . . . *le roi de Rome* . . . Oh, "a curse, a curse be upon this house!"'

'Now what on earth's going on? Why don't you want to go back home now? Why are you acting so crazily?'

'I'll explain, I'll explain . . . I'll tell you everything; don't shout, people will hear . . . *le roi de Rome* . . . Oh, I feel sick, I feel miserable! "Nurse, where is your grave?" Who said that, Kolya?'

'Don't know, don't know who said it! Come on home now, this minute! I'll smash Ganya, if I have to . . . now where are you off to?'

But now the general was tugging him towards the porch of a nearby house.

'Where are you going, that's not our porch!'

The general sat down on the porch, still tugging Kolya towards him by the hand.

'Bend down, bend down!' he muttered. 'I'll tell you everything . . . disgrace . . . bend down . . . your ear, your ear; I'll whisper it in your ear . . .'

'What on earth's the matter!' Kolya was greatly alarmed, but bent his ear all the same.

'*Le roi de Rome* . . .', whispered the general, who seemed to be trembling too.

'What? . . . Where do you get this *roi de Rome* from? . . . What?'

'I . . . I', the general was hissing again, clutching ever-more tightly at "his boy's" shoulder. 'I want . . . I . . . you . . . everything, Maria, Maria . . . Petrovna Su-Su-Su . . .'

Kolya tore himself free, took a grip on the general's shoulders, and stared at him dementedly. The old man turned crimson, his lips went blue as light tremors passed across his face. All of a sudden he leaned forward and began to fall gently into Kolya's arms.

'A stroke!' shouted Kolya for the whole street to hear, realizing at last what the matter was.

5

WHEN talking to her brother, if truth be known, Varvara Ardalionovna had rather exaggerated the accuracy of her information concerning the prince's proposal to Aglaya. Perhaps, being a perceptive woman, she had merely foreseen what was bound to happen in the near future in any case; vexed perhaps at the way the project had gone up in smoke (though she had not really believed in it herself), she, being human, could not forego the pleasure of twisting the knife a little by exaggerating the disaster to the brother she none the less loved genuinely and compassionately. At all events, she could not possibly have got such accurate information from her Yepanchin friends; there were only hints, half-spoken words, meaningful silences, and puzzling allusions. It was possible that Aglaya's sisters had deliberately let something slip so as to elicit information from Varya; it might also have been that they wished to indulge themselves in the feminine pleasure of teasing a friend a little, even one they had known since childhood: by this time they could not have failed to discern at least a glimmer of her intent.

On the other hand, the prince too, despite being perfectly truthful in assuring Lebedev that he could tell him nothing, and that nothing particular had happened to him, might also have been wrong. Really, it was as if something very odd had happened to them all: nothing had taken place, yet at the same time a great deal had taken place. It was this last that Varya had divined with her unerring female intuition.

It is very hard, however, to set down in order how exactly it came about that all the Yepanchins became possessed of the identical notion simultaneously—that something of the utmost

importance had happened to Aglaya, and that her destiny hung in
the balance. But no sooner had the idea flashed into all their
minds at the same time, than all insisted they had thought the
matter over long ago and seen it all coming; that it had all been
obvious since the 'poor knight' incident, or even before; it was
just that they had been disinclined to credit such an absurdity at
the time. So the sisters asserted; of course, Lizaveta Prokofievna
had also foreseen it, and found out before anyone else—her heart
had long been 'aching': but whether it had or not, she could not
countenance the idea of the prince now—really because it posed
her such a problem. A question was looming which demanded an
immediate solution; but not only was Lizaveta Prokofievna
unable to solve it, she couldn't even frame the question clearly,
try as she might. It was a difficult business: 'Was the prince a
good match or not? Was all this a good thing or wasn't it? If it
wasn't (and that was certainly the case), then why exactly wasn't
it? And if it might be a good thing (which was also possible), then
why was that so?' The head of the household, General Yepanchin
himself, was initially astonished, but later on he suddenly
confessed, 'honestly, he had often had visions of something of the
sort all this time, they would fade and then suddenly come back
again!' He lapsed into silence at once under the menacing eye of
his wife, but that was in the morning. In the evening, alone with
his wife and compelled to say something, he suddenly gave vent
to a number of surprising thoughts with a certain marked zest:
'After all, what does it amount to? . . .' (Silence.) 'Of course, it's
all very strange, if it's really true, and I'm not arguing, but . . .'
(More silence.) 'On the other hand, if you look the thing straight
in the face, the prince is, really and truly, a most excellent young
chap, and . . . and, and well of course there's our name, isn't
there, our family name, it will have the appearance of keeping up
the family name, so to speak, which has gone down in the eyes of
the world, that is, looking at it from that point of view, that is,
because . . . of course society; society is society; all the same, the
prince is not without means, even if they aren't as much as all
that. He has . . . and . . . and . . .' (petering out in a prolonged
silence). Having heard her husband out, Lizaveta Prokofievna
exploded.

In her view, everything that had happened was 'unpardonable, even criminal nonsense, a fantasy, stupid and absurd!' To start with, this 'wretched little prince was a sickly idiot, secondly, he was a fool, he didn't know the ways of society and had no place in it: who could he be presented to, where could one advance him? He was a kind of unacceptable democrat, he hadn't even got a civil-service rank, and . . . and . . . what would Belokonskaya say? After all, was it, was it really this kind of husband they had imagined and planned for Aglaya?' This last argument was the chief one, of course. Her mother's heart quivered at the thought, grieving and tearful, although at the same time something also stirred within that heart, suddenly saying to her: 'And why is the prince not the right man?' Well, it was these, her own heart's objections, which were the most trying for Lizaveta Prokofievna.

Aglaya's sisters were rather pleased at the thought of the prince; it didn't even seem particularly strange to them; in short, they might easily have found themselves on his side completely. But both of them decided to keep quiet. It had been established once and for all within the family, that the more insistent and pertinacious Lizaveta Prokofievna's opposition and objections became in any wide-ranging family argument, the more it served them all as an indication that she was already perhaps giving way on the point. But Alexandra could hardly keep silent altogether. Having selected her long ago as her confidante, her mother was constantly summoning her these days and asking her opinion, and especially for her recollections, on the lines of: 'How on earth had this all come about? Why hadn't anyone seen it coming? Why had nobody said anything at the time? What had that wretched "poor knight" signified? Why was she, Lizaveta Prokofievna, alone condemned to worry about all of them, keep her eye on things, and foresee everything, while the rest of them just stood gaping?' And so on, and so forth. At first, Alexandra had been very circumspect and merely observed that she thought her father's idea was quite well-founded; that in the eyes of society, the choice of a Prince Myshkin as husband for one of the Yepanchin girls might well seem most satisfactory. Gradually warming to the task, she added that the prince was by no means a fool and never had been, while as for social status—lord alone knew what the social status of a gentleman in Russia would depend on in a few years' time—obligatory advancement in the civil service as formerly, or something else altogether. To all of this her mother brusquely retorted that Alexandra was 'a free-thinker, and it was all because of that wretched woman question'. Half an hour later she set off for town, and from there to Kamenny Island to catch Belokonskaya, who fortunately happened to be in Petersburg, though soon due to depart. The princess was Aglaya's godmother.

The 'old woman' listened to all Lizaveta Prokofievna's hectic and despairing confessions and was not in the least disconcerted by the tears of the distraught mother, in fact she looked at her derisively. The princess was a dreadful tyrant; in friendship, even the oldest established, she could not tolerate equality, and decidedly regarded Lizaveta Prokofievna as her protégée, just as she had done thirty-five years before; she simply could not come to terms with the blunt independence of her character. She pointed out, however, that they all seemed to have run too far ahead of themselves as usual, and made a mountain out of a molehill; that despite listening most carefully, she had not been convinced that anything serious had really occurred, and wouldn't it be better to wait until something transpired; that the prince was, in her view, a decent young man, though an invalid, somewhat singular and socially altogether too obscure. The worst thing was that he was openly keeping a mistress. Lizaveta Prokofievna was very well aware that Belokonskaya was somewhat annoyed at Radomsky's lack of success; it was she who had recommended Yevgeni Pavlovich in the first place. She returned home to Pavlovsk in even greater irritation than when she had left, and everyone immediately felt the edge of her tongue, chiefly on account of having 'taken leave of their senses'; it was certainly only in their house that things like this happened; what was the hurry? What had happened? However hard she looked, she couldn't see that anything had actually taken place! Wait till it did! What did General Yepanchin's imaginings matter, why make a mountain out of a molehill? And so on, and so on.

It appeared, therefore, that all they had to do was calm down, take a level-headed view, and wait. Alas, the calm lasted less than ten minutes. The first blow to the level-headed view came with the news of what had happened during mama's absence on Kamenny Island. (Lizaveta Prokofievna's trip had taken place the morning after the prince had turned up after midnight instead of nine.) In answer to their mama's eager inquisition, the sisters replied in great detail that in the first place 'absolutely nothing seemed to have occurred in her absence', that the prince had come over and Aglaya had kept him waiting for a long time, a good half-hour, then she came out and, as she did so, suggested a game of chess; the prince didn't even know the moves and Aglaya had beaten him at once; she had got very gleeful and scolded the prince dreadfully for his incompetence, and made such fun of him that he was pitiful to look at. Then she suggested a game of cards and they played 'fools'. This time it was just the opposite: the prince turned out to be as expert at 'fools'* as . . . as a professor; he played brilliantly; Aglaya even stooped to cheating and swapped the cards around; she stole tricks before his very eyes, but he made a 'fool' of her every time; five times in a row. Aglaya became furiously annoyed and forgot herself completely; she said such wounding and impertinent things to the prince that he stopped laughing altogether; he had turned quite pale when she finally said to him that she would not set foot in the room while he remained sitting there, and that he ought positively to be ashamed, for his part, to come visiting, especially after midnight, *after all that had happened*. Then she had gone, slamming the door. The prince departed as if from a funeral, notwithstanding all their attempts at consolation. Suddenly, a quarter of an hour later, Aglaya had run down on to the veranda in such haste that she hadn't managed to dry her eyes, which were red with weeping; she had run down because Kolya had arrived and brought a hedgehog with him. Everyone started looking at it and Kolya explained in answer to their questioning that the hedgehog wasn't his. He was passing with a school-friend of his, Kostya Lebedev, who had stayed outside, too shy to come in because he was carrying an axe; they had bought both hedgehog and axe just now from a peasant they had met. The peasant was selling the hedgehog for fifty kopecks, but they persuaded him to sell the axe, because he might just as well and it was certainly a good axe. At this point Aglaya suddenly began pestering Kolya to sell her the hedgehog immediately, she had got very excited about it and even called Kolya 'sweet'. Kolya would not agree for a long time, but eventually gave way and called Kostya Lebedev, who actually did come in with an axe and was greatly embarrassed. Then it suddenly turned out that the hedgehog was not theirs at all—it belonged to a third boy, Petrov, who had given them both the money to buy Schlosser's *History** from yet a fourth boy who was short of money and was selling it cheap; they had gone out to buy Schlosser's *History* but had yielded to temptation and bought the hedgehog, so therefore both it and the axe belonged to the third boy, and they were taking them to him instead of Schlosser's *History*. Aglaya was so insistent, however, that they finally decided to sell her the hedgehog. As soon as she got it, she immediately placed it in a wicker basket, with Kolya's assistance, and after covering it with a napkin, began begging Kolya to take it at once to the prince, and ask him to accept it as 'a mark of her most profound esteem'. Kolya agreed, overjoyed, and promised to deliver it, but immediately began badgering her: 'What did the gift signify—and a hedgehog at that?' Aglaya told him it was none of his business. He answered that he was certain there was an allegory involved. Aglaya lost her temper and snapped that he was nothing but a young puppy. Kolya immediately retorted that if it were not that he respected her as a woman, and besides had principles of his own, he could have demonstrated to her at once that he knew how to respond to insults like that. The upshot, however, was that Kolya went delightedly off with the hedgehog, with Kostya Lebedev trotting after him; Aglaya, seeing him swinging the basket too much, could not help shouting to him from the veranda: 'Please, Kolya, don't drop it dear!' just as if they had not that minute been having words; Kolya stopped and, just as if he had not that minute been answering her back, shouted with the utmost good will: 'No, I shan't drop it, Aglaya Ivanovna. Don't worry!'—and ran on again at breakneck speed. Aglaya then burst into loud laughter and ran to her room extremely pleased with herself, and had remained in high good humour for the rest of the day.

Lizaveta Prokofievna was aghast at this news. Not that there was any real reason, but her mood prompted her to it. Her apprehension was acutely aroused—mainly on account of the hedgehog; what did the hedgehog signify? What was its agreed meaning? What kind of signal was it? A message of some kind? Moreover, poor General Yepanchin, who chanced to be present at this interrogation, spoilt the whole thing completely with his answer. In his view, there was no message involved, the hedgehog 'was a hedgehog, pure and simple—apart from the fact that it signified friendship, a burying of the hatchet, and making up, in a nutshell it was just one of her antics, in any event it was innocent and excusable'.

We should observe in parenthesis, that he was quite correct. On his return from Aglaya, derided and banished, the prince had been sitting for a good half-hour in a mood of bleakest despair, when Kolya suddenly turned up with the hedgehog. At once the heavens cleared; the prince was as if born again; he interrogated Kolya, hanging on his every word, he cross-questioned him again ten times over, laughed like a child, and kept squeezing the hands of the laughing boy who was gazing brightly at him. It undoubtedly meant that Aglaya had forgiven him and the prince could go to her that very evening, which for him was not only the main thing—it was everything.

'What children we still are, Kolya! And . . . and . . . what a good thing it is that we are!' he exclaimed at length, rapturously.

'It's purely and simply that she's in love with you, Prince, that's all there is to it!' responded Kolya with impressive authority.

The prince coloured up at that, but this time said nothing, while Kolya merely roared with laughter and clapped his hands; the prince followed suit a moment later, then kept looking at his watch every five minutes until evening, to see how much time had elapsed and how much remained.

But Lizaveta Prokofievna's mood got the upper hand of her; she finally yielded to a burst of hysterics. Notwithstanding all the objections of spouse and daughters, she immediately sent for Aglaya with the object of putting the ultimate question to her and receiving a clear and final answer. 'To be rid of the thing once and for all, so we can forget about it and never bring it up again! Otherwise', she declared, 'I shan't live till evening!' It was only now that they all realized the muddle they had allowed to develop. Apart from feigned surprise, indignation, laughter, and scoffing at the prince and all her inquisitors, they got nothing out of Aglaya. Lizaveta Prokofievna took to her bed and only emerged to take tea when the prince was expected. She awaited the prince in fear and trembling, and almost had a fit of hysterics when he did arrive.

The prince, for his part, also entered timidly, almost groping his way in, smiling strangely and gazing questioningly into everyone's eyes, since Aglaya was again missing from the room and this at once troubled him. That evening there were no outsiders present, just members of the family; Prince S was still in Petersburg in connection with the business of Radomsky's uncle. 'If only he'd been here to say something', Lizaveta Prokofievna lamented. General Yepanchin sat with an extremely anxious countenance; the sisters looked grave and seemed intent on saying nothing. Lizaveta Prokofievna didn't know how to start the conversation. At length she suddenly came out with a vigorous condemnation of the railways, and glanced at the prince with positive defiance.

Alas, Aglaya did not appear and the prince floundered. Barely able to articulate, and covered with embarrassment, he gave it as his opinion that repairing the railway was very useful; then Adelaida suddenly started laughing and the prince was crushed again. It was at that very instant that Aglaya came in, calmly impressive, favoured the prince with a ceremonious bow, and solemnly sat down in the most prominent place at the round table. She looked questioningly at the prince. Everyone realized that the resolution of all their perplexities was at hand.

'Did you get my hedgehog?' she asked firmly, almost crossly.

'Yes', answered the prince, flushing. His heart was in his boots.

'Explain your thoughts on the matter to me at once. It is essential for *maman*'s peace of mind and that of all our family.'

'Look here, Aglaya . . .', the general was suddenly nervous.

'This . . . this is beyond everything!' Lizaveta Prokofievna was alarmed all of a sudden.

'There's nothing to be beyond here, *maman*.' Her daughter's reply was prompt and severe. 'Well then, Prince?'

'What thoughts do you mean, Aglaya Ivanovna?'

'About the hedgehog.'

'Well I . . . I think, Aglaya Ivanovna, that you want to know how I took the . . . hedgehog . . . or, more precisely, how I regarded . . . the sending . . . of the hedgehog, that is . . . in that case, I think that . . . putting it briefly . . .'

He choked on his words and stopped.

'You haven't said a great deal, have you?' Aglaya waited a few seconds. 'Very well, I'm willing to drop the hedgehog; but I'm glad to be able to end all these doubts that have built up. I should like to hear from you in person: are you courting me or not?'

'Oh, good gracious!' burst out Lizaveta Prokofievna.

The prince gave a start and recoiled; General Yepanchin stood petrified; the sisters frowned.

'Don't lie, Prince, tell the truth. I am being pestered with strange questions because of you; are there any grounds for these questions? Well, come on!'

'I was not courting you, Aglaya Ivanovna', said the prince, livening up suddenly, 'but . . . you know very well how much I care for you and believe in you . . . even now . . .'

'I asked you a question: are you asking for my hand or not?'

'Yes', answered the prince, his heart shrinking within him.

A considerable general commotion ensued.

'This is all wrong, dear fellow', said General Yepanchin, greatly agitated, 'it's . . . it's almost inconceivable, if this is the case, Aglaya . . . I'm sorry, Prince, I'm sorry, my dear chap! . . . Lizaveta Prokofievna!' he turned to his wife for assistance. 'It needs . . . going into . . .'

'Don't look at me, I wash my hands of it!' Lizaveta Prokofievna waved her arms.

'Permit me to say something myself, *maman*; I do have something to do with this, after all: the crucial moment of my destiny is being decided' (Aglaya actually used this expression), 'and I want to find out for myself, and I'm glad everyone is present to hear it . . . Please let me ask you, Prince, if you do "cherish such intentions", how precisely do you propose to make me happy?'

'I honestly don't know how to answer you, Aglaya Ivanovna; is . . . is there any answer possible? And is one . . . necessary?'

'You seem to be embarrassed and gasping for breath; rest a little and recover yourself; have a drink of water; you'll be getting some tea presently anyway.'

'I love you, Aglaya Ivanovna, I love you very much; I love only you and . . . please don't be flippant about it, I love you very much.'

'But still, this is a most important matter you know. We're not children, and we must take the practical view . . . Be so good as to explain how much you are worth?'

'Come, come, Aglaya. Really! This is wrong, wrong . . .', muttered General Yepanchin, dismayed.

'Disgraceful!' Lizaveta Prokofievna said in a loud whisper.

'She's off her head!' hissed Alexandra, just as loudly.

'Worth . . . you mean money?'

'Exactly.'

'I have . . . I now have . . . one hundred and thirty-five thousand roubles', mumbled the prince, reddening.

'Is that all?' Aglaya was loudly and frankly surprised, and quite unblushing. 'Still, it's not too bad, especially if we economize . . . Do you intend to enter the service?'

'I was thinking of qualifying as a private tutor . . .'

'Most suitable; of course that will increase our means. Do you propose to be a gentleman of the bedchamber?'

'Gentleman of the bedchamber? I hadn't thought of that at all, but . . .'

But at this point the two sisters could not contain themselves and burst out laughing. Adelaida had seen for a long time the twitching of Aglaya's features, betokening the swift and irrepressible laughter which for the time being she was doing her best to control. Aglaya threw a threatening glance at her laughing sisters, but the next second she too lost command of herself and burst into a frenzied paroxysm of laughter, verging on hysteria, culminating in her jumping up and fleeing from the room.

'I knew it was just a joke from the very start, from the hedgehog.'

'No, now this I will not have, I won't have it!' Lizaveta's anger erupted as she hurried out after Aglaya. The two sisters at once ran after her. The prince and the head of the family were left alone in the room.

'This . . . this is . . . could you ever have imagined such a thing, Lev Nikolayevich?' the general cried harshly, evidently not realizing himself what he wanted to say. 'No, I mean seriously, seriously?'

'I see that Aglaya Ivanovna was making fun of me', the prince said miserably.

'Just wait a moment, dear fellow, I'll go and see, and you wait a moment . . . because . . . can you at least explain, Lev Nikolaich, you at least; how did all this come to be and what does it all mean, taking it as a whole, as it were? You must see, dear fellow, I'm her father; I am her father, after all's said and done, and I don't understand a thing; so can you at least explain?'

'I love Aglaya Ivanovna; she knows that and . . . has done for a long time.'

The general shrugged.

'Strange, strange . . . you love her very much?'

'Very much.'

'Strange, all this seems very strange to me. I mean it's such a surprise and a shock that . . . You see, dear man, I'm not talking about the money (though I had expected you to have a bit more), but . . . my daughter's happiness . . . in short . . . are you capable, so to speak, of providing for her . . . happiness? And . . . and . . . what is all this: a joke or serious, on her part I mean? That is on her part, not yours?'

Alexandra Ivanovna's voice came from behind the door, summoning papa.

'Just wait here a moment, dear fellow, wait a moment! Wait here and think things over, I'll be back presently . . .'

He found his wife and daughter in one another's arms, dissolved in tears. They were tears of happiness, tender emotion, and reconciliation. Aglaya was kissing her mother's hands, cheeks, lips; they were hugging one another warmly.

'There just look at her, Ivan Fedorovich, that's what she's really like!' said Lizaveta Prokofievna.

Aglaya turned her happy, tear-stained, little face away from her mother's bosom, glanced at her papa, laughed uproariously as she darted towards him, squeezed him tightly, and kissed him several times. Then she rushed back to her mama again and fairly buried her head in her bosom, so that no one could see, and at once began crying again. Lizaveta Prokofievna covered her with the end of her shawl.

'Now look what you're doing to us, you cruel little thing, after all that, that's what you are!' she said, but joyously this time, as if she found breathing easier all of a sudden.

'Cruel! Yes, cruel!' Aglaya quickly seized on this. 'Good-for-nothing! Spoilt! Tell papa that. Oh, of course, he's here. Papa, are you there? Can you hear?' she was laughing through her tears.

'My darling, my idol!' The general kissed her hand, positively beaming with happiness. (Aglaya did not withdraw her hand.) 'So then you love this . . . young man?'

'No-no-no! I can't stand . . . that young man of yours, I can't stand him!' Aglaya suddenly burst out and raised her head. 'And if you dare once more, papa . . . I mean it; do you hear? I mean it!'

And she really did mean it: she had gone all red and her eyes glittered. Her papa was startled into stopping short, but Lizaveta Prokofievna signalled to him behind Aglaya's back and he realized it meant: 'Don't ask questions.'

'If that's the case, my angel, then of course it's up to you, he's waiting there by himself; shouldn't I drop him a tactful hint to go away?'

The general in his turn winked at Lizaveta Prokofievna.

'No, no that's not necessary; especially if "tact" is involved; you two go out to him; then I'll come in, presently. I want to apologize to . . . the young man, because I've hurt his feelings.'

'Very much so', Ivan Fedorovich confirmed gravely.

'Well, then . . . you'd better stay here, and I'll go in first by myself, you straight after me, the very same second; that'll be best.'

She had already reached the door when she turned back.

'I'll burst out laughing! I'll just die!' she confided, dolefully. But the same instant, she turned and ran in to the prince.

'Well, what does it mean? What do you make of it?' said Ivan Fedorovich swiftly.

'I'm afraid to say it', came the equally swift reply, 'but I think it's clear enough.'

'I think so too. Clear as day. She loves him.'

'Not only loves him, she's in love with him!' declared Alexandra. 'But to think, a man like that!'

'God bless her if that's how it must be', said Lizaveta Prokofievna, crossing herself devoutly.

'It must be fated', the general assented, 'there's no running away from that.'

And they all passed into the drawing-room, where another surprise awaited them.

Aglaya, far from bursting out laughing as she had feared when approaching the prince, was so apprehensive of him that she spoke almost diffidently:

'Forgive a stupid, wicked, spoilt girl' (she took his hand), 'and rest assured that all of us hold you in high esteem. And if I ventured to ridicule your beautiful . . . sweet-natured simplicity, then forgive me as you would a naughty child: forgive me for persisting in an absurd charade which of course cannot give rise to the least consequence . . .'

Aglaya laid particular emphasis on these last words.

Father, mother, and sisters all managed to reach the drawing-room in time to hear and see everything, and they were all struck by that 'cannot give rise to the least consequence', and still more by Aglaya's grave demeanour as she spoke of her 'absurd charade'. They all exchanged questioning glances; the prince, however, seemed not to comprehend these words and was supremely elated.

'Why do you say such things', he murmured, 'why are you . . . asking forgiveness?'

He wanted to say that he was unworthy of being begged for forgiveness. Who knows, perhaps he had realized the meaning of 'an absurd charade which cannot have the least consequence', but, odd fellow that he was, he may even have been glad to hear them. It was beyond doubt though, that the very fact that he could come and see Aglaya again without hindrance, that he could talk with her, sit with her, go for walks with her, was enough to make him blissfully happy, and who knows, perhaps he would have remained content with that for the rest of his life! (It was just this contentment that Lizaveta Prokofievna feared inwardly; she could see through him; she had many secret misgivings, which she could not have put into words herself.)

It would be hard to imagine the prince's gaiety and high spirits that evening. He was in such good humour that people felt cheerful just looking at him—as Aglaya's sisters put it afterwards. He was full of talk, and that hadn't happened since the morning six months ago when he had first met the Yepanchins; after his return to Petersburg he had been noticeably and deliberately taciturn, and quite recently, he had let slip to Prince S, within everyone's earshot, that he had no right to degrade an idea by uttering it himself. He was virtually the only one who talked the whole evening, telling a great many stories; he responded to questions clearly, gladly, and in detail, but there was nothing in the least resembling small talk in all his conversation. All the ideas were serious, at times verging on the ingenious. The prince even ventured to expound some of his own views, his own private observations, and it would all have been rather ridiculous if it had not been so 'well expressed', as all his auditors later agreed. Though the general was fond of serious conversational topics, both he and Lizaveta Prokofievna found it too scholarly for their taste and towards the end of the evening became positively miserable. The prince, however, eventually went so far as to tell some extremely droll stories, at which he was the first to laugh, so that the others laughed, more at his joyous hilarity than at the stories themselves. As for Aglaya, she hardly said a thing all evening; she drank in every word the prince said, though she did not listen so much as gaze at him.

'The way she looks at him, can't take her eyes away; she hangs on his every word; not one slips by!' said Lizaveta Prokofievna to her husband. 'But tell her she loves him and she'd raise the roof!'

'It's fate—what can you do?' shrugged the general, and as he had taken a fancy to the phrase he went on repeating it. We should add that, speaking as a practical man, there was a great deal in the present situation that was not to his liking, most particularly the vagueness of it all; still, he resolved to say nothing for the present and merely look . . . into Lizaveta Prokofievna's eyes.

The family's mood of elation did not last long. The very next day Aglaya quarrelled with the prince, and so it went on ceaselessly throughout the following days. She would hold the prince up to ridicule for hours on end and make him out to be little better than a clown. True, they did sit occasionally for an hour or so in the summer-house in the little garden, but it was noticed that at such times the prince was almost always reading the paper or some book to Aglaya.

'Do you know', Aglaya said to him once, interrupting his perusal of the newspaper, 'I've noticed that you're awfully uneducated; you don't know anything properly, if anyone asks you: who it was, when it happened, or what treaty it was. You're really pitiful.'

'I told you my general knowledge is poor.'

'What have you got if you haven't got that? How on earth can I respect you after that? Go on reading; or rather don't, stop reading.'

And again that evening she gave a hint of something very puzzling to them all. Prince S had returned from Petersburg and Aglaya was making a fuss of him, asking him a good deal about Radomsky (the prince had not yet arrived). All of a sudden, Prince S ventured to hint at the 'imminent alteration in the household', picking up on some remark Lizaveta Prokofievna had let slip about it being necessary perhaps to put off Adelaida's wedding again, so that both weddings could take place at the same time. Everyone was taken aback as Aglaya flared up at 'all these stupid assumptions', and in passing, blurted out that 'she certainly had no intention as yet of taking the place of anyone's mistress'.

These words stunned them all, especially her parents. Lizaveta Prokofievna insisted, during a privy conference with her husband, that he had got to have it out with the prince about Nastasya Filippovna once and for all.

The general swore that it was only an 'outburst', attributable to Aglaya's 'shyness'; that if Prince.S had not started talking about the wedding, it wouldn't have happened, because Aglaya was well aware, knew it for a fact, that it was all a slander put about by ill-disposed individuals, and that Nastasya Filippovna was going to marry Rogozhin; far from conducting a liaison, the prince had nothing to do with her; in fact he never had, if the whole truth were told.

The prince, meanwhile, did not seem to let anything embarrass him and continued to bask in bliss. Oh, of course, even he was sometimes aware of Aglaya's sullen and fretful looks; but his faith lay elsewhere and the gloom dispersed of itself. Once having placed his trust in something, nothing could cause him hesitation. Perhaps he was too serene; that, at least, was how it appeared to Ippolit, when he chanced to encounter him in the park.

'Well now, wasn't I right when I told you back then that you were in love?' he began, coming up to the prince of his own accord and accosting him. The prince offered his hand and congratulated him on looking so well. The invalid did indeed seem brisk and cheerful, as is often the way with consumptives.

He had approached the prince intending to pass some caustic remark about him looking happy, but was distracted at once and started talking about himself. He began complaining, and kept it up at length, somewhat incoherently.

'You wouldn't believe', he concluded, 'how touchy and small-minded, how selfish, vain, and banal they all are; if you can believe it, they took me only on condition that I died as quickly as possible, and now they're all furious because I'm not dying and actually feel better. What a laugh! I'll wager you don't believe me?'

The prince was not disposed to contradict.

'I sometimes think of moving in with you again', Ippolit added casually. 'So then, you don't think them capable of taking a man in on condition that he's sure to die, and as soon as possible at that?'

'I thought they had other reasons for inviting you.'

'Oho! You're not half as simple as people make you out! Now's not the time, otherwise I'd tell you a thing or two about friend Ganya and his hopes. They're undermining you, Prince, unmercifully, and . . . it's really pitiful to see you so unconcerned. Ah well, you can't help it!'

'What a thing to pity me for!' laughed the prince. 'What, you think I'd be happier if I were more worried?'

'Better to be unhappy and *know* than happy and live . . . in a fool's paradise. It seems you aren't the slightest bit worried that you have a rival . . . in that quarter?'

'Your remarks about rivalry smack of the cynical, Ippolit; I'm sorry I don't have the right to answer you. As for Gavrila Ardalionovich, you must admit he can hardly stay unruffled after all that he has lost, if you have the least inkling of his affairs. I think it would be better to look at things from that point of view. He has time to change; he has a long life before him, and life is rich . . . but still . . . still', the prince lost the thread suddenly, 'about undermining . . . I don't really understand what you're talking about; let's drop the subject, Ippolit.'

'Yes, we'll leave it till later; besides, you have to be chivalrous about it, haven't you? Yes, Prince, you have to touch it with your finger so as not to believe it again, ha-ha! And do you despise me very much now—what do you think?'

'What for? Because you have suffered more than us, and are suffering still?'

'No, because I'm unworthy of my suffering.'

'He who can suffer more must be worthy of suffering more. Aglaya Ivanovna wanted to see you, after reading your confession, but . . .'

'She's putting it off . . . she can't, I understand, I understand . . .', Ippolit broke in, as if to change the subject as quickly as possible. 'By the way, I hear that you read all that rigmarole to her yourself; it really was written . . . and done in delirium. And I can't understand how anyone could be so—I won't say cruel, that would humiliate me—so childishly vain and vindictive to reproach me for that confession and use it as a weapon against me. Don't worry, I'm not talking about you . . .'

'I'm sorry that you're repudiating that manuscript Ippolit, it has sincerity, and even the absurd parts of it—and there are plenty of those' (Ippolit scowled), 'are redeemed by suffering, because such admissions also constitute suffering and . . . perhaps great courage. The idea that prompted you to write was certainly a noble one at bottom, however it may have seemed. That becomes steadily clearer to me as time goes by. I am not judging you, I'm merely saying what I think, and I'm sorry I didn't say so at the time . . .'

Ippolit flushed. The thought crossed his mind that this was a pretence and the prince was trying to catch him out; looking at his face, however, he could not but believe in his good faith; his own face cleared.

'And for all that, to have to die!' he said, almost adding: 'a man like me!' 'And you can't imagine how that Ganya of yours plagues me; he's thought up—by way of an objection—that perhaps three or four of those who listened to my manuscript at the time will die before me! What do you think of that? He thinks that's a consolation, ha-ha! In the first place they haven't died yet; but even if they had, that's no sort of consolation, you must admit!

He judges everybody by himself; incidentally, he goes further—now he just abuses me, saying that in this situation a
decent man would die in silence and the whole thing was just
self-conceit on my part! What do you think of that! No, but what
about his own self-conceit! What exquisite, or rather what
bovinely gross egoism they have—and can't observe it in
themselves! . . . Have you ever read, Prince, about the death of a
certain Stepan Glebov* in the eighteenth century? I happened to
read it yesterday . . .'

'What Stepan Glebov was this?'

'He was impaled in Peter the Great's time.'

'Ah, good heavens, yes I know! He was fifteen hours on the
stake in his fur coat in the bitter cold, and died most nobly; of
course I've read about it . . . what of it?'

'God can grant that kind of death to some people, but not to
us! Perhaps you don't think I'm capable of dying like Glebov?'

'Oh, not at all', the prince was disconcerted. 'I just meant that
you . . . not that you wouldn't have been like Glebov, but . . . that
you would more likely have been . . .'

'I can guess: like Osterman, not Glebov, is that what you
meant?'

'What Osterman?' The prince was baffled.

'Osterman, Osterman the diplomat, Peter the Great's Osterman', muttered Ippolit, suddenly losing his train of thought. A
certain puzzlement ensued.

'Oh, n-n-no! I didn't mean that', the prince suddenly brought
out after an interval of silence. 'I don't think you could ever have
been an Osterman . . .'

Ippolit frowned.

'Actually, the reason I say that', the prince resumed, evidently
anxious to make amends, 'is because men in those days (it's
something that has always struck me, believe me), were not at all
the people we are today, not the same race of men as we are
nowadays, really, a different breed . . . Back then, people were
driven by a single idea somehow, now they're more edgy, more
mature, more sensitive, able to cope with two or three ideas at a
time . . . the man of today has a wider apprehension and, believe
me, that prevents him from being harmoniously integrated as

they were in those days ... that ... that was the only thing I had in mind, not ...'

'I understand; now you're doing your best to mollify me after disagreeing with me so naively, ha-ha! You're a perfect child, Prince. However, I can't help noticing that you treat me like ... like a china cup ... It's all right, it's all right, I'm not angry. At all events we've had a most amusing conversation out of it; you're like an absolute child sometimes, Prince. I'd like you to know, however, that I might well prefer to be someone rather better than Osterman; it wouldn't be worth rising from the dead to be an Osterman ... However, I can see that I should die as soon as possible, or I could well ... Leave me ... *Au revoir!* Well, all right, well, tell me yourself then, what would be the best way for me to die in your opinion? ... So as to be most ... virtuous, I mean? Well, go on!'

'Pass by us and forgive us our happiness!' said the prince in a low voice.

'Ha-ha-ha! Just as I thought! I knew it would be something like that! Really, you ... really, you ... Well, well! These men of eloquence! *Au revoir, au revoir!*'

6

VERA Ardalionovna had been perfectly correct in what she had told her brother about the evening gathering at the Yepanchins' villa, where Princess Belokonskaya was expected; the guests were indeed expected that evening; but again she had put it rather more strongly than was warranted. True, things had been organized in very much of a hurry and attended with a certain quite unnecessary flurry, simply because in that family 'everything was done differently from anyone else'. It could all be put down to Lizaveta Prokofievna's eagerness 'not to be kept in suspense any longer', and the tremulous fluttering of both parental hearts over the happiness of their favourite daughter. Besides, Princess Belokonskaya really was leaving shortly, and since her patronage carried weight in society and as they hoped that she would be well disposed towards the prince, the parents were counting on society accepting Aglaya's fiancé directly from the hands of the all-powerful 'old woman'—consequently, if there was anything odd about the affair, her patronage would make it seem a good deal less so. That was the whole trouble; the parents were incapable of deciding for themselves whether there *was* anything odd in all this business, and if so, how much exactly? Or was there nothing odd about it at all? The friendly and candid opinion of influential and competent persons was just what was needed at this juncture, when, thanks to Aglaya, nothing had yet been finally settled. In any event, sooner or later the prince had to be introduced into society, of which he had not the smallest comprehension. In a nutshell, they intended to 'put him on show'. The party, however, was planned on simple lines: only a restricted number of family friends was anticipated. Apart from Belokonskaya they expected another lady, the wife of a prominent landowner and high dignitary. Radomsky was practically the only young person they counted on arriving; he had to appear as he was escorting Belokonskaya.

The prince heard almost three days beforehand that Belokonskaya would be there; he only learned of the formal party itself the day before. Naturally he had noticed the harassed looks of the members of the family, and from certain anxious insinuations when they talked to him, he realized that they were apprehensive as to the impression he might make. Every last one of the Yepanchins, however, had got it into their heads that his native simplicity would prevent him from divining that they were so worried on his account. That was why, when they looked at him, their hearts sank within them. In point of fact he attached almost no significance to the forthcoming event; he was preoccupied with something else entirely: Aglaya was becoming more fretful and sullen with each passing hour—that was what was crushing him. When he found out that they expected Radomsky as well he was delighted, and said that he had wanted to see him for a long time. Unaccountably these words were not to anyone's liking; Aglaya left the room in a huff, and it was only late in the evening, some time after eleven, when the prince was already leaving, that she seized the opportunity to say a few words to him alone as she was seeing him out.

'I would like you not to come tomorrow during the day; come in the evening when these . . . guests will be here. You know there are guests coming?'

She spoke impatiently and with exaggerated harshness; it was the first time she had mentioned the 'party'. She too found the idea of the visitors almost intolerable; everyone noticed that. She might well have been strongly inclined to quarrel with her parents about it, but pride and shyness prevented her speaking up. The prince at once realized that she too was apprehensive on his behalf (and didn't want to admit it), so suddenly took fright himself.

'Yes, I'm invited', he replied.

She obviously found it difficult to go on.

'Is it possible to talk seriously about anything with you? Just once in your life?' She had suddenly lost her temper completely, without knowing why, but was unable to stop herself.

'Yes, and I'm listening to you; I'm very glad', mumbled the prince.

Aglaya was silent for a moment, then began again with obvious repugnance:

'I didn't want to argue with them about this; there are times when you can't make them see sense. I've always detested these rules that *maman* insists on sometimes. I'm not talking about papa, you can't expect anything from him. *Maman* of course is a high-principled woman; dare to suggest anything underhand to her and you'll see. Well, but she bows and scrapes in front of that . . . trash! I'm not just talking about Belokonskaya: she's a trumpery old crone, with a character to match, still, she's cunning and knows how to keep them all in hand—you can say that for her at least. It's so sordid! And laughable as well: we've always been middle-class people, as middle-class as you can possibly get; why try to climb into high society? My sisters are the same; it's Prince S that's set them in a whirl. Why are you glad Radomsky is coming?'

'Look, Aglaya', said the prince, 'it seems to me that you're very worried on my account in case I'm a flop tomorrow . . . among the society people.'

'On your account? Worried?' Aglaya blushed furiously. 'Why should I worry on your account, I don't care if you . . . I don't care if you disgrace yourself completely. What's it to me? And how can you use words like that? What do you mean "flop"? It's a trashy word, vulgar.'

'It's . . . a schoolboy expression.'

'Of course, a schoolboy expression! A wretched word! I suppose you're intending to use expressions like that all the time tomorrow. Look up some more like that in your dictionary at home: that's just the impression you want to create! It's a pity you know how to enter a room properly, it seems; where did you learn to do that? Will you know how to accept and drink a cup of tea properly when everyone is making a point of watching you?'

'I think I can.'

'That's a pity; otherwise I'd have a good laugh. At least smash the Chinese vase in the drawing-room! It's valuable; smash it, please; it was a present and *maman* will go off her head and burst into tears in front of everybody, she thinks so much of it. Make some gesture, like you always do, knock it over and smash it. Sit close to it on purpose.'

'On the contrary, I'll try and sit as far away as I can: thank you for the warning.'

'So you're already worried about making expansive gestures. I'll wager you get talking about some "topic", something serious, learned, elevated? How . . . nice that will be!'

'I think that would be silly . . . if it wasn't relevant.'

'Listen to me, once and for all', Aglaya had lost patience at length. 'If you start talking about anything like capital punishment, or the economic state of Russia, or about "beauty saving the world", then . . . of course I'll be delighted and have a really good laugh, but . . . I warn you in advance: don't ever let me see you again! You hear: I mean it! This time I really mean it!'

She certainly delivered her threat as if she meant it—there was even something exceptional in her voice and expression that the prince had never noticed before, and of course was not in the least like a joke.

'Well, now you've made it certain I'll "start talking" and even . . . perhaps . . . smash the vase. Earlier on I wasn't afraid of anything, but now I'm afraid of everything. I'll certainly flop.'

'Say nothing in that case. Just sit and say nothing.'

'I won't be able to; I'm sure I'll start talking out of sheer nervousness, and smash the vase for the same reason. I might fall over on the polished floor or something like that, because that's happened to me before; I'll be dreaming about it all night tonight; why did you have to say anything!'

Aglaya regarded him dolefully.

'You know what; it's best if I don't come at all tomorrow! I'll report sick, and there's an end of it!' he decided at length.

Aglaya stamped her foot and went positively white with anger.

'Heavens! Did you ever see anything like it? He won't come when it's specially for him and . . . Good lord! What a pleasure it is having to do with such a . . . dunderhead as you!'

'All right, I'll come, I'll come!' the prince hastened to break in. 'And I give you my word of honour that I'll sit there the whole evening and not utter a word. That's what I'll do.'

'By far the best thing. You said "report sick" just now; really, where do you pick up expressions like that? What makes you want to use such words when you're talking to me? Are you teasing me, or what?'

'I'm sorry; it's another school expression; I shan't say it again. I'm very well aware that you're . . . apprehensive on my account . . . (don't be angry, please!) I'm very pleased that you are. You've no idea how fearful I am and—how pleased I am at your words. But I swear, all this panic is just trivial nonsense. It really is, Aglaya! But the joy will remain. I'm terribly glad that you're such a child, such a good, kind child! Ah, how wonderful you can be, Aglaya!'

Aglaya would have flown into a rage of course, indeed she wanted to, but all of a sudden an unexpected access of emotion took instant possession of her soul.

'And you won't reproach me for my harsh words just now . . . any time . . . afterwards?' she asked abruptly.

'Of course not, of course not! And why have you flared up again? You're looking grim again! You do look very gloomy sometimes, Aglaya, you never did before. I know why that is . . .'

'Don't say it, don't!'

'No it's better to say it; I've wanted to say it for a long time; I already have said it, but . . . too little, you didn't believe me. Between us there still stands one creature . . .'

'Don't, don't, don't, don't!' Aglaya interrupted him hurriedly, laying tight hold on his arm and staring at him almost in horror.

At that moment, she was called for; almost gladly, she left him and ran away.

The prince was in a fever of anxiety all night. It was odd, but he had felt feverish for several nights in a row. This time an idea came to him in his semi-delirium: what if he had an epileptic seizure in front of them all? Hadn't he suffered fits in public before? He turned ice-cold at the thought; all night he kept picturing himself in every kind of weird and unheard-of company, the oddest of people. The main thing was that he 'started talking'; he knew that he shouldn't do it, but he kept on talking all the time, trying to persuade them of something. Radomsky and Ippolit were also among the guests and seemed on excellent terms.

He woke up after eight with a headache, his thoughts in turmoil; he was haunted by strange impressions. Unaccountably, he felt terribly keen to see Rogozhin, to see him and talk to him at length—about what he didn't know himself; then he definitely made up his mind to go and see Ippolit for some reason. His heart felt vaguely troubled, so that the impact of the morning's events, powerful as it was, seemed to be somehow diluted. One of these events consisted of a visit from Lebedev.

Lebedev appeared quite early, just after nine, almost completely drunk. Although the prince had become rather unobservant of late, he could hardly help noticing that since General Ivolgin had moved out three days before, Lebedev had been conducting himself very badly. All of a sudden he had become extremely stained and grubby, his tie was askew and his coat collar was ripped. In his own rooms he would rage and bellow and the noise could be heard across the little courtyard. Vera had come over once in tears and told him something about it. As he made his entrance now, he started speaking very oddly and striking himself on the chest and blaming himself for something . . .

'I have been requited . . . requited for my treachery and baseness . . . A slap in the face!' he concluded tragically.

'A slap in the face! Who from? . . . So early?'

'So early?' Lebedev smiled sarcastically. 'The time has nothing to do with it . . . even for physical retribution . . . this was a moral slap in the face . . . moral not physical!'

He sat down abruptly, without ceremony, and began to tell his tale. His narrative was markedly incoherent; the prince frowned and felt like leaving, when all of a sudden he was dumbfounded by something Lebedev said ... Mr Lebedev was recounting some curious things.

At first, there seemed to be some letter involved; Aglaya Ivanovna's name was mentioned. Then Lebedev suddenly began vehemently accusing the prince; it appeared that the prince had hurt his feelings. At first, said he, the prince had honoured him with his trust in matters connected with a certain 'personage' (Nastasya Filippovna); later, however, he had broken with him entirely and driven him away with ignominy—and so woundingly, moreover, that last time he had rudely rebuffed 'an innocent question concerning imminent alterations in the household'. Lebedev confessed with drunken tears that 'after that he simply couldn't bear it, especially as he had been well informed ... very well informed ... both by Rogozhin and Nastasya Filippovna, and by her friend, and by Varvara Ardalionovna ... from her own lips ... and by ... and by Aglaya Ivanovna herself even, imagine that, sir, through Vera, my darling daughter, my only daughter ... yes, sir ... well, not my only one, as I've got three. And who kept on passing information to Lizaveta Prokofievna by letter, in the very deepest secrecy, sir, heh-heh! Who kept writing to her about all the relationships and ... the movements of the Nastasya Filippovna personage heh-heh-heh! Who, who is this anonymous person, may I ask?'

'Surely not you?' cried the prince.

'It is indeed I', replied the drunkard with dignity, 'and at half-past eight this very morning, a mere half-hour ... no, three-quarters ago, sir, I informed her most noble ladyship that I had an incident to report ... something important. I sent her a note through one of the maids at the rear porch. She received me.'

'You've just seen Lizaveta Prokofievna?' asked the prince scarcely able to believe his ears.

'I saw her just now and got a slap in the face ... morally. She returned the letter, flung it at me in fact, unopened ... and I was thrown out neck and crop ... morally, I mean, not physically ... it was almost physically though, not far off!'

'What letter did she fling back at you unopened?'

'But surely ... heh-heh-heh! But I haven't told you yet, have

I! And here I was thinking I'd told you . . . I'd got the one little letter to hand over, sir, to . . .'

'From whom? To whom?'

Some of Lebedev's 'explanations', however, were extremely difficult to follow or make any sense of. The prince did gather, to the best of his understanding, that the letter had been handed over early that morning through a maid to Vera Lebedeva, for delivery to an address . . . 'the same as before . . . the same as before to a certain personage and from the same person, sir . . . (one of them I designate as a "person", sir, and the other only as a "personage", as a mark of disparagement and to differentiate them; for there is a great difference between an innocent and most honourable general's daughter and . . . a *camellia*, sir), and so, the letter was from a 'person' beginning with the letter A . . .'

'How can that be? To Nastasya Filippovna? Rubbish!' cried the prince.

'It was, it was, sir, and if not to her, then to Rogozhin, sir, it makes no difference, Rogozhin, sir . . . or even to Mr Terentyev; there was a letter to him once, for delivery from the "person" whose name begins with A', Lebedev winked and smiled.

As he frequently skipped from one subject to another, and kept forgetting what he had started to say, the prince stopped speaking so as to let him finish. Nevertheless, it was all still very vague: had the letters passed through him or Vera? If he asserted that it didn't matter whether they were addressed to Rogozhin or Nastasya Filippovna, it was more likely they had not been sent through him, that is if there had been any letters at all. How this particular letter had reached him now remained completely unexplained; the most likely supposition was that he had somehow stolen it from Vera . . . slyly purloined it and taken it to Lizaveta Prokofievna for reasons of his own. Thus the prince reasoned and concluded.

'You've taken leave of your senses!' he exclaimed in profound dismay.

'Not altogether, dear Prince', replied Lebedev, not without a touch of malice. 'True, I was going to give it to you, into your own hands, as a favour . . . but I thought it might be better to do the favour elsewhere and reveal everything to her most noble ladyship . . . since I had informed her once before, by means of an anonymous letter; when I wrote this morning beforehand, to ask her to receive me at eight-twenty, I again signed it: "your secret correspondent"; I was admitted at once, immediately . . . to her most noble ladyship.'

'Well?'

'As I've already told you, sir, I was almost assaulted, I mean just a little bit, sir, so it might almost be said I did get a beating, sir. And she threw the letter at me. True, she did want to keep it. I saw that, I did notice that, but she changed her mind and flung it at me: "If they've entrusted it to a man like you, go ahead and deliver it . . ." Really offended, she was. If she did not scruple to say it to my face, it means she was offended. An irascible nature!'

'Where is this letter now, then?'

'I've still got it, here it is, sir.'

And he handed over the note Aglaya had written to Gavrila Ardalionovich, which the latter was to show triumphantly to his sister two hours later on that morning.

'You can't keep this letter.'

'It's for you, you! It's you I'm bringing it to, sir!' Lebedev explained feelingly. 'Now I'm yours again, all yours, from head to heart, your servant, sir, after my fleeting moment of treachery, sir! Punish my heart, but spare my beard, as Sir Thomas More said . . . in England, and in Great Britain, sir. *Mea culpa, mea culpa*, as the Roman Pope says . . . I mean, he's the Pope of Rome but I call him the Roman Pope.'

'This letter must be sent off at once', the prince bestirred himself. 'I'll deliver it myself.'

'But wouldn't it be better, much better, most courteous Prince, better, sir, to . . . do this, sir!'

Lebedev pulled a strange, pathetic face, accompanied by a vast amount of fidgeting about in his chair, as if he had been suddenly stuck with a needle. He kept giving crafty winks and demonstrating something with his hands.

'What is that supposed to mean?' the prince asked grimly.

'Why not open it first, sir!' he whispered ingratiatingly.

The prince leapt to his feet in such a fury that Lebedev took to his heels, but paused on reaching the door and waited in case the prince relented.

'Ah, Lebedev! Is it really possible to stoop to such depths

as you have?' cried the prince, distressed. Lebedev's face brightened.

'I'm vile, vile!' He approached the prince at once, tearfully beating his breast.

'That's abominable!'

'Abominable it is, sir. The very word, sir!'

'What's this penchant you have for acting in this . . . odd way? It means you're . . . nothing but a spy! Why did you send an anonymous letter and distress such a noble and good-hearted lady? And in any case, why hasn't Aglaya the right to write to whom she pleases? Did you go over there to complain today, or what? What did you expect to get out of it? What prompted you to turn informer?'

'Only to satisfy my curiosity, and . . . to be of service to a noble soul, yes sir!' mumbled Lebedev. 'But now I am yours to command, yours heart and soul once more! Hang me if you like!'

'Did you go to see Lizaveta Prokofievna looking like that?' enquired the prince, with distaste.

'No, sir . . . much cleaner, sir . . . and really decent, sir; I reached . . . this state after my humiliation, sir.'

'Well, all right, leave me now.'

Actually the request had to be repeated several times before the visitor eventually made up his mind to leave. With the door wide open, however, he came back again and tiptoed into the centre of the room, once again making letter-opening gestures; he did not venture to repeat his advice aloud; after that he went, smiling softly and sweetly.

All this had made very painful listening. Out of it had emerged one salient fact: that Aglaya was greatly troubled, and in deep uncertainty and mental anguish for some reason (jealousy, the prince whispered to himself). It was also clear that she was being plagued by ill-disposed individuals, and it was certainly strange that she reposed so much trust in them. Of course, in that inexperienced but impulsive and proud young head, all sorts of special plans were brewing, perhaps disastrous and . . . and extravagantly foolish. The prince was greatly alarmed and did not know what course to adopt in his perplexity. He sensed that he had certainly got to do something to forestall events. He glanced again at the address on the sealed letter: oh, he had no doubts or disquiet on that score, because he trusted her; it was something else about the letter which made him uneasy—he could not trust Ganya. However that might be, he had resolved to deliver it personally to him, and had already left his house for the purpose when he changed his mind on the way. Almost at the door of Ptitsyn's house he providentially met Kolya, and asked him to deliver the letter into his brother's hands, as if it had come straight from Aglaya Ivanovna. Kolya asked no questions and delivered it, so that Ganya was unaware that the letter had made so many stops on the way. Back at his house, the prince sent for Vera and told her as much as was needful to set her mind at rest, as she had been searching for the letter all this time and was in tears. She was horrified to learn that her father had made off with it. (The prince later found out from her that she had often run secret errands for Rogozhin and Aglaya Ivanovna; it had never entered her head that anything harmful to the prince's interests might be involved.)

The prince became so distraught at length, that when a messenger from Kolya arrived some two hours later with news of his father's stroke, he could barely comprehend at first what it was all about. But it was this occurrence which actually restored him, by providing a powerful distraction. He stayed at Nina Alexandrovna's (where they had naturally taken the sick man) practically till evening. He was of very little use, but there are people who are pleasant to see close by in time of trouble. Kolya was terribly affected and cried hysterically, but nevertheless, he was constantly on his feet: he ran for the doctor, and brought three, he ran to the chemist and the barber. The general revived, but did not recover consciousness; the doctors gave it as their opinion that, 'at all events, the patient is in a critical condition'. Varya and Nina Alexandrovna never left the patient's bedside; Ganya was aghast and deeply shaken, but didn't want to go upstairs and feared even to see the sick man; he kept wringing his hands and, in the course of an incoherent talk with the prince, he managed to say 'what a misfortune it was; it would happen just at a time like this!' The prince fancied he knew exactly what this 'time' was. The prince had not found Ippolit at the Ptitsyns'. Towards evening, Lebedev came trotting along; after that morning's 'explanations' he had slept all day without waking.

Now he was practically sober and wept genuine tears over the sick man, as if he had been his own brother. He blamed himself aloud, without, however, explaining why, and kept pestering Nina Alexandrovna, assuring her every minute that 'it was he, he was the cause, no one but him . . . solely out of idle curiosity . . . and that "the deceased"' (as he insisted on calling the still living general) 'was a man of the greatest genius!' He laid particular stress on this genius, as if some special good might come of it at that moment. Nina Alexandrovna, seeing the sincerity of his tears, said to him at length, with no hint of reproach, indeed with something approaching affection: 'Well, God be with you, there, there, don't cry, God will forgive you!' Lebedev was so overcome by these words and the tone in which they were uttered that he was unwilling to leave Nina Alexandrovna for the rest of the evening (and throughout the days following, right up to the general's death, he spent his time almost from morning till night in their house). During the day, messengers twice came from Lizaveta Prokofievna asking after the general's health. When, at nine o'clock that evening, the prince made his appearance in the Yepanchins' drawing-room, which was already crowded with guests, Lizaveta Prokofievna at once began to make sympathetic and detailed inquiries of him about the invalid's progress. She made a dignified reply to Belokonskaya's question as to who the sick man was and who Nina Alexandrovna was. The prince was much pleased at this. For his part, when explaining matters to Lizaveta Prokofievna, he spoke 'beautifully' as Aglaya's sisters expressed it afterwards: 'modest, quiet, restrained in speech, no gestures, replete with dignity; he made a splendid entrance; he was superbly dressed', and so far from 'falling over on the polished floor', as he had feared the previous day, he seemed to make a positively agreeable impression on the company.

For his part, once he had taken his seat and looked about him, he noticed at once that those present bore no resemblance to the bogies Aglaya had terrified him with the day before, or to his subsequent nightmares. For the first time in his life he was seeing a small corner of what bore the dread name of 'society'. Consequent upon certain particular intentions, ideas, and inclinations of his own, he had long wished to break into this charmed circle of people and so took a keen interest in his first impression of it. This first impression was positively entrancing. He had an immediate feeling, somehow, that all these people were simply born to be together; that the Yepanchins were not giving a party that evening at all, and there were no invited guests; they were all friends together, and he himself had long been their devoted associate and shared their opinions; he was now returning to them after a brief separation. The charming effect of elegant manners, simplicity, and seeming candour, verged on the magical. It could never have occurred to him that all this good nature and high-mindedness, all this wit and lofty sense of dignity, might only be a superb artistic veneer. The majority of the guests, their impressive outward appearance notwithstanding, comprised rather shallow individuals, who were too complacent to realize that many of their good points were simply a veneer, something they were not responsible for, since it had been acquired unconsciously through inheritance. Rapt in the delicious spell of his first impressions, the prince was not disposed to have any inkling of this. He saw, for example, that this old man, this important dignitary, who might have been his grandfather, actually broke off his own conversation in order to listen to a young and inexperienced person like himself, and not merely listen, but clearly value his opinion, so affable towards him, so genuinely good-natured, and yet they were strangers and were meeting for the first time. Perhaps it was this refined courtesy which most powerfully affected the prince's ardent sensibilities. Perhaps he was too much predisposed, won over in advance, perhaps, to a favourable view of events. Meanwhile all these people, although 'friends of the family' and of each other of course, were by no means such friends either of the family or of one another, as the prince had supposed while he was being introduced to them. There were people here who would never under any circumstances have admitted the Yepanchins as even approaching equality with them. There were people who positively detested each other; old Belokonskaya had despised the wife of the 'old dignitary' all her life, and the latter, for her part, was far from being fond of Lizaveta Prokofievna. This 'dignitary', her husband, who had been the Yepanchins' patron for some reason since their very young days and immediately assumed the chair this evening, was such a grand personage in General Yepanchin's eyes that the latter could feel nothing but reverence and awe in his presence, and would genuinely have despised himself had he for a moment considered him as an equal, rather than Olympian Jove. There were people there who had not met for several years and felt nothing for each other beyond indifference, if not actual aversion; nevertheless, they greeted one another now as if they had only met the day before, in the friendliest and most agreeable company. However, the gathering was not a large one. Besides Belokonskaya and 'the old dignitary'—certainly an important figure—and his wife, there was, first of all, a certain very imposing army general, a baron or a count, with a German name; he was a man of extreme reticence, with a reputation for being vastly knowledgeable in affairs of state and even a hint of scholarly eminence— one of those Olympian administrators who know everything 'except perhaps Russia herself'; he was a man who, once in five years, uttered a dictum 'remarkable for its profundity', certain to become an adage and gain currency in the highest circles; he was one of those highly placed officials who, after extremely (even singularly) long service, commonly die after attaining exalted rank in the highest positions in the land and considerable fortunes to go with them, though they can boast no great achievements and, if anything, have always displayed a certain hostility to such achievements. This general was the immediate superior of General Yepanchin in the service. Ivan Fedorovich, from the ardour of a grateful heart—and even a peculiar sort of vanity—regarded him as his benefactor. The general, however, by no means regarded himself as Ivan Fedorovich's benefactor, and treated him with complete unconcern, though glad enough to avail himself of his many good offices. He would have replaced him without a second thought, if some consideration, not necessarily of the highest importance, had made that desirable. There was another impressive-looking middle-aged nobleman present, who was even supposed to be a relation of Lizaveta Prokofievna, though this was quite untrue; he was a man of exalted rank and title, rich and of high birth, thickset and in robust health, a great talker, with some reputation as a malcontent (though in the most permissible sense of the word), even choleric (though even that was agreeable in him), with the habits of an English aristocrat—and English tastes to suit (as regards, for example, underdone roast beef, horse-tackle, servants, and so forth). He was a great friend of the 'dignitary' and kept him amused—besides which Lizaveta Prokofievna cherished the odd notion that this middle-aged man (a somewhat light-minded individual and quite an admirer of the fair sex) might suddenly take it into his head to make Alexandra happy by proposing marriage.

After this topmost and most worthy stratum of the gathering, came one made up of younger guests, though also distinguished by brilliant qualities. Apart from Prince S and Yevgeni Pavlovich Radomsky, this stratum boasted the celebrated and charming Prince N, sometime seducer and conqueror of female hearts all over Europe, still at about 45 preserving his splendid appearance; he was a brilliantly accomplished raconteur, a man of wealth, whose financial affairs were in some disarray, however, and who was in the habit of spending most of his time abroad. Lastly, there were those present who made up something like a third layer, who did not belong to the 'exclusive circle' of society, but who could nevertheless be encountered in that circle on occasion, just like the Yepanchins themselves. Prompted by a certain sense of fitness, and regarded by them as a rule of conduct, the Yepanchins, on the rare occasions when they gave a formal party, liked to mingle the highest society with people from a lower stratum, along with selected representatives of 'the middle class of people'. The Yepanchins were even lauded for this and were spoken of as people of tact who knew their place, and they took pride in this opinion. One of these middle-class representatives at this party was a colonel of engineers, a grave individual and a very close friend of Prince S, who had brought him along to the Yepanchins. He was a taciturn man in society, however, and wore a large and conspicuous diamond solitaire on the forefinger of his right hand, most likely presented to him. Finally, there was actually a literary man, a Russian poet of German extraction, moreover a perfectly decent chap who could be introduced into polite society without a qualm. He was of handsome, though somehow repellent, appearance, about 38, impeccably dressed. He belonged to a family which was extremely bourgeois but extremely respectable; he had an eye for the main chance, and could contrive to secure the patronage of highly placed personages and retain their goodwill. At one time he had translated some important work by an important German poet, knew how to dedicate the translation in verse—and to whom; knew how to boast of his friendship with a celebrated, though deceased, Russian poet (there is a whole cluster of writers who are terribly fond of proclaiming in print their friendship with great but deceased writers), and had been introduced quite recently to the Yepanchins by the wife of the 'old dignitary'. This lady was given out to be the patroness of literary men and scholars, and one or two writers actually had got a pension through highly placed persons with whom she had influence. And influence of a kind she did have. She was about 45 (and thus a very young wife for such an old stick as her husband was), a former beauty, with a mania even now, as many ladies of her age have, for dressing up a touch too grandly; she was of small intelligence and her knowledge of literature was extremely dubious. Patronizing literary men, however, was as much a mania with her as overdressing. A great many compositions and translations had been dedicated to her; two or three writers had, with her permission, published the letters they had written to her on matters of great moment . . . And it was all this society that the prince took for the genuine article, the purest, unalloyed gold. This evening, however, as luck would have it, all these people were also in the most genial of spirits and well pleased with themselves. Every last one of them knew they were doing the Yepanchins a great honour by being there. Alas, however, the prince had no suspicion of subtleties such as these. He had no suspicion, for example, that the Yepanchins, in contemplating such a weighty step as their daughter's future, would never have dared not to exhibit him, Prince Lev Nikolayevich, to the old dignitary, the acknowledged patron of their family. The latter too, though for his part he could have borne with equanimity the news of the most dreadful disaster which might have befallen the Yepanchin family, would assuredly have been offended if they had consented to the engagement of their daughter without consulting him and, as it were, without his permission. Prince N, that charming, that incontestably witty, that utterly open-hearted individual, was totally convinced that he was a kind of sun, rising that night over the Yepanchin drawing-room. He regarded them as being infinitely far beneath him, and it was this simple and generous notion which prompted his wonderfully gracious ease and cordiality towards these same Yepanchins. He was well aware that he had to tell some story that evening without fail for the delight of the company, and prepared himself for it with a touch of positive inspiration. Prince Lev Nikolayevich, on hearing the story later, felt that he had never heard the like of such brilliant humour, such wonderful, artless merriment, almost touching to hear on the lips of such a Don Juan as Prince N. And yet, had he but realized how old and stale the story was, how it was known by heart, a hackneyed bore in every drawing-room—and only at the innocent Yepanchins' did it seem the fresh, unexpected, spontaneous, and brilliant recollection of a brilliant and splendid man! Even the German poetaster, though he behaved with great courtesy and diffidence, virtually considered that he was honouring the house with his presence. But the prince didn't notice the reverse of the medal, or see any undercurrent in all this. This was a misfortune Aglaya had not foreseen. For herself, she was wonderfully pretty that evening. All three young ladies were smartly dressed, though without overdoing it. They had had their hair done in a special way. Aglaya was sitting with Radomsky and talking and joking with him in very friendly fashion. For his part, Yevgeni Pavlovich was perhaps a little more formal than usual; this too might have been out of respect for the grandees. He had long been known in society, however; though still a young man, he was no stranger there. He had arrived at the Yepanchins' that evening with a crêpe band round his hat, and Belokonskaya had complimented him on it: not every nephew about town perhaps, in the circumstances, would have worn mourning for such an uncle. Lizaveta Prokofievna had also been gratified by that, but on the whole she seemed extremely anxious. The prince noticed Aglaya glancing closely at him once or twice and seeming to be satisfied with him. Little by little, he was beginning to feel terribly happy. His 'fantastic' thoughts and misgivings of the previous day (after his conversation with Lebedev), seemed to him now, as they darted swiftly into his mind every now and then, altogether impossible, inconceivable, an absurd figment! (In any case, his primary, if unconscious, desire and inclination then, and all during the day, had been somehow to render that dream incredible!) He spoke little, and then only in answer to a question; finally he lapsed into silence altogether, just sitting and listening, but obviously blissfully content. Gradually, something akin to inspiration began welling up in him too, ready to burst out when the occasion arose . . . He began speaking quite by chance, also in reply to a question, and seemingly without any special intent.

7

WHILE he was lost in the delightful contemplation of Aglaya chatting gaily to Prince N and Radomsky, all of a sudden the middle-aged anglophile nobleman, who had been entertaining the dignitary in another corner of the room and relating something to him in a very lively manner, let fall the name of Nikolai Andreyevich Pavlischev. The prince swiftly turned in their direction and began to listen.

The conversation concerned present-day management regulations and the muddles there were on the landed estates in a certain province. The anglophile's stories must have contained something amusing, because the old chap eventually began to laugh at the peppery vehemence of the speaker. He was speaking suavely, with a kind of peevish drawl, tenderly stressing his vowels, about why he had been forced by these new regulations to sell his splendid property in that province for half its value, despite not being pressed for money, while at the same time having to keep another estate that was ruined, a drain on resources and the subject of a lawsuit—and even have to spend money on it. 'To avoid another lawsuit over the Pavlischev property, I got out of it. One or two more inheritances like that and I'll be ruined, won't I? I should have got eight thousand acres of first-class land, incidentally.'

'This . . . Ivan Petrovich fellow is a relation of the late Nikolai Andreyevich Pavlischev', said General Yepanchin to the prince in an undertone. 'You were looking for his relatives, weren't you?' He had suddenly materialized by the prince's side, noticing his intense interest in the conversation. Up till now, he had been entertaining the general, who was his service superior, but having been aware of the prince's conspicuous isolation for some time now, he had grown uneasy; he wanted to get him to take some part in the conversation and thus show him off a second time to the 'superior persons'.

'Lev Nikolayevich was Pavlischev's ward, after the death of his parents', he put in, catching Ivan Petrovich's eye.

'Ho-ow do you do-o', drawled the latter. 'I remember you very well, actually. When General Yepanchin introduced us earlier on I recognized you at once, it was the face. You've hardly changed at all to look at, though I only saw you as a child, you'd be about 10 or 11. There's something about the features . . .'

'You saw me as a child?' asked the prince, with marked surprise.

'Oh, a very long time ago now', Ivan Petrovich went on, 'in Zlatoverkhovo, where you were living at the time with my cousins. I used to drop by Zlatoverkhovo quite often—you don't remember me? Qui-ite possibly you don't . . . At the time you were . . . you had some illness, at the time; I remember being quite taken aback once . . .'

'I don't remember anything at all!' the prince reiterated, with some emotion.

A few more words of explanation, supremely unruffled on the part of Ivan Petrovich, strangely agitated on the part of the prince, and it transpired that the two ladies, old maids both, relatives of the late Pavlischev, who were living on his Zlatoverkhovo estate, having charge of the prince's upbringing, were also Ivan Petrovich's cousins. Like everyone else, Ivan Petrovich was at a loss to explain the reasons which had prompted Pavlischev to take so much trouble over the little prince, his adopted child. 'Well, I didn't take much interest in it at the time.' All the same, he turned out to have an excellent memory, since he even recalled how strict his elder cousin, Martha Nikitishina had been with the little boy, 'so that I had words with her once over you and her way of bringing you up, because birching and birching a sick child, it's . . . you have to admit . . .', and how affectionate, on the other hand, the younger cousin, Natalya Nikitishina had been . . . 'Now both of them', he

went on, 'are living in —— province, where Pavlischev left
them a very nice little property indeed; I don't know if they are
still alive though. Martha Nikitishina wanted to enter a convent, I
believe; I wouldn't swear to it though; perhaps it was somebody
else I heard about . . . oh yes, it was a doctor's wife, the other
day . . .'

The prince drank this in, eyes glistening with rapturous
emotion. He declared with unwonted feeling that he would never
forgive himself for not having taken the opportunity, during his
six months of travelling round the central provinces, of seeking
out and visiting his old guardians. 'He had intended going every
day, but something had always cropped up . . . but now he
pledged his word . . . most certainly . . . even if it was in ——
province . . . So you know Natalya Nikitishina? Such a beautiful,
such a saintly woman! But Martha Nikitishina too . . . I'm sorry,
but I think you're wrong about her! She was strict, but . . . she
was bound to lose patience . . . with an idiot such as I was (hee-
hee!). After all I was a real idiot, you wouldn't believe it (ha-ha!).
Still . . . still, you saw me at the time and . . . How comes it that I
don't remember you, can you please tell me that? So you . . . ah,
good heavens, can you really be a relation of Pavlischev's?'

'I ass-ure you I am', smiled Ivan Petrovich, gazing at the
prince.

'Oh, I didn't mean to say that I doubted your word of
course . . . how could one doubt it in any case (heh-heh!) . . .
even a tiny bit!! (heh-heh!) I just said it because Nikolai
Andreyevich Pavlischev was such a splendid man! The noblest of
men, really, I assure you!'

The prince was not so much breathless as 'choked with
goodness', as Adelaida expressed it next morning, when talking
to her fiancé, Prince S.

'Why, good heavens!' laughed Ivan Petrovich. 'Now why
shouldn't I be related even to the no-blest of men?'

'Oh, goodness!' cried the prince, embarrassed, hurrying on in
mounting animation. 'I . . . I've said something stupid again,
but . . . that's to be expected because I . . . I . . . I, still that's not
the point either! And what is there in me, pray, compared with
such interests . . . such vast interests! And compared with the
supreme nobility of the man, because that's what he was, really
and truly, the noblest of men, wasn't he. Wasn't he?'

The prince fairly shook. It would have been hard to say why he had suddenly become so wrought-up and gone into such rapturous emotion for no apparent reason, and, as it would seem, out of all proportion to the topic under discussion. He was simply in that sort of mood; it was almost as if, for some reason, he felt the warmest and most heartfelt gratitude to someone—perhaps to Ivan Petrovich, but practically to all the guests present. His cup of happiness was truly running over. At length Ivan Petrovich began to regard him a good deal more closely; the dignitary too was staring at him most intently. Belokonskaya directed an irate look at him and pursed her lips. Prince N, Radomsky, Prince S, the girls—everyone broke off their conversations to listen. Aglaya seemed alarmed, while Lizaveta Prokofievna simply quailed. The girls and their mama were being rather perverse in fact: they were the ones who had proposed and resolved that the prince would do better to sit through the evening in silence; but no sooner had they espied him in a corner in perfect isolation and perfectly happy with his lot, than they were at once filled with disquiet. Alexandra had been about to go over to him and fetch him discreetly across the room and attach him to their own group, that is Prince N's group around Belokonskaya. But now that the prince had started talking of his own accord, they were even more alarmed.

'You're right when you say he was a most excellent man', declared Ivan Petrovich weightily, by now no longer smiling. 'Yes, yes . . . a splendid man! Splendid and worthy', he added after a slight pause. 'Worthy, one might say, of every regard', he added, even more impressively, after a third pause, 'and . . . it's certainly nice to see that you . . .'

'Wasn't it the same Pavlischev involved in that . . . odd business . . . with the abbé . . . the abbé . . . I've forgotten which one, everybody was talking about it at the time', said the dignitary, as if striving to recall.

'The Abbé Goureau, the Jesuit', Ivan Petrovich reminded him. 'Yes indeed, there are our most excellent and worthy people for you! After all, he was a man of birth and fortune, a Court Chamberlain, and if he'd . . . gone on being a public servant . . . But there he goes and throws it all up to join the Catholics and become a Jesuit, and made very little secret of it either, practically gloried in it. Of course he died just in time . . . yes; everybody said so at the time . . .'

The prince was beside himself.

'Pavlischev . . . Pavlischev converted to Catholicism? That can't be possible!' he exclaimed in horror.

'Well now, "impossible" is going a bit far, don't you think, my dear Prince?' Ivan Petrovich mumbled gravely. 'Still, you think so highly of the deceased . . . certainly he was a most kindly natured man, to which I mainly ascribe the success of that old fox Goureau. But just ask me how much trouble and fuss I had to contend with over this business . . . with this selfsame Goureau! Imagine', he addressed the old man suddenly, 'they even wanted to make a claim under the provisions of the will, and I had to resort to the most energetic measures . . . to get them to see sense . . . because they're past masters at this sort of thing! They're a-mazing! Still, thank the Lord it happened in Moscow, I went straight to the count, and we . . . made them see sense . . .'

'You have no idea how much you have shocked and distressed me!' the prince cried again.

'I'm sorry about that; but when all's said and done, really it's all a lot of nonsense, and that's what it would have come to in the end, as usual; I'm sure of that. Last summer', here he addressed the old man again, 'Countess K went into a Catholic convent as well, somewhere abroad; our people seem not to hold out once they give an inch to those . . . sly rogues . . . abroad especially.'

'I think it all stems from our . . . weariness', mumbled the old fellow with an air of authority. 'The way they preach as well . . . it's elegant, all their own . . . and they know how to put the fear of God into people. They tried to scare me too, in Vienna back in thirty-two, believe you me; only I didn't succumb, I ran away from them, ha-ha!'

'I heard tell, my dear sir, that you gave up your post that time and ran away from Vienna to Paris with the beautiful Countess Levitskaya, not to escape the Jesuits', put in Belokonskaya suddenly.

'Well, yes, but it was from the Jesuit wasn't it, it means I was escaping from the Jesuit!' the little old man responded, laughing heartily at the fond memory. 'You seem to be very religious, which is so rare in a young man nowadays', he said gently to the prince, who was listening open-mouthed, still in a state of shock; the old man was evidently eager to know more of the prince, who had begun to interest him greatly for some reason.

'Pavlischev was a man of unclouded intellect and a Christian, a true Christian', the prince brought out abruptly. 'How on earth could he have submitted to a faith that is ... unchristian? ... Catholicism is the same as an unchristian religion!' he added suddenly, eyes flashing as he stared straight ahead, seeming to include them all in his gaze.

'Well, that is going too far', muttered the old man, glancing at General Yepanchin in surprise.

'How can Catholicism be an unchristian religion?' enquired Ivan Petrovich, swivelling on his chair. 'What sort is it then?'

'First of all, it is an unchristian religion!' the prince began again, very much agitated and speaking with undue harshness. 'That's the first thing, and the second thing is that Roman Catholicism is even worse than out-and-out atheism, that's how I see it! Yes, that's how I see it! Atheism just preaches negation, but Catholicism goes further than that: it preaches a distorted Christ, traduced and abused by itself, the opposite of Christ! It preaches the Antichrist, I swear it, I can assure you of that. It is my own long-held conviction and it has indeed tormented me ... Roman Catholicism believes that without universal temporal dominion, the Church cannot survive on earth: '*Non possumus*',* they cry. In my opinion, Roman Catholicism is not even a faith, it's a continuation of the Western Roman Empire, and everything in it is subordinate to that idea, beginning with their faith. The pope seized the earth, an earthly throne, and took up the sword; since that time everything has gone the same way, except that to the sword they've added lies, intrigue, deceit, fanaticism, superstition, and evil-doing. They have trifled with the most sacred, truthful, innocent, and ardent emotions of the people and bartered them all, all of them, for money and paltry temporal power. Is not this the teaching of Antichrist? Atheism was bound to come from them! Atheism did come from them, from Roman Catholicism itself! Atheism first came into being through them: could they believe in themselves? It gained strength from the abhorrence in which they were held; it is the spawn of their lies and spiritual impotence! Atheism! In our country it is only the social élite who do not believe, as Mr Radomsky put it so splendidly the other day, they have lost their roots; meanwhile in Europe, great masses of the common people are themselves losing their faith—at first from ignorance and falsehood, but now through hatred of the Church and Christianity!'

The prince stopped to catch his breath. He had been speaking terribly quickly. He was pale and panting. Everyone exchanged glances; but at length the little old man openly burst out laughing. Prince N took out his lorgnette and regarded the prince fixedly. The little German poet crept out of his corner and edged closer to the table, smiling ominously.

'You do ex-ag-gerate a lot', drawled Ivan Petrovich, a touch bored, almost as if he were ashamed of something. 'Their Church also has representatives who are worthy of high regard and are most vir-tuous . . .'

'I never mentioned individual members of the Church. I was speaking of Roman Catholicism as such, the essence of it; I'm talking about Rome. Can a Church disappear entirely? I never said that!'

'Agreed, but all that is well known and—beside the point and . . . belongs to the realm of theology . . .'

'Oh no, oh no! Not just theology, I do assure you, it isn't! It concerns us much more closely than you think. That's where we make our mistake, not seeing that this is not just something that has to do with theology! After all, socialism too is the spawn of Catholicism and its essence! Like its brother, atheism, it too was born out of despair, in moral opposition to Catholicism, to try to replace the lost moral power of religion, to assuage the spiritual thirst of parched humanity and save it, not through Christ, but again through violence! This too is freedom through violence, unification through sword and bloodshed! "Don't you dare believe in God, don't dare to possess property, don't dare to have individuality, *fraternité ou la mort*,* two million heads!" By their works ye shall know them—it is written! And don't go thinking that all this is innocent and poses no danger for us; oh no, we must repel it and quickly, quickly! Our Christ must shine out in opposition to the West, the Christ we have preserved and whom they have not known! Not slavishly taking the Jesuit hook, but carrying our Russian civilization to them. We must stand before them now and let it not be said among us that their preaching is elegant, as someone said just now . . .'

'No, I'm sorry, I really am sorry', Ivan Petrovich was beginning to get dreadfully nervous, even fearful, as his eyes roved the room. 'All your ideas are laudable of course and highly patriotic, but it's all greatly exaggerated and . . . perhaps we'd better leave it there . . .'

'No, it's not exaggerated, it's an understatement if anything; yes, an understatement because I can't express myself properly, but . . .'

'No, rea-lly!'

The prince stopped short. He was sitting bolt upright and motionless, staring at Ivan Petrovich, eyes blazing.

'I think this business about your benefactor has been too much of a shock', suggested the old man gently, retaining his composure. 'You're over-excited . . . perhaps because of your solitary way of life. If you had more to do with other people, society, I hope, would welcome you as a splendid young man, and of course, you would calm your excitement and come to see that all these things are much simpler . . . and as I see it, such rare cases . . . occur partly because of our surfeit and partly from . . . boredom . . .'

'That's it, that's it exactly', cried the prince. 'A magnificent idea! It is from boredom, our boredom, not from surfeit, on the contrary, from our thirst . . . not surfeit, you're mistaken there! Not only thirst, but fever, burning thirst! And don't think this is so trifling a matter we can afford just to laugh at it; I'm sorry, but one must be able to see ahead! As soon as our people get to the shore, as soon as they're sure it is the shore, they're so overjoyed they lose all sense of proportion; why is that? You're surprised at Pavlischev now, you put everything down to his madness or goodness of heart, but you're wrong! And this passionate Russian intensity astonishes all Europe, not us alone: if a Russian goes over to Catholicism, he's sure to become a Jesuit, and a most assiduous one at that; if he becomes an atheist, he's bound to start demanding the violent extirpation of religious belief, meaning, of course, by the sword! Why is this, why such fury all of a sudden? Don't you know? It's because he has found the motherland he missed here, and he is overjoyed; he has found the shore, dry land, and flings himself down to kiss it! It is not just out of exhibitionism; Russian atheists and Jesuits are not merely born out of sordid feelings of vanity, they spring from spiritual anguish, spiritual thirst, a yearning for higher things, a firm shore underfoot, a homeland they had ceased to believe in, because they had never known it! It's so easy for a Russian to become an atheist, easier than for anyone else in the world! And Russians don't just become atheists, they positively believe in it. As if it were some new faith, oblivious of the fact they are believing in a negation. Such is the thirst we have! "He who has not firm ground beneath his feet, has no God either." Those aren't my words. They are the words of a merchant, an Old Believer, whom I encountered on my travels. True, he didn't put it that way. What he said was: "He who has renounced his native land, has renounced his God also." And just to think that some of our most cultivated people have even turned flagellant! . . . But still, in this sense, are flagellants worse than nihilists, Jesuits, or atheists? They may be more profound than any of them! But that's what their yearning has brought them to! . . . Show the shores of the New World to the thirsting and parched crewmen of Columbus, show the Russian World to a Russian, let him seek out the gold, the treasure hidden away from him in the earth! Show him the future renewal of all mankind, and its resurrection, perhaps through Russian thought alone, the Russian God and Christ, and you will see what a mighty, truthful, wise, and gentle giant he will rise before an astonished world, astonished and frightened, because all they expect from us is the sword, the sword and violence, because, judging by themselves, they cannot imagine us as other than barbarians. That is how it has been up till now, and as time goes on, the more it will be so! And . . .'

Here, however, something happened to cut short the orator's speech in the most unexpected fashion.

All this hectic tirade, all this outpouring of passionate, agitated words and rapturous ideas, jostling and tumbling over one another in a kind of turmoil, foretold something ominous, something peculiar in the mental state of this young man who had so suddenly broken out for no apparent reason. Of those present in the drawing-room, all who knew the prince wondered uneasily (and some with embarrassment) at this outburst of his, so out of keeping with his usual almost timid reserve, his rare and singular tact on other occasions, and his instinctive feeling for the decencies of behaviour. They couldn't understand how it had come about: the news about Pavlischev couldn't possibly have been the cause. In their corner, the ladies were looking at him as if he had gone mad, and Belokonskaya confessed afterwards that 'another minute and I would have run for safety'. The 'elders' were disconcerted by the initial surprise of it all: the general-superior looked on with stern disapproval from his chair. The engineer colonel was sitting stock-still. The little German had turned positively pale, but still retained his counterfeit smile, glancing at the others to see how they would respond. Actually all this, the whole embarrassing scene in fact, might have been resolved within the minute in the most ordinary and natural fashion; General Yepanchin, considerably astonished, but recovering himself quicker than the rest, had tried several times to halt the prince; after failing to do so, he was now making his way towards him, intent on firm and resolute action. Another moment and, had it been necessary, he would have nerved himself, perhaps, to lead the prince away in a friendly manner, on the pretext that he was ill; Ivan Fedorovich certainly believed he was, and it might well have been the case in fact . . . But events took a different turn.

At the very start of the evening, as soon as the prince came into the drawing-room, he had seated himself as far as possible from the Chinese vase that Aglaya had so alarmed him about. Could one really believe that, after Aglaya's words of the day before, a kind of indelible conviction had imprinted itself on the prince's mind, a sort of amazing and impossible presentiment that he would smash the vase the following day, no matter how he tried to steer clear of it and avoid disaster? But so it was. As the evening wore on, other powerful and luminous emotions began to flood his soul; we have already spoken of these. He forgot about his presentiment. When he caught the conversation about Pavlischev, and General Yepanchin had brought him up to introduce him to Ivan Petrovich for the second time, he had moved his seat nearer the table and sat himself down in an armchair close to a huge and beautiful Chinese vase, standing on a plinth almost level with his elbow and a little behind.

As he spoke his last words, he suddenly rose from his seat and waved his arm carelessly, moved his shoulder somehow—and . . . there was a sudden cry from all present! The vase tottered, as if initially undecided whether to fall on the head of one of the old men, but abruptly yawed in the opposite direction, where the little German barely leapt aside in horror, and fell to the floor. The crash, the shouts, the precious shards scattered over the carpet, the dismay, the astonishment—it would be difficult, indeed unnecessary, to describe what the prince was feeling. We must mention, however, an odd sensation that came over him at that instant and stood out sharply from all the other strange and confused emotions that came crowding in upon him: it was not the embarrassment, the disgrace, the fear, not the suddenness of it all that struck him most forcibly, it was that the prophecy had come to pass! He would have been at a loss to explain what was so arresting about this notion; he simply felt stricken to the heart and stood there in a terror that was almost mystical. A moment passed and everything before him seemed to expand; instead of horror—light and gladness, ecstasy; he began to struggle for breath and . . . but the moment passed. Thank God, it wasn't that! He took a deep breath and looked about him.

For a long time he seemed not to comprehend the commotion seething all around, or rather he understood perfectly well and saw everything, but kept standing there like a man apart, who had had no hand in it all; like the invisible man in the fairy-tale, he had made his way into the room and was observing people he did not know, but whom he found interesting. He saw the fragments being cleared away, heard the sound of rapid conversation, saw Aglaya, pale and looking strangely at him, most strangely: there was no hatred in her eyes and not a trace of anger; she was gazing at him with a frightened but affectionate expression while her eyes flashed at the others . . . all at once he felt a sweet pang in his heart. At length, he saw with an odd amazement that everyone had resumed their seats and were even laughing, just as if nothing had happened! A minute passed and the laughter grew louder: now they were laughing as they looked at him, at his mute stupefaction, but the laughter was friendly and cheerful; many of them spoke to him and they spoke so gently, Lizaveta Prokofievna above all: she was laughing as she spoke, and saying something very very kind. Suddenly he became aware that General Yepanchin was patting his shoulder in friendly fashion; Ivan Petrovich was also laughing; but better still, most agreeable and affectionate of all was the little old man; he took the prince's hand and, pressing it gently and patting it lightly with his other palm, urged him to pull himself together, as if he were a little frightened boy (which appealed to the prince very much), and then sat him down close by his side. The prince gazed into his face in sheer pleasure, but still found it hard to speak for some reason, his breath failed him; he liked the old man's face so much.

'What?' he murmured at length. 'You really do forgive me? And . . . you, Lizaveta Prokofievna?'

The laughter swelled. Tears started into the prince's eyes; he could not believe it, and he was enchanted.

'Of course it was a beautiful vase. I remember it being here for the last fifteen years or so, yes . . . fifteen . . .', Ivan Petrovich began.

'Well, what a calamity! Every human being comes to an end and here we are fussing over a clay pot!' said Lizaveta Prokofievna loudly. 'You didn't let it alarm you, Lev Nikolayevich, did you?' she added, with real apprehension. 'It's all right, dear, it's all right; you frighten me, you really do.'

'And do you forgive me for *everything*? Apart from the vase?' The prince made as if to rise suddenly, but the old man at once tugged at his arm. He was reluctant to let him go.

'*C'est très curieux et c'est très sérieux*',* he hissed across the table to Ivan Petrovich, rather loudly however; the prince might indeed have heard it.

'So I haven't offended any of you? You won't believe how happy that thought makes me; but that's how it should be! How could I possibly offend anyone? I should be offending you again if I thought so.'

'Calm yourself, my friend, you're exaggerating this. You have no reason at all to thank us; it's a fine feeling to have, but exaggerated.'

'I'm not thanking you, I'm only . . . feasting my eyes on you, it makes me happy just to look at you; perhaps what I say is stupid but—I have to say something, I have to explain . . . if only for the sake of my own self-esteem.'

Everything about him was jerky, confused, and feverish; often the words he uttered were possibly not those he wished to say. His expression seemed to ask permission to speak. His gaze fell upon Belokonskaya.

'It's all right, dear sir, do go on, only don't get out of breath', she remarked. 'You started when you were panting just now and look what happened; don't be afraid to speak up: these gentlemen have seen things a lot queerer than you, you won't astonish them, you're not so difficult to fathom, it's just that you smashed that vase and gave them all a fright.'

The prince heard her out, smiling.

'Wasn't it you', he addressed the old man abruptly, 'wasn't it you who saved the student Podkumov and Shvabrin the official from exile in Siberia three months back?'

The old man blushed a little and muttered something about calming himself.

'And wasn't it you I heard about', he at once addressed Ivan Petrovich, 'when you gave timber free to the peasants in —— province after their village was burned down, even though they were free and had caused you trouble?'

'Now that's ex-ag-gerating it', murmured Ivan Petrovich, assuming a pleasurably dignified air all the same. This time, however, he was absolutely right about it being an exaggeration: the rumour that had reached the prince was untrue.

'And you, Princess', he turned suddenly towards Belokonskaya with a bright smile, 'was it not you, six months ago, who received me like her own flesh and blood, on Lizaveta Prokofievna's written recommendation, and gave me some advice I shall never forget. Do you remember?'

'Why make such a fuss about it?' cried Belokonskaya, vexed. 'You're a good fellow, but you're silly; somebody gives you a penny and you thank them as if they'd saved your life. You think that's commendable in you, but it isn't, it's distasteful.'

She was ready to lose her temper in good earnest, but all of a sudden burst into laughter, this time good-natured. Lizaveta Prokofievna's face cleared; General Yepanchin beamed.

'I was telling you that the prince was a man . . . a man . . . anyway, just as long as he doesn't go losing his breath, as the princess observed . . .', mumbled the general blissfully, repeating the princess's words, which had struck him forcibly.

Aglaya alone seemed cast down, though her face was still flushed, perhaps with indignation.

'He really is very endearing', the old man murmured to Ivan Petrovich again.

'I entered this room with anguish in my heart', the prince resumed, with rising emotion, speaking ever more rapidly, more strangely and eagerly. 'I . . . I was afraid of you, afraid of myself. Myself most of all. When I came back here, to Petersburg, I resolved that I must see our foremost men, senior people, those of old-established families, to which I belong myself, men among whom I am one of the first in lineage. Now I sit among princes like myself, don't I? I wanted to get to know you, and I had to do it; I had to, had to! . . . I had always heard a great deal more that was bad about you than good, about your petty and exclusive interests, your backwardness, your shallow culture, your absurd habits—so much is written and spoken about you! I came here today in curiosity and perplexity: I needed to see for myself and make up my own mind as to whether all this upper stratum of Russian society was effète, had outlived its time and exhausted itself through its prolonged existence, and was only fit to die out—but still engaged in a petty and envious struggle against the people . . . of the future, obstructing them, unaware that it was itself dying. I never fully supported that opinion myself, because we have never really had an upper class in Russia, except for the courtiers, the military men, or . . . by accident and now it has disappeared altogether, that's so isn't it? Isn't it?'

'Well, no it's not like that at all', Ivan Petrovich gave a caustic laugh.

'Well, now, he's off again', Belokonskaya could not resist saying.

'*Laissez-le dire!** He's positively trembling all over', admonished the little old man again in an undertone.

The prince was fairly beside himself.

'And what happened? I saw people who are elegant, unaffected, and intelligent; I saw a venerable old man who makes a fuss of a boy like me and lets me have my say; I see people capable of understanding and forgiveness, good-hearted Russian people, almost as good-hearted and warm as those I left behind abroad, practically as good as those. Judge for yourselves what a glad surprise that was! Ah, let me tell you this! I had heard a great deal that I willingly gave credence to—that in high society it was all outward show, nothing but antiquated forms of behaviour from which the substance had withered away; but I can actually see for myself that it cannot possibly be the case with us; it may be so elsewhere but not here. Are all of you here really Jesuits and deceivers? I heard Prince N telling a story just now—wasn't that unaffected, inspired humour? Genuine good nature? Could words like that come from the lips of a man who is . . . dead, a man whose heart and gifts have withered away? Could dead men behave towards me as you have? Could such men fail to understand and fall behind the times?'

'I would ask you again, dear fellow, do calm yourself, we'll discuss all that some other time and I shall be delighted . . .', smiled the dignitary.

Ivan Petrovich gave a grunt and swivelled round in his chair; General Yepanchin stirred; his superior-general was talking to the wife of the dignitary, by now ignoring the prince completely; the dignitary's wife, however, kept listening in and glancing over at him.

'No, it is best if I talk, you know!' the prince resumed, with a fresh access of feverish energy, addressing himself to the old man in a trusting and oddly confidential kind of way. 'Yesterday Aglaya Ivanovna forbade me to talk— and even listed the topics I shouldn't talk about; she knows what a poor figure I cut if I do! I'm going on for 27 but I know I'm like a child. I don't have the right to express what I think, I've always said that. The only time I've ever talked frankly was with Rogozhin in Moscow . . . We read Pushkin together, everything; he didn't know a thing, not even Pushkin's name . . . I'm always afraid my odd appearance will detract from the thought and the *main point*. My gestures are all wrong. I always use them in the opposite way to what I am saying, and that raises a laugh and takes away from the idea. The sense of proportion just isn't there either, that's the main thing; that really is the main thing . . . I know it would be better just to sit and say nothing. When I do resolutely keep quiet, I seem very sensible and it gives me time to reflect as well. But it's better that

I should speak now. I started talking because you look at me so pleasantly; you have a wonderful face! I gave Aglaya Ivanovna my word yesterday that I'd keep quiet all evening.'

'*Vraiment?*' The old man smiled.

'But at times I think I'm wrong to think that way: sincerity is worth more than mere gestures, that's right, isn't it? Isn't it?'

'Sometimes.'

'I want to make it all clear, everything, everything, everything! Oh yes! You think I'm a utopian, an ideologist? Oh, no. All my ideas are very simple, believe me . . . You don't believe me? You smile? You see I am sometimes mean-spirited because I lose sight of my faith; on my way here earlier I was thinking, how on earth shall I talk to them: "Well now, how am I going to strike up a conversation with them? What words shall I begin with, so that they understand something at least?" I was greatly afraid, but more afraid on your account, terribly, terribly afraid! And yet how could I be afraid, was it not shameful for me to be afraid? What does it matter if there's a bottomless pit of backward and wicked people for every one progressive man? That's the reason I am so happy now—I'm convinced now that it isn't a bottomless pit at all, it's all living material! There's no need to be embarrassed if we're absurd, is there? It's a fact that we are absurd, light-minded, addicted to bad habits, we're bored, we don't know how to look at or understand anything, we're all like that, aren't we, all of us, you, I and everyone else! You don't take offence because I tell you to your face that you're absurd, do you? And if that's the case, then you are good material aren't you? You see, I think being absurd is actually all right sometimes, better than that in fact: it makes it easier to forgive one another and be properly humble; one can't understand everything in a flash, after all, you can't start off with perfection! To attain perfection you have to start off by being ignorant of many things! If we understand things too quickly we may not understand them properly. I am saying this to you, you who have been capable of understanding so much already . . . and failing to understand. Now I am not afraid on your account: you're not angry, are you, that a mere boy is saying such things to you? You're laughing, Ivan Petrovich. You think I was afraid on *their* account, I was *their* advocate, a democrat, a propounder of equality?' he broke into a hysterical laugh (he had been breaking into short, rapturous laughter at intervals). 'I am afraid for you, for all of you and all of us taken together. After all, I am a prince of ancient lineage and I sit among princes. I am saying this to save you all, to prevent our class disappearing pointlessly into the darkness, blind to the situation, constantly at odds, and so forfeiting everything. Why disappear and yield the place to others, when it is possible to stay in the front rank and be leaders? Let us stay in that front rank and so be leaders. Let us become servants in order to be masters.'

He started to pull free and get up from his chair, but the little old man kept holding him back, regarding him with growing uneasiness, however.

'Listen! I know it's wrong to talk: better to show an example, just to start . . . I've already started . . . and is it really possible to be unhappy? Ah, what are my grief and misfortune to me, if I have the capacity to be happy? Do you know, I can't understand how one can pass a tree and not be happy at seeing it! Talk to a man and not be happy at loving him! Oh, it's just that I can't find the words . . . and so many beautiful things at every step that even the most desperate man finds beautiful! Look at a child, look at God's dawn, look at the grass growing, look into the eyes that look at you and love you . . .'

He had been standing for a long time, as he spoke. The old man was by now looking at him in frank alarm. Lizaveta Prokofievna was the first to guess what was amiss and cried out: 'Oh, good God!' as she flung up her arms in dismay. Aglaya swiftly ran to him and managed to catch him in her arms, and, horror-stricken, her face distorted with pain, heard the wild cry of 'the spirit that cast down and racked'* the wretched man. He lay on the carpet. Someone hastily managed to put a cushion under his head.

This was something no one had expected. A quarter of an hour later, Prince N, Radomsky, and the little old man attempted to resuscitate the party, but half an hour after that everyone had dispersed. Many words of sympathy were spoken, a good many disgruntled remarks and various other comments were passed. Ivan Petrovich said, among other things, that 'the young man was a slav-o-phile, or something of the sort, but not dangerous'. The

old man said nothing. True, some two or three days later they
were all a little cross. Ivan Petrovich even felt offended, but not a
great deal. The superior-general behaved somewhat coldly to
General Yepanchin for a while. The family 'patron', the
dignitary, mumbled something sententious to the father of the
family, but spoke flatteringly at the same time of his very keen
interest indeed in Aglaya's future. He was actually rather a kind-
hearted man, but one of the reasons for his curiosity about the
prince during the evening had been the old story of the prince
and Nastasya Filippovna; he had heard something of the story
and was very much interested, and would have liked to question
him closely.

Belokonskaya said to Lizaveta Prokofievna, as she was leaving:

'Well, there's good and bad in him; but if you want my opinion,
more bad than good. You can see for yourself what he is, a sick
man!'

Lizaveta Prokofievna finally resolved that the prince was
impossible as a fiancé, and during the night vowed that while she
lived he would never become Aglaya's husband. Thus resolved,
she rose the next morning. But that same morning, during
breakfast at twelve, she lapsed into the most astonishing self-
contradiction.

In reply to a very guarded question from her sisters, Aglaya
suddenly responded with chilly hauteur, almost snapping:

'I have never given him a promise at any time and never in my
life considered him as my fiancé. He is as much a stranger to me
as anyone else.'

Lizaveta Prokofievna suddenly flared up.

'That I did not expect from you', she said, distressed. 'He's
impossible as a fiancé, I know, and thank God it's turned out as it
has, but I did not expect to hear words like that from you of all
people! I thought to hear something quite different from you. I'd
have turned everybody out who was there last night apart from
him, that's the kind of man he is! . . .'

Here she stopped short, afraid herself of what she had said.
But if she had only known how unfair she was being to her
daughter. Everything was settled by now in Aglaya's mind; she
too was awaiting the hour which must decide everything, and any
hint, any incautious touch, wounded her to the heart.

8

FOR the prince too, that morning began with grim forebodings; they might have been accounted for by his medical condition, but his misery was too ill-defined for that, which only made it the more tormenting. He was certainly confronted by clear-cut, painful, and galling facts, but his wretchedness went beyond anything he could grasp or call to mind; he realized that he could not compose himself on his own. He gradually arrived at the settled expectation that something special and decisive was going to happen to him that very day. The fit he had suffered the night before had been a minor one; apart from a sense of depression, a certain heaviness in the head and aches in his limbs, he felt no particular ill effects. His mind was working with reasonable clarity, even if he was sick at heart. He got up quite late and at once clearly recalled the previous evening; he also recalled, though not so clearly, being taken home half an hour after his fit. He learned that an emissary had already been over from the Yepanchins to ask how he was. At half-past eleven, another messenger arrived; he felt pleased at that. Vera Lebedeva was among the first to visit and wait upon him. The moment she saw him she suddenly started crying, but when the prince at once reassured her, she burst out laughing. He was quite suddenly struck by the powerful compassion of this girl towards him; he clutched her hand and kissed it. Vera blushed.

'Oh, don't do that, don't!' she cried out in alarm, swiftly withdrawing her hand.

She left soon after in an odd sort of embarrassment. Meanwhile, she had managed to tell him that her father had rushed off at first light to 'the deceased', as he kept calling General Ivolgin, to find out whether he had died in the night, and that she had heard it said that he would probably die soon. Lebedev himself came home after eleven and went to the prince, 'only for a minute', to inquire as to his precious health and so on, and rummage about in the 'cupboard'. He did nothing else but moan and groan, and the prince soon dismissed him, but all the same he had tried to ask a question or two about the previous night's seizure, though it was obvious he already knew all the details. Kolya trotted in after him, also just for a minute; he really was in a hurry and his mood was one of gloom and disquiet. He began by bluntly insisting on an explanation from the prince of all that people had been concealing from him, adding that he had already found out almost everything the day before. He was profoundly shaken.

With all the sympathy he was capable of the prince related the whole story, establishing all the facts with absolute precision; the poor boy was thunderstruck. He was unable to utter a word and wept in silence. The prince sensed that this was one of those moments which leave a permanent impression and mark a turning-point in the life of an adolescent boy. He hastened to give him his own view of the matter, adding that, in his opinion, the old man's imminent death might be due mainly to the horror he felt in his heart of hearts at his own delinquency, and that it was not everyone who was capable of such feeling. Kolya's eyes began to glitter when the prince had concluded.

'They're a rotten lot, Ganka, Varya, and Ptitsyn! I'm not going to quarrel with them, but from this moment forward our paths lie in different directions! Ah, Prince, since yesterday I've learned a lot that was new to me; it's a lesson to me! I also regard myself as directly responsible for my mother; I know she's provided for at Varya's, but that's not the same thing.'

He jumped to his feet, remembering that he was expected, asked hurriedly after the prince's state of health, and on hearing the response, swiftly added:

'Isn't there something else as well? I heard yesterday . . . I don't have the right I know, but if you ever need a loyal servant for anything, he's standing before you. It doesn't look as if either of us is exactly happy, does it? However . . . I'm not prying, I'm not prying . . .'

He went out and the prince pondered even more; everybody was prophesying disaster, they had all drawn their conclusions; everyone was looking as if they knew something he didn't; Lebedev was interrogating him, Kolya was making blunt hints, and Vera was crying. At length, he gave up in annoyance: 'It's my accursed morbid imagination', he thought. His face cleared when, soon after one o'clock, he saw the Yepanchins coming in to visit him, 'just for a moment'. With them it really was just a moment. Getting up from breakfast, Lizaveta Prokofievna had announced that they were all going out at once for a walk together. This notification was issued in the form of an order, abrupt, cold, and without explanation. They all went out—mama, the young ladies, and Prince S. Lizaveta Prokofievna at once set off in the opposite direction from the one they took every day. They all realized what was going on, and no one said anything for fear of irritating their mama, while she, as if to avoid any reproaches and objections, walked ahead of them all without looking back. At length Adelaida remarked that there was no need to run when out for a walk and they couldn't possibly catch up with their mother.

'So then', Lizaveta Prokofievna abruptly turned round to them, 'we're passing his house now, and whatever Aglaya may think and whatever happens afterwards, he is not a stranger to us, and now that he is wretched and ill into the bargain, I at least am going in to visit him. Whoever wants to go with me can do so, anyone who doesn't can walk on past; the path is clear.'

They all went in, naturally. The prince, predictably, hastened to apologize again for the vase and . . . yesterday's scene.

'Oh, that doesn't matter', replied Lizaveta Prokofievna, 'it's you I'm concerned about, not the vase. So you realize now that there was a scene: that's what "the morning after . . ." means, I suppose. Still, that doesn't matter either, since anyone can see that you're not to blame. Well, *au revoir*, then; if you feel up to it, go for a walk and then have another sleep, that's my advice. If you feel like it, drop in on us as before; you can be sure once and for all that, whatever happens and whatever transpires, you will still be a friend of the household, mine at any rate. I can answer for myself at least . . .'

They all rose to the challenge and confirmed their mother's sentiments. They left, but in this unaffected eagerness to say something kindly and encouraging, there lurked a good deal that was cruel, of which Lizaveta Prokofievna was unaware at the time. In the invitation to visit 'as before' and the words 'mine at least' there was an ominous ring. The prince tried to recall Aglaya; true, she had given him a wonderful smile on entering and leaving, but hadn't uttered a word, even when they were all declaring their assurances of friendship—though she had looked intently at him once or twice. Her face had been paler than usual, as if she had slept badly. The prince decided he would certainly go and see them that evening 'as before', and glanced feverishly at his watch. Vera came in exactly three minutes after the Yepanchins' departure.

'Aglaya Ivanovna has just given me a secret message for you, Lev Nikolayevich.'

The prince fairly quivered.

'A note?'

'No, sir, a verbal message; she only just managed that. She asks you particularly not to stir from the courtyard for a single minute today, right up to seven this evening, or nine even, I didn't quite get it all.'

'But . . . what for? What does it mean?'

'I don't know anything about that; she just said to make sure and tell you.'

'She said "make sure"?'

'No, sir, not in so many words: she hardly had time to turn round and say it, it was lucky I ran up to her myself. But I could see from her face that she meant it: make sure or not. She gave me such a look, my heart stood still . . .'

After further questioning, the prince's agitation increased, though he had learned nothing more. Left alone, he lay down on the sofa and began brooding again. 'Perhaps they're entertaining some guest till nine o'clock and she's afraid I'll get up to my tricks again in front of them', he concluded at length, and once more began glancing at his watch and waiting impatiently for the evening. The solution of the mystery came long before evening, however, also in the form of another visit, a solution in the form of a new, poignant mystery: some half-hour after the Yepanchins, Ippolit entered his room, so weary and exhausted that, without a word, he literally fell into a chair, as if unconscious, and instantly burst into an unbearable paroxysm of coughing. He coughed till the blood came. His eyes glittered and hectic spots reddened in his cheeks. The prince mumbled something to him, but he made no answer and for a long time kept waving the prince away. At length he recovered himself.

'I'm going!' he brought out with difficulty at last, in a hoarse voice.

'I'll see you home if you like', said the prince, half rising, then stopped, recalling the recent prohibition on leaving the court-yard.

Ippolit laughed.

'It's not you I'm going away from', he went on, gasping for breath and coughing slightly. 'On the contrary, I've found it necessary to come to you, and on business . . . otherwise I wouldn't have troubled you. I'm going *there*, and this time, I do believe, it's certain. *Kaput!* I'm not looking for sympathy, I assure you . . . I lay down this morning at ten intending not to get up until *the time* came, but I went and changed my mind and got up again to come and see you . . . that means I had to.'

'I'm sorry to see you like this; you should have sent for me, instead of giving yourself the trouble.'

'Well, that's enough then. You've expressed your regrets and that should cover the social amenities . . . Yes, I forgot: how is your health?'

'I'm all right. Yesterday I was . . . not very . . .'

'I heard, I heard. The Chinese vase caught it; pity I wasn't there! Anyway to business. Firstly, I had the pleasure today of seeing Gavrila Ardalionovich meeting Aglaya Ivanovna this morning, at the green bench. I was amazed to see how silly a man can look. I said as much to Aglaya after Gavrila Ardalionovich had gone . . . You seem not to be surprised at anything, Prince', he added, looking mistrustfully at the prince's impassive face. 'Not to be surprised at anything is a sign of great intellect, they say; in my opinion, it could just as well serve as a mark of great stupidity. I didn't mean you actually . . . I'm not having much luck in my expressions today.'

'I knew yesterday that Gavrila Ardalionovich . . .', the prince stopped short, evidently embarrassed, although Ippolit was annoyed that he had not been surprised.

'Knew! Now there's a novelty! Still, there's no need to tell me . . . But you didn't witness the meeting this morning?'

'You saw I wasn't there, since you were there yourself.'

'Well, sitting behind a bush somewhere perhaps. Still, at all events I'm glad, for your sake, naturally, otherwise I might have thought that Gavrila Ardalionovich was—the lady's preference!'

'I beg of you not to speak of it to me, Ippolit, especially using such expressions.'

'Especially as you know everything already.'

'You are wrong. I know practically nothing, and Aglaya Ivanovna certainly knows that. Even about the rendezvous I knew precisely nothing . . . You say there was a rendezvous? Very well, let's leave it at that . . .'

'Now how can that be, you knew and didn't know? You say very well, let's leave it . . . Oh no, don't be so trusting! Particularly when you don't know anything. That's why you are trustful, because you don't know. And do you know what those two, brother and sister, are reckoning on? You do suspect something in that direction, don't you? . . . All right, all right, I'll leave it there . . .', he added, noticing the prince's gesture of impatience, 'but I came on business of my own and that's what I want to . . . discuss. Damn it all, you can't even die without giving an account of yourself; it's awful the amount of explaining I do. Do you want to hear it?'

'Go ahead, I'm listening.'

'Still, I've changed my mind again: I'll start with Ganya after all. Can you believe that I also had an appointment by the green bench this morning? However, I have no wish to lie: I insisted on the meeting myself, I forced it on her by promising to reveal a secret. I don't know whether I arrived a little too early (it seems I actually did), but I had just taken my place next to Aglaya, when I saw Ganya and Varya coming along arm in arm, as if out walking. It seemed they were both astonished at seeing me. They certainly didn't expect that and they were really taken aback. Aglaya Ivanovna turned red and, believe me or believe me not, she rather went to pieces, whether because I was there or just at seeing Gavrila Ardalionovich, that most handsome man, but all she did was blush crimson and settled the matter inside a minute, very funny it was: she half rose, answered Ganya's bow and Varya's ingratiating smile, then suddenly snapped out: "I am here merely to express my pleasure personally for your sincere and friendly sentiments, and should I ever have need of them, be assured . . ." At this she bowed, and they both went off— whether in triumph or feeling like fools I don't know; Ganya of course felt foolish; he could make nothing of it and went as red as a lobster (what a wonderful expression his face has sometimes!), but Varvara Ardalionovna, I think, understood that they had better make themselves scarce quickly and that this was quite enough from Aglaya Ivanovna; so she dragged her brother away. She's cleverer than he is and I'm sure she's feeling gleeful now. I had come to have a talk with Aglaya Ivanovna about arranging a meeting with Nastasya Filippovna!'

'Nastasya Filippovna!' cried the prince.

'Oho! I do believe you're losing your sang-froid and beginning to be surprised? I'm very glad you mean to act like a human being. I'll amuse you as a reward. That's what comes of doing a good turn for high-minded young ladies: I got a slap in the face from her today!'

'M-moral?' the prince couldn't help asking.

'Yes, not physical. I don't think anyone would raise a hand against someone like me; even a woman wouldn't strike me now—even our Ganya wouldn't! Though for a moment yesterday I thought he would pounce on me . . . I'll wager I know what you're thinking at this moment. You're thinking: "Supposing he can't be thrashed, he could easily be smothered with a pillow or a wet cloth in his sleep—and ought to be . . ." That's what you're thinking, it's written all over your face.'

'I've never thought that!' the prince said in disgust.

'I don't know, I dreamed last night that somebody had smothered me with a wet rag . . . a certain person . . . well, I'll tell you who: just imagine—Rogozhin! What do you think, can a man be smothered with a wet rag?'

'I don't know.'

'I've heard it's possible. All right, let's leave it. Well then, why am I a scandalmonger? Why did she call me a scandalmonger today? And bear in mind, that was after she'd listened to every last word I had to tell her, and even asked me to repeat some of it . . . Still, that's women for you! It was on her account I got in touch with Rogozhin, that interesting man: it's for her sake I've arranged a personal interview with Nastasya Filippovna. Was it because I hurt her pride when I hinted she was glad of Nastasya Filippovna's "leavings". But it was in her own interests, I kept telling her that, I don't deny it; I wrote her two letters in that strain, and a third today, the meeting . . . I began this morning by telling her that she was degrading herself . . . And besides, that word "leavings" wasn't mine in actual fact, it was somebody

else's; everybody was saying it at Ganya's at any rate; she even
confirmed it herself. So how on earth can she call me a
scandalmonger? I can see, I can see, you're very amused as you
look at me now and I'll bet you're applying those stupid lines to
me:

> And it may be—upon my sad declining
> True love will smile, a valediction shining.

Ha-ha-ha!' He went into a paroxysm of hysterical mirth suddenly
and started coughing. 'Take note', he gasped through his coughs,
'Ganya's a fine one: he talks of "leavings" but he doesn't mind
doing the same himself!'

The prince was silent for a long time; he was horror-stricken.

'You spoke of a meeting with Nastasya Filippovna?' he
muttered at length.

'Oh dear, can it really be that you don't know there's to be a
meeting today between Aglaya Ivanovna and Nastasya Filippovna—who has been specially summoned from Petersburg,
through Rogozhin, at Aglaya's invitation and by my own efforts?
And that she is with Rogozhin now, not a million miles from you,
at her former address, Darya Alexeyevna's house . . . her
questionable lady-friend, and that Aglaya is going there today, to
that dubious residence, for a friendly chat with Nastasya
Filippovna and to sort out a number of problems? They want to
do some arithmetic. Didn't you know? Honestly?'

'It's incredible!'

'Well, have it your own way, it's incredible; anyway, how on
earth could you know? Although if a fly moves, everybody
knows—it's that kind of place! But I've forewarned you and you
can thank me for it. Well, *au revoir*—in the next world, likely. Oh,
and something else: although I've behaved like a swine to you,
because . . . why on earth should I go sacrificing my own
interests, kindly answer me that? For your advantage? I dedicated
my confession to her (you didn't know that?). And if you only
knew how she received it! Heh-heh! But towards her I haven't
behaved badly, I've done her no harm at all; it's she who's
snubbed and betrayed me . . . I've done you no kind of harm
either; if I referred to "leavings" just now and all that sort of
thing, I'm now telling you the day, the hour, and the address of

the meeting and exposing the whole game—out of spite, of course, not generosity. Goodbye, I'm chattering away like a stammerer or a consumptive; be on your guard then, take steps and quickly, if you deserve to be called a man. The meeting is this evening, that's certain.'

Ippolit headed for the door, but the prince shouted to him and he halted on the threshold.

'So according to you, Aglaya Ivanovna will be going to see Nastasya Filippovna herself today?' asked the prince. Red spots stood out on his cheeks and forehead.

'I don't know exactly, but very likely', answered Ippolit, half turning. 'Still, it can't really be otherwise. Nastasya Filippovna won't be going to her, will she? And not at dear Ganya's either; they've practically got a dead man on their hands. What do you think about the general?'

'It's impossible for that reason alone!' the prince pursued. 'How could she go out even if she wanted to? You don't know the . . . customs of that household: she can't get away alone to Nastasya Filippovna; it's all nonsense!'

'Look Prince: nobody goes jumping out of windows, but if there's a fire then the finest ladies and gentlemen will jump out of the window. Needs must when the devil drives, and our young lady will go off to see Nastasya Filippovna. Don't they ever let them out to go anywhere, those ladies of yours?'

'No, I didn't mean that . . .'

'Well if not, then all she has to do is step down off the porch and go straight on, and she needn't go back home. There are times when boats have to be burnt and there's no going home: life isn't just made up of breakfasts and dinners and princes called S. It seems to me you regard Aglaya as a young lady or a schoolgirl; I've already told her about that and I think she agreed with me. Wait till seven or eight o'clock . . . In your shoes I'd send somebody there to keep an eye on things and catch her the very minute she comes down the steps. You might send Kolya; he'd be delighted to do a bit of spying, believe me, for you at any rate . . . because everything's relative, isn't it . . . Ha-ha!'

Ippolit went out. The prince had no need to ask anyone to spy for him, even if he had been capable of making such a request. Aglaya's instruction for him to stay at home was now almost explained: perhaps she wanted to call on him. True, perhaps she didn't want him to turn up there, and had therefore commanded him to stay at home . . . That might be it too. He felt giddy; the whole room was going round. He lay down on the sofa and closed his eyes.

One way or another, this was to be finally decisive. No, the prince did not regard Aglaya as a young lady or a schoolgirl; he was aware now that he had long been afraid of something precisely like this; but why did she want to see her? A cold shiver ran through his frame; he felt feverish again.

No, he didn't regard her as a child! Some of the looks and words she had employed recently had horrified him. It occurred to him at times that she had been too reserved and controlled, and he recalled that this had alarmed him. True, he had been trying not to think of it all this time and had dismissed his gloomy imaginings, but what lay hidden in that heart of hers? This question had tormented him for long enough, though it was a heart he trusted. And now all of that was bound to be revealed and resolved that very day. A horrible thought! And again—'that woman!' Why did he always feel that she would appear right at the very last moment to snap his destiny in two, like a rotten thread? He was willing to swear that he had always thought this way, though he was half-way to delirium. If he had been trying to forget about her lately, it was solely because he was afraid of her. Well, then: did he love this woman or hate her? He had not posed himself that question once that day; here his mind was clear: he knew whom he loved . . . It was not the meeting of the twain he feared so much, not the strange circumstances, not the mysterious reasons for the meeting, nor its outcome, whatever that might be—it was Nastasya Filippovna herself that he feared. He recalled afterwards, several days later, that virtually all through those feverish hours he kept picturing her eyes, her glance, kept hearing her words—strange-sounding words, though little enough remained in his memory after those fever-ridden and anguished hours. He barely remembered, for example, Vera bringing him dinner and him eating it; he did not remember whether he slept after dinner or not. All he knew was that he began to have a clear picture of that evening only after the moment when Aglaya suddenly came on to the veranda and he started up from the sofa to greet her in the centre of the room: it was a quarter past seven. Aglaya was quite alone. She had dressed simply and apparently in a hurry, in a light cloak. Her face was pale, as it had been that morning, but her eyes glittered with a dry brightness. He had never known such an expression in her eyes before. She inspected him carefully.

'You're quite ready', she observed softly and with seeming composure, 'dressed and hat in hand; you must have been warned, and I know by whom. Ippolit?'

'Yes, he told me . . .', muttered the prince, feeling more dead than alive.

'Let's go then: you know you have to escort me there. You're well enough to leave the house, I suppose?'

'Yes I am, but . . . can this be happening?'

He broke off on the instant and was unable to say another word. It was his only attempt at stopping the possessed girl; after that he followed her like a slave. However confused his thoughts, he was well aware that she would go there without him if necessary, therefore he had to follow her in any event. He realized the strength of her determination; he was not the man to stop this wild impulse. They walked on in silence, scarcely exchanging a word the whole way. All he noticed was that she knew where she was going, and when he suggested taking a longer route through a side-street, because it was less frequented, she listened to him as if straining her attention and replied abruptly: 'It doesn't matter.' When they had almost reached Darya Alexeyevna's house (a sizeable old wooden building), a gorgeous lady accompanied by a young girl came down the steps; both got into a splendid carriage waiting by the porch, laughing loudly and talking. They did not once glance at the arrivals, seeming not to notice them. As soon as the carriage had driven off, the door immediately opened a second time and the waiting Rogozhin ushered Aglaya and the prince inside before closing the door behind them.

'There's nobody in the whole house now, apart from the four of us', he remarked aloud, and gave the prince an odd look.

Nastasya Filippovna was waiting for them in the very first room they entered; she too was dressed very simply and all in black.

She rose to meet them, but did not smile and didn't even give the prince her hand.

Her intent and troubled gaze eagerly sought Aglaya. Both sat down some distance apart: Aglaya on the sofa in a corner of the room, Nastasya Filippovna by the window. The prince and Rogozhin did not sit down, nor were they invited to do so. The prince glanced at Rogozhin in bewilderment and seeming pain, but Rogozhin merely smiled his usual smile. The silence lasted a few more moments.

A kind of ominous expression crossed Nastasya Filippovna's face at length; her gaze, which had never wavered from her visitor, became obstinate, hard, and almost hateful. Aglaya was obviously disconcerted but not intimidated. As she came in she had barely glanced at her rival, and for the time being was sitting with downcast eyes, apparently deep in thought. Once or twice, as if by chance, she threw a glance round the room; distaste was clearly depicted in her face, as if she feared contamination here. She automatically adjusted her garments and once even changed her place, moving to the corner of the sofa. She could hardly have been aware of all her own movements, but the very fact made them the more insulting. At length she looked Nastasya Filippovna firmly and directly in the eyes, and at once read everything that her rival's embittered stare conveyed. Woman understood woman; Aglaya shuddered.

'You know, of course, why I asked you to come', she brought out at last, but very softly, pausing once or twice even in this short sentence.

'No, I don't', answered Nastasya Filippovna, cold and abrupt.

Aglaya flushed. Perhaps it had suddenly struck her as most strange and incredible that she was now sitting with 'that woman' in the house of 'that woman' and hanging upon her answer. A shiver seemed to pass through her body at the first sound of Nastasya Filippovna's voice. All this was, of course, most carefully noted by 'that woman'.

'You understand it all . . . you're deliberately pretending that you don't', Aglaya almost whispered, staring grimly at the floor.

'What would be the point of that?' Nastasya Filippovna asked with the faintest hint of a smile.

'You want to take advantage of my position . . . that I'm in your house', Aglaya went on, absurdly awkward.

'You're to blame for your position, not I!' Nastasya Filippovna suddenly flared up. 'I didn't invite you, you invited me, and I still don't know why.'

Aglaya raised her head haughtily:

'Hold your tongue; that is your weapon and I haven't come to fight you with it . . .'

'Ah, so you have come to "fight" at any rate? Just think, I had imagined you were . . . more intelligent than that . . .'

They looked at one another, by now not bothering to disguise their hostility any longer. One of them was the very woman who had so recently been writing such letters to the other. And now all of that had melted away at their first encounter and their first words. But why not? At that moment, it seemed, not one of the four people in that room found anything odd in the fact. The prince, who the day before would not have believed it possible even to dream of such a scene as this, was now standing and listening as if he had foreseen it all long ago. The most fantastic of dreams had suddenly been transformed into the most vivid and sharply defined reality. At that moment, one of these women already despised the other so profoundly, and so longed to tell her as much (perhaps that was the only reason she came, as Rogozhin put it next day), that however fantastical the other might be, with her deranged mind and diseased soul, she would not have been able to withstand the venomous, purely feminine scorn of her rival, whatever preconceived plan she might have devised. The prince was confident that Nastasya Filippovna would not mention the letters unprovoked; he could guess from her glittering stare what those letters might cost her now; but he would have given half his life for Aglaya not to bring them up now either.

All of a sudden, however, Aglaya appeared to pull herself together and at once recover her self-possession.

'You misunderstand me', she said. 'I have not come to . . . quarrel with you, though I do not like you. I . . . I have come to talk to you as one human being to another. When I asked you to meet me I had already decided what I was going to talk about, and I shall not retreat from that decision, even if it means you do not understand me at all. That will be the worse for you, not me. I wanted to reply to what you wrote me, and make that reply in person, because that seemed more convenient. Listen, then, to my reply to all your letters: I began to feel pity for Prince Lev Nikolayevich the first time we were introduced and when I found out all the things that had happened at your party. The reason I was sorry for him was that he was a naive person who believed, in his simplicity, that he could be happy ... with a woman ... having a character like that. What I feared for him indeed came to pass: you weren't able to love him, you made his life a misery, and then cast him aside. You couldn't love him because you were too proud ... no, not proud, that's not it, because of your vanity ... not even that either: you're self-obsessed to the point of ... mania, and your letters to me prove it. You couldn't love a simple man like him, perhaps deep down you even despised him and mocked him. The only thing you were capable of loving was your own shame and the constant idea of how you had been dishonoured and humiliated. If your dishonour had been less, or had not existed, you would be more unhappy than you are.' Aglaya took considerable pleasure in these words which tripped all too lightly from her tongue, but which had been prepared and pondered over long ago, when the present meeting had not even been dreamed of; with venomous eyes she watched their effect on Nastasya Filippovna's face, as it contorted with emotion. 'You remember', she went on, 'he wrote me a letter at the time; he says you know about the letter and have even read it. Because of that letter, I understood—and correctly understood—everything. He recently confirmed that to me himself, that is, everything I am saying to you now, word for word. After the letter, I started waiting. I guessed you would be bound to come here, because you can't do without Petersburg: you're still too young and pretty for the provinces ... However, those aren't my words either', she added, blushing dreadfully: from that moment on the colour never left her face until the very end of her speech. 'When I saw the prince again, I felt angry and hurt on his behalf. Don't laugh; if you laugh, it means you're unworthy of understanding ...'

'You can see I'm not laughing', said Nastasya Filippovna, with sad severity.

'Still, it doesn't matter, laugh away, just as you like. When I began asking him myself, he told me he had stopped loving you long ago, that even the memory of you was torture to him, but that he pitied you and, when he recalled you, it "pierced his heart for ever". I must also tell you that I have never met anyone like him in my life for noble simplicity and infinite trustfulness. I guessed, from the way he talked, that anyone who wanted to could deceive him, and he would forgive anyone who did so deceive him, and that was the reason I fell in love with him . . .'

Aglaya stopped for a moment, apparently stunned and unable to believe herself capable of uttering the word; but at the same time an almost boundless pride began to shine in her eyes; it was as if nothing mattered to her now, not even if 'that woman' were to start laughing at the blurted avowal.

'I have told you everything, and of course you realize what it is I want from you.'

'Perhaps I do; but say it yourself', replied Nastasya Filippovna softly.

Anger flared in Aglaya's face.

'I wanted to find out from you', she said firmly and distinctly, 'what right you have to interfere in his feelings towards me? By what right do you dare to write me letters? By what right do you constantly trumpet the fact both to him and to me that you love him, after you cast him aside yourself and ran away from him in such an insulting . . . and disgraceful fashion?'

'I have never trumpeted the fact that I love him, neither to him nor you', Nastasya Filippovna brought out with an effort, 'and . . . you're right, I did run away from him . . .', she added, barely audible.

'What do you mean, "him nor you"?' cried Aglaya. 'What about your letters, then? Who asked you to play the matchmaker and persuade me to marry him? Isn't that trumpeting? Why are you forcing yourself upon us? At first I thought that, on the contrary, by meddling in our affairs you wanted to provoke revulsion in me towards him, so that I would reject him, and only afterwards did I realize how things stood: you simply imagined you were doing something noble by all these posturings . . . Could you really have loved him if you loved your own vanity so much? Why didn't you simply go away from here instead of writing me silly letters? Why don't you now marry the generous man who loves you so much and who has done you the honour of offering you his hand? It's very obvious why not: if you marry

Rogozhin, what becomes of your grievance? You would be receiving too much honour in fact! Radomsky said of you that you had read a lot of poetry and were "extremely cultivated for your . . . position"; that you were a bookish woman with lily-white hands; add to that your vanity and there are all your motives . . .'

'And aren't your hands lily-white?'

Things had reached this unexpected juncture much too quickly and crudely—unexpected because Nastasya Filippovna, on her way to Pavlovsk, still cherished certain dreams, though of course she anticipated things to turn out badly rather than otherwise; Aglaya was really carried away by the emotional surge of the moment, as if rushing down a mountainside, and couldn't resist the dreadful satisfaction of revenge. It was strange for Nastasya Filippovna to see Aglaya like this; she was looking at her as if she couldn't believe her eyes, and was decidedly at a loss for the first moment or two. Whether she was a woman who had read too much poetry, as Radomsky had supposed, or simply mad, as the prince was convinced, at all events this woman, whose behaviour was sometimes cynical and insolent, was in reality far more shy, gentle, and trusting than might have been assumed. True, there was in her a good deal that was bookish, dreamy, self-enclosed, and fantastical, but it existed along with qualities of strength and profundity . . . The prince understood this; his distress showed in his face. Aglaya noticed it and quivered with hatred.

'How dare you speak to me like that?' she said with an indescribably imperious air, as she responded to Nastasya Filippovna's remark.

'You must have misheard', marvelled Nastasya Filippovna. 'How have I spoken to you?'

'If you had wanted to be an honest woman, then why didn't you get rid of your seducer, Totsky, just . . . without histrionics?' said Aglaya suddenly, out of the blue.

'What do you know of my situation that lets you presume to sit in judgement on me?' Nastasya Filippovna trembled and went pale.

'All I know is that you didn't go to work, you went off with a rich man like Rogozhin, so you could play the fallen angel. I'm not surprised Totsky wanted to shoot himself to escape a fallen angel!'

'Stop it!' Nastasya Filippovna said with revulsion and seeming anguish. 'You understand me no better than ... Darya Alexeyevna's maidservant, who took her fiancé to court the other day for breach of promise. She'd have understood better than you ...'

'Most likely she's an honest girl and works for a living. How can someone like you speak of a maidservant with contempt?'

'I don't regard work with contempt, just you when you talk of work.'

'If you'd wanted to be an honest woman, you'd have taken in washing.'

Both rose to their feet and stared at one another, ashen-faced.

'Aglaya, stop it! This is unfair', the prince cried despairingly. Rogozhin listened with lips pursed and arms folded, no longer smiling.

'There, just look at her', said Nastasya Filippovna, shaking with anger, 'at that noble young lady! And I used to think she was an angel! Have you come visiting without your governess, Aglaya Ivanovna? ... Do you want ... do you want me to tell you now bluntly, without mincing words, why you've come here? You were afraid, that's why you came to see me.'

'Afraid of you?' asked Aglaya, beside herself with naive and haughty amazement that the other should address her in this fashion.

'Of course of me! If you've made up your mind to come and see me, it means you're afraid of me. If you fear someone you don't despise them. To think I've respected you up to this very moment! And let me tell you why you're afraid of me and what your chief anxiety is now. You wanted to make sure personally whether he loved me more than you or not, because you're dreadfully jealous ...'

'He's already told me he hates you ...', Aglaya just managed to falter.

'Perhaps he has; perhaps I'm not worthy of him, but ... but you're lying, I think! He can't possibly hate me and he couldn't have said that! However, I'm willing to let it pass ... bearing in mind your situation ... I did think better of you, though; I thought you were more intelligent, and prettier too, honestly I did! . . . Well, take your treasure then . . . there he is, looking at you, he can't take it all in, take him home with you, but on one condition: get out of here at once! This very minute!'

She fell into a chair and dissolved into tears. But all of a sudden something new glittered in her eyes; she stared fixedly at Aglaya and rose to her feet:

'Or would you like me to . . . or-der him this minute, you hear, one or-der from me and he'll leave you at once and stay with me for ever, and marry me, while you run home on your own! You want that? You want that?' she shouted like a mad creature, perhaps not fully believing herself capable of uttering such words.

Aglaya made to rush for the door, but halted on the threshold as if rooted to the spot and went on listening.

'If you like, I'll get rid of Rogozhin. Did you think I was going to marry him to suit you? I'll shout out now in front of you: "Go away, Rogozhin!" and I'll say to the prince: "Remember what you promised?" Lord, why have I humiliated myself so before them? Wasn't it you, Prince, assured me that you'd marry me, whatever happened to me, and would never leave me, that you loved me and forgave me everything, and that you res . . . resp . . . Yes, you said that as well! And I ran away from you just to set you free, but now I don't want to! Why has she treated me like some loose woman? Ask Rogozhin whether I'm a loose woman, he'll tell you! Now that she has put me to shame before your very eyes, will you too spurn me and walk away arm-in-arm with her? Well curse you then, because you were the only one I trusted. Go away, Rogozhin, you're not wanted!' she shouted, frenzied, forcing the words out of her breast, face contorted and lips parched, clearly not believing a word of her tirade but at the same time wanting to prolong the scene, if only by a second, and keep up the self-deception. The paroxysm was so intense that she might have died, so at least thought the prince . . . 'There he is, look!' she cried at last to Aglaya, pointing to the prince. 'If he doesn't come up to me, now, take me, and give you up, then you can have him. I'll let you have him. I don't want him! . . .'

Both she and Aglaya stood still, seemingly in suspense, then both looked at him as though demented. He, however, perhaps did not comprehend the full force of that challenge; indeed he certainly did not. All he saw before him was the distracted, despairing face which, as he had let slip to Aglaya once, 'pierced his heart for ever'. He could bear it no longer, and he turned to Aglaya with a look at once beseeching and reproachful, as he pointed to Nastasya Filippovna:

'How could you! She's really . . . so unhappy!'

But that was all he managed to utter, as he was struck dumb by a terrible look from Aglaya. It contained so much anguish and at the same time such limitless hatred that he threw up his arms, uttered an exclamation, and darted towards her, but it was already too late! She had not been able to endure even an instant of hesitation; she covered her face with her hands, cried out: 'Oh, my God!' and rushed out of the room, followed by Rogozhin to unbolt the front door for her.

The prince also pursued her, but was clasped on the threshold by two arms. The ravaged, contorted face of Nastasya Filippovna was staring at him and her bluish lips stirred, asking him:

'After her? After her?'

She fell unconscious into his arms. He raised her and bore her into the room, and stood over her in numb suspense. There was a glass of water on the table; on his return to the room, Rogozhin seized it and sprinkled some water in her face; she opened her eyes, and for a moment failed to realize what had happened; then she suddenly looked round, gave a start, cried out, and rushed to the prince.

'Mine! Mine!' she cried. 'The proud young lady has gone? Ha-ha-ha!' she laughed hysterically. 'Ha-ha-ha! I was giving him up to that noble lady! But why should I? Why? Mad! Mad! . . . Get out Rogozhin, ha-ha-ha!'

Rogozhin stared at them wordlessly, picked up his hat, and left. Ten minutes later the prince was sitting beside Nastasya Filippovna, his eyes fixed on her as he stroked her head and face with both hands, like a little child. He laughed when she laughed and was ready to cry when she cried. He said nothing, but listened intently to her jerky, rapturous, incoherent babbling, barely understanding anything, but smiling gently; as soon as he thought she was starting to fret or weep, reproach or complain, he immediately began stroking her head again and passing his hands tenderly over her cheeks, comforting and soothing her like a child.

9

A FORTNIGHT had passed since the events related in the last chapter, and the situation of the characters in our story had altered to such an extent that we should find it difficult to continue without making certain things clear. We feel, however, that we should confine ourselves to a simple recital of the facts without any particular elaboration, as far as that is possible. The reason is a simple one: we ourselves find it difficult to explain what happened, in many cases. Such a statement on our part must appear very vague and strange: how can one tell a story if one has no clear notion of events or personal opinion regarding them? To avoid placing ourselves in a still more false position, it would be best if we attempted to clarify matters by giving an example and then, perhaps, the indulgent reader will understand where our precise difficulty lies, particularly as this example will not be a digression; on the contrary, it will be a direct continuation of our story.

During the subsequent two weeks, bringing us to the beginning of July, the tale of our hero, particularly the latest episode, had become transformed into a strange, vastly entertaining story of scandal, almost incredible and yet plain for all to see. This story had gradually spread through all the streets close to the villas belonging to Lebedev, the Ptitsyns, Darya Alexeyevna, and the Yepanchins; in short it was all round the town and even the surrounding districts. Virtually every element in society—locals, villa folk, music visitors—began telling one another the same story in a thousand different versions; how a certain prince, after creating a scandalous scene in a well-known and respectable household, had thrown over the daughter of the family, to whom he was already engaged, and was now besotted with a cocotte. He had severed all his former ties and despite everything, regardless of threats and universal public indignation, intended to marry this fallen woman in the next few days here in

Pavlovsk, openly, in public, with head erect and looking everyone in the eye. The story became so embellished with scandalous details, so many celebrated and important figures were involved in it, and so various were the fantastic and mysterious nuances given to it, while on the other hand it was presented in such incontrovertible and concrete detail, that the general curiosity and gossip were, of course, very pardonable. The most subtle, ingenious and, at the same time, most plausible interpretation of the event was left to a few really serious gossip-mongers from that judicious section of the population who are invariably eager to explain events to others, whatever level of society they move in; this is where they find their vocation and often their consolation too. According to their version, a young man of good family, a prince, very nearly a rich man, something of a booby but a democrat and crazy over the modern nihilism revealed by Mr Turgenev,* and barely able to speak Russian, had fallen in love with one of General Yepanchin's daughters and had reached the point of being regarded in the household as the girl's fiancé. However, it was like that French seminarist in the papers recently, who deliberately allowed himself to be consecrated as a priest; having begged to be thus consecrated, he had then gone through all the rites, genuflections, kissings, vows, and so on, only to declare publicly in a letter to his bishop the very next day that, as he didn't believe in God, he regarded it as dishonourable to deceive the people and live at their expense; he therefore renounced the priesthood he had assumed the day before. He had published his letter in the liberal newspapers. The prince had seemingly perpetrated some such subterfuge as had this atheist. The story went that he had deliberately waited for the formal engagement party at his fiancée's parents' house, where he was presented to great numbers of extremely important persons, only to trumpet his opinions, abuse the respectable dignitaries, reject his fiancée publicly and insultingly and, while resisting his ejection by the servants, smash a beautiful Chinese vase. They added, as an illustration of his contemporary mores, that the blockheaded young man really did love his fiancée, the general's daughter, but had renounced her purely out of nihilism and for the sake of the subsequent scandal, so as not to forego the pleasure of marrying a fallen woman in front of the world, thus demonstrating his conviction that there were no such things as fallen women or virtuous women, there were only free women; that he did not believe in old-fashioned society divisions, all he believed in was 'the woman question'. In his eyes, a fallen woman stood, if anything, slightly higher than one who was not. This explanation seemed wholly plausible and was accepted by the majority of the villa community, particularly as it was confirmed by day-to-day events. True, numerous things were left unaccounted for: it was said that the poor girl loved her fiancé (her 'seducer', some called him), so much that the very next day after he had rejected her, she ran to see him when he was sitting with his mistress; others asserted that, on the contrary, she had been lured on purpose to his mistress's house, purely out of nihilism, that is, to heap shame and insult upon her. However that might be, interest in the affair increased daily, especially when there remained no shred of doubt that the scandalous marriage really was going ahead.

And so, if we had been asked for an explanation, not about the nihilistic aspects of the affair, but just about how far the forthcoming wedding accorded with the prince's actual desires, what his desires actually were at any given moment, how one might describe our hero's state of mind, and so on and so forth, we should have had great difficulty in replying. We know only one thing—that the wedding was definitely fixed and that the prince himself had entrusted Lebedev, Keller, and some acquaintance of Lebedev's, whom the latter had introduced to the prince for the purpose, to undertake all the arrangements, religious and otherwise; that money was not to be stinted; that Nastasya Filippovna was insisting on the wedding and hurrying things along; that Keller had been chosen as the prince's best man, at his own ardent request; that Burdovsky, ecstatic at his appointment, was to give the bride away, and that the day of the wedding had been fixed for early July. But apart from these perfectly precise details, we know of several other facts which we are at a loss to account for, since they run counter to the previous ones. We strongly suspect that, after entrusting Lebedev and the others to oversee all the arrangements, the prince almost forgot the very same day that he actually had a master of ceremonies, a best man, or a wedding, and that if he had been in such a hurry to arrange for others to undertake the bothersome details, it was solely because he did not want to think about it himself, indeed, wanted perhaps to forget all about it as quickly as might be. What was he thinking of himself in that case then, what did he prefer to remember and what was he trying to achieve? Undoubtedly there was no question of any coercion involved either (from Nastasya Filippovna, for example). She really did want the wedding to take place as soon as possible, and it was her idea and certainly not the prince's; but the prince had acquiesced of his own free will, almost absently in fact, as if he had been asked to do something quite usual. We have a great many such odd facts before us, but so far from clarifying matters, in our view they actually cloud the issue, no matter how many are adduced; however, let us consider another example.

Thus, we know for a fact that during that fortnight the prince passed whole days and evenings with Nastasya Filippovna; that she took him with her for walks and to listen to the music; that he rode about with her every day in her carriage; that he began to get anxious about her if an hour passed without seeing her (which meant, to all appearances, that he genuinely loved her); that he listened to whatever she had to say for hours on end, with a meek and gentle smile, saying almost nothing himself. But we also know that during those same days he went off several, indeed many, times to the Yepanchins, without concealing the fact from Nastasya Filippovna, which drove the latter almost to despair. We know that while they remained in Pavlovsk the Yepanchins did not receive him, and steadily refused to allow a meeting with Aglaya; that he would go away without a word, then return the very next day, as though completely forgetting the previous day's refusal and, of course, receive another refusal. We know, too, that an hour after Aglaya Ivanovna had run out of Nastasya Filippovna's house, or perhaps even sooner, the prince was already at the Yepanchins', naturally confident of finding Aglaya there, and that his appearance had occasioned considerable alarm and dismay in the household, because Aglaya had not yet returned home and it was only through him that they even learned she had gone out with him to Nastasya Filippovna's. It was said that Lizaveta Prokofievna, her daughters, and even Prince S had been hostile and dealt harshly with the prince, and it was at this point that they denied him their further acquaintance and friendship in the strongest terms, especially when Varya suddenly appeared and announced that Aglaya Ivanovna had been in their house for an hour or more in a dreadful state, and seemed reluctant to return home. This last piece of news shocked Lizaveta Prokofievna most of all, and was perfectly true: coming out from Nastasya Filippovna, Aglaya really would have consented to die rather than face the people at home, and so had rushed to see Nina Alexandrovna. Varya, for her part, had at once found it incumbent upon her to inform Lizaveta Prokofievna of all this without delay. Mother and daughters at once rushed round to Nina Alexandrovna, with the head of the household, General Yepanchin, who had just arrived home, following on behind; Prince Lev Nikolayevich trailed after them as well, notwithstanding his expulsion and the hard words; by Varya's orders, however, he was not allowed to see Aglaya there either. The upshot was that, when Aglaya saw her mother and sisters weeping over her without a word of reproach, she flung herself into their arms and returned home with them at once. The story went, though the rumours were not precisely accurate either, that Ganya was very unlucky on this occasion too; seizing the opportunity after Varya had run off to the Yepanchins to be alone with Aglaya, he had thought to broach the subject of his love; in spite of all her anguish and tears, Aglaya had burst out laughing as she listened and suddenly made him a strange proposition: would he prove his love by burning his finger in the candle there and then? It was said that Ganya was dumbfounded by this proposal, and was so disconcerted and registered such bewilderment that Aglaya had burst into hysterical giggles at the sight and fled upstairs to Nina Alexandrovna, where her parents found her. This story reached the prince through Ippolit next day. Ippolit, now confined to bed, deliberately sent for the prince to pass on the news. How Ippolit had come to hear of it we do not know, but when the prince heard about the candle and the finger, he laughed so much that he surprised Ippolit; then he suddenly began to tremble and dissolved in tears ... Altogether, at that time he was in a state of considerable agitation and vague but agonizing distress. Ippolit bluntly declared that he considered him to be out of his mind;

but that could not yet be said with any certainty.

In presenting all these facts and refusing to explain them, we are by no means trying to justify our hero in the eyes of our readers. Moreover, we are quite willing to share the indignation he aroused against himself even among his friends. Even Vera Lebedeva was angry with him for some time; even Kolya was indignant; even Keller was too, until such time as he was chosen to be best man, not to mention Lebedev, who even began scheming against the prince, also out of a perfectly sincere indignation. But we will speak of that later. In general, then, we are wholly in sympathy with certain forceful and psychologically profound remarks of Radomsky's, which he made to the prince bluntly and without mincing words during a friendly conversation on the sixth or seventh day after the episode at Nastasya Filippovna's. We should mention, incidentally, that not only the Yepanchins themselves but everyone who had any connection with the Yepanchin household, either directly or indirectly, found it necessary to sever completely all relations with the prince. Prince S., for example, even turned away on meeting the prince and refrained from returning his bow. But Radomsky was not afraid of compromising himself by going to see the prince, despite the fact that he had begun to frequent the Yepanchin household again every day and was received with noticeably increased cordiality. He came to see the prince the day after all the Yepanchins had left Pavlovsk. When he entered, he was already aware of all the rumours that were circulating and might well have had some hand in assisting the process. The prince was terribly glad to see him and at once started talking about the Yepanchins; such a direct and artless beginning put Yevgeni Pavlovich completely at his ease, so he came straight to the point without beating about the bush.

The prince did not yet know that the Yepanchins had gone; he was startled and went pale; a minute later, however, he shook his head, bemused and thoughtful, and admitted 'it was to be expected'; then he quickly enquired where they had gone to.

Yevgeni Pavlovich, meanwhile, was watching him closely; all of this, the swift series of ingenuous questions, the embarrassment coupled with an odd sort of candour, the agitation and excitability—all this surprised him a good deal. However, he told

the prince everything in detail in a very amiable fashion: there
was a lot the latter did not know, and Radomsky was the first
bearer of news from the Yepanchins. He confirmed that Aglaya
really had been ill, that she had not slept for three days on end
and had been running a high temperature; that she was feeling
better now and out of all danger, though still in a nervous and
hysterical condition . . . 'It's a good thing there's perfect peace in
the household', he said. 'They try not to refer to the past at all,
even among themselves, not just in Aglaya's presence. The
parents have already talked between themselves about a trip
abroad in the autumn, straight after Adelaida's wedding; Aglaya
said nothing when she heard the first mention of that.' He,
Radomsky, would also go abroad, possibly. Even Prince S
intended to go for a month or two with Adelaida, if work
permitted. The general himself would remain behind. They had
all gone over to Kolmino, their estate about fifteen miles out of
Petersburg, where there was a large manor-house. Princess
Belokonskaya had not yet left for Moscow, and had apparently
stayed behind deliberately. Lizaveta Prokofievna had strongly
insisted that it was impossible to remain in Pavlovsk after all that
had happened; he, Yevgeni Pavlovich, had kept her informed
every day about the rumours circulating in the town. They had
not found it possible to go to their dacha on Yelagin Island either.

'And really', added Radomsky, 'you have to admit, they could
hardly have hung on . . . particularly when they knew everything
that was going on in your house here all the time, and after your
daily trips over there, despite being turned away . . .'

'Yes, yes, yes, you're right, I wanted to see Aglaya
Ivanovna . . .', the prince nodded again.

'Oh, my dear Prince', exclaimed Yevgeni Pavlovich suddenly,
with heartfelt sadness, 'how could you have allowed . . . all that to
happen? Of course, of course, it was all so unexpected for you . . .
I agree, you were bound to lose your head and . . . you certainly
couldn't have stopped that mad girl, that was beyond your
capabilities! But you must have realized, mustn't you, how
intensely and seriously that girl . . . felt towards you. She didn't
want to share you with another woman, but you . . . could throw
away and smash a treasure like that!'

'Yes, yes, you're right; yes, it's my fault', the prince began again, in great anguish. 'And you know, she was the only one, Aglaya was the only one who looked on Nastasya Filippovna in that light . . . Nobody else did, did they?'

'But that's what makes all this so exasperating, that there was nothing serious in it!' cried Yevgeni Pavlovich, carried away in real earnest. 'I'm sorry, Prince, but . . . I . . . have been thinking; I've thought it over a lot; I know everything that took place earlier, I know all that happened six months ago, everything, and . . . it was all to do with your head, not your heart, a figment, a fantasy, passing clouds; only the frightened jealousy of a completely inexperienced girl could regard it as anything serious!'

At this point Yevgeni Pavlovich, dispensing with the niceties altogether, gave full vent to his indignation. Clearly and sensibly and, we repeat, with great psychological insight, he unfolded before the prince the whole story of his former relationship with Nastasya Filippovna. Radomsky had always had a way with words, but now he rose to real eloquence. 'From the very start', he declared, 'it was a lie; what begins with a lie must end with a lie; that is a law of nature. I don't agree, in fact I feel positively indignant, when somebody—oh, whoever it might be—calls you idiot; you are too intelligent for a name like that; but you are sufficiently odd, you must admit, not to be like other people. I have decided that the fundamental cause of what has happened is due in the first instance to your inherent inexperience, as it were (note the word "inherent", Prince); secondly, to your extraordinarily ingenuous nature; thirdly, to a phenomenal lack of any sense of proportion (which you have admitted yourself several times); and lastly, to that enormous accretion of intellectual convictions which you, with that amazing honesty of yours, have hitherto taken to be genuine, natural, and spontaneous. You must admit, Prince, that in your relationship with Nastasya Filippovna from the very beginning there was something conventionally democratic (to put it shortly), some infatuation, so to speak, with the "woman question" (to put it even more briefly). You see, I know all the details of that strange and scandalous scene that took place at Nastasya Filippovna's when Rogozhin brought his money. If you like, I'll analyse you to yourself, point by point, I'll show you to yourself in a mirror, so accurately do I know how it was and how it turned out the way it did! You, a young man in Switzerland, were homesick for your native country; you longed for Russia as an unknown but promised land; you read a lot of books about Russia, perhaps excellent books, but for you—pernicious; you arrived in the first flush of eagerness for action, so to speak, and flung yourself into it! And then, on your very first day, you are told the sad and heart-rending tale of a wronged woman—to you, a chaste knight-crrant—and about a woman! The very same day you see the woman; you're captivated by her beauty, her fantastic, demonic beauty (I do agree she's a beautiful woman). Add to that your nervous state, your epilepsy, add in our Petersburg thawing weather, which can be such a shock to the system; add to it the whole of that day, in an unknown and to you almost fantastic city, a day of encounters and scenes, a day of unexpected acquaintances, the day of the three Yepanchin beauties, among them Aglaya; add to that fatigue, light-headedness, Nastasya Filippovna's drawing-room and the atmosphere there, and . . . what else could you have expected of yourself at that moment, do you think?'

'Yes, yes; yes, yes', the prince was nodding his head, beginning to flush, 'that's almost how it was, you know; and do you know I really had hardly slept at all the night before, on the train, or the night before that either, and I was feeling very unsettled . . .'

'Well, of course you were, that's what I'm trying to say', Yevgeni Pavlovich pursued eagerly. 'Obviously intoxicated by the thrill of it all, so to speak, you clutched at the opportunity to proclaim publicly your noble-hearted notion, that as a prince of lineage and a man without stain, you did not regard a woman as dishonoured who had been shamed by a disgusting high-society libertine and not through any fault of her own. Why heavens, of ' course it's understandable! But that's not the point, dear Prince, the point is whether the emotion you experienced was genuine and authentic; did it come from nature or was it simply a mental transport of enthusiasm? What do you think: the woman taken in adultery was forgiven, the same kind of woman, but she wasn't told she had done well, was she? That she was worthy of honour and esteem? Surely after three months your own common sense must have suggested to you what the real situation was? Suppose she is innocent now, I won't press the point as I don't wish to, but could all her adventures justify such intolerable demonic pride, such brazen, such voracious selfishness? I'm sorry, Prince, I'm getting carried away, but . . .'

'Yes, all that may well be so; you may well be right . . .', the prince began murmuring again, 'she really is very prone to anger of course, but . . .'

'Deserving of compassion? That's what you mean to say, my soft-hearted Prince? But for the sake of compassion and to satisfy her, how could you have put to shame another girl, high-minded and pure, and degrade her in those arrogant and hate-filled eyes? What lengths will compassion go to after that? Why, it's incredibly out of proportion! How could you, if you loved a girl, humiliate her in front of her rival, reject her in favour of the other, after you'd proposed to her yourself . . . and you did propose to her, didn't you, you told her in the presence of her parents and her sisters! After that, may I ask if you are an honourable man, Prince? And . . . didn't you deceive that heavenly girl by telling her you loved her?'

'Yes, yes, you're right, oh, I do feel it's my fault!' said the prince, inexpressibly anguished.

'Is that really enough?' cried Yevgeni Pavlovich indignantly. 'Is it really enough just to cry out: "Ah, I am to blame!" and then persist in what you're doing? And where was your heart that time, your so "Christian" heart! You could see her face at that moment, couldn't you? Was she suffering less than the other one, your other woman, the one who has come between you? How could you see that and let it happen? How?'

'But . . . you see I didn't . . .', mumbled the wretched prince.

'What do you mean, you didn't?'

'Honestly, I didn't let anything happen. I still don't know how it all came about . . . I—I did run after Aglaya Ivanovna, but Nastasya Filippovna fainted; and after that they won't let me see Aglaya.'

'It doesn't matter! You should have run after Aglaya, even if the other one was lying in a faint!'

'Yes . . . yes, I should have, but she would have died! She would have killed herself, you don't know her, and . . . anyway, I'd have told Aglaya everything afterwards and . . . You see, Yevgeni Pavlovich, I can see that apparently you don't know

everything. Tell me why they won't let me in to see Aglaya? I
would explain everything to her. You see, at the time neither of
them were talking about what mattered, absolutely not, that's why
things turned out as they did. I'm afraid I can't explain it to you at
all; but I could have explained it to Aglaya, perhaps . . . Oh dear,
oh dear! You talk of her face at the moment she ran out . . . oh,
heavens, I remember! . . . Let's go, let's go!' He tugged at
Radomsky's sleeve as he jumped up hurriedly from his chair.

'Where to?'

'Let's go to Aglaya Ivanovna, let's go at once!'

'But she's not in Pavlovsk, is she? I was telling you, and why go
anyway?'

'She'll understand, she'll understand!' mumbled the prince,
clasping his hands beseechingly. 'She'll understand that all this is
beside the point, what matters is something quite, quite
different!'

'Something quite different? But you are still getting married
aren't you? So you're persisting . . . Are you getting married or
not?'

'Oh yes . . . I'm getting married; yes, I am getting married!'

'So how is it "beside the point"?'

'Oh no, that's what it is, that's just what it is! It doesn't matter,
my getting married, that means nothing!'

'What do you mean it doesn't matter and it doesn't mean
anything? It's hardly a trifle, is it? You're marrying a woman you
love, to make her happy, and Aglaya Ivanovna sees that and
knows it—so how can it not matter?'

'Happy? Oh no! I'm just getting married; she wants that; and
what does it matter if I do . . . I . . . but it's all of no consequence!
She would certainly have died, that's all! I can see now that her
marrying Rogozhin was madness! I realize now what I didn't
before, and you see: when they were both standing facing each
other, I couldn't bear to see Nastasya Filippovna's face . . . You
don't know, Yevgeni Pavlovich' (he lowered his voice mysteriously), 'I've never told this to anyone, never, not even Aglaya,
but I cannot bear Nastasya Filippovna's face . . . You were right
just now when you were talking about that evening at Nastasya
Filippovna's; but there was one other thing you missed, because
you don't know about it: I was looking at her face! Even that

morning, looking at her portrait, I couldn't bear it . . . Now Vera, Vera Lebedeva, has quite different eyes; I . . . I'm afraid of her face!' he added, greatly terrified.

'Afraid?'

'Yes; she's mad!' he whispered, ashen-pale.

'You're sure about that?' asked Yevgeni Pavlovich with keen curiosity.

'Yes, I am; now I'm really sure; now, over these last days, I've found out for certain!'

'Then what are you doing to yourself?' cried Yevgeni Pavlovich in alarm. 'You mean you're getting married out of fear of some kind? It's absolutely incomprehensible . . . Not even loving her, I dare say?'

'Oh, no, I love her with all my soul! You see . . . she's an absolute child! Oh, you just don't know!'

'And at the same time you were assuring Aglaya of your love?'

'Oh yes, yes!'

'But how? You mean you want to love both of them?'

'Oh yes, yes!'

'Please, Prince, think what you're saying, do come to your senses!'

'Without Aglaya . . . I simply have to see her! I . . . I shall soon die in my sleep; I thought I was going to do it last night. Oh, if only Aglaya were to know everything . . . absolutely everything, I mean. What matters here is to know everything! Why can't we ever know everything about another person, when we ought to, when that other person is to blame . . . Really, I don't know what I'm saying, I'm all muddled-up; you've shaken me terribly . . . Surely her face can't be the same now as when she ran out? Oh yes, I'm to blame! I'm most probably to blame for everything! I still don't know what for, but I'm to blame . . . There's something involved here which I cannot explain to you, Yevgeni Pavlovich, and I don't have the words, but . . . Aglaya would understand! Oh, I always believed she would understand.'

'No, Prince, she wouldn't! Aglaya Ivanovna loved you like a woman, a human being, not like . . . some disembodied spirit. Look here, my poor Prince: most probably you've never loved either of them!'

'I don't know . . . perhaps, perhaps; you're right about many things, Yevgeni Pavlovich; oh, my head is starting to ache again, let's go to her! For God's sake, for God's sake!'

'But I'm telling you, aren't I, she isn't in Pavlovsk, she's in Kolmino.'

'Let's go to Kolmino, then, straight away!'

'It's im-poss-ible!' drawled Yevgeni Pavlovich, getting to his feet.

'Listen, I'll write a letter; take a letter for mc!'

'No, Prince, no! Spare me such commissions, I can't do it!'

They parted. Radomsky left with some odd impressions: in his opinion, too, the prince was not entirely in control of his faculties. And what did this face mean, that he was so much afraid of, and yet so loved? At the same time, he might actually die without Aglaya, so that perhaps Aglaya would never know he loved her so much! Ha-ha! And what was that about loving two of them? Two different kinds of love somehow? That was interesting . . . poor idiot! And what would become of him now?

10

THE prince, however, did not die before his wedding, awake or 'in his sleep' as he had predicted to Radomsky. Perhaps he really did sleep poorly and have bad dreams; but during the day, in the company of other people, he appeared kindly and even content; at times he was somewhat pensive, but that was when he was alone. The arrangements for the wedding proceeded apace; it was fixed for a week or so after Yevgeni Pavlovich's visit. In view of such haste, even the prince's best friends, if he had any such, must have despaired of their efforts to 'save' the foolish wretch. It was rumoured that General Yepanchin and his wife, Lizaveta Prokofievna, were partly responsible for Yevgeni Pavlovich's visit. But even had they both desired, out of the limitless goodness of their hearts, to rescue the pitiful madman from the abyss, they were bound of course to restrict themselves to this feeble attempt; any more serious attempt would not have been appropriate to their position, nor even perhaps to their hearts' inclination (naturally enough). We have mentioned that even those closest to the prince had, to some extent, turned against him. Vera Lebedeva, however, confined herself to solitary weeping and stayed more in her part of the house, looking in on the prince less frequently than before. Kolya, meanwhile, was occupied with his father's funeral; the old man had died from a second stroke, about a week after the first. The prince had participated fully in the family mourning, and in the first few days spent several hours at a time with Nina Alexandrovna; he was at the funeral and the church service. Many people noticed that the church congregation couldn't help whispering at the prince's arrival and departure; the same thing happened in the street and the park: whenever he walked or drove by, conversation would well up, his name would be mentioned, people would point, Nastasya Filippovna's name would be heard. People looked out for her at the funeral too, but she was not there. The captain's widow was not there either, Lebedev having succeeded in catching her in time and preventing her from coming. The funeral service made a powerful and painful impression on the prince; he whispered to Lebedev while still in the church, in answer to some query of his, that it was the first time he had attended an Orthodox funeral service, and the only other such service he could recall had been in some country church when he had been a child.

'Yes, sir, it doesn't seem to be the same man in the coffin that we chose to be our chairman not so long ago, remember, sir?' Lebedev hissed to the prince. 'Who are you looking for, sir?'

'It's nothing, I just thought . . .'

'Not Rogozhin?'

'He's not here is he?'

'In the church, sir.'

'That's why I thought I saw his eyes', muttered the prince, perturbed. 'But what . . . why is he here? Was he invited?'

'They never thought of it, sir. They don't know him at all, sir. All sorts of people are here, sir, the public, sir. Why are you so surprised? I often meet him nowadays; I've run across him three or four times in the last week here in Pavlovsk.'

'I've never once seen him . . . since that time', muttered the prince.

Since Nastasya Filippovna had also not once mentioned

meeting Rogozhin 'since that time', the prince concluded that Rogozhin was keeping himself out of sight for some reason. All that day he was plunged in thought; Nastasya Filippovna, on the other hand, was unusually cheerful all that day and evening.

Kolya, who had been reconciled with the prince before his father's death, suggested he choose Keller and Burdovsky to assist at the ceremony, as the matter was vital and pressing. He could vouch for Keller's behaving properly, adding that he might 'come in handy'; there was no difficulty about Burdovsky, who was a quiet and unassuming individual. Nina Alexandrovna and Lebedev kept pointing out to the prince that, if the wedding was indeed decided upon, then why have it in Pavlovsk, at the height of the fashionable holiday season, why so public? Would it not be better in Petersburg, or even at the house? The prince knew perfectly well what prompted all these misgivings, but responded briefly and simply, that such was Nastasya Filippovna's express wish.

The next day Keller came to see the prince, after being informed that he was to be best man. Before entering, he halted in the doorway and, as soon as he saw the prince, raised his right hand with the index finger away from the rest, as if taking a vow, and cried:

'I won't drink!'

Then he went up to the prince, squeezed and shook both hands firmly, and announced that when he had first heard of the wedding he was against it, of course, and had declared as much over billiards, and for no other reason than that he had hoped and waited daily, with a friend's impatience, for him to marry a Princess de Rohan, no less; but now he could see for himself that the prince's view of things was at least ten times as high-minded as the rest of them put together. Because what he wanted was not glitter, not riches, not even honour, but simply—the truth! The sympathies of exalted persons were very well known, but the prince, because of his education, was too exalted not to be an exalted person himself, taking it all in all! 'But the rabble and various sorts of riff-raff look at it differently; in the town, in the houses, at the assemblies, in the villas, at the music, in the taverns and billiard-halls, all the talk and shouting is of nothing else but the forthcoming event. I've heard they even want to organize a tin-pan serenade under your windows, and that on your, so to speak, first night! If you need the pistol of an honourable man, Prince, I'm ready to exchange a good half-dozen shots of honour before you rise the morning after from your honeymoon couch.' He also counselled the prince to have a fire-hose ready in the yard, in the event of a sizeable invasion of dry throats after the church ceremony; Lebedev had opposed this, however: ' "If you turn the fire-hose on them", says he, "they'll smash the house to matchwood." '

'This Lebedev is scheming against you, Prince, I swear he is! They want you put under legal restraint, if you can imagine such a thing—involving everything, your freedom of action and your money, the two things that distinguish every one of us from the quadrupeds! I've heard it, heard it for a fact! It's the honest truth!'

The prince recalled having already heard something of the sort himself, but had ignored it of course. Now too, he merely burst out laughing and forgot about it immediately. Lebedev really had been active for some time; the man's calculations were invariably conceived as the fruit of inspiration and, out of an excess of zeal, grew steadily more complicated and ramified as they spread away in all directions from their original starting-point; that is why he had had so little success in life. When, almost on the wedding day, he came along to the prince to confess his guilt (it was his invariable habit to come and confess his guilt to those against whom he had been scheming, particularly if he had been unsuccessful), he declared that he had been born a Talleyrand but for some unaccountable reason had remained a mere Lebedev. He then proceeded to disclose his entire strategy, at the same time intriguing the prince enormously. According to him, he had started out by seeking the good offices of highly placed persons, on whom he could depend in case of need, and had gone to see General Yepanchin. The general was much perplexed; he wished 'the young man' well, but stated that, despite his 'willingness to save him, it would be improper for him to act in the matter'. Lizaveta Prokofievna wished neither to see nor to listen to him; Radomsky and Prince S simply waved him away. Lebedev, however, had not lost heart, and consulted a certain shrewd lawyer, a venerable old man, a good friend and quasi-benefactor to him; the latter concluded that the business was perfectly feasible, provided that competent people could be found to testify to the prince's mental derangement and undoubted insanity, with the involvement of eminent persons to lend their support, this last being the most important thing. Even this did not dampen Lebedev's spirits, and he went so far as to fetch a doctor, a villa resident, along to the prince on one occasion. Another worthy old gentleman, with the St Anne ribbon,* he was to spy out the land, so to speak, make the prince's acquaintance, and let him, Lebedev, know what his conclusion was, not officially for the moment, but as a friend, so to speak. The prince recalled the doctor's visit; he remembered Lebedev kept telling him the day before that he looked unwell, and when the prince refused any treatment he had suddenly appeared with the doctor, under the pretext that they had both just come from Mr Terentyev, who was very poorly, and that the doctor had something to tell the prince about the sick man. The prince thanked Lebedev and greeted the doctor with the utmost geniality. They at once got talking about Ippolit's illness, and the doctor asked the prince for a detailed account of the suicide scene. The prince utterly captivated him with his description and interpretation of the incident. They went on to talk about the Petersburg climate, the prince's own illness, about Switzerland, and about Schneider. The doctor became so interested in the prince's stories and his description of Schneider's system of treatment that he sat there for two hours, smoking the prince's excellent cigars; Lebedev, for his part, regaled them with a most delicious liqueur, which Vera brought in. Here the doctor, a married man with a family, began paying her such high-flown compliments that he provoked her intense indignation. They parted friends. As he was leaving, the doctor informed Lebedev that if every such person was placed under restraint, who on earth would be left to do the supervising? In answer to Lebedev's tragic account of the forthcoming marriage, the doctor wagged his head, knowingly roguish, and remarked at length that, leaving aside the fact that 'there's no knowing who will marry whom', 'the seductive creature, at least as far as he had heard tell, apart from her matchless beauty, which might of itself attract a man of fortune, possessed means of her own from Totsky and Rogozhin—pearls and diamonds, shawls and furniture—so that the dear prince's choice, so far from being, as it were, evidence of any outstanding foolishness, rather testified to a shrewd and calculating worldly intelligence. It therefore pointed to the opposite conclusion, one highly favourable to the prince . . .' This idea had impressed Lebedev as well; that was the end-result of his labours, and now, he added to the prince, 'now, you will see nothing from me, apart from devotion and the readiness to shed my blood; that is what I came to tell you.'

Ippolit too helped to take the prince's mind off things during these last days; he sent for him on many occasions. The family was living in a little house close by; at least the little children, Ippolit's brother and sister, were glad of the country existence, because they could escape from their ailing brother into the garden; his poor mother, however, was always at his beck and call and had no life with him; it was the prince's task to separate and pacify them every day, and the sick man went on calling him 'nanny', at the same time, apparently, not daring to despise him for his role as peacemaker. He had a considerable grievance against Kolya for hardly coming to see him of late, first staying by the side of his dying father, and then with his widowed mother. At length he made the prince's imminent marriage to Nastasya Filippovna the target of his sneers, ending up by offending the prince and eventually causing him to lose his temper: the prince stopped visiting him. Two days later, Ippolit's mother came trailing along in the morning and tearfully beseeched the prince to visit them, otherwise *he* would eat her alive. She added that he wanted to disclose a great secret. The prince went. Ippolit wanted to make it up and started crying, but after the tears, of course, he was more spiteful than ever, though afraid to give vent to his ill humour. He was very ill and all the signs indicated that he would now soon die. There was no secret at all, apart from intense appeals, gasping with emotion so to speak (perhaps put on), to 'beware of Rogozhin'. 'He's the sort of man who will never give up what is his; we're no match for a man like him, Prince: if he wants something he wouldn't bat an eyelid . . .', and so on and so forth. The prince began questioning him further, trying to elicit some facts; but there were no facts beyond Ippolit's own feelings and impressions. To his own immense gratification, Ippolit ended up by scaring the prince thoroughly. At first the prince refused to answer some of his peculiar questions, and only smiled at his advice to 'run away, abroad if necessary. There are Russian priests everywhere', Ippolit went on, 'and you can get married there.' But at length Ippolit concluded with the following thought: 'The only person I'm afraid for is Aglaya: Rogozhin knows how much you love her; a love for a love; you've taken Nastasya Filippovna away from him and he'll kill Aglaya Ivanovna; she's not yours now, of course, but it would be a heavy blow for you, wouldn't it?' He had achieved his object: the prince left with his mind in turmoil.

These warnings about Rogozhin came on the day before the wedding. That evening, the prince saw Nastasya Filippovna for the last time before the ceremony; she, however, was in no mood to reassure him; on the contrary. Recently she had been making him more and more distraught. Before that, several days earlier that is, she had done all she could to cheer him up during their meetings and greatly feared his mournful looks: she even tried singing to him; above all, she tried recounting to him every funny story she could think of. The prince almost always pretended to be vastly amused, and indeed he did occasionally laugh at her brilliant wit and the vivacious manner of the telling when she was carried away by the subject, as she often was. Seeing the prince laugh, and seeing the effect she had on him, she would go into ecstasies and begin to feel proud of herself. But these last days, her musing sadness intensified almost by the hour. His opinions about Nastasya Filippovna's state were by now firmly fixed; otherwise everything about her would have seemed to him puzzling and incomprehensible. But he genuinely believed that she could still recover. He had been perfectly truthful when he had told Radomsky that he loved her genuinely and wholeheartedly, and his love for her really did contain the kind of bond one has with some pitiful, ailing child whom it is difficult, if not impossible, to leave to its own devices. He had never explained his feelings for her to anyone, unless it was inescapable; when he was alone with Nastasya Filippovna they never spoke of their 'feelings'; it was as if they had agreed not to do so. Anyone could participate in their normal, cheerful and lively conversation. Darya Alexeyevna used to say afterwards that all this time she did nothing but marvel and be glad, just looking at them.

But it was this view he had of Nastasya Filippovna's spiritual and mental state which relieved him to some extent of many another perplexity. Now she was a totally different woman from the one he had known three months before. He no longer brooded, for example, over why she had run away from marrying him back then, with tears, imprecations and reproaches, and was now herself insisting on having the wedding as soon as possible. 'She mustn't be afraid any longer, as she was then, that marriage to me would mean my ruin', thought the prince. Such a swiftly restored self-confidence could not, to his way of thinking, be natural to her. It couldn't simply have arisen out of her hatred for Aglaya alone: Nastasya Filippovna was capable of feeling more deeply than that. Could it stem from her fear of a future with Rogozhin? In fact, all those reasons together with others might have contributed to it; but what was most obvious to him was what he had suspected for a long time, that her poor, sick mind had given way. All this, though it did in a way save him from worrying about other possibilities, could not give him rest or peace of mind throughout this period. Sometimes he seemed to try not to think about anything: he certainly regarded his marriage as a sort of minor formality; he felt little concern about his own future. As for objections and discussions like the one with Radomsky, he would most certainly have been unable to answer them, and felt himself totally incompetent to do so, and for that reason he steered clear of any discussion of that sort.

Still, he did observe that Nastasya Filippovna knew and understood very well what Aglaya had meant to him. She didn't say anything, but he saw her 'face' at times when she came across him at the very beginning, getting ready to go to the Yepanchins. When the Yepanchins left, she was literally radiant. However unobservant and lacking in intuition he might have been, the idea had begun to nag at him that Nastasya Filippovna would make her mind up to create some sort of scandalous scene, in order to drive Aglaya out of Pavlovsk. The uproar and commotion among the villas about the wedding was to some extent kept going by Nastasya Filippovna herself in order to exasperate her rival. Since it was difficult actually to meet the Yepanchins, Nastasya Filippovna on one occasion had sat the prince in her carriage and given orders for him to be driven past the very windows of their villa. This had been a dreadful surprise for the prince; as usual, he had realized what was going on too late to avert it, and the carriage was already driving past the windows. He had said nothing, but was ill for two days afterwards. Nastasya Filippovna did not repeat the experiment. In the final days before the wedding she was beginning to brood a great deal; she always ended by overcoming her melancholy mood and recovering her cheerfulness, but was somehow more subdued, not so noisy, not so happily cheerful as she had been before, not so long ago. The prince redoubled his attentiveness. He found it curious that she would never speak to him about Rogozhin. Just once, about five days before the wedding, Darya Alexeyevna sent for him to come at once as Nastasya Filippovna was feeling very unwell. He found her in a state bordering on complete derangement: she was crying out, shuddering, shouting that Rogozhin was hiding in the garden of their house, that she had just now seen him, and that he was going to kill her in the night . . . cut her throat! She was unable to calm down all day.

But that same evening, when the prince had dropped in to see Ippolit for a minute or two, his mother, the captain's widow, who had just returned from town after attending to some small matters of her own, told him that Rogozhin had called at her flat that day and questioned her about Pavlovsk. In response to the prince's question, she said that Rogozhin had been there at virtually the same time when he was supposed to have been seen by Nastasya Filippovna in the garden. The whole business was therefore a simple case of imagining things; Nastasya Filippovna went to see the captain's widow herself to inquire in more detail, and was greatly reassured.

On the eve of the wedding the prince left Nastasya Filippovna in a great flutter; her finery for the morrow had arrived from the Petersburg dressmakers—the bridal gown, the veil, and so on. The prince had not anticipated that she would be so excited by the garments; for his part, he praised everything and that made her happier still. But she did let something slip: she had already heard that there was indignation in the town and that some scallywags were going to organize a tin-pan serenade, with music and possibly even verses specially composed for the occasion—and that this more or less had the support of the rest of the townsfolk. Thus it was that now she was even keener to hold her head high before them and eclipse them all with the splendour and style of her wedding finery: 'Let them shout all they like, let them whistle if they dare!' The mere idea made her eyes sparkle. She also cherished one more secret dream, but did not speak it aloud; she hoped that Aglaya, or at least some emissary of hers, would be in the throng, incognito, in the church, and would be watching and noting everything: she was inwardly preparing herself for that. She parted from the prince, much exercised by these and similar thoughts, at about eleven in the evening. Midnight had not yet struck, however, when a messenger from Darya Alexandrovna came hot-foot to the prince, asking him to come 'as fast as he could, it was very bad'. The prince found his bride locked in her bedroom in floods of tears and hysterical despair; for a long time she could hear nothing said to her through the locked door, but she finally opened it to admit just the prince, then closed it after him and fell on her knees before him. (Such, at least, was the story Darya Alexeyevna, who had contrived to catch a glimpse, gave out later.)

'What am I doing! What am I doing! What am I doing to you!' she cried out, embracing his legs convulsively.

The prince sat with her for a whole hour; we don't know what they talked about. Darya Alexeyevna said that they parted an hour later, reconciled and happy. The prince sent again to enquire after her during the night, but Nastasya Filippovna was asleep by then. In the morning, before she woke, two more messengers arrived at Darya Alexeyevna's and a third was instructed to convey to the prince that 'Nastasya Filippovna was surrounded by a veritable swarm of dressmakers and hair-stylists from Petersburg; that there was no sign of the previous night's alarms, that she was busy with her toilet as only a beauty like her could be on her wedding morning, and that at this very moment a grave conference was taking place about which of her diamonds she should wear and how best they should be displayed'. The prince was completely reassured.

The whole of the succeeding account was given by people present at the wedding, and appears to be accurate.

The ceremony was due to take place at eight in the evening;

Nastasya Filippovna was ready by seven. Since as early as six o'clock, gaping crowds had gradually started congregating around Lebedev's villa, but more particularly near Darya Alexeyevna's house; from seven onwards the church too began filling up. Vera Lebedeva and Kolya were extremely concerned on the prince's account; however, they had a good many chores to see to at home; they were organizing the reception and hospitality arrangements in the prince's rooms. In fact, nothing much in the way of a reception was planned for after the ceremony; in addition to the essential people who were assisting at the ceremony, Lebedev had invited the Ptitsyns, Ganya, the St Anne doctor, and Darya Alexeyevna. When the prince enquired of Lebedev why he had thought to invite the doctor, whom he hardly knew, Lebedev replied complacently: 'He wears a decoration, a respectable man, sir, for the look of the thing, sir', and made the prince laugh. Keller and Burdovsky looked very smart in their evening dress and gloves; but Keller still worried the prince and his well-wishers by a certain unconcealed readiness to do battle, as he regarded the onlookers who had gathered near the house with considerable hostility. Finally, at half-past seven, the prince set off in his carriage for the church. We should observe, incidentally, that the prince made a deliberate point of abiding by all the accepted ceremonies and customs; everything was done 'properly', out in the open for all to see. Inside the church, having somehow or other made his way through the crowd amid ceaseless whispering and comments from the public, the prince, escorted by Keller, who was glowering menacingly to right and left, concealed himself temporarily in the sanctuary. Keller set off to fetch the bride, where, by the porch of Darya Alexeyevna's house, he found a gathering not only two or three times as numerous as at the prince's but perhaps three times as free and easy. As he went up the porch steps, he heard such comments that he could no longer restrain himself, and was about to address the public in appropriate language when he was fortunately prevented by Burdovsky and Darya Alexeyevna herself, who ran down from the porch and dragged him inside by main force. Keller was irritable and in a hurry. Nastasya Filippovna rose, glanced at herself in the mirror, remarked with a 'wry smile', as Keller later recounted, that she was 'as pale as death', bowed reverently before the icon, and went out on to the porch. A hubbub of voices greeted her appearance. True, there was some initial laughter, applause, and something like hissing, but in an instant other voices were raised:

'How beautiful she is!' came from some in the crowd.

'She's not the first, and she won't be the last!'

'A wedding-ring hushes everything up, fools!'

'No, try finding a beauty like that anywhere, hurrah!' cried those in front.

'A princess! I'd sell my soul for a princess like that!' shouted some clerk. ' "My life for just one night . . ." ', he sang.

Nastasya Filippovna was certainly as white as a sheet when she emerged, but her great black eyes blazed out at the crowd like burning coals; the crowd could not withstand a look like that; their indignation turned to rapturous shouting. The carriage doors were already opened and Keller had already offered the bride his arm, when she suddenly screamed and rushed straight down from the porch into the throng. All those accompanying her froze in astonishment, the crowd parted before her, and half-a-dozen paces from the porch appeared Rogozhin. It was his eye among the crowd that Nastasya Filippovna had caught. She ran to him like a mad thing and seized both his hands.

'Save me! Take me away! Wherever you like—now!'

Rogozhin took her in his arms and almost lifted her into the carriage. In an instant, he took out a hundred-rouble note from his purse and proffered it to the coachman.

'The railway station, and if we're on time, there's another hundred in it for you!'

Then he sprang into the carriage after Nastasya Filippovna and closed the doors. The coachman didn't hesitate for an instant and lashed his horses forward. Keller afterwards blamed the unexpectedness of it all: 'Another second and I'd have recovered my wits and stopped them', he explained when recounting the incident. He and Burdovsky were about to take another carriage which chanced to be standing there and hurtle off in pursuit, but had second thoughts, as 'it was too late in any case! We couldn't very well bring her back by force!'

'And the prince wouldn't want that either!' decided a stunned Burdovsky.

Meanwhile, Rogozhin and Nastasya Filippovna reached the station in time. As he got out of the carriage and was about to board the train, Rogozhin managed to stop a girl wearing an old but presentable dark shawl and a silk kerchief over her hair.

'Fifty do for the shawl?' He suddenly held out money to the girl. Before she had time to be astonished or realize what was happening, he had thrust the fifty roubles into her hand, removed the shawl and kerchief, and thrown them over Nastasya Filippovna's head and shoulders. Her magnificent gown was too conspicuous and would have arrested everyone's attention on the train; only afterwards did the girl realize why her old rags had been purchased at so much profit to herself.

News of the incident was noised abroad and reached the church with extraordinary rapidity. When Keller was making his way through to the prince, great numbers of total strangers rushed up to question him. A loud hubbub of voices rose, with wagging of heads and even laughter; no one left the church, everyone was waiting to see how the groom would take the news. He turned pale, but received the news quietly enough, saying in a barely audible voice: 'I was afraid it might happen, but I didn't think it would, all the same . . .', adding after a pause: 'Still . . . in her state of mind . . . it might well have been expected.' Keller himself later described the comment as 'unprecedented philosophy'. The prince left the church, apparently calm and in good spirits; that, at any rate, is what many people observed and afterwards recounted. He seemed very anxious to get home and be alone as soon as possible; this, however, was denied him. Several of those invited followed him in, among them Ptitsyn, Ganya, and the doctor, who also had no plans to leave. Besides which, the whole house was literally besieged by a festive crowd. Even from the veranda the prince caught the sound of Keller and Lebedev commencing a fierce argument with several complete strangers, respectable-looking people who were determined at all costs to reach the veranda. The prince went up to the disputants, inquired what was the matter, politely dismissed Lebedev and Keller, and tactfully addressed a stout, grey-haired gentleman standing on the steps at the head of a number of other desirous individuals, inviting him to do him the honour of paying him a visit. The gentleman sheepishly did so, followed by another and a third. Out of the whole crowd, about seven or eight people came in, trying to appear as much at ease as they were able; no more volunteers came forward, and the crowd even started criticizing the intruders. The newcomers were seated, and conversation got under way as tea was served. All of this was done very decorously and modestly, to the surprise of the newcomers. There were attempts made, of course, to enliven the talk and turn it towards the topic of the moment; several tactless questions were asked and a few 'pointed' remarks passed. The prince answered everyone so simply and genially, and at the same time with such dignity and faith in the integrity of his guests, that the indiscreet questions subsided of themselves. Gradually the conversation took an almost grave turn. One gentleman, picking up someone else's remark, vowed with great indignation that he would not sell his property whatever happened; he would wait and see, 'business assets are better than money; there, sir, is my economic system, and I don't care who knows it'. Since he was addressing his remarks to the prince, the latter warmly applauded him, despite Lebedev whispering in his ear that the gentleman had neither house nor home and had never possessed an estate of any sort. Almost an hour had passed, the tea had been drunk, and after that the guests began to feel embarrassed at staying any longer. The doctor and the grey-headed man said a cordial goodbye to the prince, and indeed they all took their leave cordially and noisily. Good wishes were expressed and opinions passed to the effect that it was no use crying over spilt milk, perhaps it was all for the best, and so forth. True, there were attempts made to request champagne, but the older guests restrained the younger ones. When they had all gone, Keller leaned over to Lebedev and said: 'You and I would have had a shouting match, got into a fight, disgraced ourselves, and had the police brought in, but here he's made some new friends, and what friends; I know them!' Lebedev, who was 'well primed', sighed and said: '"Thou hast hidden these things from the wise and prudent and vouchsafed them to babes",* I've said that before about him, but I'm adding now that God has preserved the babe himself, saved him from the abyss, He and all his saints!'

At last, around half-past ten, the prince was left alone. He had a headache. Kolya had been the last to leave after helping the prince change out of his wedding clothes into his everyday garments. They parted very affectionately. Kolya did not talk much about what had happened, but promised to call early on the following day. He testified later that at their last parting, the prince had not forewarned him of anything, so must have been concealing his intentions even from him. Soon there was almost no one left in the house: Burdovsky had gone to Ippolit's; Keller and Lebedev had also set off somewhere. Only Vera Lebedeva remained for a little while in his rooms, hurriedly setting everything to rights after the reception. As she left, she glanced into the prince's room. He was seated at the table leaning his elbows on it, his head buried in his hands. She went softly up to him and touched him on the shoulder; the prince looked at her bemusedly and spent almost a minute apparently trying to recall something; once he had done so and it had all sunk in, he suddenly became extremely agitated. All he did, however, was to implore Vera earnestly to knock on his door the following morning at seven o'clock, as soon as the trains started running. She promised to do so; the prince began begging her earnestly not to tell anyone about it; she promised again, and when at length she opened the door to leave he stopped her for the third time, took her hands, kissed them, then kissed her on the forehead and, with a sort of 'peculiar' expression, uttered the words: 'Till tomorrow!' This was Vera's account afterwards at any rate. She left greatly concerned about him. Next morning she felt somewhat more cheerful when she knocked on his door a little after seven as arranged, and informed him that the Petersburg train would be leaving in a quarter of an hour; when he opened the door she thought he looked perfectly cheerful and even smiling. He had hardly undressed that night; however, he had slept. He thought he might be coming back that day. It would appear, therefore, that she was the only person he had considered it possible and necessary to tell, at that moment, that he was setting off for town.

11

AN hour later he was already in Petersburg, and was ringing at Rogozhin's house some time after nine. He went in by the main entrance, and for a long time no one opened the door. At length the door of Rogozhin's old mother opened and a pleasant-faced old maidservant appeared.

'Parfion Semyonovich is not at home', she announced from the doorway. 'Who is it you want?'

'Parfion Semyonovich.'

'He's not at home, sir.'

The maid was regarding him with intense curiosity.

'At least tell me whether he spent the night at home. And . . . did he come back alone last night?'

The maid kept on staring at him, but made no reply.

'Wasn't . . . Nastasya Filippovna here with him yesterday . . . evening?'

'May I enquire, sir, who you may be yourself?'

'Prince Lev Nikolayevich Myshkin, we know one another very well.'

'He's not at home, sir.'

The maid dropped her eyes.

'And Nastasya Filippovna?'

'I don't know about that, sir?'

'Wait, wait! When will he be back?'

'I don't know that either, sir.'

The door closed.

The prince decided to return in an hour. Glancing into the courtyard, he encountered the porter.

'Is Parfion Semyonovich in?'

'Yes, sir.'

'Then why was I told just now he was out?'

'Did his servant tell you that?'

'No, the mother's maid, I rang Parfion Semyonovich's bell, but nobody answered.'

'Perhaps he has gone out then', decided the porter. 'He doesn't say, sir, you know. Sometimes he takes the key with him and the flat stays locked for three days.'

'You're certain he was at home yesterday?'

'Yes he was. Sometimes he uses the front entrance though, and you don't see him.'

'Nastasya Filippovna wasn't with him yesterday, was she?'

'That I don't know, sir. She doesn't come visiting often, at that; think I'd have known if she'd come.'

The prince left and spent some time walking the pavement sunk in thought. The windows of Rogozhin's rooms were all shut; the windows of his mother's flat were all open; it was a hot and sunny day; the prince crossed the street on to the opposite pavement and stopped to look again at the windows; not only were they closed, but white curtains were drawn almost everywhere.

He stood for a moment and strangely enough, all of a sudden, he thought he saw a corner of one of the curtains being lifted and for a moment caught a fleeting glimpse of Rogozhin's face, one fleeting glimpse, then it vanished instantly. He waited for a while and was on the point of going over and ringing again, but changed his mind and postponed it for an hour: 'Who knows, perhaps I just imagined it . . .'

What decided him was that he was in a hurry to get to the Izmailovsky Regiment district, to the flat Nastasya Filippovna had occupied recently. He knew that, when she had left Pavlovsk at his request three weeks previously, she had gone to live with an old friend of hers, a schoolmaster's widow, a respectable woman with a family, who rented out a well-furnished room and virtually lived on the proceeds. Most likely, Nastasya Filippovna had kept the flat on after moving to Pavlovsk; at any rate it was perfectly conceivable that she had spent the night there, where Rogozhin, of course, had brought her the previous evening. The prince took a cab. On the way it occurred to him that he should have started here in any case, as it was highly unlikely that she had gone straight to Rogozhin's that night. Now the porter's words came back to him too, that Nastasya Filippovna did not often go there. If she didn't go there often in any case, why should she be staying with Rogozhin now? Cheering himself with reflections of this kind, he arrived in Izmailovsky at length, in a state of fearful anxiety.

To his absolute amazement, no one at the widow's had heard of Nastasya Filippovna either that day or the previous one, but they all ran out to peer at him as if he were some sort of prodigy. All the widow's numerous family—all eight girls from 7 to

15—spilled out after their mother and surrounded him, open-mouthed; behind them came a gaunt, sallow aunt in a black kerchief, and finally the grandmother put in an appearance, a little old lady in spectacles. The widow earnestly requested him to go in and sit down, which he accordingly did. He realized at once that they were perfectly well aware of who he was and knew that his wedding should have taken place the day before; they were dying to ask him both about the wedding and the extraordinary fact that he was enquiring about the woman who should have been nowhere else but with him in Pavlovsk, but were too tactful to mention it. He briefly satisfied their curiosity about the wedding. There followed a chorus of astonishment, cries and groans, so that he felt obliged to tell them practically everything else, in broad terms of course. At length the advice of the sage and agitated ladies was that he should first of all knock up Rogozhin and find out definitely what was going on. If he was really not at home (which he must ascertain) or refused to say anything, then he must go to the Semyonovsky quarter and see a German lady, a friend of Nastasya Filippovna who lived with her mother: perhaps, in her excitement and anxiety to conceal herself, she might have spent the night with them. The prince got up feeling absolutely crushed; they said afterwards that he 'had gone terribly pale'; indeed, his legs were almost giving way. At length, through the terrific babble of voices, he made out that they were agreeing among themselves to act in his interest and were asking him for his address in town. As it turned out that he didn't have one, they advised him to put up at a hotel. The prince thought for a moment and gave them the address of his former hotel, the one where he had had his seizure some five weeks previously. After that he set off for Rogozhin's again.

This time not only Rogozhin's door but even that of his mother remained shut. The prince went down to seek out the porter and found him, after some difficulty, in the yard; the porter was busy with some task and would barely answer him, or even look at him, but he did announce positively that Rogozhin had gone out very early that morning, to Pavlovsk, and would not be back that day.

'I'll wait; perhaps he'll be back this evening?'

'And perhaps not for a week, who can tell?'

'So he must have spent the night here, then?'

'Spent the night, yes indeed . . .'

All of this was suspicious and sinister. It was highly likely that the porter had had time to get fresh instructions in the meantime: earlier, he had been quite talkative, but now he simply turned his back. Still, the prince decided to call again in a couple of hours and even keep watch on the house if necessary; now there remained the hope of the German lady, and he set off post-haste for the Semyonovsky Regiment district.*

But at the German lady's they didn't even understand him. Gleaning a few words here and there, he was able to gather that about a fortnight previously, the beautiful German lady had quarrelled violently with Nastasya Filippovna, and so had heard nothing of her, 'even if she had married all the princes in the world'. The prince left hastily. It had crossed his mind, meanwhile, that she might have gone to Moscow as before, and Rogozhin of course after her, or perhaps with her. 'At least let me find some trace of her!' He remembered, however, that he had to stay in some hotel, so he hurried off to Liteinaya, where he found a room at once. The servant enquired if he would like something to eat; he replied absently that he would, then, recollecting himself, was furious because the meal delayed him half an hour, and it was only afterwards that he realized that nothing had prevented him leaving untouched what they brought him. An odd feeling possessed him in that dim and stuffy corridor, a sensation that strove tantalizingly to take the form of thought, but he just could not grasp what the insistent notion was. He emerged from the hotel at last, feeling dizzy and thoroughly out of sorts. But where could he go now? He rushed round to Rogozhin's again.

Rogozhin had not returned; no one answered the bell; he rang the old mother; the door was opened and he was informed that Parfion Semyonovich was not at home and might not be back for three days or more. It disturbed the prince that, as before, he was scrutinized with such avid curiosity. On this occasion the porter was nowhere to be found. As he had done earlier, he crossed over to the opposite pavement, looked at the windows, and walked about in the stifling heat for half an hour or more; this time nothing stirred; the windows had not been opened, the white curtains were motionless. He came to the definite conclusion that he had been imagining things earlier; it was obvious that the windows were so grimy and long unwashed that it would have been hard to make out even if someone actually did peer through the panes. Cheered by this reflection, he drove back to the widow's in Izmailovsky.

They were already expecting him there. The widow had been to three or four places, and had even called in at Rogozhin's: no trace. The prince listened in silence, went in, sat down on the sofa, and began looking at them, seemingly unable to understand what they were talking about. It was odd: one moment he was sharply observant, the next he would become incredibly absent-minded. The whole family stated later that he was 'an astonishingly strange person' that day, so that 'perhaps all the signs were there already'. He finally got to his feet and asked them to show him Nastasya Filippovna's rooms. These were two spacious, light, high-ceilinged rooms, very decently furnished and not cheap. All these ladies said afterwards that the prince went round examining every object in the rooms; he noticed an open library book on the little table, the French novel *Madame Bovary*, bent the corner of the opened page, and asked their permission to take it with him; ignoring their objections that it was a library book, he slipped it into his pocket. He sat down by the open window and, seeing a card-table with chalk marks, asked who played. They told him that Nastasya Filippovna used to play cards with Rogozhin every evening—'fools, preference, millers, whist, own trumps, all the games'—and that they had started playing just lately, on their return to Petersburg from Pavlovsk, because Nastasya Filippovna kept complaining of being bored, and Rogozhin sat all evening without saying a word and couldn't talk about anything; she often wept. The following evening Rogozhin suddenly brought out a pack of cards from his pocket; Nastasya Filippovna had laughed at this and they had started to play. The prince asked where the cards were that they had played with, but they could not be found; Rogozhin always used to bring the cards in himself, a new pack every day, then take them away with him.

The ladies advised him to go and try Rogozhin again, and give a good hard knock, not now but during the evening: 'Perhaps he'll be there.' The widow volunteered to go to Darya Alexeyevna's in Pavlovsk and find out if they knew anything.

They asked the prince to call again at ten that evening, if only to make arrangements for the next day. In spite of all their heartening and reassuring words, the prince was overwhelmed by despair. He reached his hotel in a state of unutterable despondency. The dust and heat of a Petersburg summer crushed him like a vice; he had been jostled by hard-faced or drunken men as he stared aimlessly at passing faces and perhaps walked much further than he need have done; it was almost evening by the time he entered his room. He decided to rest for a while before following the ladies' advice and going to Rogozhin's again. He sat down on the sofa and, leaning his elbows on the table, began to ponder the situation.

Goodness knows how long he sat there, or what he was thinking about. There were many things he dreaded, and he sensed painfully and poignantly that he was horribly afraid. He thought of Vera Lebedeva; then it struck him that perhaps Lebedev knew something about all this, and if he didn't he could find out quicker and more easily than he, the prince, could. Then he remembered Ippolit and that Rogozhin used to go and visit him. Then he recalled Rogozhin himself, recently at the memorial service, then in the park, then—suddenly here in the corridor, when he had hidden that time in the corner and waited for him with a knife. He was remembering the eyes now, the eyes watching in the darkness. He shuddered: the tantalizing thought of earlier in the day now suddenly entered his mind.

It was partly that, if Rogozhin was in Petersburg, then even if he did conceal himself for a while, the inevitable upshot would be that he would come to him, the prince, with good or evil intent, as he had done then. At least if Rogozhin wanted to see him for any reason, there was nowhere for him to come but here, to this selfsame corridor. Rogozhin didn't know his address, so he might very well assume that the prince would be staying at the same hotel; at any rate he would try looking for him here ... if he needed him badly enough. And who knew, perhaps he would need him badly?

So his thoughts ran, and the idea seemed quite a plausible one for some reason. He would not have been able to say why, had he tried to explore his thinking. Why, for instance, should Rogozhin need him all of a sudden, and why was it out of the question that they should never meet at all? But the thought was a painful one. 'If he's all right, he won't come', the prince pursued his train of thought, 'he's more likely to come if he's unhappy; and he will surely be unhappy.'

Of course, if he was convinced of that he ought to wait for Rogozhin at home, in his hotel room, but this new thought of his wouldn't let him sit still; he seized his hat and ran. Out in the corridor it was already almost dark: 'What if he suddenly comes out of that corner and stops me by the stairs?' flashed through his mind as he was approaching the familiar spot. But no one emerged. He went down and out through the gates on to the pavement, and stood astonished at the dense crowds of people spilling out into the street at sundown (as always in Petersburg at holiday time), and walked in the direction of Gorokhovaya Street. Fifty yards from the hotel, at the first crossroads, someone in the throng suddenly touched his elbow and spoke in an undertone just by his ear:

'Lev Nikolayevich, come this way, friend, I need you.'

It was Rogozhin.

It was odd: the prince was so pleased to see him that he suddenly started babbling and hardly finishing his words, as he told him of how he had expected to see him just now in the corridor.

'I was there', Rogozhin replied unexpectedly. 'Come along.'

The prince was taken aback by this answer, but that was at least two minutes later, when he had absorbed its import. When he did, he took fright and started flicking glances at Rogozhin, who was already walking half a yard ahead, staring straight in front of him, without glancing at passers-by as he let them go past him with automatic consideration.

'Then why didn't you ask for my room . . . if you were in the hotel?' the prince asked suddenly.

Rogozhin halted, looked at him, thought for a moment, and said, as if he hadn't understood the question at all:

'Now then Lev Nikolayevich, you go straight on to the house, you know? And I'll go on the other side. Just watch that we keep together . . .'

So saying, he crossed the street on to the opposite pavement, glancing over to see whether the prince was proceeding; seeing him standing gaping at him, he waved his arm in the direction of Gorokhovaya Street and walked on, turning every minute to look at the prince and urge him on to follow. He was evidently relieved to see that he had understood him and wasn't coming over to his pavement. It occurred to the prince that Rogozhin was looking out for someone, and had crossed over so as not to miss them. 'Only why on earth didn't he say who it was?' They went on in this way some five hundred yards and, all of a sudden, the prince began shaking; Rogozhin had not stopped glancing back, though he did it less often; the prince could contain himself no longer and beckoned to him. Rogozhin at once crossed the street.

'Nastasya Filippovna isn't at your house is she?'

'Yes.'

'And was it you I saw earlier on, looking at me from behind the curtain?'

'Yes . . .'

'Then why on earth did you . . .'

But the prince didn't know what more to ask or how to finish his question; besides, his heart was pounding so violently that he could scarcely speak. Rogozhin said nothing either, and regarded him as before, almost pensively.

'Well, I'm going', he said abruptly, making as if to cross the street again, 'and you walk on this side. Just as long as we aren't together in the street . . . it'll be better for us . . . on opposite sides . . . you'll see.'

When they finally turned off on their opposite pavements into Gorokhovaya Street and got closer to Rogozhin's house, the prince's legs began to give way, making it quite difficult to walk. It was ten o'clock in the evening by now. The windows on the old woman's side stood open as they had earlier in the day, those on Rogozhin's were closed, and the white curtains seemed even more conspicuous in the fading light. The prince approached the house from the opposite pavement; Rogozhin on his side went up on to the porch and waved to him. The prince crossed over and joined him on the porch.

'Even the porter doesn't know I've come back. I said earlier on I was going to Pavlovsk, and told mother's servants too', he hissed, with a crafty smile, almost pleased. 'We'll go in and no one will hear anything.'

By now there was a key in his hands. As he went up the stairs, he turned round to warn the prince to walk more quietly, then gently opened the door to his rooms, admitted the prince, cautiously entered after him, then closed the door behind him, pocketing the key.

'Come on', he whispered.

Ever since the Liteinaya pavement he had been speaking in whispers. Despite his apparent composure, he was inwardly in a state of profound agitation. When they had entered the drawing-room, prior to going on into the study, Rogozhin went over to the window and beckoned the prince mysteriously over to him.

'You see, when you started ringing this morning, I realized it was you straight away; I tiptoed to the door and heard you talking to Pafnutievna; I'd given her orders at first light that if you, or anyone sent by you, or anybody at all, was to start knocking on my door, she was under no circumstances to say I was in—especially if you had come in person asking for me; I told her your name. Then, after you went, it crossed my mind: what if he's standing there now keeping a look-out or patrolling the street? So I went over to this very window, drew back the curtain, and there you were standing and looking straight at me . . . That's the way it was.'

'But where . . . is Nastasya Filippovna?' the prince brought out, gasping.

'She's . . . here', said Rogozhin slowly, seeming to hesitate for the faintest instant.

'But where?'

Rogozhin raised his eyes and stared at the prince:

'Come on . . .'

He still spoke in whispers, slowly, unhurriedly, and, as before, strangely thoughtful. Even when he was talking about the curtains, it was as if he had wanted to say something else, for all the seeming spontaneity of the story.

They entered the study. The room had undergone a change since the last time the prince had been in it: a green damask curtain, with gaps at both sides, was suspended across the entire breadth of the room, cutting off the study from the alcove where Rogozhin's bed was. The heavy curtain was drawn right across and the gaps closed. But it was very dark in the room; the 'white nights' of the Petersburg summer had begun to get darker, and had there not been a full moon it would have been difficult to make anything out in Rogozhin's darkened rooms. It was still possible to pick out one another's faces, but very indistinctly. Rogozhin's bore its habitual pallor; the eyes were fixed on the prince, intent and shining brightly.

'Couldn't you light a candle?'

'No, no need for that', replied Rogozhin, and taking the prince by the hand, pressed him into a chair; he seated himself opposite, shifting his own chair forward, so that the two sat almost knee to knee. There was a small circular table between them, a little to one side. 'Sit down, let's sit here for a while!' he said, as though trying to persuade the prince to remain where he was. They were silent for a minute or so. 'I knew you'd be staying at that hotel', he began, the way people sometimes prepare the ground for the main issue by starting with irrelevant details off the point. 'As soon as I got to the corridor, I thought to myself, you know, maybe he's sitting waiting for me now, just as I'm waiting for him at this same moment. Have you been to the teacher's widow?'

'Yes.' The prince could hardly speak for the fierce thudding of his heart.

'I thought of that too. People will start talking, I thought . . . then I had another thought: I'll bring him here for the night, so this night, together . . .'

'Rogozhin! Where is Nastasya Filippovna?' the prince whispered suddenly as he rose to his feet, his whole body shaking. Rogozhin also got up.

'There', he whispered, nodding towards the curtain.

'Asleep?' whispered the prince.

Again Rogozhin stared at him intently, as he had earlier.

'All right, come on then! . . . But you . . . well, come on then!' He half-raised the curtain, halted, and turned again to the prince.

'Come through!' He nodded at the curtain, inviting the prince to pass him. He did so.

'It's dark in here', he said.

'You can see', muttered Rogozhin.

'I can just make out . . . the bed.'

'Go closer, then', Rogozhin suggested softly.

The prince walked still closer, one step, another, then stopped. He stood there taking it in for a minute or two; neither uttered a word all the time they were standing by the bed; the prince's heart was beating so loudly, it seemed to be audible in the deathly silence of the room. But he had by now peered closely enough to make out the whole of the bed; someone lay asleep upon it, absolutely motionless; not the slightest rustle could be heard, not the faintest breath. The sleeper was shrouded from head to toe in a white sheet, but the limbs were somehow only vaguely discernible. All that could be seen from the raised outlines was that a human figure was stretched out there. All about, in disordered heaps on the bed, the foot of the bed, the armchairs, the floor even, discarded garments were scattered—the rich white silk gown, flowers, ribbons. On the small table by the headboard, glittering diamonds lay discarded and scattered about. At the foot of the bed, lace of some kind had been crumpled up, and on this white lace the end of a bare foot peeped out from under the sheet; it looked as if it had been carved out of marble, and was horribly still. As he gazed, the prince felt that the longer he went on looking the more still and death-like the room became. Suddenly a fly began buzzing and flew about over the bed before settling down near the headboard. The prince shuddered.

'Let's go back', Rogozhin touched his hand.

They went out and sat down in the same chairs, again facing one another. The prince was trembling with increasing violence and kept his eyes fixed questioningly on Rogozhin's face.

'I see you're trembling there, Lev Nikolayevich', said Rogozhin at length, 'almost the way you do when you're ill, remember how it was in Moscow? Or once just before a fit. I can't think what I would do with you . . .'

The prince listened hard, straining his utmost to understand, his questioning expression unaltered.

'It was you?' he finally got out, nodding towards the curtain.

'It was . . . me . . .', whispered Rogozhin, and dropped his eyes.

They were silent for some five minutes.

'Because', Rogozhin resumed, as if the interruption had not occurred, 'because if you were to be ill now, and have a fit and shout out, someone might hear you in the street or the yard and realize there's someone spending the night in here; then they'll come knocking and come in . . . because they all think I'm not at home. I haven't lit a candle so they won't guess out there in the street or the yard. Because when I go out, I take the keys with me as well and nobody comes in to tidy up if I'm not here for three or four days, that's how I've arranged things. So nobody finds out we're here for the night . . .'

'Wait a moment', said the prince. 'Earlier on I asked the porter and the maid whether Nastasya Filippovna had spent the night here? They must know already.'

'I know you asked them. I told Pafnutievna that Nastasya Filippovna called in yesterday and only stayed ten minutes before she went back to Pavlovsk the same evening. They don't know she stayed the night here—nobody does. Last night we came in as quietly as you and I did today. On the way here I thought she'd never come in on the quiet—but not a bit of it! Whispers, walks on tiptoe, gathers up her skirts round her, holds them in her hands to stop them rustling, wags her finger at me on the stairs—it was all because she was afraid of you. On the train she was out of her mind, she was so scared, and it was she who wanted to spend the night at my place; at first I thought to take her to the widow's flat—not a bit of it! "He'll find me there first thing in the morning, you can hide me and first thing tomorrow, it's off to Moscow." Then she wanted to go to Oryol for some reason. As she was going to bed, she was still saying we'd go to Oryol . . .'

'Wait a moment; what are you going to do now, Parfion, what is it you want to do?'

'You see, I'm not sure about you, you're all of a tremble. We'll spend the night here, together. There's no bed in here besides that one, so I thought we'd take the cushions off the two sofas and I'll make them up here by the curtain, for you and me, so we can be together. Because if they get in, they'll start looking round or searching; they'll see her at once and take her away. They'll start questioning me, and I'll tell them it was me, and they'll take me away straight away as well. So let her lie there near us, near you and me . . .'

'Yes, yes!' the prince assented fervently.

'So no confessions and no taking her away.'

'N-not for anything!' resolved the prince. 'No, certainly not!'

'So I've decided not to give her up on any account, my lad, not to anybody! We'll spend a quiet night. I've just been out for an hour this morning; the rest of the time I've been with her. And then I went to fetch you this evening. The only thing is the smell in this hot weather. Can you smell anything or not?'

'Perhaps I do, I don't know. There'll probably be a smell by morning.'

'I've wrapped her in oilcloth, good quality, and a sheet on top of that, and put four opened bottles of Zhdanov fluid by her, they're there now.'

'Like they did ... in Moscow?'*

'It's because of the smell, friend, and you see how she's ... lying. In the morning, when it gets light, have a look. What's the matter, can't you even stand up?' Rogozhin asked in nervous surprise, seeing the prince trembling so badly that he couldn't get to his feet.

'My legs won't carry me', mumbled the prince. 'It's from fright, I know ... Once the fear passes, then I'll get up ...'

'Wait a minute though, you just wait there till I make our bed up ... then you can lie down ... both of us ... and we'll listen ... because I still don't know, lad ... I still don't know everything yet, so I'm telling you in good time, so that you know all about it in advance ...'

Mumbling these obscure words, Rogozhin started making up the bed. It was evident that he'd thought up the idea of the beds possibly as early as that morning. He had lain down on the sofa the previous night. But the sofa couldn't accommodate two, and he was resolved they should lie side by side, which was why, with much effort, he now dragged cushions of all shapes and sizes from the two sofas right across the room and placed them right by the end of the curtain. Somehow or other the bed was made ready. He then went over to the prince, took him tenderly and rapturously by the hand, raised him up, and led him over to the bed; it seemed, however, that the prince was able to walk by himself, so his fear was 'passing'; however, he still continued to shake.

'Because, friend', Rogozhin began abruptly, placing the prince on the left and better cushion, while himself stretching out on the right side, hands clasped behind his head, but without undressing, 'it's hot now and of course there'll be a smell . . . I'm afraid to open the windows; mama has some vases of flowers, they smell lovely; I thought I might bring them in but Pafnutievna would guess something, because she's inquisitive.'

'Yes, she is', assented the prince.

'Should I buy some—set bouquets and flowers all round her? But I think it would be a pitiful sight, all flowers, eh?'

'Listen . . .', said the prince, seeming to get muddled as he sought the right question to put, and kept forgetting it at once. 'Listen, tell me: how did you do it to her? A knife? That knife?'

'That knife.'

'Wait, wait! I want to ask you something else, Parfion . . . I want to ask you a lot of things, about everything . . . but better tell me to begin with, first and foremost, so that I know: did you mean to kill her before my wedding, before the ceremony, at the church door, with the knife? Did you or not?'

'I don't know whether I did or not . . .', Rogozhin replied coldly, seemingly rather surprised at the question and not understanding its import.

'Did you never take the knife to Pavlovsk?'

'Never. I can only tell you this about that knife, Lev Nikolayevich', he added after a pause. 'I took it out of the locked drawer this morning, because it all happened this morning, some time after three. I had kept it as a bookmark all this time. And . . . and there's another strange thing: the knife only went in about three or four inches . . . just under the left breast . . . and there was only about a spoonful of blood came out on her chemise, no more than that.'

'That, that, that', the prince sat up in fearful agitation, 'that, that I know, I've read about it . . . it's called an internal haemorrhage . . . Sometimes there isn't a drop. That's if the blow goes straight to the heart . . .'

'Wait, did you hear that?' Rogozhin broke in swiftly, sitting up fearfully on the cushions. 'Did you hear?'

'No!' the prince replied just as quickly and fearfully, looking at Rogozhin.

'Footsteps! You hear? In the drawing-room . . .'

Both strained their ears.

'I can hear', whispered the prince firmly.

'Footsteps?'

'Yes.'

'Shall I bolt the door or not?'

'Bolt it . . .'

The door was bolted and both lay down again. For a long time neither spoke.

'Ah, yes!' hissed the prince in his former rapid and agitated whisper, as if he had caught the thread of his thoughts and greatly feared to lose it again; he even sprang up in bed. 'Yes . . . that's what I wanted . . . those cards! Cards . . . They say you played cards with her?'

'Yes, I did', said Rogozhin after a short silence.

'Where are those . . . cards, then?'

'Here they are . . .', Rogozhin said, after an even longer pause, 'here . . .'

He drew out an old pack of cards, wrapped in paper, and held them out to the prince. He took them, but seemed bewildered. A new feeling, melancholy and desolate, oppressed his heart; all at once he had become aware that at that moment, and for some time past, he had not been saying what he ought to have been saying, not doing what he should have been doing, and that these cards he held in his hands and had been so pleased about, could avail nothing, nothing at all now. He got to his feet and flung up his arms. Rogozhin was lying stock-still and seemed not to hear or see his movements; yet his eyes shone brightly through the darkness and were wide open and unmoving. The prince sat down in a chair and began regarding him with terror. Half an hour passed; all at once Rogozhin uttered a loud and abrupt shout and began to laugh, apparently oblivious of the need to whisper:

'That officer, that officer . . . remember, how she lashed that officer at the music with a riding-crop, remember? Ha-ha-ha! And the cadet . . . cadet . . . that came running up . . .'

The prince sprang from his chair in fresh alarm. When Rogozhin subsided (which happened suddenly), the prince bent quietly over him, seated himself close by, and with heart thumping and breathing heavily began to look closely at him.

Rogozhin did not turn his head towards him, and indeed seemed oblivious of him altogether. The prince watched and waited; time passed, and it began to grow light. From time to time Rogozhin began muttering, loudly, harshly, incoherently; he began to utter short screams and laugh; the prince reached out his trembling hand and gently touched his head, his hair, stroking them and his cheeks ... there was nothing more he could do! He began shaking again himself, and his legs again suddenly gave way under him. A totally new sensation of infinite anguish was oppressing his heart. Meanwhile it had grown quite light; at length, he lay down on the cushions, as though in utter exhaustion or despair, and pressed his face against the pale and motionless face of Rogozhin; tears flowed from his eyes on to Rogozhin's face, but perhaps he was no longer aware of his tears and knew nothing of them ...

At all events, when, many hours later, the door opened and people came in, they found the murderer totally unconscious and in a raging fever. The prince was sitting motionless beside him on the cushions, and every time the sick man went into bouts of delirium or shouting, he hurriedly passed his trembling hand gently across his hair and cheeks, as though caressing and soothing him. But he no longer understood the questions that were put to him and did not recognize the people who had come into the room and surrounded him. And if Schneider himself had arrived from Switzerland at this moment to see his former pupil and patient, remembering the state in which the prince had sometimes been during his first year of treatment, he would have washed his hands of him and said, as he had then: 'An idiot!'

12

THE teacher's widow, who had rushed off to Pavlovsk, went straight to Darya Alexeyevna, still upset after the previous day's events, and by telling her everything she knew contrived to alarm her thoroughly. Both ladies decided to get in touch with Lebedev, who was also much agitated, being his tenant's friend as well as his landlord. Vera Lebedeva recounted everything she knew. On Lebedev's advice, it was decided that all three of them should go to Petersburg in order to avert, as quickly as possible, 'what might well happen'. Thus it came to pass that, at around eleven o'clock the following morning, Rogozhin's apartment was opened in the presence of the police, Lebedev, the ladies, and Rogozhin's brother, Semyon Semyonovich Rogozhin, who lived in one of the wings of the house. The greatest assistance in the matter was furnished by the porter, who stated that he had seen Parfion Semyonovich and a friend entering by the porch in what looked like a surreptitious manner. After this statement there was no hesitation in breaking down the door when it failed to open in answer to their ringing.

Rogozhin suffered from brain fever for two months, and when he recovered, the investigation and trial followed. He gave straightforward, precise, and entirely satisfactory evidence on all points raised, as a result of which the case against the prince was dropped at once. Rogozhin remained silent throughout his trial. He did not contradict his skilful and eloquent lawyer, who demonstrated clearly and logically that the crime was a consequence of the brain fever, occasioned by the prisoner's personal distress, which had set in long before the perpetration of the crime. He did not, however, add anything on his own behalf in confirmation of this view; as he had throughout, he confirmed and recalled, clearly and precisely, every tiny circumstance pertaining to what had taken place. In view of the extenuating circumstances he was condemned to fifteen years' hard labour in Siberia, and heard his sentence 'thoughtfully' and in grim silence. The whole of his immense fortune, with the exception of the comparatively insignificant portion he had squandered during his early debauches, went to his brother Semyon Semyonovich, to the latter's considerable satisfaction. Old Mrs Rogozhin is still alive and seems to recall her favourite son, Parfion, from time to time, but only vaguely: God has spared her mind and heart from any awareness of the horror which has befallen her melancholy house.

Lebedev, Keller, Ganya, Ptitsyn, and many other characters in our tale are carrying on living as before, and there is almost nothing for us to say about them. Ippolit died in a state of dreadful agitation, somewhat earlier than he had expected, about a fortnight after Nastasya Filippovna's death. Kolya was profoundly shaken by what had happened, and finally grew very close to his mother. Nina Alexandrovna worries about him being too thoughtful for his years; perhaps he will turn out a good man. It was partly due to his efforts, incidentally, that the prince's future was settled; a long time before, Kolya had singled out Yevgeni Pavlovich Radomsky from all the people he had recently got to know; he was the first to go to him and give him a fully detailed account of the crime and the prince's present condition. He had not been mistaken. Radomsky played a most energetic part in the future of the unfortunate 'idiot', and as a result of his care and effort the prince once more found himself abroad, in Schneider's Swiss clinic. Yevgeni Pavlovich himself, who went abroad with the intention of making a long stay in Europe, openly calling himself 'an utterly superfluous man in Russia', quite often visits his sick friend at the Schneider clinic, at least once every few months; but Schneider frowns more and more and shakes his head: he hints at complete destruction of the reasoning faculties; he does not definitely speak of incurability, but he allows himself the gloomiest insinuations. Yevgeni Pavlovich takes this very much to heart—and he has a heart, as he has demonstrated by receiving letters from Kolya and even answering them occasionally. But besides this, an odd side of his character has become apparent—and since it is a laudable side, we will hasten to describe it: after each visit to the Schneider clinic, besides the letter to Kolya he sends off another one to a certain person in Petersburg, in which he gives the fullest and most sympathetic account of the prince's present condition. As well as the most respectful expressions of devotion, these letters sometimes—and with increasing frequency—contain some candid statements of his own opinions, ideas, and feelings—in short, something approaching an expression of friendly and intimate feelings. This person who corresponds with Yevgeni Pavlovich (though the letters are rather infrequent) and has won so much of his attention and respect, is Vera Lebedeva. We were unable to discover with certainty how such a relationship could have grown up between them; it arose, of course, in connection with what had happened to the prince, when Vera had been grief-stricken to the point of falling ill; but the details of how their acquaintance and friendship came about, we do not know. We have mentioned these letters mainly because some of them contained news of the Yepanchin family, and in particular, of Aglaya Ivanovna Yepanchina. Radomsky wrote of her in a rather incoherent letter from Paris, that after a brief and intense attachment to a certain *émigré*, a Polish count, she suddenly married him against her parents' wishes. If they eventually did give their consent, it was only because the affair threatened to develop into a full-blown scandal. Then, after a silence of almost six months, Radomsky informed his correspondent, once again in a long and circumstantial letter, that during his last visit to Professor Schneider in Switzerland he had encountered the whole Yepanchin family there (except, of course, for General Yepanchin, who was detained in Petersburg by his business affairs), as well as Prince S. It was a strange reunion; they all greeted Yevgeni Pavlovich with something approaching rapture; Adelaida and Alexandra regarded themselves as being beholden to him for some reason over his 'angelic solicitude for the unfortunate prince'. Lizaveta Prokofievna wept unrestrainedly at the sight of the prince in his sick and humiliated state. Evidently all had been forgiven him. Prince S uttered several apposite and intelligent truisms. Yevgeni Pavlovich gained the impression that he and Adelaida did not yet fully see eye to eye; but it seemed inevitable that, in the future, Adelaida's spirited nature would submit voluntarily and wholeheartedly to Prince S's intellect and experience. Moreover, the lessons absorbed by the family, particularly Aglaya's affair with the *émigré* count, had made a deep impression on her. Everything the family had feared in giving Aglaya to this count had come to pass within six months, along with some surprising developments they had never even thought of. This count turned out to be no count at all, and if he really was an *émigré*, he was one with a shady and dubious past history. He had captivated Aglaya by the extraordinary nobility of his soul, tortured by anguish for his native land—so captivated her, in fact, that before she married she became a member of some committee in exile for the re-establishment of Poland, and furthermore had found her way into the Catholic confessional of a celebrated priest, who had gained an almost fanatical ascendancy over her mind. The count's vast fortune, of which he had furnished Lizaveta

Prokofievna and Prince S almost incontrovertible evidence, turned out to be wholly fictitious. Not only that; within six months of the wedding, the count and his friend, the celebrated priest, had caused Aglaya to quarrel violently with her family, so that they had not seen her for several months . . . In a word, there was a great deal to talk about, but Lizaveta Prokofievna, her daughters, and even Prince S had been so shaken by all this 'terror' that they were positively afraid to refer to certain matters when talking to Yevgeni Pavlovich, though they were aware that he knew of Aglaya's latest enthusiasms without their telling him. Poor Lizaveta Prokofievna would have preferred to return to Russia, and according to Yevgeni Pavlovich, she criticized everything she saw abroad bitterly and unfairly: 'They don't know how to bake decent bread anywhere, and they freeze in winter like mice in a cellar', she said. 'At least I've had a good Russian cry over this poor fellow', she added, agitatedly indicating the prince, who had not recognized her at all. 'There's been enough getting carried away with things, it's time to listen to common sense. And all this, and all this abroad, and all this Europe of yours, it's all just an illusion, and all of us abroad are nothing but an illusion . . . mark my words, you'll see!' she concluded, almost angrily, as she took leave of Yevgeni Pavlovich.

EXPLANATORY NOTES

6   *Fredericks ... Hollanders*: 'Fredericks' were Prussian coins worth five silver thalers. 'Hollanders', 'Dutch *arapchiki*', are actually Russian gold coins worth three roubles. They were minted in St Petersburg but called Dutch because they resembled the old ducats of the Dutch States.

56   *the Horde*: most of the Russian principalities were conquered by the Mongols in 1237–40, and the vassal-princes and other dignitaries were obliged to travel to Saray on the Lower Volga to transact business with the Golden Horde, a state set up by Batu, grandson of Genghis Khan in 1236, and comprising the major part of present-day European Russia and western Siberia.

63   *for political offences*: a reference to the incident in 1849 when Dostoevsky, along with others of the Petrashevsky circle, was led out to be shot then reprieved at the last moment.

96   *not in the government service*: by order of Tsar Nicholas I in 1837, members of the civil service were forbidden to wear beards or moustaches.

99   *Avis au lecteur*: 'Advance warning!'

103   *Mon mari se trompe*: 'My husband is mistaken.'

111   *se non e vero ...*: part of an Italian saying which continues '... e ben trovato'—'If it is not true, it is well thought-up.'

115   The *Indépendance Belge* was published in Brussels from 1830 to 1937. The newspaper carried extensive coverage of political and public life in western Europe. It appears that Dostoevsky read the paper himself in 1867–8.

126   *Masquerade*: a highly melodramatic play, written in regular rhymed verse. As with Lermontov's other plays, the main focus of interest lies in the hero's violent self-expression.

132   *Rira bien qui rira le dernier*: 'He who laughs last laughs longest.'

142   *it was in the papers*: a reference to Danilov's trial. Danilov was a young Moscow University student found guilty of murdering a money-lender in 1866. Dostoevsky followed the case with intense interest, finding, as did many of his contemporaries, a

good deal in common between Danilov and Raskolnikov, the hero of Dostoevsky's earlier novel *Crime and Punishment*.

167   *Marlinsky*: the pseudonym of A. A. Bestuzhev (1797–1837), a romantic poet and novelist. He took part in the Decembrist Uprising of 1825 and was exiled to the Caucasus as a private soldier. His style was passionate but high-flown and rather forced.

172   *to make it firm*: a reference to the murderer Mazurin (see note to p. 481 below).

175   *merchant of the Third Guild*: before 1863 there were three guilds of merchants, after it only two. The wealthier First Guild was for those engaging in foreign commerce while the other guilds were for less-exalted traders. If a merchant or businessman was unable to meet his dues, he was liable to revert to the burgher or peasant class.

179   *Yekaterinhof*: a pleasure-garden, like Vauxhall Gardens in London.

194   *rural-council policy*: land reforms had been in progress since January 1864. Members of the nobility were in charge of the rural councils or *zemstva*. These were responsible for the smooth running of their district or province, including such matters as road-upkeep, agricultural development, trade and industry, and education.

196   *Izmailovsky Regiment quarter*: the district of St Petersburg where the companies of the Izmailovsky Lifeguards were billeted was known colloquially as Izmailovsky Regiment. This is the area now occupied by the Red Army streets. Dostoevsky lived in Third Izmailovsky Company from March 1860 to September 1861 (now Third Red Army Street, Block no. 5).

202   *the Zhemarin family killing*: refers to the killing of six members of the merchant Zhemarin's household in March 1868 by a young nobleman, Vitold Gorsky, a student who was tutoring Zhemarin's little son. At the trial Gorsky, a Pole by nationality, professed himself an atheist, though he was of Catholic background. In Dostoevsky's eyes he was a typical representative of the young men who had been corrupted by the 'nihilist' doctrines of the 1860s in Russia.

214   *the castrate sect*: Dostoevsky mentions the castrate sect in several of his works. It had been founded in Oryol province in the late eighteenth century by Kondrati Selivanov and many of

its members were said to be rich merchants and businessmen. It was thought that their vital energies, denied a natural outlet, were diverted towards the miserly accumulation of wealth through money-changing, trading in silver and gold, and the like.

217 *Old Believer*: the Old Believers were a numerous sect which split off from the Russian Orthodox Church in the seventeenth century because of their refusal to accept the new service books as edited and corrected by the Patriarch Nikon. They also rejected the use of three fingers when crossing, instead of two. The schism reflected an abiding Russian distrust of foreign ideas. Until the middle of the nineteenth century, the Old Believers were persecuted by the state.

230 *and took his watch from him*: Dostoevsky changed the circumstances of this crime to suit his thesis. The peasant Balabanov did not kill Suslov merely for his watch; he intended to sell the watch for money to feed his starving family in the country.

238 *the Petersburg Side*: St Petersburg is built on a large number of islands in the mouth of the River Neva. The Petersburg Side refers to Petersburg Island, where the building of the city commenced, close to the St Peter and Paul fortress.

265 *N.F.B.*: the initials stand for Nastasya Filippovna Barashkova.

270 *Gorskys and Danilovs*: a reference to the cases mentioned in notes to pp. 142 and 202 above.

277 *Krylov's Cloud*: a reference to a fable of Krylov (1769–1844), about a cloud which floats over a parched field but discharges its rain into the sea.

298 *in order to rob them*: another reference to the Vitold Gorsky case.

300 *I got married . . . goodbye!*: a reference to Chernyshevsky's celebrated novel on the 'woman question', *What is to be Done?*

312 *Princess Maria Alexevna won't scold*: refers to lines spoken by Famusov, the voice of convention in Griboyedov's celebrated play *Woe from Wit*. Princess Maria Alexevna may be regarded as the equivalent of Mrs Grundy: 'what will people say?'

326 *Archbishop Bourdaloue*: (1632–1704), one of the most popular preachers in the France of Louis XIV. This first mention is really a pun by Keller on 'Bordeaux' wine. He later refers to

the archbishop's fame as a castigator of human vices.

351 *typically pre-Famusov*: see note to p. 312 above.

373 *d'Anthès*: Baron Georges d'Anthès was a Frenchman in the Russian service. Pushkin took offence at the attentions he was offering his wife and challenged him to a duel. Pushkin was fatally wounded and died on 29 January 1837.

391 *the 'star Wormwood'*: Revelation 8: 11.

429 *les extrémités se touchent*: 'extremes meet'.

430 *Talitha cumi!*: 'Maiden arise!' (Aramaic), a reference to Mark 5: 41.

435 *ferme les yeux*: actually the misquoted original is by the French poet Nicolas Gilbert (1751–80):
> Oh, let them see thy holy beauty
> Those friends deaf to my departure!
> Let them die full of years, let their death be mourned,
> Let some friend close their eyes!

444 *home-grown Lacenaires of ours*: Pierre François Lacenaire (1800–36), thief and murderer, was the leading figure in a notorious criminal trial in France in the 1830s. In a volume of memoirs published after his execution he depicted himself, with extreme vanity, as an enemy of society.

454 *Paul de Kock*: French novelist (1794–1871), whose hugely popular works had the reputation of being rather coarse and *risqué*.

481 *that Moscow murderer*: a reference to Mazurin, who murdered the jeweller Kamykov with a razor in July 1866, having bound the handle to ensure a better grip. He wrapped the body in oilcloth and filled two bowls with Zhdanov antiseptic fluid (named after its inventor) to hide the smell. Dostoevsky modelled Rogozhin on Mazurin, who was also of merchant stock and had inherited two million roubles. In Mazurin's house, where the murder was committed, the police found a bloodstained knife which had been specially purchased for 'domestic use'.

485 *Podkolyosin*: the hero in Gogol's comic play *Marriage*.

Tu l'as voulu, George Dandin!: 'That is what you wanted, George Dandin!', from Molières play *George Dandin*.

487 *Lieutenant Pirogov*: the hero of Gogol's story 'Nevsky Prospect'.

498 *Nozdrev*: a ludicrous character in Gogol's *Dead Souls*.

523 *one of Chornosvitov's* . . .: Chornosvitov was, like Dostoevsky, exiled in 1849 for his involvement with the Petrashevsky circle. He invented an artificial leg and later published a book on the subject (1855).

524 *the Archive*: *Russian Archive*, a magazine of the time.

   it's in the papers now: another reference to the Balabanov case (see note to p. 230 above).

525 *Voilà . . . ton père?*: 'Here's a lad of spirit! Where is your father?'

   Le fils . . . petit?: 'The son of a boyar—and a brave one too. I like the boyars. Do you like me, little one?'

527 *Charasse's book*: *Histoire de la campagne de 1815. Waterloo.* Jean Charasse (1810–65) was active in public life as well as being a military historian. Dostoevsky had read this book in Baden-Baden in 1867.

528 *Conseil du lion*: 'The lion plan.'

529 *Bah! Il devient superstitieux!*: 'Bah! He's getting superstitious!'

530 *Petite fille, alors*: 'Still just a little girl.'

   Ne mentez jamais!: 'Never tell lies!'

538 *fools*: a rather simple card game for two, in which the object is to get rid of one's cards quicker than one's opponent.

539 *Schlosser's* History: a three-volume work on world history which had been translated into Russian (1844–56) and which Dostoevsky had read.

551 *Glebov*: Stepan Bogdanovich Glebov (*c.*1672–1718) was the lover of Peter the Great's first wife, Yevdokia Lopukhina. He was condemned to a cruel death for his part in a plot against Peter and for his connection with Lopukhina, now a nun. After severe tortures he refused to confess and was impaled.

574 *Non possumus*: 'We cannot' (Latin).

575 *fraternité ou la mort*: 'brotherhood or death.'

580 *C'est très . . . sérieux*: 'It is very strange and very serious.'

582 *Laissez-le dire!*: 'Let him speak!'

585 *the spirit . . . racked*: Dostoevsky uses biblical language here in referring to Mark 9: 17–27; Luke 9: 42.

607 *revealed by Mr Turgenev*: Turgenev's novel *Fathers and Children* (1862) had popularized the use of the term 'nihilist' for young

people of radical opinions. The hero of the novel, Bazarov, was the subject of heated debate, and Turgenev had to endure criticism from both ends of the political spectrum.

622 *the St Anne ribbon*: instituted in 1797. Originally of three classes, this was normally a decoration for officials in the public service. It was less exalted than the Order of St Vladimir. Chekhov's story 'An Anna round the neck' refers to this connection.

631 *vouchsafed them to babes*: an imprecise quotation of Christ's words; see Matthew 11: 25 and Luke 10: 21.

636 *Semyonovsky Regiment district*: the common name for the district along Zagorodny Prospect, where the barracks of the Semyonovsky Lifeguards were situated.

645 *Like they did . . . in Moscow?*: another reference to the Mazurin case, see note to p. 481 above.